PENGUIN BOOKS
Belle

Belle

LESLEY PEARSE

PENGUIN BOOKS

PENGUIN BOOKS

Published by the Penguin Group

Penguin Books Ltd, 80 Strand, London WC2R 0RL, England

Penguin Group (USA) Inc., 375 Hudson Street, New York, New York 10014, USA

Penguin Group (Canada), 90 Eglinton Avenue East, Suite 700, Toronto, Ontario, Canada M4P 2Y3
(a division of Pearson Penguin Canada Inc.)

Penguin Ireland, 25 St Stephen's Green, Dublin 2, Ireland (a division of Penguin Books Ltd)

Penguin Group (Australia), 250 Camberwell Road,
Camberwell, Victoria 3124, Australia (a division of Pearson Australia Group Pty Ltd)

Penguin Books India Pvt Ltd, 11 Community Centre,
Panchsheel Park, New Delhi – 110 017, India

Penguin Group (NZ), 67 Apollo Drive, Rosedale, Auckland 0632, New Zealand
(a division of Pearson New Zealand Ltd)

Penguin Books (South Africa) (Pty) Ltd, 24 Sturdee Avenue,
Rosebank, Johannesburg 2196, South Africa

Penguin Books Ltd, Registered Offices: 80 Strand, London WC2R 0RL, England

www.penguin.com

First published by Michael Joseph 2011
Published in Penguin Books 2011

10

Printed in England by Clays Ltd, St Ives plc

ISBN: 978-0-241-95036-4

www.greenpenguin.co.uk

MIX
Paper from
responsible sources
FSC   FSC™ C018179
www.fsc.org

Penguin Books is committed to a sustainable
future for our business, our readers and our
planet. This book is made from paper certified
by the Forest Stewardship Council.

To Harley McDonald, my new and
gorgeous grandson, born 5 March 2010.
And to Jo and Otis for making me such
a happy and proud Granny again.

Acknowledgements

Evelyne Noailles for all your invaluable help and research into all things French. Bless you, it was above and beyond the call of duty.

Jane Norton my dear friend and wise woman who put me in touch with Evelyne. I will try to budget someday.

Jo Prosser for being willing to listen endlessly to the plot and showing remarkable fortitude as we tramped around Paris for the research. What would I do without you?

Al Rose, for his great book *Storyville, New Orleans*, which helped me so much in writing about the notorious red-light district. A fantastic read which brought to life a fascinatingly naughty place and time.

Finally, last but by no means least, my dear editor at Penguin Books, Mari Evans. Without your encouragement, support and friendship I might have floundered in writing *Belle*. At times it seemed as long and hard as an elephant's gestation period, but you kept me focused with your enthusiasm and advice.

Chapter One
London 1910

'You must be a whore. You live in a brothel!'

Fifteen-year-old Belle took a step back from the red-haired, freckled-faced boy and looked at him in consternation. He'd run after her down the street to return her hair ribbon which had fallen off. That in itself was unusual enough around the teeming streets of Seven Dials, where practically everyone would pocket anything not nailed down. But then he'd introduced himself as Jimmy Reilly, the recently arrived nephew of Garth Franklin who owned the Ram's Head. They chatted for a while and Jimmy asked if he could be her friend. Belle was thrilled; she liked the look of him and she guessed he was close in age to her. But then he had to spoil it by asking if she minded being a whore.

'If I lived in a palace I wouldn't necessarily be a queen,' she retorted angrily. 'It's true enough that I live in Annie's Place, but I'm not a whore. Annie's my mother!'

Jimmy looked hard at Belle, his tawny eyes repentant. 'I'm sorry if I got it wrong. My uncle told me Annie's was a brothel, so when I saw you come out of there . . .' He broke off in embarrassment. 'I really didn't mean to hurt your feelings.'

Belle was even more confused then. She didn't think she'd ever met anyone before who cared whether they hurt her feelings. Her mother certainly didn't, or any of the girls in the house. 'It's all right,' she replied somewhat uncertainly. 'You weren't to know, you haven't lived around here long enough. Is your uncle treating you well?'

Jimmy shrugged.

'He's a bully,' Belle stated, guessing that Jimmy had already been introduced to his uncle's fists, for it was common knowledge Garth Franklin was hot-tempered. 'Do you have to stay with him?'

'My mother always said I was to go to him if anything happened to her. She died last month and Uncle paid for her funeral and said I was to come here to learn the trade.'

Belle surmised by his gloomy tone that he felt obligated to stay. 'I'm sorry about your mother,' she said. 'How old are you?'

'Nearly seventeen. My uncle said I've got to do some boxing to build up muscle,' Jimmy responded with a cheeky grin. 'Ma always said it were better for a man to have brains than muscle, but maybe I can have both.'

'Just don't assume all girls are whores or you won't live to build up muscle,' Belle said teasingly. She was warming to him; he had a lovely smile and a softness to him which was very different to all the other boys around the area.

Seven Dials wasn't far from the smart shops of Oxford Street, the theatres of Shaftesbury Avenue or even the grandness of Trafalgar Square, but it was a million miles from gentility. Great swathes of its higgledy-piggledy tenements and rookeries might have been demolished in the last twenty years, but with Covent Garden fruit and vegetable market still at its heart, and so many narrow lanes, courts and alleys all around, the newer buildings had soon become just as shabby as the old. Its residents were in the main the underbelly of society – thieves, prostitutes, beggars, rogues and thugs – living alongside the poor who worked in the very lowliest of jobs – street sweepers, scavengers and labourers. On a grey, frosty January day, with many people bundled up against the cold in little more than rags, it was a depressing sight.

'Next time I rescue a pretty girl's hair ribbon I'll be really careful what I say to her,' Jimmy said. 'Your hair is lovely, I've never seen such shiny black curls before, and you've got pretty eyes too.'

2

Belle smiled because she knew her long, curly hair was her best feature. Most people thought she must curl it up nightly and put oil on it to make it shine, but that was the way it was naturally – all she did was brush it. Her blue eyes had come from Annie, but Belle had to assume she had her father to thank for her hair for her mother's was just light brown.

'Well, thank you, Jimmy,' she said. 'Go on flattering girls like that and you'll be a huge success around here.'

'Back in Islington, where I come from, girls wouldn't talk to someone like me.'

Belle had barely been out of Seven Dials, but she knew Islington was where the respectable, middling sort lived. She assumed by his last remark, and what he had said about his uncle paying for the funeral, that his mother had been in service there.

'Was your mother a cook or housekeeper?' she asked.

'No, she were a dressmaker, and she made a good living at it till she got sick,' he said.

'And your father?'

Jimmy shrugged. 'He cleared off around when I was born. Ma said he were an artist. Uncle Garth called him an arse-wipe. Anyways, I don't know him and don't want to. Ma always said it was lucky she were a skilled seamstress.'

'Or she might have had to come and work at Annie's Place?' Belle said impishly.

Jimmy laughed. 'You're quick, I like that,' he said. 'So can we be friends?'

Belle just looked at him for a minute. He was an inch or two taller than her, with fine features and a good way of speaking. Not posh like a gentleman exactly, but he didn't have the rough speech peppered with London slang that most lads around Seven Dials adopted. She guessed he'd been close to his mother, and had been protected from the kind of excesses of drinking, violence and vice which went on around here. She liked him, and she was as much in need of a friend as he was.

'I'd like that,' she said, and held out her little finger in the way that Millie back at Annie's Place always did when offering friendship. 'You have to give me your little finger too,' she said with a smile, and as his little finger wound round hers, she shook his hand. 'Make friends, make friends, never, ever break friends,' she chanted.

Jimmy responded with a soppy-looking grin which told her he liked what she'd said. 'Let's go somewhere,' he suggested. 'Do you like St James's Park?'

'I've never been there,' she replied. 'But I should get back really.'

It was just after nine in the morning, and Belle had done as she often did, slipped out for some fresh air while everyone else in the house was still sleeping.

Maybe he sensed that she wasn't anxious to go home and was tempted by an outing because he caught hold of her hand and tucked it into his arm, then started walking. 'It's really early still, we won't be missed,' he said. 'The park's got a lake and ducks and it will be good to have some fresh air. It isn't far.'

A little bubble of excitement welled up in Belle. All that was waiting for her at home was emptying slop buckets and hauling coal for the fires. She didn't need any further persuading to go with Jimmy, but she wished she'd put on her best royal blue cape with the fur-trimmed hood. She felt so dowdy in her old grey one.

As they hurried through the back alleys to Charing Cross Road, then down to Trafalgar Square, Jimmy told her more about his mother, and made her laugh with little stories about some of the wealthy women she made dresses for.

'Mrs Colefax was the one that used to make Ma really mad. She was colossal, hips like a hippopotamus, but she made out

4

Ma charged her for too much material and used the leftovers to make something for herself. One day Ma couldn't hold back any longer and she said, "Mrs Colefax, it takes all my ingenuity to make a dress for you out of six yards of crêpe. What's left over wouldn't make a jacket for a grasshopper."'

Belle giggled, imagining the fat woman standing there in her corset being fitted for a dress. 'What did she say to that?'

'"I've never been so insulted."' Jimmy imitated Mrs Colefax by speaking in a high, breathless voice. '"You would do well to remember who I am."'

They paused to look at the fountains in Trafalgar Square, then hurried across the road towards the Mall.

'Isn't the Palace grand?' Jimmy said as they walked through Admiralty Arch and saw Buckingham Palace in all its pale splendour ahead of them at the far end of the Mall. 'I love to get away from the Ram's Head and see beautiful places. It makes me believe I'm worth something more than being my uncle's errand boy.'

Until that moment Belle had never considered that beautiful places might inspire anyone, but as they walked into St James's Park and she saw how the frost had turned bare branches, bushes and grass into a glittering spectacle, she understood what Jimmy meant. Weak sunshine was breaking through the thick cloud, and the swans, geese and ducks on the lake were gliding effortlessly through the water. It was a different world to Seven Dials.

'I want to be a milliner,' she admitted. 'I spend all my spare time drawing hats. I daydream of having a little shop in the Strand, but I've never told anyone that before.'

He took her two hands in his and drew her closer to him. His breath was like smoke in the frosty air, warm on her cold face. 'Ma always said that if you want something hard enough you can have it,' he said. 'All you have to do is work out how you'll achieve it.'

Belle looked at his smiling, freckled face, and wondered if he wanted to kiss her. She had no experience of such things; boys were something of a mystery to her as she'd grown up with only women. But she had such an odd feeling inside her, like she was melting, and that was ridiculous as she was freezing cold.

'Let's just whizz round the park, then I really must go home. Mog will be wondering where I am,' she said quickly, for the strange feeling was making her nervous.

They began to walk fast across the bridge over the lake. 'Who's Mog?' he asked.

'I suppose you'd call her the maid or the housekeeper, but she's more than that to me,' Belle replied. 'She feels like mother, aunt, older sister all rolled into one. She's always been the one who took care of me.'

As they walked briskly round the park, Jimmy talked about how nice it would be in summer, about books he'd read and about the school he went to in Islington. He didn't ask Belle anything about her home; she guessed he was afraid to, for fear of saying the wrong thing.

All too soon they were back in grimy Seven Dials, and Jimmy said his first task when he got in would be to wake his uncle with a cup of tea, and then scrub the cellar floor.

'Can we meet again?' he asked, looking anxious as if he expected her to refuse.

'I can get out most mornings at this time,' Belle replied. 'And usually about four in the afternoons too.'

'I'll look out for you then,' he said with a smile. 'It's been nice today. I'm really glad your ribbon fell off.'

Chapter Two

Belle felt a bit flat as she watched Jimmy walking on down Monmouth Street. For the last hour she'd felt free and happy, but she knew as soon as she went in it would be back to a series of chores, including emptying chamberpots and clearing and lighting fires.

They had more in common than Jimmy realized. He had his bad-tempered uncle to contend with; she had a bad-tempered mother. They were both surrounded by people, but it was clear that Jimmy was as lonely as she was, with no friends of his own age to talk to.

The sun that had come out fleetingly while they were in the park had vanished behind black clouds, and as they'd passed the man who sold matches on the corner, he'd called out it was going to snow later. Reluctant as Belle was to go in, it was too cold to stay outside any longer.

She knew very little about the world beyond Seven Dials. She'd been born in the same house she still lived in. The story was that her mother had delivered her alone upstairs, put her baby in a drawer wrapped in an old quilt and gone down to the parlour again with the other girls as if nothing had happened.

Belle had learned at a very early age that she had to be virtually invisible. Her place, once she was too big to sleep in the drawer, was down in the basement of the house, and she must never, ever venture up the stairs after five in the evening, or ask her mother questions about what went on up there.

She had gone to a little school in Soho Square from the

age of six until she was ten, where she learned to read and write and do sums, but that ended abruptly after some kind of disagreement between her mother and her teacher. She then had to go to a much bigger school which she hated, and was very relieved when she was allowed to leave at fourteen. But since then she'd found the days long and dreary. Yet when she voiced this thought aloud one day her mother rounded on her and asked how she'd like to be a scullery maid or selling flowers on the streets as so many girls of her age were forced to do. Belle wouldn't like to do either job: the girl selling flowers further along the street was so thin and ragged that she looked as though a gust of wind could blow her away.

Annie didn't approve of Belle doing what she called 'raking the streets' either. Belle wasn't sure whether this was because her mother thought she'd get into mischief, or because she didn't want her daughter to hear gossip about her.

In one of her rare nostalgic and communicative moods, Annie had told Belle that she'd been the favourite of 'the Countess', who ran the house at the time Belle was born. If it had not been for the woman's affection Annie would have been thrown out on to the streets and ended up in the workhouse. She explained that the Countess was given the nickname as she had a grand manner, and because she'd been a real beauty in her younger days, with male admirers in high places. It was one of these, rumoured to be a member of the royal family, who had set her up in the house in Jake's Court.

When Belle was still just a small child, the Countess became ill and Annie nursed her for over a year. Before the woman died, she made a will and left everything she had to Annie.

Annie had run the house ever since. She hired and fired, acted as hostess and took care of the money. It was often said around Seven Dials that she ran a good house, even if she was as hard as nails.

Belle had heard the word 'brothel' all through her childhood but she didn't know its precise meaning, only that it was something you didn't talk about at school. Annie's Place was also known as a 'whorehouse': years ago Belle had asked her mother what that meant and was told it was a place of entertainment for gentlemen. Just the way Annie rapped out her reply told Belle she shouldn't question her further.

Around Seven Dials any common woman or girl who dressed in a vulgar manner, acted a bit flighty or saucy, and liked a few drinks and a dance was likely to be called a whore. It was a derogatory term, of course, but as it was used so often there was an almost affectionate ring to it, in the way people called someone 'a minx' or 'a witch'. So until a few months ago Belle had believed that her mother's business was just a nightly party where gentlemen could meet saucy, fun girls for drinking and dancing.

But recently, through bawdy songs, jokes and overheard conversations, Belle had come to realize that men had some kind of urge and it was for the satisfaction of this urge that they came to places like Annie's.

The details of what this entailed Belle hadn't discovered. Neither Annie nor Mog could be drawn on the subject, and the girls themselves were much too afraid of incurring Annie's wrath to divulge any secrets to Belle.

At night, lying in her bed down in the basement, sounds of merriment filtered down to Belle; the piano played with spirit, clinking glasses, guffaws of male laughter, thumping, dancing feet and even singing – it sounded such fun. Belle sometimes wished she dared creep up the stairs and peep around the door.

Yet however much she wanted to know the entire truth about her mother's business, something told her that there was also a dark side to it. On occasions she'd heard crying, pleading and even screaming, and she was well aware that the girls were not always happy. There were many days when

9

they came down for their dinner with red-rimmed eyes, and ate their meal in sullen, heavy silence. Occasionally one of them would have a black eye or bruises on their arms. Even on the best of days the girls were always pale and wan. They were not very kindly disposed to Belle either. Mog said this was because they felt she was Annie's spy, and that they were jealous of her. Belle couldn't imagine what they were jealous for – she didn't get anything more than they did – but they never included her in their conversations and would stop chatting to one another when she came into the room.

Only Millie, the oldest girl, was different. She smiled at Belle and liked to chat. But then Millie wasn't the full shilling; she flitted from one subject to another like a butterfly, unable to sustain a meaningful conversation with anyone.

Mog was in reality Belle's only friend, and far more of a mother to her than Annie. Her real name was Mowenna Davis, and she came from the Welsh valleys. Belle hadn't been able to say Mowenna when she was a baby and had called her Mog, and the name had stuck with everyone. She had told Belle once that if she were called Mowenna now she wouldn't recognize it as her name.

A plain, slight woman in her late thirties, with dull brown hair and pale blue eyes, Mog had worked in the house as a maid since she was twelve. Maybe it was her plainness that kept her cleaning rooms and lighting fires, wearing a black dress and white apron and cap rather than the gaudy satin and berib-boned hair of the girls upstairs. But she alone in the house was constant. She didn't throw tantrums, argue or fight. She went about her household duties with serene happiness, her loyalty and devotion to Annie and her love for Belle unwavering.

The front door of Annie's Place was in Monmouth Street, at least tucked back in a small alley off it, but it was only the gentlemen callers who entered that way, up four steps to the front door and into the hall and the parlour. The entrance used by all the residents was around the corner in Jake's Court, and they came into the small yard, then down six steps to the back door into what was a semi-basement.

Mog was cutting up some meat on the kitchen table as Belle came in through the scullery. The kitchen was a big, low-ceilinged room with a flagstone floor, dominated by the vast table in the centre. A dresser along one wall held all the china and on the opposite side was the stove, saucepans and other pans hanging above it on hooks. It was always warm because of the stove but a little dark because it was in the basement. During the winter months the gas lighting was on all the time. There were also several other rooms on this floor, a laundry room, Belle's and Mog's bedrooms, and several storage rooms as well as the coal cellar.

'Come and warm up by the stove,' Mog said as she saw Belle. 'I don't know what you find to do out on the streets! I can't bear all that noise and pushing and shoving.'

Mog seldom went further than the immediate area because she had a fear of crowds. She said that when she went to watch Queen Victoria's funeral procession nine years earlier, she was so hemmed in by people that she got heart palpitations and thought she was going to die.

'There's a lot of noise here too but that doesn't seem to bother you,' Belle pointed out as she took off her cape and scarf. From upstairs she could hear Sally, the newest girl, screaming about something.

'That one won't last long,' Mog said sagely. 'Too much fire in her belly!'

It was rare for Mog to make any comment about the girls and Belle hoped that as she'd said this much, maybe she could get her to continue.

'What do you mean by that?' she asked, warming her hands on the stove.

'She thinks she ought to be the top girl,' Mog replied. 'Always arguing, always pushing herself forward. The other girls don't like that, or the way she plays up to the gentlemen.'

'In what way?' Belle asked, hoping she didn't sound too obvious.

But Mog stiffened visibly, clearly suddenly aware she had been talking about something her charge shouldn't know of. 'That's enough, we've got jobs to do, Belle. As soon as I've put this stew on I want to give the parlour a real bottoming. You'll help me, won't you?'

Belle knew that she didn't really have a choice, but she liked the way Mog always put orders to her as if they were requests.

'Of course, Mog. Have we got time for a cup of tea first?' she replied. 'I've just met Garth Franklin's nephew. He's a really nice boy!'

Over the tea Belle told Mog all about Jimmy, and how they'd gone for a walk in the park. She always told Mog everything, for she was far closer to her than to Annie. In most people's eyes Mog was an old maid, but Belle saw her as very modern in many ways. She read the newspapers and was keenly interested in politics. She was a supporter of Keir Hardie, the socialist MP, and of the suffragettes who were campaigning for votes for women. Hardly a day passed when Mog didn't comment on their latest meeting, march on Parliament or story about them being force-fed in prison because they'd gone on hunger strike. She often said she'd like to join them.

'I'm glad you've found a friend,' Mog said fondly. 'But you mind he don't take no liberties with you or he'll have worse than Garth Franklin to deal with! But we'd best get on with the parlour now.'

Annie boasted that she had the finest parlour outside of Mayfair, and it was true that she had spent vast sums of money on the Italian mirrors, crystal chandelier, Persian carpet and beautiful velvet curtains at the windows. But with upwards of twenty gentlemen a night visiting, the girls in and out and cigars and pipes being smoked, along with drinks spilt, it needed spring-cleaning frequently.

Belle thought the parlour might look good by night, but she didn't think much of it by day. The curtains were hardly ever drawn back or the windows opened, and the gold paper on the walls just looked a dirty yellow when daylight entered. Likewise, the plum-coloured curtains had dust and cobwebs on them, and a stale odour of tobacco clung to them. But Belle liked spring-cleaning the room. There was something really satisfying about removing a month of dirt from the mirrors and seeing them sparkle, or beating the rug outside until the colours became bright again. And she liked working alongside Mog because she was a happy soul who worked hard and appreciated the help of others.

As always in a spring-clean, they stacked up the sofas and tables in one corner first, then rolled up the Persian rug and carried it downstairs between them.

The parlour took up most of the ground floor. There was a small area for hats and coats by the front door, which Mog answered when the bell was rung. Behind the staircase which led to the other three floors was what they called the office, which was an L shape, and was also Annie's room. Tucked in here too, behind a door, were the stairs to the basement. Mog had often remarked that the layout of the house was ideal. Belle supposed she meant that Belle never saw who came calling, and the gentlemen never saw how they lived.

There was a lavatory on the ground floor too. It had only been installed a couple of years ago; before that everyone had to use the outside privy.

Belle often felt aggrieved that the girls didn't always go to this lavatory, using their chamberpots in their rooms instead. She felt that if she could make her way on a wild, cold night to the outside privy and not use the pot under her bed, they could at least go down a couple of flights of stairs inside the house.

Yet Mog never backed her up when she grumbled about having to empty the pots. She just shrugged and said perhaps the girls had been caught short. Belle thought that was absurd; after all, if they were entertaining the gentlemen in the parlour it would take far longer to go to their bedrooms for a pee in a chamberpot than to use the lavatory by the parlour.

It was bitterly cold as they lifted the rug over the washing line in the back yard, their breath like smoke in the icy air. But once they began beating the rug with the bamboo paddles, they were soon warm again.

'We'll leave it here till the floor's dry,' Mog said when they'd finished and they both had a grey film of dirt all over them.

It was only as they went back upstairs that Belle saw her mother. As always in the mornings, Annie was wearing her dark blue velvet dressing-gown over her nightdress and she had her curlers covered by a lace cap.

Mog was close in age to Annie, both being in their late thirties, and they had formed what Mog called an alliance as young girls because they came to this house when it was owned by the Countess at around the same time. Belle often wondered why Mog didn't say they had become friends, but then Annie was not a very warm person, so perhaps she didn't want a friend.

Dressed up, with her face painted, Annie was still beautiful. She had a tiny waist, a firm, high bosom and a queenly air. But in her dressing-gown her complexion looked grey, her lips thin and bloodless, her eyes dull. Even the shapely body was gone without her corset. The spiteful way she often spoke to her girls suggested she resented that her own looks were fading while they were still in their prime.

'Hello, Ma,' Belle said from her position on her knees

scrubbing the floor. 'We're giving it a spring-clean, and not before time, it's filthy.'

'We'll leave the rug outside till we've finished,' Mog added.

'You should give the girls some instruction on cleaning,' Annie addressed Mog tartly. 'Their rooms are like rats' nests, they do no more than make the bed. It's not good enough.'

'That's not good for business,' Mog replied. 'No point in keeping the parlour beautiful, then taking a gentleman into a midden.'

Belle was still looking at her mother as Mog was speaking, and she saw Annie's eyes widen in shock at the remark about taking gentlemen into a midden. Mog saw the look too and blanched, and as Belle glanced from one to the other she realized her mother hadn't wanted her to know the gentlemen went to the girls' rooms.

Belle had learned long ago that if she wanted to keep on the right side of her mother it was best to pretend she was too dumb to understand much of what was said around her. 'I could spring-clean the girls' rooms,' she offered. 'I could do one each day and get them to help.'

'Let her do it,' Mog said. 'She likes to keep busy.'

For a few seconds Annie just stood there, looking down at Mog and Belle, not saying a word. It seemed to Belle she was trying to find a way of dealing with the information which had slipped out.

'A good idea. She can make a start on Millie's today because that's the worst. I doubt Millie will be much help though, she can't stick at anything for long.'

By half past one, with the parlour now gleaming and smelling fresh, Belle embarked on cleaning Millie's room at the top of the house. Millie had gone out somewhere with Sally, and the other girls were in one of their rooms downstairs. Belle had had a huge bowl of soup for dinner, followed by treacle tart, and the appeal of spring-cleaning was waning fast. But it had just started to snow so she couldn't go out, and Millie's room was the warmest in the house as all the heat from the many fires wafted up there.

Millie held a unique position in the house. Although she was much older than all the other girls, around twenty-eight, she was still outstandingly lovely, with silky, long blonde hair, wide blue eyes and a soft, childlike mouth. Being slow-witted, she had everyone's affection: indeed it was perhaps because of her childlike, naive nature that everyone cared about her.

Millie was also the only girl remaining from the days when the Countess ran the house. Belle sensed that both Annie and Mog tolerated her laziness because of a shared past. It had also been said on many an occasion that she was very popular with the gentlemen because of her sweet nature.

Belle was equally fond of Millie. She liked her sunny, friendly temperament, and her kindness and generosity. She often gave Belle little presents – a few beads, a hair ribbon or some chocolates – and would hug her tight if she was hurt or sad.

Millie's room reflected her childlike nature. She had cut up chocolate box lids with pictures of kittens and puppies and tacked them to the walls. She had tied a lace parasol to a chair back with a length of pink ribbon and beneath it sat several dolls. Some were rag dolls in gaudy cotton dresses which looked as if she might have made them herself. But there was also a rather grand doll with a porcelain face, wavy blonde hair and a pink satin gown.

As Belle looked around she saw that Millie had ten times more possessions than any of the other girls: china ornaments, silver-backed hairbrushes, a wooden toy train, a cuckoo clock that didn't work, and many ribbon-trimmed cushions.

Belle got to work, making the big brass bed first, then covering it with a dust sheet before piling on to it as much of the furniture and other items as she could.

The floor was thick with dust, and the only rug a small one

which could be shaken from the window. Once she'd cleaned out the fire grate and swept and washed the floor, she laid a fire and lit it to dry the floor more quickly.

An hour later she was almost finished, shelves cleaned and dusted, mirrors and windows gleaming, all Millie's possessions arranged carefully again.

It was dark now and still snowing hard. Looking out of the window on to Jake's Court, Belle saw the snow had transformed it. Seven Dials was notorious in London for having the most brothels, gambling dens, public houses and other low dives within a square mile. With the Covent Garden market starting its day in the middle of the night just as the drinkers and gamblers were going home to their beds, there was never a silent time. It was always being said that the slums in London would soon be a thing of the past, and it was true that many such areas were being cleared, but no one in the government took into account where the residents of a cleared slum would go. At present they were flocking here, finding a modicum of shelter with hundreds of other desperate men, women and children in the many courts, fetid alleys and narrow winding lanes. Even to Belle, who had never known anywhere else, it was a dirty, stinking, noisy place, and she could understand how terrifying it must be to anyone who stumbled into it by accident when they'd taken a wrong turning from the neighbouring smart streets.

But now, in the yellow glow of the gaslight, the Court looked enchanted and beautiful under a thick blanket of snow. It was also deserted, a very unusual occurrence, and Belle guessed the house would remain very quiet tonight.

The room was very warm now and, with the curtains closed and just the light of the fire and the gaslight turned down low, it was so cosy that Belle couldn't resist lying down on the bed for a rest. She expected Millie to come in at any minute, and be thrilled to find her room looking so nice.

She felt herself growing drowsy and attempted to rouse herself to go back downstairs, but she was too warm and comfortable to move.

The sound of feet on the stairs woke her with a start. She had no idea what the time was, but the fire was almost out, which suggested it was now evening and she'd been asleep a long time. Her stomach lurched with anxiety, for the rule that she was never to go upstairs after five was one of Annie's strictest. Belle could still remember the beating she'd got at six years old for daring to disobey it.

It was just blind panic which made her jump up, straighten the covers and slip underneath the bed. Once there, she told herself that if Millie was alone she could explain why she was there and get her to smuggle her back to the kitchen without anyone else seeing her.

But her heart sank as the door opened and Millie came in, followed by a man. Millie turned up the gaslight and lit a couple of candles too. From her position beneath the bed, Belle could see no more than the lower half of Millie's pale blue dress with its lace flounces, and the man's dark brown trousers and side-buttoned boots.

'Why did you pretend not to be here last week when I called?' the man asked. His voice was gruff and he sounded cross.

'I wasn't here,' Millie replied. 'I had a night off and went to see my aunt.'

'Well, I've paid for the whole night with you tonight,' he said.

Belle's first reaction was shock that he'd paid to share Millie's room. But then her stomach lurched when she realized that meant she was trapped. How was she going to get out? She couldn't possibly stay here, but then she couldn't possibly come out from under the bed, apologize for intruding and then leave, either.

'The whole night,' Millie repeated, and it sounded as if she was as horrified by the idea as Belle was.

There was silence then, and Belle guessed they must be kissing as they were standing close together. She could hear heavy breathing and the rustling of clothes and all at once Millie's dress was tossed to the floor just a few inches away from Belle. A petticoat fluttered down too, and then the man's boots and trousers came off, and it finally dawned on Belle exactly what a whore was. Men paid whores so they could do that thing they were only supposed to do to their wives to have children. She couldn't understand why she hadn't worked that one out before. But now she had, it sickened her to think that Jimmy and other people she knew believed she was allowing men to do that to her too.

Millie was down to her chemise, stockings and white lace-trimmed drawers. The man had removed his jacket along with his trousers and boots, but he'd kept his shirt on and it came down almost to his knees, exposing very muscular, hairy legs.

'Let me put some more coal on the fire, it's nearly out,' Millie said suddenly. As she bent over to put the shovel into the coal bucket, Belle thought of trying to signal to her so she'd get the man to leave the room, but before she could even attempt it, the man moved and grabbed Millie around the waist from behind, pulling her drawers off so roughly that they ripped.

Belle was so shocked that she felt her heart might stop beating. From her position she could still only see the couple from the waist down, but that was far too much. She didn't want to see Millie's plump, dimpled thighs and buttocks, or the man forcing her to bend over so he could push his cock into her. Belle had only seen a couple of cocks in her life, and they had belonged to small boys being cleaned up by their mothers under a street pump. But this man's had to be seven or eight inches long and as firm as a barber's pole. She could see by the whiteness of Millie's knuckles as she supported herself on the fireplace that he was hurting her.

'That's better, my lovely,' he said breathlessly as he hammered into her. 'You love it, don't you?'

Belle closed her eyes to shut out the sight but heard Millie reply that she loved it more than anything else in the world. This was clearly a lie, for when Belle opened her eyes again Millie had moved enough so she could see her face sideways on, and it was strained with pain.

Suddenly Belle understood why the girls so often looked sullen and dejected. She had been mystified by this for the parties sounded so much fun. But clearly they didn't get a jolly time in the parlour for long. Instead they were whisked away to their rooms to be subjected to this kind of ordeal.

As the man bent down further over Millie's back, Belle saw his face in profile. He had dark hair, slightly grey at the temples, and a thick, military-style moustache. His nose was quite prominent, with a slight hook. She thought he might be around thirty-two, though she always found it hard to guess men's ages.

The couple moved on to the bed then, and the twanging sound of the springs just inches from her head, and the foul things he was saying to Millie, were horrible. Worse still, she could see them reflected in the mirror above the fireplace. Not their faces, just from their necks down to their knees. He had a hairy, very bony backside and he was holding on to Millie's knees and seemed to be forcing them further apart so he could drive himself further into her.

It went on and on remorselessly, the slapping sound of flesh against flesh, squeaking springs, grunting, swearing and panting. From time to time Millie would cry out in pain – at one point she even urged him to stop – but he carried on regardless.

Belle realized that this was what 'fucking' was. She heard

the word daily out on the streets where it was mostly a swear word – some men used it in every sentence they uttered – but she had heard it used in relation to men and women too, and now she understood this was its real meaning.

She hated being witness to it and was tempted to take a chance and crawl out from under the bed to the door. But common sense told her there would be hell to pay if she did, from the man and Annie too. She wondered as well why Mog hadn't noticed she was missing and come looking for her.

Just when she thought Millie's ordeal was never going to end, all at once the man appeared to be reaching some kind of crescendo, for he was panting furiously and moving even faster. Then it stopped abruptly and he rolled off Millie and sank on to the mattress beside her.

'Wasn't that splendid?' he asked.

'Oh yes, dear,' Millie replied, her voice so weak and feeble it was hardly there at all.

'So let's have no more of this shilly-shallying,' he said. 'You'll leave here tomorrow morning and come with me to Kent?'

'I can't,' she said weakly. 'Annie won't let me go, she needs me here.'

'Rubbish! Whores are ten a penny, and most far younger than you. And why did you lie to me about last week?'

His voice, which had never been tender with her, was now becoming positively menacing.

'I didn't lie to you,' she said.

'You did. You never have a night off from here and you have no aunt. You purposely avoided me last time I came. And you never intended to come and live with me.'

Millie denied it. Then a sharp crack punctuated by a cry revealed that he'd hit her. 'That will show you what happens when I'm lied to,' he hissed at her.

'I avoided you because of this,' she cried out. 'Why do you hurt me when you say you want me to live with you?'

'A whore must expect such things,' he said, as if surprised by her protest. 'Besides, you love me fucking you.'

All at once Millie jumped off the bed and Belle saw she was wearing nothing but a little lace-trimmed camisole, her big soft breasts billowing over the top, and her abundant pubic hair showing beneath. 'I don't love it at all. I pretend to because that's what I'm supposed to do,' she said defiantly.

Belle instinctively knew such a statement was not going to please this man, and that Millie might even be in danger from him. She willed her to run to the door and get out now while she could.

But before the girl could even think of fleeing, his arm reached out to grab her and he hauled her back to him on the bed.

'You bitch,' he snarled at her. 'You led me on with your sweet talk, fed me lies and more lies. I've made plans for us, and now you say you were pretending!'

'Us girls are told to be nice to our customers,' Millie argued.

He hit her again and this time she yelped with pain and begged him to let her go.

'I'll let you go all right,' he responded. 'Straight to the devil where you belong.'

Just the crazed way he spoke suggested to Belle that he was going to kill Millie. She so much wanted to be brave, to get out from under the bed and whack him over the head with the chamberpot before alerting Annie to what was going on. But she was frozen with fear and unable to move a muscle.

'No, please!' Millie pleaded, and there was a sound of thrashing around as if she was trying to get away from him. But gradually the sound abated, and as Belle could hear heavy breathing above it she thought her fears had been groundless because he was kissing Millie again.

'That's better,' he said softly as finally the struggling stopped. 'Just give in to me. That's how I like it.'

In her fear Belle had retreated to the centre of the bed, so she could no longer see them in the mirror. But the way the man spoke suggested that the nastiness was completely over and he was about to start fucking Millie again. Belle thought she would wait for the thumping, slapping sound to begin again and then she would creep out and make a run for the door.

But some little time passed and there was no thumping, just the heavy breathing, so she wriggled to the side of the bed so she could see their reflections in the mirror. What she saw was so shocking that she almost cried out.

The man was kneeling up on the bed, completely naked now and rubbing his cock while holding it to Millie's face. Her chin was jutting upwards, exposing her white neck, but she wasn't reacting to what he was doing. Her eyes seemed to be almost popping out of her head and she looked as though she was screaming, only there was no sound coming out of her open mouth.

Belle forgot her own terror in her fear for Millie. Silently she turned beneath the bed until she was facing the door, crawled down to the end of the bed, then gathered herself while still out of his line of vision for the last dash to the door.

In one swift movement she leapt to her feet and to the door to pull back the bolt. She heard the man roar out something, but by then she had the door open and she raced down the two flights of stairs two at a time.

'A man is hurting Millie! Save her!' she shouted as she got to the last landing and saw Annie coming out of her office.

For just the briefest second her mother's expression was so fierce Belle thought she would strike her. But without saying a word she moved swiftly towards the parlour.

'Jacob!' she called out. 'Come with me to check on Millie.'

The bald, burly man was a newcomer to the house, Belle had seen him just once about a fortnight earlier when he was putting a new washer on the tap in the scullery. Mog had said he'd been hired to do odd jobs, but also to make sure there was no rowdiness upstairs during the evenings. He looked smart tonight in a dark green jacket, and he responded swiftly to Annie's order, racing up the stairs.

Annie followed, but she paused, looking down at Belle and pointing to the door to the basement. 'Down there, and stay there. I'll deal with you later,' she barked.

Belle sat at the kitchen table, her head in her hands, wishing that Mog would come down because she knew she could explain how this had all come about much more easily to her.

The kitchen clock said it was ten past ten. Clearly she'd been asleep in Millie's room for much longer than she'd imagined. But she couldn't understand why she hadn't been woken up by the girls getting ready for the evening, or why Mog hadn't come upstairs to find her when she didn't return from cleaning the room. Mog was like a mother hen; she normally got frantic if Belle was missing for just an hour, and they always had tea together around six, before Mog had to go upstairs to prepare for the evening ahead.

The evenings were normally very tedious to Belle because she had to spend them alone. She would wash up the tea things, then read a newspaper if one of the gentlemen had left one upstairs on the previous evening. If there was no paper to read, she sewed or knitted. But she was usually in bed by half past eight because she couldn't stand her own company any longer. Tonight, however, she wasn't just lonely, she was terrified. Not for herself, though she was scared of what Annie would do to her, but for Millie. She could see her face so clearly in her mind's eye, that silent scream, the way her head was tipped back and her eyes bulging. Had the man killed her?

There was no sound coming from the parlour upstairs, so

maybe there had been no one but Jacob in there as she came down the stairs. That was understandable considering the snow, but she wondered where the girls and Mog were. Aside from Millie there were seven other girls, but even if they were all in their rooms, with or without a gentleman, surely some of them would have looked out when Annie and Jacob went running up the stairs?

Yet over and above her fear for Millie, and the possible repercussions of tonight's events, were the shock and disgust she felt about what had been going on nightly above her head. How could she have been so stupid as not to know what was going on in the house she lived in?

How was she ever going to be able to hold her head up out on the streets now? How could she be friends with Jimmy without wondering if he'd want to do the same thing to her? No wonder Mog had said he wasn't to take any liberties with her!

Belle heard a loud yell from out the back, quickly followed by banging and clattering, as if someone had knocked over the dustbins, then even more shouting from several different people. She ran into the scullery and towards the back door. She didn't unlock it and go out, for she knew she was in enough trouble already, but she looked out of the window next to it.

There was nothing to see, just the snow covering all the old crates and boxes out there, and it was still coming down hard, the wind blowing it into drifts.

'Belle!'

Belle wheeled round at her mother's voice. She had come into the kitchen and was standing by the table, one hand on her hip.

'I'm sorry, Ma, I fell asleep in Millie's room. I didn't mean to be up there.'

Annie always wore black in the evenings. But this long-sleeved silk dress had a wide swathe of ornate silver embroidery from her shoulders right around the low neckline. She had her hair fixed up with silver combs, and with diamond bobs in her ears she looked regal.

'Come with me. I want you to quickly tell me exactly what you saw,' she said hurriedly.

Belle thought it very strange when instead of shouting at her or accusing her of wrongdoing, Annie took her hand and led her into Belle's tiny bedroom. She ruffled up the bed and indicated that Belle was to undress, put on her nightdress and get into it. She even helped Belle with the buttons on the back of her dress and slipped her nightdress over her head. It was only once she'd got her daughter beneath the covers that she sat down on the bed beside her.

'Now tell me,' she demanded.

Belle explained how it had come about that she was there when Millie came in with the man, and that in panic she'd hidden under the bed. She didn't know how to tell Annie what the couple were doing, so she referred to it as kissing and cuddling. Annie waved her hand impatiently and asked that she move on to what the man had been saying to Millie.

Belle repeated everything she could remember and how he had struck Millie, then how it all went quiet and she looked out from under the bed. 'He had his . . .' Belle broke off to point at her belly. 'It was in his hand, by her face. She wasn't moving, and that's when I ran for it. Is Millie all right?'

'She's dead,' Annie said curtly. 'It looks as if he strangled her.'

Belle stared at her mother in horror. She might have already wondered if the man had killed Millie, but it was something very different to have it confirmed. She felt her head might explode with the shock, for this was the worst kind of nightmare.

'No! She can't be dead.' Belle's voice was just a whisper. 'He hurt her, but surely that wouldn't kill her?'

'Belle, you know me better than that, I wouldn't say it if it wasn't true,' Annie said reproachfully. 'But we haven't got much time. The police will be here soon, I sent Jacob for them. You have to forget that you were in that room, Belle!'

Belle didn't understand and could only stare at her mother blankly.

'Look, I'm going to tell 'em that I found Millie. I'll say I went up to her room because I heard a noise of someone climbing out the window,' Annie explained. 'You see, I don't want them to question you. So I'm going to say you were in bed down here. So if they do ask to speak to you, that's what you must say. You got into bed here at half past eight and you only woke up a little while ago because of a noise outside. Can you do that?'

Belle nodded. It was such a rare thing for her mother to speak to her in a kind and gentle fashion that she was prepared to say anything she asked. Of course she didn't understand why she couldn't tell the truth, but she supposed there had to be a good reason.

'Good girl.' Annie put her arm around Belle's shoulders and squeezed them. 'I know you've had a shock, you've seen things I never wanted you to see. But if you were to tell the police you were in that room and saw what happened it would turn into the worst nightmare you can imagine. You'd have to be a witness at the man's trial and be interrogated. They would say all kind of vile things to you. You would be in the newspapers. And you could be in real danger from the man who did this to Millie. I couldn't put you through all that.'

Having expected to be punished severely, only to find instead that her mother wanted to protect her from further harm, made Belle feel a little better.

'Where's Mog?' she asked.

'I let her go and see her friend in Endell Street as I knew

it'd be quiet because of the snow,' Annie said, pursing her lips. 'A good thing, as it turned out. But she'll be home soon. Now, just you mind you stick to the same story to her too.'

Belle nodded. 'But when the police catch the man he might say I was in the room,' she whispered.

'They won't catch him because I shall say I didn't know him,' Annie said. 'But you mustn't concern yourself with anything about this business. Only Jacob and I know you were up there, and Jacob won't tell.'

'But if the police don't catch the man he won't be punished for killing Millie,' Belle said.

'Oh, he'll be punished, make no mistake about that,' Annie said fiercely.

Chapter Three

Belle was still wide awake when she heard Mog's distinctive step on the stairs. She had a stiff knee and came down slowly.

'Mog!' Belle used a stage whisper because she wasn't sure whether the police were still upstairs. She'd heard them clonking around earlier and had braced herself for them coming down to her at any minute. 'Will you come and see me?'

'Oh ducks, what a to-do!' Mog exclaimed as she came into the room. There was no gaslight in Belle's room so she struck a match and lit the candle. 'Yer ma told me what happened tonight. The police had just gone when I got back. Fancy Millie being murdered! All the girls are scared now, I dare say some of 'em will scarper tomorrow. But I told 'em this place is safer than anywheres else, lightning don't strike twice in the same place.'

Mog's lack of hysteria was predictable; she never got really worked up about anything. 'Poor Millie,' she went on, her eyes glinting with unshed tears. 'She were a sweet, good soul, it ain't never right she were took.'

She perched on the edge of Belle's bed then and smoothed back her hair from her face. 'You all right, my lovely? Must 'ave shaken you up sommat chronic.'

'I didn't know nothing about it until Ma came down here with the policeman,' Belle lied.

Mog looked at her sharply. 'Never! You with ears like a bat! You didn't even hear the geezer shinning down the drainpipe into the back yard?'

'Well, I did hear sommat,' Belle admitted. 'But I just thought it were a cat getting scraps from the bins.'

Mog sat on the bed silently for a moment or two, her face looking younger and softer in the candlelight. 'You was still up in Millie's room when I left. What time did you come down?' she asked eventually.

Belle shook her head. 'Don't rightly know, I didn't look at the clock. It wasn't late, the house was quiet.'

'Annie let the girls go to the music hall, 'cos of the snow. She only kept Millie and Dolly back. I was still here then and the girls made enough noise to wake the dead when they was leaving, all excited and that. Funny you never heard that and come on down!'

Belle felt very uncomfortable now. Mog knew she was lying, just as she always did.

'You fell asleep up there, didn't you?' Mog said worriedly. 'I was going to come up and find you, but I thought yer ma might larrup you if she saw you up there. Reckoned you'd slink down later when it was all quiet.'

Belle could feel tears welling up. She could never be sure her mother had any real feelings for her, but she had always felt Mog's love thick and strong just by the way she spoke and looked at her. It was hard to lie to her, even though Annie must have had good reason to insist she should.

Suddenly Mog's eyes widened in horror. 'You saw what happened!' she exclaimed, clamping her hand over her mouth. 'Oh, sweet Jesus! And your ma told you to say nothin'?'

'Don't,' Belle said weakly. She so much wanted to blurt it all out, to cry and let Mog cuddle her till the fright went away. But when Annie gave an order, everyone had to obey. 'Just accept I was here asleep.'

Mog caught hold of Belle's two hands and her small, normally twinkly eyes were cold and serious. 'No good will come of lying about a killing,' she insisted. 'I shall tell Annie that tomorrow and I don't care how much of a fuss she makes. Aside from it being wicked to let a murderer get away with his crime, any woman should know a young girl needs to talk about something like this, or it will give her nightmares. But I understand you made your ma a promise and I won't force you to break it tonight.'

Belle took that to mean she was going to give up questioning her for now and she felt both relief and disappointment in equal measures. The relief was because she knew if Mog was to keep on asking her things she would buckle and tell her the whole story, and Annie would be furious with her. But at the same time she was disappointed Mog wouldn't go against Annie's wishes because she so much wanted to talk about what she'd seen.

'Go to sleep now.' Mog nudged her back on to the bed and pulled the covers up to her ears, tucking them in so tightly Belle could barely move. 'Tomorrow things may look different for everyone.'

The snow lay even thicker the next morning as there had been a fresh fall during the night, concealing any tracks made by the killer. Millie's body was collected by the mortuary van early in the morning, and the first lot of policemen arrived soon afterwards to search her room thoroughly.

Annie ordered Belle to stay in the kitchen. She didn't even want her upstairs to clean, lay the fires or empty chamberpots. She was grim-faced and sharp-tongued, though Mog pointed out that this was partly because she'd been forced to get up and get dressed at what she considered an unearthly hour.

Mog remained upstairs, whether this was because she was asked to do so by the police or because she chose to keep a close eye on the girls, Belle didn't know. She heard the girls being called into the parlour for questioning, one after another, and when Ruby, one of the youngest, came down to the kitchen to get a cup of tea, she said the police were asking about the men who especially liked Millie.

'I told 'em they all liked Millie,' Ruby said with just a touch of bitterness. She wasn't very pretty, her skin was bad and her brown hair dull. 'I'm buggered if I know why they chose someone as old as her. And she were soft in the head!'

'She were nice though,' Belle said. 'Kind and smiley.'

Ruby grimaced. 'Smiling shows she were soft in the head, there ain't a lot to smile about in this place, I can tell you! The bluebottles had Dolly in there for ages just because she didn't come with the rest of us last night. She said she went to bed 'cos she had one of her bad heads and never heard nothin'.'

It was unusual for Belle to get this long talking to any of the girls; Annie discouraged it. Now that Belle had a chance to talk to Ruby she was determined to find out more about the activities upstairs.

'Funny she didn't hear anything,' Belle said.

'Well, she likes her la-la medicine, don't she! A coach and horses could come galloping through the house when she's on that and she wouldn't wake up.'

'La-la medicine?' Belle asked.

'Laudanum,' said Ruby, looking quizzically at Belle as if surprised she had to ask what it was. 'The brown stuff what makes the day a bit smoother.'

Belle had heard of laudanum, but she thought doctors only gave it to people when they were in pain. 'Does it hurt a great deal when you do the thing with the gentlemen then?' she asked.

Ruby tittered. 'Ain't you done it with nobody yet?'

Belle was about to retort that of course she hadn't when Annie appeared at the top of the stairs and ordered Ruby upstairs again.

'I just wanted a cup of tea,' Ruby replied.

'You'll have one when I say you can have one,' Annie snapped. 'So come on up. Belle, you can iron that pile of bed linen.'

32

Belle put the flat iron on the stove and laid the thick blanket over the table ready to start ironing. But on hearing a policeman call Annie into the parlour, she crept up the stairs and opened the door into the hall just a crack so she could listen to what was being said.

The policeman asked several general questions, about who lived in the house, what Annie knew about each of them, and how long they'd worked there. After that he moved on to ask her about the gentlemen callers and whether they picked out the girl they liked best, or if she selected a girl for each man.

'When it's the man's first visit he's often shy, so I usually pick someone for him,' Annie replied. 'But by the second or third visit they mostly like to come in here and have a drink and a chat with the girls. If I've got a pianist they dance too. Then they pick who they want out of the ones that are free.'

'And Millie, did she get chosen often?' A different, gruff-voiced policeman asked this question; until then Belle had thought there was only one policeman with her mother.

'Oh yes, she was my most popular girl,' Annie said without any hesitation. 'I'd say nearly all of my gentlemen have asked for her at some time. But I told you last night she wasn't killed by any of my regulars, the man that done it had never been here before.'

'Will you describe him for me?' the gruff policeman asked. 'And try and think about it a little harder than you did last night,' he added sarcastically.

'I already told you it wouldn't do to study a man too closely on his first visit or he'd never come again,' Annie said sharply. 'He weren't no more than twenty-five, I'd say. Slender, well-dressed, with brown hair and clean-shaven. Looked like he worked in an office – he wore a bowler hat and a wing collar.'

Belle frowned in puzzlement at her mother's description of the man as it was about as far from the truth as she could possibly get. She sort of understood why her mother didn't want her to tell the police about what she'd seen, but now she seemed to be sending them off on a wild goose chase looking for a man who was nothing like the real killer.

Mog came stomping down the main stairs at that point, so Belle had to close the door and rush back to her ironing. Strangely, Mog hadn't said anything more to Belle yet, no questions, no warnings, nothing. Whether that was because Annie had warned her against it, or because she didn't want to say anything while the police were in the house, Belle didn't know.

Another strange thing was that Jacob was nowhere to be seen, and although Belle couldn't be certain, she didn't remember him being there last night when the police arrived. It seemed to her that Annie must've told him to call the police, then clear off and not come back until this blew over.

It struck Belle that in the last twenty-four hours her whole life had changed. Yesterday morning she hadn't even understood the nature of what went on upstairs. She understood that now and it disgusted and shamed her. She'd also witnessed a murder which had terrified her. But now she was hearing her mother lie through her teeth and that didn't make any sense at all to her.

The police tramped in and out of the house until after four in the afternoon, and Mog grumbled bitterly about the snow they kept bringing in with them.

'Up and down the stairs, in and out the parlour, not a thought to what they're doing to our carpets. Why can't they come in and stay in? Men! Useless articles! I wouldn't give them house room!'

Belle sensed that Mog wasn't worried so much by the mess as about everyone she felt responsible for. Belle had found herself jumping at sudden noises, feeling weepy and scared.

She'd gone over what she'd seen again and again, and still it didn't make sense that the man would kill Millie just because she didn't want to go and live with him. She really needed to talk about it, to rid herself of the ugly pictures in her head, and the one person who should be there to listen, to comfort and to explain things, was her mother.

Anger was building up inside Belle minute by minute. She felt let down and bitter that Annie appeared to care more about 'her girls' than her own daughter, and that Belle was expected to act as if nothing had happened and get on with normal chores.

'Ma wouldn't have much of a business without men,' she sniped, half hoping that would provoke Mog into continuing what she'd started last night.

Mog didn't rise to it and continued stirring the chicken stew she was making for supper, but her pale, strained face showed that she was every bit as troubled as Belle.

'Good girl,' Mog said appreciatively when she looked round to see Belle was folding up the ironing blanket having finished the huge pile of laundry. 'We'll have a sit down and a cup of tea now, I think we've earned it.'

Throughout her short life Belle had observed that Mog's way of dealing with any problem was to make a pot of tea. If the girls upstairs fought, if it rained on washday, the kettle went on. She never spoke out about the problem until she'd gone calmly through the ritual of laying out the cups and saucers, the milk jug and sugar basin, and filled the teapot. It was only once the people involved were sitting down at the table and she was pouring the tea that she felt ready to air her views.

But she wasn't calm this time, for as she took the cups from the cupboard they rattled because her hands were shaking; even her walk across the kitchen was slightly unsteady. When she opened the drawer under the table to take out the teaspoons, she dropped one on the floor. Belle guessed that she was struggling to control her emotions, and that she was every bit as confused, afraid and perplexed as she herself was.

Mog was just putting the red knitted tea cosy over the filled teapot when they heard Annie come through the door at the top of the basement stairs. They both jumped as if they had been caught red-handed in some wrongdoing.

'It's all right, I'm not going to bite,' Annie said. She sounded bone-weary. 'A cup of tea is just what I need, I'm all in.'

Belle hurried to get another cup and saucer from the cupboard.

'Are we open tonight?' Mog asked cautiously.

Annie sat down, looking thoughtful for a second or two. 'No, I think we'll stay closed. Out of respect. Millie was a good girl and we're all going to miss her.'

'What about her folks?' Mog asked. 'I know she had a family. Who's going to tell 'em?'

Belle noted the sharp tone to Mog's voice and sensed she had things she wished to say to Annie, so she took the tea poured for her and went over to sit in the easy chair by the stove to let the two women talk.

'Not me, I suppose the police will,' Annie replied, and for once she sounded very unsure of herself. 'Will they have to tell the truth about how and why she died? That's a terrible thing for a mother to hear.'

'It certainly is,' Mog agreed.

Now that Belle understood what Millie was, and that her mother made a business out of girls like her, she found it somewhat surprising that Annie cared about what Millie's family would be told.

'Maybe you could write a few words to them?' Annie asked Mog.

'Even if I knew where they lived, what could I say that

would make it any better for them?' Mog asked plaintively, and Belle saw that a tear was rolling down her cheek. 'I did write a letter for Millie once when she first come here making out she were my housemaid and that she was a good girl. Millie begged me to do it as her mother would worry about her and she couldn't write herself. But her ma never wrote back and although Millie was always saying she was going to go home when she'd saved some money, she always spent it.'

'I was thinking you could say she took a fever, or was knocked down by a cab,' Annie suggested. 'But if you don't remember where her folks lived you can't do that anyway.'

'This is the kind of gory story that gets slapped on the front page of all the newspapers,' Mog reminded her in a sharp tone. 'They'll find out the truth anyway!'

'Don't be like that, Mog,' Annie said reprovingly. 'I feel bad enough about this without you sniping at me.'

'That's right, you feel so bad about it that you won't let your daughter tell the police what she saw, and told them a pack of lies about what that killer was like too.'

Belle was astounded that Mog could be so bold and brave. She looked ready for a real fight, sticking her chin out defiantly. Luckily Annie just looked crumpled, as though she hadn't got the energy to make a scene.

'I didn't say a word to Mog,' Belle blurted out, afraid her mother would blame her for telling tales. 'Mog guessed.'

'That's right, I did. As soon as I saw Belle I knew – she can't lie convincingly like you can.'

'Watch what you're saying,' Annie warned.

'What are you gonna do? Throw me out? I could go to the police and tell them what I know, and you'd be for the high jump then. Just tell me why you are shielding this man. I take it he is the one the girls call Bruiser?'

'I don't want to talk about it in front of Belle,' Annie hissed.

'She's already found out in the worst possible way what

goes on in this house,' Mog said fiercely, holding a clenched fist up at Annie. 'I begged you to send her away to school, I told you again and again that it were only a matter of time before she found out. But you knew best! You thought if you kept her down here she'd never know. God knows it never crossed my mind she'd find out in such a terrible way, but even someone with half a brain would see that a girl as smart as Belle would figure it out for herself any day.'

'You're taking liberties, Mog,' Annie warned, but the usual starch in her voice was missing.

'I dare take liberties because I love you and Belle.' Mog's voice rose. 'In case you've forgotten, it were me what talked the Countess into not throwing you out when you found you were up the duff. I helped Belle into this world, washed and fed her, loved her like she was me own to leave you free to soft-soap the Countess. I've been with you both every step of the way, worked for you, lied for you, cried for you, and supported you when things were blackest. You might be the mistress of this house, Annie Cooper, but I'm the glue that's held your life together.'

Belle had never heard quiet, gentle Mog stand up to anyone before. It made her feel braver too.

She moved until she was standing right in front of her mother. 'Give me a good reason why I shouldn't tell the police what that man really looked like and that I saw every-thing,' she asked, looking her mother in the eye.

Annie dropped her eyes first. 'Because he's a very danger-ous, well-connected man. Even if the police were to catch him tonight and lock him away, he'd find a way of hurting us. I can't take that risk.'

A cold chill ran down Belle's spine. That wasn't what she had expected to hear.

'Why didn't you refuse to let him in after the first time he was rough with one of the girls?' Mog asked, but her voice had lost its hard edge as if she already felt defeated.

'I tried, but he threatened me,' Annie replied, eyes still cast down and winding her fingers together on her lap. 'He'd found out something about me. When he kept asking for Millie and she didn't seem to mind his roughness I thought he'd get bored in time and move on to another house.'

'I think he loved her,' Belle volunteered. 'He said he wanted her to go and live with him.'

'Men like him don't love anyone,' Annie exclaimed contemptuously. 'A pretty, dumb girl like Millie would be used and then discarded once he'd grown tired of her. She's better off dead than in a life with him.'

Belle couldn't help feeling her mother was talking with the voice of experience.

'What's his name?' Mog asked.

'He called himself Mr Kent, but I happen to know the name he's known by in other circles is "the Falcon". But enough of this. The girls have been cooped up in their rooms all day with nothing to eat. It's time they came down for supper. Not a word to any of them about this, either of you. I shall speak to the police sergeant tomorrow and ask whether they know where Millie came from. If they don't, I'll arrange a funeral for her. That's the best I can do for her.'

Chapter Four

It was four days after the night of Millie's murder before Belle got a chance to leave the house again. The police had kept calling round at different times to ask more questions and Annie was a bag of nerves. Her fright was not merely about the police, but also that a newspaper man was said to be sniffing around Seven Dials asking questions. She was afraid he might try to get into her place undercover and print a sordid story about it, so she hadn't opened up for business again.

Rose and May had left two days after the murder. They said they were afraid and were going home to their mothers but Mog was convinced they'd just gone to another brothel to work. As for the other girls, with too much time on their hands they veered from saying they were afraid to be alone with any man to complaining because they weren't earning any money. Every hour or so there was a heated argument or squabble for Mog to sort out. She said they were behaving like children.

Belle felt she'd held herself quite well in the immediate aftermath of the murder. She hadn't become hysterical or blurted out anything she shouldn't. She hadn't even felt afraid either, despite everyone else in the house being convinced they were all in mortal danger. But it seemed as if the shock had just been delayed, for on the third day she woke before it was light from a nightmare of Millie's death. It had been as if it was in slow motion, every little detail magnified and stretched out, making it a thousand times more terrifying. All that day she'd found herself dwelling on it further, not just the murder but the nature of the house she lived in.

The word 'fucking' kept running through her mind, just a swear word she had heard daily since she was a tiny child, but now she knew that was what men came to the house for, it had a sinister ring to it. Some of the girls were only a few years older than she was, and she couldn't help but wonder if her mother intended her to become a whore as well.

Before Millie's death she scarcely ever gave a thought to her mother's business. Maybe that was just because she'd grown up with it, the same as children of a butcher or a public house landlord. Yet now that business was on her mind constantly. She found herself looking at the girls differently, wanting to ask them how they felt about it and why they chose to do it.

It seemed to Belle that her mother must have been a whore too, and in all probability her father was one of her customers. That sickened her, yet it could be the explanation as to why Annie was always so chilly with her. Young and inexperienced as she was, Belle realized that a baby had to be the last thing any whore wanted; it would just make their life twice as hard.

Before all this had happened Belle had felt secure and even a little superior to her neighbours. Her home was clean and tidy, she could read and write well, she was well dressed and healthy and everyone remarked on how pretty she was. Her dream of having a little hat shop had always seemed attainable, for she'd filled a whole pad with sketches of hats she designed. She'd intended to go into the milliner's in the Strand one day and beg them to take her on as an apprentice so she could learn how to make hats.

But her confidence was gone now. She felt as low and worthless as any of the street urchins who slept underneath the railway arches in Villiers Street or in the abandoned boxes around Covent Garden market.

As if the hat shop owner would take on the daughter of a brothel keeper!

It struck Belle too that all this time she'd been acting a bit superior, many of the shopkeepers in Seven Dials must have found it hilarious that a brothel keeper's daughter had the cheek to put on such airs and graces. She blushed to think of what they were saying about her; maybe they were even laying bets on how long it would be before she was selling herself.

She tried to talk to Mog about this, but Mog was quite short with her. 'Don't take that attitude about your mother, Belle, you've got no idea how hard it is for a woman to make a living,' she said tartly. 'Cleaning, dressmaking, serving in a shop, they all pay so little and the hours are so long. I don't always approve of what your mother does, but I won't have you turning your nose up at her running this place. She did what she had to do, to get by. I hope you never find yourself in a position like that.'

The walls of the house seemed to be closing in on Belle; however hard she tried to banish it, the image of Millie's eyes popping out of her head, and that dreadful man holding his cock against her cheek, wouldn't leave her. She desperately needed fresh air, the sound of something other than the girls squabbling upstairs, or the sight of Annie's haunted expression.

Above all she wanted to see Jimmy. For some reason she couldn't attempt to rationalize, she felt he would understand what she was going through.

She put on her old grey, fur-trimmed cloak and her stoutest boots, and slipped out of the back door. No more snow had fallen in the last three days, but it was still too cold for the snow and ice to melt. It was no longer a beautiful sight; the snow on the roads and pavements was now black with filth, strewn with horse droppings and furrowed by wagon and cab wheels. Many of the shopkeepers had sprinkled sand and salt outside their establishments for safety, and that added to the ugliness.

Belle picked her way carefully along Monmouth Street, lifting her skirts up a little away from the filth. It was just on nine in the morning, another grey, very cold day, and it seemed to her that the sun hadn't shone for weeks.

'Belle, wait on!'

At the sound of Jimmy's voice from behind, her heart quickened and she turned to see him racing recklessly along the street towards her, then going into a slide on an icy section of hard-packed snow.

He was wearing a shabby blue jumper that looked a couple of sizes too small for him, and his grey trousers were a little too short. He had a checked muffler round his neck but no coat. Belle suspected he didn't own one.

'How are you?' he panted out as he reached her. 'It's a terrible thing about the girl being murdered, everyone is talking about it. But someone said you'd been sent away. I would've been glad for you if it made you feel better, but I didn't like that I might never see you again.'

Belle's eyes filled with tears involuntarily for he was the first person to sound concerned about her. Even Mog had avoided all reference to her ordeal, and she knew just how much Belle had seen.

'Yes, it was terrible,' she admitted. 'I liked Millie and it's all been such a huge shock.'

'Don't cry,' he said, stepping closer to her and taking one of her gloved hands in his. 'Wanna talk about it? Or shall I try and distract you?'

His tawny eyes were full of concern for her yet he gave an impish grin which showed a dimple in his chin.

'Distract me,' she said.

'Then let's go down to the Embankment,' he suggested. 'The snow's still pretty there in the gardens.'

Holding her hand tightly, he made her run and slide with him down through Covent Garden, past porters carrying boxes of fruit on their heads and others wheeling trolleys laden with sacks of vegetables. He took her into the flower section of the market and the banks of brilliant colour along with the perfume immediately lifted her spirits.

'Where do they get flowers in the middle of winter?' she asked. He had picked up a pink rosebud from the floor and was sniffing it.

'Hot countries maybe,' he replied, coming closer to her and pushing the flower through the fastener of her cloak. 'Or perhaps they grow them in hothouses. I dunno really. But I love to come here and see 'em an' smell 'em. It makes me forget all the ugliness around me.'

'At your uncle's?'

He nodded and looked thoughtful. 'Yeah. The men who drink away the money they ought to take home for their wives and children. The ones who boast of hitting their wives to keep them in line. The thieves, pimps, liars and thugs. I'm beginning to think there isn't an honest, good-hearted man in Seven Dials. I don't even know that Uncle Garth is one.'

'He can't be all bad. He took you in and paid for your mother's funeral,' Belle reminded him. 'My mother isn't what you'd call a good woman either, but perhaps neither of them had any choice in it.'

'You might be right. I suppose it is pretty hard to claw your way up to get a business of your own. Don't suppose many people could do it and remain whiter than white,' Jimmy said with resignation.

As they walked across the Strand and then down to the Thames Embankment Jimmy told her how in the Ram's Head they'd got news of the murder the same night it happened.

'We didn't know what girl it was then, but someone said they hoped it wasn't Millie because she was a good girl. If I hadn't met you I wouldn't have thought anyone from a brothel could be good. I kept thinking about you that night, wondering if you were safe, how it would be for you and your mother.'

The little garden on the Embankment looked very pretty. The snow on the paths was trampled but it was thick, crisp and white on the trees, bushes, grass and iron railings. It was a reminder for Belle that just a few short days ago she'd been as innocent as a fresh snowfall, but that evil man had trampled on that purity of mind and shown her harsh reality.

She needed to try to make Jimmy understand how it was for her, but it was so hard to put into words.

'I really didn't know what went on in the house,' she said hesitantly, blushing furiously. 'I mean, not until that night. I just thought it was a kind of private party that men paid to come in to.'

Jimmy nodded in understanding. 'I told my uncle I'd met you, and he said you'd been kept well away from it. He said it was credit to your ma that she brought you up so well. But maybe she should have explained a bit about it. It must have been an awful shock to find out the truth?'

'It was, and worse still because it was Millie. She was the only one of the girls I felt I really knew,' Belle said, her voice shaking.

Jimmy swept snow off a bench and suggested they sat down as Belle launched into the story that she'd been told to give. Jimmy was very attentive and it was so good to be out in the fresh air, but the prettiness of the gardens, even a little robin who kept hopping about in front of them, made her feel she would choke on her lies about being in bed when it happened. She stopped mid-sentence, tears welling up in her eyes.

'Don't cry,' Jimmy said, putting his arm around her shoulder comfortingly. 'It must have been so shocking to have all that going on over your head. But don't say any more if it's upsetting.'

She leaned her face into his chest. 'It's telling lies I find upsetting,' she said in little more than a whisper. 'If I tell you the truth, will you promise not to repeat it to a living soul?'

He put his finger under her chin and lifted her face so he could see it better. 'I would never tell anyone anything you told me in confidence,' he said. 'My ma was real hot on keeping promises and telling the truth. So fire away, it might make you feel better.'

Belle blurted out the true story then. It was disjointed at times; she couldn't find the right words and was embarrassed by what the man had been doing with Millie before he killed her. Finally she explained that it was her mother who insisted she must say she was asleep in bed through it all.

Jimmy looked both shocked and dismayed.

'I didn't even know what the girls did with men until that night,' she whispered, putting her hands over her face to hide her shame.

She began to sob then, shedding the bitter tears which should have come soon after it happened. Jimmy seemed to sense this, for he put his arms around her, held her tightly to his shoulder and let her cry.

Finally she managed to stop and she wriggled away from him and found her handkerchief to blow her nose. 'Whatever must you think of me?' she said, blushing with embarrassment.

'I think you're lovely,' he said, taking the handkerchief from her to wipe her eyes. 'I've thought of nothing but you since we met. I just wish I could do or say something to make you feel better about all this.'

Belle peeped at him through her lashes and saw the sincerity in his eyes. 'I've wanted so much to see you since it happened,' she said softly. 'It's been so horrible, and no one at home will let me talk about it. I felt you would understand, but then that seemed a silly thing to think when I hardly know you.'

'I don't think how long you've known someone is important. I've known my uncle all my life, but I couldn't confide in him. Yet I'd only talked to you a few minutes and I was telling you things about my mother,' he replied.

He put his icy-cold finger under her chin and lifted her face up to look at him. 'My opinion is that your ma is wrong not to tell the police who it was and that you saw it. Yet I can understand why she doesn't want to, because she's scared of what might happen to you. So that proves she cares about you.'

'What made you think she didn't?' Belle asked.

'Just the way you spoke about her,' he said with a shrug. 'Sort of like you're scared of her.'

'Everyone's a bit scared of her.' Belle gave a watery smile. 'She's not an easy person to be with. Not like Mog. I often wish she was my mother.'

Belle talked generally about how it was to grow up in a house of women. 'If I didn't read books and newspapers I don't suppose I'd even know what it would be like to have a father,' she ended up.

'It was a bit like that for me too,' Jimmy said thoughtfully, moving his arm to put it round her shoulders. 'It was always just me and Ma, and the visits from the ladies she sewed for. Uncle Garth came round every few months, and he used to say she was making me soft. I didn't know then what he thought men ought to be like, and now that I see them in his bar, I don't want to be like that. You wouldn't want a father who was like the men who come in your ma's place, would you?'

47

Belle half smiled. 'I expect he was one of them. But I've never seen any of the men, except the murderer, and they can't all be like him.'

'Do you know what the man's name was?'

'He called himself Mr Kent, but I heard Ma say he was known as the Falcon. You wouldn't get a name like that unless you were dangerous.'

They walked on then to keep warm, going right along the Embankment towards Westminster Bridge. When Belle was about nine Mog had taken her to see Trafalgar Square, the Horse Guards, Westminster Cathedral and the Houses of Parliament. Back then Belle had believed she'd walked miles – it wasn't until Jimmy had taken her to St James's Park that she realized that all these splendid, historical places were very close to home.

Jimmy knew much more than she did about London. He explained about the ceremony of the changing of the guard at the Horse Guards, and what went on in Parliament.

'When the spring comes I'll take you all over London,' he said. 'We'll go to Greenwich, Hyde Park, St Paul's Cathedral and the Tower of London. That is, if you're still my friend?'

Belle giggled. 'Of course I will be,' she said, suddenly aware he had made her feel hopeful and happy again. 'I really like being with you.'

He stopped walking suddenly and turned to her with a smile of pure delight.

'I think you are lovely,' he said, a blush staining his cold, pale face. 'But we'd better go back for now or we'll both be in trouble.'

As they were walking back to Seven Dials he told her that his main job was to collect and wash glasses, keep the beer cellar clean, and check all the deliveries, but his uncle kept him busy with a great many other things too, from washing their clothes and keeping the floors above the bar clean, to cooking meals. Belle got the idea that he was working from around eleven in the morning till gone twelve at night, without ever a kind word.

'A smart boy like you could get a better job,' she said, feeling very sorry for him.

'Yes, I could,' he agreed. 'But hard as Uncle Garth can be, he didn't hesitate to take me in when my mother died, and she thought a lot of him. Besides, I'm learning a great deal from him. He's shrewd, hard-nosed, you'd have a job to fool him about anything. I'm going to bide my time, learn everything I can from him, make myself indispensable, and then I'll find a better job.'

'Perhaps that's what I should do too at Annie's,' Belle said.

Jimmy stopped, turned to her and took her two hands in his. 'I think the less you learn about that place the better,' he said. 'Read books, Belle, including ones about history and geography. Practise your letters, and go on dreaming of your little hat shop. You don't have to become a whore, just as I don't have to be a barman who serves thieves and pimps and wife beaters. Let's be really good friends and support one another. We could get out of Seven Dials if we helped one another.'

Belle was deeply touched. She looked into his tawny eyes and wished she had the right words to tell him how much better he had made her feel about herself. He made hope flicker inside her again, made her feel she could have a good life away from Seven Dials. She thought he might even have the power to erase the memory of the ugly side of men that she'd learned in Millie's room. She didn't feel that kind of threat in Jimmy, in fact she wished he would hold her tight again, perhaps even kiss her.

'That's something nice to think about,' she said, and leaned forward and kissed his cheek. 'Thank you, Jimmy, for cheering me up. I'll do what you said.'

They hurried back then, aware they'd both be in trouble for being gone so long, but as they parted at the way into Jake's Court, Belle waved and he blew her a kiss.

Chapter Five

'Where have you been?' Mog asked indignantly as Belle walked into the kitchen after saying goodbye to Jimmy. 'You should have asked me before you went out alone.'

'Sorry,' Belle said. 'I only wanted some fresh air.'

'You're lucky your ma is still in bed,' Mog said. 'I've got to go out in a minute to arrange Millie's funeral. The peelers say they've had no luck in finding out where her folks live, but I don't suppose they even tried.'

'Is there anything I can do to help?' Belle asked. It was clear Mog was a bit overwrought.

'Not really, ducks. It will just be Annie and me going. We don't want no one else tagging on.'

'Will her family ever find out what became of her?' Belle asked, thinking how sad it was that such a lively, sunny person should be buried almost in secret.

'Well, they knew where she was when she first come here,' Mog said with a disapproving sniff. 'But they've never written. I'd say that meant they had no feelings for her.'

Belle had to agree it looked that way. 'When's it to be then?' she asked.

'Friday afternoon at four,' Mog said. 'At Holy Trinity. We'll have a little tea here for us and the girls afterwards. Just a little send off, nothing fancy. I'll make a few cakes and sandwiches. It's all we can do for her.'

Belle thought witnessing a murder must have made her grow up suddenly, for she sensed Mog was holding in her grief about Millie because everyone always expected her to cope with whatever life threw at her. Belle was used to thinking of

Mog as being old, but in reality she was just ten years older than the dead girl, and she'd spent over half her life in this house, rarely going out, at everyone's beck and call and mostly unappreciated.

She moved closer to Mog, put her arms around her and hugged her tightly.

'What's that for?' Mog said gruffly.

'Because you're so special,' Belle said.

'Get off!' Mog responded, but the playful way she pushed Belle away and the tremor in her voice said she was touched.

On Friday at three-thirty, Mog and Annie, in black clothes and veiled hats, left the house to go to the undertaker's in Endell Street. Millie's body had been taken there after it had been examined at the mortuary. The two women would follow the horse-drawn hearse on foot the short distance to the churchyard for the burial. During the morning two wreaths and a couple of bouquets had been left at the door in Jake's Court. There were no cards with them, but Mog thought they were probably from gentleman admirers. Annie had bought a wreath of evergreens with wax red roses, which she said would last longer than a wreath with fresh flowers. She had been very spiky during the morning, and Mog said it was to be expected as she'd been fond of Millie. Belle thought it was more likely she was afraid the funeral would draw further unwanted attention to her.

Lily and Sally, the two eldest of the remaining girls, had been left in charge. Mog told them they were to put the kettle on at four-thirty and lay out the tea things in the kitchen. She and Annie would be back soon after.

As soon as Mog and Annie were out of sight, Belle put on her cloak and left by the back door. The girls were all upstairs – she could hear them shrieking at one another. Dolly's necklace had gone missing and she had claimed one of the others must have stolen it.

They had been bickering constantly since Millie was killed. Mog said it was because they were bored, but whatever was causing it, Belle was sick of hearing their nastiness to one another. She was going out to find Jimmy.

She didn't dare go into the Ram's Head to look for him, so she walked slowly past it, hoping he might see her. He had said he could usually get out around four o'clock, so she crossed over the road to look in a second-hand clothes shop window while she waited for him to appear.

The temperature had risen slightly during the day and the heaps of dirty ice in the gutters were melting fast. She waited at least fifteen minutes till it was dark, then, feeling really chilled, she walked down towards Covent Garden market, keeping an eye out for Jimmy.

As always, the narrow streets were a seething mass of humanity, and Belle's ears were assaulted by street vendors' cries, buskers playing accordions, violins and even the rapping spoons on a thigh, rumblings of carts over cobblestones, and people shouting to one another over the din. It was not just her ears, but her nose too. Horse dung, toffee apples, fish, rotting vegetables, hot bread and cakes all mingled together and hung like a stinking, foggy web in the cold air. She dejectedly noticed the buildings all around her in a bad state of repair, the rubbish-strewn street, men and women in various states of drunkenness, and filthy children swarming around wearing nothing more than a few rags. The only places which appeared thriving and well kept were the public houses and pawn shops.

It seemed odd to her that she'd grown up here, yet until now she'd never really noticed how squalid, depressing and broken down it was. Maybe she wasn't quite herself, for the noise was making her head ache, the smells were turning her stomach, and she sensed danger lurking in every alleyway and court. She began to walk faster, anxious to get home to safety.

Belle heard a carriage behind her as she approached Jake's Court, but she didn't even turn her head as it was a common enough sound. All at once, however, she felt herself jerked off her feet by someone who had pounced on her from behind. Her arms were caught in a tight grip and twisted up behind her back, and at the same time a hand slapped her mouth to silence her. She struggled and tried to kick out, but her male attacker was a great deal bigger and stronger than she was, and she was lifted bodily into the black carriage which was now alongside her, filling the narrow street.

As it was dark, the gas street lighting murky, and darker still inside the carriage, Belle didn't realize there was another man inside, not until he caught hold of her arms while the first man leapt in after her. One of them rapped on the carriage wall to tell the driver to go on.

Belle was terrified, but she still shrieked as loud as she could, and struggled to reach the carriage door to escape. A hard blow to the side of her head knocked her down on to the seat.

'Another sound from you and I'll kill you,' a familiar gruff voice said.

Belle knew instantly that it was Millie's murderer. And she had no doubt he'd carry out his threat if she disobeyed him.

'Where is she, Mog?' Annie asked peevishly. They had been home for some fifteen minutes. As her girls were already in the kitchen when they got back, all clamouring to hear about the funeral, she hadn't noticed immediately that Belle wasn't there. It was only as she poured everyone a small glass of sweet wine that she missed her.

'I don't know. I expect she just went out for a breath of fresh air, you know how she is,' Mog replied. 'Did she say anything to any of you?' she asked the girls.

'Last time we saw her was just afore you went out,' Lily replied. Lily and the other four girls were only half dressed, with shabby wraps over grubby-looking chemises and drawers. Not one of them looked as if they'd used a hairbrush in days. Lily's fair hair looked like a bird's nest.

The girls' slovenly appearance, along with their vacuous expressions, made Mog angry. 'You could have made an effort to look nice to show some respect,' she snapped at them.

'But we ain't opening tonight,' Lily said in an insolent tone. 'What's the point of getting done up if there's no one calling?'

'I just hope someone makes an effort at your wake,' Mog hissed at her. 'And you could show more concern over Belle.'

'She'll be all right,' Amy chimed in as she twiddled a rat's tail of greasy hair and chewed the end of it. 'What can happen to her around 'ere where everyone knows 'er ma?'

By eight that evening Annie was down at Bow Street telling the police she thought her daughter had been snatched and maybe even killed. She and Mog had been all over Seven Dials, asking everyone they knew if they'd seen Belle. But to their distress no one had seen her that day.

The sergeant behind the desk, a big man with a bristling moustache, seemed to find Annie's claim amusing. 'That ain't likely, lady,' he said, a smirk playing at his lips. 'Girls of that age, they go wandering. Might even have a young feller for all you know.'

'She wouldn't go wandering after dark, and surely you know a girl was murdered in my place just a few days ago? It is possible that same man was watching the house and snatched my Belle.'

'Now, why would he want her? She ain't a workin' girl,'

the policeman said. 'You said yerself she was in her bed at the time of the murder and you never lets her upstairs of an evening. He probably don't even know you've got a young daughter.'

'He's done it to mark my card,' Annie insisted. 'It's like a warning he can do whatever he wants. Kill one of my girls, snatch my Belle, what's he going to do next?'

The sergeant got up from behind his desk, stretched and yawned. 'Look, lady, I understand you're worried, but you can bet yer life she went off to meet a pal and forgot the time. She'll be scared stiff to come home now 'cos she knows you'll be mad with her. But she will come back when she gets cold and hungry.'

'Please start searching for her,' Annie begged him. 'At least ask about to see if anyone saw her this afternoon.'

'Fair enough, we'll do that starting tomorrow if she don't come home tonight,' he agreed. 'But she will come back, you'll see.'

At eleven that same night Annie and Mog sat together in the kitchen, both too worried to think of going to bed. They had not been reassured by the policeman's opinion. They both knew Belle would never have willingly missed Millie's little wake; to her that would have looked as though she didn't care about the dead girl. If something else had happened to her, if she'd been knocked down in the street or taken ill, she would have made certain a message was sent to them.

'I don't know what to do for the best,' Annie admitted. 'If I tell the peelers that I knew the murderer and that Belle saw it happen, they'll think I was somehow in with him and maybe charge me with obstruction. Yet if I don't tell 'em they aren't going to take me seriously enough to look for her. But the worst thing is that if I tell 'em it's the Falcon and he gets word that I've fingered him, he'll kill Belle and then come for me.'

Mog knew Annie could be right. No one else in Seven Dials would kidnap Belle. Annie was part of the community, and however villainous some of their neighbours were, they didn't rob or hurt their own.

But this man Kent, or the Falcon as he was known, knew his liberty depended on making sure Belle and her mother kept their mouths shut. He had probably got contacts everywhere, in fact Mog would bet he already knew Annie had been to Bow Street tonight. But after the cold-blooded way he'd killed Millie, Mog was only too aware that he wouldn't even need the excuse that the police were closing in on him to kill Belle.

'I think you must tell the police the truth,' Mog replied after weighing it all up. 'But along with that I think you should call in a few favours and get some help to find out where the evil bastard has taken her.'

Annie was silent for some while, chewing on her nails thoughtfully.

'I'm scared he might sell her,' she finally blurted out.

Mog blanched. She knew exactly what Annie meant by 'selling'. A young and pretty virgin would fetch a high price in some circles. 'Please God, not that,' she whispered, crossing herself. Her eyes filled with tears and she reached out for Annie's hand, for she knew this was what had happened to her friend when she was the same age as Belle.

Annie's lips were trembling. She squeezed Mog's hand and tried hard to prevent herself recalling the horror of what had happened to her twenty-five years earlier.

It was the most painful, disgusting and humiliating experience, and even now, after so many years, she could smell that man's sweat, the whisky on his breath, and feel once again that sensation of being crushed alive by his heavy body on top of her. She screamed, it hurt so much, but he seemed to like that, and when it was finally over he examined her private parts and took pleasure in seeing blood.

She was just a child then. She had no breasts – just a skinny little body like a boy's!

Annie knew now that she was just one of thousands of children snatched from the streets. All over London unscrupulous brothel keepers paid people, often motherly-looking women, to procure pretty young girls for this trade. Mostly the girls were treated much like Annie, imprisoned and semi-starved to make them compliant. Sometimes they were beaten too until their spirit was completely broken.

Mostly, once children had been abused in this way, they felt ruined both mentally and physically, and they stayed in prostitution because they couldn't face going home. Annie was the same; she knew that if her mother learned what had happened to her, she'd never get over it. So she lost her family for ever; she thought it was preferable for them to think she didn't care about them than know what kind of work she did.

She did find enough spirit a couple of years later to run from the evils of that brothel, and luck shone on her in as much as she found the comparative safety of the Countess's place in Jake's Court. There she learned to tolerate, if not like, the profession she'd been thrown into. Sometimes, in the company of the other girls, she was even happy.

At the time the Countess passed the house on to her, Annie did consider selling it and using the money to open a shop in a respectable area. But it was all she knew by then, and if she started another business and failed, losing all her money, how would she and Belle live?

She thought about it long and hard and it seemed to her that as long as men had the urge for sex, there would always be people making money from it. So she made the decision to stay in the business but promised herself that her house would be a good one. She would only ever take on willing, experienced girls. She would feed them well, check their health and cleanliness, and not take all the money they earned. That seemed to be the perfect compromise.

She had never, and would never, offer a child to anyone. Men had often asked her to find them one, but she had always showed such men the door, making them quite aware what she thought of such sick practices.

Now that Belle was missing and maybe on the verge of being molested by a brute, she realized how stupid she'd been not to have foreseen something like this. How could she have imagined she could keep Belle safe when she lived in a brothel?

'You were right, I should've sent her away to a boarding school,' Annie said, her voice cracking with emotion. 'It was stupid to keep her here with me.'

Annie knew exactly why she hadn't sent Belle away. It was because she was the one good thing in her life, in truth her only reason for living. She had felt that by keeping her close she could prevent any harm ever coming to her daughter.

She looked at Mog with tear-filled eyes. 'Even if this hadn't happened, sooner or later she would've become aware what was going on.'

'Stop blaming yourself and start thinking who we can get to help us.' Mog took no pleasure in being right about sending Belle away. Besides, although she'd pushed for it, she had felt nothing but relief when Annie refused to do it. Belle was so precious to her that even a day without her was too long.

'What's the name of that man that was sweet on Millie? The youngish one with the red cheeks. Wasn't he some kind of investigator?'

Annie frowned. 'Noah Bayliss! I think you're right. Millie said he wrote for a newspaper too. But how will we find him?'

'We can start by looking in the house book,' Mog said. 'I know they all put false names, but Noah weren't what you'd call a regular gaming man, he might have put his real address.'

Chapter Six

A rapping at his door penetrated Noah's deep slumber and made him open his eyes cautiously. He couldn't see anything; the heavy curtains were drawn. 'What is it?' he called out feebly, for he'd drunk a great deal the previous night.

'There's a lady to see you,' Mrs Dumas, his landlady, called back. 'She said she was sorry to call so early, but she wanted to catch you afore you went to work.'

'I haven't got any work today,' Noah murmured. 'What's this in connection with?' he asked in a louder voice.

'She said it was Millie.'

Noah was suddenly wide awake. He knew only one Millie, and although he couldn't imagine why anyone would be calling on him here about her, he was intrigued. 'I'll be right down,' he called as he threw back the bedcovers.

Noah Bayliss was thirty-one, unmarried and living a somewhat precarious life financially because although he was both a freelance journalist and an investigator for an insurance company, neither paid very much or even offered work on a regular basis. Journalism was Noah's real love; he dreamed constantly of getting the big scoop, so that *The Times* would offer him a permanent position on their staff. Often he projected that daydream even further to becoming editor of the paper. But to his disappointment he was never sent to cover exciting or important news stories like a sensational trial or an inquest. Mostly he only got ordered to report on very dull council meetings, or other news stories that would be given less than an inch of space at the back of the paper.

Even claiming he was an investigator for insurance companies was something of an exaggeration. Mostly he was just sent along to see claimants in their own home and report back anything which could be suspicious. He usually had to call after a death to see the grieving widow or widower. He hadn't as yet met anyone where there was the slightest whiff of poison, a push down the stairs or anything which might point to the death being other than a natural one, though he couldn't help but hope that one day he might.

He washed his face in cold water from the jug on the washstand, slipped on a clean shirt and rescued his trousers from the floor where he'd dropped them the previous night. He was fortunate in his lodgings in that Mrs Dumas was a widow who wanted company and something to do, rather than just money. Her terraced house in Percy Street, just off Tottenham Court Road, was very clean and comfortable, and she treated her three lodgers almost like members of her own family. Noah appreciated this, so he took it upon himself to do any small maintenance jobs, and always filled the coal buckets each day for her. As he ran lightly down the stairs he hoped that Mrs Dumas would keep her distance from the caller; he wouldn't want her to know he'd been to a brothel.

'Miss Davis is in the parlour,' she said as he reached the hall. She was a tiny little woman of well over sixty, reminding Noah of a little bird with her sharply pointed nose and bright and beady eyes. She was standing by the door which led through to the kitchen, wearing the white frilly apron she always put over her dress in the mornings. 'Come on into the kitchen when you've finished and I'll make you breakfast,' she said, her face alight with curiosity.

The name Miss Davis meant nothing to Noah, but as he walked into the parlour, he recognized the slight woman in a black coat and rather severe cloche hat as the maid at Annie's Place, whom Millie had called Mog.

'I'm sorry to call so early, Mr Bayliss,' she said, standing up and offering her hand. 'I think you know where I'm from.'

Noah nodded and shook her hand. 'My landlady mentioned Millie.'

'I'm sure you heard the terrible news about her murder?' Mog said.

Noah reeled back in shock. 'Murder?' he gasped.

'Oh dear.' The woman frowned and took a step nearer to him, reaching out her hand to touch his arm in a gesture of comfort. 'I am so sorry, Mr Bayliss, to give you such a shock. It never occurred to me you wouldn't know already, not with you being a reporter and it being in all the papers too.'

Noah was so horrified and appalled that his wits left him temporarily and he couldn't think of anything appropriate to say. He'd been out on insurance investigation for the past week and hadn't bothered to buy a newspaper. He could feel tears welling up in his eyes and that embarrassed him. 'I can't believe it! Who would kill such a lovely girl? When was this? Has the killer been caught?' he croaked out eventually, and had to hope Mog wouldn't realize he'd had romantic dreams about Millie.

Mog gently suggested they sat down and she told him the whole story. Noah found it curious that a woman who worked in a brothel should be so sensitive and kindly. She explained how she had been out for the evening and arrived home just after the police left, and she told the murder story through the eyes of the young girl who had witnessed it. As she got to the point where Annie, the girl's mother, had lied to the police and said Belle slept through the whole thing, she had to dab tears from her eyes with a handkerchief.

Noah hadn't imagined Annie having a child, much less a

fifteen-year-old living on the premises. Just from the way Mog spoke of her it was clear this young girl was very innocent and he could hardly bear to think she should have witnessed something so shocking.

'But to make it even worse, now Belle has been snatched!' Mog exclaimed, her voice rising in her distress. 'Snatched right off the street! It were yesterday while we were at Millie's funeral.'

'Oh, my good God,' Noah burst out. 'You went to the police, I'm sure?'

'Yes, of course, though little good it did us as they don't know Belle saw the murder and they won't be rushing around on our account. So we don't know what to do. Then Annie remembered that you were an investigator and that you really liked Millie. So we hoped you might be willing to help us.'

Noah the journalist couldn't help but think this could be the scoop he'd always hoped for to make his name. But he immediately felt ashamed of such a thought. He had been very fond of Millie, and though he would like to be the man who brought her killer to justice, he couldn't possibly exploit her death to further his career.

He hadn't known she was a whore when he first met her. He had been in the Strand shortly after a child had been run down by a hansom cab, and hoping to be first with the story, he began asking people if they'd seen what happened. Millie was just one of these people. She was so pretty and helpful, concerned for the child and its parents, and when she said she had to get home, he walked with her. Just as they got to Jake's Court she blurted out what she was. He said he didn't care, he still liked her just as much.

He had only been to a brothel once before he met Millie, and he wouldn't have gone then but for a friend dragging him there when he was drunk. He disliked the concept that a man could buy a woman as if she were a bag of sugar or a sack of coal. But he was desperate to see Millie again, and nervous as he was about going into Annie's Place, it was the only way to see her.

On that first visit, he didn't even want to have sex with her. He told her he just wanted to be with her, so they went to her room and simply talked and kissed.

On the next and subsequent visits he did have sex with Millie – he couldn't hold back once he was up in her warm, cluttered room and she took off her dress and stood there in her underclothes with her full breasts billowing over the top of her chemise. It was wonderful, the most thrilling thing he'd ever experienced, yet it wasn't just the sex, he liked everything about her – her sweet, kind nature, her silky skin and her vivid smile.

Maybe he was fooling himself, but he believed she liked him as much as he did her, and over the period of the next six or seven weeks he went to see her every Monday night, the quietest night at Annie's. But the last time he went, she had someone in with her already and he felt so dejected and hurt he stayed away the next week. Now she was dead and he'd never get to hold her again.

'Look, Miss Davis, I'm not a detective,' he explained, his voice trembling with emotion. 'I was fond of Millie and I'd like to see her killer swing for it. I'd like to help find Belle too, but I haven't any idea of how to go about it.'

'I'm sure you could find out,' Mog said, pleading with her eyes.

Noah sighed. 'I suppose I could start by talking to people around Seven Dials – some of them might know something. Maybe I can find someone at the newspaper too that knows the right policeman in Bow Street to tap for information.'

'Mrs Cooper wouldn't expect you to do it for nothing,' Mog hastened to tell him, guessing that like most young men his money was spent as fast as he earned it. Right from the first time he came to Annie's she knew he was a good man. She liked his rosy cheeks, the way his fair hair didn't want to lie down flat, however much oil he put on it. He wasn't handsome – his squat nose reminded her of a Pekinese dog, and his ears stuck out – but there was honesty in his face, and she liked the fact that he was sweet on Millie, rather than just lusting after her.

When she found he had put his real address in the house book, that confirmed what she'd sensed about him, that he was an honest man. And to find he lived in such a respectable house was further evidence that he was all she believed.

'It goes without saying that the Falcon, or Mr Kent as we knew him, is very dangerous. We think too that he's probably got many people in his pay, so you'll have to be careful what you say.'

'Have you got any idea where he might have taken Belle?' Noah asked. 'I mean, has he got a house or business address you know of? Any relatives, lady friends?'

'We don't ask such questions,' Mog said reprovingly, as if he should know that. 'Belle said he was asking Millie to go away with him to Kent, so he must have a place there. I dare say that's why he used the name Kent as an alias too. But Annie is afraid he's going to sell her. You know what we mean?'

Noah blushed, his already ruddy cheeks turning fiery. 'A fifteen-year-old?' he said in horror.

'It happens to girls even younger,' Mog said, wincing with distaste. 'It's difficult to believe men can take pleasure in a child. If I had my way they'd be hung up by their feet and a bit chopped off them every day, starting with the offending part.'

Noah half smiled. He believed Mog was capable of inflicting that punishment on the man who had taken Belle. It was clear from the way she spoke of her that she loved her dearly. She had also cared deeply for Millie and that endeared her to him too. 'But why would he do that? She'd still be able to inform on him.'

'Most girls sold that way never recover their wits,' Mog said and her eyes filled with tears. 'They do what's expected of them and escape from reality with drink or laudanum. Others become hard, just as ruthless as those that sold them, and they often go on to become equally evil. Either way they are lost souls.'

Noah gulped hard, not liking the images Mog had created for him. 'I'll try to get some information for you,' he said. 'Now, just tell me about Belle's friends. I don't for one moment think she's off with any of them, but she may have told them something she didn't tell you about this man Kent.'

Mog shrugged. 'She don't have no real friends. When she left school well over a year ago we kept her home. But we never let her mix with our girls because we didn't want her tainted. As for the neighbours' children, they're either raga-muffins, or their folks wouldn't let them mix with our Belle.'

'Surely there must be someone?' Noah said. It sounded such a sad and lonely life for a young girl.

Mog put her head on one side as if she were thinking hard. 'There is a lad called Jimmy who lives at the Ram's Head with his uncle, name of Garth Franklin,' she said. 'She ain't known him long, in fact she only met him the morning of the day Millie was killed. I remember because she come home full of it, telling me all about him. Seems his mother had died recently and his uncle took him to the pub to live. Belle was really taken with him. But I don't think that's the only time she saw him. After Millie was killed she disappeared one morning, even though her ma said she were to stay in. I think she met up with him.'

'I'll start with him then. Is the Ram's Head in Monmouth Street?'

Mog nodded. 'But I never told Annie about this Jimmy. She wouldn't have liked Belle being friends with any boy, and truth to tell I'd clear forgotten about him until you asked about friends. The boy's uncle is a hard, difficult man. But if you could get him on our side, he might know people who'd help us.'

'I can't make you any promises, but I'll do my best,' Noah said. 'You and Belle's mother must be very frightened.'

'We are sick with worry,' Mog admitted. 'Most people think because of the work we do that we don't have feelings. That ain't so.'

'Millie told me that Annie's was a good place to work and that you were very kind to her,' Noah said. 'I know she'd want me to help you.'

Mog reached out and touched his cheek, a gesture of appreciation and trust. 'I must go now,' she said. 'Annie will be wanting to go back to Bow Street to tell the peelers Belle still hasn't returned. She's decided to admit Belle witnessed the murder, but we'll beg them to keep that quiet.'

Noah went straight out as soon as he'd eaten his breakfast. Mrs Dumas had been very inquisitive about his visitor, so he had to lie and say Miss Davis was a relative of someone he'd had to check out for the insurance company and she'd given him some information which implied there had been a fraudulent claim. When his landlady kept on asking him more questions he had been curter than he'd have liked to be, just to stop her in her tracks.

It was a raw, windy day and as he made his way down Tottenham Court Road he tied his wool muffler tighter round his neck and turned up the collar of his overcoat. Noah knew that many people thought Seven Dials was a terrifying place where they were likely to be attacked and robbed, or catch some nasty disease even by passing through it. This might have been true a couple of decades earlier, before some of the worst rookeries were pulled down, but it wasn't that bad now and Noah liked going there. While he could appreciate that it was a deprived, overcrowded, squalid and vice-ridden area of London, it was also lively, colourful and fascinating, and nowhere near as ground-down and depressing as parts of the East End.

The natives were friendly, laughed easily and didn't complain about their lot in life. They were wily of course, never missing an opportunity to snatch a pocket watch, handkerchief or wallet, and he'd been told hard-luck stories by the score that would soften a heart of stone. But then he wasn't a target for robbing: his clothes were cheap ones and he had no fat wallet or pocket watch to snatch.

An old hunchbacked man was washing down the pavement outside the Ram's Head.

'Good morning,' Noah said politely. 'Is Jimmy in?'

'Well, I don't rightly know,' the hunchback replied. He spun the words out in a curious manner. 'I mean, I don't know if he's "in" to you!' he added after a dramatic pause.

'Then perhaps you wouldn't mind asking him if he'd see Mr Bayliss, about Belle Cooper,' Noah retorted.

The hunchback went inside the pub with a crab-like sideways scuttle which was even odder than his way of speaking. Noah followed him but kept well back.

The Ram's Head was one of the better public houses in Seven Dials. It hadn't seen a lick of paint for years, the wood panelling was cracking and the floor creaky and uneven, yet even at ten on a Saturday morning, too early for customers, it had a welcoming atmosphere. A fire was lit at the far end of the room, and the bar had been polished. Noah wasn't surprised it was such a popular place; it was probably far more comfortable and warmer than most of the homes in the neighbourhood.

'Jimmy!' the hunchback called out at the back of the bar. 'Someone here to see you about Belle Cooper.'

There was a clatter of feet on stone steps and a young, freckled-faced, red-haired lad came bursting into the bar. His trousers were wet below the knees, as if he'd been washing down a floor.

'Have you found her?' he asked breathlessly.

Noah shook his head. He realized the lad thought he was a plainclothes policeman.

Jimmy's face fell. 'Have you got proof yet that she was kidnapped then?'

'What makes you think she might have been kidnapped?' Noah asked.

Jimmy stared at Noah for a moment or two. His expression had become wary as if he was afraid he'd said the wrong thing. 'You tell me who you are first,' he said.

Noah walked over to a table by the fire. 'Will you come and sit down with me?'

Jimmy did, but sat on the edge of the seat as if poised for flight. The hunchback went back outside.

Noah explained that he wasn't police, but a friend of Millie's, and that Miss Davis had called on him to ask for help. 'I agreed to because I really liked Millie,' he said. 'I'm hoping you'll help me because you like Belle. Anything you can tell me will just be between us.'

Jimmy's sharp, suspicious expression vanished, replaced by eagerness. 'I heard that Annie and her maid were out yesterday about half past five asking everyone if they'd seen Belle. I wanted to go and help them but my uncle – he's the landlord of this place – said Annie would eat me alive if she knew Belle had been talking to me,' he rattled out quick-fire. 'Later that evening Uncle told me he'd seen Belle outside the pawn shop opposite here at about four o'clock. He thought that meant Belle might have been pawning something to run away.'

'Why didn't he go and tell Annie that?' Noah asked.

'Well, I'm glad he didn't, 'cos I knew she was there waiting for me and everyone would've been mad about that. But I weren't here at the time, I'd been sent up to King's Cross to take a message to someone.'

'So why do you think she was kidnapped rather than just running away?'

'Because of what she told me after Millie was killed.'

'What was that?'

'She made me promise not to tell.'

Noah liked that the boy was honest and loyal. 'I think she told you what Miss Davis told me too, about seeing the murder,' Noah said. 'If I'm right, you must tell me what you know because the man who killed Millie is almost certainly responsible for Belle's disappearance.'

'Do you think he might kill her too?' Jimmy asked fearfully.

Noah nodded. 'I won't lie to you. I think that's more than likely. He could hang with what she witnessed. Desperate men do desperate things.'

Jimmy blanched, but quickly revealed everything Belle had told him. 'We have to save her,' he said breathlessly as he finished. 'Have you got any idea where she might have been taken?'

'None,' Noah admitted. 'I was hoping you and your uncle might have some ideas. Where would your uncle stand on this? Would he want to help find Belle?'

'Why don't you ask me yourself?' a deep voice rang out behind them.

Noah turned on his seat to see the landlord standing there, and his stomach turned over, for the man looked the kind who could twist someone's head off his shoulders just for looking at him the wrong way. He was big, six foot at least, with massive shoulders and arms like a prize fighter's. Noah guessed he was somewhere around his mid- to late thirties, with a thick, dark red beard, and a high colour as if he drank a great deal.

'I'm sorry, sir.' Noah leapt to his feet and held out his hand. 'My name is Bayliss, I was a friend of Millie's. Now I've been asked to help find Belle Cooper, and as I was told your nephew was her friend I came here to see if he could tell me anything more.'

'More than what?' Garth asked sneeringly.

'More than that she just disappeared while her mother was at Millie's funeral! I was also hoping you'd come in on our side too, sir.'

'A pub landlord has to remain impartial,' Garth said curtly.

'Of course,' Noah agreed. 'But let me tell you the whole story, as Miss Davis told it to me. If you don't wish to help after that I'll go about my business.'

Garth remained standing and crossed his arms, a stance that said he wasn't likely to be swayed.

Words were Noah's livelihood, and he told the story of Belle hiding under the bed and witnessing Millie's murder eloquently, adding dramatic and graphic details of things Miss Davis had only hinted at. He knew he was striking home when Garth uncrossed his arms and sat down on a chair, his pale blue eyes wide with shock.

'I'm sure you can imagine how terrifying such a scene would've been to such a young and innocent girl,' Noah finished up. 'And she must have been even more shocked that her mother didn't immediately tell the police the whole truth.'

'Well, I have some sympathy for Annie in that,' Garth said, dropping his harsh tone. 'She's done her best for the girl all these years; she wouldn't want her questioned by the police and having to stand witness when they caught the murdering bastard.'

Noah felt more hopeful of the man's help now his aggression had faded and been replaced by sympathy.

'But if she'd told the police the truth, they might have caught him right away,' he said. 'Or at least they might have posted one of their men to watch the place.'

'By the looks of you I'd say you ain't that familiar with criminals,' Garth said scornfully. 'Or how useless the police can be.'

'That's why I need help from someone like you who knows the area, the people and how things work,' Noah said.

Garth sucked in his breath. 'Like I said, a landlord has to be impartial, wouldn't do my trade no good if people thought I was passing out information.'

'I'm not sure you can be truly impartial,' Noah said, looking the big man right in the eye. 'Not as Belle told Jimmy that she witnessed the murder, and the name of the man who did it. That puts Jimmy in danger too.'

Garth's eyes widened. 'Is that so, Jimmy?' he asked. 'And if it is, why didn't you tell me this last night?'

'I was tempted to, Uncle Garth,' the lad replied nervously, hanging his head. 'But I'd promised Belle to keep the secret. It's only because Noah here thinks it's the murderer who snatched her that I told him.'

Garth put his fist against his forehead as if in deep thought. 'The girl knew the murderer?' he asked eventually.

'No. She'd never seen him before she saw him kill Millie, but Annie knew him as Mr Kent, he'd been to her place a few times,' Noah explained. 'She believes he's also known as the Falcon.'

Garth's big ruddy face blanched. 'Holy damnation!' he exclaimed. 'He's an evil one and no mistake, and he'd go to any lengths to save his own neck.' He took a step nearer to his nephew and put one big hand on his shoulder. 'From now on, son, I don't want you setting foot outside the door on yer own.'

'You know him then?' Noah's heart quickened.

'Only by his reputation, never actually met him. But I know what he's capable of. Reckon I'll have to come in with you now, you don't look capable of taking on that turd on yer own.'

Jimmy looked up at his uncle with an expression of shock and admiration with some delight thrown in. Noah guessed that the lad was more surprised by his uncle's concern for him than by him offering his help in finding Belle.

'I was told he wanted to take Millie to his place in Kent,' Noah said. 'Have you any idea where in Kent that might be?'

Garth sucked on his teeth thoughtfully. 'I dunno, but he was a sailor, so I've heard tell. Sailors often make their home near the port they used to sail from. Could be Dover.'

'Could you possibly find out for me?' Noah asked. 'Any information would be useful.'

'I expect it would be,' Garth said in a dry tone. 'But before you go off half-cocked asking folk questions and talking wild, remember this cove is a vicious brute. He'll slit yer throat in a back alley soon as look at yer, and he'll 'ave my Jimmy too if he thinks he's in on it.'

'What would you suggest I do then?' Noah asked nervously.

'Start with Annie's other girls. He'll have been with one or two of 'em when Millie weren't free. He may have dropped a pal's name, mentioned family, places he drinks, or where he lives.'

'Miss Davis said the girls nicknamed him Bruiser,' Noah said. 'She thought that was just because he liked to hurt them, but can't "bruiser" also mean a prize fighter?'

'If he was I never heard tell of it,' Garth said, rubbing his beard thoughtfully. 'But they say he's a flash geezer, good clothes, handmade shoes, gold watch.'

'I'll ask the girls what they know about him,' Noah responded.

'Just make sure they don't start blabbing all around about him,' Garth said warningly, making a gesture of a knife slitting his throat as he walked out and left Noah with Jimmy.

'Do you think he's killed Belle already?' Jimmy asked, his voice shaky with emotion.

Noah's heart went out to the young lad. Anyone could see he had been gently brought up, and being made to live and work in a rough place like the Ram's Head was hardly ideal for a sensitive boy still grieving for his mother. But sadder still in Noah's view was that he sensed from the way the lad spoke about Belle that she was the best thing that had happened to him since his mother's death. Now she too had been snatched away from him.

Considering what he'd been told about Kent, and that Belle was the one person who could get him hanged, Noah couldn't help but think he had probably already killed her. But he couldn't bring himself to tell Jimmy that.

'What do I know?' Noah shrugged. 'I'm not a detective. But it strikes me that if he took her with the intention of killing her, he'd have done it straight off and dumped her body. I'm going down to Bow Street now, to ask if they've found a body, but if they haven't, then we can be hopeful she's still alive. They do say that the longer a kidnapper keeps his victim, the less likely he is to kill them.'

'But it ain't long yet, not even twenty-four hours,' Jimmy said. 'And if he has killed her he ain't likely to leave her body on a street corner in Seven Dials so the police can find her easily, is he?'

Noah gulped and thought fast. 'No, of course not, but the police keep in touch with the ones from other areas, and we must hope every hour that passes without them finding a body means she's just that bit safer. But I've got to go now. I want you to try and talk to your uncle. Get him to think about everything he's heard about the Falcon, places he drinks, who his friends are, anything might be useful. Perhaps you could write it all down for me?'

'I'll do all I can,' Jimmy said, fixing his tawny eyes on Noah. 'You'll let me know what's happening, won't you? I won't be able to sleep until I know Belle is safe.'

'You're sweet on her,' Noah said teasingly, hoping to lighten the mood.

'I am,' Jimmy said with blinding sincerity. 'She's the nicest, prettiest girl I've ever known. I won't rest until she's safe again.'

Chapter Seven

Belle shrieked at the top of her voice, only to be silenced instantly by Kent pressing on her vocal chords with his thumbs and shoving his face so close that his moustache touched her nose.

'Be silent,' he snarled at her. 'Or I'll kill you here and now.'

'But why do you want me?' she whimpered when he'd loosened his grip on her. 'I haven't done anything to you.'

'You know who I am, that's enough,' he said. With that he forced her face down on to the carriage seat, holding her there while his companion tied her ankles together. Then he jerked her up to a sitting position and tied her wrists together in front of her.

Nothing in Belle's life had come close to being as terrifying as hurtling through London, the prisoner of these two men. She could hear her heart pounding, she was bathed in cold sweat, and her stomach was churning alarmingly as if she might be sick. Even the way she felt when she saw what the man was doing to Millie wasn't as bad as this. Yet a small voice inside her told her she mustn't do or say anything to make the men get angry with her. She'd seen what Kent could do when he was really angry.

As the carriage rattled through the crowded streets she could hear other cabs and carts, along with street vendors calling people to buy their wares. Yet although the familiar sounds encouraged her to hope for rescue, in her heart she knew that the two men wouldn't have snatched her unless they were determined to silence her permanently. They were probably just waiting until they were clear of the city to do it.

Terrified as she was though, she didn't scream. Instead she cried quietly in the hope they might take pity on her, or at least delay their plans. That way an opportunity to escape might present itself.

It was some little while before it occurred to Belle that they'd merely hobbled her ankles, leaving them far enough apart for her to be able to walk very slowly. This gave her another tiny beam of hope, for surely if they were going to kill her they would have tied her up tightly, then carried her to the place of execution.

But it was only a tiny beam. After all, they might be planning to take her to some deep dark woods or across a marsh, somewhere the carriage couldn't go.

The two men didn't speak to each other. Belle was facing the front of the carriage, Kent next to her, though he kept his distance from her, leaning against the window. He lit a pipe, but he appeared very tense, jerking when the carriage hit any bumps in the road.

His companion, sitting opposite her, was much more relaxed. He sat in the centre of the seat, knees wide apart, and seemed to ride with the bumps and swerves. It was too dark in the carriage to make out much detail about him, but she was sure she'd never seen him before. He had a swarthy appearance like a gypsy, with dark, frizzy hair and thick lips. He was wearing a greatcoat, the kind favoured by carriage men, and Belle could smell a strong, musty smell coming from it, as if it had been kept in a damp place.

Belle tried to work out when her mother and Mog would begin to worry about her being missing and how long it would be before they would start to search. She thought they'd just be angry when she wasn't there when they got back from the funeral, but by eight or nine they would start to think something must have happened to her, and then they would start a search. Belle hoped someone might have noticed her being bundled into the carriage, but she didn't remember seeing anyone around just before it happened, so that wasn't likely.

Under the circumstances, would her mother tell the police who killed Millie? Perhaps, but that didn't mean the police would know where to find him. She glanced sideways, and seeing his face in profile she thought she knew why they called him the Falcon, for his nose was like a hooked beak. She suspected he'd got the name for other reasons too, maybe the speed and ruthlessness he showed in going after his prey.

The journey went on and on and Belle grew so cold she felt she might just die of it even before the men attempted to kill her. All sounds of London had ceased a long while ago and all she could hear was the horses' hooves and the wheels of the carriage, nothing else. It seemed as if she'd been travelling all night but she clearly hadn't, for Kent pulled out his pocket watch and told his companion they should be there by nine that evening.

Belle had no idea how many miles it was from London to Kent or any other destination. Even if she had known, she couldn't possibly have worked out what distance could be covered in four and a half hours by a team of four horses.

She was too frightened to feel hungry, but not only was she icy cold, she desperately needed to urinate. She didn't dare mention this though, in case that was enough of an excuse for them to kill her and throw her out of the carriage.

Later Kent pulled up the window blind to look out. Belle could see nothing but inky darkness, not even a glimmer of a light to show that they were passing houses. But he appeared to know where they were, for a few minutes later the carriage slowed slightly and swung round sharply to the left on to what sounded like loose stones.

All the way here Belle had been tempted to ask what he was intending to do with her, but she was too scared to speak. Maybe it was best to keep silent anyway; Kent might hit her if she annoyed him.

'I need to go,' she finally blurted out in desperation. She didn't know how ladies were supposed to tell men they needed to go to the lavatory. Back home the girls used the word piss, but Mog said that wasn't a ladylike word.

'We'll be there soon,' Kent said curtly.

About five minutes later the driver reined in the horses. The gypsyish-looking man got out first and beckoned to Belle that she was next. The rope between her two ankles wasn't long enough for her to step down from the carriage, but he reached up, caught her by the waist and lifted her down.

Frost lay as thick as a light fall of snow on the ground, sparkling in the light from the carriage lanterns. It was too dark beyond the little pool of golden light to make out the surroundings, but Belle felt it was a farm, for the smell of animal dung was very strong. It looked like a very old place, but then the only light came from one lantern by the front door.

Belle could hear Kent speaking in a low voice to the carriage driver as the gypsy man took her arm and made her hobble along beside him to the house. He didn't have to unlock the front door, he just pushed it and walked in. It was pitch dark within and he fumbled around, muttering under his breath for a few moments. But then he struck a match and lit a candle, and Belle saw they were in a wide hallway with a stone floor.

Clearly it was a house he was entirely familiar with for even in the gloom of the single candle he found an oil lamp and lit it. Suddenly there was enough light to see an imposing oak staircase before them and several doors on both sides of the hall. To Belle it seemed to be a rich person's home, but a smell of damp and a film of dust on the huge sideboard spoke of long-term neglect.

Belle was just opening her mouth to ask the gypsy man if she could go to the lavatory when Kent came in through the front door. From behind him Belle could hear the carriage leaving.

'Through to the kitchen,' gypsy man said. 'Tad will have lit the stove and left us something to eat.'

He picked up the oil lamp and carried it down the hall past some very gloomy paintings of horses, leaving them to follow.

The kitchen was warm and there was an appetizing smell of soup or stew, but the room was very dirty. There was a loaf of bread on the table in the centre of the room, and presumably the good smell came from the blackened saucepan on the top of the stove.

Belle plucked up courage to ask if she could go to the lavatory, Kent nodded and told the other man to release her hands, but not her feet, and take her out there.

It was the most stinking privy Belle had ever been in, and as it was pitch dark in there, and the gypsy man pacing around outside, she didn't linger. He whisked her back indoors quickly but didn't retie her hands.

Kent ladled out the stew into three bowls and placed them on the table, shoving the smallest one towards Belle. He then poured some wine from a bottle into two glasses for him and his companion and gave Belle a glass of water.

At first Belle was far too scared to eat, then when she cautiously tasted the stew she found it wasn't very nice, for the meat was fatty. But she forced herself to eat it anyway; if nothing else it warmed her.

The two men ate in silence but now and again Belle felt them glancing at her and then looking at each other as if making a silent comment. It was agony not knowing what was going to happen to her. Part of her thought they wouldn't bother feeding her if they were going to kill her right away, but the way the gypsyish one kept looking at her, she thought maybe he intended to have his way with her. That thought was almost worse than dying. Her stomach knotted up again, the cold sweat came back and she couldn't stop tears running down her cheeks.

Seeing Kent now at close quarters, she realized he was older than she had thought back at Annie's: late thirties, maybe even older. If it hadn't been for his hooked nose, cold, dark eyes and sullen expression, he would have been handsome. He wasn't a big man, perhaps only five foot eight, and quite slender, but he looked strong and she remembered that when she saw him undressed his legs had been very muscular. He had dark hair greying at the temples and a dark moustache, all so ordinary, yet his clothes were good ones and he spoke like a gentleman, which was why his brutality seemed even more appalling.

Belle didn't think he owned this farm. She felt it belonged to the gypsy man. He had mentioned supper and someone called Tad, and he'd taken Kent's coat and hung it up with his own on the back of the door in the way people did in their own house. He also had a bit of a country burr to his voice. Apart from his greatcoat, which was shabby and smelled musty, all his other clothes were good and well-fitting, in fact his boots, though mud-splattered, were the kind she'd seen stylish gentlemen in Regent Street wearing. She thought he must be a bachelor for it was plain by the dirty kitchen that there was no mistress in this house. She wondered if he was a kinder man than Kent, and if it would be possible to get him on her side.

'Take her up, Sly,' Kent said brusquely as Belle pushed the bowl away unfinished.

The name 'Sly' frightened Belle even more, and she shrank

away from him as he came over to her. But he ignored that, lit a new candle, caught hold of her wrist and led her out of the kitchen.

It took some time to get up the stairs because of the way her ankles were hobbled, but Sly was patient with her, which was encouraging. Scared as she was, she felt she had to say something to him.

'Are you a bad man like Mr Kent?' she blurted out as they reached the top of the stairs. 'You don't look as if you are.'

She was speaking the truth in this respect, for he had a pleasant face, with many little laughter lines around his soft brown eyes. She found it difficult to judge men's ages but she thought he was a few years older than Kent.

'Being bad means different things to different folk,' he replied, and she thought she heard a hint of laughter in his voice.

'Killing people is bad to everyone,' she said.

'Well, I haven't killed anyone,' he said, and sounded a little surprised. 'Nor do I intend to.'

'So what are you going to do with me?' she asked.

He opened a door and led her in, putting the candle down on a wide window seat. The room was empty of furniture except for an iron bedstead with a thin, somewhat stained mattress and a chamberpot beneath it. On top of it was a small pile of blankets and a pillow.

'You can make it up yourself,' he said. 'I won't tie your hands again because you can't get out of here. The window is boarded up on the outside and I shall be locking you in.'

'How long for?' she asked. 'And what are you going to do with me?' she repeated.

'That will be decided tonight,' he said.

'If this is your house and you helped him to bring me here and then he kills me, you'll be as bad as he is,' she said, looking at him intently with the look Mog had always called her 'begging eyes'.

'You, little girl, are smart beyond your tender years,' he said with a half smile. 'I expect that's all part of growing up in a brothel. Your mother failed you, she should've sent you away. But perhaps she was intending to train you.'

Belle frowned, not understanding what he was getting at.

'Get some sleep,' he said. 'Goodnight!'

When the door slammed shut and was locked outside, Belle broke down in tears. She was cold right through to her bones, with no idea where she was, and even if her captors hadn't raped her or hurt her tonight as she'd expected, they certainly weren't going to let her go home unscathed tomorrow.

But if they were going to kill her, why hadn't they done it as soon as they got here?

Belle wanted so much to believe that wasn't their plan and that maybe they were going to demand a ransom for her release. But it was far more likely that they needed daylight to take her to wherever they were going to kill her, some forest or marsh where her body would never be found.

She had never before spent a night away from her mother and Mog. She had often felt a bit lonely and cut off being down in the kitchen while they were upstairs, but she'd never been frightened, because she always knew Mog checked on her from time to time.

But there was no Mog now to help her make up the bed, to tuck her into it and blow out her candle. Although she could barely see through her tears she selected the two softest blankets to lie between as there were no sheets, then spread the rest out on top, with her cloak over them. Sitting on the bed, she reached down and took off her boots, then swung her hobbled legs up on to the bed and wriggled down under the blankets. They felt clammy and smelled of mildew, and the mattress was thin and lumpy too.

'Please God, don't let them kill me,' she begged as she sobbed into the pillow. 'Make Ma get the police to come and get me. I don't want to die.'

She repeated the prayer over and over again in the hope that God would hear it.

Chapter Eight

Sly returned to the kitchen after seeing Belle into her room. Kent was still sitting by the stove, bent over in his chair as if mulling something over in his mind. Sly didn't speak, but took a bottle of whisky from the cupboard, poured two large glasses, and sat down by the stove too, handing one of the glasses to Kent.

Belle had been right in thinking the house belonged to Sly. His real name was Charles Ernest Braithwaite, but he had acquired the nickname of Sly because he was a gambler who appeared to have almost telepathic powers which told him which game to play and which ones to walk away from. Like any gambler, he did lose sometimes, but not as often as others, and never large amounts.

Belle had also been correct in thinking he had gypsy blood, for his mother, Maria, had been a Romany. She had turned up at this remote farm near Aylesford in Kent late one winter night when she had run away from her family. Frederick Braithwaite, Sly's father, was a forty-year-old bachelor at that time, struggling to look after his sick mother along with the farm.

Fred was not a generous or benevolent man, but when Maria begged him to give her food and let her sleep in his barn, he saw this could be to his advantage, and he agreed she could have both in return for help in nursing his mother.

Maria was equally hard-headed. She had run out on her family because they were forcing her to marry a man she hated. It didn't take her long to discover that most people were prejudiced against gypsies, and no one would give her work or shelter. She didn't really want to nurse a sick old woman who meant nothing to her, nor did she want to end up in Fred's bed, but she was desperate and she liked the look of his farm. She took the view that she could fare far worse than looking after an old lady, and she might grow to like Fred.

They were married within four months. Within a year of their marriage Charles was born and the old lady died peacefully in her bed.

It may have started out as a marriage of convenience, but Maria worked hard at being a good wife to Fred and a loving mother to Charles and they became a happy little family. Fred died of a heart attack when Charles was only nineteen, but Maria kept everything going while allowing her son to play the part of the young gentleman around town.

Charles had been twenty-seven when his mother died and it was only then that he turned to illegal enterprises to make more money. The farm was his, and it was profitable, but he had very little interest in it. Knowing it would make a good front to hide his questionable sidelines, all he had to do was pay someone else to run it.

He had always been able to justify any action of his which society would frown on by asking himself whether it harmed anyone or not. Gambling and drinking harmed no one but himself, even though his mother might have disagreed. So when he embarked on procuring young women for brothels, he reasoned that he was helping them out. Most of them had been pushed out, or run away from home; many had been brought up in orphanages. He felt that but for his intervention they were likely to starve or die of cold on the streets.

He could find young women and girls at the train stations, lurking outside public houses, in markets, anywhere in fact where they hoped to be offered food or a drink by a kindly stranger. He was that kindly stranger. He truly believed that he was giving them far more than a hot meal and sympathy;

he was getting them work in some of the best bawdy houses in town.

Charles was not a cruel man, and he didn't like the circumstances of acquiring this latest girl one bit. He had never before taken anyone against their will, and certainly never snatched an innocent from the streets.

'She ain't like my usual ones,' he said as he downed the last of the whisky in his glass and then topped it up again. 'I don't like it.'

'Don't be a fool, what's so different about her?' Kent asked, somewhat surprised at his friend's view. 'She's older than some you've taken, and her home wasn't good. Besides, you know that I had no choice but to take her. She could've got me strung up.'

Kent had admitted that he had strangled a whore in Seven Dials, but Sly wasn't entirely sure he believed that the girl who witnessed it was about to blow the whistle. People in Seven Dials learned at an early age not to squeal on anyone. Kent was his partner, though, and aside from being the kind of man no one would want to cross, he was also the one who liaised with the brothel owners when they had a new girl to sell. Sly needed to keep him sweet, but he also hoped he could talk him round.

'She's smart and it won't be easy to mould her,' Sly argued, for Kent planned to sell Belle to a brothel in France. 'I tell you, she'll be more trouble than she's worth. Let's take her back to London tomorrow night and drop her off near her home?'

'Don't be bloody stupid. We can't do that, you know why.'

'But she's got no idea where this place is,' Sly argued. 'Neither does she know anything about you. And her mother ain't going to make a fuss if she gets her back unharmed. We can go straight on to Dover after dropping her off and catch a boat to France like we planned.'

Sly might not have been lucky enough to be born with good looks, for he was short, stocky and pug-nosed, but he did have a certain charisma which served him well with both sexes. Other men saw him as an entertaining companion, admiring his wily nature, determination and strength. Women liked the way he made them feel they were the most important person in the world when he spoke to them. He had the manners and bearing of a gentleman, but with an animalistic undercurrent they found very attractive. Such was his charm that many a girl who ought to have seen him as her destroyer stubbornly defended him to all who criticized him.

Kent, or rather Frank John Waldegrave, which was his real name, was born to landed gentry in the north of England. But although the family estate was large, as the third son and the one his father liked the least, he knew at an early age that he was not going to inherit anything of value. Jealous of his favoured older brothers, and hurt that his mother and sister never took his part, Frank took himself off to sea with a chip on his shoulder which grew larger with each slight or humiliation he encountered.

Joining the merchant navy was possibly the worst possible career choice for a young man who didn't like taking orders, found it difficult to make friends and had been used to the wide open spaces of the Yorkshire Moors. He had a sharp mind which would have been far better suited to accountancy, law or even medicine, but instead he found himself forced to share all his waking hours with the kind of uneducated men who had worked as labourers on his family estate.

Frank wasn't any more successful with women than he was at making friends with his own sex. Back on dry land in Dover, a well-educated gentleman who was just an ordinary sailor was neither fish nor fowl. He liked to think that the shop girls and housemaids he ran into thought him too far above them, but the truth was that he didn't know how to talk to women. The kind of middle- or upper-class girls he might have felt more comfortable with didn't frequent the saloons and dance halls where sailors gathered.

He was in his early twenties when one night in Dover he was taken to a brothel and found that the girls there liked him. He chose to believe this because they listened attentively to him and were willing to give him exactly what he wanted. He'd even proved it to himself dozens of times when he'd been rough with one of them because he felt angry. They didn't complain or refuse to see him the next time his ship docked. They liked it.

Then ten years ago, when Frank was twenty-eight, his Uncle Thomas, his father's younger brother, died. To Frank's surprise he had made his nephew his sole heir. Frank had no real idea why this was, for he'd never had much to do with his uncle, but he could only suppose Thomas had felt ill-treated by his family, and sympathized with Frank.

Thomas wasn't a very wealthy man; he owned no large estate in the country, just a couple of tenements in Seven Dials and a dozen squalid houses in Bethnal Green. Frank was horrified the first time he saw the place they called the Core. The dilapidated buildings in Seven Dials were filled to capacity with the desperate human flotsam and jetsam that ends up in inner cities. The houses in Bethnal Green were as bad – even as shelters for animals they'd have been inadequate. Frank covered his nose, closed his eyes to the appalling sights all around those mean streets and retreated to a comfortable hotel.

But by the next day any qualms of earning a living off the rents of such places had left him. He realized that it meant he could give up the sea and live a very comfortable life with the minimum of effort. He'd grown tough in his time in the navy, and become well used to pushing others around. The prospect of becoming a slum landlord excited him.

That was when he took the name Kent.

Down in the pretty Kentish village of Charing, not far from Folkestone where he intended to make a permanent home, he would be a quiet, respectable gentleman of leisure, Frank Waldegrave. But in London, as John Kent the ruthless property manager, he could play out all his fantasies – whoring, villainy, gambling and extortion. He didn't need friends if he had people doing his bidding because they were afraid of him.

Ironically, just when he truly believed friendship wasn't for him, he met Sly at a card game in the back room of a saloon in the Strand. Something clicked between them; they were in tune with each other. Sly had once laughingly said it was because they both had traits that were missing in the other. Perhaps he was right, for Kent admired Sly's easy way with people, and Sly in turn admired Kent's ruthlessness.

Whatever the reason for their friendship, they both had the same goal, although at the time neither of them had known what that goal was. But it soon manifested that this was to take control of the vice and gambling in Seven Dials and make themselves extremely wealthy in doing so.

It was Sly who dubbed Kent the Falcon. He claimed he'd never before met any man quite as sharp-eyed and predatory. And Kent liked the name to be bandied around, for he knew it would make others fearful of him.

Belle woke to hear a cock crowing somewhere close by and her first thought was that it must be a crazy cock for it was still the dead of night. But as she lay there, filled with dread about what the coming day would bring, she noticed three tiny strips of light across the freezing room and realized she was looking at cracks on a boarded-up window and that it was light outside.

She had forgotten about her ankles being hobbled and as she got up to use the chamberpot, she almost fell over. She managed to peep through the biggest crack on the window boards, and although her view was very limited, she could see trees close by and beyond them open countryside with patches of snow still lying on bare earth. To a city girl who had grown up surrounded by houses and bombarded with the noise of traffic, it was bleak and frightening.

As she had slept in her clothes and had no hairbrush or water to wash in, she got back into bed to await whatever fate the men had in store for her.

Despite her terror she must have fallen asleep again, for the next thing she knew, she was being told to get up by Sly.

'I've brought you hot water to wash,' he said, and in the gloom she could see steam rising from a ewer on the wash-stand. 'There's a comb there too. I'll be back for you in ten minutes.'

Her terror abated a little for surely no one would give hot water and a comb to someone they were going to kill. She started to plead with Sly for an explanation but he quickly backed out of the door and locked it behind him.

Sly was back as he said he would be. He picked up her cloak from the bed, then held her arm as far as the stairs, but once there he picked her up and flung her over his shoulder instead of making her walk.

Now Belle got a chance to see more of his house because daylight was streaming in through the windows. It was a fair size – she thought about six rooms on each of the two floors. It was a very old place with low ceilings, beams and uneven floors, without even gas lighting. Through a window up on the landing she'd caught a glimpse of cows being herded into a shed next to the house, and realized she was in the farm-house. But it was also clear Sly didn't run it, someone else, probably the man called Tad did, and she didn't think any women ever came in here for it was all so dusty and neglected.

Belle looked from one man to the other as she ate the bowl of porridge Kent had given her. Both men were silent, she sensed they were in disagreement about something, and it was probably to do with her.

'Can you read and write?'

The question from Kent took Belle by surprise.

'Why do you want to know?' she asked.

'Just answer me!' he snapped.

It occurred to her that it might be a very good idea to play ignorant, that way he'd be less wary of her. 'No, I can't,' she lied. 'I never went to school.'

He made a scornful face as if that was what he had expected, and Belle felt she'd won a point.

'What are you going to do with me?' she asked.

'Don't ask so many questions,' he replied. 'Finish that porridge – you won't be getting anything else for a while.'

At that Belle felt she must eat as much as she could and not only finished the porridge but had two thick slices of bread which she spread generously with butter. Sly poured her a second cup of tea and winked at her companionably.

The wink lifted her spirits, for it did seem he was on her side.

She had barely finished drinking the tea when Kent put on his greatcoat and wound a scarf around his neck. He then picked up her cloak and passed it to her, curtly ordering her to put it on.

Within less than ten minutes she was ushered out of the front door where a carriage, probably the same one from the previous night, was waiting. Sly escorted her out to it, lifting her in, while Kent went back into the house for something. The sun had come out, and although it was weak and wintry and the trees surrounding the farmhouse were bare of leaves, it made a pretty scene.

'Did you live here when you were a boy?' she asked Sly.

He half smiled. 'Yes, I thought there was no finer place until I was your age and was expected to milk cows and help with the harvest.'

'What made you go from farmer to helping a murderer?' she asked boldly.

He hesitated for a second before replying, and she hoped that was because she'd pricked his conscience. 'I would suggest you didn't ask that sort of question,' he said, looking stern. 'Or say anything which might make Kent mad. He's got a short fuse.'

Belle's hands were tied again before the carriage left the farm, and she was placed by the window facing the front. The blind was pulled down so she couldn't see where she was going. Once again Kent sat beside her. Sly sat opposite, but he had his window blind up so he could see out.

The rolling of the carriage and the constant clip-clopping of the horses' hooves made Belle sleepy, but although her head kept drooping she was sufficiently awake to hear the two men talking quietly. Mostly they were discussing things which meant nothing to her, but she pricked up her ears when she heard Sly mention Dover and a ship.

'I'd have preferred to sail at night, and just say she was tired or sick,' Sly said.

'This is better, no risk at all. We just take her straight into the cabin and keep her there,' Sly replied.

From that little exchange Belle gathered not only that they were taking her out of the country on a ship, but that they were worried about someone seeing her and guessing she was being abducted. While the thought of being taken out of the country made her as frightened as she'd been on the previous night, knowing they were anxious pleased her. She thought that meant there might well be an opportunity to get help or indeed to escape. She continued to pretend to be asleep in the hope that they would say more. But nothing more was said, and Belle braced herself to shout and scream when a good opportunity came along.

All at once the carriage rolled on to gravel, then stopped. Belle continued to pretend to be asleep, but when she was hauled out of the carriage by Kent, she struggled with him and screamed.

'Shut your noise,' Kent hissed at her, putting his hand over her mouth.

Belle saw they weren't at Dover docks as she'd expected, but on the short drive of a small but very pretty clapboard house which was painted white with a blue front door. She'd seen such picturesque houses depicted on chocolate boxes, the garden usually bright with flowers as though in high summer. But even in January this garden was still attractive, with hedges cut into different shapes and several bushes covered in red berries.

At first glance she'd thought the house was isolated, but now as she looked around she saw it was sandwiched between two others, just a fence separating them. Clearly Kent was afraid someone would hear her and come to see what was going on. But he held on to her mouth too tightly for her to scream again as he dragged her towards the front door.

No sooner were they in the house than Kent gagged her with a white scarf. 'I can't trust you to keep quiet,' he said.

Belle was left standing in the hall, gagged and still bound hand and foot, while the two men went upstairs. She thought it must be Kent's house for he'd pulled a keyring from his pocket and selected the right key out of a bunch just by looking at it. If this was the house he'd been intending to take Millie to, she would have liked it, for it was a very pretty place.

Belle couldn't see the whole house of course, not from just standing in the hall, but what she could see was lovely and quite feminine in style. The hall had a shiny polished wood floor, with a shaggy blue rug in the middle, and there was a glass dome with little stuffed birds perched on a tree inside it. The stairs had a thick blue and gold carpet and a small crystal chandelier sparkled above her head. She shuffled forward a few steps so she could see into the sitting room, which was decorated and furnished in shades of blue and green, with hundreds of books in a floor-to-ceiling bookcase.

It didn't seem right for a brute like Kent though. Puzzled, she was just about to shuffle forward again so she could see more, when the men reappeared at the top of the stairs, carrying a big red trunk between them. Belle's heart sank because it was obvious what it was for. Shuffling backwards towards the door, she begged Sly with her eyes not to do it.

'It won't be for long,' he said apologetically.

They brought the trunk right down the stairs, then opened it in the hall.

'There's no air holes,' Sly said, looking at his companion.

'Then make a few,' Kent said churlishly and walked off towards the back of the house.

Just the thought of being locked into a small space sent Belle into a panic and she could hardly get her breath. She could see she'd need to keep her knees bent to fit in it, but if they were prepared to go to these lengths to conceal her on a ship, what were they going to do with her when they got her to France?

Kent came back up the hallway with a glass of something in his hand. He put it down on the hall table, nudged her towards a chair, then removed her gag. 'Drink this,' he ordered, holding the glass to her lips.

'What is it?' she asked.

'There's always questions with you,' he said, looking irritated. He caught hold of the back of her head and held it while pressing the glass to her lips. 'Drink!' he ordered.

Belle sensed he would hit her if she didn't comply so she

sipped at it cautiously. It tasted very like the aniseed medicine Mog gave her when she had a bad tummy ache, only very much stronger. 'Go on, all of it,' Kent prompted.

There was nothing for it but to do as he said. As she drank it down she saw Sly had a brace and bit tool in his hands and he was making small holes in the trunk's sides.

Some quarter of an hour later, having been taken upstairs by Sly to use the lavatory, Belle was carried back down and put into the trunk. Sly removed the rope around her ankles, then took off her boots. He put a blanket beneath her, placed a cushion at her head as a pillow, and then laid another blanket over her. Terrified as she was, she was also touched that Sly was trying to make her comfortable. She didn't think Kent would care if she was in pain, cold or hungry.

'You'll be fine in there,' Sly said gently. 'You'll be asleep in no time, and we'll be there by the time you wake.'

'Just tell me what you are going to do with me,' she pleaded.

'We're taking you out of the country, that's all you need to know,' he said. 'Now, shush.'

Belle was still awake when they carried the trunk with her in it back to the carriage. She felt the carriage move forward, she could hear the rumble of the wheels, smell Kent's pipe and even hear the two men's voices, although they weren't speaking loudly enough for her to hear what they were saying. But all at once she felt as if she was being sucked down and down into some dark place and was unable to stop herself.

'Try the smelling salts,' Kent suggested.

Sly pulled the small vial out of his pocket and pulled out the cork, then leaned over the open trunk and wafted it under Belle's nose. Her nose twitched and she involuntarily turned her head away. 'You gave her too much,' Sly said accusingly. 'A child like her only needs a few drops; she could have died in there.'

The ship had been delayed by three hours because of bad weather and the crossing took much longer than they had expected. Sly had tried to waken Belle once they were in the cabin on the ship. He had intended to give her a hot drink and some food, but she wouldn't wake up and he'd begun to fear she never would. They had left Calais in a hired carriage, and as it was now two in the morning, they were worried that the brothel would be closed for the night by the time they got there.

'She's coming round now,' Kent said, moving the candle he was holding closer to the trunk. 'Look, her eyelids are fluttering.'

Sly breathed a sigh of relief when he saw Kent was right. 'Belle!' he said, patting her cheek. 'Wake up now, wake up!'

He so wished he'd refused to help Kent with this girl. He might have known he hadn't told him the whole truth. Before they'd snatched her, Kent said she was a whore who'd witnessed him kill her friend and she just needed removing from London for a time. They had arrived in the carriage near the brothel half an hour before the dead girl's funeral, Kent expecting that the girl he wanted would go to the funeral. But only two older women in black clothes came out carrying a wreath, and just as Kent was saying they'd wait a few minutes and barge in and grab the girl he wanted, she came out.

Sly only saw her from a distance, enough to see she was lingering near the Ram's Head, as if waiting for someone, and there were too many people around to snatch her there. Then she went down towards the market and they couldn't follow her in the carriage. But Kent said she'd be back before the two older women returned from the funeral, and so they waited.

It was only during that wait that Kent told him of his plan to sell the girl to a French brothel. Sly wasn't averse to that, after all they'd taken girls to France and Belgium before, and he assumed that the whore in question was eighteen or more. By the time Kent announced she was coming and told Sly to get out and grab her, darkness had fallen.

It wasn't until she was in the carriage and Kent hit her for screaming that Sly saw she was little more than a child, and a very pretty, well cared for one at that. He wanted to demand that Kent stop the carriage and let her go, but Kent had pointed out earlier that if he was to be charged with murder a great many others' crimes would surface too, many of which Sly was involved in. He felt he had no choice but to go along with it, and hope that later he could talk Kent out of it.

Last night, after the girl was locked upstairs, Sly had pleaded with Kent not to go ahead with his plan. But he could not be persuaded. He said there was too much money at stake, and besides, if they did back out they'd have no choice but to kill her as she knew too much.

It was bad enough that they were taking her to France, but Sly was sickened when Kent wanted her put in the trunk. Waiting so long at Dover had been one of the most agonizing times he'd ever known. If she'd woken up and started hammering on the trunk and alerted people, Sly knew he'd be facing a very long stretch in prison.

But looking at her now in the candlelight, his heart ached and he wished to God he'd never got involved with Kent. She was very pale now, but he still thought he'd never seen a prettier girl. She had such shiny dark hair, curling delightfully all around her face, and plump red lips. But it wasn't just her looks, he admired her pluckiness too, for most girls of her age would have cried continually from the moment they were snatched. She hadn't been afraid to try to appeal to his better nature either, and now, when he thought of what lay in store for her, he wished he'd been brave enough last night to help her escape from his farmhouse.

Kent hadn't told him how much he was going to get for

her in Paris, but Sly knew that young virgins were worth a great deal to anyone who had such tastes. And one as pretty as Belle, who still had a childlike, underdeveloped body, would fetch a small fortune.

Sly's personal taste was for well-rounded, grown women with some experience and he had no time for men who wished to ravish children. But he could guess that the kind of brothel owner who was a party to this unpleasant trade was likely to be cruel and mercenary too. She would almost certainly pass Belle off as a virgin several times, then later, when the girl was just another whore, and an unwilling one at that, she was likely to be beaten, starved, drugged and constantly ridiculed until her spirit was broken.

His stomach lurched and he had to take deep breaths to avoid being sick.

'Where are we?' Belle asked as she opened her eyes.

'In France,' Sly said, and put his hand beneath her back to help her sit up in the trunk. 'Are you thirsty?'

She ran her tongue over her lips and frowned. 'I don't know. I feel very strange.'

Sly made no comment. He wished that he could be a real man and stand up to Kent. But he averted his eyes from Belle's pretty face and tried to tell himself that it wasn't his fault she was here.

It was some time before they reached a town, Belle couldn't guess how long as she'd kept dropping off to sleep, but she knew they were in a town for the carriage slowed right down, which suggested it was going along narrow streets. She could hear laughter, bursts of different kinds of music, singing and shouting, and there were also pungent cooking smells.

'Will anyone speak English where I'm going?' she asked.

'I doubt it,' Kent said, and smirked as if that thought pleased him.

Because she'd been so groggy after she woke, she didn't really feel scared, but all at once she was jolted out of her doped state by Kent's smirk. It said that he had something lined up for her that was really bad. Her terror came back tenfold, and when she looked to Sly for reassurance he wouldn't meet her eyes.

'You might as well admit where you're taking me,' she said, her voice quivering with fright. 'After all, if they don't speak any English I won't understand them, so how will I be able to do whatever it is you are planning?'

The men exchanged glances.

'Am I to be a servant?' She directed her question at Kent, and when neither of them answered she asked, 'Or is it something far worse than that?'

She waited for some response, but there was none. Sly was living up to his name and looking everywhere but at her.

'Do you think because you're leaving me here in a strange country I won't be able to find my way back to England and go to the police and tell them you killed Millie?' she said to Kent, trying to sound braver than she felt. 'I bet I could even work out where your house was, those clapboard houses are unusual. People in Seven Dials will break their normal code of silence for my mother, you know. They'll soon talk about who this man the Falcon is and his stooge called Sly. They won't like it that you snatched me off the street.'

Kent reacted then, reaching out and slapping her hard around the face. 'Shut your mouth,' he hissed. 'Where you're going you'll do exactly as they tell you or you won't live to be disobedient a second time. As for getting back to England, you won't ever get the chance.'

Belle's face stung, it felt as if it was swelling up, and she wanted to cry, but she was determined not to give him that satisfaction.

'Don't be so sure,' she said.

He moved to hit her again, but Sly leapt forward and stopped him. 'Don't damage the merchandise,' he said.

That word 'merchandise' told Belle everything. She was just a commodity to these men, like a bale of cloth, a crate of whisky or a joint of meat, to be sold on to someone else. What's more, she could guess who they would be selling her to. She might have only recently worked out what brothels were really about, but she knew with utter certainty she was going to one. She wanted to believe that she would just be a maid to the girls, as Mog was, but no one would smuggle someone on a ship and drive them so far just for that. So the reality was that she was being sold to be a whore!

She wanted to scream out her terror and to lash out at the two men, but she knew that would only antagonize Kent further and he might even throttle her if he was mad enough.

Mog had always claimed she had more tricks up her sleeve than a magician, so she took a deep breath to calm herself. She wasn't going to be killed, and she didn't think anyone would beat her, not if they wanted her to look good. All she had to do was use her wits to find a way to escape. Not protesting or making a fuss would be a start – maybe then they'd give up watching her constantly.

Only a few minutes later the carriage stopped. Kent got out first and reached up to lift Belle down, holding her arm very tightly so she couldn't run off. Sly followed immediately. They were in a gloomy, gaslit terrace of tall houses, but around fifty yards away down the street light spilled out on to the cobbled street from the windows of a bar. The place was almost pulsating with music, dancing feet and laughter.

'No one sleeps here, it seems,' Sly said, and he sounded relieved.

Kent said something to the driver. Belle presumed he was speaking French because she didn't understand a word. Then, with Kent still holding her right arm and Sly her left, they led her down a narrow alley and into a small square. Belle looked questioningly at Sly, but he turned his face away.

Another small bar in the square was still open, golden light spilling out from the small windows, but all the other shops were closed and there was no one around except a couple of men staggering drunkenly across the square. Simultaneously both men tightened their grip on Belle's arms and Kent slapped his other hand over her mouth.

The house the men led her to was in the corner of the square and set back from its neighbours. The square was dimly lit by just a couple of gaslights but even so Belle could see the house well enough to feel chilled. It was larger than most of its neighbours, with four floors and pointed, gothic-looking eaves. The windows were long and narrow and most of them appeared to be shuttered. Sitting on the two posts which flanked the five or six steps up to the front porch were stone griffins. A dim red light shone above the front door in the gothic-style porch. It reminded Belle of a witch's house she had seen in a picture book when she was small.

The door was opened immediately they rang by a big man in evening clothes. He looked down at Belle in some surprise, but Kent spoke in rapid French and the man indicated they were to come in.

Belle could hear music, chatter and laughter coming from the room on their left, but as the door was closed she couldn't see who was in there. The man who had let them in disappeared into the room on her right; Belle got the briefest glimpse of a dark blue patterned carpet, but nothing else.

Waiting in the wide hall with an ornately carved staircase straight ahead of her, Belle noticed that the hall and stair carpet was threadbare, and that the dark wallpaper was stained with age. Only a chandelier above her was impressive; it was twice the size of the one back home, and the crystals were quivering and twinkling in the draught from the front door, but no one had bothered to fill all the holders with candles. Belle found the paintings on the walls very odd; they were all of naked women, but the artist had given them animal faces.

The doorman came out again and said something to the men, and still holding Belle's arm in a vicelike grip, Kent led her into the room, with Sly taking up the rear.

Mog would have described the woman at a large, highly polished desk as 'hatchet-faced'. No smile of welcome broke her long, thin face. She was tall, slender and very elegantly dressed in a midnight-blue taffeta dress, her dark hair elaborately curled and piled up on top of her head, but the eyes studying Belle were dead, like those of a fish on a marble slab at the fishmonger's.

She spoke quickly, using her hands to express herself. Belle couldn't understand a word, and she didn't think Kent understood it all either, for every now and then he would stop the woman who would sigh deeply and roll her eyes, then repeat what she'd said more slowly. He whispered something to Sly a couple of times too, but Belle had a feeling this was so she wouldn't hear, rather than him hiding something from the woman.

They eventually appeared to come to some sort of agreement, for the woman came round her desk to shake their hands. She then came closer to Belle, who was still standing between the two men, put her hand under her chin and lifted it to study her face more closely. '*Très jolie*,' she said, and Belle guessed that was a compliment for both the men smiled.

There was a little more talking, and the woman poured the two men a brandy each, then she rang a little bell on her desk.

An older woman with greying hair in a plain black dress came in; Belle felt she must be a maid or housekeeper.

The woman at the desk rattled out some instructions and the older woman turned to Belle, smiled and held out her hand. Belle ignored her, even though the woman reminded her a little of Mog.

'Madame Sondheim wants you to go with her housekeeper who is called Delphine,' Kent translated. 'She will give you some supper and put you to bed. She expects that you are very tired and hungry. Madame will speak to you later today when you are rested.'

'You are leaving me here then?' Belle directed her question at Sly. She hated Kent, but Sly didn't seem anywhere near as cruel and ruthless, and he was at least English and her last contact with home.

'Yes, Belle.' As Sly spoke, his voice sounded a bit odd, as though he had something in his throat. 'Do as you are told and you'll be all right.'

'Please could you get a message to my mother that I'm well?' she begged him. 'Only she and Mog will worry.'

Even as she made that plea, she knew how absurd it was. Two men who could snatch a young girl and sell her to a brothel weren't going to lose any sleep about her mother's anxiety. Tomorrow, though, when it was light, she'd find some way to escape.

But as Delphine caught firmly hold of her wrist and pulled her towards the door, Belle saw Sly's sorrowful expression. 'Please, Sly?' she called out. 'Just a note through the door, anything so they know I'm alive!'

Chapter Nine

After his talk with Jimmy and Garth, Noah Bayliss spent the rest of the day in their neighbourhood talking to people. The girls at Annie's were disappointing; they knew nothing personal about Kent, they couldn't even agree in their descriptions of him. But they were all unanimous in that he was a cold, hard man who thought nothing of knocking women around.

Elsewhere Noah had been told that the man mostly known as the Falcon managed properties near Bethnal Green, and the tenements here in Seven Dials known as the Core. Everyone looked nervous even saying that much about him and several people told Noah he shouldn't go looking for trouble.

Later, at five in the evening, Noah called into the *Herald* offices in Fleet Street and had a word with the sub-editor, Ernie Greensleeve. He had always admired the wild-haired, skeletally thin man for his enthusiasm for investigative journalism. Ernie liked nothing better than digging out sordid truth, and the more gruesome or tragic that truth was, or the better-known those involved were, the more excited he became.

Noah told him the gist of the story about Millie's murder and Belle's disappearance and asked Ernie where he could go next for information about Kent.

'I've heard rumours about the man,' Ernie said, scratching his head and making his wild hair even wilder. 'A couple of years ago there was a whisper that he was involved in trafficking girls. But I drew a blank in every line of enquiry. That could've meant the whisper wasn't true, or that he had friends in high places, or even that he's just smart enough to leave no trail. But I'll ask around again and see if there's any change.'

'Have you got any way of finding out if the police are investigating properly?' Noah asked. 'After all it is a murder, and now an abduction which may lead to a second murder. Surely a serious crime can't just be brushed under the carpet, not even if the murder victim was a prostitute?'

'One of the biggest problems this country needs to face is the incompetence of the police force,' Ernie said with a sigh. 'It makes it so easy for corruption to flourish. We've got fingerprinting now, which should have doubled the number of convictions a year, but so far it's not happening. I'll see what I can do though, and you carry on trying to get folk to talk around Seven Dials.'

When Noah came into the Ram's Head at seven in the evening, Jimmy thought he looked tired and dejected.

'No luck then?' he said.

'Well, I did discover he's involved in some slum housing in Bethnal Green and the Core. As both places are hell come to earth, that's at least evidence he's got no scruples about human suffering.'

The Core was the name given to the terrible tenement building here in Seven Dials. Jimmy had a kind of horrified fascination with the place. It was said there were as many as twelve people sleeping in many of the rooms and the sanitation consisted of a tap in each yard and a latrine which was a health hazard. He had always wondered why the place was known by such an odd name, but no one seemed to know. Uncle Garth had said he thought someone had just said it was 'rotten to the core' and the name had stuck.

Jimmy couldn't imagine how anyone could bear to live in such a dreadful place. They might be the destitute, the old, the drunks, the sick and the feeble-minded who lived there, plus a fair proportion of criminals and children who had either run away or been turned out of their homes, but no one should have to live that way. They begged on the streets, scavenged or picked pockets and the place was a hotbed of disease.

'What d'you mean he's involved?' Jimmy asked. 'Is he the landlord, or just a rent collector?'

'That I don't know,' Noah said. 'But I've got someone at the paper looking into it.'

Noah stayed in the bar talking until around half past nine, and after he'd gone home, Jimmy went to help Peg Leg Alf as he washed up some glasses. Alf had lost his leg in the Crimea War back in the 1850s, when he was little more than a boy, and was then invalided out of the army. He had spent the rest of his adult life as a beggar and doing odd jobs for anyone who would take him on.

Alf lived in the Core. The man was around seventy and he shared a room with several others in a similar plight to himself. If it wasn't for the kindness of inn keepers like Garth who let him wash a few glasses and sweep the floor in return for a hot meal and a shilling or two, he wouldn't be able to survive.

'Do you know this man they call the Falcon?' Jimmy asked as he dried some glasses for Alf.

'Aye, and a nasty piece of work he is too,' Alf said, then looked over his shoulder as if the man might be there. 'You don't want no truck with him, son.'

'Why are you scared of him?' Jimmy asked.

Alf pulled a face. 'When you're my age and a man can throw you out on to the street because he doesn't like the look of you, it's as well to be scared of him.'

'He's your landlord?' Jimmy asked, hoping Alf would tell him more.

'I don't know if he actually owns the place, but he certainly sends out the slimy bastard who comes to collect the rent. He's got his spies everywhere, anyone gets in another person to help with the rent, and next thing you know you've got to pay more.

I didn't have the rent one night and he said if I didn't take it to the office the next day I'd find myself out on the street.'

'Did you get it by then?' Jimmy asked. Alf was so thin and frail that he looked as though a gust of wind would blow him over. He usually smelled bad, but he couldn't help that when he lived in such an awful place. And Alf was a good man, honest as the day.

'Yeah, I got it to him.' Alf rolled his eyes. 'He was sitting there with his feet up on the desk, lording it over me. Bet he's never done a real day's work in his life.'

'So where is his office?' Jimmy asked.

Jimmy could hardly contain his joy at finding out that Kent's office was in Mulberry Buildings in Long Acre. Knowing his uncle wouldn't approve of him breaking and entering, not even the office of a murderer, Jimmy waited until the bar was closed for the night and Garth gone to bed, then he crept out the back way.

Long Acre was near Covent Garden market, a street which was mainly offices and small businesses rather than homes. Because the market was at its busiest during the night, and there were many young lads working there, Jimmy felt confident he wouldn't look suspicious being around that area. He found Mulberry Buildings easily, and when he looked at the signboard outside it, he noted that most of the tenants were printers and allied tradesmen. Hoping this meant the security would be lax as the premises were hardly likely to be attractive to burglars, he went round to the back alley to try to find a way in.

He couldn't believe his luck when he found a window open just a crack on the ground floor. But sadly, once he was inside the printer's, he found the internal door that led to the rest of the building was locked. He had taken the precaution of bringing his uncle's spare bunch of keys with him, but although he tried them all, none would open the door, so he had to climb back out through the window and try elsewhere.

When he reached the second floor by shinning up the drainpipe he saw a small transom window open within easy reach. He climbed over on to the sill, put his hand in the small window and opened the larger one beneath it.

He found himself in what seemed to be a storeroom. When he lit the candle he'd brought in his pocket he saw hundreds of boxes of printing paper stacked in piles all around the room. He wriggled through them to the door, and to his delight this wasn't locked.

The storeroom led on to a narrow landing on which there were five other doors and as he walked along the landing he saw a small sign on the one at the end to the front of the building. Holding his candle closer, he read, 'Kent Management'.

The door was locked and he had to put his candle down to try the keys on his bunch. To his disappointment, again none of them worked. But as he bent down to pick up the candle, intending to give up and leave the building, he noticed the doormat. Remembering this was where his mother always left the key for him, he pulled it back, and there to his surprise and excitement was a key.

Once in the office he felt very scared. There were no blinds at the window and a policeman out on his beat would immediately be suspicious of a small light in a closed office. But on the other hand there wasn't much to search – the room held only a large desk, two chairs and a wooden filing cabinet almost identical to the one his uncle kept all the paperwork in at the pub.

The drawers in the desk revealed nothing more than pens, pencils, a receipt book and various other notebooks which, although written in, had no meaning to Jimmy. He turned his attentions to the filing cabinet.

There was little in these, just a couple of folders with some papers in them, a bottle of whisky and what could only be a knuckleduster, as it had four holes to slot fingers through. He tried the spiky iron thing on his hand and realized it was clearly made for a grown man with big hands. It made him shudder, for the damage it could do to someone's face was too horrible to contemplate.

He lifted out the folders and taking them to the candle on the desk quickly flicked through them. In the main they were letters of complaint from various sources about the state of the Core buildings, some of them dating back twenty and thirty years and addressed to a Mr F. Waldegrave. He assumed this was the actual owner of the building, although there were some similar in tone with recent dates, and addressed to Kent. There were substantial numbers of letters relating to various properties in Bethnal Green too, again complaints, mostly about rat infestation, sanitation and overcrowding.

But then he found a letter from a solicitor's in Chancery Lane, dated just a year ago, which was nothing to do with the Core, but about the purchase of a house in Charing in Kent. This was addressed to Mr F. J. Waldegrave.

Jimmy pocketed this letter. It wasn't recent enough to be missed and he needed to study it more carefully. As there appeared to be nothing more of interest in the office he decided to get home.

He didn't leave the same way as he came in, but walked down the stairs and out through the front door which conveniently had one of the new types of lock, which needed no key to get out, and locked it again behind him.

At eight the following morning Jimmy slipped out of the pub, despite not getting to bed until nearly three. His uncle rarely surfaced before ten and Jimmy hoped to get to see Noah Bayliss and be back home long before that.

It was very cold and he ran most of the way to keep warm.

Mrs Dumas, Noah's landlady, seemed rather surprised at her lodger having a visitor so early, but said Noah was having his breakfast and asked if Jimmy would like to sit with him over a cup of tea.

'I broke into the Falcon's lair last night,' Jimmy whispered to Noah the minute he had been shown into the breakfast room and Mrs Dumas had gone off to the kitchen. 'I found this,' he said, passing the solicitor's letter to him.

'But it's addressed to a Mr Waldegrave,' Noah said as he scanned the contents.

'I think that's Kent's real name,' Jimmy said excitedly, keeping his voice down as there was another lodger sitting at the far end of the table. 'You see, I found really old letters of complaint about the Core addressed to a Mr F. J. Waldegrave, and then more recent ones to Kent. So I reckon Waldegrave is his real name, not Kent at all, and the earlier letters of complaint were addressed to his father, or another relative. But he don't have much imagination in picking an alias, do he?' The boy sniggered. 'Not if he lives in Kent! I wonder why he needs to have a false name?'

Noah smiled. 'To do dark deeds under. Maybe I should call myself Warren Street because I live near there.'

'Or I could be Mr Ramshead,' Jimmy laughed. 'But look, we've got his address – Pear Tree Cottage, High Street, Charing. He might be holding Belle there.'

'I can't somehow imagine it being that easy,' Noah said slowly and thoughtfully. 'He wouldn't take her to a place he knew people could find out about.'

'Maybe not, but we can tell the police that's where he lives. They could check it out.'

Noah looked at young Jimmy's excited, hopeful face and wished he could assure him that the police would act to find Belle. But Noah's experience in calling at Bow Street had not been encouraging, in fact he'd encountered total disinterest in the girl's disappearance. The truth of the matter was that the police didn't see a whore's daughter as being of any importance.

But that wasn't all. When Noah insisted Belle had been taken by the man dubbed the Falcon, the police sergeant pretended that name meant nothing to him. He wasn't a convincing liar, for he couldn't meet Noah's eyes, and he became quite belligerent in the way men did when covering up something. As almost every adult in Seven Dials had heard of the Falcon, even if they'd never met him, it was inconceivable that a policeman wouldn't know something about him.

Under the circumstances, to go back to the police station with evidence of where the man had a house was likely to be self-defeating. If this sergeant was in Kent's pay, as Noah suspected, he would tip the man off, and that could result in Jimmy and his uncle being targeted by hired thugs.

'I think we need to talk to your uncle first and get him on our side,' Noah said, giving himself time to think this through. 'But we won't tell him you broke into those offices. We'd better say it was me.'

'Could you come to the pub today?' Jimmy begged.

'Not now,' Noah said, then nodded at Mrs Dumas who was coming in with a fresh pot of tea and toast for them. 'I could come around six if Garth could speak to me then.'

'I'll make sure he does,' Jimmy said. He grabbed a slice of toast and buttered it while Mrs Dumas poured his tea. He didn't give the tea a chance to cool down, but drank it eagerly, then got up to go, the toast in his hand. 'I've got to get back. But what if he's already killed her, Noah?'

The stricken expression on the boy's face made Noah's heart swell with sympathy.

'I still think he would've killed her in a back alley here if that was his intention,' he replied with as much conviction as he could muster. 'You did well to get this letter, Jimmy, it was very brave of you.'

Noah continued to eat his breakfast after Jimmy had gone, but he had little enthusiasm for it. He was speaking the truth when he said he didn't think Belle had been killed, but he couldn't bring himself to tell the lad what he suspected was going to happen to her. Nor could he spell out why the police weren't going to help to find Kent and punish him both for killing Millie and this abduction.

Sometime before Noah had met Millie, he received information about several serious crimes where the person arrested was suddenly released from custody and all charges dropped. There was some compelling evidence that police officers had been bribed, and witnesses to the crime threatened. Noah had written what Ernie Greensleeve said was a superb article on the subject, but when he took it to Mr Wilson, the editor, he said he couldn't print it because it was too inflammatory.

Noah argued that the general public had a right to know there was corruption in the police force, but the editor responded by reminding him there were plenty of other eager young journalists only too happy to take his place. Noah had to back down then. He knew that if he attempted to sell the story to one of the more sensational papers, he would never write for the *Herald* again.

Later that same morning Noah was sent out to interview a fruit wholesaler in Covent Garden. It was a rather amusing story, for a tarantula had crawled out of some bananas and on to one of the employees, a portly middle-aged man. It was spotted sitting on his shoulder by another woman employee who nearly fainted with shock. Once the poor man realized what was sitting on him, he was stricken with terror, but a young boy of only eleven who helped with odd jobs stepped forward fearlessly with a glass and a piece of stiff card and scooped it off him.

The victim passed out on the floor when the young boy

gleefully tried to show off his trophy to everyone in the wholesalers. Eventually the spider was transferred into a pot with a lid, and a message was sent to London Zoo for some-one to come and collect it.

All this had happened early in the morning, but by the time the story had reached Fleet Street and Noah had been dispatched to interview the people involved, the spider had been collected and the victim had downed so many brandies he wasn't making a great deal of sense. But the boy was the hero of the story anyway and was thrilled he was going to be mentioned by name in the newspaper.

As Noah was in Seven Dials he decided to go and talk to Annie Cooper before he went back to Fleet Street. He had spoken to her briefly the previous day, along with everyone else in the house, but now, as he had some new develop-ments to tell her of, thanks to Jimmy, he hoped that by passing them on, she might respond with something she had kept back before.

He went round to the back of the house in Jake's Court and knocked on the door. It was opened by Miss Davis wear-ing a flour-splattered apron.

'Good morning, Miss Davis,' Noah said politely. 'I'm sorry to trouble you again so soon, but I've found out a bit more about this man Kent. I wanted to tell Mrs Cooper about it.'

'Call me Mog, no one calls me Miss Davis,' she said, urging him to come in. 'Annie's in a bad way, I'm afraid.'

Judging by Mog's red-rimmed eyes she had been crying a great deal herself, but despite this she said she'd just made a pot of tea and offered Noah a cup. She had been in the middle of rolling out pastry on the table, and there was a good smell of stewing beef filling the room. She urged him to sit by the stove and asked him if she could get him something to eat.

Sitting there in the warm kitchen with Mog fussing round him, Noah could now understand why Belle hadn't become fully aware of the nature of her mother's business. The basement was entirely separate from the rest of the house, a cosy, homely place, and Mog a kindly, motherly woman. On the previous day she had shown him Belle's little bedroom, where there were old dolls, books and games on a shelf, the bed covered with a colourful quilt, and though it was a dark room with only a tiny window, it was pretty and reflected that she was a well-loved and cared-for girl.

'Annie ain't normally one for letting her feelings show,' Mog said as she offered him an iced bun with his tea. 'But this has hit her so hard I'm frightened for her. She needs to talk to someone about it, and if you've got a bit of news, that just might help her to open up.'

Leaving Noah to drink his tea, Mog went up the stairs to speak to her mistress. She returned a few minutes later and said he could go up.

Annie was in the room behind the parlour, which Millie had always referred to as 'the office'. It was in fact Annie's bedroom, but the room was L-shaped and the bed was in the smaller section and hidden by a fancy screen. It was a very feminine room, with a rose pink velvet couch in front of the fire. The small round table, the chairs and Annie's desk were all of dainty black lacquerware and hand-painted with pink and green flowers and leaves. There were many pictures on the walls, all romantic ones, whether they depicted a soldier and his lass taking a walk across a cornfield, or a woman waiting on the quay to meet her sweetheart off a ship.

Millie had said she often had tea in here by the fire with Annie in the afternoons and she'd said when she had a home of her own she wanted a room just like it. Noah could understand why now. It was a warm, welcoming room which hinted that Annie was not as stern, cold and humourless as she appeared.

But the Annie sitting here by the fire, barely able to turn her head to greet him, was changed from the elegant, haughty woman he'd met on several occasions while visiting Millie before. Even the previous day she'd managed to maintain her cold and aloof manner and indeed her elegant appearance. If Noah hadn't been told by Mog then that Annie was distraught at her daughter's disappearance, he would never have known it, for she showed no emotion.

She couldn't have looked more different today. She was grey-complexioned and gaunt, as if she'd lost a lot of weight suddenly, and her eyes were sunken and dead. Her severe black dress with its high neck and leg of mutton sleeves made her look far older than she was, and her hair, which until today Noah had only ever seen in artfully piled curls, was now pulled brutally back from her face, with streaks of grey very noticeable amongst the brown.

'I am sorry to disturb you again so soon,' Noah said. 'But I thought you might like to know that I've found out a little more about the man Kent.'

There was a slight flicker of hope in Annie's eyes as she looked at him. 'Then I am indebted to you,' she said, but her voice was flat and expressionless as if speaking was an effort.

'It wasn't just me, but Jimmy too. He's Garth Franklin's nephew at the Ram's Head. He's as keen as I am to try and find your Belle and bring that monster to trial for killing Millie.'

'Mog told me he was Belle's friend. Please pass on my appreciation for his help.'

Noah thought it odd she didn't ask more about how Jimmy knew her daughter, or even jump out of her seat to demand the news he'd brought with him. He thought she was a very cold fish.

He went on to explain how he knew where the man lived now, and that in his opinion Kent had the police in the palm of his hand. 'Short of entrapping the man and forcing him to tell us of Belle's whereabouts, I really don't know how to proceed,' he admitted. 'But I can't really believe he has killed her. I am absolutely sure he is holding her alive somewhere.'

'Sometimes that can be worse,' Annie said, half turning on the couch to look at him. 'I have discovered from my informants, as I'm sure you have too, that he is known to be a procurer of young girls.'

'That was said by a couple of people,' Noah admitted. 'But they found him responsible for so many ills, I really hoped that one was exaggeration.'

'It is one of the most lucrative sides of our trade.' She sighed and turned pain-filled eyes on Noah. 'It disgusts me, and I have never had any girl working for me who didn't come here willingly, and old enough to know what she was doing. But the thought of my Belle being used that way is too much to bear.'

Noah saw that her lower lip was quivering and she looked close to breaking down. 'I'm sorry, Mrs Cooper.' He reached out and took her hand to comfort her. 'But Jimmy tells me that she is a brave and clever girl, so maybe she'll escape it.'

'I was brave and clever too, I could be a little hell cat,' she said, her voice cracking. 'But they captured me too, imprisoned and starved me. Even without the beating or withholding food, no young girl, however plucky, is any match for an aroused fully grown male.'

'So it happened to you?' Noah asked gently. She was shaking with emotion and he didn't know whether it was better for her to talk it all out, or if he should try to move her on to something else. 'I am so very sorry.'

'I was just a little younger than Belle and I so much wanted to see London that I begged a ride on the carter's wagon to get there,' she explained. 'You know how you are as a youngster, you don't think things through. I wandered around looking in all the shop windows, and suddenly it was getting dark and I had no idea how to get back. I began to cry and a woman came up to me and asked what was wrong. She looked just like any other wife or mother, not someone to be wary of. So I told her how it was, and she said I could come home with her and she'd show me the Tower of London in the morning before she arranged for someone to take me home.

'Well, I did see the Tower of London the next day, but it was through a crack in the boarded-up windows of an old warehouse on the river.'

'She locked you up?' Noah exclaimed.

Annie nodded grimly. 'One minute she was promising all the things she was going to show me the next day, the next I was locked in that place. I screamed and cried but she shouted back through the door that there was no one to hear me. She left me there with no food, just a straw-filled sack to sleep on and one thin blanket. I was so cold that night I couldn't sleep. The next day, when a man came to give me some food, I tried to fight him. So he gave me a thrashing and took the food and the blanket away. I didn't see him for another three days, by when I was ready to promise anything just for food and a blanket. Isolation, starvation and fear are the three things which can annihilate even the toughest person's will.'

Noah was deeply shocked. 'Especially when you are young,' he agreed. 'I doubt I'd last one day without food or warm blankets.'

Annie nodded her agreement. 'Well, finally they came and got me and took me over to Tooley Street. It's still a brothel now, though I didn't know what it was then. I was bathed, my hair washed and brushed, and I was put in a clean shift, then taken down to a larger room with a big bed on the floor below. They had given me something to drink that made me feel a bit woozy, but when the first man came into the room and started in on me it hurt so much I screamed.' She paused, her eyes welling up with tears. 'He liked me screaming,' she whispered. 'He really loved that.'

'I am so sorry,' Noah said with the utmost sincerity. He felt ashamed that he was male and thought about bedding women so often.

'It didn't end with just him. There were three others too that night. The woman who'd seen to bathing me came into the room after each man to wash me. Then the next came in. I thought I would die that night, for surely no child could suffer such pain and degradation and survive.'

Noah put his hand on her shoulder as she broke down in tears. He thought of taking her in his arms as he would almost any other woman who was breaking her heart, but he was afraid to overstep the mark.

'They were what most people would call gentlemen,' she spat out viciously. 'They had good clothes and linen, rings on their fingers. They were probably professional men, lawyers, doctors, politicians, scientists. Intelligent men with money and almost certainly with wives and children at home. But they found their pleasure in raping a girl too young to even know what the act was.'

Noah couldn't speak, for the picture she'd painted was too awful to contemplate.

'It goes on everywhere,' she said, her eyes burning with anger. 'Every single day there are pretty young girls going missing, usually from the slums and back streets where their parents don't have the power or money to have a voice. But there's plenty of little country girls like I was too. Sometimes these girls end up dead, killed once their usefulness is over, or sent abroad. The rest are ruined, they can't return to a respectable life, they are too damaged.' She paused to gather herself.

'And that is what I'm afraid Belle is going through right now,' she went on, her voice sharp with pain. 'Her life is going to become a replica of mine. And it's all my fault. I should've sent her away to school. Why didn't I?'

'Because you loved her and wanted her near you?' Noah suggested.

'That is the truth, but the saddest thing is that I never showed it.' Annie sobbed. 'She was always closer to Mog than me. That was the real curse of what those men did to me all those years ago – I couldn't love, I was an empty shell with no feelings, and I stayed working as a whore because I felt it was the only thing open to me.'

Noah sighed deeply. He had a feeling Annie had never said all this to anyone before, and he wondered if she would despise herself afterwards for revealing so much.

'I'll do whatever I can to get Belle back and see that bastard hang for what he's done,' Noah said fiercely. 'Young Jimmy is beside himself with worry about her, he really cares, you know, and his uncle will do what he can too. I feel I haven't done anything yet, but come what may I will get my newspaper to speak out about the police sheltering criminals. And maybe if we told people about these beasts that abduct young girls and children they would rise up and wish to lynch such men.'

Annie looked at him with tear-filled eyes for what seemed a very long time. 'You have helped already, Noah,' she said eventually, wiping her eyes with a lace-trimmed handkerchief. 'You let me say what was in my heart. It had been stuck inside for so long that it was poisoning me. Thank you.'

Chapter Ten

Belle was confused. She had been in the house in France now for four days. She was locked into a room at the top of the building like a prisoner, yet the two women who came in and out to bring her food, put coal on the fire, empty the slop bucket and bring water to wash in were kind to her.

They didn't speak English, but the way they looked at her, brushed her hair, and tutted when she hadn't eaten the food they'd brought, showed they cared about her. She wondered if they were whores – they didn't appear to be as they wore dark blue plain dresses, caps and aprons. Back at Annie's the girls wandered around in a state of undress most of the day.

Belle had tried with sign language and miming to ask them what was going to happen to her, and to try to make them understand she wanted to write a letter to her mother, but they just shook their heads as if they had no idea what she meant.

So Belle fluctuated between thinking that she was like the children in Hansel and Gretel, being kind of fattened up before being presented to a man. Or alternatively, and ideally, that nothing was happening because Madame Sondheim hadn't liked her or considered her unsuitable and was planning to send her back to England as soon as she could arrange it.

The room she was being kept in was an attic room, and the ceiling sloped down sharply to the floor by the window. It was small, rather dark and simply furnished with just a small iron bed, a washstand and a little table and chair under the window. But it was warm and quite comfortable, though she found the food she was brought a bit strange. There was also a stack of jigsaw puzzles which helped to make the time go a little faster.

Escape was absolutely impossible. On the very first morning Belle had climbed out of the window to see if she could get down to the street that way, but once on the window sill she found it was a sheer drop down the back of the house. Looking up at the roof, she was far too afraid of trying to climb up those slippery old tiles to see if there was a way down the front of the house. Besides, if there had been a way she doubted Madame Sondheim would have left the window unbarred.

Listening at the door revealed nothing. She would hear voices and footsteps from time to time, but the people always spoke in French. During the evening she could hear music and occasional guffaws of laughter coming from downstairs, the same kind of sounds she'd heard back in London. But at home Mog had always come down to her a couple of times during the evening, the last time usually to tuck her into bed and kiss her goodnight. But here no one came up to see her after she'd had her supper, and twice the oil in the lamp had run out during the evening so she'd been forced to leave her jigsaw and get into bed.

They usually brought her supper quite late in the evening; once she'd heard the church clock strike eight as she was eating. So on her fifth night, when her supper was brought well before it was dark, she sensed something was finally going to happen.

The soup was vegetable, very tasty, with some chunks of bread, followed by a fish pie and boiled potatoes. There was the usual glass of red cordial too, but tonight it tasted different. She thought perhaps they'd put some wine in it, and she drank it down anyway.

When the door opened again she assumed it was one of the maids to collect her tray. It was the shorter of the two maids, with Delphine the housekeeper who had brought her up here on the first night. She spoke in very fast French and when Belle merely stared back at her, not understanding, she beckoned, as if to come with her.

Belle was pleased to have an opportunity to get out of the room, but also afraid of what it might mean. Delphine took her down two flights of stairs and led her into a bathroom.

The bath was already run, and the two women began undressing Belle.

'I can do that myself,' she said, irritably pushing them off her. 'Leave me be!'

They had taken her own dark blue serge dress away her first night here and given her a much nicer lightweight green one with a frill around the hem, and a collar and sash in a green spotted silky material. Scared as she was at the time, she was pleased by the dress because it was very pretty and it made her think they wouldn't do anything bad to her if they cared about how she looked. Now she saw on the bathroom stool what appeared to be a clean, lace-trimmed white chemise and drawers, so maybe they were intending to take her out somewhere.

Belle didn't like the way the women stayed with her till she was naked, clearly intending to wash her like a small child. But, unable to make herself understood, she had to let it go and allow it.

They scrubbed her as if she was a filthy tramp brought in from the street. Then, once they'd pulled out the bath plug, they rinsed her hair with several large ewers of warm water. It was only as they were drying her vigorously that Belle suddenly realized she'd been drugged. It wasn't like the sleeping draught Kent had given her, she didn't feel as if she was going to fall asleep. But she felt sort of numb and carefree, so much so that she started to giggle helplessly when the two women began drying her and helping her into the new clean underwear.

It took ages for them to dry her hair. They rubbed and rubbed it with a dry towel, then twisted her curls till they were like long black corkscrews all around her face. Someone shouted something outside the door, and Delphine shouted back.

Clearly the call had been a hurry up, for suddenly the two women seemed flustered and concerned that Belle's hair was still damp. But they forgot to help her put on her dress again, just opened the bathroom door and, holding each of her hands, hurried her barefoot up the stairs again in her underwear.

Four days earlier, when she arrived here, Belle had noticed very little about the house other than that the carpet was threadbare, but then she was scared and most of the gaslights had been turned off. They were all lit now, however, and she saw that the house was much bigger than she'd imagined, with five or six doors on every landing, and that the wallpaper was so old and stained it was impossible to see a pattern on it any longer.

The two women opened a door on the third floor, inside which was a short passage as if it led to a separate wing of the house. At the end of this passage was another door.

Delphine opened it, and inside was Madame Sondheim. Delphine said something which appeared to be an apology, gave Belle a little push forward and left, shutting the door behind her.

It was another sparsely furnished room. There was an iron bed which was unmade except for a sheet and a couple of pillows, shutters at the windows, a washstand and nothing else. But while the room in the attic appeared quite cosy because it was small with sloping ceilings, this room was big and stark.

Sitting on the edge of the bed was a big man with a fat, florid face. He was wearing a grey suit with a grey and black striped waistcoat beneath it and he was smiling at her.

Madame was clearly introducing her for Belle recognized her name. She had butterflies in her stomach now and she tried to run back to the door, but Madame got there first and waved a key at her to show it was locked already.

Without any further ado, Madame turned to Belle and yanked the new chemise off over her head. With another swift movement the drawers came off too and she was left completely naked.

Belle began to cry and wrapped her arms around her naked body, but Madame slapped her hands away, then ran her hands down over Belle's body, talking all the while, the way Belle had observed horse traders do when they were trying to sell an animal.

But the man's expression was what was really frightening. He was looking at Belle as if he hadn't eaten for weeks and she was a hot steak dinner. His eyes were gleaming, he had sweat on his forehead and he was licking his lips. Madame had finished talking about her and she pulled Belle over to the man, then pushed her down on to the bed.

With one last remark which Belle felt meant 'She's all yours now', Madame was gone, locking the door behind her.

'*Ma chérie*,' the man said, and Belle knew it was an endearment, for the two maids had used it. He bent over her on the bed and kissed her on the lips. Belle turned her head away because he had a nasty smell on his breath and whiskers on his chin. But that didn't seem to deter him for his hand was on her private parts and he was pulling the lips apart and peering at her.

All at once he was flinging his clothes off like a man possessed until he was down to just a woolly undershirt. His legs were short, fat, very white and hairy, but much more terrifying to Belle was his penis because it looked huge, with a glistening purple tip.

She tried to wriggle off the other side of the bed as he got on, but he grabbed hold of her arm and hauled her back, opening her legs and kneeling between them while he poked his fingers inside her with one hand, holding her arm tightly with the other. She was crying but he didn't seem to care for he was muttering things as he touched her intimately and seemed as though he was in a world of his own. He kept playing with his penis too, rubbing it up and down and putting the tip on her in a way that revolted her.

But suddenly he was pushing it into her, grabbing hold of her legs and pulling them up, while thrusting himself further in.

Nothing in all her short life had hurt that much. It was as though he was tearing her in two. She screamed and screamed but he didn't even seem to hear her. It was only when she tried desperately to get free that he actually took notice, and slapped her hard on the buttocks, pulling her even closer to him. He was talking constantly, at least saying the same words over and over again so she assumed they were dirty ones. But then his movements became faster and faster, the bed springs protesting almost as loudly, and the pain increased to the point where Belle felt she would die of it. She couldn't even scream any more, her mouth and throat were too dry. She cried for her mother and Mog and prayed to God to make it end quickly.

At last it was over and he sank down on to the bed, sweating like a pig. Belle got away and crouched down in the corner as far away from him as she could get. She had blood running down her legs and there was a horrible stickiness and smell too. She was shaking all over and she felt sick.

The man fell asleep almost immediately. Belle could hear him snoring, but she was unable to move from her crouched position in the corner. Then the door opened and in came

Madame. She looked at the man on the bed, and then down at Belle. She said something but Belle didn't understand, so she caught hold of her wrist and pulled her up.

The woman's eyes ran down Belle's body but her hard expression didn't soften at all, she just turned to the door where a wrap hung behind it on a nail, took it down and gave it to Belle to put on. With that she picked up the new set of underwear, caught hold of Belle's wrist again and made it clear she was taking her back to her room.

There was not one kind word. Back in the room Madame pointed to the washstand and mimed washing herself. Then she turned and left, locking the door behind her.

Later, washed and in bed wearing the nightdress she'd been given, Belle was too hurt and shocked even to cry. She just lay there, the aching and soreness inside her making it impossible to think of anything else. Seeing Millie doing that act had been horrible, but she'd been able to reconcile herself to it in a way by thinking Millie had chosen to be a whore, as all her mother's girls had. It was just a job to them, not as bad as being a skivvy, and better paid, with shorter hours, than most jobs.

But it must have been like this for all of them the first time. How did they keep going after it? How could they dress up in their best frock, do their hair and smile at the next man who wanted to do this to them?

All the following day Belle stayed in bed, crying into her pillow. The maids came in with food, and the younger one said some words which Belle was sure were ones of sympathy, but she didn't feel in the least comforted. Then again after the supper which she hadn't eaten, she was taken downstairs and pushed into the bath. They didn't wash her hair this time, and she was given the same set of underwear again, then taken to the room just like the night before.

The man was a different one, older and thinner, and his penis was much smaller. After Madame Sondheim had left the room he tried to put it in her mouth, but when she gagged and then screamed at him he went straight to the main event. It didn't hurt quite as much as the night before, but it was every bit as vile. She lay under him wishing she had a knife and could stick it in his skinny ribs and kill him.

For three more nights it was the same routine, with a different man each time. She had another who made her hold his penis in her mouth, one who took her from behind like a dog, and the final one made her keep her underwear on and sit on his lap, as if she was his daughter or niece. But he wasn't showing fatherly affection, his hands were under her drawers touching her, and she knew he was playing out some sick little game in his head. He too took her from behind finally and he was so long at it that she thought the pain and soreness would stay with her for a lifetime.

The day after the fifth man Belle began vomiting and couldn't stop. By the evening there was nothing left in her stomach to bring up, but she kept retching. As she became weaker, the housekeeper tried to make her eat and drink something, but she brought that up too.

Belle lay in bed unable even to want to get better for she felt dead inside. She was only vaguely aware of day turning to night, then back to day again. She had no idea how much time had passed, but she did pick up on the maids' concern for her when she could no longer use the chamberpot unaided. They must have spoken to Madame Sondheim about her, for a doctor came in to examine her.

He spoke a little English, and the mere fact that he was attempting to communicate with her made Belle cry.

''Ow you come to France?' he asked once he'd sounded her chest, taken her blood pressure and felt her stomach.

'In a box, with bad men,' she sobbed out, and caught hold of his hands so he would listen to her. 'My mother in England must think I am dead. Help me!'

He looked round at Madame Sondheim enquiringly, but she just shrugged.

'She is bad woman, make five men do this.' She pushed down the covers and indicated her vagina because she didn't know how else to explain.

'I weel see what I can do,' the doctor said carefully, and put his hand gently on her cheek as if to reassure her that he meant it.

Belle felt just a little better after the doctor had gone, not because of the medicine he'd left for her, but because she felt help was at hand. She fell asleep imagining herself back home in the kitchen with Mog and her mother.

She woke later at the sound of someone coming into the room. On seeing a man advancing on the bed she screamed at the top of her voice. But Delphine was with him and she darted forward and put her hand over Belle's mouth, making hushing sounds. She then gabbled away in unintelligible French, but the way she waved her hands at the man, then sat Belle up and wrapped a blanket tightly around her implied that he was going to carry her somewhere else.

Belle hoped it was a hospital for the shock of seeing the man was making her retch again even more violently.

She thought she was dreaming the ride in the carriage, yet the whirring of the wheels and the clip-clop of horses' hooves seemed very real.

It was the silence which alerted her when she woke that she had indeed been moved somewhere else. In the other house there had been constant sounds – people's voices, horses' hooves out on the street, music, and by day a distant sawing and banging which might well have been a factory or workshop. Not necessarily loud noise, but always there like the buzz of insects in summer.

This place was graveyard quiet, as though there was no

other human being or even animal for miles. Belle turned her head towards the source of the pale gold light and saw there was a large window with drawn, thin, peach-coloured curtains undulating in a slight breeze.

Her bed was warm and comfortable, but a slight fusty smell coming from beneath the covers suggested to her she'd been in it for some time, perhaps even days. She struggled to sit up, but found she felt so weak she fell back on to the pillow. The room was almost monastic in its bareness. Her bed was a narrow iron one, there was a simple wooden chair, a felt-covered card table next to her bed, and on it was a jug of water and a glass. The walls were whitewashed and there was a crucifix above her bed. No mirror, pictures, not even a washstand. She wondered where she was.

It came back to her that she had been very sick and a doctor had come to see her. She didn't feel sick now, and as she moved herself a little in the bed she found that her private parts were no longer sore. She managed to reach out and pour herself some water: it felt good to drink, her mouth was so dry.

The sound of the door opening startled her and she cowered down involuntarily, hiding her eyes.

A woman spoke in French, a gentle voice that was as soothing as the silence here.

'You are feeling better now, *ma chérie*?' she asked then in English.

Belle's eyes flew open to see a very pretty woman of about thirty. She had light brown hair in a chignon and wide grey eyes and was wearing a high-necked, grey wool dress with a pearl brooch at her throat.

'You speak English?' Belle said, and she thought her voice sounded cracked.

'Yes, a leetle. I am Lisette, I have been nursing you since you came here.'

'What is this place?' Belle asked fearfully.

Lisette smiled. Her lips were plump and she had the kind of smile that would warm anyone.

'A good place,' she said. 'Nothing for you to fear.'

'No more men?' Belle asked in a small voice.

Lisette took one of her hands in both of hers. 'No more men. I know what they did to you. It will not happen again. You will get strong and well.'

'Then I can go home to England?'

She knew just by the look on Lisette's face that wasn't going to happen. 'Not England, no. Madame Sondheim has passed you on, so you will not go back there.'

That was good enough for Belle for now. She felt hungry, she needed to wash herself, and if she could sleep peacefully in this quiet place without threat of violence, that would do.

Chapter Eleven

Mog woke from a strange, somewhat disturbing dream, and lay for a moment in the darkness wondering what exactly it had been about, and if she should get up and make herself a cup of tea. But all at once she smelled smoke and leapt out of her bed.

Fire was an ever-present danger all over London, but especially in places like Seven Dials where the houses were so close together and so many of them in a bad state of repair. Mog had always made a point of making the girls aware of how easily a fire could start with a hot cinder falling on a rug, a lighted candle knocked over, or even long skirts catching on an open fire.

But by the time Mog had got three-quarters of the way up the stairs from the basement and saw the fire was by the front door, she knew it hadn't started in any of those ways.

It was obvious that a flaming rag or something similar had been put through the letter box. It didn't take much to deduce who was responsible either, but for now her only concern was getting everyone out of the house to safety.

Although the fire hadn't yet reached the staircase which led to the upper floors, it would only take a few more minutes, so Mog knew it was foolhardy to go up there. Racing into the parlour, she grabbed the bell which they rang twenty minutes before closing to remind clients what time it was. She picked it up and rang it as hard as she could.

Annie's room was on the ground floor just behind the staircase and she appeared almost the moment Mog had started to ring the bell. She shrieked in horror to see the hall on fire, but Mog knew there was no time for hysterics or explanations.

'Take this!,' she said, shoving the bell into Annie's hands. 'Ring and scream till the girls get down here. But don't you go up, you might get trapped. I'm going down to get some buckets of water to try and slow the fire down. Tell the girls to go out into Jake's Court and make them scream so the fire engine comes.'

As Mog disappeared down to the basement, Lily came running down the stairs. Sally shouted from the first-floor landing that she was going to make the others hurry. By the time Mog had staggered back up with two buckets of water, the fire was only three feet from the staircase and very hot, Annie snatched the buckets and threw the contents on to the fire, ordering Mog to refill them.

The fire retreated a couple of feet, but it was clear it was only a temporary reprieve. Lily and Ruby came running down the stairs with Amy, coughing from the smoke.

'Outside,' Annie yelled, pushing them towards the basement. 'You too, Lily,' she yelled to the girl who was just standing there gawping. 'And raise the alarm!'

Sally still hadn't reappeared with Dolly and Annie shouted for them to come at the top of her voice.

The fire was roaring now. It filled the hallway, licking up the walls. Mog came back with another two buckets of water, and she was just throwing it at the fire as Sally and Dolly appeared at the top of the stairs. They were clinging to each other and crying, afraid to come down because they thought they'd got to go through the fire.

Annie bravely ran up to them, took their hands and pulled them down. The fire suddenly licked forward to the bottom of the staircase, effectively blocking it off.

'Over the side and jump,' Annie ordered, bundling first Sally and then Dolly over the banister. Mog stood beneath to encourage and catch them, and Annie leapt nimbly after them.

The two young girls were coughing violently from the smoke, bent over double, and Mog had to take their arms and practically drag them down the stairs to the basement.

Mog was so caught up with getting the girls out into the yard, grabbing blankets, coats and anything else that would keep them warm out on the street, that she didn't notice immediately that Annie wasn't with them.

Horror-struck, Mog ran back up the stairs. She guessed Annie had darted back to her room to collect the cash box they kept the takings in. But as she got to the door she could hear gas mantles exploding in the heat on the other side of it, and she realized the fire must now be in the parlour and sweeping down the passage to Annie's room, trapping her in there.

Mog's heart was racing with fear for her friend, but she ran back downstairs, snatched up a blanket to cover her nightdress and ran outside, screaming at the top of her lungs for Annie to open her window and jump to safety.

The kitchen was only a semi-basement at the back of the house. From the back door six stone steps led down from Jake's Court into a small yard. This meant that the windows of Annie's room were not very high up, in fact the wall around the yard was just three feet lower than her window. But sadly the wall wasn't close enough to the window to gain access that way. A ladder was needed.

The noise and commotion had brought quite a crowd out, but unlike Mog and the girls they had put coats, hats and boots on over their nightclothes. Mog glanced round at the girls and saw they were huddled together sharing blankets, just watching her.

'Someone get a ladder!' she yelled at the crowd, astounded

that they were making no effort to help. 'Annie's still in there, we've got to try and get her out!'

But not one of them moved. There were big, able-bodied men among them, yet they stood there like so many sheep staring up at the house and pointing out that flames were already licking out of the parlour window which was right next to Annie's window.

Terrified Annie would burn to death, Mog tossed aside her blanket, leapt on to a dustbin, and scrabbled up on to the yard wall. In bare feet she ran along it and on reaching the house wall tried to stretch out to reach the window sill of Annie's room. But it was at least three feet too far away.

'Let me through!' a loud male voice suddenly rang out, and Mog turned to see to her surprise and relief that it was Garth Franklin carrying a ladder, assisted by young Jimmy.

'Annie's in there!' Mog pointed to the window and came back along the wall to get down again. 'I think she must be overcome by the smoke.'

Garth moved at great speed. He practically threw the ladder against the window sill of the room and charged up it. He took something from his pocket and bashed it against the glass, then banged it several more times around the edge to knock out the remainder. Then he climbed in. Jimmy shinned up behind his uncle and leapt inside equally quickly, then all at once Garth was out on the ladder again while Jimmy helped hoist the unconscious woman over the older man's shoulder.

As Garth came down the ladder with Annie, the sounds of popping glass from within were as loud as fire crackers. Mog held her breath because Jimmy had disappeared from view. But just as Garth reached the ground, and Mog was twisting her hands in agitation because she feared Jimmy was overcome too, he climbed out of the window carrying the cashbox and Annie's fur coat.

At that very moment the clanging bell of the fire engine

rang out. The crowd cheered and moved back as the four horses pulling the fire engine behind them galloped into the Court at breakneck speed.

But Mog could only think about Annie, and took her from Garth, wrapped her in a blanket and laid her down on the ground, kneeling beside her.

She had no idea what you did for people who were overcome by smoke, but all at once Annie began to cough of her own accord and opened her eyes.

'Oh, my sweet Jesus!' Mog exclaimed breathlessly, clutching her friend in her arms. 'I thought you were dead.'

'I thought I was going to die too when I couldn't get the window open,' Annie wheezed out before another coughing fit overcame her.

Mog sat Annie up, patting her back to help her cough out the smoke, and wrapped the blanket round her more securely. Mog was freezing too in only her nightdress but her sole concern was for her friend.

'Has the whole place gone?' Annie managed to croak out a few minutes later.

Until then Mog hadn't even considered what the loss of the house meant; to her it was the people who lived in it that mattered. But as she turned her head to look at it, her eyes filled with tears. Every window had flames coming out of it. She remembered how excited she and Annie had been when they went to buy the chandelier and the Persian rug for the parlour. She had loved polishing the piano and arranging fresh flowers on the hall table. Almost everything, bedding, china, pictures and just about everything else in the house, had some little tale attached to it.

Even the basement, which was her domain, was well alight now. All those little treasures, her sewing basket, a photograph of Belle in a tortoiseshell frame, the silver-backed hairbrush that Annie had given her one Christmas, a china cat and other little bits and pieces she'd collected over the years that made her room her home, had been burned.

Mog supposed most people would think it shameful to work as a maid in a brothel, but she never had – in fact she'd taken a pride in keeping it clean and comfortable. Annie and the girls were like her family; the brothel had become her life, and now it was gone.

'Yes, it's all gone.' Mog struggled not to break down. 'But let's just be glad no one died in there. Someone was trying to kill us all.'

Garth came over and put a blanket around Mog's shoulders as she knelt beside Annie. 'You two had best come back with me,' he said gruffly.

Mog looked up at the big, bearded, red-headed man in surprise. She had always heard that he was hard and mean-spirited. 'That is so kind, Mr Franklin,' she replied. 'But you've done more than enough for us tonight. We couldn't possibly impose on you. We'll go to a rooming house.'

'You'll do no such thing,' he said firmly. 'Someone tried to kill you tonight, and there's no prizes for guessing who that could be. You need to be somewhere safe, and you will be safe with me.'

People were drifting away now, for the firemen had the blaze under control and it was too cold to hang around. Mog saw that all the girls had gone – she supposed neighbours had kindly offered them a bed for the night. But she did think they might have come and asked how she and Annie were.

'Come on, you'll catch your death out here,' Garth said impatiently, and picking Annie up in his arms as if she weighed no more than a small child, he began to walk towards the Ram's Head.

'Come on, Miss Davis.' Jimmy smiled at Mog, putting the cashbox down on the ground and holding out Annie's fur for her to slip into. 'Home with us? Your feet must be frozen!' He picked up the cashbox again and offered her his arm. Mog was glad to take it, for after the shock and exertions of the night it felt good to be able to leave decision-making to someone else, even if he was only a young lad.

Three days after the fire, Mog stood at the side of the bed, looking down at Annie in despair. She had steadfastly refused to have a bath, so she still stank of smoke and her hair fell in greasy rat's tails on the shoulders of her soiled nightdress. Apart from getting up to use the chamberpot occasionally, she hadn't left the bed since the night Garth put her in it.

'I'm ruined,' she sobbed. 'What's going to become of me?'

Mog automatically put a comforting hand on her friend's shoulder, but she was finding it hard to feel much sympathy, for physically there was nothing wrong with Annie. She ate everything put in front of her, and she'd stopped coughing. Mog had lost her home and livelihood too, but she wasn't lying around crying and wailing, in fact she was trying to make the best of a bad situation by making herself useful around the Ram's Head.

The room they were sharing was grim, very small, dingy, and until Mog got to grips with it, very dirty. But even if it didn't have the comfort and style they'd been used to, it was very kind of Garth to take them in.

In return, Mog had turned to cooking and cleaning from the first morning in the Ram's Head. And although Garth was a man of few words, and not given to praise, she sensed he was enjoying the home-cooked meals, and having cleaner living quarters. Jimmy had confided in her that his uncle had been much easier on him since they'd arrived and Mog had made it feel like a real home.

Mog liked being there. Jimmy was such a nice lad, and it was good to live without all the petty squabbles she'd been used to with the girls. But with Annie refusing to pull herself together and not even making a decision about her future, it was very likely Garth would soon feel he was being used, and would ask them to leave.

'What do you mean, "What's going to become of you?"' Mog retorted. 'You've got your life. You will also get something from the insurance company. And there's the cashbox!'

Mog had no idea exactly what the box contained, but it was heavy, and she knew Annie well enough to be sure she wouldn't have risked her life to go back for it unless there was a considerable sum in it.

'You wouldn't understand, you've never had to furnish a house or take responsibility for the running of a business.'

'I don't recall you furnishing it either. Aside from the chandelier and the Persian rug, mostly everything else was left from the Countess,' Mog snapped back. 'As for me not running it, I've been there night and day, organizing the food, the laundry, cleaning the rooms, making the girls toe the line and looking after you and Belle. If it hadn't been for me you would all have perished in your beds. So how can you suggest I know nothing of running a business?'

'You've only ever been a maid.'

Mog looked hard at Annie. She had never been a beauty. She had been attractive, with a good figure, but her skin was sallow and her brown hair dull. What she had was presence. She had only to walk into a room and people turned to her; she was cool and poised, with a hint of something exotic about her. Back in the days when she was one of the girls, this presence made men feel they were getting something extra special, and as men asked for her over and over again, perhaps she did really have it.

Then, once the house was left to her, she made the transition from whore to madam seamlessly. Her natural dignity and poise commanded respect. She used just the right amount of frost with men who had once been her customers to make them know she was now off limits, yet they were still welcome in the house.

But now she was wallowing in self-pity her dignity was all gone. She looked and smelled as rancid as some crone in the workhouse. The sad truth of the matter was that women on the wrong side of thirty weren't likely to get many new opportunities, and even though there was sympathy for Annie now because of Belle's disappearance and the fire, that would soon wither and die if she didn't get up and start fighting back.

'Only a maid!' Mog said with a deep sigh. 'Thank you for that, Annie. It's nice to know I'm valued. I have dealt with the police for you since the fire, I've emptied your chamber-pots, brought you meals, got you clothes, and all the while I've been grieving about your daughter too, as if she were my own. Yet I haven't heard you say one word about her!

'Only a maid, you say! Well, I sure as hell don't know any other maid who has done all I've done for you. So maybe it's time I looked out for myself, and stopped fretting about you and yours.'

'Oh, you know I didn't mean it like that,' Annie said with a toss of her head. 'I'm down, what do you expect?'

'I hoped you might be glad we've still got one another,' Mog retorted. 'I expected that you'd start to think about what we can do to that bastard who took Belle and burned us down. Young Jimmy, Garth and Noah are all on your side, but it's time you got yourself up and looking good again, and fought back.'

'I can't,' Annie whimpered. 'I've got no fight left in me. I wish you'd left me to die in the fire.'

'There's far worse things than losing a house,' Mog said in bewilderment. 'Having Belle snatched by a murderer was one. But you didn't fall apart with that — surely the house don't mean more to you than her?'

'You don't understand.' Annie looked up at Mog with tear-filled eyes. 'Owning that house compensated for all the other horrible things that were done to me. When the Countess left it to me it healed my wounds. I could stop dwelling on the men who raped me, and all the men I had to pretend to want because they were paying me. Now it's gone, all those memories have come back. I'm nothing now.'

'You *are* nothing if you can't fight for your Belle,' Mog retorted, tempted to slap some sense into Annie. 'You should be down at Bow Street now making a fuss about the fire, not lying here festering. Demand to see the most senior man there, insist he investigates the fire and Belle's disappearance. Why not use some of that money in the cashbox to offer a reward for information? There's bound to be some little weasel around here who knows something – money always brings them out of the woodwork.'

'The Falcon will just do something else to me,' Annie said weakly.

Mog rolled her eyes in exasperation. 'What else can he do? He's already done the two worst things I can think of, there is nothing else to do.'

'He could kill me.'

'Well, you said you wished I'd left you to die in the fire, so that won't be so bad,' Mog said tartly. 'Now, I'm going to fill up a bath for you down in the scullery. If you don't get up to have it then I'm afraid you and I will have to part company.'

Chapter Twelve

Mog leaned across the counter and aggressively stuck her face up close to the police sergeant's.

'Why haven't you been to Kent's house or office and questioned him?' she demanded to know. 'He's murdered a young woman, abducted a child and burned our house down. What more does he have to do before you act?'

It was two days since Mog took Annie to task for not fighting back, and finally this morning Annie had agreed to come down to Bow Street to stir the police into action. But as she wasn't being anywhere near assertive enough, Mog felt she had to take over.

'We have already called at both Mr Kent's home and office. He's out of the country, so he couldn't have set the fire.' The fat, red-faced sergeant smirked as he relayed this information, clearly thinking that would make Mog back down.

'Oh really!' she sneered. 'As if I'd believe that!'

The policeman's face darkened. 'You should believe it because we have evidence he was a passenger on a boat leaving Dover on the fourteenth of January.'

'That's the day after Belle was snatched,' Annie exclaimed. 'So he took her out of the country! Where to?'

'He was travelling to France with another man, no child with them,' the sergeant said airily.

Mog gasped. 'Then he must have killed her,' she said.

'There is absolutely no evidence that he abducted the girl, killed her or set the fire.' The sergeant rolled his eyes and looked wearily at the ceiling. 'Mr Kent's rent collector confirmed he is still out of the country. Now, be off with you, I've got work to do.'

Annie turned away, but Mog wasn't going to give up that easily. 'Have you got a heart?' she asked. 'How would you feel if your daughter was stolen and your house burned down? It is a fact that Millie was murdered by this man Kent, an act witnessed by our Belle. So don't you try to tell us he didn't take her, or that he didn't burn our house down to try and scare us into silence. And what is even more frightening is that you are taking the word of a man who owns some of the worst slum properties in London. He's hardly likely to be reliable!'

'Whores are even less so,' the sergeant snapped back at her. 'Now, get out before I think up something to charge you both with.'

If Annie hadn't grabbed Mog's arm and pulled her out of the police station, Mog would have tried to slap the policeman's face.

'Did you hear what he said?' she spat out as they reached the street. Her face was purple with fury.

'Yes, I heard it, and I didn't like it any more than you did,' Annie said, taking hold of both Mog's arms and shaking her gently to try to get her to snap out of it. 'But he was spoiling to lock us up for something, and that wouldn't help anyone. Noah will be round later, let's talk to him and see what we can do next.'

Mog slumped against Annie. She knew she was beaten for now and getting herself arrested would serve no purpose.

It was another very cold day and the icy wind whipped even more colour into Mog's cheeks as they walked back towards the Ram's Head. Annie glanced sideways at Mog and saw by the way her mouth was set in a straight line that she was still angry, and that some of that anger was directed at her.

Annie knew that Mog didn't think she felt as deeply as she

did about all the recent events, but she was wrong. It was just that Annie found it impossible to talk about her feelings. She wished she could be different, she would have liked to be able to spill out her anger and fear, but she couldn't. Instead, Millie's murder and Belle's abduction were locked inside her head, going round and round, paralysing her so she felt unable to do anything. That was the reason why she stayed in bed for so long following the fire.

If everyone thought she was suffering from shock at being trapped by the fire, she was glad of that, for she certainly didn't want to admit how guilty she felt that she'd failed to protect her own daughter. Not once, but twice. She'd failed to check where Belle was on the night of the murder, and then failed to foresee that Kent might try to silence her permanently because she'd seen it.

Why on earth did she try and hush it all up instead of reporting who killed Millie immediately and sending Belle away to a place of safety?

There was no real answer to that question. She'd behaved like an ostrich, hiding her head in the sand, imagining it would all blow over, and she would always feel ashamed of that. But she wished too that she was able to tell Mog that she loved her like a sister. She was always so constant, kind, honest and loyal, which was astounding when Annie was so often nasty to her. But then, she could always justify her nastiness by telling herself that Mog had a charmed life. She'd never been forced to sell herself, she'd always had a secure home and job where she was valued, with no real responsibility. Furthermore, Belle had always loved her too, far more than she did her own mother.

But deep down Annie knew Mog had earned that love, and she had to concede that Mog was also right to lay into her for staying in bed feeling sorry for herself. So she had made herself get up, take a bath, wash her hair and put on the clothes that Mog had so thoughtfully been out and bought for her. And as soon as she saw herself in the mirror looking much the same as she had before all her troubles began, she felt more like her old self too.

She was very grateful to Jimmy for rescuing her beautiful red fox coat along with the cashbox. An admirer had bought the coat for her five years ago, and now that her future looked so uncertain she couldn't help but wish she'd taken him up on his offer of marriage too. But that was all water under the bridge, and she was determined to pull herself out of this abyss she'd sunk into. Yesterday she'd spent a whole pound on a little russet velvet hat which went perfectly with her coat. Mog probably saw that as an entirely frivolous purchase, and would claim that she could have got a second-hand one for less than sixpence, but then Mog didn't have a reputation for elegance herself, and she certainly wouldn't understand Annie's desire not to lose hers.

'Do you think the two men really went alone to France?' Mog asked, suddenly breaking the silence.

'I'm sure that was what the policeman was told,' Annie said. 'But then Kent could've bribed someone to say it. They might even have smuggled Belle on to the ship. I'd be interested to know who the other man was.'

'How can we find out?' Mog asked.

'I could ask Noah to take the train down to Dover and ask in the shipping office,' Annie said. 'He seems to be a resourceful young man, I'm sure he'd be glad to go.'

Mog seemed a little cheered at this and it was some time before she spoke again. 'What are we going to do for ourselves, Annie?' she asked. 'I mean about making a living, and a new home. We can't stay with Garth much longer.'

Annie had been asking herself similar questions earlier that morning. It would be some time before she could expect any insurance money, and she doubted she'd get enough to rebuild the house or buy another. But putting that aside, she didn't feel able to make any decisions about the future yet. She needed time on her own to consider all her options.

'Maybe you should just make plans for yourself,' she replied. 'I'm not going to be able to keep a maid, at least not in the immediate future.'

The moment the words were out of her mouth, Annie realized she had implied that Mog wasn't first and foremost a trusted friend, but just an employee.

'If that's how you feel,' Mog replied, her tone revealing how hurt she was.

Annie tried to rephrase what she'd said, but she could see from Mog's expression that it made no difference.

Mog didn't speak to Annie again that morning. Each time Annie tried to start a conversation she pretended she had something to do in another room. But at noon, when Noah arrived at the Ram's Head, Mog appeared to forget her grievances.

Noah had called the day after the fire to offer his sympathy and to ask if there was anything he could do for them, but this time he'd come laden with a bag of clothes, bed linen and towels from his landlady.

'How very kind!' Mog exclaimed, asking him to come through from the bar into the small parlour behind and offering him refreshments.

'Mrs Dumas is a very kind lady,' Noah said. 'She felt very sorry for you and hoped these things might prove useful. She also wished she could offer you both a room in her house, but sadly they are all taken.'

Annie asked him to thank Mrs Dumas for both herself and Mog, then launched into telling him what had been said at Bow Street. 'I don't think the police sergeant would lie about Kent going to France, do you?' she asked, frowning deeply. 'But there might be more information to add to that, like the name of his companion, how they arrived at Dover and so forth.'

'I think the police must be convinced he's gone to France, but I agree there is probably more we could find out.'

'I think you could, Noah, after all, you are an investigator,' Annie said, and went on to offer him a daily rate of pay plus his expenses.

Noah beamed. 'I can go to Dover and come back in one day,' he said.

'Could I go with you, Noah?' Jimmy piped up from the doorway. 'We could call at Kent's house in Charing afterwards, it's on the way back. I could climb in a window and look around for you!'

Noah smiled. 'I'd love your company, Jimmy, that's if your uncle can spare you for a day. But I don't think we'll break in anywhere.'

Jimmy looked a bit disappointed at that. The fire had brought it home to all of them that Kent was extraordinarily vicious and capable of killing anyone who tried to cross him. Jimmy was desperately worried about Belle; deep in his heart he felt she was alive, but in a way that was worse for he kept dwelling on what Kent might be doing to her. Having gone as far as searching his office, now he was ready to do whatever else was necessary to find Belle.

Annie and Noah carried on chatting and Mog, still feeling bruised by Annie, went into the bar to see if she could help Garth. There were only a couple of men sitting in by the fire over a drink, and Garth asked her to mind the bar while he nipped down to the cellar.

Another two men came in while he was gone and Mog served them with a pint of beer each. Garth came back just as she was giving them their change.

'You're good to have around,' he said appreciatively. 'I'm going to miss you when Annie decides to move on.'

Mog was really surprised by the warmth of his remark. The previous day he'd praised her cooking and he'd thanked her for sewing buttons on his shirts, but she hadn't imagined he was capable of missing anyone.

'I won't be moving on with her,' Mog said sadly. 'She wants to be on her own.'

'Well, there's a surprise,' he said. 'What's she planning to do?'

Mog shook her head glumly. 'I don't think she knows yet.'

'And what about you?'

Mog shrugged. 'I'd make a good housekeeper, but who would want me when I've only worked in a brothel?'

'I would,' he replied.

Mog half smiled, thinking he was joking, only so far she hadn't found him to be one for jokes. 'Go on with you!' she said.

'I mean it. You've made it more homely here in the short time you've been staying. I like that, and I know Jimmy likes you being here.'

'He misses his mother,' Mog said.

'Yes, he does. I thought he'd spent too much time with her in the past, and said as much, but he's not namby pamby, he's a good lad.'

Mog hadn't expected to ever hear the big, red-headed man compliment anyone, let alone Jimmy, as he was the kind who acted as though he thought compliments were softness.

'So are you saying you'll take me on as your housekeeper? I mean, and pay me?'

'Well, I can't manage much. Will three shillings a week all found suit you?'

Mog was used to five shillings, and she knew a housekeeper in a big house would get far more, but after what Annie had said this morning, she was just glad to be wanted by someone.

'It will suit very well, Garth,' she said with a smile. 'So as housekeeper you won't mind if I do some serious organizing and spring-cleaning around here?'

He smiled then, and it was such an unusual sight it was like the sun coming out. 'You can organize as much as you like back in the house,' he said. 'But the bar stays the way it is, I like it well enough.'

'I'm really glad Uncle Garth asked Mog to be our house-keeper,' Jimmy said to Noah as they walked down to Charing Cross station the next morning to catch a train to Dover. 'I like Mog a lot and I didn't want her to leave.'

'What about Annie?' Noah asked. He'd already been told she intended to go her own way.

'Annie's not so easy to like,' Jimmy said thoughtfully. 'Do you think she'll get another brothel?'

Noah gulped. He didn't feel comfortable talking about such things to such a young lad. 'I've no idea. But I think she'd do better to get some other kind of business so that if she gets Belle back she won't be drawn into that.'

'She might've already been forced into it.'

Noah looked round at Jimmy and saw his eyes were filling with tears. 'Let's hope not,' he said, squeezing the lad's bony shoulder. 'You've got the advantage over me, Jimmy – you see, I didn't get to meet Belle. Tell me what she's like.'

'She's real pretty with dark, curly hair, shiny as wet tar, and deep blue eyes. Her skin's got a kind of peachy glow too, not like most of the girls around here. She smells good as well, clean and fresh, and her teeth are small and white.'

Noah smiled. That detailed description showed just how badly Jimmy was smitten with her.

'But it ain't so much what she looks like as the way she is,' Jimmy added for good measure.

'And how is she?'

'Bouncy, bright, she's got a mind of her own. I met her the

first time on the morning of the day Millie was killed. I asked if she was a whore 'cos she lived in a brothel.'

'What did she say to that?'

Jimmy smiled. 'She was very indignant. She said you could live in a palace and still not be a queen. But it turned out she didn't really know what a whore was then. She only found that out when she saw Millie get killed.'

Noah blushed, for he had a sudden recollection of Millie standing in front of him in just her chemise and taking his hand to put it on her breast. His memories of Millie were all sweet and he didn't like to hear her called a whore, or think what that word meant.

'Girls like Millie don't get much choice in what they end up doing for a living,' Noah said. 'Annie was the same, she was forced into it. So speak gently about such women, it is men just like us that turn them into what they are.'

'I know that,' Jimmy said with indignation. 'Anyway, the next time I saw Belle was when we went down to the Embankment Gardens and she told me what she'd seen, blurted it all out, and cried about it. I reckon that's a real bad way for a girl to find it all out.'

'Were those the only times you met Belle?'

Jimmy nodded glumly. 'She made a big impression on me, I was so happy she wanted to be my friend. Then she was snatched before I could get to know her better.'

They were approaching the station now and Noah stopped to buy a paper as he wanted to look at a couple of short pieces he'd written which were supposed to be in there today.

'Have you been on a train before?' he asked, glad to change the subject for something lighter as he could see Jimmy had become upset by talking about Belle.

'Just once. Mother took me to Cambridge when she had to do a fitting for a lady she made clothes for. I thought it was marvellous, but it was a very, very long way.'

'I don't think Cambridge is much farther than Dover, that's about sixty-five miles, but when you're very young, just sitting for an hour can seen interminable.'

'I've never seen the sea before. Will we be able to see it at Dover?'

'Yes, of course.' Noah laughed at the boy's enthusiasm. 'Shame it will be too cold to paddle.'

It did seem an incredibly long way to Dover and it was very cold in the carriage too. By the time they got there Jimmy's nose was as red as his hair.

'You need a warm coat,' Noah said. Jimmy was only wearing a threadbare tweed jacket and a grey muffler round his neck.

'I don't like to ask my uncle,' Jimmy said. 'Mog said she was going to broach the subject, and ask for some new boots too – mine have got holes in them – but I guess she's forgotten.'

'I've got a coat back at my place that's too small for me,' Noah said. 'I'll bring it round when we get back. But I wear my boots till they fall apart.'

'You're a real dandy dresser,' Jimmy remarked, looking with admiration at Noah's dark, knee-length coat, his bowler hat and stiff-winged shirt collar.

'I have to be in my line of work,' Noah explained. 'You couldn't expect the people I have to question about insurance claims to take me seriously if I looked like a costermonger. My mother is always saying "Clothes maketh the man".'

'My mother used to say that too,' Jimmy said as they walked down the road towards the harbour. 'I was always very well dressed until she got sick. Then we had to spend the money on the important things like her medicine and food. I used to wish I would stop growing so I didn't need new things.'

Noah put one hand on the lad's shoulder. 'She'd be really

proud of you,' he said. 'I suspect you've even got your grumpy uncle to like you!'

Jimmy chuckled. 'He's not so bad once you get used to him. His bark's worse than his bite. My mother told me that he only became the way he is when his woman ran off with another man. I think now Mog is going to stay with us he might even get jolly because he really likes her!'

Jimmy fell silent when he saw the sea. The wind had whipped up huge waves that were crashing on to the shingle beach with immense force.

'It's very different on a summer's day,' Noah explained, realizing Jimmy felt a little frightened by the sight. 'It takes its colour from the sky, that's why it's dark grey now, but on a sunny day it would be a lovely clear blue and the waves really gentle. Maybe we can come again later in the year for you to see it.'

'It's so big,' Jimmy said in an awed voice. 'It just goes on and on for ever.'

'Yet this is the closest bit to France, it's only twenty-one miles away. People have swum it!'

'Not on a day like today,' Jimmy laughed. 'You can see how cold it is just looking at it.'

Jimmy was very impressed by the way Noah charmed the clerk in the ticket office. He was a thin-faced, rather miserable-looking man who had started out belligerently saying he couldn't give out any information about passengers. But Noah said that he was an investigator for an insurance company and that he had police approval to continue his investigations, which made the clerk open a ledger and look back on the passenger list for the day in question.

'Mr Kent and Mr Braithwaite,' he said. 'I remember them now because they wanted a cabin.'

'Did they have a young girl with them?'

'Oh no! It was just the two of them.'

'Can you remember what Braithwaite looked like?' Noah asked.

The clerk frowned. 'He had curly hair and he was more pleasant than the other man, but that's all, it was dark, the light in here isn't too good.'

'Is there any way they could have smuggled a girl on to the ship without anyone noticing?'

'No. Passengers' tickets get checked again as they go up the gangway to the ship. We're all vigilant for that.'

'How did the men arrive at the ferry, do you know?'

'I can't see from here, but I imagine it was in a cab or a carriage as they had a trunk with them.'

'A trunk!' Noah exclaimed. 'How big was it?'

'I don't know, they didn't bring it in here. I just heard one of the porters ask if they wanted help with it.'

'So that was it, they had her in a trunk,' Noah said as they left the ticket office.

'You can't be sure of that,' Jimmy said.

'I am,' Noah insisted. 'Men don't take a trunk unless they are emigrating, they're more for women's things and house-hold linens. A man would just take a suitcase or bag.'

'Would she be alive in the trunk?' Jimmy asked fearfully.

Noah sucked in his cheeks as he thought. 'I'd say so,' he said eventually. 'Would anyone take the risk of being caught leaving the country with a body? That wouldn't make any sense. But if that is how they got her out, then they must have drugged her to keep her quiet.'

'That means they had something special lined up for her,' Jimmy said with a tremor in his voice. 'What could that be?'

Noah didn't need to give a reason, he could see that Jimmy already knew the answer. He reached out and squeezed the lad's shoulder, wishing he could think of a less horrifying alternative. 'You said Belle has guts and spirit, so she might very well outwit her captors,' he said. 'Let's get to Kent's house and see if we can find any clues there to where he's taken her.'

'You mean break in?' Jimmy asked, his eyes lighting up.

'I guess so,' Noah smiled.

At just after eleven that same night, Noah and Jimmy got back to the Ram's Head. Garth was chasing out the last few drinkers from the bar and he told Jimmy to go through to the back and get Annie and Mog to join them in the bar.

The two women came rushing out, their faces bright with expectation. Noah wished he had more to tell them.

He went through what they'd discovered at Dover and then moved on to how they took the train back to Charing and broke into Kent's house.

'But it revealed nothing unusual but a brace and bit left in the hall,' Noah said gloomily.

'It wasn't the kind of house we expected though, was it?' Jimmy said, looking at Noah. 'It was all nice and perfect, not the kind of place you'd expect for a man that owns slums.'

Noah smirked at Annie. 'He's right, it made me think of a doll's house. Every bit of furniture, every ornament, rug and cushion looked as though it had been picked and put in place with great care. Jimmy's a good little burglar, he prised a small window open round the back and wriggled in like an eel. But when he came and opened the back door for me, I was almost afraid to go in, it was so neat.'

'Funny though, it looked more like a woman's house,' Jimmy said. 'I used to deliver clothes Ma had made to two women in Islington. Their place was like that, like no man had ever walked in there. It gave me the creeps. We checked upstairs but there was no women's stuff anywhere.'

'What's a brace and bit?' Annie asked.

Noah demonstrated with his hands that it was a tool for

making screw holes, mostly used by carpenters. 'All his other tools were in the shed in the garden, placed neatly in a strap with leather loops to hold them. I think he used the brace and bit to drill breathing holes in the trunk. But we didn't find anything else. So I think he may have taken Belle there just to collect the trunk and put her in it, then went on to Dover.'

'Did you look through his papers?' Annie said.

'Yes, but there wasn't much, only tradesmen's bills for that place, all in the name of Mr Waldegrave, and I looked at every last one,' Jimmy said earnestly. 'You know you said Belle heard Kent asking Millie to go away with him? Well, do you reckon he did that place up for her? 'Cos that's what it looked like.'

Annie shrugged her shoulders. 'Who knows? You can't imagine a man who strangles a woman for saying the wrong thing caring enough about her to make his home nice for her. Maybe he never intended to keep her living with him. He might have been planning to ship her out somewhere else too.'

Noah looked thoughtful. 'Maybe that's why he keeps his house like that. A good place to take girls to so they think they're going to be on easy street, then he sells them on.'

'Was there any sign of Belle being kept there? Dirty dishes, things out of place, unmade beds?' Annie asked.

Noah shook his head. 'Nothing. Not a dirty cup and saucer or a rug that had been rucked up. Beds all neat with quilts just so. He must have a housekeeper. No man would keep it like that. But it didn't feel damp or cold, like no one had been there for ages. So maybe someone goes in and lights a fire now and then for him?'

'Did you ask around in the village about that?'

'We didn't dare. It was such a small place we were afraid we'd look suspicious,' Jimmy said.

'Strange that a man could live in a perfect house and earn his living from a place like the Core,' Mog said thoughtfully. 'If they didn't keep Belle there, then maybe they stayed at the other man's home. Braithwaite, was that his name?'

Garth suddenly looked animated. 'I've just remembered that I know of a man called Braithwaite,' he said. 'I don't know him personally, just stories about him. He's a gambler. Goes by the name of Sly!'

'You've seen him?' Noah asked.

'Nah.' Garth shook his head. 'Just heard men in here mention him. But I can ask around about him.'

'It might not be the same Braithwaite,' Mog said.

'It's not that common a name,' Annie pointed out. 'What's the chances of there being another around here?'

'But Kent might not know this man from here,' Mog argued.

Annie pursed her lips. 'Well, I can't see him recruiting help for a kidnap down in a little village. Can you?'

Mog ignored Annie's sarcasm. 'What now?' she asked. 'I mean, if Belle's in France we'll never find her.'

'I've got a few ways of getting Kent and Braithwaite to talk,' Garth said darkly. 'Kent won't stay away from here for long while he's got rents from the Core to bank. I'll get word when he reappears, don't worry about that.'

'What if he gets someone to start a fire here?' Jimmy said in a small, frightened voice. 'He's not going to give in easily, is he? After all, he'll hang for killing Millie.'

'The one thing a bully is scared of is a bigger bully,' Garth said with a tight little smile. 'Trust me, I'll make that bastard squeal when I get hold of him.'

'But how long have we got to wait?' Mog said, wringing her hands. 'Every day Belle is gone she's in more danger. I can't bear the thought of what might be happening to her.'

'Nor can I,' Jimmy said in a small, tense voice. 'Come what may, I'm going to find her and bring her home.'

All the adults turned to look at him and saw determination written across his freckly face. Garth opened his mouth to scoff, but saw steel in the lad's eyes and only nodded approval.

'Good for you!' Noah exclaimed. 'If I had acted on what was in my heart about Millie, maybe she would be alive now.'

'Bless you,' Mog said softly. 'You, Jimmy, and Noah and Garth have redeemed my faith in men.'

Chapter Thirteen

'Tell me where I am, Lisette, and what's going to happen to me,' Belle begged. 'I know you are a kind woman, so please tell me the truth.'

On the face of it there seemed little to be worried about. Her room was bright and comfortable, a fire was lit each morning, Lisette brought her food and drink three times a day, there was even fruit in a bowl to eat, and she'd been given some English books to read and new clothes. But outside the window, farmland in its drab winter colours of grey, brown and black stretched into the far distance without a house in sight, and the door of her room was always kept locked.

'I feel for you, *ma chérie*,' the Frenchwoman replied, her pretty face full of sincerity. 'But I am just a maid, and I was told to tell you nothing. I can tell you that you are in a village near Paris, but that's all.'

'Paris!' Belle exclaimed.

Lisette nodded.

'I don't want to get you into trouble,' Belle said. 'But surely you can tell me if men are going to come here and rape me again?'

'No, no, not that, not here.' Lisette looked horrified at the suggestion. 'Thees house is like hospital, for sick women.'

'But I am not sick now. What do they intend to do with me?'

Lisette glanced round at the door as if half expecting someone to be eavesdropping. 'You must not tell I told you. But they plan for you to go away to America soon.'

'America!' Belle exclaimed in disbelief. 'But why?'

Lisette shrugged her shoulders. 'They buy you, Belle, you are, how I say, their property.'

Belle suddenly felt sick. She knew what 'their property' meant.

'What shall I do?' she asked.

Lisette didn't answer immediately but looked down at Belle sitting on the low chair before the fire. 'I think,' she said eventually, 'that it is best for you to be what they want.'

Belle looked up, her eyes sparking with anger. 'You mean I have to be a whore?'

Lisette frowned. 'There are worse things, *ma chérie*. To be starving, to 'ave no home. If you fight them they will punish you; one girl brought here had her arm cut off. Now she cannot do any job but let men take her in alleys for a few centimes.'

Belle's stomach churned at the graphic picture Lisette had painted for her. 'They'd do that?' she asked in a horrified whisper.

'They'd do worse too,' Lisette replied. 'My 'eart goes out to you, but listen to what I say. If you go along with what they want, learn to play the game the gentlemen want, they will not watch you so closely.'

'I don't know how you can tell me to do this,' Belle cried out.

'It is because I like you, Belle, and must tell you the best way to save yourself. I get taken to 'ouse when I am young just the same as you. I know 'ow bad it is. But in time I don't mind no more. I make friends, I laugh again.'

'Do you still do it now?'

Lisette shook her head. 'No more, I work here, nurse the sick people. I have a little boy of my own.'

'You are married?'

'No. Not married. I tell people my 'usband die.'

Belle silently digested all this information as Lisette tidied her room. The thought of any man even coming near her, let alone doing that awful thing to her, made her shudder, but common sense told her that most women didn't fear sex, or loathe it, or there would be no romance or marriage. She didn't remember any of the girls back at Annie's Place saying they hated men; some of them even had sweethearts they went to meet on their nights off.

'How can I learn to tolerate it then?' she asked after a little while.

Lisette came closer to her and put her hand on her shoulder. 'You might have a young man you like, then it is very different. Many of the girls will share their tricks to make the men so excited it is all over quickly. But I promise you, it won't ever hurt the way it did the first few times.'

Tears came up in Belle's eyes because she sensed the woman really did care about her. 'I miss my mother and Mog who used to look after me,' she blurted out. 'They must be so worried. Can't you help me to escape?'

Lisette looked stricken. 'I weesh I could be brave enough, but they would hurt my Jean-Pierre. A mother with no 'usband must not take risks,' she said. 'But listen to me, Belle, even if you could get out somehow, without money you couldn't get 'ome. Maybe very bad people get you, worse than here.'

Belle was far from stupid, and from what she'd already been through she realized that her 'owners' would turn very nasty to anyone attempting to set her free. So it was entirely understandable that Lisette should fear for her son's safety. She knew too that even if she could find her way to the coast, she couldn't get across the English Channel without money. 'It's all right,' she said, giving Lisette a weak, sad smile. 'You've been so kind to me, and I wouldn't wish to get you into trouble. But why will they take me to America? That's so far!'

Lisette shrugged. 'I don't know. Maybe English girls are special there. But you will be with people who speak your language, that is good.'

Belle nodded.

'If you keep your 'ead, you act sweet and good, while you watch the people around you. You find their weakness, and you use it,' Lisette added.

Belle remembered how Mog claimed Annie discovered people's weaknesses, then played on them. At the time it hadn't made much sense to her, but now it was beginning to.

'Is it Madame Sondheim that is sending me to America?'

'*Non.*' Lisette shook her finger. 'She sell you on when you are sick. She made much money already, she have no weesh to keep you in her house.'

Belle struggled against bursting into tears for it was horrible to think she was being passed around like a side of beef in Smithfield market. 'Then my new owner could be worse?' she asked.

'Your new owner pay for you to be here. They see you get good food, soft bed and nursed back to health. You are valuable to them, they will not harm you unless you fight them.'

Belle was too dismayed to ask any further questions. She couldn't believe that anyone who could buy a sick young girl who had been systematically raped by several men and then plan to ship her to America to be a whore, could have even a shred of decency.

She hung her head and cried.

Lisette put her hand on her shoulder. 'I have taken care of many girls like you in this house, but already I can see you are one of the strong ones. You are beautiful too, and I think a clever girl, so use your head. Talk to the older girls, learn from them, and wait for your chance.'

She left the room then, swiftly and silently, leaving Belle crying.

Belle had lost track of exactly how long it was since the day of Millie's funeral when she was snatched from the street. She remembered that it was 14 January, and she supposed she could ask Lisette for the present date, but she hadn't done so because knowing exactly how long it had been might make her believe she'd never see her mother or Mog again.

She missed everything about London so badly her heart ached. There was Mog, the smell of baking in her kitchen, that snug feeling when she tucked her into bed at night with a kiss, the knowledge that she'd always love her. And her mother too, she might not have had Mog's warmth, but there was that little smile she'd give sometimes when Belle had made her proud. And her pretty, tinkling laugh that Belle knew was a rare sound, yet she got to hear it more than anyone else because her mother found her funny.

But it wasn't just the people she missed, it was the cries of the street vendors, the way people spoke, the noise, the crowds, the smells. Paris might well be a fine city, but it wasn't her city. She wanted to be with Jimmy again in the flower market, or racing down to the Embankment Gardens sliding on the ice. She had felt something special about him that day when he'd held her to comfort her, and she had no doubt he would have become her sweetheart if she hadn't been snatched away.

That was almost the worst part of this: they'd taken all those simple things away from her, a sweetheart's kiss, her daydreams of owning a hat shop, of marriage and children. All rubbed out, never to happen, for there would never be another boy like Jimmy looking at her in that special but innocent way which had told her she was the girl of his dreams.

As she stood at the window watching snow falling over the fields as the afternoon light faded, she guessed she'd been gone at least a month. Therefore it must be nearly the end of February.

She suspected it was the snow which was preventing them sending her on to America. She had woken the day after that talk with Lisette to a heavy snowfall, and for three days it had remained below freezing so the snow hadn't melted. Now that it was snowing again the roads would probably be impassable.

Maybe she ought to be glad she couldn't be moved, but she wasn't. Being locked in this room, however comfortable it was, still felt like a prison cell. She wanted to move on, for there at least was a chance of escape, far better than looking out at frozen fields and wondering what was in store for her.

The move, when it came, was sudden and frightening. One minute she was sound asleep, the next she was being shaken by a woman she'd never seen before, and ordered to dress. It was pitch dark outside, and the woman kept saying, '*Vite, vite*,' as she stuffed Belle's spare clothes and nightdress into a bag.

For a brief moment Belle thought the speed was required because the woman was rescuing her, but that hope was soon dashed. As the woman was rushing her down the stairs, the housekeeper who sometimes came up to the room with Lisette came into the hall to hand over a basket which appeared to contain provisions for the journey.

Before leaving the house Belle was given a dark brown fur coat, knitted mittens, and a bonnet which was lined with rabbit fur and came right over her ears. They smelled musty and looked old, but it was so cold she was very glad to have them.

A man was waiting in the carriage outside, and although he spoke in French to Belle's companion, and took her hand to help her in, he didn't say anything to Belle, not even to introduce himself. It was too dark to see him clearly but Belle thought him to be middle-aged as he had a grey beard.

The couple spoke to each other just occasionally on the very long drive. Belle remained hunched up in the fur coat, a rough blanket over her knees, but she was unable to sleep for the cold.

As it grew light the woman opened up the food basket. She handed Belle a large chunk of bread and a piece of cheese. She said something sharply, and although Belle couldn't understand her French, she thought it was an order to eat it up as she might not get anything later on.

There was less snow in this part of France, and it was more hilly than the place they'd come from, but it appeared to be just as sparsely populated, for she only saw the odd cottage here and there. Belle spotted a signpost at a crossroads, and saw the road they were taking led to Brest. She seemed to remember seeing that name on a map of France and she was sure it was up on the left-hand side, by the sea. She supposed they were to go on a ship from there.

She tried not to panic at the prospect of a long sea journey in mid-winter, and made herself daydream of finding a friendly sailor on the ship who could be persuaded to help her, if not to escape, at least to get a message to her mother and Mog. She accepted another lump of bread and cheese gratefully, smiling at the couple in the hope of winning their trust, but they did not reciprocate.

The carriage came to a stop in a harbour, and the door was opened by a tall man with cold blue eyes wearing a black greatcoat and a homburg hat. He stared at her for a few moments as if puzzled, then looked at the couple. '*Je ne savais pas qu'elle était aussi jeune*,' he said.

Belle didn't know what he'd said except for the word *jeune* – Lisette had used it sometimes and she knew it meant 'young' – so she surmised that as he looked puzzled he had said he hadn't expected her to be so young.

The couple gabbled something back and shrugged their shoulders as if that had nothing to do with them.

'You will come with me to the ship,' he said to Belle in perfect English with just a slight French accent. He held out his hand to help her down. 'My name is Etienne Carrera, you will call me Uncle Etienne all the time we are on the ship. I will tell anyone who asks that you are my brother's daughter, brought up in England, and that I am taking you to my sister because your mother is dead. You understand?'

'Yes, Uncle Etienne,' Belle answered cheekily, hoping to disarm him because he looked grim-faced.

'I would say before we take another step,' he said, catching hold of her wrist in a grip that felt like a vice, his icy blue eyes boring right into her in a chilling manner, 'that if you make a fuss, try to get anyone to help you escape, or anything else I don't like, I will kill you.'

Belle's blood ran cold, for she sensed he meant it.

It seemed the steamship was sailing to Cork in Ireland first, to pick up more passengers and to refuel, then on across the Atlantic to New York.

Etienne led Belle down a companionway on the ship, along a short corridor and then down more stairs to their cabin.

'This is it,' he said brusquely as he opened the door. Belle stepped into the tiny space, which was less than eighteen inches from the narrow bunk beds to the small porthole. Beneath the porthole was a foldaway washbasin, a narrow shelf and mirror above it. At the end of the bunks were a couple of hooks to hang up clothes and beneath the lower bunk was a cupboard for everything else.

Belle didn't mind that it was so small, but she was horrified that she was to share it with Etienne.

'There is no reason to fear me touching you,' he said, as if reading her mind. 'My job is to deliver you without sampling the merchandise. You can have the top bunk and pull the curtain across to give you privacy. I will only come back here to collect you for meals, to take you for some exercise and fresh air, and of course to sleep.'

He took from his shoulder her bag and his own. He handed Belle's to her and put his own on the lower bunk. 'I will leave you to settle in. We sail very soon. I'll come for you when we are underway.'

He left the cabin then, locking her in behind him.

Two days later, as the ship left Cork with a great many more passengers, Belle stood at the porthole watching Ireland's coastline grow smaller and smaller until she couldn't see it any more, and the surprising thought occurred to her that she had already travelled much farther than either her mother or Mog had in their lifetime.

She wasn't scared as she'd expected to be. She was bored, frustrated by being kept locked in until Etienne came to escort her, and lonely too. But not scared. Etienne was very respectful: if she wanted to use the lavatory he didn't make her wait till it suited him but came down the corridor with her and waited outside. He would leave the cabin so she could get washed and dressed. He was even solicitous about how she felt, if she'd had enough to eat and drink, and found her a couple of books to read.

But he didn't talk much. Not a word about his own situation or where she was bound for. In the dining room he replied if another passenger spoke to him but didn't start conversations. Belle guessed he was afraid she would entreat someone to help her, and of course she *was* watching out for the right person.

They were second-class passengers, as everyone was who had a cabin on the same level as them. There were only about twelve first-class passengers, whose cabins were on the deck above, and they ate in their own dining room where the food was probably much nicer.

At Cork they'd taken on a hundred or so third-class or steerage passengers. They were housed down in the bowels of the ship, and Belle had heard one of the officers informing them very curtly that they were only allowed on certain parts of the deck at certain times. From the glimpses Belle had got of them as they embarked at Cork, she could see by their worn clothes and boots that they were poor. She remembered from school being told about the early Irish immigrants to America, and that they suffered terrible conditions on the voyage; she hoped these poor people wouldn't be treated so badly.

Almost as soon as Belle had found herself locked in the cabin, she'd made a plan. Realizing that Etienne was not going to tolerate disobedience or rudeness, she decided to try to soften him up with charm. Each time he came back to the cabin she greeted him warmly, asking how cold it was on deck, who was up there and other such things. She made his bunk for him, kept her things tidy and as far as was possible treated him as if he really was her uncle.

She felt he was responding to this too, for he came back to the cabin often to suggest they had a stroll around the deck or went and sat in the comfortable chairs in the lounge on the top deck to look at the sea.

She turned away from the porthole as she heard Etienne coming in. 'Hello, come to liberate me?' she said with a smile.

'There's a storm brewing,' he said. 'Some folk are already feeling seasick. It's usually better to be closer to the fresh air when the sea's rough. Would you like to go up to the lounge?'

Belle had decided that Etienne was an attractive-looking man. His icy blue eyes might have been a little frightening at first, as was his threat to her, but he had a well-proportioned nose and a generous mouth, and his skin was smooth, clear and golden as though he'd been in the sun recently. Unusually, he didn't have a moustache or beard, and she liked that. His hair was good too; she was so used to seeing men with thinning hair slicked down with oil, or around Seven Dials they left it unwashed and untrimmed. But Etienne's hair was clean, thick and fair, the kind she was sure Mog would say was made to ruffle.

Belle had peeped out from behind the curtain earlier today to see him stripped to the waist to wash and shave, and had been quite taken aback to see he had a hard, powerfully built muscular body like a prize fighter's. He was younger than she had first thought too, she would guess only about thirty-two or thereabouts. It was all this, his comparative youth and good looks, that made her feel hopeful she could get him on her side.

'That would be nice, Uncle,' Belle said with a grin. 'Maybe we could have a cup of tea too?'

Etienne did order them tea and a cake, and as they sat by the window looking out at the sea, Belle noticed three smartly dressed young women sitting together. They were no more than twenty-three or -four and they must have come on board in Cork for she hadn't seen them before. Two of them were quite plain, but the third was very pretty, with flame-red curly hair.

'That red-headed girl would be just right for you,' Belle said. 'She's really pretty.'

'And what makes you think I want to find a young lady?' Etienne replied, a faint smile playing at his lips.

'All men do, don't they?' she retorted.

'Maybe I've already got a wife,' he said.

Belle shook her head. 'I don't think so.'

'What makes you say that?'

She wanted to reply that no wife would like a husband

who took young girls to work in brothels, but that was likely to anger him.

'You look lonely,' she said instead.

He laughed for the first time and his eyes seemed less cold. 'You are a funny girl, old beyond your years. How does someone look lonely?'

'Like they've got no one to care about them,' she said, and she thought of Jimmy and how his face had lit up when she said she'd be his friend. She wondered if he had asked Mog where she was. If he knew she'd been snatched, was he worried about her?

'I do sometimes feel lonely, but then everyone does,' he said.

'Back home there was a lady who looked after me when I was small. She said that it was good to feel lonely sometimes because it makes you appreciate what you have,' Belle said. 'I didn't appreciate anything at all, not until I was snatched off the street and taken away. Now all I can think of is back home, and that makes me lonelier still.'

'You were snatched off a street?' Etienne's brow furrowed and he looked very surprised.

Belle had assumed that he knew everything about her background and why she was in France. To find he didn't gave her a ray of hope that she could gain his sympathy.

'Yes, I witnessed a murder, and the man that did it brought me to France. I was sold to a brothel and I was raped by five men in as many days before I became ill. It seems the madam in that house sold me on then, and my new owners, whom you must work for too, nursed me back to health.'

He looked a bit shaken by this.

'It's no good you looking like you didn't know this, you must have known what I'd been through, and what's ahead of me,' she said tartly.

'I never ask anything, I just do what they require,' he said.

'But then, I've never before been asked to take one of their girls anywhere. This is the first time.'

'Do you think it is right to force a young girl into such a thing?'

'No, no, of course not,' he said hurriedly. 'But that is my personal view. You see, in my line of work I have to do many things I would rather not do, but that is part of the job. I have no choice in the matter. They gave me this job because I know America well.'

'But aren't you ashamed of doing bad things for money?'

He looked at her hard for a moment and then smiled. 'You have been so composed so far that I thought you were eighteen at least, but I see now that you still have the idealistic mind of a child. What did your father do for work? I'm sure that even he had to do some tasks he didn't like.'

'I don't know who my father is,' Belle said truthfully. 'But I know what you are getting at because I was brought up in a brothel. My mother ran it. Some people would say that was bad, but I know she didn't hurt anyone, and none of the girls who worked for her were forced into it.'

He looked so surprised at her coming from such a background that she went on to tell him a little more about it, and how she was kept unaware of the exact nature of her mother's business until that fateful night when Millie was killed. 'My mother wouldn't have made me be a whore,' she finished up. 'She and Mog wanted me to have a respectable life and they must be in agony not knowing where I am or what has been done to me.'

'I haven't hurt you, have I?' he said, as if that made his part in this all right. 'Like your mother, I had little alternative but to do what I do, and I always try to use the minimum of force. You are a smart girl, Belle. I know you have decided to try and win my trust, which is always the best ploy in a situation like we have. But however much I sympathize with you, I have to follow the orders I've been given, or I will be maimed or killed.'

He said this so casually that Belle knew it had to be true.

That night a storm blew up and the ship was tossed around like a stick in a flooded river. Belle felt fine, even though it was disconcerting to be almost thrown out of her bunk and to be in a cabin that felt like a mad fairground ride.

But Etienne wasn't faring so well. When Belle heard him groaning, she jumped out of her bunk to get the slop pail kept in the small cupboard under his bunk. He was violently sick several times in close succession, until he had nothing left to bring up but bile.

She finally had the opportunity to leave the cabin without his supervision to empty the slop pail, but she was so concerned for him she did nothing more than that, and then went to find a steward to ask if the ship's doctor could come to him.

The doctor never arrived. It seemed there were so many sick passengers that he concentrated on seeing the most vulnerable ones, the very young and the very old. So Belle was Etienne's nurse. She held the bucket for him to be sick in, sponged him down, made him sip water, and changed the sheets on his bunk when they became soaked with sweat. She barely slept at all and had very little to eat either for she didn't like to leave him for more than a few minutes.

But on the evening of the fourth day, the rolling and pitching of the ship eased and Etienne was more peaceful. Belle went up to the dining room then, wolfed down a hearty meal herself and got some soup and bread for Etienne.

'You've been very kind,' he said weakly as Belle helped him to sit up and put pillows behind him to support him.

'It was lucky I wasn't seasick too,' she said, spooning the

soup into his mouth as though he was a baby. 'Practically all the passengers are ill. The dining room was empty.'

'Did you seize the opportunity to get help for yourself?' he asked, catching hold of her wrist.

He was still terribly pale, but the green tinge to his skin had gone. She looked down at his hand gripping her and frowned. He removed it at once and apologized.

'That's better,' she said starchily. 'But no, I didn't seek help, I was too busy looking after you.'

His relief was palpable, and it crossed her mind she should have lied and said she'd told the purser or someone.

'Then I'd better pull myself together quickly, before you take off in a lifeboat,' he said with a smile. 'You'd make a first-class nurse, for you have a strong stomach and an iron will, but you are kind too.'

Belle smiled because she was happy to see him so much better. But at the same time she was confused as to why she should care how he was when to all intents and purposes he was her enemy. 'Eat up, you've got some way to go before you'll be strong enough again to bully me. I'll leave my escaping until then,' she retorted.

In the days that followed the sea grew calmer and gradually the normal routine on board returned. Etienne recovered very quickly and was soon eating well again. But his manner to Belle had changed: he was much warmer, and instead of locking her in the cabin for long periods he suggested they played cards and board games in the lounge to pass the time.

'What's the place like in New York where you're taking me?' she asked while they played chequers.

'It's not in New York. It's in New Orleans.'

'But that's right at the other end of America, isn't it?' she asked.

Etienne nodded. 'In the Deep South. You'll be a whole lot warmer there.'

'But how will we get there?'

'Another ship.' He went on to tell her that New Orleans was completely different to anywhere else in America, as prostitution was legal and it had non-stop music, dancing and gambling. He explained that the natives were French Creoles but there was also a huge population of negroes. This was because they had flocked to the town after the Civil War and the abolition of slavery. The Union Army had destroyed most of the big cotton and tobacco plantations in the South and the displaced workforce had to find some other line of work.

'New Orleans is a fine-looking town too,' he said with obvious appreciation. 'It was built by the French with elegant mansions, beautiful gardens and squares. I think you will grow to love it.'

'Maybe I will once I get over the hurdle of selling myself,' she said tartly.

He gave her a wry little smile. 'You know something, Belle, I've got a feeling that you are just smart enough to persuade the people who've bought you that you'd be more beneficial to them in a different role.'

'What sort of role?' she asked.

Etienne sucked in his cheeks thoughtfully. 'Dancing, singing, front of house, hat-check girl. I don't know, but you think on it and see what you can come up with. Did your mother have anyone working in her house who didn't go with the men?'

'Well, there was Mog, who I've already told you about,' Belle said. 'My mother called her the maid, but she was housekeeper and cook too. In the evenings she worked upstairs. I think she showed the men in and poured them drinks – she never talked to me about what she did.'

'A maid in a brothel usually looks after the money and minds the girls,' Etienne explained. 'It's a crucial role, for she has to be diplomatic and sensitive, but tough too if necessary. Why do you suppose she didn't go with any of the men?' he asked, one eyebrow raised.

'Well, she wasn't very pretty,' Belle said, and instantly felt disloyal to Mog.

Etienne laughed and reached out to smooth a stray curl from her cheek. 'No one will ever be able to say that of you! But you are definitely sharp-witted, Belle, and that could well be a bonus in a town that has hundreds of pretty, but lazy, greedy and rather stupid girls.'

Belle had already worked out that whoever owned her now must have paid a very high price for her. The travelling expenses alone would be more money than she could ever imagine earning. She was puzzled, because it didn't make any sense to buy an English girl they didn't even know, when there had to be countless prettier and more amenable girls already there in the Southern States of America.

But it did mean she must be seen as some kind of prize. So if she put that with what Etienne had said about offering herself as something else, maybe it would work.

But what could she offer herself as? She could sing in tune, but she wasn't brilliant; the only dance she knew was the polka, and she couldn't play a musical instrument either. She couldn't think of anything she could do which would make anyone sit up and take notice.

Mog had said just after Millie was killed that she'd been the favourite of the house, and Belle had always been aware that Mog and Annie had given her more praise, affection and little treats than any of the other girls. She knew now that this meant Millie brought them in more money, but what was the difference in how Millie treated her clients to how the other girls did it? Belle certainly didn't want to be a whore, but if she had no choice, then she'd rather be a great one that men paid far more for.

How on earth could she find out what made a great one? She had a feeling Etienne would know, but she was far too bashful to ask him such a thing.

Two days before they were due to disembark in New York, Etienne took Belle for an afternoon stroll around the deck. It was cold and windy, but the sun was shining, and it felt good to be out in the fresh air, watching seagulls swoop and swirl around the ship.

'We've got two days in New York before we have to board the ship for New Orleans,' he said as they leaned on a rail up by the bow, watching the sea curl away as the ship ploughed its way through. 'I'm going to give you a choice. Either stay locked in the boarding-house room with me. Or, if you promise me you won't run off, I'll take you to see the sights.'

Belle had already learned that Etienne was a man of his word, and she liked that he was prepared to take her on trust too.

'I'll promise I won't run off as long as you let me send a letter home to tell them I'm alive,' she replied.

He turned, leaning his back against the ship's rail. The wind was ruffling his fair hair and it made him look boyish and totally unthreatening. He stared at her without replying for what seemed an eternity.

'Cat got your tongue?' she asked cheekily.

He smiled. 'I never understood that English phrase. Why would a cat take anyone's tongue? But I've decided I'll allow you to write a postcard home. All it can say is that you are in New York and in good health. I read it, and post it!'

Belle gave a whoop of delight. It wouldn't get her rescued, but it would stop Mog and her mother fretting that she was dead. 'A deal,' she said. 'I won't try to run off.'

It was night as the ship sailed up the East River to dock in New York. It had been announced earlier that they would be disembarking in the morning and instructions about what they could expect when they went through immigration on Ellis Island had been given. Belle had only half listened to the officer, as she knew Etienne would know what to do. But as she was packing away her things into her bag ready for the morning, she did wonder how he intended to deal with any immigration officer who asked them awkward questions, for the captain had announced that there was a medical examination and several kinds of tests to be passed before entry into America.

She was just about to start getting undressed to go to bed, when Etienne came back into the cabin.

'We're leaving,' he said sharply. 'Put the last of your things in your bag and hurry.'

He had that tense, steely-eyed look again that he'd had when they first met in Brest.

'How can we leave?' she asked in puzzlement as he pulled his bag out from beneath his bunk and put the last of his things into it. 'The ship hasn't docked.'

'Someone has come alongside to take us off,' he said. 'Now, be quick and don't argue.'

The ship was lying at anchor, waiting for a tug to take it in at first light. It was very quiet as they left the cabin and made their way up to the lower deck. Belle thought most of the passengers must be packing or getting an early night to be ready for the morning. Holding her arm, Etienne led her to the port side of the deck where she saw Petty Officer Barker was waiting. This man had been very solicitous to Belle when Etienne had been ill. She understood why now, for he was clearly getting paid for helping them to evade the immigration officers.

In great haste, Barker grabbed her and pushed her on to a bosun's chair, putting their bags in her lap. Etienne jumped on then, standing astride her with his feet wedged beneath her legs and holding on to the rope. Suddenly the chair was pushed out over the side and Barker began to lower it. The seat spun round crazily in the cold wind and Belle had to close her eyes for she was afraid she'd fall out into the water.

'Don't be frightened,' Etienne said in a low voice. 'You're quite safe. We'll be on the other boat in seconds.'

He was right – almost as he spoke she felt a bump as the seat reached the other boat. Etienne jumped off and helped her out too. They were on what looked and smelled like a fishing boat. The bosun's chair was hauled back up, and before Belle had time to adjust to the rocking motion of the little boat, it began to chug away from the big ship.

A small, stocky man in waterproofs came over to them. 'Into the wheelhouse with you,' he said curtly. 'Sit down on the floor out of sight.'

Belle might not have felt seasick during the storm on the big ship, but she felt very queasy once she was squashed up in a corner of the wheelhouse. It wasn't just the smell of fish, or the rocking motion of the small boat, but fear, for she had no idea what was in store for her. The man at the helm didn't speak to them, or even turn to look at them as they scuttled into the wheelhouse. It was as if he thought that by not acknowledging their presence, he could pretend he didn't know they were aboard.

Belle was scared. If she was entering the country illegally, what would happen to her if she tried to leave it? She felt angry with herself that she hadn't run away from Etienne instead of going along with his escape plan. How could she have been stupid enough to believe he was going to show her the sights of New York or send a postcard home? Wasn't it far more likely that he was going to take her to some terrible place, even worse than the brothel in Paris? Why on earth had she started to trust him?

Etienne didn't speak to her at all as they sat hunched up on the floor, and as Belle felt she might endanger herself even more by saying anything, she stayed quiet too. They had been on the boat for about twenty-five minutes when suddenly there was bright light coming in through the wheelhouse windows, and Belle could hear men shouting to one another.

'We're approaching the docks. They'll be mooring any minute,' Etienne whispered. 'We stay here until they tell us it's safe to go.'

'Where do we go?' she whispered back fearfully.

'To a hotel, just like I told you,' he said. 'I didn't tell you this was how we were going into New York, just in case you panicked.'

'What if we get caught?' she whispered. 'Won't they shove us in prison?'

He took her two hands in his and lifted her fingers to gently kiss the tips of them. His eyes were full of mischief. 'I don't ever get caught. Back in France they call me L'Ombre, which means the shadow.'

'You make a very good guide,' Belle said as they came down the gangplank of the little boat which had taken them out to see the Statue of Liberty. 'Maybe you should take that up instead of working for bad men.'

It was dusk now, and growing very cold, but the last two days had been bright and sunny and they'd walked miles and seen so much: the Flat Iron Building, the first of New York's skyscrapers, the Brooklyn Bridge, Central Park . . . they'd travelled on the 'E', a train which ran high over houses and offices. Belle had eaten her first hot dog and marvelled at the grand shops on Fifth Avenue, but also seen enough grim, over-crowded tenements to realize there were even more desperately poor people in America than there were back home.

Etienne had been as good as his word, getting her safely from the fishing boat to a guest house on the Lower West

Side. Although the neighbourhood looked every bit as squalid as Seven Dials, and certainly didn't live up to the way people back in England imagined Americans lived, the guest house was comfortable and warm, with steam heat, hot baths and indoor lavatories.

'It's been good to show you round,' Etienne said. 'I just wish we had a couple more days for there's a great deal more I'd like to show you. When I get back to France I shall have to continue in the same line of work, for I have no choice, but when we get to New Orleans I will try to influence your new mistress into taking very good care of you.'

Belle was holding his arm and she squeezed it, knowing he really did feel badly about his part in her capture. She also knew why he had to go through with it, because he'd finally told her his story.

He was born and grew up in Marseille, but his mother died when he was six, and his father turned to drink. Etienne stole first out of necessity. His father spent every penny he made on drink, and someone had to put food on the table, clothes on their backs and pay the rent on their two rooms.

But by the time he was fourteen he had become a skilful burglar, and targeted the grand hotels all along the Riviera where the very wealthy stayed. He went after jewellery which he then fenced for a fraction of its real value in one of the many little jewellers in the narrow street down by the harbour.

He was eighteen when he was caught red-handed one night in the room of a man who had become a millionaire through, it transpired, extortion. He was offered a choice: work for this man, whom Etienne chose to call Jacques because he couldn't reveal his real name, or be thrown to the police, who would no doubt make sure he got an extremely long prison sentence as he'd been a thorn in their side for years.

Etienne explained to Belle that at the time he thought he was the luckiest man alive to be offered work with Jacques.

'I could hardly believe it. He sent me to London where I was given English lessons. I stayed in a nice place called Bayswater, and I had further lessons on the habits of the English aristocracy so that I could rob them. But whereas in the past I would be stealing a diamond ring or some emerald ear bobs, left on the dressing-table, now I was to be clearing out a safe containing hundreds of pounds worth of jewels, or conducting a confidence trick on someone which would make them part with thousands of pounds.'

He said that for a few years it was good to have hand-tailored suits and silk shirts and stay in the best hotels, and he was making more money than he'd ever dreamed of. But a scare with the English police had made him go back to Paris to lie low for a while, and during that time he went home to Marseille and met a girl he fell in love with. He wanted to marry her, and he felt it was time to put the money he'd made to good use and start a legitimate business, before his luck ran out.

'So I told Jacques my plan, and he asked that I give him another two years. When that was up I went back to Marseille and married Elena, and in partnership with her brother who is a chef, we opened a restaurant there. But I was wrong to think I could just say goodbye to Jacques; he didn't like anyone to escape from his net. Every now and then he would send word that he had a job for me, and I couldn't refuse him.'

'Was that jobs like collecting me?' Belle asked.

'No, I told you I had never done anything like escorting girls before. It was always strong arm stuff,' Etienne explained. 'Mostly I have to threaten someone who isn't toeing the line, or maybe is standing in Jacques' way. Often I have to use violence, but you must understand these people were all thugs and gangsters, so it is nothing to me. But I wish now that once I had the restaurant I had refused point blank to do any more work for him.' He sighed. 'He wouldn't have liked it, he would have made things tough for me, but by going along with it I've just got in deeper and deeper.'

Belle listened to him attentively and asked if there was any way he could get out of it now.

'By escorting you here I have put myself in an even worse position,' Etienne replied glumly. 'Strong arm stuff between thugs and gangsters is understood and accepted by most people, but now Jacques has involved me in trafficking such a young girl, he has got an even stronger hold over me.'

'What does your wife think about this?' she asked.

'She thinks I am an aide to a businessman with many companies, and although she doesn't like me to be away from her, she likes the extra money I bring home. If I am truthful, I always enjoyed being the big man who sorted out grievances between criminals. But I don't feel that way now, not now Jacques has made me do this job. Trafficking young girls is wicked, and I do not wish to have any part in it, nor would I want my wife and children to ever discover that I have done.'

'We're kind of in the same position, aren't we?' Belle said glumly. 'I can't run away from you now because I'd be afraid what would happen to you. And you can't help me go either because of what might happen to your wife and sons.'

He turned to her and cupped her face between his hands. 'Belle, I would take that risk if I could be certain you'd be safe, for I could easily tell Jacques the immigration people caught you, and he'd believe that for he'd have no way of checking. But what would become of you? You would either have to find work here, with all the risks that go with being a young girl alone in a dangerous city. Or you'd tell the authorities that you were brought here illegally, and get them to send you back home.'

Belle knew that hope must have registered on her face, for he shook his head.

'That might seem the perfect solution to you, but this man

Kent you tell me about back in England, he will hear from New Orleans what has happened and he'll have to get to you and kill you to save himself. I know how these men work, as he will be much the same as Jacques.'

'Is there no other way?' she asked.

'You are a remarkable young lady,' he said sadly. 'It is this which makes me sure you will conquer New Orleans on your own terms. It is many things, a corrupt, dangerous place, but it also has a soul, and I think on balance you will be safer there and get the opportunity to select your own path in life.'

Chapter Fourteen

As the ship sailed south down the coast of America, the wind dropped, and gradually it became a little warmer and the skies bluer. On Belle's sixteenth birthday Etienne bought a bottle of French champagne for them to celebrate.

'I wish you'd told me that your birthday was so soon while we were in New York and I would have bought you a little present,' he said apologetically. 'You must be thinking of your mother and your Mog so much today?'

Belle *had* been thinking of home. Mog had always made her a special iced cake with candles, and there would be little presents from everyone in the house. Last birthday her mother had given her the grey cloak she was wearing when she was snatched, but even that had gone now, left back at Madame Sondheim's.

'It doesn't matter,' she said, even though she did feel very sad. 'In years to come I'll remember where I was when I had my first glass of champagne.'

A few days later they were standing on deck looking at the coast-line in the distance.

'New Orleans is much warmer than England all year round,' Etienne explained. 'It has very mild winters and hot, sticky summers. But it has quite heavy rain too, and hurricanes, mostly at the end of August or the beginning of September.'

'What else can you tell me about it?' Belle was growing very scared now, for within twenty-four hours Etienne would be handing her over and he'd have to return to France.

'It's a place for fun,' he said, his eyes lighting up as if he had good memories of there. 'People come over the weekend to let their hair down, to dance, gamble, find a woman, and hear the music. The music is what stays in your head long after you've left New Orleans. It wafts out of every bar, club, dance hall and restaurant, follows you up the street and into your dreams.'

'And if they make me do that thing?' She blushed scarlet for she couldn't bring herself to speak openly of what she knew would be expected of her. 'Is there anything you can tell me that would make it easier to bear?'

He put his hand on her cheek, his eyes tender now as if he wished he could reassure her that wasn't going to happen. 'If I was you I'd try and think about the money. Slavery is dead, and you should get half of what you earn, if you stand up for yourself. And put the money somewhere safe, it's your future you are saving for.' He paused for a moment as if thinking what he could say about the actual act.

'I think the real trick to it is making the men think they are getting something unique and wonderful,' he went on. 'This is easy because men can be fools, they'll look at your pretty face and see how young you are, and before you so much as hold their hand they'll believe you are a dream come true.'

Belle smiled. She loved hearing Etienne talk, even if the subject wasn't all that agreeable. That hint of French accent was so compelling, and the more she looked at him, the sadder she was that she was soon going to lose him.

'But above all you have to believe you are the best,' Etienne said earnestly. 'The top girls in New Orleans get as much as thirty or forty dollars a time, they wear the latest silk gowns, have a maid to arrange their hair, some even have their own carriage to drive around in. Many of these girls have wealthy patrons who pay them not to go with any other man. There are other top girls who get booked for all night, every night, yet often their clients only want to go to sleep with them in their arms. And so it goes right down the scale to the cheaper sporting houses, girls who rent out a room by the hour, until you finally get to the girls who do their work in back alleys. They are filthy, depraved and disease-ridden hags, charging only a couple of cents.

'You must always remember that you are a top end girl. You will look beautiful, be sweet and charming to your clients even when you want to cry. You must try to love the men for the short time you are with them, and soon you will find that you really can love them a little and you won't feel bad about your life.'

'You sound as if you really know what goes on. Have you been to these houses?'

'Belle, I was a burglar, I always mixed with people on the wrong side of the fence. I got to know the girls in cat houses in Marseille like they were my sisters. They would tell me about their lives, their clients, the other girls and the madams, and I know from this that you must always keep the madam on your side. She is the one who can make your life hell if she doesn't like you.'

'You said sporting houses and cat houses – are they the same as brothels?' she asked curiously.

Etienne smiled down at her. 'They use these words more in New Orleans than the word brothel. Sporting houses are usually quite grand places, often with a band playing in the drawing room. They put a screen round the musicians so they can't see the identity of the men who come in to dance and have fun with the girls.'

All at once Belle was overcome by emotion and she began to cry.

'What is it?' Etienne asked, putting his arms around her and drawing her to his chest.

'I am going to miss you so much,' she sobbed.

He held her tightly and stroked her hair. 'I'm going to miss you too, little one. You have taken a part of my heart. But I may get sent here again some day and you will be so grand and important you won't want to talk with me.'

'I would never be too grand for you.' She sniffed back her tears and almost laughed because she knew he was only teasing her. 'But my admirers might be jealous as you are so handsome.'

He put his hands on either side of her head and bent down to kiss away her tears. 'I think it might be better for me to stay away when you are older, for you will surely break my heart,' he said softly. 'Now, just remember what I told you, that you are beautiful and clever, and you must use that sharp mind to outfox any that would try to trap or hurt you.'

A little later Etienne left Belle on deck while he went down to their cabin for something. Aside from when he was suffering from seasickness, it was the first opportunity she'd had to speak to anyone she chose. There were dozens of other people on deck – respectable married couples, groups of young men, a few elderly people, and even two plainly dressed women who she felt might be the churchy kind. They would be ideal people to ask for help, and she had no doubt that if such an opportunity had arisen on the steamer from France, she would have gladly snatched it.

But she didn't want any help now. While it was true that being delivered to a brothel wasn't her ideal start in life, would London have been any better for her? While she was absolutely certain her mother and Mog would not have wanted her to become a whore, what else was there for a girl of her background except going into service or working in a factory? To stay at home for ever was an even worse prospect, for she'd never make any friends and the days would be endless.

Belle had often looked at the grand department stores like

the new Selfridges which had opened just the year before in Oxford Street, or Swan and Edgar's in Regent Street, and wished she could work in one of them. But even had she been able to get a good reference from someone, which was unlikely, everyone said the girls in those shops worked very long hours for very little pay and were bullied by the floor managers. She remembered how the other girls at the school she went to in Bloomsbury whispered about her. She had no doubt that kind of whispering would follow her to any job she might find. Just as Jimmy had assumed she had to be a whore because she lived in a brothel, so would everyone else.

So she had decided she was going to do exactly what Etienne had suggested and use her wits to make a good life for herself. She wouldn't fight being a whore, just go with it and aim for the top spot. They wouldn't lock her in or watch her like a hawk if they saw that she was willing. And it would be good to wear silk dresses and drive in her own carriage. In fact it might even be the greatest of adventures. She was after all in America, a country where dreams could come true.

One day, when she'd saved enough money, she'd sail home to England and open that little hat shop she used to dream about.

That evening in the dining room with Etienne, Belle felt oddly lightheaded because she'd become resolved about her future. It was warmer, and she'd put on a lighter, pale blue taffeta dress which she'd been given in Paris and hadn't worn before because it had been too cold. It was very pretty, with white lace ruffles on the bodice and sleeves, and she'd put a blue ribbon in her hair to match. When Etienne offered her some red wine, she accepted it eagerly for it was all part of moving on to her new way of life.

'You seem different tonight,' Etienne said as he poured it. 'You aren't planning to bolt the moment the ship docks tomorrow, are you? Only New Orleans is a very dangerous place for an unescorted young lady to be.'

Belle giggled. 'No, I'm not going to bolt. That would be silly. I'm feeling better about everything now.'

He smiled, and put his hand over hers on the table. 'I'm glad of that. You know I will do everything I can tomorrow to make sure they understand how special you are.'

Etienne went out on deck to smoke a cigar after dinner, and Belle went down alone to their cabin and lit a candle to undress by. She realized that she was just a little tipsy, but she liked the feeling, just as she'd liked the touch of Etienne's hand on hers.

As she started to unbutton her dress she was thinking of what it would be like to be kissed by Etienne. Not a kiss on the cheek, but a real grown-up one on the lips. The thought made her feel all hot and shaky.

She glanced at his bunk, and suddenly she knew she wanted to be in it, with him. With trembling fingers she undid the remainder of the buttons and stepped out of her dress, then took off her boots. Her two petticoats came next, falling on to her blue dress in a white froth. She paused then in her chemise, drawers and stockings, wondering how much more she should remove. She liked the chemise, it was the one which had been given to her in Paris, soft white cotton with pin tucks and rows of lace around the low neckline. Decided, she whipped off her drawers and stockings, threw all her clothes up on to her bunk, and climbed into Etienne's.

Her heart was thumping, every nerve, muscle and tendon braced for his return, but fortunately she didn't have long to wait before she heard his familiar footsteps coming along the corridor.

The cabin door opened and he came in, then stopped abruptly as he saw her in his bed. 'Now, what are you doing there?' he asked. 'Too tipsy to climb on to the top one?'

She liked that he hadn't assumed she was in his bed to be with him. 'No, I'm in here because I want your arms around me,' she whispered nervously.

He took off his jacket and hung it on one of the hooks at the end of the bunks, then he knelt down by the bunk. 'Beautiful Belle,' he sighed. 'You are enough to tempt even the most holy of men. But what makes you do this? Are you practising being a temptress? Or maybe you think if you do this I won't be able to take you to the house tomorrow?'

'I know you will still have to take me,' she said, a little daunted by his concerned expression. 'But Lisette said to me in Paris that if I found a man I really liked, I would change my mind about it.' She didn't know what word to use, she couldn't bring herself to use the word sex, or fucking, and if there was a less graphic word she didn't know it.

'With a man you really like it is called making love,' he said, leaning forward so his face was very close to hers. 'I am flattered that you like me, Belle, I never met a young girl I liked more than you. I will hold you and kiss you but that is all, for I have a wife at home who I cannot be unfaithful to.'

He leaned still closer and his lips met Belle's, touching them with the softness of a butterfly's wings. Belle's arms came up to hold him and his tongue flickered into her mouth, making a little tremor run down her spine.

'How was that?' he said teasingly. With only one candle alight she couldn't see his face clearly. But she reached out her hands and cupped it, using her thumbs to caress his lips gently.

'It was good enough for me to want more,' she whispered.

He moved and slid on to the bunk beside her, scooping her into his arms. 'You are a little temptress,' he sighed. 'You will do well in New Orleans!'

He kissed her again and again until her whole body was aching to be caressed too. But though he kissed and nuzzled at her neck, her arms and fingers, he didn't attempt to go any further.

Belle knew he desired her, she could feel his cock straining to be released from his trousers, but when she tentatively put her hand on it, he gently removed it.

'Time for both of us to sleep,' he said, kissing her forehead softly and getting off the bunk.

He took her clothes from the top bunk, blew out the candle and leapt up there, and Belle stretched out in the space he'd vacated and smiled to herself as she smelled him on the pillow.

No man would be so frightening now she knew how sweet it could be. She felt sad that Etienne wasn't prepared to be the one to initiate her in the arts of lovemaking, but he had made her understand what desire was.

'*Bonsoir, ma petite,*' he said softly from above her.

'Goodnight, Etienne,' she whispered back. 'If the gentlemen of New Orleans are all like you I won't have any trouble loving them.'

Chapter Fifteen

Gold cherubs holding up an alabaster table, turquoise velvet couches strewn with gold and pink satin cushions, a white piano, and a life-size painting of a naked lady lying on a couch hanging above the white marble fireplace – these were just a few of the marvels in the drawing room of Martha's *maison de joie*, as the woman had called it. Belle had to force herself not to be distracted by the splendour and to pin her ears back so she could hear what Etienne was saying to Madame Martha.

She was a very big woman of around forty-five. Belle thought she must be five feet nine inches or so, and at least fifteen stone; her hair was bleached a golden blonde and piled up on her head in elaborate coils. But however big or old she was, she was still beautiful, her skin like ivory satin, eyes so dark Belle could see no iris. She was wearing an apricot-coloured, loose-fitting tea dress with elaborate bead-work around the low neck, and her huge breasts billowed up and threatened to spill over. Her feet were tiny, encased in embroidered slippers the same colour as her dress, and her equally small hands had a ring on every finger.

'Belle is very different from your usual girls, madame,' Etienne said very politely. 'She is intelligent, she has the poise and communication skills of a fully grown woman; she is also a kind, caring and sensitive girl. I wouldn't dare to try and tell you how to run your house. But I got to know Belle well on the long journey here, and I believe it would be more fruitful for you to hold her back. Let her learn from the other girls and perhaps even tease the gentlemen a little with her.'

'If I wanted your opinion, honey, I would've asked for it,'

Madame responded. Yet despite what she'd said, she looked amused at his cheek.

'I wouldn't dream of offending such a beautiful woman,' Etienne said silkily. 'It was just that I know sometimes girls are whisked so quickly into working that their true assets are not noticed. Belle has been treated very badly, abducted from her home and taken to Paris where she was subjected to the kind of thing I know you abhor. She could do with more time.'

Madame was nodding her head as Etienne was speaking, but once he reached the part about her being badly treated in Paris, she turned to look at Belle appraisingly.

'Is that so, honey chile?' she asked.

'Yes, it is,' Belle replied, surprised to be spoken to. 'I was abducted because I witnessed a murder. In Paris I was raped by five different men, and then I became very ill,' she admitted. But not wanting to look as though she was permanently damaged, she smiled at the older woman. 'I'm all better now of course, and I would make a very good maid and I could help you all around the house with cleaning, laundry and even cooking.'

'I sure didn't pay for you to be brought all the way from Paris to be a maid,' Madame said. Her tone was sharp but her dark eyes were twinkling. 'My house is one of the best in town because my girls are happy, and I guess I can wait a little while to see how things go with you, and see if you can be happy too.'

'You are a good woman,' Etienne said, taking her hand and kissing it.

'I think you are sweet on her,' Madame said lightly, raising one eyebrow suggestively.

'Any man would be,' he replied. 'She's a little pearl.'

Etienne said he had to go then and Belle followed him to the front door to say goodbye.

The hall was almost as grand as the drawing room, with a huge chandelier, a black and white tiled floor and walls covered in an ornate red and gold raised paper. Everything Belle had seen so far seemed fine, but she was aware that appearances meant little, and once Etienne had left she would be on her own, in a strange country, without anyone to turn to.

Perhaps Etienne sensed how she felt for he stopped at the door and turned to her. 'Don't be scared,' he said, caressing her cheek tenderly. 'Although I've never met Martha before, I have it on good authority she is a good woman. You will be safe here.'

Belle didn't want him to go, but she was too proud to cry or look distressed. 'Tell me something, would you have killed me if I'd run away or sought help?'

He grinned boyishly. 'How could I kill you if you'd run away? And I couldn't have done it if you'd got help either. But I had to scare you into behaving. I'm sorry if I frightened you.'

'I'll never be sorry I met you,' she said, and blushed a becoming pink. 'You've got a piece of my heart now.'

'Stay as beautiful and as sweet as you are now,' he said. 'I believe you will come to see New Orleans as your home, and you'll forget the past. Just make sure you never let anyone push you around, and put some money away for a rainy day too.'

Belle moved forward so she could kiss him on the lips. 'Safe journey home and think of me sometimes.'

His eyes, which had seemed so hard and cold when she first met him in Brest, were now soft and sad.

'It will be hard to think of anything else,' he said, then kissed her with such feeling that she felt her legs were going to give way.

*

By the time Belle fell exhausted into bed at first light the follow-ing morning, she almost felt she was at home. The atmosphere in Martha's was similar to Annie's Place, overcharged with expectancy, faintly hysterical, yet warm and welcoming too. It even smelled and sounded much the same – perfume, cigars, the rustle of taffeta petticoats and girlish giggling. She might not have spent an evening upstairs back home, but the sounds and smells permeated the whole house.

There were only five other girls here, all around eighteen or nineteen and exceptionally pretty: Hatty, Anna-Maria, Suzanne, Polly and Betty. In the early evening when Belle saw them coming down the stairs, each in a different vivid-coloured silk dress that revealed enough of their charms to tease any man, it was like looking at five rare and beautiful hothouse plants.

They hadn't looked that way at their first meeting. Although it was the middle of the afternoon, they'd only just got out of bed, and they wore only a loose wrap over a chemise, with their hair all bedraggled.

As the girls ate fruit and pastries and drank coffee, Martha had introduced Belle. She suggested she tell them something about herself, and as Belle wanted them to become her friends and allies, she told them that she had been brought up in a brothel and about the murder she'd witnessed.

Afterwards she wondered if she'd said too much, and that it might have been better to have kept her own counsel, but they had hung on her every word, full of sympathy for her, and wanted to know all about England. She had been sur-prised at their concern for her, remembering that whenever a new girl arrived back home there was always backbiting and bad feeling.

Raven-haired Anna-Maria was Creole, and her French accent was comfortingly like Etienne's. Hatty and Suzanne had come from San Francisco, and as with Belle, Martha had paid to have them come and work for her. They were quick to say they hadn't got any regrets, and although their year's contract with Martha had ended months ago, they wanted to stay on.

Polly and Betty had worked together in an Atlanta bordello but it was closed down by the police and so they came to New Orleans. They said they were fortunate in being directed to Martha's, and in being taken on immediately.

All five were white girls. It seemed that mixed houses weren't allowed, so the coloured girls were in different houses.

The pianist sat down to play in the drawing room in the early evening, the girls arranged themselves prettily on the couches, and soon afterwards gentlemen began to arrive. To Belle's surprise they really did appear to be gentlemen. They were astoundingly well-mannered, they didn't use any profanities, and treated the girls like real ladies. They all wore well-cut suits, boiled white shirts, highly polished boots, and had neatly trimmed beards and moustaches. There were a few who sported the kind of loud checked waistcoats and ostentatious gold watch chains that Etienne had pointed out as being markers of 'white trash' while they were on the ship from New York. But though these men were a little brash and flashy, they were still very polite. Belle thought it rather sweet that they asked the pianist for special tunes so they could dance with the girls.

The pianist's name was Errol, and he was a negro, but apparently all pianists here were called 'the Professor'. He knew hundreds of tunes, just playing them by ear without any music. Some got Belle's toes tapping and made her want to dance. Betty told her it was called jazz, and she would be hearing a great deal more of it for it was *the* music of New Orleans. But the Professor sang too – he had a lovely deep, husky voice – and in some of the songs he'd changed the words to rather naughty ones about Martha's house which made everyone laugh.

Belle offered the gentlemen whisky, wine or champagne, which seemed awfully expensive at a dollar a time, especially as she knew the 'wine' they bought for the girls was just red-coloured water. She thought it was nice that the men weren't rushed up the stairs and that the girls sat around chatting and flirting with them, just as if they were at a party. But she realized later that all the drinks they bought added up to quite a lot, so that was why Martha encouraged the girls to keep them in the drawing room.

Asking a girl to dance appeared to be the discreet way the men picked their girl, and when they left the room together, hand in hand, they could have just been going to take an innocent stroll around the garden.

Belle wondered how the money changed hands, for apart from charging for the drinks, and seeing the gentlemen tipping Errol, she saw no other money. But Suzanne explained that the first thing the girls did when they got to their room with the gentleman was to ask for the twenty dollars. This they handed to Cissie, the upstairs maid, who passed it on to Martha who kept a record of what all the girls earned in an evening.

Cissie was a negro, a tall, thin woman with a cast in one eye. She had a very stern expression and rarely smiled, but the girls had said she was kindness itself, especially when they were sick.

Belle had been very surprised by what a short time the men spent upstairs with the girls, especially as they usually stayed in the drawing room chatting and drinking for over an hour. She thought the average time they spent in a girl's room was only about twenty minutes; if they stayed as long as thirty minutes Martha began to look tense. Then as soon as the men came down they left the house. Belle had always assumed the sex act lasted at least an hour, for that was how long it seemed to be for her in Paris, and when Kent was with Millie. Now she was beginning to see that it had been a much shorter time than that, it was just the horror of it which had made it appear so long.

As each girl entertained about ten gentlemen during the evening, at twenty dollars a time, they were making a small fortune, even if Martha took half of it. Belle had thought it marvellous when Martha said she'd give her a dollar a day to serve drinks, and just this first evening she'd been given a total of two dollars, fifty cents in tips. That of course was small beer in comparison to what the girls got, or the tips the Professor received – almost every gentleman gave him a dollar. But it seemed to her that this was a place where anyone with the right attitude could get very rich very quickly.

The girls had said that tonight was a quiet night, and that on Saturdays it was packed out. Yet having watched the girls, seen their ready smiles, heard the peals of laughter, it obviously wasn't as vile a job as Belle had imagined.

But she didn't want to think about that just now. It was better to allow herself to sink into her soft feather mattress with just a thin comforter over her because it was so warm, and remember how cold it was back home.

She hoped that by now the postcard she had sent Annie and Mog in New York had reached them. Etienne hadn't let her say where she was bound for, or what she was expected to do, just as she hadn't said what had happened to her in Paris. But considering her mother ran a brothel, they were bound to realize the truth. All Belle could hope for was that they sensed she was happy when she'd written the postcard and that would stop some of their anxiety.

She had planned to write a proper letter home once she was settled here, but she wasn't so sure now if that was the right thing to do. It might just make things worse; after all, her mother couldn't afford to come here and get her, and even if she could, Martha would be bound to insist that she paid back however much she'd paid for Belle.

She wondered too about Jimmy. She so much wanted to write and tell him the whole story, but if she did, he might want to go after Kent, and then his life could be in danger.

So on reflection Belle thought maybe it might be better for everyone if she didn't write at all. The truth would only make them fret. Yet if she was to lie and tell them she was working in a shop or as a maid, they wouldn't believe that. After all, no one would ever abduct someone and then give them a nice, respectable life!

She fell asleep pondering on the problem.

Belle found herself wide awake the next morning at ten o'clock. It seemed odd that there was barely a sound from the street outside. The previous evening it had been even rowdier than Monmouth Street on a Saturday night.

She was dying to go out and explore, as all she'd seen of New Orleans so far was from the cab on the way from the ship. It had been quiet then too, as it was only nine in the morning, and all she saw were delivery carts, road sweepers and negro maids scrubbing doorsteps and polishing door brass. But she had been impressed by how old and attractive the city was. Etienne told her that the part they drove through from the dock was called the French Quarter, because back in 1721 the first twenty blocks were laid out by the French.

All the houses were right on the street with no front gardens, like many of the Victorian terraces back home, but these houses weren't all the same: there were colourful Creole-style cottages with shuttered windows right next to houses of the Spanish style with dainty wrought-iron balconies on their upper floors, often with a profusion of plants and flowers growing there. Belle had glimpses of pretty little courtyards, there were squares with a central garden, and she saw many exotic-looking flowers and tall palm trees.

Etienne had gone on to explain that until 1897, New Orleans

was a terrifying, lawless place, with prostitutes plying their wares or posing nearly naked in doorways all over town. With it being such a busy port, sailors of every nationality poured into town nightly to gamble, drink, find a woman and usually end up in a fight too. The death toll from stabbings and gunshot wounds was high, and countless others were found unconscious in back alleys having been beaten up and robbed. Ordinary, respectable people trying to bring up their children had this going on all around them and they demanded that something must be done about it.

Alderman Sidney Story came up with a plan to take the area of thirty-eight blocks on the far side of the railway track, behind the French Quarter, and make prostitution legal there. This would mean that all the city's ills were housed in one place, making it easier for it to be policed. Ordinary law-abiding people were happy to vote for a bill that would mean an end to whores and rowdy, drunken sailors around their homes. Gambling and opium dens would be out of sight, and they would no longer have to fear the violence of vice-related crime.

Sidney Story sponsored the bill and got it passed, and so the area was given the name of 'Storyville'. But most people just called it the District.

Belle had been somewhat amused as Etienne explained how it had been before the bill was passed. It sounded so much like Seven Dials! She told him about that and said that although she'd been surrounded by all kinds of criminal activity and vice, she hadn't really been aware of it, nor touched by it, not until Millie was murdered.

'It amuses me that the very people who complain about the vice are mostly the ones who benefit most from it,' Etienne said with a wry smile. 'Shops, hotels, saloons, laundries, cab drivers, dressmakers and milliners couldn't survive without all the visitors the District brings to New Orleans.

Even the local council, the hospitals and schools benefit from the taxes that come from it. But everyone likes their dirty income to be hidden.'

Belle got out of her bed to go over to the window and see this place the good people of New Orleans wanted hidden away.

Her room was on the fourth floor, just a small, sparsely furnished room intended for a maid, very different from the opulent rooms the girls had downstairs. The window looked out on to the railway tracks which separated Basin Street from the French Quarter. As she understood it, Basin Street was the first in the District, and the one with the most prestigious sporting houses, the most beautiful girls, the best food, drink and entertainment. The establishments in the streets running behind Basin Street, be it saloons, restaurants or sporting houses, became cheaper and rougher as they got to the end of the District. By the last block and Robertson Street, the bars were hovels and the working girls down there turned tricks for just a few cents. Some couldn't even afford to rent one of the cheap cribs.

Betty had told her about the cribs. They were a series of tiny rooms with no space for anything more than a bed. Men stood in line outside, and as one came out the next went in. Betty said they could service as many as fifty men a night. But these girls were controlled by pimps, who took most of what they earned and were often beaten if they didn't earn as much as their pimp wanted. For these girls there were no such luxuries as a bath or indoor lavatory. Their lives were unspeakably hard, and most took refuge in drink or opium. Betty said that the men who used them were the very roughest kind, and the girls had no hope of anything improving for them, and most saw death as a happy release.

To Belle's disappointment she couldn't see anything more than the railway tracks opposite, even when she craned her neck out of her small window. For now she would have to be satisfied with what she'd seen fleetingly as she arrived on the previous day – big, solidly built houses, not a single one dilapidated the way they'd been around Seven Dials. She'd been told by Hatty that they mostly had electric lighting in every room, and steam heat.

Even though it was only April, the sun was warm on Belle's bare arms and face, just like a summer's day back home. She thought of how grey, cold and windy it was in Seven Dials at this time of year, and she surprised herself by being more glad than sad that she was here.

She wished she could go out now, walk around and see the District for herself. But she had a feeling Martha might not approve of her going without first asking permission.

Opening her door and going out on to the narrow staircase which led to the next floor, she listened for signs of anyone else being up. But there wasn't a sound aside from gentle snoring which seemed to be coming from Hatty's room.

She could smell the cigars from the previous night and there was a blue satin garter lying on the red and gold carpet on the landing below her. She wondered which of the girls it belonged to, and why it had been dropped there. A window on the landing had a pretty white lace blind over it, and as the bathroom door was slightly ajar she could see the black and white floor, and part of the claw-footed bath.

It all looked so clean, bright and pretty, and she smiled to herself, thinking back to how she had thought of nothing but escape when she was in Paris. She could leave here right this minute, get dressed, walk down the stairs and out the front door. But she realized she really didn't want to.

And it wasn't just because all she had in the world was the two dollars and fifty cents in tips she got last night. She actually liked it here.

'Better start behaving like the other girls then,' she murmured to herself, turning to go back into her room and into bed.

A week later, about three in the morning, Belle was alone in the drawing room collecting up glasses and ashtrays, when she heard screaming coming from out in the street.

It had been a quiet night at Martha's. The last gentleman had left half an hour earlier, and the girls had gone up to bed as there clearly weren't going to be any more callers. Martha had gone to her room on the first floor, and Cissie was in the kitchen making a cup of tea.

Belle put the tray of glasses down and went over to the window to look out. She could see a small crowd gathered some twenty yards away, further down the street by Tom Anderson's, for they were standing in a pool of bright light from his place.

Belle had been astounded when she first saw Tom Anderson's by night for it was lit with so many electric lamps it almost hurt her eyes. Anderson ran everything here – he settled disputes, punished those who needed it, and owned more than his fair share of the town. His dazzling, half-block-long saloon was all ornate carved cherry wood, mirrors and gilt, and was run by twelve bar tenders round the clock.

Basin Street was never completely silent. There might be a lull after five in the morning until nine or ten but the rest of the time music blasted out of dozens of bars, clubs and sporting houses, there were buskers in the streets and on top of that all the carousing and shouting which went hand in hand with a red light district. Sometimes Belle would look out to see gangs of sailors lurching drunkenly down the street towards the Few Clothes Cabaret. The other girls said they'd probably had a drink in most of the bars they'd passed since leaving their ship. They would be making for the cribs in Iberville Street where the whores cost a dollar, but by the time they got there they'd probably be unable to perform and their money would be gone.

Men who came into New Orleans by train were better placed to get to the women before they were too drunk, for the trains stopped right there at the start of the District and the passengers would have seen girls in some of the sporting houses posing seductively in windows for their benefit.

Unable to see from the window, Belle went to the front door and out on to the porch. She assumed the gathered crowd were watching two brawling men as there were cheers and shouts of encouragement. But suddenly the crowd broke away, and to her astonishment Belle saw it was two women fighting, going at each other like two savage dogs.

She had seen the big woman with dyed red hair the previous day, for she'd been shouting out in the street. Hatty had said she expected it had something to do with the woman's pimp, who'd been seen with another woman or something similar. If that was the case and the slightly smaller woman with bleached hair was the one who'd stolen the red-headed woman's lover and protector, she was in danger of being killed.

They rolled together on the ground, got up and leapt at each other again. The blonde fought like a woman, scratching the other's face with her nails, but the big red-head fought like a prizefighter, using her fists, and each time one connected with the blonde's face or body the crowd cheered.

All at once they were locked together, and Belle moved out along the sidewalk to get a better look. A sudden wail of pain and outrage from the blonde made everyone move closer still, and the red-head spat something out of her mouth on to the pavement.

She had bitten three fingers off the other girl's hand.

Belle was transfixed to the spot in horror. The three bloody fingers were there on the sidewalk about ten yards in front of her.

'That'll do!' a man in the crowd roared out. 'C'mon, Mary, yer can't bite lumps off folk.'

'I'll bite the ear or the nose off anyone who tries to stop me killing the bitch,' the red-head screamed out, blood dripping from her mouth.

Four or five men leapt forward and restrained the woman, while others took care of the injured one.

Belle backed off and went indoors, feeling queasy at what she'd seen.

'What was all that commotion?' Martha asked, coming down the stairs just as Belle locked the front door.

Belle told her, and retched as she explained.

'That'll be Dirty Mary,' Martha said, and taking Belle's arm drew her into the drawing room and poured her some brandy. 'She took an axe to another woman a few years ago, sliced her arm right off below the elbow. She got acquitted too. She's got the luck of the devil himself.'

'Why would she do something as bad as that to anyone?' Belle asked, feeling very shaky and wishing she hadn't gone outside.

'She's got syphilis, that's why they call her Dirty Mary. It can affect the brain, you see.'

'But won't she infect people?' Belle asked in horror.

'Oh, she don't fuck no more,' Martha said as calmly as if she were discussing what they would have for breakfast. 'She only does French now.'

'What's that?' Belle asked, though guessing she'd rather not know.

'She takes it in her mouth.' Martha wrinkled her nose with distaste. 'A lot of the girls do that, no danger of getting pregnant and you can't catch nothin' either. You'll have heard the girls speak of the French House further down the road – that's what they do there.'

Belle winced.

'Now, don't you go looking that way,' Martha said with a smile. 'It's quick, don't make no mess, nor need no bed. There's a whole lot of advantages to it.'

Belle had heard more than enough about 'French', but she did want to know what was going to happen to Mary and the blonde with the missing fingers.

'Mary will go to court; she probably won't get no more than a fine though. The other girl will go to hospital.'

'But without fingers how will the blonde girl manage?' Belle asked.

Martha smiled and patted Belle on the shoulder. 'You stop worrying about other people and go to bed. Tomorrow I want to talk to you about your future.'

Chapter Sixteen

'You just stay there and watch what Betty does,' Martha said firmly. She indicated the low chair behind the screen and the small hole in the screen's fabric which Belle could look through from a sitting position. 'Mind you take it all in! How she checks he's got no pox, washing him and all. You stay quiet there and learn!'

Belle had been given prior warning that this was how Martha prepared new girls, so it wasn't a total shock to her. And Betty had been astoundingly open when she spoke of how she viewed her work.

Belle liked the saucy girl from Atlanta. She was funny, warm-hearted and always keen to chat.

'We all make out we're having a good time,' Betty said with a wicked grin. 'I mean, that's the job. But I think naughty thoughts when I'm doing it, and guide them to pleasure me, and you know, honey, sometimes it's real good.'

While Betty was unusual in being eager to discuss such things, Belle could sense that none of the girls actually hated their work or were unhappy about their life. They all laughed a lot, and they took a great interest in everything and everyone around them. All of them had come from poor families, yet while each of them had mentioned that, poverty didn't appear to be the only reason they'd ended up as whores. Belle felt it was a combination of a craving for adventure, enjoying being lusted after, greed and laziness too, because they knew respectable work was hard.

Belle was grateful that Martha had given her almost two weeks' reprieve before throwing her to the lions, for in that time the languid, sensual atmosphere in the house had got to her. Over and over she'd found herself daydreaming of how she had felt when Etienne held her and kissed her, she looked at men appraisingly, and wanted them to want her too. She longed to wear a beautiful silk gown like the other girls, to have Cissie help her dress her hair, and to earn more money too.

It might have been that the atmosphere in the house had soothed the traumas of the past, and indeed made her actually look forward to the day she would become what Martha called 'a courtesan'. Yet it was taking walks around New Orleans that had made her see she had choices. She didn't have to think of herself as trapped for ever in a place and an occupation she loathed.

At first all she saw was the colour, music and decadence of New Orleans: one huge party that went on round the clock, seven days a week. It was only when she looked a little closer that she saw it was all about making money. Right from the rich men who owned the ritzy gambling saloons where thousands of dollars changed hands nightly, the madams running exclusive sporting houses, down to the cab drivers who charged just a few cents for a ride, and the musicians in every bar or busking right on the street, money was the hub the whole District revolved on.

But unlike London and New York where it was mainly men who ran the show, here women could have starring roles. They came from all over America and beyond. Many were madams of course, but still more had shops or other businesses – they owned hotels, bars and restaurants. Belle had been told that a big proportion of them had arrived in town flat broke, and used prostitution as a way of getting started, but that impressed her all the more because it proved that with drive and determination anyone could make good.

Belle felt she could do it too. She had the cachet of being English to start with, which was a curiosity here. Without being boastful she could see she was also prettier than most other girls, and she had youth on her side too. But above everything else she was intelligent. She hadn't really been aware of this back home because she had no one much to compare herself with. Here, she saw daily that she was streets ahead of the other girls in the brains department. As Etienne had said, most were dumb, lazy and greedy.

Both Mog and Annie were keen readers, and they had directed Belle towards books and the better-quality news-papers, but she hadn't realized that was unusual for a girl of her background. She remembered in the house in Paris that the maids had seemed surprised she read the books left in the room. Etienne had been equally surprised to find her reading. Reading had given her knowledge about so much – history, geography, and different kinds of lives to her own.

None of Martha's girls read, in fact Belle sensed that they couldn't, for they would flick through magazines just looking at the pictures. They had very little knowledge or interest in anything beyond the latest fashions and the District gossip. Betty had believed that England was by New York. Anna-Maria thought that Mexico was just beyond the Mississippi. The only thing they all aspired to was love and marriage. They all wanted a husband who would give them a pretty house and children, and though Belle thought that was understandable, she wondered how they thought they were going to achieve it. Surely they knew that few men would want to marry a working whore?

Belle had no ambition to be kept like some little pet. She wanted to be equal to any man. She didn't know yet how she was going to achieve it, but for now she was going to study men very closely and learn all about them.

It was some ten minutes before Betty came into the room leading her gentleman by the hand. Betty was a short, curvy red-head, with pale, creamy skin and wide blue eyes that held an innocence her ribald conversation belied.

Her apple-green silk dress barely covered her ample breasts, and as she shut the door she pulled down the bodice to expose them, and took the man's hands and placed them on her. 'You like them, honey?' she asked, looking up at him with the sauciest of expressions.

'Love them,' he said, his dark eyes feasting on her breasts, his voice thick with lust. 'I sure can't wait to see what else you've got for me.'

He was no more than twenty-four, slender and dark-haired, with a moustache and suntanned skin. He was not perhaps really handsome, but he had a nice face.

'Well, honey, you just give me the twenty dollars, then slip off your trousers and get ready to visit paradise.'

Belle wanted to laugh, for Betty knew she was there watching, and it seemed like that last line was straight out of a whore's instruction manual.

The man gave her the money, Betty opened the door and handed it over to Cissie, then closed the door, leaned back on it and smiled seductively at her man.

'Let's see what you've got for me then,' she said.

He had his shoes, trousers and underpants off in the blink of an eye, and Belle could see his penis was already erect as it was pushing his shirt out in front of him.

'A lovely big one,' Betty said, and she nudged him down on to the bed, pulled his shirt up and took hold of his penis, squeezing it and looking at it closely.

Only the day before the girls had been talking about checking for pox while they were drinking coffee in the kitchen. They spoke of looking for 'gleet', a yellowish pus, and any sores or lesions around the genitals. If there was any evidence of infection they turned the man away.

After Betty had examined her man she took a cloth from a

bowl of water and disinfectant and washed him vigorously, but all the time making ribald remarks about his manhood and how much she was looking forward to having him inside her.

She got the man to unfasten her gown once she'd finished washing him, and tossed it and her petticoat aside on to the chair, leaving herself wearing only a lace-trimmed chemise which exposed her breasts and ended at her bottom. Belle had been told that in other sporting houses the girls only ever wore lingerie, some danced with their men when they were almost naked. But Martha liked to maintain an illusion of purity in her house, so although the girls' necklines were low and they wore no drawers, they were dressed while in the public rooms.

The young man was growing more and more excited as Betty stripped off her clothes, and as she climbed up on to the bed and knelt beside him, she lifted her chemise to show him her private parts. Belle could see she had a very luxuriant mound of dark curly hair there, and as the young man reached out to touch it, Betty groaned and arched her back, inviting him to take liberties with her.

It was the oddest thing to Belle. She had imagined that she would feel revulsion at witnessing such things, and indeed reminders of what she'd been through in Paris, but instead she felt a curious excitement, and a warm sensation in her own private parts.

The man's fingers had disappeared right into Betty and she was undulating her body as if loving it, making little low moaning sounds.

'Umm, that sure feels good, honey,' she said. 'You're getting me good and ready for riding your big cock.'

Belle looked at the man's face and saw his eyes were feasting on Betty's breasts, and the excitement he was feeling as he touched her was evident in his high colour and the stiffness of his penis.

'Ride me now!' he said suddenly, and Betty moved quickly to straddle him, slowly moving down until he was right inside her. She leaned forward, supporting herself on her hands, and the man played with her breasts as she rode up and down on him.

He was almost delirious in his pleasure, his head tossing this way and that on the pillow, his hands moving down over Betty's curvy body with evident delight. And Betty seemed to be controlling the act, rising almost off him, then sinking down again while his gasps and groans of pleasure got louder and louder.

Then all at once it was done. The man let out a kind of frenzied roar and then he was still, reaching up to cup Betty's face tenderly.

Betty wasn't sharp with the man but she wasted no time in slipping off him, washing his penis and handing him his underpants and trousers. As he was putting on his shoes, she was washing herself, and by the time he was ready to leave, she was at the door waiting to stand on tiptoe to kiss his cheek to say goodbye.

'Bye, sugar,' she said. 'You come back to me real quick now.'

There had been no kissing at all until that one brief goodbye, and as Betty closed the door on her man, Belle came out from behind the screen rather sheepishly.

'See, there ain't nothin' to it,' Betty laughed. 'You gets 'em all excited even before you gets to the bed and they is a marshmallow in your hands. You know I'd do it with that young man for free, he's nice and I reckon he'd pleasure me all night if I asked him to.'

Belle helped Betty back into her dress and fastened up the hooks and eyes. 'Why didn't you kiss him?' she asked.

''Cos that's what sweethearts do, honey,' Betty said. 'Kissin' gets you goin', but it's for making love, not turning a trick. You save that for the man you love. You understand?'

Belle did understand, far better than she'd expected to. She couldn't claim that she was eager to take her place as one of the girls, but she was far less reluctant now, and she even thought if she got a young man like that one, it wouldn't be too bad at all.

During the next week Belle watched each of the girls with a client, and one evening she watched Anna-Maria and Polly with just one man.

'I make 'em pay a great deal more for this,' Martha explained. 'It's usually the old, rich ones that want it, but you'll see the girls don't mind it at all; the hardest thing for them is not to laugh.'

Belle had already found that laughter was a plentiful commodity in Martha's house. During the afternoons the girls loved to sit out in the small shady back yard sipping iced tea or lemonade and discussing the previous night's highlights. They held little back, descriptions were vivid and graphic, and mostly very funny, especially those given by Betty and Suzanne. Sometimes the girls laughed so much they complained of getting a stitch.

At first Belle just sat back and listened, but gradually she had been coerced into telling the girls about her experiences in Paris. Yet those nightmare scenes which she had tried so hard to forget became almost comedy when she relayed them to her new friends. She found herself exaggerating the fatness of one man or the great age of another, that way it hurt less. Maybe her voice did crack and her eyes fill with tears on occasions, but the girls would take her hand and squeeze it, and make some comment that not only showed they understood what she'd been through, but often turned her tears to laughter.

'If you can laugh about the pathetic old devils who can only get it up with someone young and frightened, then you've scored over them,' Suzanne said, with a touch of bitterness that suggested she knew what she was talking about. 'Don't you let them ruin your life, Belle. One day you'll meet a man who will show you sex can be beautiful. But while you're here we'll show you it can be fun, and very profitable.'

Suzanne's words proved true when Belle watched the girls performing with the client. Both of them, raven-haired Anna-Maria and blonde Polly, were completely naked, their young, firm bodies and lovely faces in strong contrast to the big, boastful Texan with the ruddy face and huge, flabby belly. His penis was very small, but when Anna-Maria knelt with her knees either side of his neck and let him watch her at close quarters as she stroked herself, it leapt to attention. Polly jumped on to it, leaning back to play with his balls as she moved on him, then Anna-Maria moved forward so the man could lick at her.

Belle could hardly believe what she was seeing, for it was quite clear that the girls had the upper hand, not the man. She watched their faces. Polly was trying hard not to laugh, yet at the same time stroking him and gyrating her hips to make it as erotic as possible so he would ejaculate quickly. Anna-Maria did in fact seem to be really enjoying being licked by the man; she was telling him it was thrilling and sexy and that she was coming. She certainly looked as if it was for real, her face was flushed, eyes half closed and mouth partially open.

The Texan bellowed like a bull when he came, and Polly put her hand over her mouth to stop herself laughing. Anna-Maria was still undulating against the man's big tongue; she caught hold of his head at the point when she said she was coming, and sweat was glistening on her forehead and running down her breasts.

Belle sat back in her chair as the two girls said their good-byes to their client. He was grinning from ear to ear, insisting they'd taken him to the ends of the world and back.

'I sure would like you two little fire crackers in my bed every night at home,' he said, putting his arms around them both and squeezing them hard. 'I reckon I'll be taking my cock in hand every night and thinking of you both.'

After they'd let the man out and closed the door, Belle came out from behind the screen. Polly started to giggle. 'How was that, sugar? You like it?'

Anna-Maria was sitting on the edge of the bed, struggling to put her chemise back on. She looked a bit stunned.

'That sounded as though you really liked it,' Belle said to her.

'I did,' she said in her faint French accent, and she giggled and blushed. 'That ees the first time that ever happened to me, I really did come.'

Belle had heard that expression many times since arriving at Martha's. She understood it in the male sense, but she hadn't until now known it could happen for women too. However, it obviously struck a chord with Polly as she went off into a fit of giggles. 'Imagine him cock in hand thinking of us,' she chortled.

Belle went off up to her room to let the other two girls get washed and dressed again. She sat on her bed and realized she was confused. Not about what she'd just seen, but all the things life had thrown at her, for surely there had to be some plan behind it, if she could just work it out.

She'd grown up in a brothel but hadn't known what that meant. She'd seen a girl murdered and her mother had lied about who did it. Then there was her abduction and the horrible events in Paris. But then she met Etienne, by whom she'd been terrified at first, only to get to like him, maybe even love him a little. She ought to have been horrified at being brought here to be a whore, yet she wasn't. She ought to be appalled by New Orleans, yet she liked it. She didn't feel even the slightest resentment that Martha was going to push her into the work she'd bought her for.

Was this because she was born to be a whore? Was it possible you could inherit the disposition for such a job in the same way you inherited your mother's nose or colouring?

Part of her believed that it was bad for any woman to sell her body, yet the other part denied it. She'd seen the delight on that man's face tonight, the girls had made him happy, so how could it really be bad?

But there were other things which puzzled her too. She missed Mog, and would always have a special place for her in her heart, but she felt more at home here with Martha and her girls than she had back in London. Why was that? Didn't that make her disloyal?

If Etienne had tried to have his way with her she suspected she wouldn't have resisted him. That was surely further proof of a loose nature. In fact it seemed to her that she couldn't define what was good or bad any more, for everything had become mixed up and blurred around the edges.

A soft rap on her door startled Belle, and she was even more surprised when Martha put her head around it.

'Can I come in, honey?' she asked.

'Yes, of course,' Belle said, feeling awkward at being caught out. 'I was just going to come downstairs again. I'm sorry.'

'Pay no mind to that,' Martha said, sitting herself down on the narrow bed. 'You needed to gather yourself, I understand.'

Belle had noticed the older woman seemed to understand almost everything people did. She hadn't heard her raise her voice in anger once.

'I dare say what you saw tonight was a little surprising?' Martha went on.

Belle would've expected her to use the word shocking rather than surprising, yet in fact her word was exactly how it was.

'Yes, ma'am,' Belle whispered, dropping her eyes.

'You didn't expect the girls to have so much fun, or the gentleman to be so pleased?'

Belle nodded.

Martha sighed deeply. 'Respectable, church-going folks don't tend to see that we were made to enjoy sex. It ain't just about gettin' babies, honey. Lovin' one another in the physical way is good for all of us, it's the glue that can hold a marriage together and make it a happy one. If the wives of the men we service here were to let themselves go and learn to love fuckin', there'd be no need for places like mine.'

Belle blushed. Martha and all her girls used that word a great deal, and she found it disconcerting.

Martha tilted up Belle's chin with one finger. 'Look at you blushing! That's what it is, honey chile, might as well learn to say the word and be done with being bashful. Once you knows how good it can feel to be loved by a man, you'll see things clearer. I reckon I ought to have suggested that Etienne stayed the first night with you here. He's the kind to awaken any woman.'

'He was married,' Belle said indignantly.

Martha laughed. 'Now, honey, do you think I worry about married men coming in this house?'

Belle smirked, for she guessed that more than half the men who came here were married. 'No, I suppose not.'

'Etienne had, how shall I say?' Martha paused to choose the right word. 'Charisma! I doubt he's ever paid for a woman.'

'He was very proper with me,' Belle retorted.

'And that makes a woman even more inclined to be improper,' Martha chuckled. 'But honey, I think it's time I got you awakened.'

Belle had the most vivid, disturbing dream that night. She was naked, lying on a big bed surrounded by men who were all reaching out to touch her. They weren't grabbing at her roughly, just gentle strokes that made her feel like she was on fire. She woke from it to find she was dripping with sweat, her nightdress up around her armpits, and she was fairly certain she had been stroking her private parts in just the way she'd seen Anna-Maria do earlier in the evening.

Chapter Seventeen

Jimmy dodged behind a pile of flower boxes in the market as the man stopped to speak to someone. He waited a second, then peeped out round the edge of the boxes to see what they were doing.

He was absolutely certain the man was Kent. He'd spent hours over the last few weeks watching his office building, at all different times of the day, gradually eliminating the men who worked in the printer's on the ground and first floor as they went in or out. There was never a light up in Kent's office, and Jimmy had begun to think he'd given up using the place, when suddenly today he appeared.

There was something about the way the well-dressed man walked up Long Acre, purposeful, self-assured, which made Jimmy stiffen even before the man got close enough for him to see that he had the prominent nose, the thick, military-style moustache, and the wide, muscular shoulders which fitted the description he'd been given of Kent.

When he went into the building, this confirmed it was him, but it also put Jimmy in a quandary. It was just after ten in the morning, he'd already been out for over an hour, and he knew he must get back to the pub. But his need to know more about this man was greater than his fear of his uncle. He decided to wait for another hour and see if he came out again and where he went. To his delight, Kent reappeared after only ten minutes.

Jimmy followed him down through the flower market towards the Strand, but before he got there, Kent turned right into Maiden Lane. Jimmy kept well back, only too aware that his red hair, even though it was covered by a cap, was memorable. Like most of the old lanes in the area, Maiden Lane was narrow and squalid, with old buildings like rabbit warrens on both sides. There were also the back doors of two theatres in the Strand, and when Kent suddenly disappeared, Jimmy thought at first that he'd slipped into the Vaudeville. But as he reached the theatre door he found it was locked. The door next to it was slightly ajar though, and it seemed very likely that was where he'd gone.

Jimmy hesitated. Above the door was a hand-painted sign of a woman's face half concealed by a fan. There was no name, nothing to say what the business inside was, but he was fairly sure it was some kind of drinking club, probably with dancing girls. Maybe Belle had been brought here if Kent owned the place.

His heart was hammering with nerves, but he pushed the door open a little further and went in. Aware that if he was caught prowling he'd be in big trouble, he decided the only way to behave was as if he had real business there. So he walked boldly down the narrow corridor and up the bare wooden stairs as all the doors on the ground floor had padlocks on them.

At the top of the flight of stairs was another door with a small pane of glass in it. He peeped through and saw the room inside was more or less as he'd expected, large, dingy and windowless and furnished with tables and chairs. The floor was just rough boards. The bar was on the right-hand side, a small stage and a piano on the left. It would have been in total darkness but for an open door at the far end, and Jimmy could hear men talking in there.

He opened the door a crack and the smell hit him like being slapped round the face with a stinking floor cloth. It was a gut-wrenching mixture of stale beer, tobacco, dirt and mildew. He asked himself then whether he was really brave enough to go in, for if he was stopped he couldn't claim to have a valid reason for being there. But scared as he was, he felt compelled to hear what the men were talking about and see what the room they were in was like.

With a hammering heart, he crept round the edge of the room, staying close to the wall and ready to duck down under a table if anyone came out. All the time his ears were straining to hear what was being said.

'They said they want two more, but I can't get the kind they want,' one of the men said. He was well spoken, so Jimmy thought it was probably Kent.

'Surely Sly can come up with a couple?' a man with a rougher London voice answered.

'No. He's gone yellow-bellied on me since that other one. There's a cove over in Bermondsey who I hear can do it, but I don't know if I can trust him.'

Jimmy crept closer, right up to the door, and peeped through the crack on the hinges side. It was an office, with a big window which looked out on to the Savoy Hotel in the Strand. Kent was standing facing the window, and the other man was sitting in a chair behind a desk. He looked very like the pictures of King Edward, big, bald, with a bushy beard, but he had a vicious-looking scar on his cheek, and he wore a red waistcoat under his jacket and a gold watch chain.

'We don't have to fret over whether we trust him,' the bald man said with a mirthless chuckle. 'Once he comes up with the girls we can dispose of him.'

Jimmy knew he'd heard enough to be torn limb from limb if he was caught, so he sidled away from the door and crept back round the room on tiptoe. When he reached the outer door he was through it and down the stairs in the blink of an eye, nervous sweat dripping from him.

*

'You damn fool! What on earth did you think you were doing?' Garth roared at Jimmy.

He had been annoyed when he got up at nine and found his nephew had gone out, for he had an errand he wanted him to run. But when Jimmy still wasn't back at eleven he became angry. A delivery of beer was expected, the fireplace in the bar needed clearing and the fire lit, plus dozens of other jobs. When Jimmy came running into the bar, red-faced and out of breath, Garth had jumped to the conclusion that the lad had been up to some mischief and had fled from whoever was chasing him. But when he questioned him and found that he'd been spying on Kent, fright made him even angrier.

Despite all his bragging, Garth had failed to find the man Sly, and indeed to get any further information about Kent. Noah had drawn a blank as well, and it said reams about Kent's reputation that no one dared talk about him. With the police showing absolutely no interest in apprehending anyone for the crime, it was over three months now since young Belle went missing, which almost certainly meant she was dead too. Garth had mentally given up, even though he wouldn't admit that to Mog.

To discover his nephew was still trying to do something both shamed him and made him feel inadequate. And it was his way to strike out when he felt like that.

'I have to find out more about the man,' Jimmy said defiantly. 'And from what I heard today, I'd say they were snatching other girls and taking them away somewhere. I'm going to break into that office and see what else I can discover.'

'You'll do no such thing,' Garth roared. 'You get caught by anyone involved with that club and you'll be killed and thrown into the river.'

'I won't get caught, I know how I'm going to do it,' Jimmy said stubbornly.

'You won't go near that place again,' Garth bellowed at him.

Jimmy was scared when his uncle yelled like that, but he stood his ground and looked up defiantly at the older man. 'We've found nothing new for ages now, Uncle. Mog is grieving, Annie's gone away because she can't bear to think about the fire taking all she held dear, and I want to see that bastard hang for killing Millie, and get Belle back.'

'She'll be dead by now,' Garth shouted in exasperation. 'Surely you realize that!'

Jimmy shook his head. 'I feel she's alive, and so does Mog. But even if we're wrong and she *is* dead, I still want to nail Kent.'

Garth was pulled up short by his nephew's courage and determination. It made him feel ashamed of himself. 'You be very careful then,' he said. 'The last thing Mog and I want is to have you disappear too. And next time you want to play detective, for God's sake tell us where you're going.'

Jimmy scuttled off then to do his chores, but he was grinning. He'd half expected his uncle to give him a thrashing; he certainly hadn't expected to find concern.

Garth slumped down on to a chair after Jimmy had gone, confused by his feelings and by the way his life had changed since his sister died and he took Jimmy in. In fact he didn't remember having much feeling about anything, he was too busy taking care of the Ram's Head, and he supposed the past had made him bitter.

He and Flora had not been close as children. He'd only been six and his sister fourteen when she was apprenticed to a fashion house and went to live in there. Flora finished her apprenticeship and stayed in that same fashion house as a seamstress until she married an Irish artist, Darragh Reilly, when she was twenty-five.

Garth was seventeen at the time of the wedding and he could remember his father saying Flora had picked a broken reed. It soon became evident that his father was right, because Darragh believed himself to be far too talented an artist to soil his hands doing any other kind of work to bring in some money. Soon after Jimmy was born he disappeared, never to return, and Flora had to become the sole breadwinner.

Garth did what he could to help her in the early days of her abandonment, but Flora was such a good seamstress that she soon began to make a living for herself. Garth always admired her for that, but he often fell out with her about how she was with Jimmy. He felt she was too soft with him, and that the lad would end up being a waster like his father.

He had to concede now that he'd been wrong there. Jimmy was a hard worker, honest and loyal and a credit to his mother. He could do well in life if he just put this thing about Belle aside. But with Mog around he wasn't likely to do that, she kept the flame burning.

Annie had moved out six weeks earlier. She'd rented a house up in King's Cross and was intending to take in boarders. While she'd been here she'd been idle, acted superior and walked about like she had a bad smell under her nose, so Garth was glad when she left. Mog might be grieving for Belle still but she kept it to herself and was a superb housekeeper. He really liked her, and he knew Jimmy did too.

Mog came into the bar just as Garth was pouring himself a small whisky.

'You're starting early today!' she said sharply. She glanced round at the fire which hadn't been cleared from the night before. 'It's another cold day, it should be lit before customers come in.'

'I'm the landlord here,' Garth pointed out. 'I do know what needs doing, and that's Jimmy's job.'

'He's doing his work in the cellar and trying to keep out of your way,' Mog said, 'so I'll do the fire. He does so many jobs for me during the day, it's the least I can do.'

'You're a kind woman,' he said, his voice husky, for she had dropped to her knees by the hearth to rake out the cinders and for some reason the sight of that made him feel chastened. 'I really don't know how we got along before you came. Now we've got laundered shirts, good food and a clean house.'

Mog sat up, dropping back to sit on her heels. She wore her grey apron over her dark dress; the apron would be changed to a snowy-white one once she'd finished all the morning's dirty work. 'I'm just doing my job,' she said. 'But mostly it don't seem like a job, not as your Jimmy is such a lovely lad. I know you're vexed because he won't give up on Belle, and maybe you even think that's my influence, but I can't take any credit for his determination, he's like a young bulldog with a bone.'

Garth couldn't help but smile for he remembered his mother saying that about him when he was a young lad. 'I worry he'll get himself beaten up,' he admitted.

'You should smile more,' Mog said boldly. 'It makes you handsome.'

Garth laughed then. It occurred to him that he had become inclined to smile and laugh a great deal more since Mog had come to live here – she had a way with her.

'If I should smile to make me more handsome, I think you should wear something prettier than a black dress day after day,' he said teasingly.

'You can't make a silk purse out of a sow's ear,' she said, looking right at him with those steady grey eyes. 'And if I started dressing up, folk would say I'd set my cap at you.'

'Since when did you care what folk say?' he asked, amused by her response.

'I knew exactly who I was when I worked for Annie,' Mog said thoughtfully. 'I was her maid, housekeeper, mostly mother to her child too. I might have known all the comings and goings in her place, learned stuff about our gentlemen that would curl your hair, but everyone round here knew I wasn't a whore. I was proud of that, it gave me dignity.'

'You still have that dignity,' Garth said. 'Nothing's changed.'

'Folk are waiting for me to slip up,' she said. 'Few people around here really liked Annie, she was too cold and haughty. They thought the same of me too, without ever knowing me. Now Annie's moved on, they want to gossip about me. Believing I was warming your bed to keep a roof over my head would give them plenty to chew on.'

It was a surprise to find Mog was so astute. Garth already valued her for her homemaking skills, but he had been guilty of assuming she was a simple soul. In a flash of intuition he realized she was sharper than he was, and that she'd only stayed working for Annie because she loved Belle.

'I would never give anyone the idea you were warming my bed,' he said, surprised at himself for caring what his customers and neighbours thought about Mog.

'But I'll keep wearing the black dresses and aprons to spare you the embarrassment of them thinking you are,' she retorted, and got back to clearing the fireplace.

Garth busied himself straightening up bottles behind the bar but all the time he was watching her busily shovelling up the ash into a tin box. It was clear she believed herself to be unattractive, and no doubt Annie had reinforced that view for her own ends. But Garth was attracted to her curvy little body, and he saw a sweetness in her face that came from within. As a younger man he'd always gone for the kind of saucy, pretty women who use their feminine wiles to get what they want. But he knew to his cost that their kind were mostly insincere. They turned into treacherous harpies if the presents, attention and drink didn't flow their way fast enough. Maud, his last woman and the one that set his heart on fire, had been a fine example. He'd vowed when she skipped off with another man, taking his savings with her, that he'd never let another woman into his life.

Two days later at four in the morning, with the sounds of his uncle's snoring reverberating through the Ram's Head, Jimmy slipped out through the back door into the dark streets. He ran all the way down to the market, only slowing down to side-step the porters pushing heavily laden carts of fruit, flowers and vegetables.

He went to Maiden Lane first, but as he expected the club door was padlocked. He then went round to the Strand, crossed over the road by the Savoy Hotel and looked up at the windows on the opposite side. Most of the windows above the rank of shops were part of the shop or storeroom beneath; in some cases the owners lived there. The office Jimmy wanted to reach was very obvious because the windows hadn't been cleaned in years, and furthermore the smallest pane of glass on the end had been broken sometime and a piece of wood put over it, something he'd noticed when he was peering through the crack in the door.

There was a stout-looking drainpipe running from the top of the building right down to the street, and it was only a foot or so from the first-floor window sill. Even from across the street in darkness, Jimmy could see that the sill was a wide one. Stuffed into his coat pocket he had a bunch of keys, a couple of candles and a few tools for picking locks and prising doors open. He also had a length of stout rope wound round his chest beneath his coat. But he thought he could get into the office without using any of these things.

Checking first to see there was no one about, he crossed over, jumped to get a grip on the drainpipe and then began shinning up it. He had always been good at climbing; his mother had said he was like a cat.

Once up on the window sill, he examined the broken window and found to his delight that the wood was only tapped tightly on to the frame, to keep the rain and cold out rather than burglars. A little prise and a yank and it was off, but before leaving the window sill Jimmy took the rope from his chest and secured it tightly around the drainpipe in case he had to make a hasty exit.

Inside the office Jimmy lit his candle, then pulled the curtains across the window. They were very old, stiff with dirt and smelled bad, but at least they were thick and would stop anyone noticing the light from the street. Once they were pulled he lit the overhead gaslight, for he could be quicker if he could see well.

It was an untidy, jumbled office, and very dirty, with ashtrays piled high with cigar stubs, used glasses, cups and plates everywhere. The waste bin was overflowing with paper and there was cigar ash all over the floor. It didn't look as if the place had been cleaned for months.

The drawers in the desk revealed nothing of interest, only some account books which appeared to be the club's. In an unlocked cashbox there was close on fifty pounds, perhaps a few days' takings. But he closed that up and put it back where he'd found it, for he wasn't there to steal.

Next he opened the filing cabinet, but there was no organization there, just piles of papers shoved in on top of one another. Clearly the man who owned the place didn't understand the concept of filing.

Jimmy lifted out a pile of papers and put them on the desk to go through. There was a variety of reasons for the correspondence. Some of the letters were about this building; it seemed Mr J. Colm was renting the property in Maiden Lane from a company in Victoria. They were writing to him to warn him they'd had complaints from other tenants about noise, drunks leaving the building and violence spilling out into Maiden Lane. Some of the letters threatened him with eviction, but Jimmy saw such threats went back over four or five years, so it seemed Mr Colm was either ignoring them, or paying his landlords something to keep them sweet.

The other correspondence was mainly from suppliers of drink. There was also a list of women's names and addresses who Jimmy thought might be dancers or waitresses. He put that in his pocket.

He trawled right through the contents of the cabinet, but there was nothing that proved a link or partnership between him and Kent, or indeed anything other than stuff directly to do with running the club. He pulled the curtain back a little and guessed by a faint light in the sky that it was getting on for six, and he must leave before the Strand became busy with people.

He was just going to open the curtain before turning off the gas when he saw an address tacked on to the wall by the window. It was one in Paris, and he probably wouldn't have thought anything of it, but the name was Madame Sond-heim, and to an eighteen-year-old boy with imagination, that sounded like a brothel keeper's. So, just in case, he snatched it down and stuffed it in his pocket, then opened the curtains and turned out the light.

Once out on the window sill Jimmy saw several people walking along the Strand. But it was raining and dark and they had their heads down, and delaying his descent to the street would do him no good as more and more people would soon be about.

He let the rope drop down over the sill, then nimbly went down it hand over hand. A man coming towards him looked shocked and surprised, and called out for him to stop. But Jimmy took off at speed, belting round the corner, then doubling back along Maiden Lane to Southampton Street. The man must have decided against giving chase, for there was no hue and cry or pounding feet following him, and by the time he reached the market, Jimmy slowed down to a mere stroll.

'Where have you been, Jimmy?' Mog asked as he walked in the back door. She had a wrap over her nightdress and her hair was loose on her shoulders. 'You're soaking wet! What time of day is this to go out?'

'A good time if you want to get some information,' Jimmy said with a grin.

'You haven't been getting into that man's office again?' she asked in alarm.

'Not the one you mean,' Jimmy said. 'Why are you up so early anyway?'

'I heard you slip out,' she said reproachfully, and wagged her forefinger at him. 'I was that worried I couldn't get back to sleep. So I came down to make a cup of tea in the end.'

For just a brief second Mog had an expression on her face that was so like his mother's it made a lump come up in Jimmy's throat. 'Don't look like that,' he whispered.

'Like what?'

'Like my mother used to.'

Mog came closer to him, took off his cap and ruffled his hair. 'Looks like I've got to take her place,' she said. 'We'll have a cuppa and you tell me what you found.'

Some half an hour later over a second cup of tea Jimmy had told Mog everything.

'This Madame Whatsit might not be anything to do with Belle,' Mog said sadly, but she continued to stare at the piece of paper as if willing it to answer her questions. 'As for the list of girls or women, it's far more likely they are girls that work for him.'

'But I did hear him talking about getting girls, and he said someone had turned yellow-bellied on him. Garth said the man called Braithwaite was known as Sly, and we know Braithwaite went to France with Kent, so maybe it was him who turned yellow-bellied. If we could just talk to him!'

'A man like that wouldn't admit anything he'd done, not even after he was sorry he'd done it,' Mog said sadly. 'He'd probably cut your tongue out to shut you up if you got anywhere close to him. But this Madame Whatsit, she might be worth following up. Noah might be game for going there and finding out about it.'

'Shall I run round to his place and leave a message for him?' Jimmy asked.

Mog sighed. 'I think we'd better talk it over with your uncle first. But let's have another look at that list of girls. Some of them live close by here – I could make a few enquiries about them myself.'

Later that morning, with her chores completed and a steak and kidney pudding simmering in a pan on the stove, Mog went round to Endell Street to the first address on the list.

Endell Street was a mixed area. Some of the buildings and houses were in a bad state and poor people lived in them in overcrowded and insanitary conditions, but the rest of the houses were neat and tidy, homes to decent, hard-working people – cab drivers, carpenters and the like. Mog was very surprised to find that number eighty was one of the tidy ones, with snowy-white lace curtains at the window and a well-scrubbed doorstep.

She knocked at the door, uncertain about what she was even going to say, and when the door was opened by a plump woman around the same age as her, wearing a spotless white apron over her print dress, Mog was tongue-tied for a moment.

'I'm sorry to call on you, but does Amy Stewart live here?' she asked once the woman had enquired what she wanted and forced her to say something.

'She did,' the woman replied, but all at once her lips began to quiver and her eyes filled with tears.

'Oh, please don't take on,' Mog begged her in alarm, assuming the girl had done something to upset her mother.

'Why are you asking?' the woman said, and there was a kind of plea in her eyes that Mog could identify with. 'My Amy disappeared two years ago. She went to the shop for me and she never came back. She was only thirteen, too young to go anywhere on her own.'

Chapter Eighteen

'I'm charmed to meet you, Belle. You must know your name means beautiful in French? You were well named for you are truly beautiful.'

Belle felt she was blushing from her hair to the tips of her toes, for this handsome man paying her such an extravagant compliment had a French accent like Etienne, with a deep, velvety tone that made her tingle inside.

'Well, thank you, Mr Laurent, you are very kind,' she said breathlessly.

'You must call me Serge. Will you come for a little walk with me?' he asked. 'We could go to Jackson Square and get an ice cream.'

Belle realized as soon as Martha called her downstairs to introduce her to this man that he had to be the one Martha hoped would teach her to like lovemaking. She had come downstairs in trepidation, expecting him to be old and ugly. When she was confronted by a slim, tall man, beautifully dressed in a pale grey suit, with a captivating face, her heart lurched. His hair was black, his eyes like pools of melted chocolate, and his full mouth that turned up at the edges made him look as if he was smiling even when he wasn't. She had never seen such a perfect-looking man; he even had a dimple in his chin and his teeth were flawless.

For a moment she could only stare at him. She might be scared stiff at the prospect of making love, but surely no woman in the world would be able to resist Serge Laurent. Even his name made her heart flutter.

'I'd love to go for a walk with you,' she said breathlessly.

As they walked to Jackson Square, Serge told her many little stories about people who had lived in the houses they passed in the French Quarter. He introduced her to pirates, gamblers, Voodoo queens, madams and villains, along with a smattering of famous writers and poets. He made it all so colourful she felt sure he was making some of it up, or at least exaggerating, but that didn't matter – she was enjoying his company and it was a lovely warm day.

Martha had said earlier today that soon it would turn very hot, and that was when people got too lazy to work, tempers flared, and sometimes people went mad because the heat got to them. Belle couldn't imagine heat like that; back home the hottest days she remembered was when the milk turned sour and the butter melted in a dish. But hot weather in England never amounted to more than perhaps only seven or eight days in a whole year.

Serge bought them both an ice-cream cone and they went into the gardens on Jackson Square and sat on a bench in the shade to eat them. Belle had only been to this part of the French Quarter a couple of times and she really liked it. It was gentle, quiet and serene, at least compared with Basin Street which was always loud, hectic and rough.

There were a couple of musicians busking, a black girl was tap-dancing on a piece of board, and a strange-looking mulatto woman wearing a red satin cape over what looked like an old lace wedding dress was telling fortunes with some sticks she was throwing.

Many of the men walking round the square were likely to be down in the District later in the day; perhaps many of the pretty younger women walking under their frilly parasols were in fact whores by night too. But it didn't seem that way. If Belle looked up she could see people sitting out in the afternoon sun on their pretty wrought-iron balconies, mothers nursing their babies. She could hear couples chatting together, and children squealing as they played ball games with their mothers, and it felt as if nothing bad could ever happen in the French Quarter.

Serge didn't ask her any questions, not even about her background or how she came to be with Martha. He talked about general things and told her even more amusing stories, but all the time he was holding her hand and caressing it, and all she could think of was how much she wanted to be kissed by him.

They had come out of Martha's at about three, and it was nearly five when he said he'd take her to his place to make her some mint tea. By then Belle felt she might just pass out with longing if he didn't kiss her soon.

She didn't have long to wait. They were barely in his small apartment with dark wood shutters at the windows, when he took her in his arms. As his lips came down on hers she felt as if she was losing all sense of her own will. She wanted nothing more than to be possessed by Serge.

'Beautiful, beautiful Belle,' he whispered as he nuzzled at her neck while unhooking her dress. 'You know you were made for love, your hair, your skin, your body, all so perfect. And I will make you see how good lovemaking is for you. You might have come in here a young girl, but you will go out a woman.'

Belle wanted to believe him as he bent his head to kiss her breasts, murmuring that they too were perfect, that he'd never said this to another girl, and that he was falling in love with her. But she knew that wasn't how it was, that he was just an actor who played his part superbly, and she didn't really mind, for he was making her feel things she couldn't have imagined before.

He removed all her clothes easily and quickly and moved her over to his bed while still fully dressed himself, apart from his jacket which he'd taken off as they came in. Then on the bed he kissed her ever more passionately while his fingers caressed her private parts. The astounding thing was that the stroking and probing which those other men had done back in Paris and had seemed so vile and painful, were now exquisitely lovely.

His lips moved down her body, kissing her breasts, her arms, her belly, and she was arching her back for more of his caresses for he had found a spot in her vagina which felt so wonderful when he circled it with his finger that she thought she might scream out loud.

He moved away from it, turning her over to kiss her back and her buttocks, then slid his hand beneath her again to play with her and make her gasp out that it was wonderful.

Belle didn't remember him removing his clothes, he did it so seamlessly. One minute he was dressed, the next naked, and when she saw his erect penis, she wasn't scared, she wanted it inside her.

She was beyond caring about how she was behaving or what he would think of her. She pulled him towards her by his hips, wrapping her legs around him like a vine, and as he slid into her she screamed out in pleasure.

Belle had witnessed the sex act many times now, but what she felt at this moment had nothing in common with the quick, unemotional procedures she'd observed. Both she and Serge were bathed in sweat, every stroke, squeeze, kiss or caress was intended to please, and it did, so much. He withdrew from her several times, on each occasion finding that little sensitive spot again. Then all at once she felt herself exploding under his fingers, and he drove himself in again, harder and harder, until it happened for him too.

Half dozing, lying in the security of Serge's arms, Belle

felt that at last she understood all those jokes the girls made. This was the state everyone wanted to attain, but perhaps few did, for she was sure not many men understood a woman's body like Serge did.

He half sat up, leaning over her, his dark hair flopping over his tanned face. 'You were made for love, Belle. And now you know how good it can be, make sure you have lovers worthy of you, for most men are selfish, thinking only of their own pleasure.'

Belle frowned. She remembered Millie saying something like that one day in the kitchen. Mog had shushed her, mouthing something to remind Millie that Belle was listening.

'I doubt the men who will be paying me will want to please me,' she said lightly.

'Many will if you encourage them,' he said with a smile, bending to kiss her again. 'I learned all I know in cat houses. It is a fallacy that all men just want to spill their seed and leave. They may do that because it is expected, but a good courtesan will give them much more than that. Martha sees your promise, and I sense you wish to become rich. Is that so?'

Belle nodded.

'Then be the best of the best,' he said. 'When a man wants you, you ask him if he wants heaven, or just a little release. You fulfil his fantasies and he will come back again and again to you, paying more each time.'

'But how do I know what his fantasies are?' Belle asked, puzzled because she didn't really know what he meant by the word.

'It is simple, you ask him.' Serge laughed, his dimple deepening. 'You see, my fantasy is just what I had, an inexperienced girl whom I take to heaven and back. Many men share that one, especially with a young, pretty girl like you. But some men, they like a girl dressed as a maid or a waitress. I have a friend who likes his lady to dress in a nun's habit.

'It doesn't have to be about dressing up or acting though. Some men like a girl to be a tease, to walk around naked and show herself to him. Even to touch herself there so he can watch her do it.' Serge put his hand on her vagina again and smiled down at her. 'I would like to see you do that, just as I would like to see you suck my cock, and I would like to lick you there too. But I have to get you back now, and I have to leave something for other men to be the first with.'

Martha only smiled at Belle when she got back to Basin Street. Serge had brought her back at ten in the evening, kissed her goodbye at the door, and she knew deep down that it would be the last she'd see of him. She wondered as he walked away through the crowds on the street, so light on his feet, back straight, head held high, how much money he was paid for the time he spent with her.

She felt she ought to be ashamed, but she wasn't. Serge was after all just doing as she herself intended to do. And if he could make her feel so good when he was being paid to do it, then she was sure she'd be able to do likewise.

She felt she understood all the mysteries of life now. Martha might have taught her the practical things like putting a little sponge deep into her vagina to prevent getting pregnant, the douching out afterwards, and what male infections looked like. But even if the men who paid her for sex could never make her feel the way Serge had, at least she knew now how good it could be with the right man.

The following afternoon Martha called Belle up to her room. 'I think you are ready now,' she said with a warm smile. 'So tonight you make your debut.'

Belle's heart fluttered nervously, wanting so much to ask for a bit more time. But Martha had already been incredibly patient and kind, and she had a feeling that might end if she didn't get some return for her investment very soon. 'If that's what you'd like,' she said.

'Brave girl,' Martha said. 'The first time is always the worst, awkward and embarrassing, but let me show you the gown I've picked out for you. That should make you feel better.'

She went behind her dressing screen and brought out a red silk gown. Belle couldn't help but gasp for it was beautiful. Sleeveless, with a low neckline, it looked as if it was designed to cling to the body rather than conceal it.

'Try it on,' Martha said. 'Go on! There's a new chemise behind the screen too.'

As soon as Belle had shed her own clothes and put on the new chemise, she sensed Martha didn't want her wearing any drawers. The new chemise was red and white spotted crêpe de chine, barely covering her nipples and short, reaching only about two inches below her bottom. It made her feel wicked; she wished she could see herself in a mirror because she could imagine how Serge would have reacted to seeing her that way.

The dress was whisper-light, with whalebones in the bodice to support and shape her breasts. There were several rows of ruffles beneath the hem of the skirt which created the swishing sound and movement of petticoats, but the soft red silk clung to her body like a second skin.

'Come out and I'll fasten it for you,' Martha called out.

She said nothing as Belle came out hesitantly. She secured the gown at the back in silence, tucking the straps of her chemise out of sight on her shoulders. 'Take a look,' she said then, pointing at the large cheval mirror.

Belle could hardly believe what she was seeing. She looked so shapely, so adult, she hadn't known her body was so curvy and womanly. It was of course the cut of the dress, which clung to places that were normally well covered with petticoats and drawers. She hadn't even realized her breasts had become so big; they were threatening to pop out of the bodice.

'Aren't I indecent?' she whispered, looking at Martha.

The woman laughed. 'Sure would be if it was church you were goin' to. But for our gentlemen you'll look like first prize. I think you like yourself a little in that gown, don't you?'

Belle did a twirl in front of the mirror. All that she'd felt with Serge the previous day was still with her, and this dress made her feel giddy with expectancy. 'I like myself a lot in it,' she admitted, and laughed. 'I think I already am a whore at heart!'

Martha came over to her and, putting a jewelled hand on each shoulder, kissed both of Belle's cheeks. 'Most women are, but they repress it and deny it,' she said. 'You'll be one of the great ones, I sensed it when you first arrived. Now, let's get that dress off, you can put it on later after you've bathed and Cissie has arranged your hair. You can have a little brandy tonight to calm your nerves, but don't let Cissie tempt you into laudanum, that's a bad road to take.'

Belle was astounded by how nice the other girls were to her when she came down to the parlour dressed ready for her first gentleman. She had expected sniping – after all, she was competition and younger than all of them – but they complimented her on how lovely she looked and everyone had a bit of advice.

'Don't let them stay over their time.' 'At the first hint of trouble, call Cissie,' 'Don't kiss them, or forget to wash and examine their cock. Make sure you get the money before you undress.'

'You look scared,' Hatty said in sympathy. 'Remember that we all were. You'll be fine, the men are going to be so eager for you, they'll come as soon as look at you.'

Martha watched when the first three men of the evening came in. Two of them were friends who had been here before, the third one she didn't know, but he was young, no more than twenty-five, fresh-faced and fair-haired. She decided he was ideal for Belle, for he looked as nervous as she was.

Belle looked beautiful. The dress was a triumph, enhancing both her figure and her skin tone. Cissie had coaxed some of her hair back and fastened it with a thin red ribbon, then used curling tongs to give her ringlets bouncing on her almost bare shoulders. A touch of rouge concealed that she was pale with nerves.

Martha felt indebted to her associate in the hospital in Paris. She had been honest enough to admit Belle had been ill used, and the price she asked for reflected that. But she had said too that she thought Belle could be brought round, and she had that special quality which made great courtesans.

It had been a gamble depositing a large sum of money in a bank with no certainty the girl would ever arrive here, and even if she did, the associate in Paris might have been totally wrong in her assessment.

But the moment the Frenchman arrived here with Belle, Martha knew she'd found her little golden goose. She wasn't just pretty, she was beautiful, with a perfect body, and her English voice would set many a man's pulse racing even before he saw her other assets. At fifty dollars a time, more than double what she asked for the other girls, she would recoup what she'd paid out for her in just weeks.

Many people claimed there was aphrodisiac in the very air of New Orleans, and maybe that was partially true, for this young English girl had opened out like a flower to the whole idea of sex and seduction since she'd been here. Maybe it was Etienne who had healed her wounds on the way here, perhaps created the first sexual stirring in her, and being made to watch the other girls with their clients and listening to their ribald tales had stirred her up still more. But it was Serge of course who had achieved her ripening into womanhood. Martha had seen the expression on the girl's face when she returned home. Serge had definitely taken her to a place she was going to want to return to.

Now that Belle was one of her girls, Martha had got Esme in to serve drinks in her place. Esme was in her thirties, a mother of three now and no longer inclined to sell herself, but she was a very good maid, intuitive, discreet and excellent at putting the right girl with the right man. She didn't take any nonsense from the girls either. If they had their way they'd spend all night in the parlour drinking, dancing and flirting, but one look from Esme and they high-tailed it off up those stairs.

Esme didn't have to recommend Belle to the fair-haired young man. He gazed at her with his mouth hanging open and Belle moved towards him as though she'd done this a thousand times before.

'I'm Belle,' she said with that delightful, wide-mouthed smile she had. 'Would you like a drink?'

It was Esme who informed the young man that the fee would be fifty dollars, and Martha smiled when he didn't even look shocked and took out his pocket book to pay then and there. Esme shook her head. 'Not here, give it to Belle when you get upstairs, she passes it to the maid.'

Belle was still sipping the brandy Martha had given her for Dutch courage, but the young man, who said he was called Jack Masters and was from Tennessee, gulped his down in one, then took Belle's hand and walked with her to the stairs.

Martha slunk back into the shadows as they walked up the stairs. She didn't want to see Belle's pretty face tight with fear. She could still recall her own first time, it was in a cat house in Atlanta and the man she'd got was no pussy cat like the one Belle had landed. He was such a brute she felt she'd been torn in two.

*

'Well, Jack, if you'll just take your pants off, I can wash you,' Belle said, trying hard to sound as if she'd said that a hundred times before. He'd given her the money as they got into the room, and she'd opened the door again and handed it to Cissie who was waiting outside. As she poured the water from the jug into the basin on the washstand, her hand was shaking so hard she thought she might drop it.

'You sure are lovely,' he said as he unbuttoned his trousers. 'Why, I can't believe I've found an angel like you.'

'That's very kind of you, sir,' Belle said, suppressing a giggle. 'Is that because you haven't been to a sporting house before?'

His pants were on the floor, along with his underpants. He was very pale-skinned and his legs were very thin. 'This is my third time,' he said with some pride. 'I come to New Orleans on business with my uncle once every three months. He's in tableware.'

Belle knew she had to hurry him along, so she parted his long shirt, took hold of his penis and went to wash it with the cloth. His penis instantly reared up, and thankfully it looked very healthy, with no sign of any discharge.

'He's pleased to see me,' she said, copying what she'd heard Hatty say to one of her gentlemen.

'He sure is,' Jack gasped.

'Well, you'd better unfasten my dress for me,' Belle said.

His breath was hot on the back of her neck, and she could feel his fingers trembling. That he wanted her so badly made her feel a faint stirring of desire for him too. She didn't think it was going to be too bad.

Once she had stepped out of her dress and thrown it on a chair, she stood there in her short chemise, stockings and shoes and, smiling at him, reached out and took his hand, placing it on one of her breasts.

She was just going to ask him how he wanted her, when he

lunged forward, pulling her chemise down to expose her breasts, and took one nipple in his mouth to suck. His hand slid between her legs, and holding her that way he nudged her towards the bed and bent her back down on to it. He wasn't rough, just passionate, and again Belle felt that stab of desire, so she moved under him, telling him she liked it. All at once he was on her, pushing into her, while his mouth was still glued to her breast. She was only half on the bed, and he was standing on the floor fucking her.

He came after just four or five thrusts, then collapsed on top of her with a sob. She looked at the little clock on her mantelpiece and saw he'd been with her less than ten minutes. It was almost a comic situation; he'd spent more than most people earned in months on her, and it didn't even last as long as a glass of beer. But she saw the sad side of it: a nice but lonely young man who probably thought coming to a whorehouse made him a real man.

She cuddled him for a couple of minutes, telling him he was marvellous, then eased him up from her and said he must get dressed. She half expected him to say he hadn't had long enough, but he looked stunned and happy, not a bit disgruntled.

'Could I call on you next time I get to New Orleans?' he asked.

'Of course, I'll be waiting for you,' Belle replied.

He was gone in a trice. She shut the door behind him and leaned back on it, closing her eyes. She didn't feel bad at all, for Jack had seemed really delighted with both her and himself. If they were all like Jack, she might even find herself begging one of them to stay a while longer so she could teach him a thing or two about pleasure.

She laughed to herself then. She was officially a whore now. A fifty-dollar-a-time one at that. She wondered what her mother and Mog would think of that.

*

244

'You've made a mistake, Martha,' Belle said at the end of the evening. All the girls had received their pay, and Belle had hung back till everyone else had gone. She wanted to query why she'd only been given two dollars. 'I went with twelve men. I should be getting three hundred dollars.'

'No, honey. New girls under contract to me get just two dollars a day until their fee has been repaid and the cost of any gowns, shoes or underwear recovered.'

Belle didn't know what to say. Two dollars for a night's work would be as much as she could expect in most other lines of work. But Etienne had said she'd get half of what was taken, and she didn't like being cheated.

'Well, I'm sure you won't mind showing me the books you're keeping?' she said after a second's thought. 'Show me what you paid for me, what you've spent on me so far. That way I'll know how long I have to go until the debt is paid off.'

She saw Martha's face tighten, and knew being smart probably wasn't such a good idea. But she had no intention of retracting anything.

'Go to bed,' Martha said in a voice like ice. 'I'll talk to you in the morning.'

Belle lay awake for a long time that night, listening to the sounds of Basin Street. A jazz band was playing just along the street and she could hear dancing feet pounding on a wooden floor somewhere close by, shouts, laughter, muffled conversations, drunks calling out and bottles being thrown into a bin. It was much the same kind of noise she'd grown up with in Seven Dials, and that made her consider what her mother's response would have been if any of her girls had questioned what they were paid.

She suspected Annie would have told them they could sling their hook if they didn't like it and there were plenty more girls to take their place. But then, Belle had no idea how many men each of her mother's girls serviced in an evening. Nor did she know the price they charged. But she doubted that they went for more than five pounds a time, top whack. She also had no doubt that if the girls had only got one pound a night all found, they'd have been ecstatic.

But knowing that didn't make Belle feel any better. It was she who had to put up with men groping her, gawping at her, saying crude things, pawing her, fucking her and finally maybe even giving her the pox or making her pregnant. All Martha did was sit on her fat backside and watch the money flow in.

Belle was sore too, not so much from the sex, as none of the men lasted long enough to hurt or bruise her, but from the disinfectant Martha made them use. It smelled strong enough to kill a grown man, let alone a sperm or a germ.

It was clear there was big money to be made from whoring, but now Belle had a sick feeling that she wasn't going to make it here working for Martha. The woman was unlikely to ever admit how much she paid for her, and that meant the time would never come when Belle didn't owe her.

But Belle wasn't finished yet. These Southern Americans thought they were all so smart, but they couldn't beat the cunning of a girl from Seven Dials. She'd go along with everything for now, but she'd be watching, listening and learning, then when the right opportunity came along, she'd grab it with both hands.

Chapter Nineteen

Mog looked at Mrs Stewart in astonishment. 'You say your Amy's gone missing?' she gasped.

'Yes, that's right. It were two years ago now. I nearly lost my mind with grief and worry.'

'I'm so sorry,' Mog said with utter sincerity. 'We lost our Belle the same way so I can understand what you've been through. Could I come in for a moment and talk to you?'

'You know something?' Hope sprang up in Mrs Stewart's face and for a brief second she looked ten years younger.

'Not exactly, but if we put our heads together . . .' Mog said.

Mrs Stewart opened her door wider. 'Come in, Mrs . . .' She paused, realizing she didn't know the name.

'Miss Davis,' Mog said as she stepped over the threshold. 'But everyone calls me Mog. Belle is my friend's daughter, I don't have any children of my own, but I helped bring Belle up from a baby.'

'I'm Lizzie.' Mrs Stewart led the way down a narrow passage into a large, warm kitchen. 'I'd take you in the parlour but it's so cold in there. I always lit the fire in there until Amy disappeared, but there doesn't seem any point now.'

'I live in the kitchen too,' Mog said. She glanced round the room, noting that it was spotlessly clean, and the table and floor well scrubbed. Two easy chairs by the stove made it very homely. 'No point in wasting good coal on a fire you can't sit in front of. You say your Amy was thirteen when she went. Did the police have any suspects?'

Lizzie shook her head sadly. 'They were worse than useless,

kept telling me she'd come home in her own good time. I knew my girl, she wouldn't go off like that and frighten me.'

'What do you think has happened to her?' Mog asked.

'It's my belief she's gone to the white slave trade,' Lizzie said.

In the more sensational newspapers there were always stories about young women being captured for this trade. In the past Mog had thought it was scaremongering, lurid stories made up to sell more newspapers. Yet however much she had once laughed at fanciful tales about young English girls being sold to become concubines in the harems of Persian princes, now that Belle was gone, she no longer found it amusing.

'I don't think the white slave trade exists, at least not in the way it has been portrayed in the press,' Mog said gently. 'But I do think your Amy may have been taken by the same people that took our Belle.'

She didn't want to say too much. 'You see, a friend of mine has been doing some snooping to try and find Belle, and he came across a list of names and addresses. Your Amy's was on it, that's why I called on you.'

'We must take it to the police then,' Lizzie said.

Mog became a little frightened then; she didn't know if she could trust Lizzie Stewart. She was a respectable woman, and if Mog began telling her about a girl being murdered in a brothel she'd probably run down the street squealing like a stuck pig.

'We think the man behind this has the police in his pocket,' she said. 'So I daren't go to them until I've got real proof that he's snatching young girls. But I'm going to call on the other addresses on the list, and if all the girls have disappeared then we'll have a case that the police won't be able to ignore.'

'Are you saying the police are corrupt?' Lizzie's pale blue eyes opened wide with childlike innocence.

'Let's just say they look the other way sometimes, especially if villains are strong, powerful men,' Mog said, not wishing to disillusion the woman entirely. Lizzie was comfortably off, and although she lived close to Seven Dials she was probably blissfully unaware of what went on there. 'Do you have a picture of Amy you can show me?'

Lizzie went straight over to the dresser and brought over a framed family group picture taken in a studio. She was sitting on a couch with her husband, a tall, slender man with a large moustache, and Amy was sitting on a low stool by their knees.

'Amy was twelve then.' Lizzie's voice trembled. 'Isn't she pretty?'

'She is indeed,' Mog agreed. The girl was slender like her father, her fair hair plaited and wound round her head like a crown.

'When I took her hair down it reached her waist.' Lizzie's eyes filled with tears and her lip trembled. 'The day she disappeared she was wearing a cornflower-blue coat, the same colour as her eyes, I made it for her myself. Larry, my husband, he said it was a daft colour for a coat because it would show the dirt. But I didn't care, she looked so pretty in it . . .' She stopped short, overcome by emotion.

Mog put her hand on the other woman's arm in silent sympathy.

'She's my only child. The pain of losing her was so bad I thought I'd die,' Lizzie sobbed. 'Sometimes I wish I *had* died because there's nothing else left in this life for me.'

'I've felt the same way about Belle,' Mog admitted. 'It's the not knowing if they are alive or dead which makes it even worse. But I'm staying strong because I don't believe Belle is dead, not in my heart. And I'm going to find her. How about you? Do you think Amy has been killed?'

Lizzie shook her head. 'No, I'm sure I'd sense it if she was. Larry doesn't trust my intuition, he says it's just wishful thinking, but I think he's wrong.'

'Then there's hope,' Mog said, and put her arms around the other woman and hugged her. Lizzie hugged her back and they stood that way for some little while, two strangers united because of fear for their girls.

Mog broke away first, her eyes damp with tears now. 'I can't promise you anything, but I will come and tell you if I find out anything at all. If you think of something that might help us, or you just want to talk to me, you can find me in the Ram's Head in Monmouth Street.'

The second name on the list was Nora Toff of James Court. Mog knew that it was over by Drury Lane, and she remembered people often called it Gin Court for it was said to be home to hard drinkers. But, unconcerned whether this was true or not, she hurried off there, anxious to have some kind of case to put before Garth and Noah.

James Court was very squalid. Mog picked her way carefully through refuse, ignoring the stares from snotty-nosed urchins wearing only rags and found her way to number two, which had a door that appeared to have been kicked in many times. She rapped firmly on it.

'Bugger off, you little bastards,' a male voice bellowed from within, and Mog stepped back from the door in fright.

It was flung open by a man wearing only trousers and a dirty vest. His feet were bare and he smelled of drink. 'If you're from the church you can bugger off too,' he snarled at her.

'I'm not from the church,' Mog said, indignation at being spoken to so rudely making her bolder. 'I came to ask you about Nora Toff. Is she your daughter?'

'And what's it to you?' he said.

Mog took that to be confirmation that he at least knew Nora, even if he was not her father.

'I hope she has nothing to do with me, but my friend's daughter has disappeared, and also another girl under very similar circumstances. I'd just like to know if Nora is safe at home.'

'She went off six months ago,' the man said. 'What are you saying? What's happened to those other girls?'

'We don't know, they just disappeared,' Mog said. 'Both of their mothers know they wouldn't run off of their own accord, they were good girls.'

'You'd better come in,' the man growled. 'Our Nora weren't flighty neither, she never done nothing like that afore.'

Mog did not want to go into the man's home alone; the dank, festering smell wafting out was enough to know it would be even worse inside. He looked a desperate character too; it really wasn't safe. 'I'd like to talk about it to you,' she said carefully, 'but not here. Could you come to the Ram's Head in Monmouth Street early this evening? Ask for Mog.'

She slipped away quickly, even as he was calling after her. Once around the corner in Drury Lane she looked at the list of names and addresses and decided that she'd done enough for one day.

When Mog walked into the pub, she found Noah there talking to Jimmy and Garth. They all looked round expectantly as she came in and obviously had been discussing the list of names.

'Amy Stewart disappeared two years ago,' Mog said quietly, aware some of the drinkers might be listening. 'Only thirteen and she's got very respectable parents.' She went on then to tell them what had happened when she asked about Nora Toff.

'I'm not sure if the man was her father,' she explained. 'He was a rough sort, and he'd been drinking, but I suggested he came here in the early evening. I don't feel inclined to try any more today – Lizzie Stewart drained me.'

'I'll go and ask about some of the others,' Noah offered,

taking the list from her and looking at it. 'There's two from near Ludgate Circus, I'll check them as I've got to go to Fleet Street this afternoon anyway.'

'What about going to Paris? To check out that Madame Sondheim,' Jimmy said, his eyes sparkling with excitement. 'If you go, Noah, can I go with you?'

'You aren't going anywhere, son,' Garth said firmly.

Jimmy stuck out his lip.

'Your place is here,' Noah said, reaching out to ruffle the lad's hair. 'You've done a fine job getting this list, and the address in Paris, but if I take anyone there with me, it will have to be someone who speaks French.'

'Seems to me,' Garth said ponderously, 'that we should double our efforts to find that man called Sly and kick some information out of him.'

'Oh, Garth!' Mog exclaimed.

Garth folded his arms defiantly. 'Look, Jimmy heard him mentioned again, they said he'd turned yellow-bellied, so ask yourself why that is.'

'Disgusted with what the others were doing?' Noah suggested.

'Possibly,' Garth said. 'But it's more likely he found himself in deep water and got scared.'

'You said no one round here had seen him in ages,' Jimmy said.

Garth nodded. 'That's right, but I know a man I could lean on who might tell me where he hangs out.'

Mog didn't like it when men spoke of giving people a kicking or leaning on them, and said so. Garth merely grinned. 'Some folk just don't respond to being asked nicely,' he retorted.

Two weeks later Mog, Garth, Noah and Jimmy gathered round the table in the kitchen behind the saloon. It was wet and very windy outside, and at six in the evening the bar was still quiet.

Noah had a sheet of paper in front of him on which he'd written out the names and addresses from the list found in Colm's office and next to each he'd made notes of what he'd found out.

'Amy Stewart,' Noah read. 'Disappeared two years ago, age thirteen. Nora Toff, fourteen, disappeared six months ago. Flora Readon, sixteen, disappeared eleven months ago. May Jenkins, disappeared fourteen months ago.'

Noah paused and looked around the table. 'There's no need to go right through all the twenty names on this list. All but three of them have gone missing in the last four years. They were mostly between fourteen and sixteen. Amy Stewart was the youngest of all at thirteen. Every one of them was said to be pretty; in most cases I was shown a photograph which confirmed this. As for the remaining three names I can't be sure what happened to them as their families no longer live at the addresses on the list. But a neighbour of Helen Arboury said the girl had "gone off". She couldn't or wouldn't say if she thought there was anything suspicious about this, but she did say that Helen's mother was a widow and she took her other two children and went to stay with relatives.'

'So shall we go to the police now?' Mog asked. 'I mean, that's all the proof we need that Kent and the man Colm in Maiden Street are grabbing young girls and doing heaven knows what to them.'

Noah looked at Garth, who shook his head. 'We could go to the police, Mog – I'd say for any man to have a list of missing girls in his office makes it fairly certain he's heavily involved. But I'm afraid there might be an informer at the police station. If these people find out we're on to them they'll shut down their operation and then we'll never find any of the girls, or see those responsible put behind bars.' He paused, looking thoughtful. 'My plan is to stop wasting time and go to Paris immediately to check out Madame Sondheim.'

'Even if she is involved, it was probably only as the person the girls were taken to initially,' Mog said doubtfully. 'They could be anywhere in the world now.'

'Trust me to use my initiative,' Noah said with a smile. 'Obviously I'm not expecting all twenty girls to be locked up at that address. I have a friend who speaks French who'll go with me. I think together we can find out something.'

'I still think it would be more direct to find the man Sly and make him talk,' Garth said stubbornly. 'Besides, if you run into trouble in Paris you'll have no one there to call on.'

'We'll cope,' Noah said firmly. 'I've got my editor on side. He's really hoping for a sensational story, so he's come up with false identities for us and he'll pay all our expenses. We're going to pose as a couple of wealthy businessmen having a fling in gay Paree. Girls will of course come into that!'

Mog nodded. She could see what Noah meant, and if his friend was as well bred and charming as he was, she doubted they would have any trouble gaining the confidence of a brothel owner, or the girls in her house. 'But you must be careful,' she warned them. 'A great many brothels employ a thug to deal with difficult customers, and if they suspect you are investigating them, you are likely to find yourself dragged into a back alley and beaten up.'

'Don't worry, Mog.' Noah smiled at her. 'We'll be passing on every last bit of information to my editor as we go. If anything should happen to us he'll be poised to strike. He's got a copy of the list of girls' names too, and there'll be huge headlines about the police doing nothing while young girls go missing.'

'That won't bring you back to us,' Mog said reproachfully.

'I'll be back,' he said with a wide grin. 'I'm after a staff job on the paper.'

'That's it then,' Noah said to his friend James, looking up at the tall, ugly house lying slightly back off the square in the Montmartre district of Paris. 'It looks a bit forbidding, hardly a house of fun!'

'We need to ask someone about it and Madame Sondheim,' James replied. 'We should pick on someone our own age. I mean, if she does run a brothel here the people who live in this square might not want to admit it.'

'I don't think anyone living in Montmartre is troubled at the idea of a brothel,' Noah said with a grin. Walking up from the Pigalle, they'd seen dozens of street walkers, and they'd looked at the posters of the cancan girls outside the Moulin Rouge. 'Some of the artists who live here only paint girls in brothels, so there must be hundreds of them.'

'Maybe so, but this square looks like a place where ordinary people live,' James said.

James Morgan would be described by most people as 'a gentleman of leisure'. When his father inherited his grandfather's successful hardware shop in Birmingham, he sold it and sank everything into manufacturing bicycles. He was a visionary, and while most people thought him crazy to take such a risk on something which might only be a five-minute wonder, he was convinced that bicycles would become the most popular means of transport. He was right of course, and having got into the business before the rest of the world realized their value, and overcome various teething troubles, British-made Morgan bicycles had become the benchmark of good craftsmanship and reliability.

His company had gone from strength to strength, selling not just to the home market, but exporting all over the world.

James was officially employed in the London office, but his only real work was taking trips around Europe to find new outlets. This was why he had been happy to agree to come to Paris with Noah: to all intents and purposes he was just checking on some of the shops which already stocked Morgans.

Noah pulled out his pocket watch. 'Almost one,' he said. 'So why don't we go and have luncheon in that place over there?' He pointed to a restaurant across the square with tables and chairs outside. 'We can play the part of a couple of bounders and ask the waiter where we can find some girls!'

James laughed. He liked being with Noah; his warmth, good looks and confidence drew other people to them. James didn't find it so easy to make friends – he wasn't exactly shy, just unable to push himself forward. He knew he wasn't handsome, being short and a little tubby, and his hair seemed to recede further each time he looked in the mirror. People were always saying that at thirty, well-educated and wealthy, he was the most eligible of bachelors, but although his parents and their friends were always introducing him to suitable girls, they never seemed to be very keen on him. The truth was that he thought women found him boring, and he felt he must be for he was still a virgin. But he couldn't bring himself to tell Noah that.

Two hours later, after a good lunch with several glasses of wine, the two men were having a brandy each.

James had not been able to bring himself to ask outright if there was a brothel nearby, but Noah, with only a handful of French words to work with, a little sketch of a naked woman on a piece of paper, and a great many gestures with his hands, had managed to make himself understood to the little old waiter with a stooped back and a green apron almost as long as his trousers. The waiter pointed diagonally back across the square, exactly to the address they had, and held up seven fingers which they had to assume was the time the place opened.

'So we're doing fine so far,' Noah said, ordering another brandy. 'Once I knew that was a brothel I didn't think it wise to mention Madame Sondheim. If she got to hear anyone was asking about her, we might find we couldn't get into the place.'

'So we've got to go in there tonight?' James said nervously.

'How else are we going to find out anything?' Noah asked, rolling his eyes in a display of impatience. 'Come on, James, you're the one that speaks French, don't you go all reluctant on me now.'

'I've just never been in a brothel before,' James whispered, not wanting anyone to overhear him. 'I don't know the form.'

'They kind of know if you're green.' Noah laughed, remembering his first time. 'I don't suppose it's any different here. We'll both act like novices, that way we might get to chat more to the girls. As you are the one with the French, you could make out you don't really want to do it as you have a fiancée at home.'

'But I wouldn't mind doing it,' James said eagerly.

Noah smirked. 'You are a novice, aren't you?'

James hung his head and admitted it. Noah had explained everything about Belle witnessing Millie's murder when James agreed to come to France with him, but now he felt he had to tell his friend how he met Millie and how he felt about her.

'I was totally smitten with her,' he admitted. 'She was so beautiful, warm-hearted and kind, not the way people think whores are. It's because of how she was that I must find out where Belle is, and all those other girls too.'

'Did you love her?' James asked. He had agreed to come on this trip because he felt he and Noah would be rescuing girls from moral and physical danger. But his sheltered upbringing made it hard for him to accept that any decent man could have had romantic ideas about a whore.

'What is love?' Noah said with a wry smile. 'If it is having someone on your mind so continuously that you can't eat, sleep or think about anything else, then yes, I loved her. But I think my father would insist that what I felt was lust. I suppose that if I had been able to whisk her away from Annie's Place and been on my own with her, then maybe in a few weeks I might have discovered that's all it was. But I didn't get the chance to find out. So I suspect I'll always be hoping to find another woman that makes me feel the way she did. Have you ever felt like that?'

'The closest I've come to it is having very lurid dreams about one of the girls I saw in my father's factory in Birmingham,' James admitted. 'If I hadn't had one or two glasses too many I wouldn't tell you, but this girl was testing out the height of the saddle on a bicycle. Her skirt was rucked up and I could see her black-stockinged leg, right up to her knee, surrounded by the lace on her petticoat. I thought it was the most erotic thing I'd ever seen.'

Noah sniggered. 'But what did she look like?'

'Just ordinary really,' James admitted. 'I only see her leg in my daydreams, not her face.'

'Well, James, along with finding out what happened to Belle and the other girls here in Paris, we'll have to make sure you get something more substantial to dream about than a girl and a bicycle.' Noah grinned. 'Now, let's go for a walk and get to know the area before we come back here tonight.'

The two men returned to the square at eight that same evening. Darkness had fallen when they came out of their hotel on to the Pigalle, but they found themselves plunged into brilliant light, noise and action. They were astounded by the huge numbers of bars, cafés and restaurants which hadn't been apparent earlier in daylight. A tout outside the Moulin Rouge was yelling out that it was the top show in Paris, and tourists of many different nationalities were standing outside gawping at a huge poster showing a row of female legs high kicking out of a froth of net petticoats.

As they walked up the steep, winding lane, music from pianos, accordions and violins wafted out of dark, smoky bars. Cooking smells from the restaurants vied with those of street traders with their hot chestnuts or crêpes, and added into the pungent mix was the odour of horse droppings too.

James and Noah's eyes popped many times as a tout shoved a picture of statuesque showgirls wearing little more than a few sequins and a large feathered fan under their noses. There was no shortage of prostitutes either, they were accosted several times during their walk, and whatever it was that the girls said to James they got him blushing furiously.

James said that the doorman had warned they should be careful as it was still a dangerous place, full of thieves and thugs, even though many of the old dwellings had been pulled down in the last ten years as the Sacré-Coeur was being built. But Noah thought it was the most thrilling place he'd ever been to. It was picturesque, colourful and vibrant, with a strong overtone of sauciness thrown in and less squalid than Seven Dials.

'Another drink before we go over there?' James suggested as they got to the square. Madame Sondheim's place was in darkness except for a red light by the door. But Noah was sure that the lack of light inside was only because it was shuttered, not because there was no one there.

'That's just delaying tactics,' Noah teased him. 'It's best to go now, they are bound to be busier later on, and we might not get a chance to talk to anyone. Now, I'm relying on you, you're the one with the French. I'll try and get an English-speaking girl, however ugly.' He broke off laughing. 'I want you to see I am serious and committed!' he added.

James looked like a frightened rabbit as they approached the front door. 'Courage, my friend,' Noah said. 'What's the worst that can happen in a brothel?'

'That I couldn't get it up?' James replied, assuming that was Noah's worst-case scenario.

'No, for me it's a fire breaking out and I have to run out naked,' Noah grinned.

James laughed, and found it made him feel a bit less tense. 'That's easily overcome, just keep your clothes on.'

When Noah rang the doorbell a little hatch shot back and they saw a woman peering out at them. Noah lifted his hat to her. The door opened and a rather gaunt-looking woman of at least fifty, wearing a plain black dress, stood there.

James told her in halting French that they were English and a friend had given them this address. The woman made a gesture to come in with one hand, then, after closing the door, took their hats and ushered them into a room to the left of the hall.

The room was very warm, thanks to a blazing fire. There were four girls in the room, all scantily dressed, with silky negligees barely disguising their underwear. The woman who had shown them in offered them a drink; there was no choice, just red wine. She then introduced the girls as Sophia, Madeleine, Arielle and Cosette. Arielle was a dark-haired beauty, with huge, limpid eyes, and a wide, full mouth, but the other three girls were all unremarkable.

James shook their hands, which made the girls giggle.

'Do any of you speak English?' Noah asked.

'A leetle,' the small, mousy-haired one called Cosette replied.

James began speaking to Arielle and Noah noted that she seemed quite taken with him and involved with whatever he was saying to her. Noah smiled resignedly at Cosette and took her hand to kiss it.

That made all the girls giggle too, but Cosette looked as if she liked it.

A pianola in the corner of the room was playing, and Noah held out his arms to dance. Again Cosette giggled as if no man had ever suggested such a thing as a dance before. 'Does Madame Sondheim not like you to dance?' he asked. He knew many madams didn't like the girls wasting their time with such things.

'You know her?' Cosette looked alarmed.

Noah shook his head. 'No, not me. My friend came here, he said she was very fierce. Is that right?'

Cosette nodded. Noah noticed she had pretty grey eyes, and even though her hair looked in need of a wash, it was marvellous that she spoke some English.

'You tell me about it upstairs?' he said, sensing she would be very guarded in front of the other girls.

'You want me?' she asked, as if astounded.

Noah wasn't sure he wanted to have sex with her, but he smiled and said of course he did. All at once she had her hand in his and practically dragged him from the room while James was left with the beautiful Arielle, Madeleine and Sophia looking on.

Cosette took him up to the third floor, but as they went past the closed doors on the first and second floors he heard sounds which suggested there were other girls in there with clients. Cosette's room looked just like her – worn, untidy and uncared for.

'You must give me the money,' she said, holding out her hand.

Noah had not got to grips with French money, so he took a ten-franc note from his pocket and handed it to her. She frowned, so he added another to it, and this time she smiled and went to the door where she handed the money to some-one else.

She began to take off her blue wrap, but Noah stopped her. 'I can't,' he said. 'My friend wanted woman very much. I just come with him. We just talk?'

Cosette shrugged and sat on the bed, pulling the wrap back over her shoulders.

'Englishmen strange,' she said, shaking her head.

Noah laughed. 'Yes, that is so. Many of us like very young girls. I heard Madame Sondheim gets very young girls some-times.'

'Not for young men like you,' she said incredulously. 'Only old men.'

Noah came and sat on the bed beside her and took her hand in his. 'Does she get young English girls?' he asked.

Cosette nodded. 'Sometimes. It is bad. We hear them cry. Not good for us, the men who come only want this.'

Noah took that to mean trade was dropping off for her and the other girls because of it.

'Have you seen any of these young girls?'

'No, never see. They stay upstair. Not come in parlour.'

'Locked in?' Noah mimed the locking process.

She nodded.

'The men go up there?'

Again a nod. 'How much?' he asked.

She made a gesture with her hands which appeared to mean it was a huge amount of money and she pursed her mouth in distaste.

'Then where do they go?' Noah asked.

Cosette didn't seem to understand that question. Noah tried again, changing words, asking how long the girls stayed upstairs, but she still kept shaking her head and saying 'No understand'. But the strangest thing was that there were tears in her eyes.

He took out his wallet and peeled off some notes. 'For you,' he said, folding her hand around the notes. 'Madame will not know.' He lifted her chin and very gently wiped her tears away with one finger. 'Now tell me why the tears?'

A volley of French spewed out, and even though he didn't understand a word of it, he knew outrage when he heard it, and it wasn't directed at him. 'English, please,' he said. 'Where do the girls go?'

'I not know,' she said. 'I hear someone say some go to *couvent*.'

'*Couvent?*' he queried. 'Is that the same as convent?'

She shrugged, clearly not knowing if it was.

'Where?' he said, and seeing a pencil by the bed picked it up and opened his wallet to find a scrap of paper to write it on.

But she pushed his hand and shook her head. 'I not know where it is. Or what it called. I only hear them say "*couvent*".'

He began to ask her if a girl was brought here in January, but she put a finger across his lips. 'No more. I can say no more. You understand, trouble for me.'

To Noah that meant there *was* a girl brought here in January and if they could find the convent, they were on their way.

Noah couldn't bring himself to leave Cosette without making her feel better about herself.

'You are a sweet girl,' he said, taking her face between his two hands and kissing her forehead, cheeks and then her lips. 'If I was not married . . .' He paused, hoping she'd draw the right conclusion to that remark. 'But my wife made me promise to be good in Paris.'

She smiled then, and it was as though the sun had come up, for her face actually became pretty. 'Your wife lucky to have good husband,' she said.

'You talk more,' she went on, pulling him back to the bed when he walked towards the door. 'I speak the Engleesh.'

Noah felt it was more that she didn't want him to go downstairs too quickly for fear of losing face with the other girls than because she wanted to practise her English, but it would have been churlish to refuse.

She said she came from Reims, that she was the eldest of seven daughters, and her father was a farm labourer. She didn't have to say why she'd come to Paris to become a whore, it was clear it was the only way she could earn enough to send money home for her family. She blushed when she told him she'd learned her English from an English artist who lived in Montmartre. She said she saw him when she had afternoons off. When Noah asked if he would marry her, she laughed lightly and said no, because he was very old. She added that he was kind to her, and it struck Noah that if she smiled more and looked prettier, then more people would be kind to her.

When Noah went back to the parlour, only Sophia was still there. She said something in French which sounded very surly, and sat down again, turning her back on him.

Five minutes later James came down the stairs. His face was bright red and he was beaming. As the maid who'd let them in appeared from a doorway at the back of the hall to pass them their hats, the two men said nothing further until they were walking across the square.

'She was wonderful,' James blurted out. 'So kind, so giving.'

'But I bet she took the money,' Noah said archly. He was glad his friend had finally got there, but realized he was now expected to spend the evening being told how marvellous the experience was.

'I don't think she wanted to,' James said dreamily. 'She's too afraid of Madame Sondheim not to take it.'

'So you did ask her some questions then?'

'She didn't seem to understand many of them. I asked about young girls and she just said she was better for me than someone very young.'

Noah couldn't help but smile. He supposed it was an impossibility to expect his friend to interrogate a woman as lovely as Arielle when he was alone with her in a bedroom.

'Does the word *couvent* mean convent?' he asked unexpectedly.

'Yes, why?' James frowned.

'Because that is where some of the young girls go after that place. Unfortunately I would imagine that looking for an unnamed convent in Paris will be close to the proverbial needle in a haystack.'

Chapter Twenty
1911

The heat woke Belle and as usual she was bathed in perspiration. She thought nostalgically of the cool English weather all the time now for the sticky summer heat of New Orleans was exhausting.

She remembered how thrilled she'd been back in April of last year when she was given this room. It was at the back of the house, so it was quieter, large and sun-filled, and had a beautiful big brass bed. It hadn't occurred to her then that it would be like an inferno once the weather grew warmer and that was why none of the other girls wanted it.

But then, in sixteen months of being at Martha's, she'd found that she couldn't actually trust anything or anybody. What seemed good one day could become bad the next.

It had been a huge mistake to ask Martha for proof of what she'd paid for her, especially so soon after she'd arrived here. The woman had been really frosty with her and Hatty warned Belle she ought to apologize immediately.

'We are all on some kind of a contract, honey,' she explained. 'The madam of a whorehouse has to hold the whip hand or the girls take advantage. Even for those of us who weren't bought like you were, she still gives us board and lodging, she supplied us with dresses, shoes and the like, so of course she takes that back out of our money – she has a living to make. We have to earn her trust too. How would it be if she took on a girl and got up one morning to find she'd hightailed it out of town taking the silver teaspoons and a trunk full of dresses?'

Put like that, Belle could understand. 'But all I wanted to

know was how long it would be before she'd got all her money back,' she explained. 'I can't see anything wrong in asking that. How else can I plan my life?'

'Martha don't see it that way, she'd say it was her business,' Hatty insisted. 'And us girls are just like flowers, we only stay fresh for a limited period. She's got to make her pile out of us while she can. If we get pregnant, get the pox, get our face slashed by another girl, or beaten up by one of the men, we aren't any good to her.'

That sent a shiver of fear down Belle's spine. She hadn't considered that any of those things could happen to her, but perhaps they could. 'But the man who brought me here said she was a good woman, and she seemed so kind,' she said in puzzlement. 'How can she earn so much money from us and then sling us out if something bad happened?'

Hatty smirked as if unable to believe Belle was that naive. 'She *is* a good woman, at least compared with most of the madams in this town. She feeds us well; if we're sick she takes care of us. She don't expect us to work when we've got our monthlies. Afore you start complainin', honey, you gotta open your eyes and see how it is for some of the girls in this town. My! Some of 'em ain't even fed right, they get whipped, they've had their babies taken away. I heard tell there was one madam, when her top girl wanted to leave to go home to her folks, she got a tattoo put on the back of the girl's hand, which said "Whore". That way she could never go home. If you've got a coupla hours, I could tell you stories about mean madams that would make your hair fall out.'

'But I need the money to get back to England,' Belle argued, though what Hatty had said frightened her. 'I'm scared I'll be here for years and years.'

Hatty laughed at that. 'Honey chile, none of us, not even the real pretty ones of us, will be here for years and years, not up this end of the town anyway,' she said, condescendingly

267

patting Belle on the head. 'Best thing you can do is make it up with Martha, prove yourself here, then bide your time and look out for a rich man who might take you for his mistress, or even marry you. That's the only way I've seen girls get out of it, and it's what I'm gonna do.'

Belle thought about everything Hatty had said for a couple of days. The part which shook her most was the statement about flowers not staying fresh; it hadn't occurred to her that there was some kind of time limit to this work. On top of this she remembered how Etienne had said that girls should always keep the madam sweet. Her mother used to complain about certain girls, and now she came to think about it, those girls always left. Probably not by their own free will either.

There was no doubt in her mind that Martha was very annoyed with her. She turned away when Belle came in the room, and hadn't once spoken directly to her.

What with everything Hatty had told her, Belle realized she had no choice but to apologize and make everything smooth again; if not, she just might find herself sold on to someone else. Everyone in America was very eager to point out that slavery was a thing of the past, but while the slave markets for field hands and servants might be gone, here in New Orleans they still existed for whores, whether white, negro or mulatto.

Everyone accepted this arrangement; Martha's girls talked about it all the time. At the high end of the market there was even a kind of kudos for a girl who had changed hands for a great deal of money. That girl could rely on being treated with kid gloves as long as men flocked to pay a king's ransom for her. But further down the line the girls had no rights; no one cared how they were treated, least of all the police. And Belle was fairly certain that if a girl was to speak out about it, she'd probably end up silenced for good.

So Belle told herself that she must be glad she was in a

good sporting house, and that she was considered a valuable commodity because she was young, pretty and English. She must take to the work, show real enthusiasm for it, and that way she could keep herself safe until she found a way out of it.

So she went to Martha and apologized.

Belle found she barely remembered incidents that had happened just a week ago, yet she could recall everything about that day sixteen months ago when she went down to see Martha in her parlour.

She dressed for the occasion in the pale blue frilly dress she'd been given in France because it made her look innocent. She left her hair down on her shoulders, and she put just a touch of rouge under her eyes to look as if she'd been crying.

It was almost noon and Martha was sitting on her couch wearing her apricot-coloured loose tea dress, her hair covered in a matching turban.

'What is it, Belle?' she asked in a chilly tone.

'I came to ask your forgiveness,' Belle said, keeping her head down and wringing her hands. 'I know you are cross with me for asking about the money, I realize I must have sounded very ungrateful when you'd been so kind to me.'

'I do not like being questioned by my girls,' Martha replied. 'This is my house and it runs by my rules.'

'I was very wrong to question you,' Belle said. 'But I didn't understand how it all worked, I'm so new to it. I wasn't thinking about the lovely dresses and underwear and shoes you'd got for me, or how much it must have cost to bring me here. But I have thought it all through now and I realize I am very, very lucky to be in your house. Please can I make amends for upsetting you?'

'You, honey, are very fortunate I didn't sell you on to another house immediately,' Martha said sharply. 'The only reason I didn't was because you are so young, and unaccustomed to this business. I have taken time and trouble with you; no one else in this town would do that.'

'I know, ma'am,' Belle said contritely. 'You've been like a mother to me. I am so sorry.'

'Do I have your word then that there will be no further unpleasant outbursts from you?' Martha asked.

'Oh yes, I promise that I will do my best to make it up to you,' Belle said, and managed to squeeze out a tear or two, even though she would have preferred to tell the woman what she really thought about slavery. 'I truly want to put this behind me and start afresh.'

'Come here, honey.' Martha patted the seat beside her for Belle to join her. 'I am glad you came down to me today. It tells me you are at heart the sweet thing I took you for. Now, I am going to overlook your mistake this time, I think perhaps it went to your head a little that my gentlemen were so taken with you. But should you question me again I won't be so lenient a second time. You'll be out that front door before you can even say Mississippi. Have I made myself clear?'

'Yes, ma'am,' Belle said, hanging her head and forcing out a few more tears. 'I promise I will never show you any disrespect again.'

'Run along now, honey,' Martha said, patting Belle's knee as if she were a child. 'And do take off that dress, it looks like something a school marm would wear.'

Belle remembered how she left Martha's parlour that day and ran back to her room so she could seethe in private at the indignity of having to grovel just to keep a roof over her head. But she made a promise to herself that she would play the game for only as long as it suited her, and then she'd be off.

Belle hadn't reckoned on the seductive charm of New Orleans, however. Nor had she realized that the easy, luxurious life at Martha's would suck her in and make her as indolent as the other girls.

Martha reverted to being the warm, friendly woman she'd been before their little upset. Belle had made friends with the other girls and during the afternoons they went out together to Jackson Square or for a walk along the levee by the Mississippi. They always had plenty to laugh and chat about, for their work was such that often very funny things happened, and no one took it very seriously. Belle had her two dollars a night, and she saved as much every week as she could.

Mostly Belle felt really happy with the girls, as though they were the older sisters she'd never had. She learned from them about America, about fashion and beauty tips, and about men of course, for they were always a main topic of conversation.

Belle had her big new bedroom too, which although too hot in summer, was pretty, with deep pink roses on the wallpaper. She could eat what she liked, and she had developed a taste for spicy jambalaya and the other traditional Creole dishes. She could sleep most of the day if she wished to or laze on cushions in the shady back yard reading a book. She never had to scrub floors, wash clothes or do anything other than make herself look pretty.

But now and again anger and resentment would rise up inside her.

She could deal with the work; if she was completely truthful, mostly she quite enjoyed it. She preferred the older men to the younger ones. Sometimes they told her they were widowers or that their wife wouldn't sleep with them any longer. Though she knew it was quite likely that they were lying and all they wanted was young flesh and uncomplicated thrills, whether they spoke the truth or not, they were invariably polite, gentle and grateful. She was often moved by their appreciation – a few tears, a warm hug before they left, flowers or chocolates left for her later made her feel special and even loved.

Some of the younger men, on the other hand, could make her feel dirty. They could be rough, uncouth and very insensitive to her feelings. They often acted like they thought she should be grateful they'd picked her, and occasionally she'd get one who would claim she wasn't worth the money. Martha said a proportion of men always did that as they felt diminished by having to pay for sex, and she shouldn't take it personally. But it was hard not to.

In much less than two years, she'd gone from barely understanding what sex meant to knowing more than she wanted to. She knew now that no two penises were the same; she'd seen huge ones, tiny ones, bent ones and diseased ones, and every other kind in between. She'd learned the tricks of tightening her internal muscles to increase men's pleasure and make them climax quicker. She could even take them in her mouth and look as if she was loving it when she really felt like vomiting.

Some men wanted real lovemaking, others just quick release. Some wanted to believe she was really a lady, while others wanted her to act like a wanton hussy. She had developed the ability to sense which they wanted just by the way they looked at her down in the parlour. She slid from lady to hussy so often that mostly she no longer knew which was closest to her real character.

Belle knew she wasn't the same girl who had come out from England. She didn't have romantic daydreams any longer, instead she took all she was told with a pinch of salt. She had developed a certain cynicism and she could be hard too, especially to men who came close to seeing the girl she used to be.

England and all those she loved there seemed a distant blur now, like looking back on a dream. Her seventeenth birthday had come and gone, and she still hadn't written a letter home because she knew there was nothing she could say that would make her mother and Mog feel better about her disappearance. She thought it was best that they believed she was still in New York as she had been when she'd sent a card, and that she was having a far better life than she could have had with them.

Yet she couldn't help but scour the newspaper for English news. Unfortunately the American papers only wrote up an English story when it was something really newsworthy and important, like when King Edward died last May. That had been covered well, with pictures of his funeral, and Belle cried when she saw one with Westminster Abbey and the Houses of Parliament in the background and remembered when Jimmy took her there.

Mog would have been there in the crowd somewhere to watch. Even though she didn't like crowds, nothing would stop her seeing a procession, and she'd thought King Edward was a good sort. Sometimes there would be a few lines about the suffragettes too, the force-feeding of them in prison or the latest thing they'd done to push their cause. That was enough to make Belle cry as well, for Mog had always said she wished she had the guts to join them.

Yet it was the coronation of George V back in June of this year which really made her homesick. That was the kind of story from England Americans liked, and every paper and magazine was full of it. She could remember when Edward VII had been crowned, the excitement, the bunting and flags going up. Mog took her to watch the procession in Whitehall and she'd never forget the gilded coach and everyone cheering. They'd had a street party that day, someone wheeled a piano out, and the dancing and drinking went on most of the night.

When these feelings of homesickness came upon her, Belle

tried to tell herself that her life here was far better than in England, but the debt to Martha was always there in the back of her mind. Common sense and a love of figures said the money had been repaid months ago and that Martha was a greedy, conniving witch who was taking her for a fool.

Belle had enough money saved to leave town, though it wasn't enough to get back to England, but it was said that Martha had spies everywhere and word would get back to her the moment one of her girls bought a train ticket, whereupon she would immediately send someone to the railway station to stop them boarding.

Belle told herself that was just a story put about to frighten the girls, but all the same she was too afraid to chance it, for she knew if she was caught, Martha would take her revenge. She'd sell her on before the day was out, and it wouldn't be to another house up on Basin Street, but several blocks back where she might be expected to service forty or fifty men during the course of one day. And the people who owned those places watched their girls closely and beat them if they stepped out of line.

Pregnancy was another worry. So far Martha's sponges and douches had protected her, and indeed the other girls in the house, but Belle knew that in other houses the girls weren't so lucky. They had the choice then of visiting Mammy Lou, a mulatto woman who could get rid of unwanted babies, or having the baby and taking the chance on her madam letting her stay in the house. Belle knew Martha would never agree to any of her girls bringing up a baby in her place. There were cat houses in the back streets where there were several babies and small children living in an upstairs room but Belle had heard they were dosed with 'the Quietness', a cordial made by Dr Godfrey which was laced with laudanum, and when they were bigger they were farmed out. Even back in London Belle had heard of children sent away to stay with women who made a business out of minding children. They got no tender love and care there, mostly they weren't even fed adequately, and it was said to be just the same here in America.

But for now Belle felt she must concentrate on pleasing Martha, because she still had a feeling the woman didn't really like her. There was nothing tangible to confirm this, just the odd dark look or a sharp word, but the other girls often told her stories about how vindictive Martha had been in the past to girls who'd upset her in some way.

Belle didn't find it easy to suck up to her like the other girls did. She avoided letting Martha see her reading the newspaper or a book, guessing that was one thing which set her apart as different, and she never aired her opinions either. But Belle wasn't made to be subservient, and she couldn't bring herself to act dumb to please a woman who bought and sold human beings.

So it seemed to Belle that Hatty's idea of finding a man who wanted her as his mistress was the only way out of her predicament. She didn't want a husband; it wouldn't be right to marry knowing she was intending to run off. But a married man keeping a mistress was already being deceitful, so he deserved to be deceived himself.

Every night Belle jotted down in her diary all the gentlemen she serviced, and later she'd think of each one and make further notes: what she thought of him, what he looked like, how often he visited Martha's, and if she was his favourite. There were many men who visited Martha's on a regular basis and always asked for her. She separated out those she liked especially, and those who bought her presents, and finally those she thought were probably rich enough to keep a mistress.

It came down to just two men: Faldo Reiss, a jovial Texan who had an important job on the railways, and Captain Evan

Hunter, who owned several ships which sailed out of New Orleans. Faldo was in his fifties and had a wife and four grown-up children back in Houston. Evan was a little younger, around forty-seven – he'd never mentioned a wife or children but his home was in Baton Rouge.

What Belle needed to establish was whether the two men had legitimate business in New Orleans, or whether they went out of their way to come here to Martha's just to see her.

It was frustrating that Martha didn't encourage any man to stay longer than half an hour in the girls' rooms. This was because she could make far more money with a succession of men than one staying for several hours, or even all night. Half an hour was just about the right length of time for the sex, but it left no time for talking. There was time in the parlour, but the other girls and Martha always had their ears flapping, so Belle couldn't hope to have an intimate conversation with anyone.

On a Friday night right at the end of July, rain was belting down so hard that the drains couldn't carry the water away fast enough and Basin Street became like a river. The girls called it a hurricane, but then they were always talking about hurricanes and how scary they were, with roofs being ripped off houses and trees being uprooted. Martha agreed this could be a hurricane, although it was a month early, but she said the girls were exaggerating and that in all her years in New Orleans she'd only ever seen one roof ripped off.

Belle had seen rain as hard as this dozens of times in England, but there it was always cold. This rain was like a warm shower, and she wasn't surprised that people were still out on the streets regardless of getting soaked.

But the rain was keeping gentlemen away. By nine in the evening only two had come in, the Professor was wilting at his piano and the girls were so bored that they were sniping at one another.

Anna-Maria, who Belle had discovered at least a year ago was extremely treacherous, asked Suzanne why she had chosen a green dress as it made her look sallow. This wasn't true – Suzanne had glossy, coppery-coloured hair and green suited her.

'I don't mean to be unkind,' Anna-Maria simpered. 'I just think someone ought to tell you.'

'Someone ought to tell you that you're a lying bitch,' Suzanne retorted, getting to her feet and looking down at the other girl menacingly. 'You're jealous of me because that rich banker asked for me yesterday.'

'He won't ask for you again now he knows how dirty you are,' Anna-Maria snapped back, jumping out of her chair. 'I know you don't wash between clients, you stink like a polecat.'

Suzanne sprang at the other girl with her long nails poised to claw her face. Belle didn't like Anna-Maria much, and felt she deserved a scratched face for being so nasty to Suzanne, but Martha was likely to put all the blame on to the one that struck the first blow. So Belle jumped up too and stepped in front of Anna-Maria.

'That's enough,' she said in the kind of firm voice she'd often heard Mog use with the girls. 'Anna-Maria! You will apologize to Suzanne, that was an awful thing to say and it isn't even true.'

Hatty, Polly and Betty all began to add their opinions. Betty said that Anna-Maria deserved a good thumping as she was always making mischief.

'Watch out I don't claw you as well,' Anna-Maria yelled at Betty, trying to get past Belle. 'You're just jealous of me too.'

The Professor began to play louder, and at that moment the parlour door opened and Martha stood there, her double chin quivering with anger.

'What is this?' she asked, looking at each of the girls in turn.

None of them answered. It was an unwritten law that they didn't tell tales on one another.

'I suppose it was you, Belle?' Martha snapped. 'I can see by the way you are that you've been intimidating Anna-Maria.'

'I haven't,' Belle said, aware she was still standing right in front of the other girl, and maybe that did look like intimidation to someone just coming into the room. 'Tell her, Anna-Maria?'

'She was, she's always pushing me around,' Anna-Maria burst out.

By lying she'd just knocked out the code of silence, and all the other girls began to shout out what had really happened.

They were all still shouting and adding other grievances about Anna-Maria when suddenly Cissie's voice cut through the noise to say a gentleman had called.

It was Faldo Reiss, the big Texan, but although he was usually impeccably dressed in a pinstriped grey and white tail coat and stiff-winged collar, tonight, soaking wet, he looked ridiculous as he stood in the doorway of the parlour.

The girls fell silent immediately. Belle wanted to laugh, for with his wet clothes sticking to him and plump belly, hair and moustache dripping wet, he resembled a walrus.

'How good to see you, Mr Reiss,' Martha gushed. 'The girls were just having a little debate. You look almost drowned, you poor man. Cissie will take your coat and hat, and do come in and have a drink.'

Belle pulled herself up sharply and went over to Faldo, smiling a welcome. 'How nice to see you, Mr Reiss. I hope you didn't risk getting pneumonia just to see me?'

'I would risk anything to see you,' he said gallantly, taking the glass of whisky Cissie offered him and downing it in one.

'Could we dry his clothes for him?' Belle turned to Martha to ask.

Martha gave a kind of bodily quiver, as if she was trying to shake off the incident she'd broken up a few minutes earlier. 'Yes, Belle, that would be kind. Would you like to go up with Belle, Mr Reiss, or was it another girl you wanted to see?'

Belle sensed Martha hoped it was another girl he wanted. But Faldo smiled and said it was Belle he wanted.

As they went out of the room, Belle couldn't resist smirking back at Anna-Maria.

Up in her room, Belle urged Faldo to take off all his clothes. She said she'd give them to Cissie to dry down by the stove in the kitchen. 'Mind you, they won't be dry in just half an hour,' she said, as he began to peel them off.

'I'll pay to stay all night,' he said all too eagerly. 'Will that be all right?'

'I'll have to consult Madam,' Belle said, lowering her eyes coyly. She wasn't keen to have him there all night; he was a big man, and the thought of him wanting to do it over and over again wasn't inviting, but then, she had wanted an opportunity to get to know him better, and this was it.

She took his clothes and shoes downstairs, passing them on to Cissie.

Martha was still in the parlour, and as Belle went in she sensed tension and guessed she'd been telling the girls off. Belle asked if she could speak to her privately. When Martha came out into the hall she explained, and asked how much it would be if Faldo stayed the whole night.

'Five hundred dollars,' Martha said curtly.

Instinctively Belle knew that was a far higher price than was normally charged, especially in such bad weather when they were unlikely to get any other business. But she had a feeling Martha had picked on such a high price hoping Faldo would refuse it, which would make Belle lose face in front of both her and the other girls.

'I don't know if he likes me that much,' Belle said with a little grin. 'I can only ask him.'

As she went back upstairs, her satin gown rustling, she could sense Martha's eyes following her, and her animosity. It made Belle feel uneasy, but she really didn't know what she could do about it.

Faldo was in bed when she got back to her room. He had a big, flabby white chest, and where he'd rubbed his hair dry on her towel it was standing up like a porcupine.

'I don't think you'll want to stay all night, she says it will be five hundred dollars,' Belle said in a small voice.

He made a loud guffaw of laughter. 'I call it a bargain to stay with you,' he said. 'Pass me my pocketbook on the table, honey. I'll add another twenty so we can have a bottle of champagne too.'

As Belle came back up the stairs a few minutes later with the champagne in an ice bucket and two glasses, she could hardly contain her delight. Martha's face had been a picture when Belle gave her the money, struggling between pique because she'd been mistaken about Faldo, and sheer greed that she'd got so much money on a bad night.

But Belle's delight was not in making Martha eat humble pie, but in Faldo's reaction. He wanted to be with her, and he'd asked for champagne, which implied he saw this as a special occasion. She was determined to make sure it was one.

A little later, sitting up beside him in her bed drinking the champagne and laughing with him, Belle remembered what Etienne had said about loving her clients a little. Physically Faldo was not very attractive; in fact, he was very odd-looking. His head was small and egg-shaped and completely out of proportion with his big frame. His eyes were like black boot buttons and his nose was too big, and with his big flabby belly, yet skinny arms and legs, he was all wrong. Yet despite that he was a nice, good-humoured man, who'd always treated her well. He didn't appear to have any of the disturbing little fetishes other men had, and he smiled with his eyes as well as his mouth.

But now he seemed in no rush to have his way with her, she was seeing yet another side of him. It was good just to lie back on the pillows and talk; she never had a chance to do that with other men. He told her how he had to ride the railway a great deal to check that the passengers on the trains were being treated properly, that the trains ran on time, and that the stations along the routes were maintained well. But he was also involved in decision-making about new railways, negotiating the deals for the land they crossed, and buying up or building hotels and other related businesses by the railway stations.

He had the ability to make even rather mundane things interesting, but once he got on to the subject of different parts of America, the wildlife and the Red Indians, he was spell-binding. 'It's God's own country,' he said with real fervour. 'Vast plains, huge forests, wide, fast-flowing rivers and mountains so beautiful they bring a lump to your throat.'

Then he wanted to know about England, and although Belle did her best to describe London so he could imagine it, she was ashamed that she knew so little about the city of her birth.

She wanted to ask him about his wife and children, but she sensed he wouldn't welcome such questions. So instead she told him how she had been snatched off the street and eventually brought here.

He looked thoughtful as she told him the story, and when she'd finished he took her hand in his and squeezed it.

'It's men like me who make this lucrative market,' he said sadly. 'We only see the excitement, the colour and the thrill of sporting houses. We don't ever think how the girls came to be there. I sure do feel ashamed now.'

She squeezed his hand back and cuddled closer to him. 'Don't be. You are a good man. There aren't any girls in this house who aren't willing. Even if I hadn't been forced into this way of life, maybe I would've come to it anyway. You weren't the one who captured me, or one of the men who raped me in Paris. I like being here with you. I really like you.'

He turned to her and stroked her cheek. 'I like you too, Belle. You are the prettiest girl I've ever seen, with your mop of dark curls and your dancing eyes. You make me feel young again.'

When they'd drunk all the champagne Faldo scooped her into his arms in the way she felt a husband or a lover would, and he sought to please her rather than expecting her to please him.

Sex with any of her clients was quickly over and much the same whoever it was with. Faldo had been like all the other men too; there was nothing to single him out other than that he hadn't been rough, said crude things or been unpleasant in any other way. But he was different tonight, slower, sensitive and loving. It wasn't in the same league as Serge's lovemaking, but it was enjoyable.

Belle glanced at the clock on her bedside table at one point and was amazed to see it was gone twelve, yet they'd come up to her room soon after nine. But he was holding back, wanting to make it last, and for once Belle didn't try to speed things up; she was liking it, really liking it.

Daylight was just creeping around the edges of the shutters when she awoke to find herself still in his arms, and his body, which she'd thought so flabby the previous evening, now felt warm, soft and comforting. And she stretched herself along it like a cat, winding her legs over his. This, she thought, was how it must be when you were married, a cosy kind of contentment.

He made love to her again a little later and it was sweeter still than it had been the night before. She even let him kiss her, for she felt as if she should give him all that she had.

But around half past eight he looked at his pocket watch and sighed. 'I have to go, my little flower. I have a meeting at ten and I need to go to a barber's and get shaved and back to my hotel to get a clean shirt.'

'It's been really lovely,' she said, wrapping her arms around him tightly. 'I wish it could be like this all the time.' In the half-light of the shuttered room he didn't look old or ugly, just a sweet man who had made her feel happy and good about herself.

'You are good at your job,' he chuckled softly. 'For a moment I almost believed you meant it!'

Belle sat up sharply and looked down at him. 'But I did. Truly!'

He smiled and moved closer to kiss her nipple. Just that light touch sent a shiver of pleasure down her spine and she pulled him closer to her.

'I have to go,' he said reluctantly after a minute or two. 'Could you get me my clothes?'

Some ten minutes later he was dressed in his dry, pressed clothes. Cissie had even polished his shoes for him. He put his hands on Belle's waist, smiling down at her red satin and lace negligee. 'Can we do this again, sugar?' he asked.

'I would be cross if you didn't want to,' she replied, tilting her face up so she could kiss him. 'But I feel bad that you had to pay Madam all that money.'

He leaned down to kiss her. 'You're worth it, sugar,' he said with a smile. 'But now I must hit the road!'

Belle went back to bed after she'd shown him out. She wasn't sure exactly what she felt. She was pleased that she'd got closer to Faldo, maybe he would want her for his mistress now, and she was fairly certain he could afford to pay whatever

Martha asked to release her. But she also felt sad that she was planning to cheat such a good man.

'You can't think about that,' she told herself sharply. 'Your duty is to look after yourself and get back to England. Faldo will get what he wants too.'

'What was it like with him all night?' Hatty asked later that same day. All the girls were in the kitchen dunking beignets in their coffee. 'He sure must be loaded to pay so much.'

Hatty was a big, voluptuous girl with mid-brown hair, green eyes and a very kind heart. She was the one Belle confided in and sought out for company. She'd been brought up in an orphanage in San Francisco and had run away when one of the male governors tried to have his way with her. She had been forced into prostitution by a couple who pretended to befriend her, and it was these people who sold her on to Martha, along with Suzanne.

'Or he's in love with Belle?' Betty said with a wide smile.

'I think it was more because he didn't want to put his wet clothes back on,' Belle giggled.

She had noticed Anna-Maria was scowling and so she thought she'd better keep her real thoughts about Faldo to herself for now. 'I thought morning would never come,' she added for good measure.

There was a little more conversation between the girls about men who asked to stay all night. It seemed to Belle that most men backed off when they heard how much it was. From what she could gather, without seeming too interested, Hatty was the only other of them to have had an all-nighter.

'You'd better share your tricks with us, honey,' Anna-Maria said to Belle. The girl was smiling, her voice sugar-sweet, but Belle sensed the underlying venom. 'Did you pick them up in Paris? Do tell!'

'No tricks. Like I said, he just didn't want to put his wet clothes back on,' Belle repeated. 'I wouldn't mind betting that when he looks at his empty pocketbook he'll never come back again.'

In the week that followed Faldo was never far from Belle's mind. It wasn't so much daydreaming about him as the possibility of the ticket out of here and a few steps nearer to getting home to England. But meanwhile, along with the undercurrent with Martha, there was one with Anna-Maria too. She gave Belle dark looks, and often broke off conversations when Belle came into the room.

Belle knew Anna-Maria had been the house favourite when she arrived, and within weeks Belle had taken her place. Belle could imagine how galling that was; she knew even she would be jealous if Martha bought in a new girl and her position was usurped.

Anna-Maria's beauty was of the tempestuous, dramatic kind: olive skin, nearly black eyes and black curly hair, and the fiery nature to go with it. She was not only angry about Belle's popularity with the gentlemen, she resented the other girls approving of her and often siding with her.

Cat fights had been commonplace back home in London where hardly a day passed without some little altercation. Belle remembered Mog saying once that girls could be as deadly as snakes when they were jealous, so she was careful not to antagonize Anna-Maria further.

Ten days passed before Faldo turned up again, and he arrived with a beautiful box of candy for Belle. It was decorated with pink velvet roses, and so pretty it made a lump come up in her throat.

'May I stay all night again?' he asked before he'd even had a drink.

'Are you sure you want to spend that much?' she whispered

back to him, not wanting anyone else to hear. Fortunately the parlour was crowded and the Professor was playing quite loudly.

'The hell I do!' he said. 'I'd risk swimmin' through the 'gators in the swamp to be with you.'

Belle laughed, but said he must ask Martha. There were so many gentlemen in that evening that she felt sure Martha would refuse.

Surprisingly Martha agreed, though Belle didn't know how much there was in the wedge of notes Faldo handed her.

Once again he ordered champagne and Cissie followed them upstairs with it.

Once in her bedroom, Belle kissed Faldo on the lips and began to remove his jacket. 'You can't go on doing this,' she said. 'It's madness.'

'A good madness, honey,' he laughed, catching hold of her waist and kissing her again. 'I've thought of nothing else but you since I left last time. It's sure been torture thinking 'bout you with other men.'

She cupped his face in her hands and looked at him tenderly. 'I can't do anything about that, Faldo. I've been wishing I could be with you too.'

He turned her round and began unhooking her dress, bending to kiss her back as he pushed the dress down on to the floor. 'You are so lovely,' he murmured. 'So little and perfect, and I'm being an old fool in fallin' for you.'

Belle stepped out of her dress and turned to him again. 'I'm falling for you too,' she said, and she didn't feel bad saying it as it felt like the truth.

He took her with a fierce passion before they were even completely undressed, and Belle responded eagerly.

Later, as they sat in her bed drinking the champagne, with all the noise and music from the District wafting up through the open windows, Faldo sighed deeply.

'That sounds like you've got all the worries of the world on your shoulders,' she said.

'Only one worry, and that's you,' he said. 'What would you say if I asked you to give this up and come and be with me?'

Belle's heart leapt. She hadn't expected it to come to this so quickly. 'I wish I could,' she said, 'but I'm tied into a contract with Martha.' She went on to explain it and how she didn't know how much money was still owing.

'I see,' he said, sounding angry with Martha. 'But I'll sort that out, don't you fear.'

'But Faldo, she won't let me go easily,' Belle said, and she clung to him, for all at once it occurred to her that Martha hadn't risen to own one of the most successful sporting houses in the District by being soft, honest or caring about the future of her girls.

'I have influence,' he said reassuringly. 'Let me worry about Martha.'

The next morning Faldo got up and pulled his clothes on. Belle stayed in bed, but she was a little worried about his set expression. 'What is it?' she asked.

Faldo sat on the edge of the bed and looked down at her. 'I've thought it all through,' he said. 'You must act like nothing is going on between us, don't say a word to anyone.'

Belle nodded. She was afraid he'd gone off the idea of taking her away.

'I'll set up a place for us,' he said. 'It has to be here in New Orleans because this is the only place I come to all the time, but I can find somewhere away from the District. When I've got it all arranged I'll come back one evening to let you know. The next afternoon you pretend to go out for a walk, but you get a cab and come to me. Once you are out of here I'll settle up with Martha.'

Belle could tell by his serious expression that he'd thought it all through and meant it. She wound her arms around his neck and thanked him. 'You understand you'll be on your own a great deal?' he said warningly. 'And you won't be able to come back to the District and see your friends. It has to be a clean break.'

'I don't care about that,' she said. 'I only want to be with you.'

Chapter Twenty-one

'It's no good, Jimmy, we just have to accept we are never going to find Belle,' Noah said pleadingly. 'Too much time has passed, the trail has grown cold and we've run out of ideas. I can't do any more, however much I wish I could.'

It was a hot, airless day in September, and the two young men were sitting in the back yard of the Ram's Head in the early evening. It had been a hot, dry summer and Mog had gone to great lengths to make the back yard more attractive. She'd persuaded Garth to get rid of all the old crates and other rubbish out there and she'd planted geraniums in tubs and painted an old bench and small table white. For weeks now it had been a much appreciated little refuge from the hurly-burly and heat of the pub.

The prolonged drought and heat were causing problems all over London. People were tetchy, they couldn't sleep, the drains stank, food went off too fast, the streets were dusty and even the leaves on the trees were falling prematurely. Just last night Garth had said he was in two minds whether to shut the pub for a week so he, Jimmy and Mog could go and stay by the sea for a holiday.

But Jimmy's response was that his uncle and Mog could go, and he'd stay here in case there was any word from Belle. Garth had said he never knew anyone so stubborn and single-minded that they could still be hoping word would come after a year and a half.

Noah had been back to Paris three times now with James, trying desperately to find the convent the girl in the brothel had spoken of. He believed he'd called at every single one in

Paris, over forty in all, yet he had been unable to find one that would admit to having any connection to Madame Sondheim. Several of the convents acted as hospitals and they did say they'd had many patients who were prostitutes, women who'd been attacked and those who had been brought in with complications in childbirth. But they assured Noah and James that these were not English girls and not one of them had ever claimed to have been forced into their career.

Noah couldn't believe that any of the nuns he spoke to would countenance aiding the exploitation of young women anyway. They had been very open, horrified that anyone would suspect anyone in a religious order of trying to conceal such a crime.

In the light of this he felt that the people behind this trafficking in young girls were probably calling the place they used a convent as a way of deflecting suspicion from it, and that it was just a house where girls were held until they could be sent on somewhere else. But without a single clue as to the whereabouts of this house he now knew he had no hope of finding it.

Jimmy had been just as relentless in searching too. He'd broken into both Kent and Colm's offices again to check through their papers and he'd cross-examined just about half the population of Seven Dials in the hope that someone would know something. A year ago he *had* found out something, and that was where Charles Braithwaite, known by the name of 'Sly', lived.

Jimmy was only told that the man lived in Aylesford in Kent, and he went down there to find out about him. He was told that Braithwaites had farmed there for three generations, but Charles Braithwaite had been brought up to think he was a gentleman, and ever since he inherited the farm he had spent most of his time in London.

With Garth with him for muscle, Jimmy called at the farm with the intention of forcing Braithwaite to give them some information, but they found only Tad Connor, the farm manager. He said Braithwaite had gone away some three months since, and he hadn't heard from him or had any wages in all that time. Connor seemed an honest, decent man caught in the trap of being unable to leave because he had a wife and three children to provide for and his cottage was a tied one. He said he was surviving by selling produce, and if Braithwaite didn't come back soon he was going to sell some cows at the market.

Jimmy asked if he could recall Braithwaite bringing a young girl here back in January. Tad did remember his employer and his friend coming late one night and leaving early the next day, for that was the only time in January they were there. He said if there was a girl with them, he didn't see her. But he added there had been girls there in the past. He couldn't remember dates, and had only seen the girls from a distance, so he was unable to describe any of them, but he recalled feeling Braithwaite and his friend were up to no good as they hadn't let him into the house during this period as they normally did.

Because Jimmy remembered Colm and Kent talking about Sly turning yellow-bellied, he suggested to Connor that maybe he should report his employer missing to the police. Connor didn't seem to think that was necessary, but he said he'd consider it if he still hadn't heard from Braithwaite in another month.

Shortly after Jimmy and Garth had returned from Aylesford, Noah had told Jimmy he didn't think there was anything further that any of them could do to find Belle. At the time Noah thought Jimmy was in agreement. But looking at him now, it seemed as if he wasn't ever going to let it go.

'You did really good with the story in the newspaper about

all the missing girls,' Jimmy said sadly. 'I really thought that would shake up the police. But they haven't done anything.'

Noah reached out and ruffled the lad's red hair affectionately. His story earlier this year about the missing girls had been an all-out attempt to get some kind of action and justice. While it appeared to make no difference to the police, who still maintained they had done everything possible already, the newspaper received hundreds of letters from people from all over England. The story clearly touched a nerve as along with all those offering sympathy to the parents of the missing girls, some of the letters were from people who had also had a daughter who had disappeared. Some were from people who offered advice, though mostly that was impractical. And a few letters were from those who thought they knew the perpetrators of the crime; Noah handed those names over to the police for investigation.

The irony of writing this article was that while it didn't really help Belle, Noah began to get far more journalistic work, all good investigative stuff he could get his teeth into.

'The police did do a great deal,' he reminded Jimmy. 'They brought Kent and Colm in for questioning, and I really believe they tried hard to nail them. But those two are practised villains, and there was absolutely no hard and fast evidence to link them to the missing girls. Even Annie's statement about Kent killing Millie doesn't really hold water, Mog wasn't there that night to corroborate it. All they've got is hearsay, which came from a young girl who is now missing. If Annie had only told the police the truth on the night it happened it might all be different now.'

'Isn't there anything else we can do?' Jimmy asked plaintively.

'Our best hope is that one of the missing girls turns up and tells us where she's been and who captured her.'

'If only that could be Belle,' Jimmy said, his voice cracking. Noah had known Jimmy now for over a year and a half, during which time his eighteenth and nineteenth birthdays had come and gone. But it was only now that he suddenly noticed the physical changes in the lad. He'd grown at least three inches, muscles in his shoulders and arms were straining the fabric of his shirt, and he had a shadow of stubble on his chin. He'd shown his maturity in the way he'd resolutely done everything in his power to find Belle, and worked so hard for his uncle, but now he was looking like a man, and while hardly classically handsome, with his red hair and freckles, he had a good, strong face.

'You should be getting out and meeting other girls,' Noah said gently. 'You only knew her for a very short time. Even if she was to turn up one day, it's unlikely you'd have anything in common any more.'

Jimmy looked straight at him, his eyes flashing a warning to say no more on this subject. 'I will find her, Noah,' he said with conviction. 'Maybe she won't want me then, and I'll accept that. I've met a few other girls since she went, but they didn't mean anything to me, not the way Belle does.'

With that he said he had a couple of errands to run and went out through the back gate of the yard, while Noah went back into the pub. Garth hadn't opened the bar yet, and he was sitting at the kitchen table smoking his pipe, while Mog sat across from him darning a pair of socks. Noah had observed that the pair always seemed to be together now, and Mog was a good influence on Garth, for he was a lot less fierce than he used to be.

'Would you like a drink, tea or some beer?' Mog asked.

Noah declined and said he'd better make tracks for home as he was taking a young lady out to the music hall in King's Cross later.

'Jimmy ought to be doing something like that too,' Mog said.

Noah thought so as well, but he was a little surprised at Mog feeling the same.

'Well, don't look like that!' she exclaimed. 'He's nineteen, high time he had a sweetheart.'

'She's right,' Garth said gruffly. 'It's not good for him mooning over Belle all the time.'

'I just said something similar to him,' Noah admitted. 'But just because we all want that for him doesn't mean he'll take any notice.'

'Maybe I make him worse,' Mog said fearfully. 'I mean, I do talk about Belle, I can't help it. I don't understand Annie. She never comes down here to ask if there's any news, not even to see how I'm doing. And when I went up there last month the maid told me she wasn't in. I know that was a lie.'

Noah had been to see Annie twice, and he too was baffled by the stony-faced reception he'd got. The house where she was taking in lodgers was a smart one, and she'd got the kind of lodgers who would be horrified to discover their landlady had once run a brothel, but surely she didn't think Mog or he would say anything to embarrass her?

'She always were a right cold fish,' Garth said. 'There were talk she blackmailed the Countess into leaving her drum to Annie.'

'That's malicious gossip and quite untrue,' Mog said stoutly. 'The Countess cared for her and Annie looked after her right to the end like she was her own mother.'

'So why ain't she more caring about her own kid?' Garth asked. 'It's like you was Belle's ma, Mog. What went wrong?'

Noah stopped both of them by holding up his hand. 'I know Annie was forced into that line of work. It can't be easy to love a child when she was born that way.'

Mog was biting her lip as if she had something to say but didn't dare speak out. 'Well, Mog?' Noah said. 'I can see you know something.'

'It's my fault,' she whispered. 'As soon as Belle was born I took her in my arms and did everything for her. I never gave

Annie a look in. She was the Countess's top girl, and I told her she must get back to it as quick as possible to stop anyone else stepping in.' Mog began to cry, huge tears rolling down her cheeks. 'If I hadn't done that I reckon it might have gone differently. Maybe this is my punishment. I took Annie's baby all those years ago so now I've got to suffer the pangs of grief losing her,' she sobbed.

To Noah's surprise Garth got up from his chair and went round the table to comfort Mog, and as the big man bent over her, his usually stern face full of tenderness, Noah suddenly realized that Garth had fallen in love with her.

'Nothing's your fault, Mog,' Noah said over his shoulder as he began to walk to the back door. 'You've been a good friend and a fine stand-in mother to Belle. But it's time you made a life of your own, and it looks to me as if you've got the right man there to make it with.'

Noah smiled as he reached the back yard. He hoped that Mog and Garth would see for themselves that this was a bright new dawn for them.

'Don't cry, Mog,' Garth said awkwardly. He'd never been comfortable around crying women. 'Noah's right, nothing is your fault, you're a good woman.'

'What did that last thing he said mean?' she asked, drying her eyes on her apron and looking up at him. Garth felt that same butterfly-in-his-belly feeling he often got around her. He thought she had the sweetest face, he loved the way she bit her lip when she was nervous, and the gentleness of her grey eyes. He knew he had to speak now or maybe he never would be able to.

'About the right man there to make it with! Well, I reckon he knows I've got feelings for you, Mog,' he blurted out.

Her eyes widened and her hand fluttered up to her mouth. 'For me?'

'Yes, you, who else?' he said, his voice croaky because it

seemed a lifetime ago that he'd tried to woo a woman, and she hadn't meant as much as this one did. 'But maybe you don't feel the same? If so, speak out and I'll say no more.'

'Oh, Garth,' she said softly, her lower lip quivering as if she was going to cry again. 'I do feel that way, but I thought it was just on my side.'

Realizing this kind of talk could go back and forth like a tennis match and never be resolved, Garth reached down, took her hands and pulled her up into his arms and kissed her.

She tasted of the apples she'd been slicing for a pie earlier, and she smelled of soap and lavender water. He wrapped her tightly in his arms, lifting her right off her feet as he kissed her, and his heart soared because he could sense by the way her lips were yielding that she felt the same as he did.

'I reckon it's high time I opened the bar,' Garth murmured against Mog's neck a little later. He had sat down on a kitchen chair and taken her on his lap to kiss her again and again. He didn't really know how to proceed now. Courting was for young people, but he sensed Mog was likely to be frightened off if he tried to go too fast with her. Besides, there was Jimmy to think of. He couldn't just take Mog off to his bed without making it right with the lad first.

But he had a feeling that Jimmy would think marriage was the only right way to do that, and perhaps he'd be right.

'I never thought this would happen to me,' Mog said, blushing prettily. 'But we have to think of Jimmy's feelings; we can't let him walk in and catch us like this.'

Garth thought it was astounding how she always seemed to pick up on what he was thinking. 'I didn't ever think it would be my young nephew that would make me get married again,' he said.

Mog stiffened on his lap and began biting her lip again, and Garth realized that hadn't come out the way he intended.

'I meant, I can't set a bad example to him,' he said, and realizing that didn't sound so good either, he felt his face turning as fiery red as his hair. 'What I really mean is, I want to marry you, Mog. Will you be my wife?'

She laughed then, a soft little trill that sounded like water over stones. 'I'd like nothing better, Mr Franklin,' she said. 'And we'd better make it soon if we don't want to set Jimmy a bad example.'

Noah was still smiling about Mog and Garth as he walked up Tottenham Road towards his lodgings. He thought they made a perfectly matched couple, and he felt certain that Jimmy might stop fretting quite so much about Belle if they decided to marry.

But, as so often happened when he thought about Belle, his mind turned to all those other missing girls and he recalled what one of the senior policemen down at Bow Street had said to him.

'We know it goes on, young girls lured away to France or Belgium to become prostitutes. And girls there are brought over here for the same purpose. We found two French girls at a bawdy house in Stepney we raided a few months back. They were in a sorry state, stick-thin, dirty and addicted to opium. Once we got them cleaned up and got someone in to speak to them in French we found they thought they were coming to England to be ladies' maids. Seemed they'd both been interviewed in the same big house in Paris by the same woman, who told them they would be coming to England with her for a year. They were both broken in by "gentlemen" in a big house, where they were watched so they couldn't escape. Then, a few months down the line, they were taken off to various other places, each worse than the one before, until they got to Stepney and we found them.'

The policeman said that in any year there were three to four hundred young women going missing, and of that number only around a hundred and fifty were ever seen again. He pointed out that many were probably with a man they'd run off with, some might have been murdered, but he thought the rest were in brothels somewhere. He pointed out that most would be beyond saving, even if they knew where they were, for drug addiction and disease would have taken their toll. Before long they would be yet another body on a mortuary slab.

'Maybe I'd better make one more trip to Paris, and try bribing Cosette,' Noah muttered to himself, unable to bear the image of young girls on mortuary slabs.

Chapter Twenty-two

Belle felt quite sick with fear as she walked down the stairs to leave Martha's for good. It was two in the afternoon, a very hot, sultry day without even a whisper of a breeze.

It was only last night that Faldo came in to tell her he'd found a place for them. He paid for only a short time, just long enough to give her the address and instruct her on what she had to do, leaving her with a severe case of jitters. This hadn't left her; she'd lain awake agonizing about whether she was doing the right thing: it seemed to her that she was putting all her trust into the hands of someone she knew very little about.

But it was too late to change her mind now, and as Faldo had asked, she was carrying only a small reticule, which held nothing more than her savings, hairbrush and a few rolled-up ribbons. She was wearing her blue dress beneath the green one she'd been given in Paris, and beneath those she had on two sets of petticoats, drawers and chemises. She felt terribly hot with so many clothes on, but she hadn't been quite able to bring herself to leave all her belongings behind as Faldo had said she must.

Everything Martha had given her she'd left in her bedroom, and she hoped the other girls would be able to share out the few bits of jewellery and other personal things she'd left behind.

Martha came up the passage from the kitchen just as Belle got to the bottom of the stairs. 'It's very hot out,' she said, looking curiously at Belle, as if noticing she looked stouter than usual. 'The other girls are all out in the back yard drinking lemonade.'

Belle's stomach turned over. She felt sure Martha had guessed what she was up to. 'I fancied a walk,' she said. 'It's so easy to get lazy when it's as hot as this.'

'Well, don't overdo it,' Martha said. 'I've never really understood why the English always seem to want exercise.'

Martha had been making sharp little comments about the English for quite some time. Belle had the feeling she had been trying to goad her into snapping back at her. She certainly didn't have any intention of rising to the bait now, so she smiled sweetly.

'I expect I'll regret it as soon as I've crossed the railway line,' she said. 'And then I'll be right back for a sit-down in the cool and a glass of lemonade.'

Martha walked off into the parlour then, and Belle made it to the front door. She was sorry she couldn't say goodbye to the other girls, for apart from Anna-Maria she had grown to love them all and had been grateful for their company, advice and friendship. She was going to miss them for the laughs they'd had, the lovely chats, and because their presence had helped when she'd felt scared, alone and homesick.

Belle walked quickly across the train tracks into the French Quarter, then zigzagged her way across it, looking over her shoulder now and then to make sure Martha hadn't sent Cissie or someone else after her to spy on her.

Finally, when she was sure she wasn't being followed, she hailed a cab to take her down Canal Street.

Belle had rarely been out of the French Quarter and the District, so she had no idea what the Mid-City area was like. The cab seemed to go a very long way along Canal Street before it turned off. But she saw the sign for North Carrollton Avenue and felt relieved, as that was the right road. Yet when the cab stopped in front of one of the many 'Shotgun' houses, she was shocked and disappointed.

Belle knew this style of single-storey wooden-frame house was very common all over the Southern States because they were cheap to build. At little more than twelve feet wide, with the rooms leading on from one to another without a hall, there was no wasted space, plus they caught a through draught of cool air in the summer. They were said to be called 'Shotgun' because with a door at the front and one at the back a shotgun could be fired clear through the house.

There was really nothing wrong with such a house; she knew millions of people would be happy to have such a home. But she'd had the idea Faldo would get them one of the pretty Creole cottages like the ones in the French Quarter, with wrought-iron balconies and fancy shutters. She hadn't expected a shabby, poor person's house.

There wasn't even a front garden. All the houses in the street were raised up on brick posts with wooden steps up to the front door, the slightly overhanging roof making a small porch.

Faldo came out of the front door and down the steps just as Belle was getting out of the cab. He greeted her with a warm smile, paid the driver and then took her arm to help her up the steps.

'I hope you didn't run into any problems with Martha,' he said. 'I was worried for you.'

'No. She did speak to me as I was leaving but I just said I was going for a walk. I thought she'd notice how fat I look. I've got two dresses on and I'm so hot.' Belle laughed nervously. Relieved as she was to get away from Martha's without any trouble, suddenly she was really scared of what lay ahead of her.

Faldo opened the wire screen door that kept out flying insects and waved her to walk in first. Her first impression was that the room was bigger than she'd expected and the high ceiling made it seem airy, but it was very sparsely furnished with just two dark red velvet armchairs and a small table by the window. The lighting was gas, and there was a fireplace, although with the weather being so hot, she couldn't imagine New Orleans ever being cold enough to light a fire.

'I managed to get just a few bits of essential furniture delivered this morning,' Faldo said. 'But I thought you'd like to choose the rest yourself.'

Belle had no idea what to say. It looked so bare and uninviting, especially after the comfort of Martha's. She knew she was going to be living here alone most of the time and that made her shiver with fear.

'Can I see the rest?' she said, trying to pull herself together and be glad she'd managed the first step towards freedom.

'Just a bedroom and kitchen,' he said, leading her through the door into the bedroom. The bed he'd bought was a pretty brass one, and sitting on it were some new bed linen, pillows and a quilt. 'I left it for you to make, women are so much better at such things.'

There was also a dark wood dressing table with three oval mirrors, a stool sitting before it. Belle admired it and the bed, then gave Faldo a hug because she was afraid he'd sense her true feelings about the place.

'I know you are too young to have learned homemaking skills, honey,' he said, his lips against her neck. 'But I'll help you all I can, and a clever girl like you can pick up so much from magazines and books.'

The third and last room was the kitchen. It had a gas stove, a sink, shelves on the wall with some crockery and saucepans sitting there, and a small scrubbed table with two chairs in the centre. Faldo opened a cupboard lined with some kind of metal, with a lump of ice sitting in a square dish at the bottom. 'This is where you'll store milk, butter and meat to keep cool,' he explained. 'A man will come round to sell you ice each week. You just go out to him with the dish when he rings his bell.'

Belle had seen ice being brought into Martha's, but she didn't expect that ordinary people could have it too, and that made her spirits rise just a little.

'But I'm afraid the water closet is outside,' he said, looking concerned she would be offended by this.

'That's fine,' she said, though her heart sank back down again.

He filled the kettle to make some coffee for them. He'd bought a box of groceries too, and seeing a walnut cake on the top, Belle roused herself to put everything away.

'Can you cook?' he asked as he spooned the coffee into a pot.

'A bit,' Belle said. 'I used to help Mog back home. I peeled and chopped vegetables, made jam tarts and stuff like that with her. But I never made a whole meal by myself.'

'If you can read, you can cook,' he said, and smiled. 'At least, that's what my mother used to claim. Maybe you should go to a bookshop and get a recipe book?'

'That's a really good plan,' she said, wanting to sound enthusiastic and joyful, even if she didn't feel it.

They had coffee and walnut cake, then Faldo told her he was going to give her ten dollars a week pocket money. Belle was horrified it was so little – she wouldn't get far on that – but he didn't notice her stricken face. 'But I've opened two accounts for you,' he went on. 'One is at Frendlar's grocery shop down Canal Street. The other account is at Alderson's, it's a store which sells everything from stockings, sewing cotton to tables and chairs. Between these two shops you'll be able to find everything you need to make this house a home; just charge it to me. You must sign the bills as Miss Anne Talbot, and should anyone ever question you, you must say I'm your guardian. Is that all right with you?'

Belle assumed she had to have a false name in case Martha tried to find her. 'You've been very kind,' she said. 'I hope you don't come to regret this.'

He smiled and reached out to caress her cheek. 'There is no reason why I should, you are a delight. But I am concerned about you feeling lonely and bored. I will come as often as I can, but I know that isn't the same as having friends or family nearby.'

'I'll be fine. I can read, do sewing and learn to cook,' she said more bravely than she felt. 'But what do I say about myself to any of the neighbours?'

Faldo frowned. 'I think it best that you keep your distance from them,' he said. 'But if circumstances arise where you have to speak to them, clearly you mustn't tell them you've just come from the District. You could say I'm your guardian and you came because your parents back in England died. If they are curious about why you aren't living with my family you could say you like to be independent. But it would be safer to avoid having to say anything, that way it won't get back to Martha that you are here.'

'When are you going to speak to her?' Belle asked.

'I'm not, honey,' he said, and seeing the surprise on her face he went on to explain. 'She's a tough woman, she'll ask for an enormous sum for you, and could make mischief if I refused to pay her that much. So I shall call round one evening soon and ask for you, that way making myself look innocent of any part in your disappearance. But, as I'm sure you can under-stand, you mustn't go anywhere near the District or the French Quarter.'

Belle nodded, but she felt let down that he wasn't prepared to pay anything to free her. 'Of course. I wouldn't want to go there anyway,' she said.

'Well, shall we?' he said, taking her hand and leading her back to the bedroom. He lifted all the bed linen off the bed and dumped it on the floor. 'It will have to be a quick one, I've got a business meeting later.'

Some little time later, Belle heard the wire fly screen on the front door bang shut, and the sound of Faldo's feet going down the steps, and she lay back on the bare mattress and began to cry.

She felt more of a whore now than she ever had at Martha's. He had got her to take off all her clothes and then just did the act without any petting or kissing before hurrying away.

None of this was what she'd expected. She was alone in a part of town she didn't know and which could well be dangerous. She didn't have the luxury of a bathroom or an inside lavatory. Faldo was going to give her less money than she got at Martha's, and if Martha ever found out her top girl was still in town she'd probably send someone round to teach her a lesson about running off.

But what made Belle feel most upset was that she'd been stupid enough to think she could have everything her way, because Faldo loved her. That was perhaps an unreasonable expectation; after all, she didn't love him and had only turned to him in desperation. But it still hurt to think that all he wanted was a pretty girl always available for sex and somewhere to stay whenever he was in New Orleans.

He was smart too. By letting her put things on an account that made him appear very generous, but the truth was that he didn't want to give her cash to buy food and household items because he thought she might run off with it.

She had just over a hundred dollars in savings. While that seemed a lot, she had no idea if it would even get her to New York, let alone back to England.

Belle cried for so long she didn't notice it was growing dark outside. She had to pull herself together to put on her chemise, close the shutters and light the gas. She could smell food cooking close by, but it was very much quieter out on the street than it had been back in the District. Even if she didn't like anything else about this gloomy little house, that was one good point.

'You were far too hasty,' she said aloud as she went into the kitchen to put the kettle on. 'You should've got to know him better, or checked out other men before deciding on him. But you've done it now, there's no way back, so you've got to make the best of it.'

Within days of leaving Martha's, Belle discovered that boredom and loneliness were her biggest enemies. She dealt with the first by cleaning, cooking, walking, reading and sewing, but she couldn't find anything to stop the loneliness.

Almost daily she wished she were back with the other girls in Martha's kitchen over long, leisurely breakfasts, sitting around in their nightdresses with tangled hair, everyone talking at once about the night before and shrieking with laughter as one of them described a particularly odd experience. Then there were those lazy afternoons wandering the French Quarter or lying around in the back yard chatting and sipping cold drinks. She'd even give anything to hear the front-door bell tinkling, although that meant a gentleman was coming in and suddenly they all had to turn on seductive smiles and brace themselves for what was to come.

Back in the District it was almost impossible to walk down a street without someone stopping her for a chat. Street musicians always homed in on girls, often playing a tune especially for them – she couldn't count the times she had stopped to listen and laughed as they flirted with her. She could buy an ice cream or a slice of water melon from a stall and the stallholder would tell her a bit of gossip. The shopkeepers were all friendly and greeted her with smiles; there was no uppityness – they didn't consider themselves superior. All over the District there was a sense of everyone being in it together, very much like it had been back in Seven Dials.

But so far not one person in this street had spoken to her, or even smiled. She doubted this was because they knew she was a kept woman – she didn't see anyone talking to anyone else. She could only suppose this was how it was in 'respectable' areas. People kept to themselves for fear of something. Whether that was fear of involvement, or just common snobbishness, she didn't know. But whatever the reason, she didn't like it.

Sometimes she felt so alone that she cried herself to sleep. The silence pressed in on her and made her feel threatened. There had been a couple of thunderstorms at night too, such heavy rain that it drummed on the tin roof, and such loud thunderclaps that she shook with fear. She got into the habit of going out for long walks, each time going further and further to delay going home, and making herself really tired so she could sleep when she got back.

Faldo came once a week, but it was always on different days. At first she'd believed that was, as he said, because he didn't have a routine and never knew how long he'd be in one place, but now she suspected it was just so he could check she wasn't keeping company with anyone else.

On his first visit after she moved in, he arrived with a box from a fancy lingerie shop. He'd bought her a beautiful red silk chemise with a matching wrap, plus some elegant red leather slippers trimmed with black swansdown. He was so lovely that night, really affectionate, complimenting her on how nice the house looked and concerned about her being lonely.

She thought then that was how it was always going to be. She planned on making him special meals, arranging the table with flowers and candles, and that sometimes they'd go out to a restaurant or a theatre. She even imagined that perhaps one day he'd suggest taking her away for a holiday.

But the next time he came he seemed cold and distant and she couldn't make out why. It wasn't as if she looked a mess; every evening she washed, did her hair and put on her new lingerie, just in case he turned up. As she was doing all she could to please him, it was very hurtful that he didn't respond with any affection. But that night she forgave him because she thought he must have had an awful day.

Yet that was how it had been ever since. She was never able to relax entirely in the evenings because he could walk in at any moment. If he wasn't there by ten she knew he wasn't coming, so she'd take off the pretty lingerie, put on her night-dress and go to bed. And on the evenings he did come round, he didn't want to chat, ask how her day had been or tell her about his. He just took her to bed and did what he wanted to do, then fell asleep.

By day she could convince herself that even if Faldo wasn't being loving, she was still in a far better situation than she had been at Martha's. She was a mistress, not a whore; she had a comfortable home too, for she'd gone to Alderson's store and picked out bits of furniture, rugs, pictures and orna-ments and charged them to Faldo's account. She had plenty to eat and she could please herself what she did all day. But on the nights when he was with her, she would lie awake long after he'd gone to sleep, remembering that he'd said even less to her than he did the very first time he was with her at Martha's, and she felt terribly used and hurt.

She found herself thinking of Mog, her mother and Jimmy, and that was like sliding down into a dark tunnel which she knew led to nothing but despair. Again and again she thought of writing to them and asking for help to get home, but she couldn't bear to tell them what had happened to her.

One afternoon four weeks after she moved into North Car-rollton Avenue, a small hat shop a couple of blocks away caught her eye. She went out walking every day, taking a different route each time in order to learn more about the city and its different neighbourhoods. But for some reason she hadn't come this way before, even though it wasn't far from where she lived.

Belle waited for a heavily laden brewer's cart to go by, then crossed over to the hat shop. The window display was lovely, and she stood looking at it for some time. It had an autumnal theme with a branch of a tree, and gold, russet and red paper leaves lying beneath it. Several hats were perched on the tree: a jaunty red one trimmed with long golden and brown feathers, a moss-green one with a wide brim and a veil, a brown velvet bonnet and a beautiful tawny gold cloche-style one decorated with amber beads.

Since she left England she hadn't once picked up a pencil to draw hats the way she used to back home. In fact, apart from telling Etienne it had always been her dream to have a hat shop, she hadn't even thought about it once.

But now, as she peered into the shop through the display, it all came back to her. At the back of the shop was a bench, and a very small woman with white hair was standing at it working on a black hat on a stand. She seemed to be fixing a veil to it.

There were dozens of hats displayed all around the small shop, and Belle felt she just had to go in to take a better look. As she opened the shop door a bell rang, sounding exactly the same as the one in the sweet shop near her home in Seven Dials.

'What can I help you with, madam?' the old lady asked, stopping what she was doing.

She had to be at least sixty, her face was heavily lined and her back was stooped. Yet despite her drab black dress with only a cream lace collar and cuffs to lift it, she had bright eyes and a warm smile.

'I just wanted to have a better look,' Belle said. 'I love hats and your window display is so pretty.'

'Well, thank you, honey,' the old lady replied. 'And you're English too. I always think Englishwomen have such good taste.'

Belle chatted to her about the hats for some little while, then, because the old lady seemed pleased to have some company, she admitted how she'd dreamed of becoming a milliner and having a hat shop.

'Fancy that,' the old lady exclaimed. 'I never met anyone before who wanted to learn to make them. Most folk think I go somewhere and buy 'em ready-made. They don't know it's a real art doing the moulding and then the sewing and sticking.'

Belle was prepared to flatter and praise the old lady just so she could stay in the shop and feel marginally less alone for a while. She admitted she had no money to buy a hat, but tried some of them on and marvelled at how beautifully made they all were.

'It's good to see them modelled on someone as young and pretty as you,' the old lady said. 'Now, I'm Miss Frank, and I was just going to make myself a cup of coffee. Would you like one too?'

'I'm Belle Cooper and I'd love some coffee,' she replied. It was only after she'd blurted out her name that she remembered she was supposed to be Anne Talbot. She couldn't take back her real name, but she resolved not to divulge anything else.

'I always wanted to go to England,' Miss Frank said, as she opened a door at the end of the shop to reveal a small kitchen. 'I don't suppose I'll ever get there now, getting too darn old. But I'd have liked to see King Edward and his palace. Then there's that tower where they used to cut off kings' and queens' heads.'

'King Edward died last year, and King George has been

crowned now,' Belle said. 'I went to see the Tower of London once, it's a scary-looking place. They have men in red and gold uniforms guarding it called Beefeaters. But no one gets beheaded now.'

'I'm very glad of that,' Miss Frank chuckled. 'Beheading wouldn't be good for my business.'

Belle laughed, the first time she'd really done so since leaving Martha's.

'That's better, hearing you laugh,' Miss Frank said. 'I saw your face as you were looking in the window and you looked so sad and forlorn. Are you homesick?'

Belle nodded. She didn't trust herself to speak because the concerned question made her eyes prickle with tears.

'Staying here with relatives?' Miss Frank looked over her glasses at Belle as she spooned some coffee into a pot.

Belle nodded, then, noticing a head-shaped contraption in the kitchen, she asked if it was for shaping hats, just to move the conversation away from herself.

'Sure is. I fill the bottom part with water and boil it up, like a kettle. I put the felt or the canvas over the top and the steam shapes the crown. The big one at the top is called a block – I have many different kinds for all kinds of brims and crowns. I'll show you how it's done after we've had our coffee, that is, if you'd like to see it.'

Belle stayed in the shop for almost an hour, and Miss Frank showed her all kinds of things to do with millinery. She displayed drawers full of ribbons and braids, boxes of artificial flowers, and more still of feathers. It was all fascinating, and Belle admitted how she used to draw hats all the time back in England.

'If you feel like drawing some again, I'd love to see them,' Miss Frank said. 'I've been doing this for so many years I dare say I'm getting a bit stale. Angelica's, the dress shop in Royal Street in the Quarter, buys hats from me, and she did say last time I saw her that she could do with some cheekier designs. To be honest, Belle, I didn't really know what she meant by that.'

Belle smiled. 'I did see a magazine recently with fashions from Paris,' she said. 'The hats the models were wearing were smaller, hardly bigger than a flower. I saw one which was like a small nest, with a tiny fluffy bird peeping out. I think that's what she meant by cheeky.'

Miss Frank shook her head as if she couldn't imagine anyone wearing such a hat. 'Perhaps I'm getting too old? In my younger days it was sensible bonnets, straw hats with a nice ribbon and perhaps a flower trimming. Then in the fall and winter we had felt hats, fur if it was very cold. It was predictable what ladies would buy each season. It's not that way any more.'

Belle went home a bit later, but that evening she could think of nothing but hats. She found some paper and a pencil and began to draw frantically, but somehow none of the sketched hats looked right.

Three days later, having spent almost every spare moment drawing, she went back to see Miss Frank.

'I can't seem to get anything right,' she admitted to the old lady. 'I think it's because first I need to know how to construct a hat.'

Miss Frank just looked at Belle for some little while without speaking. 'I can't afford to pay an assistant, not unless trade picks up,' she said. 'But if you'd like to learn millinery, I'll teach you.'

'You'd do that?' Belle said breathlessly. 'I'd like it more than anything.'

From the first morning when Belle presented herself at Miss Frank's little shop, and was given the task of steaming a felt cloche hat on a block, she felt she had hope again. Millinery was a proper trade; once she'd mastered it she could find respectable employment. But even if that was a long way in the future, all at once she had a reason to get up in the morning, a purpose in each day other than just waiting for Faldo to turn up.

She learned fast. Miss Frank said she had nimble fingers and a flair for it. And the old lady was a good teacher, as keen to pass on her skills as Belle was to acquire them. But there were perils attached to her new role of trainee. Miss Frank was inquisitive, and so were the regular customers who'd been coming to the shop for years. They wanted to know why Belle had come to America, how and when, where she lived and what she lived on. Even when they didn't actually ask questions, their eyes enquired, and Belle guessed that when she wasn't in the shop, they would be quizzing Miss Frank.

Lying didn't come easily to Belle. She'd told Miss Frank she was sent to live with her guardian here when her widowed mother died. But as his wife and their children didn't want her living with them, her guardian had found alternative accommodation for her. It didn't sound plausible, not even to her, that any guardian would expect a girl as young as her to live alone in a strange city. Yet Miss Frank appeared to believe it; she tutted and said she thought it was disgraceful, but her sympathy only made Belle feel worse. She so much wished she could tell the truth, unburden herself with the whole sorry story. But however kindly Miss Frank was, she wasn't worldly, she was a church-going spinster who probably had never been kissed, let alone had a sexual experience. She wouldn't want a whore in her pretty little shop; she might even believe Belle had crept round her with the plan to rob her. She would find the idea of her being the mistress to a married man utterly despicable. She might even report Belle to the police, and that way it could get back to Martha where she was.

So Belle tried to keep her lip buttoned, saying as little as possible to both Miss Frank and her customers, while at the same time working really hard to master the new skills she was being taught, and practising designing hats at night.

She didn't tell Faldo about her new interest as she knew he wouldn't like it. But elated by new-found happiness in Miss Frank's shop, she tried much harder to please him.

'Tell me where you've been this week,' she would say after she'd made him a mint julep, a drink with bourbon that he'd said was his favourite. On a couple of occasions he did tell her that he'd been to St Louis, or even further away, but most of the time he didn't even bother to reply, just drank the mint julep and said it was time for bed.

One night she asked him why he didn't want to talk to her any more.

'What is there to say?' he shrugged. 'I don't come here to be quizzed, I'm tired at the end of the day.'

On each successive visit Belle felt a little more deflated and used by him, but she counteracted this by reminding herself she had a roof over her head, and blamed herself for jumping into the arrangement without getting to know him better.

By day, though, she was cheered considerably because her designs began to improve dramatically once she understood how hats were constructed. She would go rushing into the shop with them in the mornings and Miss Frank would laugh at her enthusiasm and say she would look at them carefully later.

Mostly she told Belle they weren't practical, sometimes because they would be too heavy or unbalanced, other times because they involved too much work, but finally she examined one design which looked like a large, flat rose and she said jubilantly that Belle had come up with a good design.

'It's perfect for women who don't want a hat which will flatten or spoil their hairstyle,' she said. 'I can make the base it sits on quite small; it could be secured with a hat pin. I think they'll love this at Angelica's. So we'll make one up and I'll take it in to show them.'

They made the first rose hat in pink. The stiffened, shaped base was covered in deep pink velvet, and the rose itself was made of wired silk, the underside of each petal just a shade darker. They finished it mid-afternoon, and when Belle put it on, Miss Frank clapped her hands in delight.

'Honey, it's a triumph,' she said. 'I'm going to take it along to Angelica's right away. You go on home and I'll shut up the shop.'

It was nearly four in the afternoon when Belle left the shop, and on the way home it began to rain, so she ran the rest of the way.

By the time she'd unlocked the door and gone in, the rain was coming down so heavily that the street was awash and it had become so dark she had to light the gas immediately.

She'd felt so happy back at the shop because she'd pleased Miss Frank, but now, plunged back to reality, all alone for yet another long evening with the rain drumming on the roof, she suddenly felt she couldn't stand much more of it.

It didn't feel right to be kept by a man who was so cold towards her. She should be able to tell him about learning to make hats, to show him her designs and admit her dream of having her own hat shop. She'd once told him she'd caught the tram to look at the big houses in the Garden District and his face had tightened with disapproval. Since then she only told him things like how she'd baked a cake, or started some embroidery or knitting, but it was all wrong that she felt unable to tell him anything else.

'I swopped one slave master for another,' she murmured to herself, and tears started up in her eyes. 'All he wants is a place to stay when he's in town and a girl in the bed so he doesn't need to pay for one in a brothel.'

Yet that didn't make any sense to her, for it cost more to keep her than for a hotel for the night and a whore. It was so puzzling: she knew about men, and she knew few of them would set anyone up in a house and pay all the bills unless they were smitten with the woman.

Why didn't he ever tell her when he was coming next? Why didn't he want to share a meal with her, take her for a walk or to the theatre? Why, when he'd been so warm and chatty back at Martha's, had he changed so dramatically?

As a kept woman Belle didn't feel she could challenge him about anything, and she believed she must always show enthusiasm for his lovemaking too. She had even thought that would encourage him to try harder to please her. But that hadn't worked; he made no attempt to please her, and that, along with his callous attitude that as his kept woman she should do whatever he said, made it increasingly difficult for her to pretend she enjoyed sex with him. She wondered how much longer she could keep up the pretence.

She walked into the parlour, slumped down on one of the chairs and gave way to tears. The empty fireplace was a reproach – back home at this time of year there would be a blaze in every fireplace in the house. She imagined Mog in a clean white apron preparing the evening meal, chatting as she stirred pots on the stove and laid the table. Annie would be up in her parlour going over the household accounts; the girls would be doing their hair for the evening ahead.

Belle wished she was back there, reading bits out of the paper to Mog, or just telling her gossip she'd picked up while out running errands. She missed home so much. Life had been so simple back before Millie was killed; maybe it was a bit dull, but she had felt safe, aware what was expected of her, and knowing too how Mog and Annie felt about her.

She thought back to the day she'd met Jimmy and how good it had been to make a real friend. He'd made London seem such a wonderful place, and she'd had such high hopes of exploring more of it with him.

Would she be walking out with him now if she hadn't been taken away? What would it have been like if he'd been the first to give her an adult kiss?

She sighed deeply, not just because she was sure Jimmy must have forgotten all about her by now, but because she doubted she could ever fit back into that life she'd left behind in England.

What was she to do? She couldn't afford to leave Faldo, not when she hadn't got a paying job or anywhere else to live. And her savings weren't enough to get her home.

Tears ran down her cheeks unchecked. She was trapped.

Chapter Twenty-three

'*Bonsoir*, Cosette,' Noah said to the small, mousy-haired girl. He had thought her the plainest girl in Madame Sondheim's last time, and that hadn't changed; she was like a little brown moth trapped in the parlour with five flamboyant and vivacious butterflies. '*Repellez moi?*'

He wasn't sure if that was the right word for 'remember', but she smiled as if she knew what he meant. 'Yes, I remember you, Englishman,' she replied in English. 'No friend thees time?'

Noah said he'd come alone to see Cosette, and accepted a glass of red wine. Two of the other girls were making eyes at him from across the room, but he turned to face Cosette and smiled at her in what he'd been told was his most beguiling way.

She took his hand as they went up the stairs later, and she seemed more animated and light-hearted than the time before. She was clearly flattered that he'd come back and picked her out, and he hoped that would make her amenable for telling him what he wanted to know.

'Your wife make you angry?' she said as he handed over the money. He remembered then that his excuse for not having sex with her last time was because he was happily married. He felt this time he must be more straightforward, so when she'd passed the money to the maid outside the door, he held out twenty-five francs to her.

'I asked you last time about young girls brought here. This time you must tell me more, the girl I ask about, her mother has broken heart and very sick.' Noah said putting his hands

318

on his heart to make it clearer. 'You said they take girls to *couvent*, but I checked every convent in Paris. No girls there. Please, please, Cosette. Tell me what you know. I will not betray you.'

She was frightened, looking towards the door as if imagining someone was behind it listening.

'I will never say you told me,' he assured her, taking her into his arms and cuddling her. 'This is a good thing for you to do. Belle's mother may die if she doesn't know where her daughter is. You know these are bad people!'

'I have no work but thees,' she said, tears filling her eyes. 'My mother is sick too, I can send money home to her now, but if I lose this work, she may die.'

Noah realized that he had to offer her more money. He opened his wallet and brought out fifty francs more. 'Take this for her. But tell me, Cosette, what I need to know! I promise I will not tell anyone you helped me.'

She was looking at the money, not him, and Noah thought she might be thinking it was enough for her to leave Paris and go back to her village for good.

'Change your life,' he urged her. 'Leave this work for good. God will smile on you if Belle can be saved.'

Her conflicting emotions showed in her face. She wanted the money, perhaps even wanted to do the right thing for other young girls, but she was very afraid.

'There is nothing to fear. No one will know you gave me any information. Be brave and bold, Cosette, for little Belle and others like her.'

She sighed deeply, then looked into his eyes. 'La Celle St-Cloud,' she said. 'There is a big house at far end of village, it has a big stone bird by gate. Ask for Lisette, she is a good woman, she is a nurse. She will be cautious in telling you anything too for she has a little boy. You promise you will not say my name?'

'I promise, Cosette,' he said, and pressed the money into her hand and kissed her lips. 'Get out of this work now,' he urged her. 'Go home and nurse your mother, marry a farmer and have many children. Find happiness!'

She put her hands on his shoulders and stood on tiptoe to kiss him on both cheeks.

'I will pray you find Belle, and that she too can learn to be happy again. For most of us there is no way back.' Her eyes filled with tears and spilled over. Noah was reminded of Millie and a lump came up in his throat. Millie had said something similar once; he hadn't understood what she meant at the time, but he did now.

Early the next morning Noah set off to the south-west of Paris, to La Celle St-Cloud. From what he could gather it was around fourteen miles out of the city, not far from Versailles, and fortunately he could reach it by train. He had looked up the area in a guidebook, just to get a bit of background information, but apart from farming its only other claim to fame appeared to be the Château de Beauregard, a huge old mansion.

There was a brisk wind and a decidedly autumnal nip in the air, and Noah wished he'd thought to bring an overcoat with him. As he waited for the train, being jostled and shoved on the crowded platform, he shivered and thought that it was twenty months now since Belle had disappeared. 'If you don't learn anything new today, you must give up on her,' he said to himself. 'You cannot keep up this crusade.'

Noah walked all around La Celle St-Cloud, and was charmed by its attractive central square where old men sat smoking pipes and women bustled about buying their bread, meat and vegetables. After the frantic pace of Paris it was good to be somewhere quiet and calm.

He finally discovered the house Cosette meant after following two different roads to the edge of the village and finding only small houses. But on the third road he saw a big house ahead of him, and sensed it was the one he was looking for, just by the way it stood alone, the last house in the village.

There was a stone eagle on one gate post, and just a piece of broken stone on the other to show there had once been a matching pair. The house was at least a hundred yards from its nearest neighbour and surrounded by open countryside. A man was ploughing in the distance, a few birds were circling above him, and although it was a lovely view, it struck Noah that to anyone held in the house it might look frighteningly remote.

He looked up at the house appraisingly. It was big. There were four floors with eight windows just on the front, and a rather grand, albeit crumbling, portico around the front door. But then, the whole house and what he could see of the garden from the gate was somewhat neglected.

As he stood there, considering what reason he could offer for knocking at the front door, a young woman suddenly appeared round the side of the house. She was slender, with dark hair, and he guessed she was in her early thirties. She was wearing a grey shawl over her head and a dark blue dress, and held a shopping basket on her arm.

He took a deep breath, and as she reached the gate, he swept off his hat, flashed what he hoped was his most beguiling smile, and asked if she was Lisette.

She lifted her head and smiled, and to his surprise he saw she was a very pretty woman, with soft, dark eyes, creamy skin and a wide, full mouth. 'I am, sir,' she replied in English. 'And why is an Englishman asking for me?'

Noah thought she had the sexiest of French accents; she was making him grin like a schoolboy too. 'I want to talk to you,' he said.

She tossed her head almost dismissively. 'I have shopping to do,' she said.

'Then I'll come with you and carry your basket,' he said. 'Maybe I can persuade you to have some coffee with me too?'

She looked at him appraisingly for a second, then laughed lightly. 'If Monsieur Deverall has sent you, then you will be wasting your time. The answer is no.'

She began to walk towards the village and he fell in beside her. 'I haven't been sent by anyone,' he said. 'I've come to ask you about a young girl called Belle.'

The way she stopped dead in her tracks and her face blanched was all Noah needed. He put his hand on her elbow. 'Keep walking,' he said softly. 'Don't be alarmed, you have nothing to fear from me. I just want to ask you a few questions.'

She said something in French, a hurried volley.

'I only know a few French words,' he said. 'You must speak English to me.'

'I cannot talk to you.' She sounded scared now. 'I don't know anything.'

'You do, Lisette,' he insisted. 'I know you have a little boy and you are frightened for him, but believe me, you have nothing to fear from me. I am a friend of Belle's mother – I promised her I would try to find out where Belle is, because she is grieving for her, and not knowing if she is alive or dead, or where she's being held is slowly killing her. But anything you tell me is between ourselves. I will not tell anyone else, call the police or anyone. You are absolutely safe with me.'

'Who sent you to me?' she asked, her eyes as wide as saucers and full of fear.

'Someone good and kind who believes you are too,' he said. 'But that is all I can say. I promised her too that she would be safe.'

'But it isn't safe,' she pleaded with him. 'You don't know how bad these people are!'

Noah saw there were other people around them now as they came into the village. 'Lisette, calm down, do not draw attention to us. Now, we're going to go over to the café. If anyone asks about me later today you just say I asked you the way to the station and I bought you coffee. That is entirely believable as you are such a pretty woman.'

She gave a nervy half-smile, but Noah felt he was succeeding in making her less afraid. He could hardly believe his luck that he'd found her so easily, but he knew that luck was likely to run out if he pushed her too fast or too far. So he stopped talking about Belle and spoke about the sights he'd seen in Paris while he led her to the café.

Once they were seated outside and coffee and pastries ordered, he began again. 'Lisette, I know Belle was brought to the place you work,' he said. 'And it's my guess you are the nurse who cared for her.'

She hesitated, clearly weighing up whether to admit this or not. Then she nodded. 'She was very sick, I fear for her at first.'

'She'd been raped?' Noah asked gingerly.

He sensed her distress and held his breath, fearing she would clam up. But she took a deep breath and looked him right in the eyes. 'Yes, she had been raped. Again and again,' she admitted, and he saw her reason for speaking out was because she felt so horrified. 'It was terrible they would do that to such a young girl. The body will heal, but not always the mind,' she added.

She paused then, looking at Noah as if still weighing up whether or not he could be trusted. 'But Belle was a fighter, she have strong, how you say? Spirit?' she said eventually. 'She asked me to help her escape, but I couldn't. I or my boy would be killed if I did. You understand that?'

Noah put his hand over hers comfortingly. 'I know, I'm sure you would have helped her escape if you could. But

323

I'm not here to blame. I just want to find her and take her home to those who love her. When she is there she can choose to speak out about the Englishmen who snatched her off the streets and took her to France. They will be punished then.'

'She is not in France,' Lisette interrupted him. 'She is in America. That is all I know.'

'America!' Noah exclaimed, his heart sinking down to his boots. 'Are you sure?'

Lisette nodded sadly. 'I did not see her go. I come in morning and she has been taken away. I weesh she were in France or Belgium and I could tell you where for I grow fond of Belle. But they not tell me where in America she go.'

'She was sold to a brothel?' Noah spoke almost in a whisper.

'Pretty young girls are like horses, or cows to these bad people,' she spat out contemptuously. 'Belle was prime steak. Young, Engleesh, so pretty. It was the same for me when I was young girl, they took me to English brothel, that is why I speak the English. But I am still trapped by them – too old for brothel, but they make me nurse the girls they hurt.'

'They won't let you leave?' he asked.

'Never,' she said ruefully. 'I am too valuable to them as nurse, and they know things about me which make sure I do as they say. Maybe if I had money I could take my Jean-Pierre and flee France, but that takes a great deal of money.'

'I could get you away,' Noah said impulsively.

She smiled sadly. 'No, that is not a good thing for you to do.'

'I think it is, and I will give you my address,' Noah said. 'If you want help anytime, just ask, and I promise I will come for you or meet you at Dover. You believe me?'

'Yes, I think you are a kind man,' she said.

'Is there anything or anyone you can tell me about who might be able to say where Belle was taken to?' Noah felt he had to try to push her just a little further.

'I am just one link in the chain,' Lisette said sadly. 'They don't trust me even with the next link. I don't know anything more.'

Noah believed her. She might know the names of a few people above her, but he doubted she'd ever been given real names because an organization like this wouldn't survive if that was known.

He felt in his inside pocket and brought out his list of the other girls who had disappeared. He showed it to her. 'Just tell me if you've seen any of those names anywhere before,' he said.

She looked at it carefully. 'There was an English Amy, just for one night,' she said with a frown. 'I think too there was Flora, and May.'

Those three girls were the youngest out of the twenty-odd names he had, and each of them had been reported to be exceptionally pretty. 'Were they sent to America too?'

'No, I never knew any girl but Belle be sent there. The others went to Belgium.'

She could only say that it was Brussels, no address.

'When I first spoke to you, you thought I came from Monsieur Deverall?' Noah asked. 'Who is he?'

The fear came back into her eyes. 'I cannot tell you anything about him,' she said hurriedly. 'He is the man at the top. I never met him, but I know him to be cruel and ruthless. They say many gendarmes have tried to put him in prison but he is too clever, they never find proof of what he does. But he would not take your Belle to America himself, she will never have seen him. They say he binds his men to him with black-mail. He has many other businesses too. Always the kind where he use force.'

Noah assumed by this that Deverall was a man much like Kent, with fingers in many areas of vice, extortion and gambling. 'But you thought I had come from him, so that means he does send someone to see you sometimes?'

She sighed. 'You are as smart as his man,' she said with

just a hint of admiration. 'He too is charming like you, the kind of man a woman wishes to trust. Deverall sends him sometimes to ask me to go with girls, but I always refuse.'

'Why?'

'It is bad to see how they have been hurt, but I make them well. I could not bear to take them to someone who will hurt them again.'

'I see,' Noah said. 'And this man who works for Deverall accepts that?'

'Yes, he knows how I feel, and there is always someone else who can take the girls for he pays well.'

'Would this man know where Belle was taken?'

'No, I don't think so, he was not involved that time. All I know is what I overheard, that a coach was coming to take her to Brest. I think the coach took Belle to meet someone who would take her on the ship.'

'Do you know who this person was who took her to America?' Noah asked tentatively.

She closed her eyes in exasperation. 'Have you heard nothing I've said?' she exploded. 'To tell you that is to risk my son being killed. I have helped you as much as I can. Do not ask more of me.'

'But surely just his name wouldn't hurt?' Noah wheedled, putting his hand over hers.

She slapped his hand away and got to her feet. 'I will go now before I feel I must report you to Deverall because you are asking too many questions,' she said angrily. 'I know you mean well but you are putting both of us in danger. Go back to England, leave this. Belle is a strong girl. I believe she will find a way back to those she loves.'

Noah quickly wrote down his address and went after her. 'Take this,' he said. 'I will help you get out of France if you want me to. I am so very grateful to you for talking to me, you are a brave and good woman.'

She put one hand on his arm, her lovely eyes gazing into his. 'You are a kind, good man too, if things were different I would wish to be your friend.'

Noah's heart jolted. She smiled, perhaps sensing how surprised he was. 'You are a very handsome man. And you offer me and my child safety, that is very tempting. But I should not wish you to take such risks for me.'

'I'm willing to do whatever it takes,' he said eagerly.

She put one finger against his lips to silence him. 'I will do one little thing more for you,' she said. 'The man in Brest, I know him only by reputation, but I know he is like me, caught up in something he cannot escape. He does not come here, but I may be able to find a way of contacting him. Do not expect this, I may not be able to do this. But if I can and I find out something about Belle I will write and let you know. Now go, ask no more questions and leave Paris quickly. Deverall has his spies everywhere.'

Chapter Twenty-four

'America!' Mog spoke the word as if she was confirming some-one's sudden death. Noah put his arm around her shoulder to comfort her and tried desperately to think of something to add which would make the news less devastating.

He had walked into the smoky fog of the Ram's Head saloon bar just at closing time. Garth was chasing out the last of the drinkers and Jimmy was collecting up the glasses. Garth greeted him warmly, saying Mog was out the back in the kitchen getting some bread and cheese for a late supper, and asked if he'd like a glass of whisky to warm him up as it was a chilly night.

As soon as the last drinker left and the door was locked, they all went through to the kitchen. Mog was delighted to see Noah and she took his coat and urged him to sit closest to the stove.

Noah thought Mog looked radiant; before he'd gone to France she'd told him Garth had proposed to her and it ap-peared to have made a new woman of her. She was even wearing a different dress, light grey with shadowy white stripes. While it wasn't a huge change, the colour suited her better, and she no longer looked like a down-trodden house-maid.

She badgered them all to sit down at the table and to eat up as she poured them tea. Then she asked Noah to tell them about his trip.

All the way home from France, he had told himself that it was a breakthrough to find out where Belle had been, and where she was now. But as he explained all he had discovered and saw the horror on Mog's face, he almost wished he'd never met Lisette and had no new information about Belle.

'At least America is a civilized country,' Garth said, doing his best to cheer Mog. 'She could run away from the people who took her there and ask for help from their police.'

'You're quite right,' Noah said, glad that Garth was offering a positive view. 'Lisette said that Belle was a strong-willed girl, you can bet she'll think of something to do. Maybe she's even been writing to you and the letters haven't been delivered because Annie's Place was burned down.'

Mog's face brightened just a little. 'I hadn't thought of that! I'll wait for the postman tomorrow and ask him what they do with letters they can't deliver,' she said. 'But where in America is she? It's a big country.'

'It's bound to be New York,' Noah said. 'That's where everything happens.'

'I could go there and find her,' Jimmy said.

Noah noted that the lad had that crusader look in his eyes again. 'You couldn't,' he said gently. 'New York is huge, and you wouldn't have the least idea where to start looking. The best thing we can hope for is that Lisette gets some further news from the man who took Belle there.'

Everyone fell silent. There was not a sound other than chewing and coals moving in the stove.

It was Mog who broke the silence. 'Are we going to tell Mrs Stewart that you think her Amy is in Brussels?' she asked Noah.

'I suppose I must,' Noah sighed. 'But I don't relish that chore – she'll be inconsolable. As will the other mothers.'

When Noah woke next morning at his lodgings, the first thing he thought of was Mog's stricken face. He lay there for a moment or two, wondering if there was anything further he could do for Belle and all the other missing girls.

He knew his editor would be delighted to publish a follow-up article based on what Noah had been told in Paris, but that would only please readers who revelled in white slavery stories. It wouldn't bring forth any information on where any of the girls were being held, or get them released. In fact, if anyone involved with the abductions was to read the article, Cosette and Lisette would immediately be implicated as informers. This might also happen if Noah went back to the police, and it wasn't as if he had anything concrete to give them to start an investigation.

He couldn't bring himself to risk Lisette or her son being hurt. He kept seeing her face, hearing her voice, and it was all very reminiscent of how he'd felt about Millie. He wished he'd asked for an address he could write to her at, that way he could at least say how much he'd liked her, and remind her that he'd meant what he said about getting her out of France. But it wouldn't do to write to the nursing home – a letter from England was bound to be intercepted. He supposed he had no choice but to wait for Lisette to contact him.

He wondered why it was that he seemed destined to fall for women with problems. Day after day he met girls and women who did ordinary jobs like nursing, needlework, working in a shop or an office. Girls liked him, he wasn't ugly, he had good manners. So why was it he didn't get that magical spark with one of them?

Belle was considering her fate too, for Miss Frank had been given an order by the two sisters who owned Angelique's hat shop in the Quarter for a dozen hats of Belle's rose design.

'I shall have to give you a paid position now,' Miss Frank said with a smile as wide as the Mississippi. 'Otherwise I couldn't possibly use your lovely design or ask you to help me make them up. I boasted to the sisters that I had a new designer and they're wild to see more of your work.'

Belle wanted to be thrilled and excited by this, but instead she felt a pang of sheer terror that Martha might go into Angelique's to look at their hats, and the sisters might tell her that their regular milliner had just found a new English designer.

'Did you tell them my name or say that I was English?' Belle asked.

'I wouldn't have told them you were English,' Miss Frank responded. 'They like to pride themselves on their stock being chic and French. But I was so happy they liked the hat I was quite talkative, so I might have called you Belle. But why do you ask?'

'I would just rather my name or that I'm English was kept out of it,' Belle said nervously, aware that might make Miss Frank distrust her.

'You are an extraordinarily secretive girl,' the older woman remarked, but she flapped her hands as if that didn't concern her, and began talking about which colours they should make the order up in.

A little later Miss Frank suggested she paid Belle a dollar a day, and that she would give her twenty-five cents each time she sold one of the hats she designed. 'I know it isn't very much,' she said apologetically. 'But it's the best I can do for now.'

As the weather turned cooler in October Belle could have been really happy but for anxiety about her relationship with Faldo. She loved working with Miss Frank, and she felt proud of herself for mastering the art of millinery, and that she appeared to be developing a real talent for designing hats. It was also good to be able to tuck away her earnings knowing that each dollar she got meant she was a little nearer to being able to leave New Orleans.

But however hard she tried to please Faldo, it wasn't

making him any nicer to her. She was the perfect mistress; she flattered him, asked him about his work, tried to make him relax and made sure she was always looking her best in the evenings in case he turned up. But he still wouldn't tell her when he was coming next, and now he was coming so late that he didn't even bother with a few moments of chit-chat, just wanted to go straight to bed.

He'd usually been drinking too, and if that meant he couldn't get hard, he blamed her. Time and again she'd had to bite her tongue for fear of telling him just what she thought of him. In the morning he rarely stayed long enough for even a cup of coffee.

One night she had tried to talk to him about why he was so different to her now.

'You used to be so pleased to see me, you were kind and loving,' she said, beginning to cry. 'Don't you remember what it was like those two nights you stayed all night? If you don't feel like that any more then maybe I should leave this house and try and find some work to keep myself.'

'The only place you could find work is in one of the cribs down in Robertson Street,' he said with a sneer.

'How can you say something so insulting to me?' she sobbed. 'I came here because I thought you cared about me. What have I done that is so bad you'd liken me to one of those disease-ridden hags?'

She thought he was going to strike her, for he took a couple of menacing steps towards her. But he stopped himself just in time and turned away. 'I'm going to bed,' he said. 'I'm tired, and just remember that if it wasn't for me you'd be servicing at least ten men a night.'

He left the next morning at dawn – she woke and saw him creeping out of the room, his boots in his hands. She thought he was ashamed of himself and so she pretended she was still asleep.

She fully expected that once he'd thought over what she'd said he would revert back to the way he'd been at Martha's. But it wasn't to be. Instead of improving, he'd grown steadily worse, becoming more taciturn and sharp each time he called. Belle thought he must be feeling guilty that he was committing adultery, that he wanted to end it, but didn't know how to.

She wished she had enough money just to go, and be done with it.

One Wednesday night in early November, Belle was startled to hear Faldo opening the front door with his key. She was sitting at the kitchen table sketching a hat, still in the plain navy blue dress she wore daily to the hat shop. The dishes from her supper were unwashed in the sink, and there was washing drying in front of the stove. She hadn't bothered to tidy herself or the house as he had been with her on Monday and she hadn't expected him to return again that week.

'Faldo!' she exclaimed in surprise as he strode through the living-room and bedroom into the kitchen. 'I wasn't expecting another visit this week! But how nice!'

He stood in the doorway, looking around the kitchen with a contemptuous expression. 'So this is how you carry on when I'm not here,' he said.

Belle hastily shut her sketching pad and got up from the table to go and hug him. 'I'd have cleared up and dressed in something less drab if I'd known you were coming.'

'I can't bear slovenliness,' he said sharply, pushing her away from him.

'Everywhere else but the kitchen is clean and tidy,' she said defensively. 'But what's it to you anyway whether I've done the dishes or not? You never stay in the kitchen. You're just using it as an excuse to be nasty.'

'What d'you mean by that?' he said, catching hold of her forearms.

'You've been horrible to me for weeks now. Each time you

come you are worse. You never take me out anywhere, or even talk to me,' she said, trying to get away from him because his fingertips were digging into her flesh.

'I got you this place, I come at least once a week, what more do you want?'

Belle didn't like the way his voice was rising, or his high colour.

'I told you before, I wanted it the way it was at Martha's,' she said. 'You seemed to really care about me as a person then, we used to talk and laugh together, it wasn't only the sex.'

'You expect five hundred dollars a night, do you?' he flung back at her.

She was so shocked at his words, and the spite in his voice, that for a moment she didn't know how to reply.

'You know I never got that money,' she said eventually. 'You know too how I came to be at Martha's, it was never my choice.'

'So you say, honey, so you say,' he said in a sarcastic Texan drawl. 'So are you writing a letter home, begging them to rescue you?' He snatched her sketchbook up off the table and opened it.

He looked at the first picture for a few seconds, then flicked through other pages.

'What is this?' he asked.

Faldo's features were very sharp, with a pointed nose and chin, and angular cheekbones too. But suspicion made them seem sharper still.

'I like to draw hats,' she said.

'Why?'

Belle shrugged. 'I told you once before, when I was back in London I used to dream of having a hat shop.'

She was scared now, afraid he'd somehow found out that she was never in during the day. Maybe he even thought she was seeing another man. She needed to calm him down. 'Would you like a drink, Faldo, or something to eat?' she asked, then went over to him, took away the sketchbook and put her arms around him. 'You seem very tense.'

'You are enough to make any man tense,' he said, pushing her away from him. 'What is it you want?'

Belle didn't understand what he meant, and his fierceness was frightening. 'I've got everything I want right here,' she lied. 'A nice place to live, you taking care of me. I just wish you came to see me more often and talked to me. Why do you say I make you tense?'

'Damn it!' he exploded. 'I know it's not me you want. You just went along with it to get out of Martha's. But like a fool I let myself believe you cared for me.'

Regardless of him being right about her motives, Belle had wanted a loving relationship with him, and it was he who had failed on that count. At risk of making him still angrier with her, she intended to stick up for herself.

'I did care for you when you brought me here, but you've managed to make me feel more of a whore than I ever felt at Martha's,' she spat at him. 'How can you expect me to love you when you won't come early enough to share a meal with me? When you don't even ask what I do all day, and then you just fuck me like I was a dollar whore and clear off in the morning without even saying when you'll be back? Why did you come tonight? To try and catch me with someone else?'

He moved so quickly she didn't even see his fist until it connected with her jaw. She reeled back from the impact and fell against the table, jarring her back.

'How could you do that?' she asked angrily, holding her jaw with one hand. 'I took you for a gentleman. You disappoint me.'

It hurt like mad and she thought that by morning she'd have a huge bruise.

'I didn't mean to hurt you,' he said, grabbing hold of her

shoulders and shaking her. 'You just make me mad because I know you'll never be mine, not in the way I want you to be.'

'What way do you want me?' she shouted at him, angry tears running down her cheeks. 'I'm always here for you, I do whatever you ask. What else is there?'

'I want your heart,' he shouted back, his face flushed and contorted.

Belle was too angry and hurt to respond with any assurances that he had it. 'You might have got it if you'd treated me like your sweetheart instead of a whore,' she hissed at him. 'We had something back at Martha's, it was sweet and good. But the moment you brought me here it was gone. I've been so lonely, sad and frightened, and you must have known that unless you're a complete fool. But have you ever shown any concern? Have you ever taken me anywhere to make me think you might want me for anything more than a fuck? No, you haven't.'

She flounced away from him towards the bedroom and began peeling off her clothes.

'What are you doing?' he asked as he saw petticoats dropping in the doorway.

Belle came back into the kitchen without a stitch of clothing on. 'What does it look like?' she said curtly. 'I'm a whore, you're paying for me, so let's get it over with, shall we?'

In that moment Faldo realized he'd handled her all wrong. When Belle was dressed she looked sophisticated and poised. From that, coupled with her intelligence and the ease with which she could communicate with others, anyone would assume she was in her mid-twenties. She wasn't just pretty, but devastatingly beautiful, with those black curls, eyebrows like tiny angels' wings over deep blue eyes, creamy skin and such a wide, sensual mouth. He had called at Martha's just after she had left there, and Martha had had a great deal to say about the girl, namely that she was a treacherous, conniving bitch, who would take any man for everything he had.

Faldo hadn't wanted to believe her; he tried to tell himself that Martha was just being spiteful because she'd lost her top girl, and a large chunk of income. Yet the poison she'd dripped in his ears, plus the knowledge that he was no great prize, and odd-looking too, all combined to convince him he'd made a fool of himself and Belle was just toying with him until someone richer and more influential came along. It had spoiled everything, and the only way he felt he could keep face was by treating her harshly and never displaying any affection.

There was so much about Belle which bore out Martha's opinion of her. She was such a practised courtesan, always wearing the red and black lingerie he'd given her when he called. She let him take her any way he chose without protest, and often caressed, pleasured and touched him in ways that no decent woman would do. Stimulating and sensual as this was, it hurt because it was further evidence of the hundreds of other men she must have done it to.

Martha had claimed that Belle was lying when she said she was abducted and forced into prostitution. She maintained that Belle was a cold-blooded predator who had been groomed to be a whore by her own mother who owned a brothel. She'd come to New Orleans because prostitution was legal here, knowing that she could make big money.

But now she was naked in front of him, her eyes swimming with tears, he could see for himself that she was none of the things Martha had insisted she was and that he had chosen to believe. She was just a vulnerable young girl, slender and perfect, and though she had pert, well-rounded breasts, they only emphasized her youth. She might be striking the pose of a seductress but he could see her hurt, and the decent, kindly man within him was reminded that it was a series of men not that different to him who had stripped her of her innocence.

For several weeks now he'd been noticing she had a kind of glow about her. He'd worked himself up today to believe that was because she had another man, and he'd come here tonight to catch her with him.

It was when he saw her sketches that he knew he'd got it all wrong. It wasn't another man who would take her from him, but her own intelligence and ambition.

'Come on then,' she said, 'what are you waiting for?'

He went towards her, intending just to take her in his arms and apologize for hitting her, but as his arms went around her slim, naked body he was instantly aroused and all he could think of was possessing her. He flung her on to the bed, unbuttoned his pants with one hand and then forced himself into her. He was aware she was very dry, and he knew he was hurting her by the stiffness of her body, but in that moment he didn't care. She was his woman and he wanted her.

'Faldo, no, no,' she cried out. 'Surely I don't deserve this?'

She fought to get away from him, but that only inflamed him more. He pounded harder and harder at her, digging his fingernails into the soft flesh on her buttocks, and the excitement of such a brutal and frenzied attack made his heart race.

Belle was terrified. Faldo might have been cold and undemonstrative with her for some time, he might have shocked her earlier when he struck her, but she would never have thought it possible that he could become a crazed brute pummelling into her like those terrible men did back in Paris.

First she attempted to fight him off, and when that made him even more ferocious, she tried putting up no resistance. But she couldn't stop herself from crying, not just because he was hurting her physically, but because he wanted to humiliate her. His face was buried in her neck, and as he panted and wheezed his breath was as hot as steam from the kettle.

It went on and on; his shirt was wet with sweat, and his breathing more laboured. But when he began to make a kind of strange growling, yelping noise her first thought was that at last her ordeal was almost over.

But then, while still inside her, he arched his body away from her and clutched at his chest with one hand, and although the light in the bedroom was dim she could see his face had turned a deep mottled red. Instinctively she knew something was badly wrong.

'Faldo!' she shouted, wriggling from under him and at the same time pushing him down on to the bed and rolling him on to his back. 'Mary, Mother of God, what is it?' she asked, for his eyes were rolling back into his head and he was jerking as if having a fit.

She ran to the kitchen and got a glass of water and a wet cloth. But the water just ran out of his mouth when she tried to make him drink, and putting the cold wet cloth on his forehead didn't seem to have any effect.

'Faldo, listen to me,' she pleaded with him, 'try and tell me what's wrong.' But even as she spoke she knew he was unable to answer, that this was something really serious and she'd got to get a doctor for him.

She dressed herself quickly, then turning back to Faldo she tucked his penis away in his pants and buttoned them up. Without even stopping to grab a shawl, she rushed out on to the street. As was usual at ten at night it was deserted, so she ran up to Canal Street where she hoped she might see a policeman or a cab driver who might know where to find a doctor.

Luck was with her. Two police officers were walking down Canal Street together. 'Please help me!' she shouted as she ran towards them. 'A friend has had some kind of turn. I don't know how to find a doctor.'

Less than five minutes later the younger of the two men entered Belle's house with her. The other officer had gone off to call on a doctor.

For a brief moment Belle thought Faldo had recovered, for he'd turned on to his side and in the dim gaslight he looked as if he'd just fallen asleep. But something made her stand back and let the officer go forward to examine him.

He put his fingers on Faldo's neck, then felt for the pulse in his wrist. The officer straightened up and turned slowly round to look at Belle. 'I'm very sorry, miss,' he said. 'But your friend is dead.'

'He can't be!' Belle exclaimed, clamping her hand over her mouth in horror. She couldn't believe this was happening to her, that one minute Faldo was red-hot with anger and passion, the next dead. Was she responsible?

Her cheek was throbbing where he'd hit her, and she remembered that he'd said he wanted her heart, and all at once she was sobbing.

'I'm so sorry, miss,' the officer said. 'Can you just tell me who you both are and what led up to him having this turn you spoke of?'

She looked at the young man bleakly. He had bright blue eyes and he looked very sympathetic, but she knew she mustn't let that influence her into telling him the whole truth.

'His name is Faldo Reiss, and he came round about nine to visit me,' she sobbed. 'We were talking for a while in the kitchen, then he said he felt a bit strange. He looked very flushed and hot. He stood up to go out the back way for some fresh air, but he was staggering, so I led him into the bedroom to lie down. Then he was breathing really hard and holding his chest. I tried to give him a drink of water and sponge his forehead, but when he couldn't speak I ran out to get help.'

'You did the right thing,' the officer said. 'Now, you said he's just a friend. So where does he live?'

'In Houston, Texas,' she said, 'but I don't know the address. He works for the railway, you see. He comes to New Orleans most weeks with his work.'

The officer's eyes narrowed as if considering something. 'Are you English?' he asked.

Belle nodded. She was terrified because she knew it wouldn't be long before she was asked far more probing, difficult to answer questions. Faldo had an important position with the railroad company. He might have been vile to her tonight, but she still cared enough for him to try to prevent a scandal which would hurt his wife and children. There was also Martha to worry about. If she got wind that Faldo died, and where, she might put two and two together.

'You say he was your friend?'

Belle's stomach lurched at the police officer's question because she guessed he had already surmised that Faldo was more than a friend. He was young, no older than twenty-five, at least six foot, nice-looking, with light brown hair cut very short, and the bright blue eyes she'd noticed earlier. But however nice he looked, police were by the very nature of their job worldly types and hard to fool.

'Yes, just a friend,' she said. 'He was very kind when I first arrived here and helped me get this place to live. He usually pops in to see me whenever he's here on business.'

The officer was jotting down what she'd said in a notebook and asked again for her name. She had to say she was Anne Talbot as Faldo had opened the accounts at the two shops with that name and it was possible the landlord had that name too. But before he could ask her anything further, the other officer arrived with the doctor and the three men went into the bedroom.

Belle stayed in the kitchen and put the kettle on to make

some coffee. Her heart was thumping so hard she was sure the three men would be able to hear it.

The doctor, a short, stout man with a bald head and glasses, came out of the bedroom after only a few minutes. 'Well, my dear, the signs are that your friend died of a heart attack. I am very sorry, but I will make a call to the mortuary and get them to come and collect him.'

The officer who had been asking the questions and who had told her his name was Lieutenant Rendall, stayed behind when his colleague and the doctor left.

'This must be very hard for you,' he said as Belle poured him a cup of coffee. 'Have you got any family you could go to?'

Belle told him she hadn't and began to cry again. He patted her on the hand and asked if Faldo was her lover.

'No, he wasn't,' she sobbed. 'He was a married man with children. That is why this is so terrible. I hope you can avoid telling his wife anything about me, as she'll probably jump to the same conclusion.'

'She surely would! And if you don't mind me saying, Miss Talbot, few wives would appreciate their husband coming to see someone quite as pretty as you,' the officer said, and the way his eyes twinkled suggested he didn't believe what she'd told him. 'But as long as the inquest doesn't show anything odd or unexpected, I can see no reason to tell his wife anything more than that he died in a boarding house.'

Belle thanked him.

'But I am curious as to why an English girl should come alone to New Orleans,' Rendall went on, fixing her with his bright eyes. 'New York or Philadelphia I could understand, even Chicago, but not down here. New Orleans is a dangerous city.'

'I came with someone else, then he left me,' she said impulsively. 'And as soon as I can raise enough money to go home, I shall be gone.'

'Would you like to tell me about him?'

Belle almost laughed, for this man had an engaging manner. 'No, I don't want to tell you about him,' she said. 'What I'd really like is for this horrible night to be over. But I suspect I'll never sleep well in that bed again, not after Faldo died on it.'

'I could escort you to a boarding house for the night if you wish,' Rendall said. 'There is a quiet, decent one just around the corner in Canal Street.'

'That's really kind of you,' she said. 'But I can't afford to pay for a room somewhere else. I'll manage here.'

'Do you have a job?' he asked.

'Yes, I work at a milliner's,' she said, hoping he wouldn't ask where. 'But it doesn't pay very well.'

'Was it Mr Reiss that hit you?' Rendall asked, looking at her intently. 'I thought it was a shadow on your face earlier, but I can see now you have a bruise coming up on your cheek.'

'I tripped earlier on the back steps,' she said. 'I fell against the post on the balustrade.'

Fortunately the mortuary van arrived just then, the horse's hooves sounding very loud in the quiet street. Two men came in, Rendall showed them into the bedroom and just a couple of minutes later they left with Faldo on a stretcher covered by a blanket.

Rendall said goodbye to Belle and hoped she would be all right, but he hesitated at the door, looking back at her as she sat by the stove crying.

'I don't like to leave you like this, miss,' he said gruffly.

'If you don't leave people will talk,' she said sharply. 'It will be bad enough that a man died here, without one of the police officers staying on.'

'Yes, I guess you're right,' he agreed. 'What I kinda meant to say was that you should have someone with you.'

'I've lived alone for a while now,' she said. 'I don't have any other friends in the city; Faldo was the only one.'

'Then I'm sorry for your loss,' he said, and finally opened the door and left.

Once he'd gone, Belle locked and bolted the door, and went into the bedroom. She was trembling all over and her stomach was churning. She had never felt more alone.

She could see the indentation on the quilt where Faldo's body had been and she could smell his hair oil and his sweat. She wanted to be able to cry for him, she owed him that much, but she was angry because he'd left her like this.

She remembered Suzanne back at Martha's telling her about a man who had died on her. Like Faldo, it had been of a heart attack. But the way Suzanne and the other girls told the story, it was really funny. Suzanne even admitted she'd gone through his wallet before the doctor got there and helped herself to a hundred dollars.

But then, it was easy to laugh at an undignified death in an inappropriate place, when it was a stranger. Suzanne had claimed that most men, if they could pick their way to die, would choose to be fucking her. She joked she was going to send a card with some flowers to his funeral and write on it, 'I always said I'd show you heaven!'

But even if Belle had all the other girls here right now, she knew she still wouldn't be able to find anything even vaguely amusing about Faldo's death. He was a complicated, contra-dictory man and he'd been a brute tonight. He'd said that he wanted her heart, so why was he so horrible to her?

Was this the way it would always be with men? They would want her body, but never her mind, and never be able to see past her being a whore?

She lay down on the bed and pulled the quilt over her. But all at once it dawned on her that she had far more to worry about than what men might think of her. She was in fact destitute. The few dollars Miss Frank gave her wouldn't keep her. Once the rent stopped being paid, the landlord would reclaim the house too. How on earth was she going to live?

Martha would block her being taken on by any of the good sporting houses: that would leave only the dreadful places down in Robertson Street.

Panic overwhelmed her. What was she going to do?

Chapter Twenty-five

'So that's how it is, Miss Frank.' Belle's voice quivered a little because she could see the older woman was horrified by what she'd been told. 'I felt I owed you the whole truth because you've been so very kind to me.'

She hadn't slept a wink through terror of what was going to become of her. The greater part of her just wanted to run, to throw her belongings quickly into a case and catch the first train out of New Orleans. But a small, sensible voice asked her where she thought she was going to run to, because it would be hard to start again in a strange town where she didn't know anyone.

That same sensible voice suggested she went to Miss Frank and told her the whole story. As the older woman appeared to be fond of her, Belle thought she might agree to pretend to the police that her name was Anne Talbot if they came round asking questions. Belle hoped that with the money she earned at the hat shop, and perhaps finding some waitressing work too, she could stay in New Orleans.

'You really think I would be prepared to tell lies to the police and say I know you as Anne Talbot?' Miss Frank finally exclaimed.

Belle heard the animosity in the woman's voice and her stomach flipped. While she'd seen the horror on Miss Frank's face as she was explaining, she'd made the mistake of assuming that was because the woman was distressed at the idea of her going through so much. But it was now clear she'd felt nothing but repugnance.

'I wasn't asking you to tell a lie. I have been working for you, and I can't see that it matters what name you knew me under,' Belle pleaded.

'It matters very much to me,' the older woman snapped. 'No one changes their name unless they are up to no good.'

'But I've explained why Mr Reiss made me use that name, and how I came to be here in New Orleans. Don't you think I've suffered enough by being abducted and sold into prostitution? If that happened to you, wouldn't you have got out of it any way you could?'

'I don't believe you had no choice in the matter. I think it's far more likely you got led astray and then made up this ridiculous story to make yourself look like a victim,' Miss Frank said tersely, her small face and body rigid with indignation. 'I don't even know that I believe this man who was keeping you died of natural causes. Not when it's clear from your bruised cheek that you were fighting! But setting that aside, have you any idea what it would do to my business if my customers knew what you are? They wouldn't want to step inside the shop, much less try on a hat you'd touched.'

Belle felt as though she'd been kicked in the stomach. She hadn't for one moment expected that she wouldn't be believed, nor had she anticipated that Miss Frank would see a whore as being as dangerous as someone with leprosy.

'They won't catch anything from me,' she retorted. 'Though they might from their own husbands, as you can bet most of them visit the District on a regular basis.'

Miss Frank gasped in shocked horror. 'How dare you say such a wicked, slanderous thing?'

All at once Belle saw that she had been a fool to imagine this little spinster could possibly understand and sympathize with what she'd been through. The society she had been raised in was completely blinkered, and most women like her were entirely ignorant about even their own bodies. Even if Belle had only admitted a man had kissed her, Miss Frank would probably have reached for her smelling salts.

But Belle was not going to beg her forgiveness for something that was not her fault. She certainly wasn't going to resort to tears either. And she wasn't going to let the silly woman hide behind her ridiculous, prudish views.

'Because it's absolutely true,' Belle said stubbornly. 'Why is it that people always cast prostitutes as the lowest form of life? They wouldn't exist but for men. And I can tell you first hand that it is invariably so-called "respectable" married men who use them. If their wives fulfilled their role in marriage, they wouldn't resort to it. So your outraged customers ought to look to themselves before they point a finger at me.'

'I've never heard anything so shocking!' Miss Frank gasped, her face flushing rose pink.

'Shocking! I'll tell you what's shocking,' Belle said angrily. 'That you've had me working here day after day, acting as if you liked me. Yet when I tell you the truth about how I came to be here, you turn against me. I took you for a kind woman. I actually believed you would want to help me.'

'I want you out of my shop immediately.' Miss Frank's voice was shrill and cold. 'Go on now, you little strumpet.'

Belle knew she had to leave; nothing she could say was going to overcome this woman's prejudices.

'Fine, I'll go,' she said, darting forward and snatching up a small pile of her designs from the work bench. 'But you can't keep these, and I'll just slip down to Angelique's to inform them their latest order was designed and made up by a whore. They'll probably want to return the lot if they are anything like you!'

She saw Miss Frank's small face crumple and for a split second she was tempted to say she didn't mean that. But she was too hurt to back down; she'd truly believed the affection she had felt for this woman was reciprocated.

'I'm just seventeen. I've been through hell since I was snatched from my home a year and a half ago, and I'm over four thousand miles away from there, without any idea of how to get back,' she spat out, waving the sheaf of designs she held in her hand. 'What little security I had died yesterday with Mr Reiss, but I thought I had one true friend who would listen and advise me what to do without judging me. What a fool I was!'

She took some small satisfaction in seeing shame flood across the small woman's face, but turned and walked out of the shop.

Almost blinded by tears, Belle returned home. She had no alternative now but to leave New Orleans. This was, by anyone's measure, a very juicy story and she knew Miss Frank would not be able to keep it to herself. It would get back to Martha in no time and then she'd be after Belle.

Then there was the police. They were bound to come back and ask her more questions, especially if anything odd came up at Faldo's post mortem. Once they found out about her past they might even blame her for his death. Yet even more alarming now was that the people who had been behind buying and selling her might want to silence her permanently.

She was terrified. If she went to the train station one of Martha's spies might tip her off and they'd come after her. A ship was probably the best plan, but she didn't have the first idea how to fix that up.

As she packed her suitcase, she tried to tell herself that she'd always known this day would come, because she'd bought the suitcase for this very eventuality. But still she sobbed, for she had never expected that it would be under these circumstances. She had selected things for her home with such care, and it hurt to have to leave them all behind. The blue fan decorated with gold cherubs that she'd fixed above her bed could go with her as it folded away to nothing, but she couldn't take the picture of an exotic beach because it was too big. She had idled away so many hours imagining staying in a little straw-roofed hut on such a beach, with swaying palm trees, white sand and turquoise sea. She'd dreamed too of a man like Etienne taking care of her. But the picture and the lovely red hearth rug in the living room and all the other pretty things she'd bought would have to stay here.

She had more clothes now than she'd arrived with, four dresses, various petticoats, chemises, stockings, drawers and shoes, but she no longer had a warm coat, for the old fur one she was given in France had been left on the ship when she arrived in New Orleans. The weather here might still be mild, but she knew that once she got nearer to New York it would turn very cold.

An hour later Belle was in Canal Street, her arm aching from carrying the heavy suitcase the short distance. She had pushed the keys of the house back through the letter box as she left, assuming the landlord would call once he'd been notified that Faldo had died.

Waving down a cab, she asked him to take her to Alderson's and wait while she shopped, then to take her down to the docks.

Belle felt a slight pang of conscience as she charged the expensive grey coat with black lamb collar and cuffs, plus a black lamb hat to match, and a dark blue wool dress, to Mr Reiss. But she reminded herself that she had always been careful with her spending until now, and he owed it to her anyway for the bruise on her cheek and for treating her so badly before he died.

By mid-afternoon Belle was close to tears for she was unable to get a passage on a ship. While she understood from the various agents she'd spoken to that most of the ships were merchant vessels which didn't carry passengers, the ones who did take them wanted to see her papers before selling her a ticket.

The docks were a stinking, sweltering, raucous hive of activity. Burly men sweated as they loaded and unloaded ships, shouting to one another as they lowered or lifted huge wooden cases with pulleys. Others rolled barrels down gang-planks, then trundled them over the cobblestones to waiting drays.

Overloaded carts and barrows drawn by tired old nags rumbled through the throngs of people. There were even cattle, horses, and goats being driven off ships. At one point a few steers had broken away in panic, scattering the sailors, stevedores and other people on the wharf. Belle had been constantly jostled, leered at and pestered by beggars, and a young negress in rags had even tried to snatch her hat from her head.

She was hot, tired and very anxious. She had been told a thousand times that New Orleans was a dangerous place but it wasn't until today at the docks that she really felt it. There were gangs of filthy, tow-haired, almost naked children no older than five or six darting around looking for things to steal; she had seen the very lowest kinds of prostitute with most of their breasts on show haranguing men in broad daylight. There were countless drunks, and others, she felt sure by their yellowing gaunt faces, were opium addicts. She had heard so many different languages, and seen every nation-ality from Chinamen to Red Indians. While it was true that she'd been aware from her first day in New Orleans that it housed people of every colour and creed, she hadn't until now been brought face to face with those who lived at the very lowest and poorest level.

As a precaution she had tucked most of her money into a

purse secured inside the waistband of her skirt before she left the house, but she could see from those around her that everything she had – clothes, shoes, and her suitcase – were prime targets for thieves. She didn't dare relax or allow herself to be distracted for a second. Yet as time passed she became more afraid, for if she hadn't found a ship by nightfall she would be forced to find somewhere to sleep, and the prospect of the kind of bed she'd find in this area was too horrible to contemplate.

'Here, miss, the *Kentucky Maid* is shipping out to France tonight.'

Belle was surprised by the young boy addressing her, and she was reminded poignantly of Jimmy back in London, for he had the same red hair and freckled face.

'Where? Is she carrying passengers?' she asked.

The boy pointed further down the wharf. 'She ain't really a passenger ship,' he said. 'But I knows the skipper and I reckon he'll take you.'

'Who are you?' she asked sternly for she'd never seen the boy before, and it was odd he knew what she was after.

'I'm Able Gustang, I do a few odd jobs down here on the docks. I heard you talking to the shipping agent, and reckoned you seemed like you was desperate to get away. Are you on the run?'

'Of course not,' she said, but she almost laughed, for his similarity to Jimmy was striking and it made her feel she could trust him. He was very skinny, bare-footed, and his ragged pants were cut off at mid-calf length. She thought he was probably only about twelve. 'But I came into America without any papers and I do so want to go home,' she explained.

'Was you a whore? They're the ones that usually ain't got papers,' he said.

'No, I wasn't,' she retorted, but she wasn't sure she sounded indignant enough.

'Well, I 'spect it were a man that brought you here anyways,' he said, squinting at her because the sun was in his eyes. 'That's what happens to pretty girls.'

Belle smiled. 'You remind me of someone back home. But I'm tougher than I look, so don't even think of trying to cheat me. You get me fixed up and I'll reward you.'

'Ten dollars?' he asked.

'Fair enough, as long as the ship is seaworthy and I won't have to sleep in the hold, or with the skipper.'

Able grinned then, showing several missing teeth. 'This one will want to, but he can be a real gent. I done a few jobs for him, he's all right.'

The *Kentucky Maid* was a sizable steamer, but Belle's heart sank as she got closer for it looked rusting and neglected and she doubted a freighter would offer the kind of comforts she'd had on the passenger ship she'd arrived in New Orleans on. But it was going to Marseille, which was at least a whole lot nearer England than New York. And anyway, this late in the day she couldn't afford to be fussy.

'You stay here a minute and I'll go and see the skipper,' Able said. 'Don't run away, will you?'

Belle assured him she wouldn't, and watched the boy bound up the gangplank with the confidence of a grown man. About ten minutes passed, in which she got more anxious by the minute, when suddenly Able appeared on deck with a short, stout man wearing a peaked cap and with gold braid on his dark jacket. He was looking at her and Able was talking excitedly, waving his hands as if driving home a point.

Able ran down the gangplank to Belle. 'He's scared you'll be trouble,' he said. 'He don't like carrying unaccompanied ladies because they get seasick and expect special treatment. But if you can convince him you ain't like that, maybe even give him the idea you'll be useful for a bit of cooking and what-not, I reckon he'll come round.'

Belle braced herself as she went up on deck to meet Captain Rollins. She knew she'd got to be very careful. If she was too accommodating he'd assume he could have his way with her the whole way to France, but if she was too frosty he'd find an excuse not to take her.

She gave her best wide-eyed smile and held her hand out to the man. 'I'm so pleased to meet you, captain. I am so grateful that you can take me as a passenger.'

'I haven't decided whether I will yet,' he said sharply. His eyes were so dark they appeared to have no pupils, and despite being short and stout he was quite handsome, with clear, golden skin and well-shaped features. 'I need to be sure you won't be a liability.'

'I will stay in my cabin all the time if that is better for you,' she said. 'Or I could help your cook. I'm a good sailor; on the way to America all the other passengers suffered from seasickness except me.'

'Why don't you have any papers?' he asked bluntly.

'Because I was abducted back in London,' she said. 'I was witness to a murder, and the murderer snatched me to stop me speaking out.'

'A little extreme, bringing you so far away,' the captain half smiled.

'He made a great deal of money selling me on,' she said tersely. 'However, I want to go home and bring him to justice. Please tell me how much you are going to charge me for taking me to France.'

'Two hundred dollars,' he said.

Belle rolled her eyes. 'Then I'll have to find another ship. I haven't got anywhere near that much.'

'I'm sure we can come to some arrangement,' he said.

Belle stiffened at his tone. She knew exactly what that meant. 'No, we will decide on a fare here and now,' she said. 'Seventy dollars?'

He sniffed and pursed his lips, looking away from her.

'I can just about manage eighty, but I can't pay any more,' she begged. 'Please, Captain Rollins, take me with you, I promise I'll be really useful to you.'

He looked back at her, shaking his head slowly. But then unexpectedly he smiled. 'All right, ma'am, I'll take you for eighty dollars, but if you get sick don't expect any help from anyone.'

Twenty minutes after paying off Able and saying goodbye, Belle was in her cabin. It was so small she could only shuffle sideways along the gap between the bunks and the wall with the port-hole. She couldn't imagine what it would be like to have to share it with another person.

Captain Rollins had told her to stay in her cabin until after they had sailed, in fact she got the clear impression that he actually meant for her to stay in it until he said otherwise. But she didn't mind, she was so tired with having had so little sleep the previous night that she would be quite happy to sleep the clock round.

The captain had informed her there were only two other passengers on board. Arnaud Germaine was French, but his wife Avril was American, and they were going home to his family in France. Belle had seen only a brief glimpse of them; Avril was around thirty-five, her husband at least ten years older. But even if they weren't likely to be company for her, she was glad that there was at least one other female on the ship. As the captain showed her the way to her cabin, she'd been leered at by several crew members. They had all looked unkempt, wild-eyed and dirty. She intended to keep her cabin door locked at all times.

By the third day on board Belle had settled into a routine and she'd found that the disreputable-looking crew were a mixture of nationalities. About half of them were negroes, the rest were Cajun, Mexican, Chinese, Irish, Brazilian, and the cook was Italian. But so far they had been surprisingly polite to her, perhaps because the captain had told them she was a friend's daughter.

She would walk on the deck for an hour after breakfast, then collect some coffee from the galley and take it to Captain Rollins to see if he had any jobs for her to do. So far he hadn't asked her to do much, in fact it seemed he was hard-pressed to find anything for her to do. She'd sewn some buttons on a shirt and tidied his cabin, and she'd also helped Gino the cook prepare vegetables for dinner, but he wouldn't allow her to do anything more in his galley. Talking to the captain filled up a chunk of the day, however, and she felt he liked her company.

During the afternoon she mostly sat and read in the small, shabby room they called the officers' mess. There were hundreds of books there, on shelves, stacked in boxes and piled on the floor, some so well thumbed they were in danger of falling apart. Belle, Mr and Mrs Germaine and the five ship's officers ate their meals in here too. And although shabby and cramped, it was homely and comfortable.

Arnaud Germaine studiously ignored her and she felt he knew about her background. His wife Avril looked at her curiously but had clearly been told not to talk to her. That suited Belle just fine as she didn't want to have to answer questions. Captain Rollins could and did question her, but he was gentle about it and his dark eyes twinkled. During their chats in the mornings she'd told him more about herself than she had intended to, but even when she admitted she had worked at Martha's sporting house he kept the same calm, faintly amused expression, and she felt that even if she was to disclose everything, he'd react just the same way.

The ship was due to berth in Bermuda to take on water, then cross the Atlantic to Madeira before finally docking in

Marseille. The evening before they reached Bermuda the captain told Belle she must stay on board the next day. 'The authorities are vigilant there,' he explained. 'Well, they would be, they are English,' he added with a wry smile. 'You might think that would make them sympathetic to your plight, but you'd be wrong. They'd just send you back to New Orleans and prosecute me. So stay in your cabin.'

It was stiflingly hot in her cabin once the ship had berthed. Belle knew that Bermuda had beaches just like the one in the picture she'd had to leave behind, and she so much wished she could see them. But she stripped down to her chemise and lay on her bunk with the porthole wide open and listened to the sounds of the tropical island which wafted in. Someone was playing a steel drum in the distance, and she could hear a woman calling out something, sounding just like the street traders back in London. She couldn't see the harbour from the porthole, for the ship was facing out to sea, but as it had come in to dock, she'd seen shiny-faced brown women wearing vivid dresses carrying baskets of fruit on their heads. She'd seen men in long boats, which looked as if they'd been made from the hollowed-out trunk of a tree, casting fishing nets on the turquoise water, and plump, naked brown children jumping from the dockside to swim.

All the crew were very excited about stopping here. Second Lieutenant Gregson had remarked that they would be blind drunk within an hour of going ashore. He'd told her that this was the place men often jumped ship, sometimes intentionally but more often because they got too drunk to get back to the ship before she sailed. He complained that it was part of his duties to try to round them all up at the end of the evening, which meant he had to stay relatively sober.

Once everyone had disembarked and the ship became quiet, Belle felt very sad and dejected. She tried to sleep to make the hours go faster till they sailed again, but she remained annoyingly alert. She kept thinking that by the time she got to France it would be Christmas, and shortly after that it would be two years since Millie was killed and that until that night she hadn't really understood what a brothel was. It was difficult to believe she'd ever been that naive, but then Mog and her mother had probably threatened the girls that they'd be thrown out if they talked to Belle about what they did upstairs.

How things had changed since then! She'd travelled thousands of miles and gone from virgin to whore, child to grown woman. She didn't think there was anything new to learn about men now; all those romantic ideas she'd once had about courtship, love and marriage were gone.

One of Belle's favourite ways to pass the time on the ship was studying crew members and imagining each of them in Martha's. Gregson, the second Lieutenant, was the youngest officer and unmarried. He had the blond, blue-eyed look of a story-book hero; she thought he would be the kind to get helplessly drunk, and when he finally got upstairs with one of the girls he would pass out.

First Lieutenant Attlee, a forty-year-old married man from St Louis, believed himself to be some kind of Don Juan. Belle thought he looked like a weasel, for he was slightly built yet tall, with sharp little dark eyes that darted around a room as if afraid of missing something. She sensed that he was the peeping Tom kind, one of those men who got a bigger thrill watching others having sex than doing it himself.

Captain Rollins was harder to pigeon-hole. He was very much the family man – on his desk he had pictures of his pretty wife and three children, and he spoke of them fondly. Yet she also felt there was another side to him, for when she had admitted about Martha's it was clear he knew his way about such places. She felt he was an opportunist, and that while he wouldn't force himself on to any woman, he was the kind to inveigle his way into a situation where a woman would find it hard to resist him. She suspected he was a passionate man who would be a good and generous lover.

That thought made Belle smile. He might come in useful when they got to Marseille.

Belle passed a bowl for Avril Germaine to be sick in, and wiped her forehead with a wet flannel, feeling genuine sympathy. She remembered how ill Etienne had been with seasickness, and Avril's wail that she thought she was going to die made Belle feel she must do what she could to help the woman. As she vomited again, her face was as green as the rough blanket Belle had wrapped round her after helping her out of the soiled sheets on her bunk.

'You are not going to die,' Belle said firmly, taking the bowl from her hands and emptying it in the slop pail. She sluiced the bowl with water, then handed it back in case Avril was sick again. 'The storm will blow itself out in a few hours and you'll feel better again then.'

Avril was a small, pretty woman with fair, curly hair, pale blue eyes and a complexion like porcelain. Her clothes were expensive and beautiful, and she reminded Belle of a china doll in a picture book Mog had given her when she was small. The doll had thought she was queen of the nursery because she was so pretty and the favourite toy of her owner. She was always nasty to all the other toys who she felt were beneath her. Avril was like her in every way.

'Why are you being so kind to me?' she asked in a weak voice. 'I've been so mean to you.'

Belle half smiled. Both the Germaines had ignored her at the start of the voyage, but they had become much more unpleasant since leaving Bermuda, not just shutting her out of conversations in the officers' mess, but making barbed comments about her. It was obvious they'd found proof she was a whore and felt affronted that they had to eat at the same table with her.

She had been tempted to tell Arnaud Germaine to go to hell when he begged her to help his wife when she became ill, but Belle had never been able to ignore another human being who was suffering.

'Even whores have hearts,' she said, as she reached across the bunk to tuck in the clean sheet. 'In fact, some of us have bigger ones than ordinary folk. But I don't know how you and your husband could be so hoity-toity about me. As I understand it, you've made your money from supplying sporting houses with liquor!'

Captain Rollins had let this bit of information slip. Belle suspected it was no accident either, and that he hoped she'd use it to her advantage.

Avril vomited again. Belle stopped her bed-making to lift the woman's hair from her neck and cool her neck with the damp flannel. Then, when Avril had stopped retching, she bathed her face and gave her some water to sip.

'You're right,' Avril said weakly, sagging back against the wall. 'That is how we made our money. But I guess I chose not to think about it.'

Belle saw no reason to labour her point, after all Avril was very sick. The china doll in her books had come to grief too; she fell off a shelf and her face cracked, and after that she was never played with again.

'Well, at least you are big enough to admit it,' Belle said. 'Now, let's get you washed and into a clean nightdress – that will make you feel more comfortable.'

An hour later Belle left the Germaines' cabin, taking the soiled sheets and nightdress away to wash. She was pleased that Avril's seasickness appeared to be abating. After being washed and tucked back into her clean bunk, she had fallen asleep and her colour was much improved.

Belle was washing out the linen in the laundry-room sink

when Captain Rollins put his head around the door. 'How did your mission of mercy go?' he asked with a twinkle in his eye.

'Mercifully brief,' Belle answered, and sniggered. 'Mrs Germaine is a little better now.'

She put the edge of the sheet between the rollers of the mangle and turned the handle, watching the water being squeezed out.

'You'd make a good nurse,' said Captain Rollins. 'I just saw Mr Germaine and he was very touched by the way you cared for his wife.'

Belle shrugged. 'Whoring, nursing, they are quite alike, just looking after different needs.'

'You could hold your head higher if you chose to be a nurse,' he said.

Belle glanced round at the captain and found him looking at her very thoughtfully. 'I could hold my head still higher if I had my own house, carriage and fine clothes,' she said tartly. 'But nursing doesn't pay that well.'

'So you will continue to earn money that way once you get back to England?'

Belle thought that was a strange question. 'Not if I can help it,' she said with a toss of her head. 'I want to have a hat shop with a few rooms above for me to live in and have a workshop. But I have very little money left, and it is a long way from Marseille to London. So if you have any good ideas about how I can avoid selling myself to get that money, I'd be glad to hear them.'

'It makes me sad to hear you speak like that,' he replied, his voice soft and reproachful.

Belle let go of the wrung-out sheet and stepped nearer to the captain, and she caught hold of his cheek with her thumb and forefinger and squeezed it. 'Like I said, you show me another way and I'll gladly take it. But don't trouble yourself about me, captain, as they say back in New Orleans, I'm a tough cookie.'

At nine that same night, Arnaud Germaine went up on the bridge to see Captain Rollins.

'Good evening, sir,' Rollins greeted his passenger. 'How is your wife now the sea is calmer?'

The storm had blown itself out around six o'clock and although the sea was still choppy the ship was no longer lurching up and down.

'She ees much better now,' Arnaud replied in his heavily accented English. 'We have Miss Cooper to thank for that.'

'So I hear,' the captain said. 'Ironically, I almost refused her passage because I felt she would become ill and demand attention.'

'I am embarrassed now at the way I treat 'er. My wife say she saved her life.'

Captain Rollins smiled. He hadn't imagined that the pugnacious little Frenchman was capable of embarrassment. 'Then maybe you should reward her,' he suggested. 'I happen to know she will struggle to get the train fare back to England.'

'Umm, maybe so,' Arnaud murmured. 'But tell me, captain, do you find this girl something of a puzzle?'

'You mean because she is young and beautiful, yet so kindly?'

Arnaud nodded. 'She also has a curious way of flaunting what she ees. Those knowing looks, the sharp retorts. I theenk she is laughing at us all. She pointed out to my wife that we made our money by selling liquor to sporting houses, so we were no better than 'er!'

Captain Rollins chuckled. 'If she had said that in the mess when your wife was well, that might have created a storm.'

'Yes, indeed. But I do not share your amusement. I am afraid now that she will try to gain my wife's sympathy in order to be invited to our home in France.'

'I don't think that is her way,' Captain Rollins smirked. 'I think you are judging her by your own standards.'

Arnaud puffed up with indignation. 'Why, sir, that is very rude!' he huffed.

The captain let his First Lieutenant take the helm later and went below to his cabin to write up the ship's log. But he found himself just sitting staring into space, thinking of what Arnaud Germaine had said about Belle.

She *was* something of a curiosity, bold, forthright, and brave too, for most young women in her position would never have dared travel all the way to France on a cargo ship. But what he liked most about her was that she wasn't ashamed of being a whore. It was as if she'd decided at one point that even though it wasn't her job of choice, she was going to excel at it. And he had no doubt she had, with those devastating looks and perfect body.

He wanted her himself, he had the moment he met her, but she'd made it plain enough that she wasn't available. He thought she was very honest, and he liked her sense of humour too. It made him smile to think of her putting Avril Germaine in her place by reminding her that her husband made his money by supplying brothels. It had also amused him when she'd told him how she'd settled on becoming the railway man's mistress, only to find him disappointing as her lover.

Rollins had met many men who treated their beautiful wife or mistress in the same way as a miser hoards his gold, never letting them shine in public and belittling them at every turn. He had to assume that they felt in some way unworthy, or were afraid another man would steal her from them. He could not imagine himself behaving in such a way, for if Belle was his mistress he would want to flaunt her, show her off, feel every other man envy him. What point was there in having a great treasure if you had to keep it hidden?

But he was a trifle concerned at Germaine's interest in Belle. Although the man had professed that he didn't want any further contact with her in Marseille, Rollins had got the distinct impression that the Frenchman's sole purpose in coming up to the bridge was to try to sound him out about Belle, as if he had some scheme in mind for her.

He wondered if he ought to warn her not to accept any invitations from the couple. But if he did, she was fiery enough to say something to the Germaines. Sadly, that would mean Germaine was likely to find another ship in future to take his wine to New Orleans. So perhaps it would be best to trust Belle's judgement, and say nothing.

Chapter Twenty-six

The dockside in Marseille was even noisier, more crowded and smellier than the one in New Orleans. Added to that it was dark, very cold, and everyone around her was speaking French. Belle stood at the end of the ship's gangway, suitcase in hand, terrified because she had no idea what to do or where to go.

She had expected that she could just walk off the ship and would see a guest house right off, but all she could see ahead of her was dark shapes of buildings which looked like warehouses. Men were trying to take her suitcase from her, beckoning her to go with them to heaven only knew where, and there were small boys pulling at her coat and asking for money.

Suddenly Arnaud Germaine was beside her. 'Let me get you a fiacre,' he insisted, taking her suitcase from her hand. 'You must find this frightening when you don't speak French?'

'Yes, indeed. Thank heavens you came along,' she exclaimed, assuming that 'fiacre' was French for carriage. 'I was just about to panic because I didn't know where to go. Could you ask the driver to take me to a guest house, somewhere clean but inexpensive?'

Since she'd nursed Avril, both she and her husband had become friendly with Belle. They had played cards most evenings after dinner, and Belle had got to like Avril. But she was wary of Arnaud; he had gone out of his way to be charming, but she felt it was forced.

'I know the very place, my dear,' he said with a warm smile. 'But let me take you there and I can introduce you to the owner.'

The smell of fish in the harbour was overpowering and Belle

pulled up the collar of her coat and buried her nose in the fur. The stink was coming from a brightly lit shed less than twenty yards away; she assumed by the shouting coming from it that the fish was being auctioned.

'That is an interesting place to look in by day,' Arnaud remarked, with laughter in his voice. 'But it is not pleasant to look at lobster, cod and herring when you are cold and tired. Take my arm now and I will get a fiacre.'

It crossed Belle's mind to ask where Avril was, but the noise and clamour were so great that she just held on to Arnaud and let him steer her through the crowds.

He put two fingers between his lips and whistled loudly. 'I always wished I could do that,' she said admiringly. 'But it's not very ladylike.'

Arnaud laughed in agreement and pointed out how effective it was as a cab driver was already flicking his horse with a whip to guide it over to them. 'Soon we will be out of this tumult and you will feel safe again.'

'This is incredibly kind of you, Mr Germaine,' Belle said as the Frenchman helped her into the cab.

'It is the least I can do after you nursed my wife when she was so sick,' he replied, putting her case in and leaping in after it, having said a few words to the driver.

Belle's hands were like ice, but it felt a little warmer in the cab. 'Where is your wife?' she asked.

'She told me to go after you and see you were safe,' Arnaud replied. 'My family will take her home and I will join her later. She asked me to invite you to visit us over Christmas.'

It would be Christmas Eve the next day, but Belle couldn't see Christmas as anything more than another inconvenience which would prevent her heading home to England immediately. Even if there was a train running in the morning, she didn't think she had enough money left for the ticket. Worse still, what little money she still had was going to run out fast while she was living in a guest house. She would have to find some work to earn more, but that was going to be difficult without being able to speak French.

She had wanted to ask Captain Rollins to lend her some money, but she found she couldn't do it. Likewise she wished she had the nerve to ask Arnaud.

'I'd love to visit you, but I will have to find some work as I don't think I have enough money to get back to England,' she blurted out.

'I'm sure that will all fall into place,' he said silkily, patting her on the knee.

Suddenly Belle felt uneasy. She didn't know whether it was just because she was tired, cold and anxious, but it sounded like his apparent kindness was just a ruse to make her indebted to him.

She was only too aware that there was just one sure way she could make money quickly in Marseille, and she was resigned to that. She'd already decided to use the hotel plan, an idea she'd got from a couple of girls at Martha's. But while she would be happy to slip a hotel doorman a few francs for assisting her to find the right client, she certainly didn't want to have Arnaud or any other man taking what she earned.

She couldn't speak out, however. He might have been genuinely trying to reassure her everything would turn out fine. If she said something sharp he might turn her out of the cab and she wouldn't have the first idea of where to go.

In the end she said nothing; it seemed the safest thing to do.

Madame Albertine, the red-headed owner of the guest house, fired a volley of French at Arnaud, and judging by the excitement in her voice and her wide smile, they were really good friends.

But all at once she clapped her hand over her mouth and turned to Belle. 'I should not be speaking French to Arnaud when you don't understand it,' she said in perfect English. 'I am so sorry. Please forgive me?'

Belle smiled and said she hadn't expected anything other than French to be spoken here in France, and that she would try to learn some while she was here.

Arnaud said he had to go, and that Belle wasn't to worry about the bill as he would like to settle it as a thank you for taking care of Avril. Belle felt ashamed she had been suspicious of his motives earlier and thanked him, kissed his cheek and wished him a Merry Christmas.

'Until we meet again,' he said, taking her hand and kissing it. 'I will send a carriage for you.'

Madame Albertine was around forty, very attractive with her red hair, green eyes and voluptuous figure. She wore a beautiful silvery brocade gown which Belle admired.

'I am going out to supper tonight,' she said. 'Any other day you would find me in very dull clothes, but it is Christmas, so I made an effort.'

As she led Belle up the stairs she said she hoped she wouldn't feel too lonely. 'I had a full house but my guests have gone home to their families now. In the next few days though I shall introduce you to some of my friends.'

The room she showed Belle into was small, with plain white walls and shutters on the window, but there was a vivid-coloured quilt on the brass bed and Madame Albertine put a match to a fire which was already laid in the hearth.

'It will soon be warm,' she said. 'If I'd known I was going to have a guest I would have lit it an hour or two ago.'

'It feels warm enough anyway,' Belle said gratefully. 'I was scared when I got off the boat. I'm just so happy Monsieur Germaine brought me here.'

Madame Albertine smiled warmly. 'It will be good to have some female company over Christmas. Now, I'll leave you out some bread and cheese for supper. You can find your own way down to the kitchen, I'm sure, it's just off the hall. Make yourself at home, won't you? And I'll see you in the morning. Perhaps you'd like to come to the market with me for the Christmas food?'

The last thing the older woman said before she left was that there was plenty of hot water for a bath if Belle wanted one. Back in New Orleans, she had to boil up pans of water to fill a tin bath, and on the ship she hadn't been able to have anything more than a strip wash, so to be told that there was a bath here was like being given an early Christmas present.

Belle slept like a log that night. She only woke as the shutters were opened and sunshine came into the room. Madame Albertine was there with a large cup of coffee in her hand.

'If you are to come to the market with me, we must go now,' she said with a broad smile. 'Up you get and put on your clothes.'

Belle was enchanted by the narrow winding lanes which led down to the market near the harbour. The houses were mostly rather dilapidated, with paint peeling off shutters and doors that looked ancient, and they were stuffed up together in a higgledy-piggledy fashion too. She could see the similarities to the French Quarter back in New Orleans in the shutters and the wrought-iron balconies, but this was the older, less organized sister. The lanes were narrower, the smells stronger and there were no signs in English.

When they reached the market Belle kept her wits about her so as not to get separated from Madame Albertine, fearing she could be lost in the huge crowds for ever. She had seen many markets – back in Seven Dials it was one big market daily – but she'd never seen anything like this one.

There were many hundreds of stalls filled with every kind of foodstuff she could think of, and a lot more she didn't recognize. Hares, rabbits and pheasants were hung up by their feet on poles. Ready-plucked turkeys, chickens and geese were displayed on vast shelves. There were stalls with mountains of shiny red apples, others where different fruits and vegetables were displayed so beautifully they looked like a work of art. There were splendid iced cakes especially for Christmas, Dundee cakes and other similar kinds topped with glazed fruit and nuts. Dozens of huge red, brown and white sausages were hung up, the stallholder often hacking off a slice and inviting his customers to try. There were countless jars of what Belle assumed were preserves although she couldn't recognize the contents, and stalls selling only bread, many of the loaves made into plaits and other fantastic shapes. There were herbs, spices, bottles of wine and cordials, chocolate, toffees and sweets.

Here and there was a stall selling hand-painted decorations for the Christmas tree, and there were also gingerbread biscuits with decorative icing which immediately reminded Belle of Mog. She used to make biscuits like these for Christmas and hang them by their strings on a line above the stove.

They had never had a Christmas tree at home. Annie sneered at them, and in fact she didn't seem to like any of the traditions of Christmas. At the age of seven Belle had been very disappointed to be told that the red woolly stocking Mog always got her to hang up by the stove for Santa Claus to fill with sweets, nuts and small toys, was in fact filled by Mog too. But even if Annie didn't embrace Christmas, she did enjoy the feasting element of it. As the house was closed, those of the girls who hadn't got family near enough to go home to came down to the kitchen, and Belle always remembered it being a very jolly day, with both Mog and her mother getting a bit drunk. Sometimes they had goose, sometimes a big chicken, but there were sausages too, wonderful stuffing and what Mog called her Special Christmas Roast Potatoes. Belle knew Mog would love this French market, for all around her were women who looked very like her, filling up their shopping baskets with special treats for their families.

On one stall a man was roasting a pig on a spit, and Madame Albertine bought two bread rolls stuffed with the roast pork for them to eat as they walked about.

'This is heavenly!' Belle exclaimed, rolling her eyes in ecstasy, for she hadn't tasted anything so good for a very long time. 'I'm not going to want to leave Marseille at this rate.'

Madame Albertine picked out a Christmas tree along with all the other goods she'd bought, and a young boy promised to bring it to the house later. Madame explained that she had a big box of decorations for it, and Belle could help her with it when they got home.

Belle finally went to bed at midnight, hardly able to believe what a wonderful day she'd had. After the long, lonely time since leaving Martha's, it was lovely to have female company, and to help with the shopping and cooking and decorating the Christmas tree. Madame Albertine was so easy to talk to that Belle ended up confiding in her about her time in New Orleans, Faldo's death and how disappointed she'd been that Miss Frank had been so nasty to her. Part of the reason she told her this was because she was fairly certain Arnaud would tell her Belle had worked in a sporting house, if he hadn't done so already, and she wanted to tell the story her own way, not let him put his slant on it.

When Belle asked her nervously whether she was horrified, Madame Albertine gave one of her expressive Gallic shrugs. 'Why should I be? I think you are to be admired for your courage and fortitude.'

Belle glowed and felt a great deal better about herself.

*

Christmas Day was just as lovely. First Belle went to church with Madame Albertine and even though the service was all in Latin, and the hymns in French, she loved the smell of the incense, the way everyone was dressed in their best clothes, and the old church was very beautiful.

Belle had put on her best dress, a pale blue crêpe which fitted like a glove down to her hips. It had a ruffle round the neck and another one around the hem which swept up at the back to her waist, creating a kind of bustle effect. She had bought it in New Orleans while she was still at Martha's, but she never wore it there as the girls said it made her look like a schoolmistress. Belle knew that wasn't the image it created at all; it was just that all the girls at Martha's were expected to wear low necklines.

Madame Albertine admired it and said it was the perfect dress for Christmas Day. She gave Belle a blue velvet flower to pin in her hair, which matched the dress perfectly.

After church a few friends came back to the house for a drink. It was the only time during the day that Belle felt a little uneasy and on show, for none of these people could speak English, and they all kept looking at her.

Madame Albertine's maid was preparing the roast goose while she was entertaining, but once the company had gone home, Belle went into the kitchen with Madame to help out.

The Christmas lunch was to be eaten at three, and there were just three guests, all gentlemen. Madame Albertine had explained before they arrived that they were all businessmen who were unable to get home to their families for Christmas, and that she had quite a reputation for taking in strays at this time of year.

Fortunately all three men spoke quite good English, and though they kept lapsing back into French, they spoke to Belle often enough for her to not feel left out. With champagne before lunch, and then wine, Belle couldn't retain the men's full names or what their business was, but it was enough that she could use their Christian names – Pierre, Clovis and Julien.

They all flirted with her and paid her extravagant compliments, and Madame Albertine seemed pleased that everyone was getting on well. Later they played cards, and Belle learned some games she'd never played before. The gentlemen left around eight in the evening, and when a couple of neighbours called in to see Madame, Belle went up to her room, where she fell sound asleep as soon as her head touched the pillow.

On Boxing Day Arnaud and Avril sent their carriage over to collect Belle and take her to their house for lunch.

They had a small but delightful home high on a hill on the outskirts of the city with an incredible view of both the sea and Marseille. There were several other guests, most of whom spoke good English, but Belle didn't feel very comfortable for she had a feeling Arnaud and Avril might have told the other guests about her. Nothing was said, they were all pleasant enough, but she felt she was being studied closely, and the men were a little too familiar, so she was quite relieved when it was time to go back to Madame Albertine.

The following morning Madame asked Belle if she would like to go to a dinner party that evening with Clovis, one of the gentlemen who had come to lunch on Christmas Day. 'He is expected to bring a partner with him, and as he enjoyed your company and thinks you are the prettiest girl in town, he hoped you liked him enough to agree to accompany him.'

Belle was flattered to be asked. Clovis was a man of sophisticated tastes, who had spoken about loving opera and the ballet, and though he was only about thirty she wouldn't have expected him to want the company of someone as young and gauche as she was. He was handsome too, in a

373

kind of bony, brooding way with high cheekbones, very dark, hooded eyes and an aquiline nose.

Belle said she would love to go, but she didn't think she had an appropriate dress to wear. 'I've got a couple of plain day dresses, and there's the blue dress I wore over Christmas, but the only other one is red satin. I think that might tell people what I am.'

Madame Albertine laughed merrily. '*Ma chérie*, this is France, we do not judge here, but maybe I have something more suitable tucked away. I was as slender as you once and I have never sold or given away any of my lovely gowns.'

She found Belle a black lace gown which fitted like a glove. It was a classic figure-hugging, long-sleeved style which flared out from just above the knee into a cascade of ruffles to the floor. The lining of the dress was a camisole style, so Belle's shoulders, arms and the swell of her breasts could be glimpsed through the lace.

'I have had some wonderful times wearing this dress,' Madame chuckled. 'Men always said it was alluring, I think they found the glimpse of flesh provocative.'

The dinner was in the restaurant of a very grand hotel in the centre of Marseille. Clovis said Belle looked beautiful when he came to collect her in a fiacre, and he seemed so genuinely excited to be with her that Belle didn't feel nervous at all when he swept her into the hotel on his arm to meet his friends.

They were twelve in number. The other five women were all attractive, beautifully dressed and dripping in jewellery, but somewhat older than Belle. They were charming, however, and appeared to believe the story Madame Albertine had suggested to Belle, that she had been sent to her aunt in New Orleans when her mother died. Belle added that her aunt had a milliner's shop where she worked making and selling hats. She found the story tripped off her tongue easily – after all, there were elements of truth in it – and she even made everyone laugh by describing some of the oddest customers who had come into the hat shop.

Strangely, no one asked why she got a ship bound for Marseille, but most of the company knew the Germaines, so the story of her taking care of Avril when she was seasick had preceded her. Belle felt good to be looked upon as a spirited and kind-hearted girl, and to bask in Clovis's admiration.

Had Belle been invited to a dinner party like this one in London, her accent would have betrayed that she was from the lower classes. But fortunately being away in America for so long had probably partially masked that, and of course being French, their ears weren't tuned into the finer points of English accents. Martha had always complimented Belle on her good manners – that she had to thank Mog for – but when she first saw the array of cutlery and different glasses on the table, she did have a moment of fear.

She picked up whatever everyone else did, however, and found she was able to really enjoy being in a swanky hotel, with a handsome and attentive partner, drinking champagne and eating wonderful food, and being something of the centre of attention. She knew she looked sensational in the lace evening gown; she might not have diamonds around her neck like the other women, only some red glass beads, but she was young and beautiful and the world was at her feet.

Belle realized she'd drunk too much when she got up from the table after dessert. She found it hard to walk in a straight line, and people's faces looked a little blurred. A small voice at the back of her head told her that being drunk with people she hardly knew was dangerous, but she wasn't prepared to listen to that voice, she was having too much fun.

When Belle got back from the powder room she was offered a liqueur. It tasted of coffee and she drank it down in one.

'Are you all right, Belle?' Clovis asked.

She turned to him, put her hand on his cheek and looked into his dark, hooded eyes. 'I'm fine,' she said, though it seemed hard to get the words out. 'I'd be even better with a kiss.'

'You shall have one later,' he said, and squeezed her hand.

In the room adjoining the dining room a band was playing, and hearing a waltz, Belle jumped to her feet and caught hold of Clovis's hands, urging him to come and dance. She thought she heard some of the others at the table say they would join them, but she didn't notice whether or not they came on to the dance floor later.

What she did remember was feeling very sleepy and clinging to Clovis. She heard him say something about taking her up to his room, and the next thing she knew, he had his arm around her and was helping her up a huge staircase with a thick, patterned red carpet.

'You have a room here?' she asked, trying very hard not to slur her words.

'Yes, this is where I always stay when I am in Marseille.'

'But what will they think of me going to your room?' she asked.

'Hotels as good as this one don't have an opinion about their guests' behaviour,' he said.

Belle remembered going up the stairs, but it seemed to take for ever to get to the room. Then, contrarywise, it seemed only a second or two before she was entirely naked. She had a vague memory of Clovis standing her before a huge mirror and touching her intimately in a way which was pleasurable but didn't seem quite right, not for a man who was just supposed to be taking her out to dinner.

Then she remembered him suddenly being naked too, and it was something of a shock to see that his chest and back were covered in thick black hair. At that point she tried to say that this was a mistake and she should go home, but he didn't listen, just swept her on to the big bed.

Everything was hazy after that. She heard him saying things in French which she suspected were rude, she knew too that he was penetrating her, and even in her drunkenness she felt a sense of shame that she'd let herself down by drinking so much and allowing Clovis to believe this was what she wanted.

She woke later with a raging thirst, and didn't know where she was at first for the room was so dark. But as she groped out to her side and her hand came into contact with a hairy back, it all came back to her.

She felt sick at letting herself down by getting drunk. What was Madame Albertine going to think of her now? Her head was pounding, she could smell herself, and she needed a drink of water badly. She vaguely remembered that she'd used an adjoining bathroom to this room, so she slid out of the bed and groped her way along the wall. She came to a door, but as she opened it, light flooded in from the corridor. Before she closed it, though, she was able to see there was a second door in the room.

Of all the things Belle valued most in life, a bathroom with a tub with hot and cold water, and a flushing lavatory, was top of her list. Even though there had been one at Martha's, with so many girls wanting to get in there, and the boiler to heat the water only lit at certain times, her turn for a bath didn't come as often as she'd like. Madame Albertine's was nice, she'd even had a thing she called a bidet for washing her bottom. But this hotel bathroom was the best Belle had ever seen, with a washbasin set in a marble stand, a huge bath, and a lavatory and a bidet too, with a black and white tiled floor that shone as though it was wet.

But although Belle took in this luxury, she had barely shut the door behind her before the contents of her stomach rose up, and she only just reached the lavatory in time.

It seemed as though she was retching for hours. One minute she was so cold she had to wrap herself in a bath towel, then she became hot and felt she might pass out from the heat. Finally, when there was nothing left in her stomach to bring up, she dragged herself off the floor and looked at herself in the big mirror behind the bath.

Her hair, which she'd spent an hour arranging the night before, securing curls with combs and pins up on the top of her head, was now like tangled brambles, her face was chalk-white and her lips looked swollen and bruised. She was sore below too, and she knew Clovis must have treated her roughly.

When Madame Albertine had first explained the purpose of a bidet, Belle hadn't really seen the point of it, but as she sat on this one, and the warm water soothed her lower parts, she suddenly understood. Unfortunately, along with enlightenment about bidets, came the sinking feeling she had been set up. She didn't think a cultured and intelligent man like Clovis would take advantage of a woman who'd had too much to drink, not unless he knew she wasn't in a position to make a complaint against him.

That meant Madame Albertine must have told him what she was, and that made Belle cry, for she'd liked Albertine, really liked her, and she'd thought her secrets safe with her.

Belle stayed in the bathroom for what seemed like hours. She washed herself all over, combed her hair, and drank copious amounts of water until she felt completely sober again. Then she crept back into the dark bedroom and groped around on the floor until she found all her clothes.

A peep through the curtains revealed that it was still night, with not even a hint of dawn approaching, and along with not knowing how to get back to Madame Albertine's, she wasn't anxious to be seen leaving by a night porter. So, once dressed, she took an eiderdown which had fallen from the bed, and sat down on the chaise longue by the window and covered herself up to keep warm, while she thought about how she was going to deal with her predicament.

Clovis was snoring softly, a rather endearing sound in many ways, and Belle wished she could believe that he'd only brought her up here intending to let her sleep off the drink, but then lust got the better of him. Sadly, however, she knew men too well to believe that. Ironically, she might have willingly gone to bed with him at a later date, for she had really liked him.

But thinking back to how they met at the Christmas lunch, it came to her like a lightning bolt that Madame Albertine might in fact have been displaying her, both then and earlier in the day, to her other friends, preparing to offer her to the highest bidder. Belle was horrified, for it was surely the worst kind of betrayal of all. But the more she thought about it, the more she felt she was right, and what was more, Madame Albertine wouldn't have been in this venture alone: her most obvious partner in crime was Arnaud.

Belle could see the whole picture now. Arnaud offered to get a cab and take her to a place he knew, because he'd planned ahead. It was possible Madame Albertine already ran a brothel, and she was delighted Arnaud had brought her a new recruit. Belle understood now why she felt uncomfortable at Arnaud's house; his friends had known what she was and might even have been making him offers for her.

Tonight's dinner party had been the bait to hook Belle.

And she'd swallowed it hook, line and sinker. All it took for her was a handsome, attentive escort, a stunning dress and too much to drink. By going willingly to Clovis's room she couldn't complain about whatever he did to her.

But of course Madame Albertine wasn't expecting her to complain. She would undoubtedly commiserate with Belle when she got home later this morning, but then gently suggest she might as well do it for money in future; after all, it would be the quickest way to earn enough for the train ticket home to England.

Whether it was Madame Albertine or Arnaud who found the customers, there was no doubt they'd be sharing the money she made. Belle would be back in exactly the same position she'd been in with Martha.

She knew that all ports had whorehouses, and although there were no other girls at Madame Albertine's, and the house didn't look anything like a brothel, it was more than possible that the two of them planned to put her in one nearby. She supposed that it wasn't really logical to be angry as she'd been intending to work as a whore anyway. But it was the deception that stung. Madame Albertine had paraded her around as if she just wanted Belle to have a nice time, but all the time she was seeing her simply as a piece of merchandise to be sold off to the highest bidder.

Belle sat there thinking for a moment or two, then got up and went over to Clovis's jacket which he'd tossed on the floor. She found his wallet and withdrew five twenty-franc notes. She reckoned that was worth about twenty dollars, a fair enough price for a night with a top-end whore.

Her eyes had grown used to the dark now and she stood by the bed for a moment or two looking down at Clovis. He was handsome, and it had been a fun night until she got too drunk, but he was no gentleman, behaving as he did. There had been around three hundred francs in his wallet, and he could count himself fortunate she hadn't taken it all. But she wasn't and never would be a thief.

Then, after tucking the money into her little reticule, she

stole out of the room on tiptoe, leaving Clovis still snoring softly.

Downstairs in the reception hall a night porter was dozing at the desk, and Belle crept quietly past him and went into the small cloakroom where she had left her coat hours earlier, and which luckily was still there.

As she came out and was approaching the main doors, the night porter woke, sitting bolt upright.

'*Revenez au sommeil, doux monsieur,*' she said cheekily, and blew him a kiss. Madame Albertine had said this to one of the men on Christmas Day when he'd missed something she said, Belle was told it meant 'Go back to sleep, sweet sir.' Whether it did actually mean that she'd never know, but the porter grinned bashfully, and Belle slipped out of the door.

It was very cold out on the street and still dark. Belle followed the road down the hill because logically that had to lead to the harbour. She hoped a café would be open there, where she could get a hot drink and directions to the train station. It was fortunate her coat was long enough to hide her evening dress, as she would look very odd being seen in it by day. She would need to buy a warm everyday dress with some of Clovis's money. She couldn't of course go back to Madame Albertine's to collect her belongings and her savings.

As she walked down the deserted street, she felt desperately ashamed of herself and foolish, too, that she'd taken people into her confidence and allowed them to manipulate her. She was tired and she felt like bursting into tears. That was hardly surprising as she'd had so little sleep and had had to part with all her clothes and belongings. But on the plus side she was sure a hundred francs would be more than enough to get to Paris, and she did have the lovely evening dress to keep.

*

It was late afternoon when the train pulled into Paris. Belle had been fortunate in that before she reached Marseille harbour, she saw a sign to the station off to her left, and found she was just a couple of streets from it. A train was due to leave for Paris at six, in just half an hour, and a café was just opening where she bought a cup of coffee.

She fell asleep almost as soon as the train started moving, and only woke at midday because the other people in the carriage were making so much noise. They appeared to be all from the same family, two women in their mid-twenties, a man of around thirty, and a much older couple who were probably their parents. They were arguing, but it seemed to be good-natured as there was a lot of laughter, and they were passing out food from a basket.

The mother said something to Belle, which she assumed was an apology for waking her, and a little later offered her a slice of a savoury flan from her basket, soon followed by bread and cheese. Belle smiled and thanked her in the little French she'd learned in the last few days, but she was relieved that none of the group knew any English, so she didn't feel obliged to hold a conversation.

It was only as the train gradually chugged closer to Paris that she began to worry. To find a cheap room, a change of clothing and toiletries, all without speaking French, was daunting enough. But she knew she had to make some more money too, and somehow acquire some papers to get back into England. There had been no problem in Marseille, where an official had come aboard the ship to check on the crew's papers; Captain Rollins didn't mention he had any passengers and they didn't ask. Once the officials had left the ship, she was free to go. It wouldn't be like that going into England, that much Belle was sure of.

As she looked out of the carriage window at the flat, bare fields she was reminded of a similar view in the hospital house where she'd been in Paris. She wondered whether the French police would help her get back to England if she explained to them what had happened to her.

Something told her that wasn't a good idea. Hadn't she learned yet that she couldn't trust anyone?

Chapter Twenty-seven

The streets around the Gare de Lyon station in Paris were dimly lit and crowded with people who all seemed to be in a tearing hurry. It was dirty, noisy and smelly, much worse than Marseille, and Belle felt threatened by every man who glanced at her. On top of that it was very cold and starting to rain. There were hotels everywhere she looked, but there was nothing to say which were good, bad, expensive, cheap, safe or dangerous, for they were all equally shabby. She was very aware of her evening dress beneath her coat, and her shoes, designed to be worn indoors, were not suitable for traipsing along city streets. She was also hungry and very thirsty.

This wasn't the Paris of her imagination, with wide, tree-lined boulevards, grand buildings, ornate fountains and beautiful shops and stylish restaurants. Everywhere was so grey and dreary, and it brought back the memory that this was the city where she had been raped by five men.

How could she have expected anything good to happen to her here?

She came to a restaurant and stopped to look in the window. It was as cheerless as all the others but it was very busy. Most of the customers looked like office workers, so she thought it might be good value for money.

Belle took a seat at a table with two girls who weren't much older than her. They were neatly but plainly dressed, their hair scraped back from their faces. She smiled at them, and said *bonsoir*. They greeted her too, but returned to their conversation.

The menu meant nothing to Belle, so when the waitress

came for her order she pointed to what looked like a beef stew on one of the girls' plates. '*S'il vous plaît*,' she said with a smile. The waitress frowned. '*Je ne parle bien français*,' Belle added, feeling proud of herself for remembering that phrase.

As the waitress walked away, one of the girls asked if Belle was English. She nodded.

'You one time in France?' the girl asked.

'*Oui*,' Belle said, relieved the girl spoke English, even if not very well. 'I'm scared because I don't know which hotel to go to.'

The two girls looked at each other and then gabbled away in French together. 'You want clean hotel, not too much francs?' the first girl, the one with the darker hair, asked her.

Belle nodded.

The two girls consulted each other, then the darker one pulled a small notebook out of her handbag, tore out a page and scribbled on it with a pencil.

'This one good,' she said, handing it to Belle. 'Not be scared.'

She had written Hôtel Mirabeau, rue Parrott, and drawn a rough map to show it was in the street which ran roughly behind the one they were in. She smiled at Belle. '*Bonne chance*,' she said.

The Hôtel Mirabeau was as tired and shabby-looking as everywhere else. If it hadn't been for a peeling sign swinging above the front door, Belle wouldn't have noticed it as it was in the middle of a terrace, squeezed in between a bakery shop and a boot repairer's. But it was too cold on the street to look further afield, and her feet hurt too, so she walked up the three steps, pushed open the heavy door and entered.

The front door opened directly into a small sitting-area-cum-hall with a reception desk. Belle stood there looking around her for a moment or two before ringing the bell on the desk. The room, and the staircase which led off from it, had dark red paper on the walls, which made it appear cosy, and made a good backdrop for the large collection of paintings hanging there. They were all farming scenes: men reaping corn with a scythe, men riding home on a haycart, a shepherd with a flock of sheep. They'd obviously been painted by the same person, and Belle wondered if it was the owner of the hotel.

A bony, stoop-shouldered woman came through a door by the staircase. Her grimace was presumably the nearest she could get to a smile. Belle asked for a room, holding up one finger to signify it was for one person. The woman nodded and said fifty centimes.

That sounded cheap enough to Belle, so she agreed and was handed a key attached to a six-inch-long piece of metal, then the woman beckoned her to follow and led the way up to the fourth floor. She opened a door and Belle went in. It was a small room, the furniture and rug on the floor old, but it looked and smelled clean.

'Thank you,' Belle said. 'It's fine.' She was too tired now even to try to think what the French for that would be.

The woman gave her a hard look. 'No visitors,' she said in English. 'Two nights in advance. One franc, if you please.'

Belle blushed, assuming the woman knew what she was. But as she got her purse out she realized the woman was suspicious of her only because she had no luggage.

'I had my suitcase stolen,' she lied. 'Tomorrow I must buy new clothes.'

The woman nodded, but her face remained stern. '*Petit déjeuner de sept à neuf.*'

Belle understood the words for breakfast but not the rest. 'Which hour?' she asked, holding up her fingers.

'Seven until nine,' the woman said curtly. '*Salle de bain dans le couloir.*' Then she walked out, shutting the door behind her.

Belle assumed that meant the bathroom was down the corridor. She prodded the bed. It was hard and almost certainly lumpy, but she resisted the urge to cry. Instead, she thought how good the meal she'd just eaten was, congratulated herself on finding a room, and told herself that everything would look better in the morning.

Belle woke at the sound of people in the passage outside her room. She knelt up in bed and pulled the curtain back a little. The sky was getting light, so she guessed it to be around seven-thirty, but there was no view, just the houses opposite which looked much the same as those on her side of the street.

She had slept well. The bed had been surprisingly comfortable, the sheets had smelled of lavender and the blankets and eiderdown were very warm. She put her coat over the camisole she'd slept in, picked up the very thin towel folded on the chair, and went to find the bathroom.

The bathroom was very clean, though very cold, and the water was cold too. But she took off her camisole, stood in the bath and washed herself all over. She wished she had a toothbrush as her mouth tasted nasty.

Fifteen minutes later Belle went down to the dining room. To her surprise it was an unexpectedly warm and inviting room painted bright yellow. The tablecloths on the six tables were blue check, and a stove was blazing away. She took the empty table closest to the stove, wrapping her coat tightly round her so her evening dress couldn't be seen. There were two couples eating, and one man alone who was reading a newspaper. He glanced at Belle and half smiled.

The woman from the night before came in shortly after Belle had sat down, carrying a tray. This was the breakfast, a pot of coffee, a jug of milk, some croissants in a basket, butter and jam. The woman wasn't as old as Belle had thought the previous night, probably only in her thirties, but she made no effort with her appearance. Her worn black dress fitted where it touched her and her hair was in such a tight bun that it looked as though she'd painted her head a dull brown. She also had a black and white checked scarf tied around her neck which looked very odd, almost as if it was hiding something on her neck. The previous evening she'd worn one too, but that had been plain black and less obvious.

There was nothing at all about the woman to suggest Belle had anything in common with her, but she couldn't resist attempting to befriend her, if only to discover who painted the pictures in the hall.

As she put the breakfast on the table Belle smiled at her. 'What is your name?' she asked.

The woman half smiled back, which was an improvement on the night before. 'Gabrielle Herrison,' she said.

'I'm Belle Cooper,' Belle said. 'Later, could you tell me where to buy some second-hand clothes?'

Gabrielle's face softened marginally. 'I find you leetle map,' she said. 'Good shop near.'

Belle was apprehensive as she entered Madame Chantal's little shop. Madame Herrison didn't look the kind of woman who knew anything about clothes, so she expected the shop she'd recommended to be like the second-hand clothes shops back in Seven Dials. They reeked of mildew, stale sweat and worse, and the clothes, all jumbled up together, were usually so shabby that only someone really desperate would buy them. But to Belle's surprise, in this shop the clothes were hung neatly on rails, and she could smell nothing other than freshly made coffee.

A small woman with greying hair, wearing a black dress with a mink collar and cuffs, came towards her, greeting her in French. Belle thought she was probably asking what she was looking for. She asked if the woman spoke English, but the answer was a shake of the head. So Belle took off her coat to show the lace evening dress and mimed someone running off with her suitcase. Surprisingly the woman appeared to understand as she nodded and indicated a rail of ordinary day dresses.

Belle looked through them. They were all good, plain dresses, but she needed something with a bit more flair if she wanted to hook some rich men.

Perhaps the owner noted her lack of enthusiasm as she looked through the rail of dresses because she said something Belle couldn't understand and held out a two-piece costume for her to look at.

It was pale blue with darker blue embroidery on the figure-hugging jacket. It looked as if it had been very expensive and it was much closer to what Belle had in mind. But the colour was all wrong. Belle smiled and nodded, so the woman knew she approved, then pointed to a purple dress and a red one, and back to the costume.

The woman nodded. After rummaging through the rails for a minute or two she pulled out a red costume with black frogging across the chest which made it look slightly military, and a purple one with a black velvet collar and cuffs.

Belle held the red one up to herself and looked in the mirror. It would be perfect as long as it fitted, classy and fashionable but just a bit racy, and the colour really suited her.

The woman led her to a cubicle at the back of the shop to try it on. She pointed to a silk label in the jacket which said 'Renee' and Belle realized she was trying to say it was special, not just made by an ordinary dressmaker. Belle could tell by the feel of the fabric, the stitching and even the cut of the costume that it had belonged to a rich woman. She could hardly wait to put it on.

The shopkeeper was gabbling away in French just outside the cubicle, and Belle was fairly certain she was giving it a big sales pitch, saying it belonged to someone young and beautiful just like her. The moment she had fastened the skirt at her waist, she could see the owner must have been the same height and size, for it was the perfect length, just an inch from the floor, and clung to her hips like a second skin. She held her breath as she slipped the jacket on, willing it not to be too small, and it wasn't; like the skirt, it was a perfect fit.

'*Magnifique! Il est fait pour vous,*' the shopkeeper crowed as Belle came out of the cubicle, and she had to assume that meant it was perfect for her.

It was indeed perfect in every way. The fit made her waist look tiny, the colour contrasted well with her dark hair, and the military style frogging gave it a slightly saucy air.

'*Combien?*' Belle asked. That was one word she'd learned from Madame Albertine while in the market with her.

'*Vingt francs,*' the shopkeeper replied, and put up all her fingers twice.

Belle swallowed hard. She knew that twenty francs was a very reasonable price for such a beautiful costume, but it would make a huge hole in the money she had. She needed the right clothes to make more money, but what if her plan in the hotels didn't work? What then? Besides, she also needed a change of underwear, an ordinary day dress and a better pair of shoes.

The shopkeeper was looking at her questioningly, and Belle pointed to her shoes, lifted her skirt to show she had no petticoat, and finally touched one of the day dresses. She took twenty-five francs out of her reticule and showed it to the woman.

She certainly understood what Belle was trying to tell her, but she didn't like it. She muttered and rolled her eyes, and paced up and down looking angry, but Belle held her ground and just looked crestfallen. Finally the woman calmed down and walked to the back of the shop where she had shoes, returning with several pairs, all in excellent condition. The little side-buttoned black ankle boots fitted Belle perfectly; they had a small heel and looked very elegant.

Next the woman pulled out a light grey wool dress. The bodice was buttoned down the front and it had appliquéd darker grey flowers on one side. Belle liked it because it would be warm, and suitable for almost any occasion. She indicated she would like to try it on. At that the woman went to a basket and brought out some petticoats, drawers and camisoles, which she shoved at Belle, as if saying she was to sort through them and pick what she wanted.

It was nearly an hour later when Belle walked gleefully out of the shop in the grey dress and her new shoes. The underwear she'd selected, the red costume and her evening dress and shoes were tied up in brown paper. She had got everything for twenty-five francs, but she felt a little guilty about the poor shopkeeper.

Further down the same street she noticed a shop selling feathers, beads, veiling and flowers for hats. She stood for some time looking at the window display and reminded herself that she was going to be a milliner when she got back to England. Focusing on that made her feel stronger and more determined. She wasn't just going to make enough money to get back to England, but a nest egg too, so she could hold up her head when she got home.

Along with a toothbrush and a tiny pot of face cream, Belle also bought a second-hand hat, a black fur one which was as close as she could get to the one that had matched her coat which she'd had to leave in Marseille. The previous day she'd felt only half dressed without a hat, but now once again she felt complete.

Madame Herrison was in the hall when Belle got back.

'You find something nice?' she asked.

Belle was so delighted with her purchases that she was

only too happy to show them off, and as she showed them to the hotel owner, she could feel the woman growing warmer. She held the red costume to Belle's shoulders and smiled.

'It is your colour,' she said. 'I think it will bring you good luck.'

'*Merci, madame,*' Belle said, and she was rewarded by a smile which lit up the woman's face and took ten years off her.

Everything Belle knew about working hotels came from one of the girls back in New Orleans who claimed to have lived this way for several months in Washington and made a great deal of money. But however brilliant a plan it was in theory, Belle found the prospect of it terrifying. She was well aware that prostitution was illegal in Paris, even if the city did have a reputation for tolerance. She had visions of a couple of gendarmes frogmarching her off and throwing her in a cell. Obviously there were thousands of whores in Paris, whether walking the streets, in brothels or working hotels, and she just wished she knew some of them to find out how it all worked.

On her second day in Paris Belle bought a street map and checked out some of the hotels near the Champs-Elysées, assuming this would be where the best ones were. Some turned out to be seedy-looking, others she dismissed because they had very alert-looking doormen and she felt she'd never be able to pull her plan off there. Other hotels looked smart on the outside, but while watching people coming and going she found the guests were very ordinary, and she needed a hotel that catered for the seriously rich.

In the end she asked a doorman about hotels, pretending that she was looking for a place for her aunt and mother to stay. He gave her a list of four hotels, then added the Hôtel Ritz in Place Vendôme. He smirked as he did so. '*Vous devez être très riche pour y rester,*' he said.

She was fairly certain he'd said you had to be very rich to

stay there, so she immediately felt that had to be the right place for her.

Place Vendôme was a large square, which looked almost circular as the buildings were bevelled at the corners with just two entrances to the square, one on each side. Belle knew right away that it was a very special place as the beautiful symmetrical buildings were possibly two centuries older than the ones on the wide boulevards she'd seen while she was walking about, and only four storeys high rather than the six that appeared to be the norm in the city. In the centre of the paved square was a huge bronze pillar, and as she stood there looking up at it, wondering if it was Napoleon on the top, she overheard an English gentleman in a frock coat and top hat explaining to his wife that it had been made out of hundreds of cannons that Napoleon had captured in his battles. As she watched, the couple went into one of the many jewellers around the square. Anyone could see just by looking at the displays in the windows of these shops that they were not for ordinary people: sparkling diamond necklaces, rings with huge sapphires, emeralds and rubies so magnificent they almost took her breath away.

The Ritz did not shout its presence in the square, in fact she had to look quite hard to see the discreet gold signs above the doors. She remembered Mog telling her that the very best hotels in London were the ones that had quiet dignity. The Ritz certainly had that, and she hoped that because it was so grand and expensive few other girls would have the nerve to try their hand there. Whether this was a wise plan she didn't know, but Martha had always said her girls should aim high.

By the time Belle got back to the Mirabeau to change she was tired as she'd walked miles following her map. She knew that soon she must learn to use the Métropolitain train – after all, people in London used the underground all the time and the one here couldn't be that different. But she had only been on the underground once with her mother, and she'd found it very confusing.

Yet walking had been good as she'd seen the Arc du Triomphe and caught sight of the amazing Eiffel Tower, which she remembered being told at school was the tallest building in the world. She'd also wandered into places that were every bit as squalid and frightening as their counterparts in London. She told herself she would explore the whole city bit by bit and learn to love it. She would go into milliners' shops and look at their hats to get ideas, and indeed study all aspects of French fashion. But before all that, she had to take the plunge and go back to the Ritz tonight.

Belle's nerve almost left her when she got back to Place Vendôme at seven-thirty. She knew she looked good in her red costume with her hair pinned up, but the enormity of what she intended to do, and the possibility she might be forcibly thrown out of the Ritz, made her knees knock together.

She had thought the Place Vendôme intimidating enough by day, but seen by gaslight, with dozens of private carriages waiting, some of which even had coats of arms on the doors, and a sprinkling of gleaming motor cars, she felt out of her depth. Just the way the light from the twinkling crystal chandelier in the entrance hall of the hotel shone out through the glass on the shiny wood doors, or the huge flower arrangement she caught a glimpse of as she walked by, spoke of famous guests, possibly even royalty.

Belle took a deep breath, put her head up and walked purposefully towards the door. She was terrified, but she wasn't going to back away now. Rich men always wanted women. She could do this.

'*Bonsoir, mademoiselle,*' the liveried doorman said with a smile as he opened the door for her.

She tried to act as if she frequented such places all the time, but before her was a long, wide corridor of white marble with the thickest, most sumptuous cobalt-blue carpet running down it she'd ever seen. There were marble statues, more huge displays of spectacular flowers, glittering chandeliers, and all the wood doors gleamed like looking-glasses. It made her think that this was how the Palace of Versailles must have looked back in the day of Louis XIV.

Fortunately there were dozens of people around, which made her feel a little less uneasy. Some were checking in at the desk, others just leaving or arriving for dinner. The women were all very elegantly dressed, dripping with jewels, and many sporting the kind of fur coats Belle guessed cost hundreds of pounds. She saw porters wheeling trolleys piled high with leather luggage, a poignant reminder of how she'd left her cardboard suitcase in Marseille. The richness of it dazzled her, and she felt profound envy for people who lived this way and knew no other. Yet looking at the women objectively, she saw that none were that beautiful, and some were even very plain.

Two men in early middle age were standing together talking. Out of the corner of her eye she saw them interrupt their conversation to look at her, and she turned slightly, keeping her head down, then lifted it and smiled mischievously at them before dropping her eyes again.

She knew that it would be impossible to solicit directly here in the foyer of the hotel, but that wasn't her plan. She had been told that all hotel concierges had girls they could supply to residents for a large fee, and she believed the concierge here would be no different, except that he would be more discerning than those in less grand hotels.

Belle positioned herself by an ornate gilded demi-lune table and stood there looking around as if waiting to meet someone. She caught the eye of another man and smiled, then dropped her eyes. Even with her eyes cast down she could feel he was studying her, and she sensed that he liked what he saw.

She was taken back momentarily to Martha's. She had always felt powerful when men came in and gave her that look which said they wanted her. She felt it again now and it stopped her being afraid. She felt good.

'*Est-ce que je peux vous aider?*'

Belle was startled by the question. She hadn't seen or heard the man approach her. He was around fifty, slim, with greying hair and a neatly trimmed moustache and goatee beard. His eyes were small and very dark and he wore a plain black suit. She couldn't tell from his clothes if he worked for the hotel or not, but she sensed that he did.

'I don't speak French,' she said, though she was fairly certain he'd asked if he could help her.

'I speak English,' he said, almost as if he was English himself. 'I am Monsieur Pascal, the concierge. I asked if I could help you. Are you waiting for someone?'

'Yes, maybe it's you,' she said flirtatiously, batting her eyelashes at him.

He almost smiled, but checked it. Belle guessed he had come over because he was suspicious of her, but he couldn't be sure whether she was a whore looking for business, or someone genuinely waiting for a friend or family member. She thought it was good he couldn't tell. From what she'd been told, the average concierge could always sniff whores out, so her clothes and demeanour must be pretty convincing.

'Are you waiting for someone who is a guest here?' he asked.

Belle knew she had to take a chance. It was a case of heads she would win, tails she would lose. He might have her ejected forcibly, but on the other hand he might see her as a little extra income.

'I could be,' she said, looking right into his eyes. 'I think that might depend on you.'

She saw his Adam's apple leap up and down. Gulping was usually a sign of uncertainty, and she guessed he was pausing while he considered what she'd said. She continued to look him in the eye, a confident half-smile on her lips.

'I think we should continue this conversation somewhere less public,' he said eventually, his voice dropping.

Belle felt like cheering. He wouldn't take her anywhere if he wasn't half-way interested in her. He'd just usher her to the door and tell her to leave or he'd call the gendarmes. 'That's fine with me,' she said.

Some twenty minutes later Belle was walking back to her hotel. She thought Pascal would make a good poker player as he hadn't revealed anything about himself, or even compromised his position at the hotel. He had taken her to a small room along the long corridor which looked as though it was used by guests for business meetings, furnished with a large table and eight chairs. He asked her to sit down, then sat down opposite her and asked point blank what it was that she wanted. She said she wished to be put in touch with gentlemen who wanted a partner for the evening when they were alone in Paris. He responded by asking her why she thought he or anyone else in this hotel would wish to get involved with such arrangements.

'To make your guests happy,' she said, trying to look as if she'd done this before.

He made no response to that, which puzzled Belle even more. He had no real reason to bring her to this room; he could have put these questions to her in the foyer where there were so many people milling around that they wouldn't have been overheard. She hadn't even vaguely alluded to sex, nor had she said anything about a fee for her services. If she had been more naive she might have thought he didn't understand what she meant.

But experience told Belle he not only knew exactly what she was offering, but he also wanted her for himself. His dark eyes might have no expression, and his manner was starchy, but he had very fleshy lips, something she had often observed meant a passionate nature.

'I believe a concierge can earn more than his regular weekly wage just by helping a guest out with something special,' she said with a smile. 'Isn't that enough reason to get involved?'

'So you think you are special?' he sneered.

'Of course, that's why I came here, to the place where all the most special people stay.'

He looked at her without speaking for what seemed at least five minutes, though it was probably only seconds. When he finally spoke his tone was very curt. 'Give me your address. If I have anything for you I will send a message to you.'

Belle had a moment of fear as she handed over a slip of paper with the address of the Mirabeau, realizing he could merely pass it on to the police and get her arrested. But her instinct said that was not his intention; he was interested in making some money but he just wasn't prepared to admit it yet.

It was a cold night and she shivered as she walked home, wishing she'd worn her coat. But however cold she was, walking up Rue de la Paix towards Boulevard des Capucines, she was seeing the Paris she had always imagined, with its wide, tree-lined boulevards. She thought of all those women in the hotel foyer in their fur coats and glittering jewels and how much she'd like to live their kind of life, and she felt utterly certain that Monsieur Pascal was going to contact her and make it happen for her.

'*Un message pour vous, mademoiselle,*' a young boy's voice trilled out.

It was three in the afternoon the following day, and very

cold. Belle was lying under the eiderdown on her bed, reading an English novel she'd found on a shelf in the dining room. She was almost asleep, but at the boy's call she was wide awake and leaping to her feet.

The dark-haired boy was Gabrielle's thirteen-year-old son, Henri. Belle had seen him briefly at breakfast that morning.

'*Merci*,' she said, almost snatching the envelope out of his hand. But then, remembering her manners, she beckoned for him to wait and got her purse. She gave him a centime, and thanked him again.

The note was short but to the point. 'Monsieur Garcia would like your company tonight at six-thirty for supper, followed by the theatre. Be at the hotel restaurant at six-fifteen pm and say you are meeting Monsieur Garcia. I shall come in to speak to you before he arrives.' The note was signed Edouard Pascal.

Although Belle was full of trepidation on arriving at the Ritz, she needn't have worried. She just smiled at the doorman and asked him to direct her to the restaurant, where she told the maître d'hôtel Monsieur Garcia had booked a table. Her coat was taken, she was shown to a corner table and offered a drink while she waited, and just a minute or two later Pascal came in. He greeted her for the benefit of the dining-room staff as if she were a relative he'd just dropped in to see for a minute or two. In a low voice he told her he'd already dealt with the fee with Garcia and he discreetly handed her an envelope which contained her share, a hundred francs.

While behaving outwardly in the relaxed manner of an uncle, he scrutinized her, approved her black lace evening dress and the lack of paint on her face. But then in a low voice he went on to caution her that she was to behave like a lady at all times, for a gentleman of Garcia's standing would not want anyone to guess he had paid for a companion.

Finally he said that Garcia would be bringing her back here after the theatre, but he would have a fiacre waiting to take her home at twelve-thirty. He kissed her on both cheeks as he was leaving, but whispered a barely veiled threat that if she stepped out of line in any way she would be sorry.

The threat was enough to make Belle nervous. Then, when Bernard Garcia arrived a few minutes later, her heart sank even further, for he was short and fat, with just a few strands of sandy hair trailing across an otherwise bald head. He was at least fifty-five, perhaps older, and even his expensive hand-tailored dinner jacket and gold fob watch peeping from his waistcoat pocket could never make him attractive as a partner.

But he spoke near-perfect English and he looked at Belle as if he was the luckiest man in the world, and that endeared him to her. He made small talk about how cold it was, and said he had come to Paris on the train from Boulogne that afternoon and he'd had to take a hot bath to warm up. Then, when the waiter came with the menus, he asked what she'd like to eat.

'You choose for me. I'm sure you know what they do best here,' she said, for a menu in French was far beyond her. She smiled and patted his arm affectionately as if she was utterly delighted to spend the evening with him.

Maybe it was the superb red wine he ordered, or just his courteous manner, but she soon felt relaxed and happy to be Bernard's companion for the evening. Despite his unprepossessing appearance he had a beautiful deep, melodious voice and a comfortable way about him. They talked mainly about England, which he knew very well. He didn't tell her about his personal circumstances, and didn't ask about hers.

The play he took her to after supper was *Madame Sans-Gêne*, by Victorien Sardou. Although he did explain what it was about to Belle, she couldn't really follow it. But she didn't mind. It was just wonderful to be sitting on a red plush chair in a box, knowing that many of the elegantly dressed people in the theatre were looking up at her and wondering who she was.

This was so much better than working at Martha's where she had to accommodate ten or twelve different men in one night. While she was dreading the moment when they got back to the hotel room, because she sensed Bernard had high expectations, the chances were that he'd fall asleep very quickly.

But she was totally wrong about that. Bernard ordered champagne for them when they got back to the hotel, and asked that she sit on the bed to drink it wearing only her stockings and camisole.

Sensing he was the kind who had fantasies about wanton women, she was happy to behave like one. She writhed about on the bed letting him get a good look at her, and when he still remained sitting in an armchair, she went over to him and sat astride his lap, taking one of his hands and placing it on her breast, the other on her vagina. His face was getting more and more flushed, his dark eyes glittered, and he pawed at her frantically but ineffectually, as if he had never touched a woman's body before.

She unbuttoned his trousers and put her hand in, but to her surprise his penis was terribly small, no bigger than a small boy's. It wasn't even hard, and she realized that her plan to stay astride him was never going to work.

'Come and lie down on the bed with me,' she suggested, taking him by the hand and drawing him out of the chair.

The most disconcerting thing about Bernard was not his inexperienced fumbling or his tiny penis, but the way he didn't speak. He'd talked so easily over supper in fluent English, chatted through the interval at the theatre and on the fiacre ride back to the hotel, but since asking her to undress he'd said nothing. This was something she'd never come across before; in fact she'd found men with tiny penises were usually inclined to talk more than other men. Not only did they claim it was small because they'd been drinking, but very often they were the ones who liked to talk dirty too. He remained silent, however, even when she began to undress him.

After an hour Belle seriously considered offering Bernard his hundred francs back, thanking him for the supper and theatre and making a rush for the door. She had tried so hard to get him to ejaculate, but nothing, rubbing him, licking him, worked. His cock remained flaccid, and he was still silent.

The good supper and the wine they'd had with it, then the champagne since they got back to his room were making her sleepy, yet she was cold too from being outside the bedclothes. Finally she felt she had to concede she was never going to make it happen, and sitting up in the bed she drew him to her breasts to cuddle him, with the intention of admitting she was defeated.

But all at once he began sucking at her breast like a hungry baby, and when she slid her hand down the bed towards his penis, she found it had suddenly grown hard. He groaned as she touched it, and sucked harder at her nipple. Belle was so encouraged that she held it more firmly. She thought there was something a bit unhealthy about him responding only to the combination of breast suckling and masturbation, but she was so relieved that she'd finally found the secret to get him going that she didn't care why that was.

He came within a few minutes, and it was only then that he found his voice and called her 'nurse'. When she looked down at him he had tears in his eyes.

Within ten minutes he was sound asleep, still with his face pressed to her breast. She wondered who the nurse was, and how old he was when he'd had a similar experience with her. Belle had a strong feeling he'd never had ordinary sex with a woman. She wished then that she had asked him earlier if he was married and had children. She knew nothing personal about him.

She waited until quarter past twelve, then wriggled away from him, got up and dressed herself. She scribbled a little note for him, thanking him for a lovely evening, and left it on the pillow, then silently let herself out of the room.

The doorman on duty was not the one who'd directed her to the dining room earlier that evening or opened the door when they came back from the theatre, and if he thought it odd that a woman was leaving to go home alone so late at night, he didn't show it. He helped her into the fiacre, smiled warmly when she tipped him, and so Belle thought that maybe it was commonplace to him.

But as the fiacre rumbled along the deserted streets Belle felt happy. In one night she'd earned far more than most women earned in a month, she'd had a lovely supper and been to the theatre too, plus she'd managed to give Bernard what he wanted. Respectable people might consider that distasteful and sinful, but she didn't care what they thought. As far as she was concerned, helping an inadequate man with sexual problems to find some release was a good and kind thing.

Chapter Twenty-eight

January slipped into February, then on into March, and Belle was still at the Hôtel Mirabeau, and still earning a hundred francs each time Pascal arranged for her to meet a gentleman.

She had moved into a bigger and sunnier room on the first floor which had a tiny wrought-iron balcony overlooking the back yards and gardens. She had bought more clothes, shoes and hats, learned enough French to be able to hold a simple conversation, and she could find her way around Paris like a native.

If Gabrielle Herrison had worked out for herself what her English guest did for a living, it didn't seem to trouble her. If she was up when Belle returned in the early morning, she always got her some coffee and a couple of croissants, even if it was too early for breakfast. She offered to wash her clothes too, and Belle in turn bought Gabrielle flowers each week as a token of her appreciation. Gabrielle wasn't one for conversation, just a smile and a few words now and then, but in those few words Belle sensed the woman liked her and cared about her.

Belle was very curious about her landlady. She felt there was a good story there, as Gabrielle had told her the pictures in the hall had been painted by a man friend who had died. Belle felt certain he had been Gabrielle's lover, for her eyes grew misty when she looked at the pictures. She hoped one day Gabrielle would tell her about him.

Belle went out with gentlemen three or four nights a week. It was rarely with someone staying at the Ritz; Pascal had connections in many different areas. But whether the arrangement was to meet up in another hotel, a restaurant or even the gentleman's own home, they were always very rich and possibly influential men.

Belle had assumed that Bernard, her first client, was an oddity, but in fact most of the men she met through Pascal had some kind of quirk, and they were often much stranger than Bernard. She had one who asked her to walk around naked in the moonlight while he masturbated, and another who wanted to be spanked with a slipper. She'd had a couple of men who had wanted to play rough with her too, but fortunately she'd been able to extricate herself quickly before any real harm was done. One man wanted her to order him around and liked her to swear at him if he disobeyed her. There had even been one man who liked to play horses. He crawled on his hands and knees and she had to ride naked on his back. At least half of her gentlemen didn't seem to be able to manage penetrative sex.

She remembered how Etienne had told her she should try to love her clients. That was a tall order, but she did genuinely find plenty to like about most of them, for so far they had all been intelligent and usually interesting. She never failed to act as if each of them was very special to her. And she knew she was successful at this as many of her gentlemen had asked to see her again and made further arrangements with Pascal.

Almost daily she counted up the money she'd made. Although she had enough to get home now, she felt she must earn more so that she could return in triumph, a proud survivor with a nest egg to start her hat shop. She didn't want to be dependent on her mother and Mog.

She daydreamed constantly of walking into the kitchen back home and surprising Mog. She could almost hear her shrieks of delight and imagine being enfolded in her arms. It was harder to imagine her mother's reaction: she would of course be thrilled to have her daughter home, but Annie had never been one for showing her feelings or demonstrating affection.

Then there was Jimmy. He might be married now of course, or at least have a young lady, but Belle was sure he would want to see her, if only for old times' sake, and she so looked forward to seeing him again.

Yet much as she dreamed of home, and longed to be there, she also knew she would never be able to enjoy the freedom there that she had here in Paris. She sometimes chatted to English people she met in the cafés of Montmartre and St-Germain and they all said that what they loved most about Paris was its lack of prudishness, its gaiety and sense of fun. She had noticed herself that Parisians didn't seem to care much about class; they embraced artists, poets, writers and musicians as being just as vital as doctors, lawyers or any other professionals. She had never once been asked how she made a living, and though she suspected most people she'd met assumed she had private means because of how she dressed, she felt certain that if she was to say she was a dancer or an actress they wouldn't think any less of her. Back home that wouldn't be so.

She rarely felt lonely here either. She had little chats with other guests, though mostly they were only in Paris for a few days at most, and she had got to know people in the cafés she regularly ate or had coffee in. On top of that she had wonderful nights out with her gentlemen, seeing shows at the Moulin Rouge and other cabaret clubs, plays and operas. She had eaten in most of Paris's finest restaurants, danced in night clubs and spent nights in luxurious hotels and splendid houses and apartments. It was going to be difficult to fit back into her old life, being told what to do and being looked on as a curiosity by everyone in Seven Dials because she'd been gone for so long.

That was why it was so important she went home with money so she could get her hat shop. She visited all the Paris milliners to see the latest fashions. She bought millinery magazines to study them, and on nights when she was alone in her room she was always sketching and working out how each design could be made. She had even considered finding a small apartment so she would have room to buy the necessary equipment and materials to make up her designs and sell them. That way she could go home with her head held high and announce she had become a milliner.

Happy as she was in Paris, there was one niggling problem, and that was Pascal. She had been wary of him at the start, because she sensed he wanted her, but she had come to think she was mistaken about that, because once he'd learned to trust her, she had very little direct contact with him.

Her instructions about who her client was, and where and what time he wanted her to meet him, came by messenger. Paris was full of young boys happy to deliver a letter for a few centimes. Then her client would hand her a sealed envelope containing her fee. It was only when she had to meet a gentleman at the Ritz that she saw Pascal, and even then they rarely went beyond a nod to each other.

But at the beginning of March he'd sent her a note asking her to meet him in a café in Montmartre. As he'd never asked to meet her anywhere before, she thought perhaps he wanted to stop their arrangement because he was afraid of his employer finding out, or that one of her clients had made a complaint about her.

Pascal was already in Le Moulin à Vent, which was close to the still to be completed Sacré-Coeur basilica on La Butte, drinking a glass of absinthe. Just the way he sat hunched over his drink suggested it was not his first, and he had such a sour expression she expected trouble.

'Ah, Belle,' he exclaimed as he saw her, and got somewhat

unsteadily to his feet. He called the waiter and asked for another glass of absinthe for her, but Belle refused it and asked for a glass of wine. He spent some time trying to convince her absinthe was the only thing to drink in Paris, but Belle had tried it before and didn't like it. Since then she'd noted that most of the habitual drunks never drank anything else.

'So why did you want to meet me?' she asked, once she'd got her glass of wine. 'Is something wrong?'

'Must there be something wrong for me to ask you to have a drink with me?' he said.

'Not at all,' she said. 'But it is unusual, so I thought you had a problem.'

'I do,' he said, then downed his glass in one and called rather loudly for another. 'My problem is that you spend the night with many other men, but not me.'

Belle's heart sank because she knew he wasn't a man to be flirtatious. He meant it.

'We have a business arrangement. It wouldn't do to mix business with pleasure,' she replied, smiling in the hope that he wouldn't take offence.

'I would pay you,' he said.

Belle cringed inwardly. The truth was that she found Pascal repellent. He was so slimy. She had watched him talking to the guests at the Ritz and he all but licked their backsides. He put oil on his hair which smelled sickeningly like violets, and his hands were too white and smooth for a man. But it was the way he looked at her which made her flesh crawl, so intense, so calculating. His eyes were almost reptilian, with no expression in them. He had no joy or warmth in him. It seemed strange that such a man would want a woman at all.

'No, Monsieur Pascal, I am very happy with how our arrangement has been, and I do not wish it to change.'

She didn't mind that his cut from what she earned was probably far bigger than hers. She understood too that to keep his job he had to be obsequious to important guests and the owners and managers of the hotel. But there was something more about him which she couldn't quite put her finger on, something dark and perhaps dangerous.

'You must call me Edouard,' he said, putting one of his soft white hands over hers and leaning so close to her she could smell garlic on his breath. 'I could give you so much more than you have now.'

Belle felt the only way out of the situation was to make light of it.

'I have everything I want,' she said, removing her hand from his. 'And I think, sir, that you are a little drunk and might regret saying such foolish things tomorrow.'

She left the café soon afterwards but with a heavy heart because she sensed that was not the end of it.

Everyone said Paris in the spring was not to be missed. There were already daffodils in window boxes, green shoots on trees, and the days were getting warmer. Belle resolved that night that the incident with Pascal was a timely reminder she must go home. She decided she would just stay another couple of weeks, until after Easter which fell at the end of the first week in April, then slip off without telling him she was going.

On the Tuesday morning after Easter young Henri brought her up a note which Pascal had sent round. It said that she was to be ready at seven that evening when a fiacre would pick her up to take her to meet Philippe Le Brun in Montmartre. Belle was delighted as she'd already had three nights with Philippe and liked the big, jovial man who had vineyards in Bordeaux and owned two large restaurants in Paris. She had bought a beautiful second-hand silver evening dress with matching shoes from Chantal's just the week before, which she'd been waiting for the right opportunity to wear. Philippe was the kind of man who liked to be seen in public with a pretty girl, so she knew he'd take her to a cabaret show, and the evening would be about eating, drinking, dancing and having fun, not just sex in a hotel room.

She went straight out and got her hair washed and put up at the hairdresser's near the Mirabeau, then during the afternoon had a leisurely bath as for once the water was hot.

Belle went downstairs to wait for the cab just before seven. Gabrielle was writing something at her desk and looked up and smiled as she saw Belle. '*Vous êtes belle,*' she said.

Belle blushed at being told she looked beautiful – it was the first time Gabrielle had made any kind of personal comment. She thanked her and said she was being taken out for dinner.

Gabrielle looked at her so long and hard that Belle felt a shiver of fear go down her spine. 'Be careful,' the older woman said softly, this time speaking in English. 'I fear you are playing with fire.'

There was something in the woman's eyes that told Belle she not only knew what Belle was doing, but had been on that road herself.

'I shall be going back home soon,' Belle replied.

At that she heard the clatter of the cab outside on the street and moved towards the door. Gabrielle got up from her desk and caught hold of Belle's arm. 'If you get in trouble is there anyone you trust that I can contact for you?' she asked.

The question chilled Belle still further, for she couldn't think of anyone. She shook her head, but a second later thought of Etienne. 'I once knew a man called Etienne Carrera,' she said, but made a helpless gesture with her hands. 'But he came from Marseille and I have no address for him.'

'Then you must keep safe and go home soon,' Gabrielle said. 'Tonight last time?'

Belle sensed her landlady really did care about her and nodded agreement to her wish. 'Last time.'

Gabrielle took her hand and squeezed it. Belle smiled weakly and broke away to go out to the cab.

Gabrielle's words and her manner had stripped away the happy anticipation Belle had felt earlier. It had been a very mild day, and although it was growing dark now the streets were still very busy with both traffic and people. As the fiacre made its way to Montmartre all the sounds and smells unexpectedly reminded her of the day she was bundled into a carriage in Seven Dials. It wasn't something she was in the habit of remembering – so much had happened since then that she tended only to look ahead, never glancing back over her shoulder. But now she had a queasy feeling in her belly, suddenly aware she had in fact been at risk each night she went out to meet a new man. She had trusted Pascal's judgement about all of them, yet in reality any one of them could have been another Mr Kent.

She reasoned with herself that she'd be quite safe tonight; after all, she knew Philippe Le Brun. But she decided she would keep her word to Gabrielle and tonight would be the end of it. Tomorrow she'd pack her bag and go.

Montmartre, or La Butte as many people called it, was Belle's favourite part of Paris. She loved the spectacular views of the city, the narrow, winding cobbled streets and the many cafés and restaurants frequented by free-thinking bohemians. She had been told that it had once been a very bad area full of thieves, prostitutes and anarchists, the sort of dangerous place upright Parisians steered clear of. But as artists, poets, writers and musicians moved in because of the cheap rents, it gradually became fashionable to be seen there. As a result rents went up, and many of the struggling artists moved to Montparnasse and St-Germain on the Left Bank. Now, with the beautiful Sacré-Coeur basilica near completion, and new houses replacing the earlier hovels, it was clear that a renaissance was on its way. Belle had told Philippe at their last meeting how much she liked Montmartre, and as one of his restaurants was just at the bottom of the hill in the Pigalle, she assumed this was why he'd asked her to meet him here.

The fiacre turned off the brightly lit and rowdy Boulevard de Clichy by the Moulin Rouge, then crossed another road which Belle recognized as one where she'd found a lovely hat shop. There were many good restaurants in this street and she expected the driver to stop there, but instead he turned right and drove up a steep, narrow, much darker cobbled street which was mainly just houses.

Belle was surprised when he reined in the horses almost at the top of the hill.

'*Voilà, madame*,' he said as he opened the door for her, pointing out a tall, thin house with shuttered windows on her right. She couldn't see very well as the nearest street lamp was right at the top of the street by a café; she thought it was one she'd been in just a couple of weeks earlier.

The fiacre drove off as she was ringing the bell on the front door. Although she could hear an accordion playing somewhere near, the street was very quiet, so she surmised this was Philippe's home, though he hadn't said he lived in Montmartre.

The clanging of the bell had barely died away when the door was opened, not by Philippe or his maid, but by Edouard Pascal. Belle's heart sank.

'Monsieur Pascal!' she exclaimed. 'What a surprise!' But assuming he was just visiting Philippe, because she didn't wish him to sense her dismay, or offend Philippe, she smiled, and accepted a kiss on each cheek.

'How beautiful you look tonight,' he said, once she had

stepped into the hall and the door was closed behind her. 'Let me take your wrap.'

She thanked him politely and let him take her short silver fox cape from her shoulders. This had been her one extravagance. It was from Chantal's, like all her clothes, but it had cost two hundred francs and she'd spent days agonizing over whether she should spend so much. But it was so beautiful, and when she wore it she felt like royalty. 'Where is Philippe?' she asked.

'He was called out on an urgent matter and asked me to look after you until he returns,' Pascal said. 'Come in by the fire, he won't be long.'

Most of the apartments and houses Belle had been to in Paris had been furnished and decorated in a very sumptuous manner, but she had often thought them lacking in character. The drawing room Edouard took her into was by contrast very homely, with large couches, a roaring fire, walls lined with books, a great many ornaments on low tables and a thick Chinese carpet underfoot. Yet it didn't seem to fit Philippe's exuberant character.

'This is Philippe's home?' she asked. 'He didn't say he had a house in Montmartre.'

While she could imagine Philippe sprawling on one of the couches, she was surprised he'd chosen pale blue ones, as for all the ornaments; that didn't fit his image either.

'I'm sure you understand a gentleman in his position would be wary of taking a lady to his home until he knew her better,' Pascal said silkily. 'Now, come and sit by the fire and I will get you a drink.'

He poured them both a large cognac, and sat opposite her by the fire. Belle felt the drink go straight to her head because she hadn't eaten anything since breakfast. She'd been expecting to have dinner with Philippe, and she just hoped Pascal would go as soon as he got back.

She had noticed on previous meetings that Pascal didn't hold conversations. He tended only to ask questions or give instructions, and he was no different now, firing questions at her about her lodgings, if she had any friends in Paris, and why she left England.

Since Belle had got to Paris she had avoided telling anyone anything about her past, it was safer that way. She had to answer Pascal's questions though, so she said she had come to Paris with a man she loved, but he went off and left her for another woman. She added that she didn't want to talk about that as she was trying to put it behind her.

'Yet you made the step from being a mistress to lady of the night without too many problems?'

Belle shrugged. She felt he might have found something out about her, and was trying to corner her into either lying or admitting something. 'It's surprising what you can do when necessity calls for it,' she said.

'You are very evasive,' he said, his eyes narrowing. 'Why is that?'

'I just don't like talking about myself,' she said. 'You should understand that, you don't talk about yourself either.'

Half an hour had gone by since she arrived and she was getting worried now that Philippe wasn't going to come back at all.

'You have only ever seen me at my place of business and of course I don't talk about myself there,' he replied. 'But it is different now, we are two friends having a drink together.'

'So tell me, are you married, do you have children?' she asked.

He hesitated and then said he wasn't married. Belle was fairly certain that was a lie for she'd overheard him talking to a married couple at the Ritz once, for whom he had been getting theatre tickets, and he'd told the woman that his wife had loved the play. As he was so slimy he could have just made that up to convince the woman she would enjoy it, but in

Belle's experience men didn't usually mention a wife if they were bachelors.

'I think I ought to go home, I'm not feeling very well,' Belle said, after trying some small talk about the Eiffel Tower and going on a boat down the Seine. She got up and put her hand to her head as if it hurt.

'You can't go,' Pascal said, leaping to his feet.

'Philippe will understand,' she said, making for the door.

As she reached it, Pascal caught her shoulder and pulled her back. 'You aren't going anywhere.'

'I beg your pardon!' Belle said reprovingly. 'It isn't for you to tell me what I can or can't do. It's not like I've been paid for tonight.'

'I'll pay you to be with me.'

Just the speed with which he responded told Belle that Philippe was not coming here tonight, this house might not even be his, and Pascal had set her up. A cold chill ran down her spine.

'No. We have a business arrangement, that's all,' she said quickly. 'Now, let me go, I don't feel well.'

He caught hold of her shoulders, his fingers digging into the flimsy silk which covered them. 'You were well enough when you arrived here. If you can give yourself to any man I find for you, why not me?'

His eyes were no longer expressionless, they were sparking with anger, and Belle felt a pang of fear.

'Because I like and respect you as a friend,' she lied.

His right hand left her shoulder and he slapped her hard, first on one cheek and then on the other. 'Don't lie to me. I know you scorn me because I am just a concierge.'

Belle's head did hurt now, for she was stunned by the vicious slaps. 'That isn't true,' she gasped. 'I do not scorn you for being a concierge, why would I? We've had a good arrangement together until now. Now let me go home. Please!'

'After you've given me what I want,' he snarled at her, and he grabbed hard at the neckline of her dress and ripped the bodice away.

Belle screamed and tried to get away from him but he was stronger than he looked and caught hold of her arm, swinging her away from the door and back towards the couch. Beneath her dress she was wearing a cream and pink striped camisole which barely covered her breasts, and now he'd ripped her dress she felt half naked.

As he pushed her down on to the couch she bit his hand as hard as she could, drawing blood.

'*Tu vas le regretter, salope que tu es!*' he exclaimed, and let go of her to suck on his hand. Belle seized the moment, pushed him away and ran for the door. But she found it was locked and there was no key, and Pascal was right behind her. He caught hold of her shoulder, spun her round and punched her in the face so hard her head banged back against the door.

'You can't get out!' he shouted at her. 'You will stay here until I've finished with you.'

All at once she felt she was back in that room at Madame Sondheim's, trapped and powerless. Her face was burning, she could taste blood in her mouth and she was terrified. In a flash of insight she saw that she should have realized that the competent, servile manner Pascal adopted with the guests at the Ritz was just a polished veneer. Beneath that was a volcano of intense jealousy. He probably resented everyone who was wealthy and successful, because he knew he could never be that. But he'd believed she could be his because she was only a whore.

'Please don't be like this,' she begged him, forcing herself to sound sweet and docile, and clutching her torn bodice together to hide her breasts. 'We just got off on the wrong foot tonight. You shouldn't have pretended I was to meet Philippe; I would have been happy to spend the evening with you if you'd just asked me.'

416

'Liar!' he spat at her. 'When I opened the door to you I saw your true feelings in your face. I was as welcome as a snake! You smile, you flirt with any other man. You do anything they ask as long as you are paid. But you don't even look at me.'

She looked at him squarely in the face then, although her right eye was swelling and she could barely see out of it. There was so much anger in his face, the flared nostrils, the straight set of his lips, and such cold eyes. She shuddered. 'You and I have had a business arrangement,' she said again, trying very hard not to cry. 'I thought it best for it to stay that way.'

'I don't want a business arrangement, I want you to be my mistress,' he snarled.

Realizing this argument could go on and on, and he'd only get even angrier and hit her again, Belle felt she had to try to calm him down. 'Why don't we start all over again?' she suggested. 'Go back by the fire, have another drink, and talk a little?'

'I don't want to talk, I want to fuck you,' he shouted at her.

Belle fought down a feeling of nausea. Her face was throbbing, she was scared of him, and the idea of being forced to have sex with a deranged man was utterly abhorrent. But there was no alternative, he wasn't going to let her go without it.

'All right then,' she said. 'Where would you like to go, in there by the fire or upstairs?'

He grabbed her by the arms and literally pulled her back into the drawing room, pushing her down on to the couch.

'Don't be so rough,' she said weakly, but he was already pulling the skirt of her dress up as he knelt by her and with his other hand unbuttoning his trousers.

In the last two years Belle had thought she'd encountered every type of sexual technique, from the gauche first-timers to the skilful lovers, with all the hundreds of variations in between. She'd learned to lock away the memory of being raped – she had to or she would never have been able to cope with her new life at Martha's. When she was with a man she didn't like or who was incompetent and clumsy, her trick was to imagine she was with Serge and think of the bliss he'd introduced her to.

But everything about Pascal made it impossible to imagine anything pleasant or feel anything but disgust, for he was as rough and unfeeling as the rapists, more sickening than the worst drunk. He forced his tongue into her mouth, bringing with it so much saliva that she retched. He probed roughly at her delicate parts until she cried out in pain, and she knew the things he muttered in French must be vile and was just glad she didn't understand. His penis was long and thin and as hard as a stick. She tried every trick she knew to make him ejaculate quickly, but without success. The ordeal went on and on and she felt violated in every way, for he bit her neck and breasts so hard she knew he must be drawing blood. He pinched and scratched at her thighs and buttocks as though he hated the female form and wished to disfigure it.

But finally, just when she felt it was never going to end, he came with a muffled sob. For a couple of seconds he lay panting on top of her, then suddenly got up and arranged his clothing.

'I will show you the bathroom,' he said curtly.

Belle had found that almost all men were softer after sex, but not Pascal. His face was sterner and colder than it had been before, his hair, usually so neat and oiled, was now ruffled and untidy, but that was the only evidence that he had been engaged in something out of character.

He caught her wrist and practically dragged her up the stairs, right to the top floor. 'In there,' he said, opening a door, and nudged her in.

It wasn't a bathroom as she'd expected, but a small attic bedroom. She turned to him to point out his mistake, but he had already backed out and closed the door behind him, and she heard him locking her in.

'Pascal!' she yelled at him. 'Let me out. I need the bathroom.'

'There is a chamberpot there and water to wash,' he called back. 'You are staying there.'

She yelled and pummelled at the door, but she could hear him walking back down the stairs, calling out that there was no point in screaming because no one would hear.

For a few minutes she just stood there, too stunned to react. The room looked as if it was the maid's: just a narrow iron bed with a faded flowery quilt covering it, a washstand with a ewer and basin and a chamberpot beneath it, a chest of drawers and a rag rug on the bare floorboards. There were shutters at the small window and she went to open them, only to find that there was no glass in the window behind them, only wood nailed in firmly all around the frame.

Suddenly the electric light went out, and she howled out in protest, realizing he must have turned it off somewhere downstairs. But aware he must have turned off the electricity for a reason, she fell silent and strained her ears. She heard his footsteps down on the tiled hall floor, then the sound of the front door being slammed shut.

Leaning against the door, she whimpered in fear. He was leaving her imprisoned here!

Chapter Twenty-nine

Gabrielle looked at the clock in the hall yet again. It was now two in the afternoon and still Belle had not returned. She tried to tell herself this was because her guest was with a man she really liked and maybe he'd taken her out somewhere today.

But no right-minded woman would go out by day in an evening dress and a fox cape. Gabrielle's instinct told her Belle was in trouble.

She had of course arrived here in evening clothes, though she had been wearing a warm coat over her dress. She had never said where she came from that day, but as the Mirabeau was so close to the station, it was fairly obvious she'd run away from a man and caught a train to Paris.

Gabrielle didn't normally take the slightest interest in her guests. As long as they were quiet, clean, respectful of her hotel and her other guests and paid what they owed, that was enough for her. Like any hotel owner, she'd had her share of difficult, unpleasant and troublesome guests in the five years she'd been here. She'd had gendarmes call to make an arrest, she'd had one woman commit suicide upstairs, irate husbands turn up looking for runaway wives; she'd even had a woman staying here who it transpired was in fact a man. There had been dozens of prostitutes asking for a room too. Usually she'd recognized what they were and refused them, but of those she hadn't, as soon as they tried to bring in a man, she showed them the door.

Belle was a special case, however. She had arrived dishevelled, clearly distressed, with no luggage, and Gabrielle had expected trouble to follow her, but it hadn't.

She realized what Belle was up to after the second time she arrived back early in the morning. Gabrielle was daunted then, experience, including some of her own mistakes in the same line of work, telling her that before long Belle would take liberties. But she did not, and was in fact the ideal guest, undemanding, appreciative of any little kindness, and extraordinarily discreet.

What had endeared Belle most to Gabrielle was her sparkle, good manners and warm smile. Gabrielle liked the way she learned some French and had grown to love Paris, and it was always a pleasure to see her so well turned out, stylish, pretty and ladylike.

Now it looked as if the anxiety Gabrielle had felt for her in the last week or two was not misplaced. She knew to her own cost that Paris was full of danger for girls like Belle. Not only were there thugs who would stop at nothing to get a cut of her earnings, but there were also madmen who developed fixations about girls as lovely as her.

At ten that evening Belle still had not returned and Gabrielle's anxiety was becoming ever more acute. In desperation she went up to the girl's room, turned on the light and looked around, hoping to find something which might give her a clue to where she had gone the previous evening.

As always, the room was neat and tidy, dresses hanging in the wardrobe, shoes beneath in a row, underclothes neatly folded in the drawers. There were a couple of English books beside the bed, a bottle of cologne on the dressing table, a hairbrush, a comb and a variety of hair clips and pins in a shallow tray.

A sketchbook by the bed was something of a surprise, for it just contained sketches of hats. While Gabrielle could speak quite good English she couldn't read it very well, but she assumed the notes beneath each hat were of materials and ideas for how to make each one. She found it odd that Belle had aspirations to be a milliner, but judging by her lovely designs and the copious notes, she was serious about it.

All the clothes, toiletries and oddments in the room had been acquired since Belle had come here to live. She received no letters, and there was no pocketbook or diary to give a pointer to who she was and where she'd come from, or even addresses of friends and family back in England. The only communication she ever got was when an errand boy called with a note for her. Gabrielle assumed it was the most recent one lying on the dressing table.

She picked it up to read it. There was no address or name to say who or where it came from.

'Monsieur Le Brun would like to see you tonight in Montmartre. A cab will come for you at seven,' she read, and beneath this were just the initials E.P.

Le Brun was a common enough name, the kind that could even be a false one, so that was no help, and Montmartre had many restaurants, cafés and bars Belle could have been taken to. The boy who brought the message was just a street urchin, one of hundreds in Paris that people used to deliver notes like this for a couple of centimes. Gabrielle doubted she would even recognize the boy if she saw him again, for he'd darted in, handed her the envelope addressed to Mademoiselle Cooper, got her to sign another slip of paper to say she'd received it, and darted out again. She couldn't even say if he was the same boy who had brought other messages before.

Gabrielle sat on the bed for a moment, staring thoughtfully at the note. It was on quality cream writing paper, but it had clearly been torn from a pad, as the top was a little jagged.

'Or the sender tore off the address that was on there,' she murmured to herself.

'A hotel!' she exclaimed as the thought came to her. 'Of course! That's how she gets her engagements.'

She knew it was common practice for wealthy male guests in the smartest hotels to ask a doorman or concierge to find them some female company. She didn't know why she hadn't considered this before as Belle was ideally suited for such work. She didn't look like a common prostitute, and she had the poise and good manners to hold her own with sophisticated men.

Gabrielle suddenly felt queasy, for Belle could have had the misfortune to meet someone very dangerous. While most businessmen away from home wanted nothing more than uncomplicated sex, there were always those who were perverted and cruel and saw a prostitute as fair game for any sick activity they had in mind.

She put her hand under the ruffle round the high neck of her dress and ran her fingers over the bumpy scar there. Her son Henri had just had his first birthday when she had the misfortune to meet the man who called himself Gérard Tournier. He seemed like a perfect gentleman, agreeing to fifty francs, then took her to supper first. But instead of accompanying her back to her apartment as they'd agreed, he'd taken her into a back alley and slashed her neck with a knife. She was lucky in that she was found before she bled to death, but the resulting hideous scar was a permanent reminder of what she used to be.

'Belle's smarter than you were though,' Gabrielle told herself, tucking the note into the pocket of her apron and leaving the room, locking it again behind her. She knew if Belle wasn't back by the morning she must enlist someone's help in finding her because she was sure she couldn't live with herself if the girl was found dead and she had just stayed here and done nothing.

Gabrielle had cut herself off from everyone she knew during her time as a prostitute. She wanted no reminders of her old career. And she never wanted Henri to discover what she'd done in the past. But there was just one person connected with that world that she remained in touch with, for she had nursed Gabrielle back to health following the attack in the alley, and looked after Henri. When she got up the next morning to find Belle still hadn't returned, Gabrielle resolved to go to Lisette after she'd given the guests their breakfast and Henri had gone to school. She didn't expect her old friend to have any idea of where Belle could be, but she might know people who would.

Unless she was taking Henri out for the day, Gabrielle rarely went beyond a half-mile radius of the Mirabeau, and then only to buy food, because she felt safer close to home. She never made any effort with her appearance either for by looking dowdy she attracted no attention to herself. But she felt compelled to make an effort for her visit to Lisette and changed into an old but still smart grey and white dogtooth check costume. The jacket was rather too well-fitting for a woman who liked to conceal her shape in loose clothing, but she tied a white scarf at a jaunty angle to hide her scar, added the black velvet hat with a half-veil she wore to Mass, and was pleased that she neither stood out nor looked too drab.

When Lisette had taken care of her over a decade ago they had both had rooms in the same house in Montmartre, but a year afterwards, when Gabrielle had left Paris to act as housekeeper for Samuel Arkwright, an English painter in Provence, Lisette went to live and work in a bordello. They kept in touch only by the occasional letter, for although Gabrielle cared deeply for Lisette, she had no wish to be reminded of the life she'd once shared with her.

Lisette's nursing skills were her saviour as a few years later, after she'd given birth to a little boy, she went to work in a nursing home in La Celle St-Cloud. The two women had met up only once since then, shortly after Gabrielle had returned to Paris following Samuel's death. Lisette said little about her own circumstances that day for she was more concerned with Gabrielle's grief at losing Samuel and whether she was doing the right thing in investing the money he had left her in a hotel.

Gabrielle was well aware of her own shortcomings. She didn't have a gregarious nature, in fact since she was attacked she had become a solitary soul who couldn't make small talk, and shied away from other people. Guests sometimes commented that she was sullen and uncommunicative, and had the Mirabeau not been so well placed near the station, she could have run into difficulties. Fortunately, however, there was a continual stream of people needing a small, comfortable hotel like hers and she didn't have to rely on guests returning.

Once on the train to La Celle St-Cloud, Gabrielle began to fret that Lisette might have moved on, as she hadn't heard from her for nearly a year. But she comforted herself that if that was the case, at least she had tried to do something to find Belle.

She found the nursing home easily enough and knocked on the door. It was opened by an old woman with a white apron over her black dress.

Gabrielle apologized for calling but said she needed to see Lisette urgently. The old woman told her to wait outside.

A few minutes passed before Lisette came to the door, looking anxious as if fearing she was going to hear bad news. When she saw her old friend, her pretty face broke into a wide smile.

'Gabrielle!' she exclaimed. 'How good to see you! What brings you out here?'

Gabrielle asked if there was somewhere they could talk and Lisette said she could come out for a cup of coffee with her; she'd just have to tell someone what she was doing.

Within five minutes they were walking down to the square and Gabrielle explained as briefly as possible that she had a guest who had gone missing after going to see a man. 'I've grown fond of the English girl,' she said. 'As you can imagine, once I knew how she was earning a living I started worrying about her safety, but she is just the way we were, confident that no one would harm her. I hoped you might know someone who could help me find her.'

'She's English?' Lisette said. 'How old?'

'About eighteen, I don't know for sure. Her name is Belle Cooper.'

Lisette looked startled. 'Belle? She has dark, curly hair, blue eyes?'

'You know her?' Gabrielle asked incredulously.

'Well, it sounds like the same girl,' Lisette said, and explained how she'd nursed a girl of that age, name and description two years earlier. 'She was taken to America,' she finished up. 'But I had a man come looking for her too, a friend of her family. That must be getting on for a year ago now.'

'Was his name Etienne?'

Lisette frowned. 'No, he was English, about thirty or so. But why did you ask if it was Etienne?'

'It was a name she gave me, the last evening I saw her. She said she trusted him.'

They had reached the café in the square now, and sat down at a table outside well away from other people. Lisette looked stunned.

'What is it? Do you know someone called Etienne?' Gabrielle asked.

Lisette nodded. 'He was the man who escorted her to America.'

Gabrielle had expected little of this meeting, and to find that Lisette knew Belle and the man she'd named was almost too much for her. Her heart began to race, and beads of perspiration formed on her forehead. 'Can you tell me everything you know?' she asked. 'It seems you know far more about Belle than I do.'

Lisette hesitated. 'I am not out of the business like you,' she said sadly. 'But I'm sure you remember how it is? I have only told you this much because you are an old friend and I trust you. I have my son to think of.'

Gabrielle understood exactly what she meant, and she took the other woman's hand between her own in reassurance. 'I haven't forgotten anything. But anything you can tell me will just be between us.'

Lisette told her everything she knew then: how Belle came to need nursing, how much she had liked her, and then about Noah Bayliss coming to see her.

'I liked him a great deal too,' she admitted. 'I almost weakened to take up his offer of help to get me away from here. But I was too afraid.'

Gabrielle nodded. The people behind bringing young girls to France were ruthless, and it would be hard for Lisette to trust any man enough to keep her and her little boy safe.

'But surely if this man Etienne was the one who took Belle to America he's as bad as all the others? Why would she say she trusted him?'

Lisette shrugged. 'Most of us caught up in this business have been forced into doing things we know are wrong, usually because they have a hold over us. That doesn't mean we are all bad. I would say Belle must have touched Etienne's good side, just as she did me, and you. She would've been with him for a long sea voyage, and they must have become friends. The Englishman Noah wanted me to try and contact him, to find out where he'd taken her. I tried at the time, but failed.'

Gabrielle sighed. 'I don't suppose he'd be any help with this now anyway.'

'Probably not,' Lisette said. 'Especially as I heard he'd left the business. A story went round that his wife and two children were killed in a fire and he is a broken man. Of course, that might not be true. I've heard stories like that before, it could just be to keep all of us fearful.'

'You mean someone could have done it purposely?' Gabrielle said in horror.

'Such things have been known, if someone steps out of line,' Lisette said, looking around her furtively as if afraid she might be overheard.

Both women fell silent for a few minutes. Lisette finished her coffee and said she had to go. 'I do have an address for Noah though,' she said as she signalled to the waiter for the bill.

'Really?' Gabrielle gasped. 'Will you let me have it?'

Lisette nodded. The waiter came over and Gabrielle paid him. The two women got up and began to walk away from the café. 'I'll slip in and get it for you,' Lisette said. 'I imagine your news will only make things worse for her family, but if Noah comes to Paris to see you, which I'm sure he will, please make him understand I can't be involved.'

As the two women were talking together in La Celle St-Cloud, Belle was lying on the bed in the small locked room, trying very hard not to give in to complete panic.

She could only guess at the time by looking at the one tiny hole in the board over the window. It wasn't even large enough to put her little finger through it. When she put her eye to it she could see nothing but a spot of sky. She didn't know the hole was there until daybreak when a pin-prick of light came through it. She had searched the room for something sharp to make the hole larger, but without success. She had removed the thin mattress from the bed only to find there were no springs, just rope criss-crossing the wooden frame, and she had felt all over the floor with her fingertips hoping to find a nail or screw, but there was nothing.

The tiny beam of light was brighter now, so she had to assume it was afternoon and the sun was shining on it. But time didn't have much meaning anyway, not as the rumbles of hunger increased steadily in her belly. There was water in the jug on the washstand, and she had drunk some of it earlier, but as she didn't know when Pascal would come back, she had resolved only to take a few sips now and then.

She fervently hoped he would come back tonight. But what was he going to do with her then? She doubted he would let her go, he'd be afraid she would go to the police or the manager of the Ritz. But he couldn't keep her here indefinitely. Was he planning to take her somewhere else? Or would he kill her?

She had dismissed that thought as preposterous earlier in the day; she'd even imagined him coming back and apologizing, or saying he'd done it just to teach her a lesson. But as time went on it seemed much less ridiculous, for it was the only sure way to guarantee her silence.

Who did the house belong to? She felt it was unlikely that it belonged to Philippe Le Brun as there was no possible reason why he would want her imprisoned in it. She was sure it wasn't Pascal's; a mere concierge would not be able to afford such a place. Was he in league with the owner, and the pair of them planned to sell her to another brothel? Or send her overseas again?

These thoughts went round and round in her head until she felt she would go mad with them. She'd tried banging on the walls and stamping on the floor. She'd listened intently, hoping to hear someone, if not in this house, next door, but there was just silence. She suspected this house was taller than its neighbours, and perhaps the walls in this room were not joined to another house.

She felt Gabrielle must have been concerned when she didn't return home, especially after the warning she'd given her. But would she do anything about it? What could she do? She didn't know who it was that arranged Belle's meetings with gentlemen.

She wondered though how long it would be before Gabrielle searched her room and found the money hidden in the space beneath the drawer at the bottom of the wardrobe. There was one thousand, seven hundred francs there. Enough to deter any hard-pressed landlady from reporting her guest missing.

It seemed to Belle that she was jinxed, for whenever she thought her life was about to take a turn for the better, something horrible happened.

Back in Seven Dials she'd been so happy to meet Jimmy, but that very night she witnessed Millie's murder. After the hideous ordeal in Madame Sondheim's brothel, she thought it was all over when she found herself in the nursing home with Lisette looking after her. But then she was sent to America.

There was that small window of happiness with Etienne in New York and on the way to New Orleans, but it wasn't long before she found herself trapped at Martha's and believing Faldo Reiss could be her ticket home. That turned out to be another form of imprisonment, but working with Miss Frank at the milliner's made her feel hopeful yet again. Then Faldo died, and Miss Frank turned against her.

She trusted Madame Albertine in Marseille, but she had betrayed Belle by setting her up with Clovis.

Then finally, just when she was about to go home to see her mother, Mog and Jimmy, Pascal did this. Why did he? He must have made a lot of money out of her, why wasn't that enough for him?

Would it have turned out differently if she'd been enthusiastic about going to bed with him?

Somehow she doubted that. He knew this room was up here, he must have planned to lock her into it. Maybe he'd been getting frightened that he'd lose his job if it got out about what he'd been doing on the side?

She should have known after that evening in the café in Montmartre that he wouldn't just give up on his desire to have his way with her. She'd felt deep in her bones that there was going to be trouble ahead. So why hadn't she acted on her instinct and left France then? What sort of a fool was she to think seeing Paris in the spring was so important? But if it had really been just that, she could have stopped accepting engagements and moved to another hotel so Pascal would think she'd gone for good. She had enough money, but she wanted still more because of her stupid pride and not wanting to go home empty-handed.

A sick feeling welled up inside her as she faced the truth about herself. She knew many prostitutes had been forced into the work in the beginning, and others got into it through desperate need or even plain stupidity, but every whore she'd ever met had remained one because they were either lazy or greedy.

She began to cry then out of shame. She was an innocent when she was snatched by Mr Kent and sold to Madame Sondheim, but why on earth did she allow Martha to corrupt her into believing it was fine to service ten men a night? Why did she lose her moral code?

She had always prided herself on being brave, but the brave thing to do would have been to have gone to the police in New Orleans and told them what had happened to her and why. This would have been so much better than striving to be the top girl and patting herself on the back because she'd learned a dozen ways to make her clients ejaculate quickly so she could move on to the next poor sod who hadn't got a woman of his own.

How many other girls' lives had been ruined by Kent and his associates? How many mothers and fathers were grieving over lost daughters? If she had only found the courage to speak out, she might have saved some of them.

It occurred to her then as she cried out her shame that it was all of this that had made her mother cold and seemingly indifferent to her child. Belle had no idea how and why Annie became a whore, and now she probably never would. But she could see now that Annie had done her best to shield her from what she did. All those rules about never going upstairs after six, keeping her away from the girls and encouraging her to read books and newspapers, were so she'd know about the bigger world beyond Seven Dials. Even allowing her to think of Mog as another mother was an act of unselfishness. For kind, gentle and loving Mog was the best of influences, teaching Belle right from wrong, good manners and to speak well, so that she wouldn't go the same way as her real mother.

'I've let her down,' Belle sobbed into the mattress, and the thought of that was worse than anything Pascal could do to her.

Chapter Thirty

Gabrielle looked thoughtfully at the address Lisette had given her as she rode home on the train. If she was to write to Noah Bayliss at that address it could be a week or longer before it got to him. That was too long, she'd have to send him a telegram.

But what would she say in it? 'Help needed to find Belle' wouldn't be much good if he'd already tried to find Belle and failed. 'Belle in danger come quick' would be frightening for the girl's mother. Yet whatever she put, whether she frightened him or not, it was still going to be another couple of days before he got here.

She would send a telegram anyway, but meanwhile what she needed was someone, preferably a man, who knew the smartest hotels in Paris and those who procured girls for their guests and might even be able to identify the initials on that note Belle had been sent.

There was a time when she had known half a dozen such men, but not any more. She felt certain that Belle's Etienne would have been ideal too, but if Lisette didn't know how to find him, what chance had Gabrielle got?

It was a stroke of amazing luck that Lisette had nursed Belle, yet perhaps not such a coincidence as she first thought, for after all Lisette was employed by people who bought and sold young girls. Gabrielle thought that once Belle was found she must persuade Lisette to get away with Jean-Pierre and sever all links with those terrible people.

Out of the blue, just as the train was slowing down and puffing into the station, Gabrielle suddenly remembered that Marcel, who ran the laundry two doors away from the Mirabeau, was from Marseille. By all accounts he'd had a chequered life before going into laundry work. She was a good customer of his, so even if he didn't know Etienne, he might be able to give her some advice.

Gabrielle went straight to the post office and sent a telegram to Noah. 'Contact me for news of Belle' she put and added the address of the Mirabeau.

'The pretty, dark-haired girl?' Marcel asked after Gabrielle had told him she was concerned about one of her female guests who had disappeared. 'Yes, I've seen her go past the window.'

As Gabrielle began to tell him she suspected foul play, Marcel ushered her into a tiny office just off his laundry. It was very hot and steamy in there but she was glad to talk to him in private, as people kept coming in and out of the laundry on the street.

Marcel was short and rotund, almost bursting out of his shirt. His round, shiny face glistened with sweat, and his receding black hair and drooping moustache were oily.

'She told me she had a good friend from Marseille, and knowing you were from there I hoped you might know him. His name is Etienne Carrera.'

Marcel's eyes widened. 'I know of him,' he said in a tone that suggested Etienne was to be treated with caution. 'But your young guest, how would she know such a man? He has a bad reputation.'

Gabrielle explained as briefly as possible about Belle's abduction and how Etienne escorted her to America two years ago. 'She told me she trusted him, so that would mean he was good to her. I don't care what kind of man he is, I just hope he may be able to help me find her.'

'I heard from my family in Marseille that he lost his wife and family in a fire,' Marcel said thoughtfully. 'It was the talk of the town some eighteen months ago, for most people think it was no accident and someone wished to punish him.'

'I heard that too. But do you know where he is now?'

'I could telephone my younger brother and ask him. They were friends as boys. I know Pierre went to the funeral of his wife and sons.'

Gabrielle put her hand on Marcel's arm. 'I would consider that a great kindness,' she said with sincerity. 'If he does know, will you ask him to tell Etienne that I believe Belle is in danger and that she gave me his name as a friend and someone she could trust?'

Marcel patted Gabrielle's shoulder in understanding. 'I will come along to see you just as soon as I have spoken to Pierre. I can see you are very worried about this girl. You liked her?'

'Very much,' Gabrielle admitted, suddenly aware that apart from Henri, Belle was the first person since Samuel died that she had cared about. 'She has had very hard times. I wish to see her reunited with her family. I think this man Etienne would wish that for her too.'

Marcel nodded. 'Leave it with me.'

Mrs Dumas opened her front door and blanched to see a telegraph boy standing there holding out a telegram. 'It's for Mr Bayliss,' the boy said.

Mrs Dumas felt relieved it wasn't for her. 'He's not home, I'm afraid,' she said. 'But he will be very shortly.'

She took the telegram and closed the front door, looking at the envelope and wondering what it contained. Was one of his parents sick or even dying? She fervently hoped not for she had grown very fond of Noah and he was doing so well now he'd been taken on to the staff of *The Times*.

Just half an hour later Mrs Dumas heard a key in the door, and rushed out into the hall to check if it was Noah. It was. He looked hot and bothered for it was a warm day and he must have walked home from Fleet Street.

'I'm afraid there's a telegram for you,' she said. 'I do hope it's not bad news. But I've got the kettle on, dear.'

Noah looked anxious, but smiled after he'd read it. 'I don't think it is bad news. Someone in Paris has news of Belle.'

Back in the days when he used to rush home hoping for a letter from Lisette, he had given his landlady a censored outline of Belle's story, omitting that she was brought up in a brothel and had been sold into prostitution. But that hoped-for letter never came, and once he'd been taken on as a reporter for *The Times* and worked longer hours, gradually his visits to Mog, Garth and Jimmy had become less frequent too.

Last time he went to the Ram's Head Garth had told him he and Mog were planning to get married soon. They wanted to find another public house somewhere in the country, and as Jimmy was virtually running the Ram's Head now, he could take it over if he wanted to.

Jimmy had grown into a strong, steady young man, honest and forthright, and he rarely mentioned Belle any more. Yet Noah knew he still thought about her, for though he had walked out with two or three young women, it was clear his heart still belonged to Belle.

Mog hadn't entirely given up hope of finding her, but she did her best to hide the core of sadness within her. She had a good life with Garth and Jimmy and filled her days with baking, cleaning and sewing. She had told Noah once that she felt deep inside her that Belle would reappear one day, and that thought sustained her.

As for Annie, her boarding house had become so successful she'd taken over the house next door too, but she had little contact with Mog now. Noah had written another article about Belle and the other missing girls just last December, hoping that after such a long time someone might come forward with new information. He had interviewed several of the mothers for this article, Annie included, and it had struck him that although she appeared hard and cold, in fact she probably grieved for Belle as strongly as Mog, but just couldn't articulate her feelings.

From time to time Noah had heard whispers about the Falcon. A young girl was found dead in a field on the outskirts of Dover, her death attributed to a large dose of sedative. She came from a village in Norfolk and was last seen at a local fair, talking to a man who fitted the description of Mr Kent. Noah had managed to get a look at the inquest report, and there had been rope marks on her wrists and ankles as if she'd been tied up, but the rope was removed after her death. Noah was convinced Kent was responsible and that he'd been planning to get her over to France the same way he had taken Belle, but when he found she'd died he just dumped her body and hoped the police might think she'd killed herself.

There were other girls missing too, several of them from Suffolk and Norfolk. Many of the policemen Noah talked to were in agreement that Kent was involved, and that he'd just moved his operation to a different area. But there was no evidence, and on the several occasions they had taken him in for questioning, he always had a watertight alibi. One senior police officer had told Noah that if they could just find one of the missing girls and get her to testify against him, he was sure other people would come forward with further information about his crimes.

But now this woman in Paris had news of Belle. Noah knew *The Times* would happily pay his expenses to go over there, and also get their French counterparts to offer him every assistance in the hope that he would find her and bring her home to testify about Kent and his operation. Noah's heart thumped with delight, not only at the prospect of seeing her reunited with Anne and Mog, but also because of what it would mean to him personally to get a lead story of human trafficking that every newspaper in the land would want.

And maybe he'd see Lisette again too.

In less than an hour after opening the telegram, Noah was on his way to Charing Cross to catch the last train of the evening to Dover. He considered stopping off at the Ram's Head to tell Mog the news, but decided against it in case things didn't work out as he hoped. He had telephoned his editor who, as he had expected, gave him his blessing and promised to telegraph ahead and ask the office in Paris to stand by to offer him assistance and an interpreter if necessary.

Gabrielle was laying up the breakfast tables at nine in the evening when the bell on the front door rang. She hurried to it, to find Marcel there.

'Did you find out anything?' she asked, and beckoned for him to come in.

'My brother does know where Etienne is, but it's a few miles from Marseille out in the country. Pierre promised me he'll go out there on his bicycle at first light tomorrow to see him and give him your message.'

'Bless you, Marcel,' she said, and impulsively leaned forward to kiss his cheek. 'Did he think Etienne might come?'

'All he said was that Etienne was the kind of man who would always help a friend. But he added that he hasn't been himself since the fire. So all we can do is hope.'

'Stay and have a glass of something with me?' Gabrielle asked. For the first time in years she didn't relish being alone. She had grown more and more terrified for Belle as the hours passed. She had pictured her body being thrown in the Seine or lying in a back alley. Even if Belle was still alive she couldn't bear to think of what might have been done to her. She had been down on her knees in front of a picture of the Virgin

Mary praying for her to keep Belle safe, but her faith wasn't sufficiently strong to truly believe that was enough.

Etienne stood at the door of the tumbledown cottage he lived in and watched Pierre cycling back down the rutted lane towards the road to Marseille. It was a beautiful spring morning, warm sunshine had made wild flowers spring up all along the lane, and the sound of birdsong all around him made him feel a little less despairing. It had been good to see Pierre again, they'd shared so much innocent fun as small boys, and even though their paths had taken them in such different directions as grown men, there was still a connection between them.

Etienne had wished for his own death after burying Elena and his boys. He'd hidden himself away in this cottage and spent the entire winter drinking himself into oblivion, barely eating anything, not bathing, shaving or even changing his clothes. The only time he went out was to get further supplies of drink.

It was only as the weather improved in early March that he noticed his surroundings. He woke one morning on his straw-filled mattress, and the sun shining in the window highlighted the filth he was living in: empty food cans and wine bottles everywhere, the table covered with mouldy bread, unwashed plates, the floor unswept since he moved in and covered in ash from the fire. He noticed an evil smell – whether it was coming from him, or from food that had fallen to the floor and rotted, he didn't know, but he knew it was time he did something about it.

He was so weak that he could only tackle the mess in small stages, resting in between. Just getting enough water from the pump outside, filling the old copper and lighting the fire beneath it left him breathless and aching. But he didn't open a bottle, and that night, after sweeping out the rubbish and burning it, bathing himself and washing his clothes, was the first that he'd fallen asleep sober since the fire.

He was physically strong again now; long, hard days of clearing the ground around the cottage had built up muscle. Mending the roof, cutting wood for the fire and making new shutters for the windows had stopped him drinking and eased his grief.

There were still days when rage consumed him. He wished he knew for certain if the fire in the restaurant had been set deliberately to punish him for daring to tell Jacques he wouldn't work for him any longer. If he could be sure he would have killed Jacques. But there was no proof – the source of the fire appeared to be the cooker.

The question Etienne had to ask himself now was whether it was wise to go to Paris and look for Belle. He'd made the break from Jacques, he could feel his old spirit gradually returning in just the way green leaves were unfurling in the hedgerows. But returning to Paris would undoubtedly bring him back in contact with the kind of scum he'd turned his back on.

Yet he could picture Belle's sweet face as she nursed him when he was sick on the steamer, he could hear her gasps of delight as they explored New York, and he remembered only too well how tempted he'd been that night when she got into his bunk.

She had crept into his mind so often in the months after he left her in New Orleans. He'd hoped he would be sent back there so he could check on her, and he'd felt pangs of guilt when he looked at Elena, for surely such thoughts of another woman were as much adultery as the physical kind?

But just the knowledge that Belle had cited him as the one person she trusted meant he must go to her aid. What did he have to lose? Everything he held dear was gone.

He turned to go back into his cottage. If he left now he could be in Paris tonight.

Belle sobbed when the heel of her shoe clattered to the floor. She had spent hours hammering on the board over the window, trying desperately to make a hole in it. The heel broke on the first shoe, and then she'd begun again after a sleep, but now the second heel was broken too she couldn't go on. It wasn't as if she'd even made any headway – all she had to show for her efforts was a slight indentation in the timber. But at least while she was hammering there was a glimmer of hope. Now that was gone.

Hunger was making her weak and dizzy. She was no longer sure whether it was two or three days she'd been here. Was that Pascal's plan? To make her so weak she wouldn't be able to fight him when he came back? Or was he intending to leave her here to die?

From time to time she could smell food cooking, it wafted in to tantalize her. If there was a restaurant that close, why couldn't anyone hear her shouting and banging? She'd been doing it mostly when there was no light coming through the small hole, with the idea that someone was more likely to hear when there was less noise on the streets. But she couldn't distinguish between evening and night, or how long she'd slept at one time.

Twice she had heard an accordion playing. It was a common sound in Paris, one she'd found enchanting when she had been free. If that sound could reach her ears, why oh why couldn't anyone hear her?

She shuffled back to the bed, feeling the bent and broken hairpins beneath her feet which she'd tried and failed to fashion into tools to pick the lock on the door. She had nothing more to use now; she'd taken out the whalebone stiffeners in the bodice of her dress and removed her suspenders, and broken every last one of them. She was defeated. And there was less than two inches of water left in the jug to drink.

She might as well just lie down and wait to die. It was hopeless.

Chapter Thirty-one

Gabrielle was sitting at her desk in the hall when a man walked in. She noticed his pale grey suit first, for it was sharply cut, and it was rare for any of her male guests to be that expensively dressed or to have the presence this man had. Then, as he spoke, the combination of his deep voice and his cold blue eyes stunned her for a moment. 'I'm Etienne Carrera,' he said. 'I believe you are expecting me.'

She could only gasp foolishly. 'I was hoping you'd come, but I didn't dare to expect it,' she managed to get out, feeling like a silly sixteen-year-old. After a moment's hesitation she got up and held out her hand to shake his. 'I am Gabrielle Herrison. And I'm so very pleased to see you. Can I get you some coffee and something to eat? You've had a long journey.'

'A coffee would be good while we talk,' he said.

She rang a little bell, and an older woman wearing a white apron came out of the dining room. 'Ah, Jeanne! Would you bring some coffee for us up to my sitting room?'

She led the way up to a half-landing and showed Etienne into a small room which overlooked the back yard. It was bright with the late afternoon sun, and simply furnished with a couch, a couple of armchairs and a table and chairs by the window. She removed some schoolbooks of Henri's. from one of the armchairs. 'My son's,' she said. 'He should be up here doing his homework but he's slipped out. Do sit down.

'I can hardly believe you could get here so quickly,' she went on once she was sitting opposite him. 'You must have left Marseille as soon as Marcel's brother spoke to you?'

He nodded. 'I sensed the urgency. Now tell me, how long has Belle been staying here, and where had she come from?'

'She arrived just after Christmas. I suspect she'd come from the south as Gare de Lyon serves that part of France. She didn't tell me anything about herself, just asked for a room in English. But I guessed she'd run from someone as she was wearing an evening dress under her coat, with no hat, scarf, gloves or luggage. Later she asked me if I knew a good second-hand clothes shop as she'd had her luggage stolen.'

Jeanne rapped on the door and came in with a pot of coffee and cups on a tray. Gabrielle waited until she'd left the room, then quickly launched into how she'd guessed what Belle was doing for a living.

'Normally when I realize this, I ask them to leave,' she said. 'I'm sure you will understand that trouble often follows such women. You let one in and her friends follow. I do not want this in my hotel.'

Etienne half smiled in understanding. 'So why did you let her stay?'

'Because she was a lady; quiet, polite, clean and charming. She had a warm personality, always with a ready smile, and she was appreciative. But I am quite sure you will know all this?'

'I do indeed. But did you say anything to her about what she was doing?'

'No, I think I was afraid I would frighten her away.'

Gabrielle went on then to tell him about how a boy would come with a note for Belle, then a fiacre would arrive later to take her to her appointment. She said that the girl was often out all night, coming back in the early morning. Then she moved on to tell Etienne what happened on the last evening she saw Belle leave.

'I felt she already knew the man she was meeting. That was the only time I warned her, and advised her to give it up and go home to England.' She looked right into Etienne's eyes, her lower lip quivering with emotion. 'You see, I know at first hand about the bad things that can happen to young girls like her. They may be fine for quite some time, but sooner or later they will come up against a man who is dangerous. And that is what has happened, I fear.'

Gabrielle showed him the note she'd found in Belle's room. Etienne studied it carefully. 'Monsieur Le Brun, a common enough name! What made you think she'd met this man before?'

'She looked especially beautiful, she'd gone to a lot of trouble and she was excited, as if she expected to be going somewhere smart with a man she really liked.'

'So you think he was a wealthy man?'

'She wasn't dressed for a night out with a poor man.'

'Could I look in her room?' Etienne asked.

'Of course. I was going to suggest you stayed in it.'

'I don't think I'll be doing much sleeping tonight.' Etienne smiled with his mouth but his eyes remained cold. 'I need to get started on investigating. But I must see around her room before I go out. Women's possessions often tell a great deal about them.'

Gabrielle went up to the next floor with him, unlocked the door and handed him the key. 'I'll give you another one for the front door before you go out,' she said.

After Gabrielle had gone downstairs Etienne stood still for several minutes, just looking around the room. He could smell a musky and heady perfume. He noted the row of shoes beneath the wardrobe, the hairbrush, face powder and hairpins on the dressing table, and the three hats on the chest of drawers. It reminded him of coming into the cabin they shared on the way to America for he'd been touched then by her neatness and femininity.

He had a mental picture of the way she used to curl up on

her bunk reading a book, absentmindedly twiddling with a lock of hair, and the way she'd look up at him and smile.

He shook himself and turned to the job in hand, opening drawers, examining the clothes in the wardrobe. He was impressed by them – although second-hand, they were good quality and stylish. Belle had clearly acquired a great deal of sophistication in the last two years.

Then he moved across the room to look at the sketchpad by the bed. When he saw it was all hats he felt curiously emotional, for he remembered she'd told him her dream was to have a hat shop. He read some of the notes beneath the sketches and it appeared she had also learned how to go about making her designs; he didn't think she had that knowledge two years ago.

He began to search then, for logic told him that if she'd been making money to get back to England, she would never have risked taking it out with her at night.

First he removed all the drawers and looked for anything stuck to the bottoms. When that revealed nothing he lifted up the mattress and felt beneath it. He slid his hand down the back of the headboard, turned the dressing-table stool upside down. He was running out of ideas, and stopped to look around him again. He put his hand up the chimney and found nothing but soot. Then he noticed the drawer at the bottom of the wardrobe. There was nothing in it. He pulled it right out, looked underneath it, then put his hand back into the space beneath where the drawer sat, and his hand met a tin box.

He drew it out and opened the lid. Lying inside was a thick bundle of francs. He flicked through it quickly and guessed there was well over a thousand.

Etienne returned the lid to the box and replaced it where he'd found it, then put back the drawer and stood up. It was a great deal of money and proof that Belle's clients were very wealthy men, for Gabrielle had said she never went out more than four nights a week. He was impressed that she'd saved so much – most girls in her position would have frittered it away on clothes and fripperies. Paris was a giddy place, a pretty girl could easily think she had the world at her feet and act accordingly. But she'd stayed in a cheap hotel, bought second-hand clothes and sketched hats, and no doubt when she wasn't with a client she was dreaming of going home to her loved ones and opening a hat shop. He was deeply moved by that, and it made him determined to turn Paris upside down if necessary to find her.

So who was this Monsieur Le Brun she'd left here to meet?

Etienne locked the door and went back downstairs. Just as he turned on the last half-landing by Gabrielle's sitting room there was a knock on the front door. Gabrielle hurried to answer it.

The tall, slender man on the doorstep took off his hat as he saw Gabrielle. *'Bonsoir. Je suis Noah Bayliss,'* he said with a stilted English accent.

Etienne hurried down the remainder of the stairs. Gabrielle had said she'd sent a telegram to this Englishman, but hadn't explained fully who he was.

'I speak English.' Gabrielle used the tone most French people adopt with English people who torture their language. She turned to Etienne and quickly said in French that Noah was a friend of Belle's family, and that he'd come to Paris several times in the past two years to try to find her. She then introduced Noah to Etienne, and told Noah that Belle had given her his name as someone she trusted.

Etienne moved closer and shook the man's hand. 'We are very glad you've come, we can do with all the help we can get.'

Noah looked confused. 'What do you mean? The telegram said there was news of Belle. Where is she?'

Gabrielle intervened to say how Belle had been staying

here and had disappeared. She explained she hadn't wanted to put anything alarming in the telegram but hoped for Noah's help and was grateful he'd come so quickly.

Noah turned to Etienne, his expression one of puzzlement. 'I'm sorry, I don't understand, Where do you fit into this?'

'It was Etienne who escorted her to America,' Gabrielle said.

Noah's eyes flashed. 'Then I'm surprised you had the cheek to show your face here. Have you any idea what her family and friends have been through?'

'I understand how it must look to you,' Etienne said. 'All I can say in my defence was that I had no choice but to take her. I was ordered to do it, and the people behind it are such that if you refuse, someone close to you will be hurt. But I can tell you that it was with a very heavy heart that I left Belle in New Orleans, for by then I'd grown fond of her, and I assume she felt the same about me as she gave Gabrielle my name as someone she trusted.'

Noah put his hand to his head. Clearly he couldn't quite grasp what was going on. 'I need all this explained more fully,' he said.

'Yes, you do, and Gabrielle is the one to do that.' Etienne realized that Noah didn't know what Belle had been doing here in France, and he didn't want to be the one to tell him. 'I've got some enquiries to make now, and you must be very tired after the long journey from England. So why don't you stay here with Gabrielle? She'll explain everything to you. We can all get together tomorrow morning when you are fresh and know as much as we do.'

'That is the best plan,' Gabrielle agreed. 'I have a room free for you, Noah, but first let me get you a drink and something to eat.'

*

447

Etienne caught a fiacre to the Champs-Elysées. He thought that Belle would have assumed that wealthy businessmen would find a hotel in that area because of its central position. He had the note Belle had received in his pocket, and he had a rough plan in his head.

As he stepped down from the fiacre and paid the driver off, it occurred to him that the task he'd set himself was going to be harder than he had first imagined. He hadn't been to this area of Paris for some years, and there seemed to be a great many more hotels than he remembered. He also had no idea which ones were the most fashionable now. Back in the days when he'd gone into hotels to rob the rich of their jewellery and money, there had only been a choice of about ten or so. But a great deal of building and refurbishment had been done for the Exposition Universelle in 1900 – as he recalled, the Gare de Lyon was built for it, and also the first Métropolitain train.

He walked quickly, passing by hotels and glancing in, noting the quality of the clothes and luggage of people getting out of carriages and cabs. He wasn't going to waste his time with hotels whose guests were mainly tourists; it was the select, discreet and expensive places he was interested in checking.

The first one he went into, the Elysée, fitted those criteria. Potted bay trees flanked the mahogany double doors with shiny brass fittings which were opened by a footman in green and gold livery.

Etienne walked across a white marble floor to the reception desk and smiled at the earnest-looking clerk with horn-rimmed spectacles. 'Could you tell me the name of your concierge? A colleague of mine said he'd leave a parcel for me with him, but I'm not sure if I have the right hotel,' he said.

'We have two,' the clerk replied. 'Monsieur Flambert and Monsieur Annily. Flambert is on duty now, he may be able to help you even if this isn't the right hotel.' He pointed out the concierge's desk across the other side of the lobby where a couple of guests were talking to the man.

Neither man had the right initials, but Etienne asked if a Monsieur Le Brun was staying at the hotel. The clerk checked the register and said there was no one of that name staying now.

Etienne then asked the clerk the names of other good hotels he could try. The clerk reeled off names – some were close by, others further afield, but he helpfully marked them on a street map, and even volunteered to give Etienne their telephone numbers.

One by one, Etienne called at all the hotels, but in each case there was no one with the right initials, nor was Le Brun staying there. He made a note of each one he'd tried, with the concierge's name beside it.

By eleven o'clock he was beginning to think that it might not be a concierge he was looking for but a hotel manager, even though he knew they were usually above making assignations for their guests. There was only the Ritz left to check now, and he didn't hold out much hope that the most prestigious hotel in Paris would have a man working for them who would risk being involved in anything so shady. He was also wary of even going in, for it had once been his favourite place to rob people of their money and jewellery, and the last time he'd gone there he'd been interrupted by a chambermaid coming into the room to turn down the bed. He'd fled past her and ran down the back stairs, leaving by the back door with someone in hot pursuit. He wasn't caught, of course – in those days he could run like the wind and scale walls effortlessly. But he'd never dared go back there for fear his luck would run out. However, he reasoned with himself that it was unlikely that anyone who had been working there sixteen years ago would remember a chambermaid's description of a skinny, shabbily dressed young lad she'd surprised robbing one of their guests.

He stood for a few minutes in the Place Vendôme looking at the Ritz and tried to imagine the Belle he'd got to know so well plucking up the courage to go into such a grand hotel. But reminding himself that he'd dared to rob people there, and Belle wasn't lacking in spirit, he went in to ask about his fictitious parcel.

And he was told the concierge's name was Monsieur Edouard Pascal.

E.B. It had to be him.

'But he has gone off duty now,' the clerk at the reception desk told Etienne. 'Is there anything else I can help you with?'

'No, thank you,' Etienne replied. 'I think I have the wrong hotel. I'll have to contact my friend and ask him which one he said he left my parcel at.'

Etienne was jubilant as he left the Ritz. Now he had the right name, he had contacts in Paris who would be able to tell him more about this man. For the first time since the fire he felt he had a purpose. He just hoped that Belle was still alive, for when girls of her age and experience went missing they were invariably found dead in a back alley or floating in the Seine. It was the innocent, trusting girls that got whisked off to work in brothels; they could be moulded to the owner's will. But Belle would not be like that now.

Le Chat Noir was a dark, smoky bar close to the Moulin Rouge. It was a favourite haunt for men who lived by their wits – confidence tricksters, gamblers, thieves and a variety of entrepreneurial fly-boys. Yet they were in the main the elite of their chosen profession, and Etienne by reputation was one of them.

The doorman, a thick-set ex-boxer, embraced Etienne with delight. 'We didn't think we were ever going to see you again,' he said. 'Word got around you'd retired.'

'I have, Sol,' Etienne replied, and pinched the man's cheek affectionately. 'Only in Paris on personal business, but I couldn't not come and see you all.'

'We heard about the fire,' Sol said, his face suddenly serious and sad. 'A terrible thing!'

Etienne nodded. He didn't wish to talk about it and hoped not everyone would feel they'd got to bring it up. Perhaps Sol understood, for he remarked on how fit and well Etienne looked and after making a joke about his expensive suit, let him go on into the bar.

About fifteen men were in there drinking, and perhaps five or six women too. Later, in the early hours of the morning, it would be packed and the air virtually unbreathable. Etienne heard his name called and saw a very short man in a checked jacket waving him over on the far side of the room.

Etienne smiled. It was Fritz, a very old friend and one of the people he'd hoped would be here tonight. Fritz had always been a mine of information, and Etienne doubted he'd changed in the four years since he'd last seen him.

He went through the same routine with Fritz as he had with Sol – the embrace, the sincere condolence.

'Don't let's speak of that,' Etienne said. 'I came here looking for you to pick your brains. All right?'

Fritz shrugged, which said that whatever Etienne wanted he could have, and then called the waiter for drinks.

Fritz played the part of a clown to strangers. He was less than five feet tall, and with the loud jackets, spats and bright waistcoats he always wore, and a voice to match, people automatically assumed he was a buffoon. But in fact he was one of the most intelligent men Etienne had ever met. When he was younger he'd single-handedly robbed a diamond merchant here in Paris. It was an audacious and meticulously planned robbery which baffled the gendarmes. Fritz was never suspected and only three people knew he'd done it – his wife, his brother and Etienne.

At the time the diamond merchant claimed the haul was worth four million francs, but Fritz had always smiled when that figure was mentioned, which Etienne took to mean it was far less than that. But to this day people still talked about the daring robbery, and each year they exaggerated the value.

Fritz had got away with it because not only had he left no clues behind as to who was responsible, he didn't brag about it either. Etienne knew it was just that which got most thieves caught, and that they splashed too much money around. Fritz bought a small house, and he and his wife and the children that came along later lived quite simply and happily. He had told Etienne at the time that he'd always planned to do just one big job that would keep him comfortable for ever, and he'd stuck to it.

'I want to know if you know anything about the concierge at the Ritz, name of Edouard Pascal,' Etienne asked as soon as the waiter had brought them each a large brandy and they'd moved to a table on their own.

Fritz frowned. 'Can't say it's a place I frequent. What's he done to you?'

'Nothing. But he's been arranging clients for a friend of mine who has now gone missing.'

'*Fille de joie?*'

Etienne nodded. He was glad Fritz had used that expression, it was kinder.

'But it's the client you should be looking for surely? Do you know his name?'

'Le Brun, that's all, there must be hundreds in Paris. But he'd be rich. And she was excited about seeing him again, so she liked him.'

'So we're looking for a Monsieur Le Brun, rich, charming. Any idea how old?'

'No. But I can't imagine he'd be much more than forty. She's only eighteen, girls of that age wouldn't be excited by someone very old. But could you get any information on this man Pascal? I may be forced to lean on him and I need to know what I'm dealing with.'

'See that man there?' Fritz pointed out a burly man in his thirties with a very big nose who was sitting a few tables away. 'He was a doorman at the Ritz a while back. Got the push for insulting someone. He'd know about the concierge.'

Etienne hesitated. 'But what's he like? I don't want it getting back to Pascal that anyone's been asking about him. Nor do I want anyone else knowing about this business. You know what I mean.'

Fritz nodded. He realized Etienne was concerned that the organization he used to work for might try to force him back to work for them if they heard he was active again. 'He owes me a couple of favours. I can make up some reason for asking about Pascal. I won't tell him you want to know.'

'Fair enough. Ask him when I've gone and we could meet up tomorrow. Can you think about the name Le Brun too, and see if you can come up with something?'

'I will. I'll meet you at Gustave's at ten in the morning.'

After leaving Le Chat Noir, Etienne hailed a fiacre to take him to the Marais. It was an area that had fallen on hard times, but he was fond of it for he'd lived there during a period when he had had to leave London in a hurry but couldn't go home to Marseille. It was well past midnight, but the place was buzzing with life, including dozens of prostitutes strutting up and down looking for business, and their *maquereaux* leaning on lamp-posts smoking and looking menacing.

Music wafted out of the many cafés and bars, above many of which were brothels. Etienne had worked in one briefly as a doorman, and he'd been shocked by the perversions the place offered. One room was like a torture chamber with manacles on the walls where the clients could be secured to be whipped. He'd seen men stagger out of there with their flesh so badly lacerated it was a miracle they were still conscious. He still couldn't understand how anyone would find that pleasurable.

It was here that he first learned that some men like sex with children, and it was hearing a girl of twelve screaming as she was raped that broke the spell of Paris and sent him back to Marseille. Again and again over the years he'd come up against men who abducted children and young girls to force them into prostitution, a practice he found despicable. The saddest thing was that there was no way out for these girls; once sucked into the trade, there they stayed until they were too old or too diseased for any man to pay them.

Because of his strong feelings about this trade, he felt deeply ashamed that he'd given in to pressure from Jacques and escorted Belle to New Orleans. While it was true he had no choice, not if he wanted Elena and the boys to remain safe, he had come to justify himself because Belle wasn't a child and he also believed that Martha's was a far better place to be than any brothel in Paris.

But after he left her there, thoughts of what he'd been a party to were like having a thorn in his foot that he was unable to get out. He had nightmares of Belle being ill treated, imagining brutish men forcing themselves into her. He hated himself for not being clever enough to find some way of getting her back safely to England, while still making sure his wife and children were protected.

This was why he eventually told Jacques he couldn't work for him any longer. He made out it was only because he wanted to spend more time with his family and Elena couldn't manage the restaurant alone.

He would probably never know for certain whether the fire that killed them was Jacques's revenge, or a genuine accident. But there was one thing he was certain of – if he did find Belle, then he was determined to expose this evil trade in children and young girls. He'd already lost everything that was dear to him, he had nothing more to lose other than his own life, and he'd die happy if he knew no more children would suffer that way.

The Trois Cygnes hadn't changed. There was the same faded red and white checked half curtain on a brass rail across the window, peeling paint and the same blast of cigarette smoke, mildew and garlic as Etienne opened the door. A wizened old man was playing the accordion just the way he remembered, and although the faces of the customers were different, they were the same mix of whores, pimps, struggling artists, dancers and students. A few of the older ones might even be the same he used to drink with all those years ago. But his memory of this place was that it had been bursting with life, with heated arguments about politics and art. Colourful characters, strong opinions and eccentricity used to be the order of the day, but the present customers looked surly, jaded and dull.

'Etienne!'

He looked over to where the shout came from at the back of the bar, and smiled at the delight in the woman's voice. It had to be Madeleine, even if the years hadn't been kind to her.

She wriggled her way through the close-packed tables and chairs, fat now and in her mid-forties, but she still had a smile to light up a room.

'Madeleine! I hoped you'd be here,' Etienne said and held out his arms to embrace her. He'd learned everything about lovemaking from her, and even more about life. In her thirties she'd been a flame-haired beauty, with a soul as beautiful as her face. Her hair was still red, but all too clearly dyed, and the porcelain-like complexion was muddy and lined now. Yet all the warmth she'd had was still there, and as he held her the years slipped away and he felt as he had at twenty.

'Let me look at you,' she said, stepping back a little. 'More handsome than ever, and a suit that tells me you won't need me to buy you a drink! But what brings you here? I heard you'd become a recluse.'

'I came looking for you,' Etienne said.

She took his hand and led him to a free table right at the back of the bar, calling to the barman to bring them cognac. As he had half expected, she'd heard about Elena and the boys – bad news always spread far and wide – and as she offered condolences her eyes filled with tears of sympathy.

'It is good to see your heart is still as big,' he said, taking her hand across the table. 'After the way I left you, I wouldn't have blamed you if you'd wished bad luck on me.'

'You were never for me, I always knew that,' she said, and he noticed her green eyes were still as vivid. 'If you'd stayed we would've destroyed one another, and I was too old for you too. But let's not talk about that – tell me why you are here in Paris. You weren't one for social calls, as I remember.'

'I'm sure I don't have to tell you that anything I say must stay between us?' he reminded her.

'Of course.'

Etienne outlined Belle's story. 'You were right in believing I'd become a recluse. If I hadn't got a message to say Belle had disappeared I would have finished clearing the land around my cottage and planted some crops and got some chickens.'

Madeleine laughed. 'Surely not! You a farmer?'

'Working the land suits me,' he said. 'I hope I can go back to it. But first I have to find Belle to put things right.'

'She may have just gone off on a jaunt with this client of hers.'

'No, she has left all her belongings at the hotel she was staying at.'

'Pssst,' Madeleine said scornfully. 'A few clothes would not hold a girl, not if the man was rich and could buy her new ones.'

'I would say that is true of many women, but not Belle,' he said staunchly. 'She would've sent a message to her landlady so she wouldn't worry.'

'Two years as a whore would've changed her. She won't be the girl you knew any longer.'

'It is over twelve years since I met you, but I'd say you still have the same values,' Etienne argued.

'Where you are concerned, maybe.' She shrugged, implying that he was a special case. 'But a girl who works the top hotels has to be smart and hard-headed. I did it myself, remember.'

'I know Belle is in trouble,' he insisted. 'I feel it, so does her landlady. She was a *fille de joie* too.'

That seemed to change Madeleine's mind. 'Fair enough. So what do you want of me?'

'Have you ever met or do you know anything about a man called Edouard Pascal?'

'Yes,' she said, and sat up with a jolt as if startled. 'He used to come to the Marais nearly every week. I went with him two or three times, but I didn't like him, he gave me the creeps. None of the other girls liked him either. But this was eight years ago or more. I haven't seen him since.'

'What did he work at?'

'He didn't say. He was well dressed but I don't think he had much money – an office worker maybe?'

'He's the concierge at the Ritz now. He was getting Belle clients.'

Madeleine's eyes widened in surprise. 'That makes me think you are right to be worried about her. The reason I remember him so well was because he liked it rough. He bit me very hard, and slapped me when I complained. The other girls talked about him too.'

'Do you know where he lives?'

'We don't take down addresses in this line of business,' she replied with a humourless chuckle. 'Mostly we don't even get real names. But he wanted us to know his, like it made him feel important.'

'Ever met a man called Le Brun?' Etienne asked.

'A few dozen,' she said dryly.

Etienne said that he thought this Le Brun must be very rich and good company as Belle's landlady claimed she was excited at meeting him.

'Well, that cuts out most of them,' Madeleine said. 'It wouldn't be Philippe Le Brun, would it? The millionaire that owns the restaurants? I know a girl who went with him. He took her out to supper and dancing. She said he gave her such a good time she'd have done it again for free!'

Etienne knew nothing of the man she mentioned, but then his contacts in Paris tended to be at the other end of the social scale. 'Is the girl you know around here?'

Madeleine looked amused. 'Do you think a man like him would want a street girl? She was a dancer, and got her clients through the manager at the theatre. But she married and moved away. That doesn't happen very often, she was one of the lucky ones.'

Etienne sensed that Madeleine couldn't help him any further, and he was suddenly very tired. 'I must go now, Madeleine,' he said. 'You've given me a great deal to think about. Thank you.'

'I wish I could be more help,' she said. 'But you know where to find me if there's anything else I can do.'

He paid the bill and handed her fifty francs. 'Buy yourself something pretty,' he said. 'Emerald green, you always looked lovely in that colour.' He got up and leaned down to kiss her. 'Take care of yourself.'

Over breakfast the next morning Etienne sensed Noah didn't trust him. He wasn't surprised – with what the man knew about him, only a fool would trust him. But it transpired Noah had never met Belle; his connection was that he had been sweet on Millie, the whore Belle had seen murdered. When Etienne began to explain that he'd grown fond of Belle on the sea voyage, Noah bristled.

'Did she tell you she has a sweetheart back in England?' he asked waspishly.

'You mean Jimmy, I presume?' Etienne replied. 'She told me about him, though she said he was just a friend. But whatever Jimmy was to her, there was nothing between Belle and me, if that is what you fear. She had been through a terrible ordeal at Madame Sondheim's and I was a married man who loved his wife. We were like the uncle and niece that we pretended to be.'

'Jimmy loves her,' Noah said stubbornly.

Etienne could see that carefully brought up Noah was somewhat naive. His foray into Annie's brothel was his first glimpse of London's underbelly, and though his heart was in the right place and there was no doubt about his sincerity, he had a rather idealistic view of both people and life.

'She would be a very easy girl to love,' Etienne agreed. 'And God willing, you will be able to take her back to Jimmy, her mother and Mog, the lady she told me so much about. If you think that I have come here to claim her for myself, you are mistaken. I'm merely trying to right a wrong.'

Noah seemed less wary after that and listened as Etienne told him what he'd discovered the night before. 'My suggestion is that we both go to meet my friend Fritz and see what he's come up with. I don't like the sound of this Edouard Pascal, and he and the man Le Brun are possibly in it together, maybe others too. We will have to tread very carefully and find out as much as possible about both of them before we make a move.'

'What do you mean, "others"?'

Etienne sighed inwardly. As Noah had been to Paris several times in the past and tried to investigate the other missing girls, he thought that by now he would have cottoned on that it was big business. 'Vice is universal, Noah,' he said. 'Fortunes are made out of it.'

'I see,' Noah looked very glum. 'So she may have been taken anywhere in the world?'

'That's right, but my hunch is that if she is still alive, she's here in Paris. There is a ready market for very young girls, but Belle is too old for that, so unless they had a buyer already lined up for her, it would take some time for them to offload her.'

Noah looked really alarmed now. 'Does that mean you think she's already dead?'

'No, it doesn't,' Etienne said more firmly than he really believed. 'But we do have to keep that possibility in the back of our minds.'

Gabrielle came into the dining room just as the two men were getting up to leave. Etienne had already told her about what he'd discovered the previous night. 'Be careful,' she said, looking very anxious. 'I would hate to see either of you hurt.'

Etienne put his hand on her shoulder. He had glimpsed the vivid scar on her neck earlier when her scarf slipped, and instinct told him how she had got it. 'We'll be fine, now stop worrying. You did the right thing getting us here, we'll take over now.'

Fritz was already at Gustave's when they arrived. It was a small café-bar, and Fritz was sitting at one of the tables outside. Etienne introduced him to Noah, then asked if he had anything for them.

'Yes and no. Found out that Edouard Pascal is an oily son of a bitch. He's roughed up a few women in his time, and has only been working at the Ritz for three years. Before that he worked as an undertaker.'

'An undertaker!' Etienne exclaimed.

Fritz nodded. 'Seems strange he went from that to being a concierge in the best hotel in Paris, and my money would be on him bribing or even blackmailing someone to get the job. Those men usually come up through the ranks. I smell something fishy.'

Etienne nodded. 'What about Le Brun? Someone told me last night he could be Philippe Le Brun, a restaurateur.'

'That's who I came up with too. He's larger than life, very rich, a ladies' man with a taste for whores, though by all accounts he treats them well. But my source said that on the night in question he was seen with a statuesque blonde dancer until the early hours.'

Etienne frowned. 'So we can rule him out?'

'Of seeing your girl that night, but he has been seen twice with the same girl recently, young, very pretty with dark curly hair, and my source thinks she was English.'

Both Etienne and Noah beamed. 'Is he approachable?' Noah asked.

'I couldn't say,' Fritz replied after a moment's thought. 'But I'm told he goes for coffee in Le Dôme in Montparnasse most mornings.'

Etienne thanked Fritz, then he and Noah left the café. 'Shall we go to Le Dôme and see him?' Noah asked.

Etienne was torn two ways. His gut reaction was to investigate Le Brun further before contacting him, but Belle had been gone for three days and maybe they needed to shake things up a little.

'Yes, I'll tell you on the way there how we are going to play this,' Etienne said as he hailed a cab.

*

Noah entered Le Dôme feeling decidedly nervous. He'd left Etienne further down the street.

There were only about ten people in the café, mostly men in twos and threes. One man was sitting alone at a table in the window reading a newspaper. Noah took the table next to him and while pretending to consult his diary glanced surreptitiously at his neighbour.

He was big, as tall as Noah, and well built, with the kind of ruddy face of a man who ate rather too well. The waistcoat clearly visible beneath his dark, impeccably tailored jacket was emerald green embroidered with silver thread. It seemed to match what Fritz had said about the man being larger than life. Noah watched and listened as he greeted another man at the back of the café. Noah guessed from odd words he understood that it was some light-hearted banter about a recent event. He liked the man's deep, throaty laugh, he seemed very amiable.

Noah ordered his coffee and leaned towards his neighbour. '*Excusez-moi. Etes-vous Monsieur Le Brun?*'

'*Je suis en effet,*' he replied, and smiled. 'You are?'

'Noah Bayliss and I'm sorry, I speak very little French.'

'All the English do,' he responded with a belly laugh. 'But I like to practise my English, so that is good.'

'Could I share your table?' Noah asked. 'I have things I wish to ask you.'

The man indicated that was fine, but his expression had tightened a little, as if he was apprehensive at being questioned.

Noah moved to Le Brun's table, then, to try to put him at his ease, asked him which restaurant he would recommend where Noah could take a young lady he wanted to impress.

This seemed to do the trick. Le Brun suggested that if he wanted to splash out, Le Grand Vefour was where Napoleon used to take Josephine, and the food was exquisite. He went on then to tell him a few other places which were less expensive but good, one of his own restaurants among them. Noah wrote the names down in his diary.

Le Brun asked him if he was on holiday in Paris, and then Noah took a deep breath and said that actually he'd come to try to find the daughter of one of his friends.

'I had an address of the hotel she'd been staying at, but she has disappeared,' he said. 'It's very strange as she left all her belongings behind. That isn't like Belle at all. I'm getting worried now.'

He watched the man's face, hoping that dropping her name would make him react, and he wasn't disappointed.

'Belle?' Le Brun said, his eyes widening. 'I know someone of that name.'

In Noah's time as a journalist and investigator for an insurance company he had become astute at gauging the truthful and the dishonest. This man might be a philanderer, but he wasn't a deceiver.

'You do? What does she look like?' he asked, leaning forward eagerly.

'Like her name, beautiful with dark curly hair. But the name is just coincidence for this girl is a *fille de joie*.'

Noah's heart raced.

'You understand that expression?' Le Brun asked a little anxiously.

Noah nodded. He didn't reply immediately as he needed time to plan his answer.

'I have every reason to believe that's exactly what our Belle is,' he said quietly. 'You see, she was abducted from London two years ago, and myself and her family have been searching for her ever since. We feared she was dead, but then I got a telegram telling me she was here in Paris. I arrived too late though, she had disappeared.'

'*Mon Dieu!*' Le Brun exclaimed and his face had become

less ruddy. 'I spent the evening with her just ten days ago. I hoped to see her again soon, she is very –'. He stopped short, and Noah knew he'd suddenly realized this meeting was not pure chance.

'Yes, I know, I found a note in her room from the man who makes her bookings,' Noah said. 'Forgive me if I have been underhand, but I'm sure you can appreciate I had to tread carefully. You see, that note said she was to meet you in Montmartre. Her landlady said she was excited to see you, but she never returned.'

'Now look here, I never . . .' Le Brun blustered angrily.

'I know,' Noah said soothingly. 'Clearly she was lured out under the pretext of meeting you. But if you liked her, I would be so grateful if you could tell me all you know about her, and the man who arranges your meetings. It would of course be in strictest confidence.'

Le Brun put his hands over his face for a second in the gesture of a man who felt cornered. 'I really liked her,' he said. 'She was funny, sweet-natured and interesting in every way. I promise on all I hold dear that I have not seen her since . . .' he paused to take a small diary from his jacket pocket, 'March twenty-sixth. I took her to Maxim's that night.'

'I do believe you,' Noah said. 'Tell me about Edouard Pascal. He introduced you to Belle, I believe?'

'It was because of him that I haven't seen Belle since.' Le Brun's face darkened at the mention of his name. 'The man is a snake. I wish I had never been foolish enough to go to him. You see, I first saw Belle in the restaurant at the Ritz. She was with an elderly man and I sensed by their manner that it was their first meeting. No one would think Belle was a *fille de joie*, she dressed so well, acted like a lady, but as they left the restaurant I saw Pascal go up to the man. There was something between them, and that's when I realized.'

'You liked the look of Belle and approached him?'

Le Brun sighed. 'Yes, for my sins. He wanted four hundred francs for an introduction as he called it. I should have walked away, but we men can be weak when we want a woman.'

Noah remembered how he'd been about Millie – he would have paid anything to be with her. 'So what else do you know about the man? Could he be involved with whatever's happened to Belle?'

Le Brun shrugged. 'He's not the kind of man you'd spend a minute longer talking to than you have to, so I know nothing about his personal life. But he's greedy, and if he told her she was meeting me he was up to no good. We could hire some muscle to beat it out of him!'

Noah smirked at that suggestion. 'I've got help from someone who could do that. But I'd be scared to do it in case he's in this with others. They might just kill her if they hear we're after them.'

Le Brun looked alarmed. 'Surely it won't come to that? What can I do to help?'

'You've done so much already by being honest,' Noah said. 'I can't thank you enough.'

'The only thanks I want is to hear she's safe and unhurt,' Le Brun said with complete sincerity. 'Keep in touch.' He took a card from his pocket. 'You can contact me there. Come for me if you need any help at all.'

Chapter Thirty-two

Belle shuffled over to the window and picked up a broken hairpin with which she continued trying to make the small hole in the board larger. She couldn't stand for long, she felt too weak and dizzy, but she had succeeded in making the tiny hole into one just large enough to put her little finger in. She still couldn't see much, just a tiled roof about twenty or thirty yards away. But when the sun was on the window a rod of light came into the room and she could lie on the bed watching the dust particles dancing in it, imagining it was fairies.

Mog had always made her say her prayers, something she'd abandoned a long while ago. But she prayed a great deal now, promising God she would never sin again if He'd just send someone to rescue her.

Hunger wasn't her only problem now. She'd run out of water, and hour by hour she felt herself growing weaker. Aside from brief spells making the hole bigger, she spent the rest of the time lying on the bed to conserve her strength. She just wished her mind would slow down the way her body was doing, for she was tortured by going over and over the events of the last two years, and blaming herself for her own part in most of them.

She thought of Mog, her mother and Jimmy a lot too, especially Mog. She imagined her in the kitchen, rolling out pastry, or wringing out wet washing in the scullery. Sometimes she woke from a dream where Mog was holding her in her arms the way she had when Belle was a little girl, and for a second or two she'd think Mog had been there.

She tried not to think about Pascal, or to guess what he

had planned for her. She couldn't really believe anyone would intentionally leave someone to die of thirst and starvation, and mostly she told herself he must be sick or had had an accident that prevented him from coming back. She no longer had any idea of how long she'd been here for when she fell asleep she didn't know how long it was for. But it seemed as though she'd been here for weeks, not just days.

The pin fell out of her fingers and she was too weak to pick it up so she shuffled back to the bed. She wondered what dying of starvation was like. Did you just become unconscious so you wouldn't feel anything? She hoped that was how it was.

Etienne listened attentively to what Noah had to tell him about Philippe Le Brun. 'Let's go to the Ritz and have it out with Pascal,' Noah suggested.

'I'd like to go there and kick it out of him,' Etienne said grimly as they walked down the street. 'But we don't know if he's working alone or with others. We need to know more about him, where he lives and who with, what hours he works and if he goes anywhere after he leaves the hotel. But I agree we should go over there now and see if we can find out anything.'

Etienne was growing on Noah. He liked his tough, uncompromising attitude, and was intrigued by his obviously colourful past. He wasn't boastful, he had a tender side too, especially about Belle, and he made Noah feel braver just by being beside him. So brave in fact that he decided to admit to his feelings for Lisette, and asked if Etienne thought he had a chance with her.

'I've never met her, all I know about her is what Belle told me,' Etienne said. 'She sounded like a good woman. But if you want my real opinion, once we've got Belle back, you should return to England and find yourself a girl from a background like your own. You'll be much happier.'

That wasn't what Noah wanted to hear. 'But I'm committed to exposing the trade in young girls,' he said heatedly. 'Finding Belle is my priority but I'm intending to write articles for the press to get all those involved stopped and punished.'

'That's a very laudable ambition, and I'll be right behind you with it. Just don't imagine you can stop it completely, there's too much money to be made from it. The men who pay for young girls are often those in positions of power – judges, lawyers, politicians and the like. As long as they demand young flesh, someone will provide it. Write your article, campaign if you must, but leave it at that. And don't be tempted to want a one-time whore for a wife; she'll never be socially acceptable and in the end you'll regret it.'

'Harsh words!' Noah retorted. 'Does that mean Belle is never going to be socially acceptable either?'

Etienne grimaced. 'Almost certainly. She may also be so damaged that she'll never want a husband or children. No woman could go through what she has and remain untouched by it. You say Jimmy loves her, but love is not always enough.'

Etienne hailed a fiacre then, signalling that was the end of the conversation.

'Shall I go in and engage Pascal in conversation?' Noah suggested when the fiacre dropped them close to Place Vendôme. 'I play the simple Englishman abroad quite well.'

Etienne smiled. He knew Noah was annoyed with him for what he'd said about Lisette earlier, but he had to admire him for not continuing to sulk. 'That sounds like a good plan. Ask him about cancan dancing, anything to do with girls. Hint you are eager for company. I'll stay outside; I'm going to follow him later, so I don't want him to recognize me.'

Etienne walked across the Place Vendôme and found a bench to sit on while he waited for Noah. His mind was whirling with fragments of information that he felt he ought to be able to put together to make a whole, but a vital chunk was missing. He didn't know anything about Pascal's domestic life, not where he lived or if he was married. Why would an undertaker leave such a potentially lucrative career and become a concierge? The two jobs were so different.

He turned to look at the hotel, wondering if there was a link he hadn't thought of, and noticed a couple getting out of a fiacre. There were four other cabs waiting in line to pick up passengers too.

'That's it! Find the driver who took Belle that night,' he murmured to himself. He knew it was a tall order, but it was worth a try. If Pascal did order the cab, the chances were that the driver regularly picked up fares here from the hotel.

Noah didn't emerge from the Ritz for some thirty minutes. He spotted Etienne and hurried over to him.

'He really is a snake,' he said. 'I watched him with other people for a little while, and though I couldn't understand what was being said, twice I saw him get what looked like a back-hander. He speaks good English though; when it was my turn he got out various pamphlets about shows, and pointed out they were all sold out for tonight, but he had a contact who could get me tickets for "a bit extra"! When I asked him about girls he was cautious. Said he knew someone who might be able to do something. I got the impression he was waiting for a big note to be passed over.'

'Did he ask where you were staying?'

'No, but I had a moment of inspiration and told him I was in Paris to arrange my aunt's funeral, and said I hardly knew where to begin to find an undertaker. Quick as a flash, he wrote a name down. Here it is.'

Noah gave the paper to Etienne. 'Arnaud Garrow, Directeur de Services Funèbres,' he read aloud. 'Rue Custine, that's close to Montmartre. I wonder if it's the one he used to work for?'

'It struck me as very odd, a concierge handing out an

469

address for an undertaker,' Noah said. 'Has he got a finger in every pie in town?'

'We'll go there later and check,' said Etienne, and went on to tell Noah about finding the driver who was paid to pick up a young woman from the Mirabeau in Rue St-Vincent de Paul on Thursday, 11 April. 'Let's go along and speak to them now, and then we'll hop in one to take us over to rue Custine.'

Noah waited as Etienne had a last word with their cab driver. He couldn't understand what he was saying, but he assumed he was asking the man to pass the word around other cab drivers about Belle's ride to Montmartre on the 11th, and telling him they were to come to Gabrielle's with the information where they would receive a reward.

'What if that gets back to Pascal?' Noah asked when the cab driver flicked his whip and the horse moved off.

'I had to take that risk. We need the information if we're to find her.'

Arnaud Garrow's business premises looked very shabby: a small shop with an arrangement of dusty wax flowers sitting on some faded purple satin material in the window. The two men looked at each other in surprise.

'Hardly in keeping with the splendour of the Ritz,' Noah said with a smirk.

'I'd better come in and do the talking,' Etienne said. 'I doubt they'll speak English. I'll just say who we were recommended by and see what reaction we get. It's bound to be some chum or relative of his. You must've played the simple Englishman well.'

A thin man with dark, oily hair arranged over a large bald patch came through from the back as they entered the shop. He had his shirt sleeves rolled up and wore a dark green apron which had sawdust attached to it. Noah asked if he spoke English and the man shook his head. Etienne took over then and Noah heard the name Pascal amidst the stream of French.

The undertaker nodded and appeared to be speaking about Pascal. Etienne then introduced Noah under the fictitious name of John Marshall, and continued to speak on his behalf. The conversation between the two men went on for some five or six minutes, Etienne doing most of the talking. Then he shook the man's hand before turning to Noah and telling him he'd said they would come back the next morning to make the arrangements when they'd discussed it with other family members.

Noah shook the undertaker's hand and said goodbye, and he and Etienne left the shop.

'Pascal is his wife's brother,' Etienne said once they were away from the shop. 'I think he must still be a partner because Garrow mentioned having one, then stopped himself. I suppose Pascal thinks he's moved up in the world and doesn't want it known he's still involved in a seedy back-street undertaker's.'

'I'm not surprised. I wouldn't want anyone knowing I was a partner in that place!'

'I'd bet he makes good money out of it. Poor people would go there; they tend to take pride in spending money on giving their loved ones a good send off, even if they can't afford it.'

Noah knew that was true. In his time as an insurance investigator he'd observed how the poor always seemed to spend far more than they could really afford on quite lavish funerals, and he'd wondered at the logic of it. 'You didn't find out where Pascal lived, I suppose?'

'It must be nearby. I asked Garrow casually if he saw much of Pascal, and he said he dropped in on his way home from work sometimes. But I got the impression there's a lot of bitterness there. Probably doesn't feel Pascal pulls his weight.

Then he went on to say he had a selection of fine coffins to show us, and he can give us a good price.'

The two men had lunch in a small café, and discussed the fact that they didn't seem to be making any real headway. Noah said he thought he would go to *Le Petit Journal*, where he had been given an introduction from his own newspaper back in England.

'I'll talk to the editor, he already knows a bit about why I'm here. I'll ask him if he remembers any stories involving Pascal or Garrow. He'll probably get someone to trawl through some old papers for me. They should be keen to cooperate if they think there's likely to be something juicy for them later.'

'Good plan,' Etienne said. 'Just don't mention me! I'll go back to the Ritz later and wait for Pascal to leave, then I'll follow him.'

'He said he was on duty till eight when I asked him about tickets,' Noah said. 'Could I meet you there then?'

Etienne shook his head. 'That's not advisable. Pascal knows your face. You wait back at the Mirabeau, I'll follow him.'

'But what if you need help?' Noah looked alarmed. 'I won't know where you are.'

Etienne looked hard at Noah. 'I've spent most of my adult life tracking down thugs and gangsters. I know what to expect from them and I can handle it. But Pascal is an unknown quantity, we don't know who is in this with him, or how he'll react if cornered.'

'All the more reason for me to come with you,' Noah protested.

'No, I don't want to put you at risk. You're the only one with the right influence to get the child traffickers behind bars. If I don't come back for you tonight, you go straight to the gendarmes and tell them everything we know.'

'But . . .'

472

Etienne stopped Noah's protest with a firm hand on his shoulder. 'I will not be responsible for endangering your life. Now, go to the newspaper and find out what you can. Leave me to do what I do best.'

At seven-thirty that evening Etienne had taken up a position in rue Gambon, close enough to the back door of the Ritz to be able to monitor anyone who left. Earlier he'd gone into the hotel to ask about room rates, and surreptitiously glanced towards the concierge's desk to look at Pascal so he would recognize him later.

Now, as he waited for the man to appear through the back door, his heart kept telling him just to pull him into a back alley, stick a knife at his throat and demand to know where Belle was. But his head told him that wasn't a good idea.

For one thing, Pascal might not know, if there were others involved, and as Etienne's name was known to the gendarmes, he might find himself locked up and Belle would be lost for good.

He'd been busy all day talking to fiacre drivers, old friends who might know something about Pascal, and he'd been over to introduce himself to Philippe Le Brun at the address Philippe had given Noah earlier in the day. He liked Philippe, he sensed he'd come up the hard way too as he hadn't got a snobbish bone in his body, and he'd willingly agreed to contact Pascal again to get him to make another appointment with Belle. Etienne had left him saying that unless something else cropped up now when Pascal left the hotel, they would meet up later that evening at his restaurant in the Pigalle to discuss things further.

But for now Etienne just had to wait.

A flurry of women came out of the hotel back door at a few minutes past eight. Etienne assumed they were chambermaids. A couple of men came out too, waiters maybe or maintenance men. Then, just when he was beginning to think Pascal had left by the front entrance, he appeared too.

He had changed his smart livery for a dark suit, and he stopped by the door to light up a cigarette. Etienne felt his blood rising, for everything about the man, his thin, bony face, the carefully trimmed moustache, goatee beard and oiled hair, reminded him of other weasel-like characters he'd met in the past. He knew that if he got real proof this man had hurt Belle, he would want to tear him apart, limb by limb.

Pascal threw the cigarette butt down and stamped on it, then walked up the street towards the Boulevard des Capucines. He was moving at a brisk pace, and it looked as if he was going to catch a bus.

Etienne stayed well back, and when he saw Pascal join others waiting at a bus stop, he hailed a fiacre and told the driver to wait until the bus came, then follow it until he told him to stop.

It was a fine, mild evening, the roads were busy with traffic and there were moments when Etienne feared the cab driver would lose the bus for carts and carriages kept getting in the way. But as they approached the Gare du Nord, he saw Pascal get off the bus. For a moment he thought he was going into the station to catch a train, and cursed, for that would make it hard to follow him, but as Etienne stopped the cab and paid the driver, he saw Pascal was walking up Boulevard Magenta in the direction of Garrow's, the undertaker.

He didn't go that far though. Instead he turned into a left-hand side street, then turned right again. Etienne stayed just twenty yards behind him and fortunately there were enough people out and about for Pascal not to notice he was being followed. They were in a narrow street of tall houses which were probably all apartments, and Pascal went right to the end before disappearing into one.

Etienne waited a moment or two, then slipped into the

hallway. It was like a thousand other apartment houses in Paris, gloomy, reeking of stale cooking smells, with a tiled floor, grubby-looking walls, and a winding staircase going up the six floors at the back. Beneath the staircase there were a couple of bicycles.

Twelve post boxes hung in the hall, and Pascal's name was on number four, proof that this was where he lived. Etienne supposed that as there were two apartments on each floor Pascal's was on the first.

Somewhat disappointed, Etienne jotted down the address on a scrap of paper and put it in his wallet. He had expected the man to be living somewhere fancier as he had been making so much out of Belle.

He waited a little further down the street until after nine o'clock, and as Pascal didn't reappear, it seemed likely that he was in for the night. As Etienne turned to go back down the street he decided to go to Philippe's restaurant and pay another fiacre to go and collect Noah so that the evening wouldn't be entirely wasted.

Philippe Le Brun greeted Etienne warmly at Le Petit Poulet. It was a traditional Parisian restaurant, long and narrow, and it was packed with diners. But Philippe led him to a table he had kept free and was pleased to hear that Noah would be joining them shortly.

'So did you manage to contact Pascal this afternoon and ask him if you could meet Belle again?' Etienne asked the moment they were seated.

'I did indeed, and he looked furtive,' Philippe smirked. 'I mean, more so than usual. He responded just how I'd expected, saying I was to leave it with him to contact her. Then I said I didn't know how he was going to do that because I'd already called at the hotel she lived in and her landlady said she'd been gone for a few days.'

'What did he say to that?'

'He was visibly thrown; asked how I knew where she lived. I said that the last time I was with her I took her home.'

'And?' Etienne asked.

Philippe chuckled. 'That shook him. But I'm not sure whether it was because I knew she was missing, or because he couldn't imagine any man treating a whore like a lady. Maybe it occurred to him that he could easily find himself cut out as the middle man if men took the girls home.'

'What then?'

'Well, whatever was on his mind, he blustered a bit, said, "You know how these girls are, probably met someone who has taken her away with him." I pointed out it was odd she'd taken nothing with her, and that I was considering alerting the gendarmes in case of foul play. Well, that did it – his voice rose, his eyes flashed and he said that would look bad for me. I pointed out it would look bad for him too as I'd have to tell the gendarmes how I met her.'

He stopped talking to pour both himself and Etienne a glass of claret, swirling his in the glass and sniffing it appreciatively before taking a sip. 'With that I turned and walked away. I thought it best to leave him to stew, not knowing what I was going to do.'

Etienne wished then that he hadn't left his post by Pascal's house. If the man had been panicked by Philippe, he might very well be rushing off now to tell whoever was in this with him that trouble was brewing for them.

Chapter Thirty-three

Belle could think of nothing but how thirsty she was. Each time she closed her eyes she saw water running from a tap and imagined cupping her hands and leaning forward to drink it. She tried to distract herself by thinking of Mog, but when she did Mog was holding the teapot, pouring tea into a cup.

A noise downstairs startled her out of it. She sat up to listen, sure she'd imagined the sound. But she hadn't – someone was definitely down there. She was off the bed and over to the door in a second, her thirst forgotten, and she yelled and hammered on the door with her fists.

She paused to listen, and she could hear footsteps coming up the stairs and noticed there was a beam of light around the door which meant the electricity had been restored.

'Help me!' she yelled. 'I'm in here!'

'I know you are in there,' Pascal's all too familiar voice rang out. 'Now, stand away from the door as I'm coming in with some food and drink.'

Relief washed over her and she spontaneously moved back, holding the remains of her torn bodice over her breasts. She heard the key turn in the lock, then, as the door opened slowly, much longed for light flooded into the room, making her blink. Pascal had a jug in his hand, and a bag hung over that arm, but in his other hand he held a knife.

'Don't be alarmed by the knife,' he said, using it to switch on the room light. 'I'll only use it if you try anything.'

Belle's eyes were on the jug, for now her thirst was greater than fear of a knife. 'Where have you been?' she gasped out. 'Why did you leave me so long?'

He handed her the jug, then quickly locked the door behind him. Belle lifted the jug to her lips and drank deeply. Water had never tasted so good.

'I hope by now you have decided you are going to be nice to me,' he said.

Her thirst quenched, Belle put the jug down on the washstand. 'I'll do anything you say, but don't leave me locked up in here any longer,' she said.

'Sit down and eat this,' he said, holding out the bag.

Belle snatched it. Inside was a chunk of bread with some cheese. The bread was stale, the small piece of cheese very hard, but that didn't matter, she tore at it with her teeth, gulping it down so fast she couldn't even taste it.

Pascal stood watching her. She glanced up at him a couple of times and he was smirking.

'Thank you,' she said, once the last crumb was gone. 'I thought you were never coming back.'

'I had to teach you to have some respect for me,' he said with a hint of menace. 'But I'm sure now you know what I can do to you, everything will be different.'

With her thirst gone and hunger partially sated, Belle's wits came back to her. 'What do you want of me?'

'I want your love,' he said.

Belle's heart sank. She looked into his eyes and instead of the cold, dead look she'd noticed the first time she met him, she saw the same kind of madness she'd seen in Faldo's eyes that last night with him. She hadn't handled Faldo very well, even though she had felt some affection for him, but she loathed Pascal and the thought of him touching her again made her flesh crawl.

'It takes time and patience for love to grow,' she said carefully, very aware now of the knife in his hand. It was only six inches long, with a thin blade, but it looked very sharp. 'Locking me up without food or drink isn't the way to make love happen.'

'In that case I'll settle for the pretend love you show your clients,' he said, licking his lips lasciviously as he stared at her.

She had been so intent on drinking and eating that she'd forgotten about her ripped dress and her exposed breasts. A cold shudder went down her spine and she tried to cover herself.

'There's no need to cover them up,' he said. 'I like looking at them. And I know how passionate you are with your clients. Many of them reported back to me.'

Just his oily voice, let alone what he was saying, was enough for her stomach to churn. She couldn't do it with him, she couldn't bear it.

'But you don't want me like this,' she said, backing away from him in horror. 'I'm dirty – let me have a wash and some clean clothes first.'

'I don't mind you dirty,' he said, moving towards her and reaching out to touch her right breast. 'It's a reminder that you are a whore, and besides, the smell on you is from the last time I had you. I like that.'

Belle's stomach lurched. She had always found it so easy to flirt with her clients, and to say flattering things to them to put them at their ease, even when she didn't like them. But Pascal was so deeply repulsive to her that she couldn't even attempt to switch on those well-practised lines, not even now when she knew her life depended on being what he wanted her to be.

'Take off your clothes,' he said when she made no response. 'Every stitch. I want to see you naked.'

She felt the way she had with that first man at Madame Sondheim's, stark, cold terror washing over her. But he was brandishing the knife and instinct told her he wouldn't hesitate to cut her.

Reluctantly she began to strip. Her dress was so damaged that it slid to the floor easily. She untied the waist of her petticoat and let that drop too till she was standing in just her chemise. He'd ripped off her drawers downstairs, days ago, and she'd taken off her stockings soon after she was locked in. She really couldn't bear to take off the last garment, even though it was so torn it didn't cover much.

'And that,' he said, and stepped forward, putting the knife against the shoulder straps and cutting first one, then the other, in two quick movements. The chemise fell to the floor.

'On the bed,' he said, and still holding the knife in his hand, he pulled off his jacket, tossed it to one side, flicked his braces off his shoulders and began unbuttoning his trousers.

There was nothing she could do but comply. His trousers were around his feet now, his shirt nearly reaching his bony knees, and his black socks were held up with suspenders. He took his cock in his hand to fondle it, while looking down at her. But as he was still holding the knife in his free hand she knew she couldn't escape what he wanted to do to her, and so she had to get it over with as quickly as possible.

'Come and let me hold you,' she said, trying to sound seductive, but she could hear the desperation and loathing in her voice and felt certain he could too.

'Open your legs. Show yourself to me,' he demanded, and leaned down and put the tip of his knife on her pubic hair.

Tears started up in her eyes. She'd been told by one of the girls at Martha's about a girl in another sporting house who had her belly ripped open by a man and she was afraid that was what Pascal intended to do.

She felt she had to do the lewd act he wanted, and held the lips of her vagina apart for him to see her.

'Did you do that for Le Brun?' he asked. 'Is that why he wanted to see you again?'

Belle was confused by that question. Had Philippe really wanted to see her again and Pascal was jealous?

'I don't remember,' she whimpered.

480

'Yes, you do. He liked fucking you so much he went to find you in your hotel.'

That was even stranger. She hadn't told Philippe where she lived.

'I told him you'd gone away with a man. He didn't like that. Rich, powerful men like him are used to having everything their way. But you're mine now. No one else will ever have you, and I'm going to mark you to remind you that you are mine.'

He slid the knife up her belly, piercing the skin. Belle looked down and saw the thin red line of blood appearing from her pubic hair to her navel and all at once the room seemed to swirl around and grow dark.

'There's little point in rushing back there now,' Philippe said calmly. 'If Pascal has gone out you'll just have a wasted journey, and anyway, wouldn't he have gone wherever he had to on his way home from work if he was that panicked?'

'I suppose so,' Etienne replied and allowed Philippe to pour him a second glass of wine. He glanced up and saw Noah coming into the restaurant, grinning broadly as he made his way through the diners.

Pulling out a chair, Noah sat down and beamed at the two other men. 'I've got some information,' he said.

As he began to talk excitedly about what he'd found out at *Le Petit Journal* during the afternoon neither Etienne nor Philippe could understand what he was trying to tell them. He was speaking so fast, using people's names they didn't know and making references to a newspaper article without telling them what it was about.

'We aren't following this at all. Calm down and tell us what you've found,' Etienne said reprovingly and poured him a glass of wine.

Noah blushed furiously. 'I'm sorry, I've been waiting and

481

waiting back at the Mirabeau, dying to tell you what I'd found,' he said by way of explanation, and drank half the glass of wine in one gulp.

'You see, I wasn't getting anywhere much until I mentioned to the editor that Pascal had been an undertaker and I thought he was still Garrow's partner,' he said, speaking more slowly. 'Then suddenly he remembered a story about two undertakers being arrested for brawling in the street. He said everyone thought it funny at the time as no one expects sombre undertakers to fight.'

'It was them? Pascal and Garrow?' Etienne asked.

'Yes, well, he had to look it up to check the names, but it was them. It happened three years ago. They were let off with a warning, but one of the journalists followed it up because he was curious about why they were fighting. It seemed it was over an old woman who had died and left a house to Pascal. It transpired that Garrow was livid because he'd looked after her, going round to her and doing little jobs, and his wife did her laundry. But Pascal had done nothing more than call on her occasionally with the odd bunch of flowers. He accused Pascal of tricking her into changing her will in his favour and he said he should sell the house and share the proceeds with him.'

'But he wouldn't?' Philippe asked.

'No, he refused point blank, and that appears to be why Pascal left the business and went to work at the Ritz, because of the bad feeling between them.'

'So where is this house?' Etienne asked.

'In Montmartre.' Noah passed a piece of paper with the address on to Etienne. 'So now we know where he lives. If my partner and brother-in-law came by a house like that and moved into it, leaving me to run the business alone, I think I'd be pretty damn angry about it too.'

'But he doesn't live there.' Etienne frowned. 'I followed

him home today and he lives in an apartment house in a street off Boulevard Magenta.'

Noah looked puzzled. 'Really? But I got someone to check up if he still owned it, and he does. Why wouldn't he live in it?'

Philippe took the piece of paper and looked at the address. 'I know this street, they are big, fairly new houses. He's probably rented it out.'

Etienne leapt to his feet. 'I'm going to go round there now to see.'

'But I was just going to order us all some dinner,' Philippe said, looking askance at him. 'Leave it till tomorrow?'

'You two stay and order,' Etienne said hurriedly. 'I must go and check it out.'

He left so fast the other two men looked at each other in astonishment. 'Was it really that urgent?' Noah asked.

Philippe grinned sympathetically at him. 'He nearly ran out of here ten minutes before you came, when I told him about the run in I had today with Pascal. Let me tell you about that.'

Etienne looked up at the six-storey building in rue Tholoze reflectively. It was an attractive and well-proportioned house, probably only built in the last twenty years, and though the gas street lights weren't bright enough to see very clearly it looked as if it was in very good condition. All the rooms were in darkness except for a faint glow in the fanlight window above the front door. In his experience that meant the residents were out for the evening and had left just one light on in the hall to see their way in later.

He was curious as to why Pascal hadn't moved in there. Anyone would prefer to live here rather than the dingy street his apartment was in. If Etienne was left a house like this he would have kept the ground floor for himself and let the upper rooms. Rents in Montmartre were high now, the days when it was home to struggling artists were long gone – they'd all moved to Montparnasse where it was a great deal cheaper.

Not wishing to go back to Philippe and Noah without some information to make his hurried departure from the restaurant look vital, he went to the neighbouring house and knocked on the door. A man of about sixty with a thick mane of white hair opened it and Etienne apologized for disturbing him. 'I've been trying to contact the owner of next door, Monsieur Pascal,' he said. 'I heard he had rooms to let.'

'Not him, he won't let it out to anyone,' the man said curtly.

'Really?' Etienne exclaimed. 'I was told he was anxious to let out some rooms.'

'Whoever told you that doesn't know the man. People are always asking for a room, but he won't let them have one. Always seemed crazy to me because he's hardly ever there.'

'Is that so?' Etienne exclaimed. 'How odd to let a big house like that lie empty.'

'The man is very odd. Comes for an hour and then he goes,' the man said, and his tone suggested he had a grudge against Pascal.

'I had heard he's a difficult man,' Etienne said in his most solicitous tone. 'I was warned he's slippery too. Is that true?'

'He certainly is. A jumped-up nobody who thinks he's gentry now he's got that place. And he got it under dubious circumstances!'

'How was that?'

'He tricked Madame Florette, the old lady who used to own it, into making him her heir. Absolutely disgraceful! She had two nephews who should have got it.'

Etienne was delighted that anger was making the man so indiscreet. 'But it makes no sense not to make money out of it. Would you know when he was last here?'

'The Thursday after Easter. I remember very well because I was so angry that his overgrown garden was invading my

484

small yard. I saw him walk past my window and I ran out to have it out with him.'

Etienne's heart leapt, for that was the day Belle disappeared. It could just be coincidence of course, but he knew he must get in to the house and look around. 'The Thursday, that would be the eleventh. Are you absolutely sure?'

'Completely sure. I entered it into my diary because I may have to take legal action against him. I've only got a small space out back, but I keep it nice. I used to look after Madame Florette's too, even though it's twice the size of mine, because she was old and couldn't manage it. But he's let it run to ruin and it's going to block out the light in my kitchen if he doesn't cut back before summer comes.'

'I hope he promised to do something about it?' Etienne responded.

'No, he didn't, he was rude to me, as he always is. He just hurried in and shut the door in my face.'

'You haven't seen him tonight then?' Etienne asked. 'He's left a light on in the hall. I assumed that means he's coming back later.'

'He never stays overnight. There isn't any furniture in the upstairs rooms, only in the drawing room. Madame Florette had so many lovely things and she left those to her friends and relatives. But for some reason she left the drawing room intact for that odious man. We had all the relatives calling on us after she died to collect things – we held the keys, you see – and they were very upset that she'd left the house to this ignorant undertaker. But there was nothing anyone could do.'

'On that night of the eleventh, he didn't bring a young lady here, did he?'

The older man frowned. 'He arrived alone, that's why I went out to see him. But he may have had someone there later on, I did hear a fiacre stop. But I can't be sure it was someone for him.'

Etienne felt the time had come to be more truthful. 'To be honest, sir, I'm not interested in renting that house. I am trying to find a young lady who has disappeared. I am certain Monsieur Pascal had a hand in that disappearance.'

The older man looked hard at Etienne, perhaps feeling it might have been unwise to say so much to a stranger. But then he sniffed. 'Well, he's certainly shady enough. But are you suggesting she might be in the house now?'

'It's possible. She disappeared the night of the eleventh, and he did send a cab to take her to Montmartre, I have a note in his handwriting to that effect. Have you heard any noise coming from his house?'

The man shook his head. 'But then, the walls are thick.'

'Would it be too much of an imposition to ask if I could get over into his garden from yours?'

The man hesitated. 'How do I know you aren't planning to rob my neighbour?'

'Would you care if I did?'

The older man smirked. 'No, but I don't like being fooled.'

'You'll be a hero if the girl is in there,' Etienne said. 'Take a risk with me? Please! He could have hurt her.'

'Then it's my duty to assist you. Come in.'

Etienne followed the man through a wide hall with two doors opening on to it, then on into a narrower passage which led to the kitchen, beyond which was a scullery. The man opened a door on to the yard. 'I shall deny knowing how you gained access to his garden if you are caught,' he said, but then smiled. 'Good luck. You will tell me if you find the girl?'

'You and the whole neighbourhood will know,' Etienne said. 'I am indebted to you.'

Etienne could see immediately why Pascal's neighbour was so rattled, for in the light coming from his scullery he could see the bushes and brambles on the other side of the six-foot wall dividing the two houses were thick and tall. Though not yet in full leaf, by summer they would be rambling over on to the small, neat yard.

He climbed the wall as effortlessly as a cat and chose a spot to get down to the other side where the brambles were less thick. Even in the dark he could see that the whole garden was totally overgrown. Here and there he could see almost luminous white blossom and smell a sweet, musky scent, which told him it had once been a much loved garden. He waited among the bushes until his eyes grew used to the dark, and then went down to the end of the garden where there was a large tree. He turned and looked back at the house. The three-quarter moon was bright, hanging right above the house, and he could see that it was taller than both its neighbours. There were no lights except a faint glow in a narrow window on the first floor, by which he assumed that it was the window on the stairs, and the light was coming up from the hall.

Going back to the house, he tried the back door, which he found was locked and bolted. Locks were no deterrent to him, but bolts were, so he looked around for an easier way in. The small window beside the back door looked good. He always carried a thin, sharp knife in a leather sheath attached to his belt and he took it out and slid the blade between the window and the frame. He could feel the metal of the catch and it was stiff, but it lifted after a couple of seconds of working on it, and the window opened.

He climbed in to find he was above the sink, and jumped silently to the floor. The layout was the same as the neighbour's house and he walked through to the kitchen, then opened the door through to the hall. Even though he'd known a light was on there he was still startled to find himself in such brightness. He stopped to listen before looking around. He could hear nothing but the ticking of a clock which appeared to be coming from a room at the front of the house.

The first door he opened was devoid of any furniture, and the walls were papered in dark green, with faded places where pictures had once hung. He assumed it had been the dining room. The second door nearest to the front door was to a well-furnished drawing room, the walls lined with books. The curtains were closed, and having seen it he shut the door again and started to go upstairs. He noticed that the stair carpet and the pictures hanging on the wall didn't go with the good taste he'd seen in the drawing room. The carpet was a bright red, it looked thin and cheap, and the pictures were the kind anyone could buy for twenty francs in the flea market. He guessed this was Pascal's input.

He had only reached the fifth step when he heard a sound. He stopped and listened. It was almost like a dog's growl, yet he sensed it was human, and it was coming from the top of the house. Etienne was always light on his feet – people often said he unnerved them because they never heard him coming – but up till now he'd made no effort to be silent. It seemed he wasn't in an empty house, however.

Creeping up on tiptoe, he winced as a stair creaked, and strained his ears to listen. The growl-like noise came again, and as he reached the first landing he could hear a low thumping sound too. Both sounds could be put down to the kinds of noise someone might make if they were tied up and gagged, and therefore it could be Belle, imprisoned in one of the upstairs rooms. But much as he wanted to run up there full tilt and check, he knew he must be cautious. He withdrew his knife again and continued creeping up, listening all the while, poised to strike out if necessary.

When he reached the fourth floor there was very little light coming from the hall any more, but as he looked upwards over the banisters he saw a chink coming from the top floor. The thumping sound was much louder now, and suddenly he realized what he was hearing. Furthermore he recognized the growling sound as the kind of noise a gagged person might make, and he was certain it was Belle.

Incensed, he threw caution aside, running at full tilt up the last flight of stairs, and when he reached the door he ran at it with his shoulder. The whole door and frame shuddered and creaked, he went back and did it again harder still, and this time the door crashed open, pieces of wood on the frame shattered and falling to the floor.

The scene in front of him made Etienne's stomach turn. Pascal had already leapt from the bed and backed up to the far wall, holding Belle in front of him.

She was naked, her face white and terrified, blood running down her stomach and legs. She had something stuck in her mouth as a gag. And Pascal was holding a knife to her throat.

Her eyes were wide with shock at seeing Etienne.

'Come any closer and I'll slit her ear to ear,' Pascal hissed. He was wearing just a shirt and his socks held up by suspenders, but his shirt was stained with blood. 'Who are you anyway?'

'Let her go,' Etienne commanded. He had concealed his own knife up his sleeve the moment he saw Pascal had one, and now he surreptitiously slid it back into the sheath to keep his hands free. 'You can have me as a hostage, but let her go.'

'Why would I want to do that?' Pascal said with disdain. 'I hold all the cards here. Make one move on me and I'll cut her throat.'

Etienne was aware the man did hold all the cards. If he was to turn and run for help, Belle would die. If he tried to grab Pascal, the chances were that the man would make good his threat.

Years ago when he was just a boy, an uncle of his who was a prize fighter had told him a cornered man was just as dangerous and as unpredictable as a cornered animal. Etienne had found it to be true on many an occasion. He knew he had to get his rage under control and think before making a move. 'I don't want to hurt you, and I don't want Belle hurt either,' he said as calmly as possible.

'You can't hurt me,' Pascal said smugly. 'She's my woman. I've waited a long time to find the right one, and now I've got her, I'm going to keep her.'

Belle's eyes were fixed on Etienne. Although she was clearly terrified, his sudden arrival must seem like a miracle to her. Etienne glanced around the bare room, noting that the window was boarded up. He winced when he saw her blood all over the blanket. 'Keep her in here? Like a caged animal?' he asked. 'What pleasure can there be in that?'

'You don't know anything about me,' Pascal retorted. 'This is my house, and she'll be mistress of it.'

Etienne realized then that the man must be completely deranged if he thought he could rape a woman, lock her up, slice her with a knife, threaten to cut her throat, yet imagine that she wouldn't run from him at the first opportunity. He knew he must be very cautious and try to talk him round.

'If you want a woman to stay with you then you have to show her some kindness and affection,' he said. Belle raised her eyebrows as if trying to warn him Pascal was extremely volatile.

'She's a whore, she's used to being paid for. I'll keep her and clothe her, and she'll stay with me. Who are you anyway?'

'Just one of many people who have been searching for her,' Etienne said. 'Even now there is a group of men waiting for me to report back about whether you were here or not. When I don't come back they'll come looking for me. And your neighbour knows I'm here. He let me get over the garden wall. He'll call the gendarmes soon. So let Belle go, and it won't be so bad for you.'

'I told you, come any closer and I'll cut her throat.'

Etienne saw Belle's hands moving towards her gag, but she was clearly too frightened to reach up and pull it out in case he slashed at her. 'At least let her take that rag from her mouth, she can barely breathe,' he said.

'No, I don't want to hear her voice. Every word she says is a lie. I brought her here to my house to give her a good life with me, but she wouldn't even give me what she'll give any other man who pays her.'

'I see,' Etienne said, and leaned back against the wall to create a less threatening image. 'So you love her, is that it?'

'You think a man like me can't love?' Pascal said angrily.

Belle looked straight at Etienne and winked, then blinked in an exaggerated manner while moving her hands slightly up and down. He felt she was trying to tell him that she could lift her hands to knock the knife away, if he would be ready to pounce on Pascal.

'I think love can lift any man up,' he said, hoping that she would understand that was his coded answer. 'But sometimes we think women have given us a signal that they want us, and we are mistaken.'

Belle blinked very quickly again, and he was sure then that he'd read her message right.

'What about your wife?' Etienne asked, and shuffled a few inches nearer to Pascal along the wall. 'How can you hope to keep Belle here when you already have a wife?'

'Frenchmen have always had mistresses,' he said.

'But a mistress has to be willing,' Etienne said, moving again. He was close enough to spring at the man now but he wanted to wait until he was off guard or growing weary of standing in one position. 'Belle isn't willing, is she? And the gendarmes have gone to your home to look for you. They'll go to see Garrow too. He'll tell them about this house, just as he told one of my friends today.'

Pascal's face seemed to sag a little. Etienne hoped by continuing to overload him with worrying thoughts he might lose his self-control for a second or two. 'This is all a terrible mess for you, isn't it? Your neighbour is suspicious of you, he saw Belle arrive here in a fiacre. He'll be contacting the gendarmes now as I didn't come straight out. And what about your job at the Ritz? If this gets out they'll fire you, but of course that hardly matters as you'll be sent to prison.'

'Shut your mouth!' Pascal roared at him. Belle nodded her head at Etienne as the man shifted his feet, and as her hand came up to swipe away the knife from her throat, Etienne leapt towards them, catching Pascal by his shoulders and pushing him hard against the wall.

Belle had slithered to the floor; Etienne couldn't pause to check if the knife had wounded her, he had to concentrate on beating Pascal into submission. Holding him back against the wall with his left hand, he punched him in the belly with all his strength, winding him, and heard the knife fall from his hand to the floor.

It was several years since Etienne had last beaten anyone. His reputation was such that most troublemakers or double-crossers backed down when he came after them. He had always prided himself on using only the minimum of force needed to suppress or control someone he'd been sent after. But he had stored up anger since he lost Elena and the boys, and as he looked down at Pascal holding his belly, he felt murderous at what he'd done to Belle.

He caught hold of the man's neck, bringing him up to his own height, and punched him in the face with his full force. He heard the man's cry for mercy as blood erupted from his smashed nose, and that goaded him further, so he caught hold of his head and banged it back against the wall over and over again.

'No more, Etienne,' Belle yelled out. 'You'll kill him. Tie him up and let the gendarmes deal with him.'

Hearing her voice brought him out of the dark place he'd

492

slipped into and he let Pascal slide down the wall to the floor, unconscious.

He turned to see Belle standing there, Pascal's knife in her hand, tears running down her cheeks making white tracks through the blood and grime. Her hair was matted and she was still naked.

'There's rope under the mattress,' she sobbed. 'Just tie him up and let's get out of here.'

Etienne picked up the blanket from the bed and wrapped it round her.

Suddenly they both heard the sound of breaking glass downstairs. Etienne guessed it was Noah and Philippe, but Belle quaked visibly. 'Don't be scared, that's reinforcements,' he said, holding her to him tightly. 'It's all over now. We're going to take you somewhere safe.'

Chapter Thirty-four

Etienne couldn't bear the sound of Belle whimpering any longer. Twenty-four hours had passed since he had rescued her from Pascal, and Philippe had arranged for her to be brought to this private nursing home. A doctor had attended her as soon as she got here, and he'd dressed the wound on her belly, which mercifully wasn't deep enough to need stitching. He said he thought she would recover completely with rest and good food. Etienne had taken it upon himself to keep a vigil outside her door as he felt the doctor was being too complacent about what she'd been through.

He opened the door and went in. It was a small, all-white room with an iron bed and a wooden crucifix above it. One of the nurses had lit a night-light when it grew dark, and Belle's hair stood out in stark relief against the white bed linen.

'Can't you sleep?' he asked gently. 'Would it help if I sat beside you in here? Or would you like to talk?'

'I'm afraid to fall asleep,' she whispered. 'I think I'm scared I'll wake up later and find I'd dreamt you rescued me. I don't even understand how you found me.'

After what she'd been through Etienne found it unsurprising that she'd hardly said a word after her rescue. He thought it was quite possible she'd never be able to tell anyone exactly what Pascal had done to her, though the bleeding, bruises and her terror told much of the story. But he thought it was a good sign that she had questions to ask.

'Noah and I have been like your English Sherlock Holmes,' he said lightly, perching on the edge of the bed. 'We snooped, bullied and pushed our way into finding you. What was that phrase Holmes used to say to his companion? "Elementary, my dear Watson."'

He was rewarded with a faint ghost of a smile.

'Who is Noah? He spoke as if he knew me well but I'm sure I've never met him before,' she said, frowning as if she'd been puzzled for some time.

'He was a friend of Millie's, the girl who was killed at your mother's,' Etienne said. 'Mog, the lady you told me about, went to him to ask for his help in finding you when you disappeared. You see, he's a journalist. He's been backwards and forwards to France several times trying to find you. On one of those trips he met Lisette, who nursed you before I took you to New Orleans, and she told him you'd been taken to America. But it is really Madame Herrison you have to thank for your rescue. When you didn't come home on the night of the eleventh she was afraid for you. Lisette is an old friend of hers and she went to her for advice. She was amazed to find Lisette knew you and furthermore had Noah's address in England, so she sent him a telegram, and she got word to me in Marseille.'

'Gabrielle did all that?' Belle whispered.

'She's been hurt by men herself and she is fond of you,' he said. 'But I can explain all of it more clearly when you feel better. The gendarmes have Pascal now, and Philippe Le Brun is arranging papers for you so that you can go home to England.'

'But wasn't Philippe in with Pascal? It was his house I was kept in.'

Etienne smoothed her hair back from her face tenderly. 'No, it was Pascal's house, Philippe knew nothing of it until Noah and I went to see him. He is a good man, and he's another person who likes you very much. He and Noah have spent the day with the gendarmes explaining everything. As you must be aware, my credentials are not as good as theirs, so I opted for staying here with you.'

'So Noah knows my mother and Mog?'

Etienne felt a surge of emotion at the hope in her eyes.

'Very well, from what he said your Mog has almost adopted him as family. She has never given up hope of you being found.'

'And my mother, Annie?'

Etienne had hoped Belle would wait to ask Noah about her mother. From what he gathered, she hadn't taken any part in trying to find her daughter. 'You'll have to ask Noah about her,' he said carefully. 'We only met a few days ago and we've been too preoccupied with finding you to talk about anything much else.'

'Does everyone know what I am?' she asked in a small voice.

'They know only what we told them, that you were abducted from England.'

'But Pascal will tell them how I went to him for clients.'

Etienne's heart tightened in sympathy for her. There was so much in his life that he was ashamed of, but he had chosen his path, she had been pushed on to hers. 'I think you'll find Philippe can tell a plausible tale or two, and no other man is going to come forward and say something different. Besides, Pascal is a madman, no one will pay much attention to anything he might say.'

She was silent for some little time, and he guessed she was mulling that over.

'Tell me how you have been,' she asked suddenly, as if she wanted to dispel memories of Pascal and her ordeal in that attic room. 'I didn't expect to ever see you again, but I've thought about you a great deal in the last two years.'

'I've got a little cottage now, I'm clearing the land to grow crops. I'm out of the business I used to be in.'

'I'm glad of that,' she said. 'It must be a great relief to your wife too.'

He nodded. He wasn't going to tell her about his misfortunes, she'd had enough of her own. 'Try to sleep now,' he suggested. 'I'll be close by if you need me.'

'Don't you want to know how I ended up back in France?' she asked.

'Of course I do, I just didn't think you were ready for that.'

'It might help me lay some ghosts.' She grimaced. 'I did become the top girl at Martha's, there were times I even loved it there. But Martha was a snake, she only paid me a pittance because she said she had to get back what she'd laid out for me.'

'I'm sorry to hear that. When I told you she was a good woman I was repeating what I'd heard. But even basically decent people can turn where money is concerned. So how did you get away from there?'

'I pretended I was just going for a walk, and went off to become the mistress of one of my clients,' she said. 'It was the only way I could get free, and I thought I could then save up enough to get back to England.'

'I hope he was a good man,' Etienne said, and caressed her cheek gently.

'I believed he was, he was kind and I liked him. I really wanted to make him happy,' she said as her eyes filled with tears. 'But he changed as soon as he'd set me up in a little house. He didn't talk to me, he'd never tell me in advance when he was calling, wouldn't take me out anywhere, he just used me and made me feel so bad about myself. Why did he change like that, Etienne? It was like I'd just swopped one prison for another.'

Etienne sighed deeply, and picked up her hand and kissed the tips of her fingers. 'It was probably because he'd fallen for you and he was afraid you'd deceive him. I'd say he was very unsure of himself.'

Belle explained briefly about how lonely she was and how she got to know Miss Frank in the hat shop and arranged to help her make hats.

'I never dared tell Faldo where I went every day, but learning to make hats cheered me so much. On nights when he didn't call on me I spent my time designing too. Miss Frank even got an order for one of my designs and I really thought I was getting somewhere. But then Faldo died.'

'He died? How?'

'He had a heart attack, while we were –' She stopped abruptly, dropping her eyes. Etienne guessed by that exactly what Faldo was doing when he died.

'He was hateful to me that night,' she said in a small voice, tears rolling down her cheeks. 'I asked him why he didn't talk to me or take me out anywhere, and he said all kinds of horrible things and hit me. Then he started pleading with me and saying he couldn't help himself because he wanted my heart. He said that, then he forced himself on me like a madman.' She broke down then and all Etienne could do was hold her hand and wait till she could finish.

'He had some kind of turn while he was doing it,' she sobbed. 'I ran for help, but by the time I got back with a policeman he was dead. Later, when a doctor got there, he said it was a heart attack.'

Etienne could well imagine just how terrible all that was to a young girl who had no one to turn to. He'd met plenty of young women who when anxious to get out of a brothel had put their trust in an older man. It usually turned sour, perhaps because the kind of men who offered a new life to a one-time whore were usually inadequate themselves.

'You must have been so frightened,' Etienne said.

Belle nodded. 'I went to Miss Frank, I thought she would help me, but when I told her about everything she turned against me too. So I packed up my things and got a passage on the only ship that would take me. That was bound for Marseille.'

Etienne raised one eyebrow. 'I wish I'd known.'

Belle squeezed his hand. 'I thought about you on the voyage, but I wouldn't have dared ask anyone if they knew you, in case the wrong people got to hear about it. But I was a fool there too. You'd think I would have learned by then not to trust anyone.'

'Who did you trust there?'

'Well, first it was another passenger on the ship, a man called Arnaud Germaine. He took me to the house of a friend of his, Madame Albertine. Do you know either of them?'

Etienne gave a wry half-smile. 'I don't recognize the name Germaine, but I have heard of Madame Albertine. She is well known for introducing handsome young men to rich older women.'

Belle frowned at this, wondering if the young men she had met at Madame Albertine's house, Clovis included, were potential gigolos. Afraid she might have been mistaken about the older woman's intentions towards her, and embarrassed about what happened with Clovis, she didn't wish to say anything further about Marseille.

'Well, let's just say I regretted telling her all about myself,' she said. 'So I caught the train to Paris.'

Etienne remembered that Gabrielle had said Belle arrived at the Mirabeau wearing an evening dress beneath her coat, without any luggage, so he guessed she had had some kind of humiliating experience in Marseille which she didn't wish to reveal.

'We all make the mistake of trusting the wrong people sometimes,' he said soothingly. 'I certainly have, many times. But sometimes we also put our trust in the right ones, as you did with Gabrielle, and I did with Noah and Philippe.'

'I thought I was seeing things when you came hurtling through that door,' she said with a faint chuckle. 'I even forgot to be embarrassed at having no clothes on.'

Etienne smiled back at her. 'In years to come we'll think we were in a scene in a penny dreadful. It's a shame I didn't think to say, "Unhand her, you scoundrel."'

Belle managed a real laugh at that. 'It is so good to see you again. When I was back in New Orleans I used to wonder if you were really as handsome and mysterious as I remembered or whether that was just because I was so young and naive. But you are everything I remembered.'

'I've often recalled how you took care of me when I was seasick, and how beautiful you looked that last night before we got to New Orleans. It was so hard to leave you in New Orleans, Belle, I've always wished I hadn't taken you there.'

'You had no choice,' she said firmly. 'And don't feel bad about it, for in some ways it was the making of me.'

'How can you say that?' he asked.

'I grew up, I became self-reliant,' she said with a shrug of her shoulders. 'I learned a lot about people. But don't let's do this "I wish I hadn't" stuff. All the time I was in that room at Pascal's I kept doing that, and it just drives you mad.'

Etienne had been impressed on the way to America by Belle's ability to accept things she couldn't change, and he was very glad she was still that way. 'Fair enough. So what else would you like to tell me, or ask me?' he said.

'I left a lot of money in my room at the Mirabeau. Did Gabrielle find it?' she asked.

'I found it,' he said. 'It's all still there, perfectly safe. And Gabrielle has a big heart underneath her dour exterior. Noah went back there last night and told her you'd been found and where you were. He said she lit up like the Eiffel Tower, she'd been beside herself with worry. But tomorrow or the next day you can go back to see her. She can't wait to see you.'

Belle closed her eyes then, and Etienne thought he would wait until she was sound asleep, then creep out.

But a few minutes later her eyes flew open. 'I know I said we weren't to do the "I wish I hadn't" stuff, but have you ever felt that it would be better to just die rather than live with the awful things you've done?' she asked.

'Yes, I have,' he admitted, remembering that it was only a

few months ago that he thought of nothing else. 'But listen to me, Belle. One in every five women in Paris are *filles de joie*, and a large percentage of them have had no choice but to make a living that way, just like you. You didn't steal or hurt anyone, in fact you gave your clients a great deal of pleasure, so you must not feel bad about it.'

'I didn't feel bad, not until Pascal. But he brought home to me what selling my body really meant. In his way he was right, why wouldn't I let him have me? I was up for sale. Why didn't I see just how low I'd sunk? I could have worked as a waitress, or cleaned for people. But I thought I was too good for that. How could I think being a whore was better?'

Etienne leaned forward, scooped her into his arms and held her tightly. 'He was bad, not you, Belle. Don't you dare begin to think you deserved what he did to you. Death isn't a solution, it's just the coward's way of escaping the hurt. The brave thing to do is to put the past where it belongs, behind you. I've seen those hats in your sketchbook, and you have real talent. So think of going back to England with the slate wiped clean, of becoming a milliner and achieving your dream.'

She began to cry then, not the sad little whimpers he'd heard before, but great heaving, cleansing sobs. Etienne continued to hold her as she wept, knowing that the healing process could not begin until she let it all out.

She cried for a very long time, but gradually it began to abate. Etienne got a wet facecloth and bathed her swollen eyes. 'Do you think you can sleep now? Have I convinced you that you are safe, that Pascal is locked up and that you are going home to England very soon?'

Belle gave a smile then, a weak, watery one. 'Yes, I'm convinced, but I have just one more question. Was Kent hanged for killing Millie?'

Etienne wasn't sure this was the right time to talk about that, but if he fobbed her off she would just worry about it too. 'No, he wasn't. There wasn't enough evidence to charge him with her murder. Noah has compiled quite a dossier on the man's crimes, and it wasn't just you he sold to a brothel, there were many other girls too. They are all still missing, and it's Noah's hope he can expose all those who had a part in it both back in England and here in France.'

'Then he'll need me to be a witness?'

Etienne hesitated. He was afraid if he said that her evidence was vital she would become scared again.

'No one is going to ask you to do anything you don't want to do.'

'I want him punished, for Millie's sake. And unless he is, and that horrible Madame Sondheim, then such things will just go on and on. But I wouldn't want people like you or Lisette to get dragged into it.'

'I shall be fine. I was just hired to escort you to America, you were not under age, and I had no choice either. I also have my own reasons to want the guilty punished, and I will assist the gendarmes with that. As for Lisette, she is as much a victim as you are, and Noah is sweet on her too, so she'll be looked after. Once the top people are arrested it usually follows that many others beneath them feel able to tell what they know. Noah hopes we may find the other girls too; they've all got families desperate for news of them.'

'Then I must be a witness,' Belle said. 'It would be very cowardly not to be.'

He smiled down at her, moved by her courage. 'It won't be easy for you. To be the main witness in a trial of this importance will mean your name will be in the newspapers, and people will talk,' he warned her.

'Let them talk,' she said. 'Bad men have to be stopped.'

'Were you here all night again?' Noah asked when he arrived at the nursing home the next morning to see how Belle was and found Etienne sitting outside her door looking hollow-eyed and unshaven.

'Yes, I was afraid she'd have nightmares,' Etienne said.

'Did she?'

'No, she slept remarkably peacefully. But before you go in to see her, let's go outside and talk. Then I'll introduce you properly before I go back to the Mirabeau to get cleaned up.'

Noah had long since lost all his reservations about the Frenchman, even if he had been a gangster, and for him to wait outside Belle's door for forty-eight hours was further evidence of the man's trustworthiness and his affection for her. They walked along the passage, down the stairs and out into a small courtyard garden at the back of the nursing home. It was a warm, sunny morning, and the sheltered garden was beautiful, bright with red and yellow tulips and a small tree laden with white blossom.

They sat down on a bench and Etienne told Noah that Belle was prepared to be a witness in any court proceedings.

'It turns out the police here have had some suspicions about Pascal for some time,' Noah said. 'Not only do they believe he tricked the old lady into giving him that house, but another girl, Claudette something or other, disappeared about eighteen months ago, and they think now he may have killed her.'

Etienne said that somehow it didn't surprise him and asked if she'd been a prostitute.

'No, she worked in a department store. A friend who worked at the same place and shared a room with her reported her missing when she didn't come home one night. She said that she was sure that a male customer who kept coming into the store to see her friend was responsible. She didn't know the man's name but the description she gave of him at the time fits Pascal. It was the girl's opinion that he had been waiting for her friend when the store closed and persuaded her to go somewhere with him.'

'Surely they followed it up?'

Noah shrugged. 'The police here seem almost as sloppy as in England. They did ask a lot of people whether they'd seen Claudette with anyone, but I suppose in a city the size of Paris it is difficult to find someone when they haven't even got his name. As they didn't find Claudette's body and she had no close relatives to push them harder, her details were just filed away and, until now, forgotten. Philippe translated all this to me, so something might have been lost in the translation, but they did say they intended to do a thorough search of Pascal's house and garden today.'

'Has Pascal said anything about Belle yet?'

'Apparently he refused to say a word for the first few hours they had him in custody, but around four o'clock yesterday afternoon he claimed he picked up Belle on the street, and she'd gone with him to his house willingly. He then said that after having sex with him she demanded five hundred francs, and said if he didn't give it to her she was going to tell his wife and his employers.'

Etienne shook his head in disbelief. 'So that's his excuse for locking her in a room for days and then raping her again and threatening to kill her?'

'He said he panicked,' Noah said wryly, raising one eyebrow. 'But as it turned out he played right into our hands by saying that. You see, Philippe had already said that Pascal had acted as a go-between for him and Belle, as Philippe had seen her having tea in the Ritz a few weeks earlier and he'd asked Pascal who she was. Philippe said Pascal stopped Belle as she was leaving the hotel and said there was a gentleman who wanted to meet her. And the upshot of that was Philippe taking her out to dinner a couple of times.'

'That was quick thinking,' Etienne said approvingly. 'It might make some think Belle was a bit fast, but that's less damaging to her than the truth.'

'Exactly. Philippe isn't the kind of man people doubt; he's a well-known, upright citizen who just happens to be a ladies' man, and besides, he clearly was very taken with Belle, the gendarmes must have sensed that. And as Philippe himself pointed out, if a body is found, that will be the main thrust of Pascal's trial, and Belle will only have to play a very minor part in it. And it is extremely unlikely that any other client of hers will come forward.'

'Didn't the gendarmes ask what she did for a living?'

'Yes, and Philippe said she was a chambermaid at the Mirabeau. It was Gabrielle who suggested that.'

Etienne was impressed that Philippe appeared to have thought of everything. 'Did you say anything about Belle being abducted and brought to France?'

'No. If I had brought that up, Kent might get word of it and disappear before the police have a chance to arrest him. Anyway, it wasn't a good idea to muddy the waters.'

'You did well,' Etienne said. 'I never did thank you for turning up so promptly at Pascal's house. It was a very nasty situation, and I can't tell you how relieved I was when you came charging in. What made you come so promptly? You surely hadn't had time to eat your dinner?'

Noah half smiled. 'The way you rushed out made me feel tense. Then I just got this gut feeling something was wrong. When we got to the house the man from next door was standing outside looking up at the windows. He was worried because you were still in there. So Philippe booted the door in. I don't think I've ever been so shocked by anything as the scene in that room. The blood, the smell, Belle's white, terrified face. Thank God you found her! He must have planned to kill her, he couldn't have just kept her there indefinitely.'

'I think you're right,' Etienne mused. 'But from what he said, I'd say he got her there thinking he could keep her there as his mistress. How could any man be so deluded as to think he could win a woman's heart with force and cruelty?'

'Speaking of hearts, has Belle asked about Jimmy? I think we should send a telegram to Mog saying we've found her, but I wouldn't mind betting that will make Jimmy come charging over here.'

'No. She wanted to know who you were and I explained that, but I steered clear of other things you'd told me, because she wasn't strong enough last night to be told about the fire, or her mother's apparent indifference. You are the one who should tell her about the fire. Hopefully you can gloss over about her mother.'

Noah nodded. 'I think the fire was probably a blessing in disguise. Belle will have no reminders about what she saw in the old place, and she'll have a real home with Mog, Garth and Jimmy.'

'I think it's a little unrealistic to imagine she'll pick up the pieces with him,' Etienne said tartly.

Noah looked at Etienne and laughed. 'Do I detect a jealous note?'

'*Bien sûr, je ne suis pas jaloux*,' Etienne retorted.

Noah laughed again. By slipping into his native tongue Etienne had proved he had feelings for Belle.

'No, of course you aren't jealous! How could you be?'

Noah was rewarded by seeing Etienne blush. He was pretty sure his blushes were rarer than hen's teeth.

'We'd better go in and see Belle now,' Noah said. 'And then you ought to go and get some sleep before you keel over.'

Etienne was pleased to see Belle looking a hundred times better than she had the night before. Her eyes were brighter, the dark circles that had been around them were gone, and the bruise on her cheek was less livid.

'This is Noah Bayliss, my Doctor Watson,' he said with a

wide smile. 'You were hardly in the mood for introductions last time you met.'

'I understand I have a great deal to thank you for, Mr Bayliss,' she said. 'Etienne told me you've been to Paris several times searching for me.'

'Please call me Noah,' he said with a smile. 'And no thanks are necessary; to see you now looking so much better is all the thanks I need.'

'Now, sit down and tell me all about Mog,' she said, and there was excitement in her voice and eyes.

'I'm going back to the Mirabeau,' Etienne said, turning towards the door. 'I believe you may be able to leave here later today or tomorrow, so I'll bring you some clothes when I return.'

'Give Gabrielle my best wishes,' she said. 'And tell her I am indebted to her for finding you.'

Noah pulled a chair up to her bed once Etienne had gone. 'Did you know he has been outside your door for the last forty-eight hours?' he said.

Belle looked surprised. 'But why? No one was going to harm me here.'

'He was afraid you'd have nightmares.'

'I seem to have the ability to recover from unpleasant things rather quickly,' she said. 'I slept very well last night, I didn't even dream. And I woke this morning feeling much better. But enough about me, tell me all about how you met Mog and my mother. I understand Millie was a friend of yours, so it must have been awful to hear how she died.'

'After you disappeared, Mog found out where I lived and came to see me. I was an investigator for an insurance company at the time, and Mog thought that meant I would be able to find you. I hadn't heard what had happened to Millie until she told me.'

'Didn't my mother come to you?'

Noah heard the note of hurt in her voice. 'I think Mog

acted on her own initiative, and someone had to stay home in case you returned or somebody called with news of you.'

He went on to explain that he really had no experience of finding a missing person. 'The police didn't take it very seriously and Mog was distraught. But Jimmy fired me up to want to find you; without him I might have just backed away.'

'Jimmy helped?' She looked surprised and touched. 'But how did you get to meet him? And how is he? Is he still with his uncle at the Ram's Head?'

'He practically runs it now, and he's a fine young man, one of the best. Without him I feel Mog might have fallen apart over your disappearance. And he and his Uncle Garth saved your mother's life in the fire.'

'Fire?'

Noah saw the horror come back in her eyes and wondered at the wisdom of telling her this so soon after her ordeal.

'Yes, your old home was burned down. Mog raised the alarm and got all the girls out safely, but Annie was trapped in her room. Garth and Jimmy rescued her through the window. Then they took both women back to the Ram's Head.'

'Was the fire an accident?'

'We think Kent got someone to set it,' Noah said. 'But of course we couldn't prove that, and such is the man's power that the police took little interest.'

Belle's eyes filled with tears. 'It must have been so sad for them losing their home and all their belongings. But why did Garth take them to his place? He was said to be an unpleasant man.'

'Like most people he can be something of a surprise,' Noah said, and he reached out and dried her eyes with her sheet. 'I've got to know him well in the last two years, and underneath that brusque exterior he's a kind and decent man. Of course Mog has turned him and the Ram's Head round since she became his housekeeper.'

Belle looked astounded.

'It gets better,' Noah said with a grin. 'He and Mog want to get married. And when they get my telegram to say I'm bringing you home they are going to be dancing with joy and I'm sure the wedding will be a double celebration with you there.'

'Oh, Noah!' she exclaimed, her eyes filling with happy tears. 'That is such wonderful news. Mog deserves all the happiness in the world. I thought she was destined to become an old maid.'

'Love and being wanted has made her blossom,' Noah said gleefully. 'All that was missing from her complete happiness was finding you.'

Belle asked many excited questions about Mog and Jimmy, but then her face clouded over.

'You haven't said anything about my mother.'

'She's doing just fine,' Noah said hastily and went on to tell Belle about Annie's boarding houses. 'She hasn't fallen out with Mog, they've just gone in different directions. Really, the fire was the best thing that could've happened to them both. They are respectable now, living comfortably. Work has even started on a new building where the old one was. Annie's Place is just a distant memory for most people around there.'

'And I'm a distant memory to Mother too?'

Noah took Belle's hand in his. 'You must know Annie is incapable of articulating her feelings,' he said gently. 'That doesn't mean she has none. I talked to her at length one day and because she was so upset about your disappearance, she told me about her past. She too was forced into prostitution when she was even younger than you. She is badly scarred by it, yet she kept you, and let Mog give you the mothering she felt she was incapable of. But I know she loved you, even if she couldn't always show it.'

'But she hasn't been frantic about me?'

Noah shrugged. 'She is a deep woman, Belle. It's difficult

to read her. Mog, to all intents and purposes, is your true mother, Annie has always known that. But I think that now you have so much more knowledge about the world she brought you up in, you should be able to see evidence that she did her best for you.'

Belle sniffed. Noah felt it would be best to leave it there for her to mull over.

'How do you feel about seeing Jimmy again?' he asked.

'I don't know,' she said with a glum expression. 'We were just innocent children really when we met. I liked him a great deal too. But I'm not that same girl any more, am I?'

She looked so sad that a lump came up in Noah's throat.

'We've all changed,' he said. 'I was such a prig when I met Millie, but through the last two years I've learned not to make judgments about people, or the way they live. Jimmy has grown in every way, even Garth has mellowed.'

'But Jimmy will be hanging on to the memory of me as I was, just as I have of him. We won't be able to go back to that point.'

'No, you won't. But in all the excitement of you being welcomed home, and Mog and Garth's wedding, maybe you'll discover a new starting point.'

'Etienne told me you liked Lisette,' she said. 'Can I hope for something to come of that? She was so kind to me.'

'Gabrielle has gone out there today to visit. They are old friends, you see. Along with telling her you are safe, she hopes to make some arrangements for us to meet. It would be folly for me to call there, the people Lisette is afraid of might hear of it. But the last time I saw Lisette I did offer to get her and her son away to safety. Gabrielle will tell her that offer is still open.'

'Then I hope she takes you up on it.'

Noah smirked. 'Etienne said I should go home and marry a girl from the same background as me.'

'So you can leave her at home and gallivant all over the place like he does,' she retorted.

Noah looked at her in surprise. 'He hasn't told you about his wife and children?'

'No, why should he?'

'They died in a fire last year,' Noah said. 'He doesn't know if it was arson or an accident. But he believes it was set deliberately because he left the organization he used to work for.'

Belle blanched. 'How terrible! Poor Etienne. I know he loved them a great deal.'

'He doesn't like to talk about it and of course I didn't know him before. But I'd say this is why he was so committed to finding you, and why he's prepared to name names and stand as a witness.'

Belle was so stunned by the news of Etienne's family dying that she couldn't speak. She knew enough about men to know his family was his world, or he might well have taken advantage of her on the ship when she tried to get him to seduce her.

He clearly didn't tell her about the tragedy himself because he wanted to concentrate all his energy and sympathy on her. Such kindness in the face of his own pain was almost unbearable. She had been rescued, she would go home to a good life with her family, but he would be left alone with only memories of his.

Noah looked at Belle's stricken face and not for the first time he wondered if there was more between her and Etienne than they'd said. But it wasn't appropriate to ask, he'd done enough damage for one day in giving her that news. There was nothing further he could tell her about the folk back home in England either, so he thought it better to go rather than make small talk. Besides, he had notes to be written up properly so that he had a decent record of what had gone on here in the last few days. There was also the telegram to send to Mog.

He told Belle that he must go and she looked at him blankly for a moment. 'Oh, yes. Thank you for coming to see me. I hope you work something out with Lisette.'

'And I hope you are well enough to leave here very soon.'

As the door closed behind Noah, Belle began to cry again as she thought of how comforting Etienne had been to her, and how quickly he must have come to her aid when Gabrielle had sent word to him.

Could that mean he held feelings for her? He'd said he remembered how beautiful she looked that last night on the ship. Had he also remembered those kisses they shared in the narrow bunk?

For two years now she'd conjured up memories of Etienne whenever she'd felt sad and lonely and even, if she was completely honest, when she was with her clients. It was of course shameful of her to hope that maybe they could have a future together just after hearing about such a terrible tragedy, but why had fate brought them together again if not for that?

Chapter Thirty-five

'You promise to write to me? And come to England soon?'
Belle begged Etienne.

They were at the Gare du Nord, on the platform by the
Calais train. Noah was already aboard with their luggage,
giving them the opportunity to say their goodbyes without
him looking on.

The station was extremely busy and very noisy with the
sounds of steam engines, luggage carts being wheeled and
people shouting to make themselves heard. But Belle was
oblivious to everything but Etienne as he held her hands and
looked down at her.

She wanted to lock the memory of his face into her mind
for all time. Those blue eyes which could be as cold as the
Atlantic Ocean sometimes, yet held the warmth and gaiety of
New Orleans when he looked at her. His angular cheekbones,
the curve of his generous mouth. She wanted to remove his
hat and ruffle up his fair hair because she liked that boyish
look he had when he first got up in the mornings.

Belle had been forced to stay in the nursing home longer
than expected as she developed sickness and a high temperature. The doctor said it was shock, but she thought it was
anxiety that Pascal might have made her pregnant. But fortunately her monthlies arrived a couple of days late and she
soon recovered. The scar on her stomach had healed well, but
she avoided looking at it; she didn't want any reminders of
what Pascal had done to her.

But it had been Etienne's visits that had brought on her
full recovery. He would come in with pastries, fruit or some

other little treat and sit beside her bed and tell her things he'd read in the newspapers that day. She found herself telling him some of the funnier stories about the girls at Martha's, and he told her tales about some of the villains he'd known in the past. He did eventually speak about the fire, and how low he'd sunk afterwards, but he was keener to talk about his plans for his little farm, and to get her to talk about her dream of having her own hat shop.

Mostly, however, they talked about inconsequential things, the sights they'd seen together in New York, books they'd read and other places they'd like to see. He was so easy to be with, he didn't fire questions at her, didn't ask what she was thinking. And he never gave her the idea that he was growing bored in her company.

She finally got to see Paris in the spring too, for once she was allowed to go back to the Mirabeau, Etienne had taken her out sight-seeing.

Paris had been grey and wintry in all her time there, but now trees were bright with pink or white blossom, and the sun shone down on flower beds alight with red and yellow tulips. People had abandoned their heavy, drab winter clothing, and it was good to see them strolling along the tree-lined boulevards, the ladies in elegant pastel dresses and lovely spring-like hats. Even the gentlemen sported lighter-coloured suits.

They'd enjoyed a boat trip on the Seine and a walk in the Bois de Boulogne, seen Versailles and been up the Eiffel Tower. It felt almost as if they were courting, the way other couples all around them were.

But Belle was only too aware she couldn't ever hope for that kind of sweet relationship, not after all she had done. She heard girls giggling and squealing on the platform at the top of the Eiffel Tower. She'd noted the way their men held their waists protectively as they looked down at the pano- ramic view of Paris so far below. She could giggle just as they did, Etienne could hold her the same way, but the sum total of all they knew about the seamier side of life prevented an innocent romance.

'I will write, but I warn you my written English is not good,' Etienne said. 'But it is not wise for me to come to England. I will always be a reminder of the past and that is not good for you.'

Belle looked at him in consternation. She knew by the break in his voice that his heart was saying something quite different to his words.

'But I need you,' she pleaded, her eyes filling with tears. 'Are you telling me you want me to forget you?'

'You must try, little one,' he said. 'As I must try too, for I know I am not the man you need.'

The guard blew his whistle then to warn everyone the train was leaving. Noah yelled from the train window that Belle was to hurry.

'You must go. Your family awaits you in England,' Etienne said.

She wanted to stamp her feet and refuse to go until he admitted he loved her and promised that they could be together in a few weeks. But she sensed by the sadness in his eyes that he would never say that, for he believed he was doing the right thing for her.

'Then just say one last thing in French to me,' she asked, standing on tiptoe to kiss him on the lips.

He caught hold of her face between his two hands and kissed her back with unbearable sweetness. '*Je défie les incendies, les inondations, et même l'enfer pour être avec vous,*' he whispered as he let her go. 'Now, the train. Go!'

Belle began to move towards the carriage door where Noah was standing beckoning frantically. She turned to look one last time at Etienne. '*Au revoir, mon héros,*' she said, and saw that his eyes were swimming with tears, just like hers.

'Belle, come now!' Noah yelled as the guard waved his flag for the train to leave.

Etienne had to bundle her into the train as it began to move. She leaned out of the window and blew him a kiss. He ran alongside the train saying something she couldn't hear, and the smoke belching from the engine almost hid his face.

She waved until he was just a dot in the distance, and only then was she ready to join Noah.

He had found an empty compartment. As she came through the door he laughingly said how he had strewn their belongings around to deter anyone from joining them. But then he noticed she was crying and handed her his handkerchief.

Belle mopped her eyes and wiped specks of soot from her cheeks. 'Putting my head out of the window always makes my eyes water,' she said by way of an explanation.

'My eyes water at odd times too, especially saying goodbye to people I like,' Noah said with a wry smile.

It took every ounce of determination Belle had not to break down and tell Noah she loved Etienne and she didn't think she could bear to go back to London. But Noah was full of excitement at the family reunion ahead of them. It wasn't fair to make him disappointed or worried, not after the lengths he'd gone to to find her. And it would be cruel to Annie, Mog and Jimmy who were probably frantically preparing for her joyful return.

There was Gabrielle too. She had seen how much the older woman cared for her this morning when they said their goodbyes, and she had such high hopes for Belle's future back in England.

Belle owed her so much; in fact, but for Gabrielle's actions her body might have been hauled out of the Seine or lain in a shallow grave for all eternity. Yet it wasn't just gratitude she felt towards this woman who said so little but had done so much for her. Gabrielle had shown her that it was possible for even the most damaged people to start a new and better life. She told Belle about her time as a whore, about the man cutting her throat and Lisette taking care of her and young Henri. She'd had heartbreak too when the artist she loved died; she said she would have taken her own life too if she hadn't had Henri to care for.

'Maybe we will never meet again,' she said as she embraced Belle. 'You will always be welcome here of course, but I understand there may be too many bad memories for you to return. But take away in your heart my affection for you, and my hopes that your dreams will come true. You did more for me than you'll ever know.'

There was no way Belle could turn back now as the train was picking up speed. So she sat down and focused her attention on Noah to prevent herself thinking of Etienne's tears.

'Is Lisette going to come to England?' she asked. Noah had met up with her twice in the past week but he hadn't said anything much about the meetings.

'She said she wanted to, but it may prove too daunting for her.'

'That's because she may not think you are entirely serious,' Belle said. 'A woman with a child needs to feel secure. You must make her feel that way by bombarding her with letters telling her all the best things about London. Promise her that she's under no obligation to you, yet say you are looking forward to getting to know her son. That should do it.'

Noah smiled. 'You make it sound so easy. But we had so little time together for me to show her that I am dependable and not a rake.'

'She would be able to see that just by looking at you,' Belle said. She had come to look upon Noah as a brother; she liked his openness and enthusiasm, and the way there was nothing hidden or complicated with him. 'And she'll have me nearby to tell her about women's stuff and for her to confide in. Then there's Mog – she's going to welcome her with open arms for being so kind to me.'

'And what about you and Jimmy?' Noah asked pointedly. 'That telegram he sent sounded like he was counting the minutes till he saw you.'

Belle winced. She too had sensed that Jimmy was expecting a great deal, and in the light of how she felt about Etienne, that was a huge worry. 'You must promise me you won't say much about Etienne to him. Let me find a way to let him down gently.'

'Give him a chance,' Noah said pleadingly. 'As I see it, Etienne is like a tiger; he's strong, brave and noble, but he's dangerous too. Jimmy may be more like a domesticated cat, but he's smart, affectionate, proud, loyal, and he'd fight tooth and nail for you. Don't shut your heart down to him before you've seen him and got to know him again.'

'No, I won't,' Belle said. Then, sitting back in her seat, she closed her eyes and pretended she was going to sleep. She wanted to remember those words Etienne had said in French.

She could understand the first part, that he would brave fire, but she couldn't translate the rest. The speed with which he came up with the sentence, together with his tears, suggested it was something she'd want to hear, yet if fire was the first thing that came into his head, surely that proved his wife was on his mind?

Belle would never be able to forget her shock and joy when Etienne came hurtling through the door at Pascal's house. Even in her wildest hopes of rescue she had never once thought of him being her saviour, or that she'd ever see him again. But there were moments too when Philippe came into the room, and he and Etienne were tying Pascal up, that she thought she was dreaming it all. Then all at once she was in the hospital bed, with a doctor giving her something to sleep, and she thought she'd gone mad and imagined it all.

In the days that followed Etienne had been the one who brought her out of shock, distress and hopelessness. Once Noah told her about his wife and children she understood why he was the one person who had the power to help her deal with it all.

She couldn't help but hope he held deep feelings for her. But perhaps that was just nature's way of trying to compensate for the trauma she'd suffered. He certainly hadn't said anything to encourage her hope.

In the last few days as he took her about Paris, he hadn't so much as hinted that his affection for her was anything more than that of a friend or brother. He hadn't kissed her again like he had on the way to New Orleans either.

Realistically she was also aware that her own feelings were possibly distorted. She might be placing him on a pedestal because he'd rescued her; he was also the only man who was never likely to throw her past back at her, and that was comforting.

Yet for all she knew, Pascal might have cast such a dark shadow over her that she might discover she was unable to give herself to any man ever again.

It was no good thinking Etienne's tears meant he had fallen in love with her. He was still grieving, just as she was still haunted by her ordeal with Pascal. They had helped each other in their time of need, and perhaps that was all there was to it.

Belle and Noah walked out of Charing Cross railway station on to the concourse in the Strand in the early evening of the following day. They had stayed the night in Calais because Noah thought it would be too tiring for Belle to attempt to do the journey all in one day.

From the ferry she saw the white cliffs of Dover for the first time. She wondered how many English people over the years had felt choked up at the sight because it meant they were nearly home.

As the train chugged through the Kentish countryside, Belle marvelled at how lush and green everywhere was, and realized that the nearest she'd ever got to countryside before was in parks. It seemed extraordinary that she'd been to America and France, but had never seen a grazing cow or sheep until on this journey home.

As they drew closer to London Belle's heart started to race, but as the train rattled over Hungerford Bridge and she saw the Thames gleaming pure silver in the sun, the dome of St Paul's and Big Ben on the Houses of Parliament, she found it hard to stay in her seat for excitement.

The Strand was as busy as it always had been, but Belle noted there were far more motorcars now. Noah had been saying on the train that he wanted one, and he thought it would only be a year or two before they were more common than horses.

As they walked along the Strand and then crossed the road to go up through Covent Garden, Belle began walking faster and faster. 'Slow down,' Noah groaned, with a suitcase in each hand. 'I can't race with the luggage.'

Belle hardly heard him. She was back on home turf and in wonderland. 'Everything looks smaller than I remember,' she said breathlessly. 'I thought the public houses were so big, the streets so wide, but they are small, even the people seem to have shrunk and grown quieter.'

Noah could only laugh. It all looked, sounded and smelled just the same to him, mucky and weary, wafts of stinking drains and horse droppings. The beggars, drunks, ragged children trying their hand at begging and the street vendors shouting out their wares were all just the same as when he left.

When Belle saw the Ram's Head she started to run. People stopped to stare at her, and Noah thought that was hardly surprising, for she looked far more Parisian in her grey and white striped dress and jaunty little grey hat than like a girl from Seven Dials.

She hesitated at the saloon door, looking back at Noah as if for encouragement.

'Go on in,' he urged her.

Belle pushed open the door, her heart thumping so hard she felt anyone passing would be able to hear it.

The smell of beer and cigarette smoke slapped her in the face. She saw people turn to look at her and for a second she wanted to back away.

But then she heard Mog scream out her name, a sound of absolute joy, and tears came so suddenly that Belle was momentarily blinded.

The small figure in a dusty-pink dress pushing her way through the crowded bar didn't look like the woman who had mothered her. 'Belle, my beautiful Belle,' she said, and the mist of tears cleared enough for Belle to see that Mog was crying too, arms outstretched wide to embrace her.

A loud cheer went up, fifty or so male voices raised in welcome. Mog's arms were round her, hugging her so tight that any trepidation vanished.

'Let me look at you!' Mog said.

Silence fell and all faces turned to the two women holding hands, crying and laughing at the same time as they studied each other.

'Welcome home, sweetheart!' someone shouted out, and a roar went up with a great stamping of feet.

Belle didn't recognize anyone, though she supposed they were all men who had seen her growing up. But she knew their delight was really for Mog. The woman she'd loved all her life was loved by all these people too.

Garth came forward then, but he had changed too. He was just as big as she remembered but his red hair and his beard which had been so unkempt were now neatly cut. He wore a dazzling white shirt, the sleeves rolled up above his mighty forearms, and an emerald-green waistcoat with small brass buttons. But the real difference was his wide smile; she'd seen him throughout her childhood, but he'd always looked so sour and mean.

'My, you've grown into a beauty!' he exclaimed. 'It's good to have you home. Now, where's Jimmy? He's been pacing up and down all day, checking the time and looking out the door, and now he isn't even here!'

'I am here, Uncle,' Jimmy's voice rang out, and everyone turned to see him standing quietly by the window where he'd clearly been all along. 'I just wanted Mog to be able to greet her first.'

His voice had deepened and he was a good three or four inches taller than Belle remembered. His shoulders were almost as broad as his uncle's, and his once spiky, carroty hair had grown darker and he'd let it grow a little longer which suited him far better.

The picture Belle had held of him in her mind was of a skinny, freckled-faced boy with tawny eyes, a polite manner and the look of a street urchin, but this Jimmy was a man, handsome, poised and confident. Only his tawny eyes were the same.

'He never gave up on you,' Garth said, and the look he gave his nephew was one of pride. 'Well, come on, you great lummox, come and give her a hug!'

Belle felt that the Jimmy she'd once known would have shrivelled up with embarrassment at such an order, but this new one didn't. He came towards her in three or four strides, swept her up in his arms and swung her round.

'I thought this day would never come,' he said as she squealed in surprise. 'You can't know how good it is to see you again.'

Garth stepped behind the bar and rang the bell for silence. 'This is the day we've all been waiting for,' he said, his voice booming out around the bar. 'It's time for celebration with our Belle home safe and sound. I only really know her through Mog and Jimmy, but I'm looking forward to getting to know her as family. Before I give the order for drinks on the house for everyone, I just want to offer very special thanks to Noah. Without his help and tenacity Belle would have been lost to us for ever.

'He isn't family, he hadn't even met Belle before she was snatched. But Mog asked him for his help, and he gave it willingly. For two years he's been our rock, comforting Mog, supporting Jimmy, advising, writing articles, badgering the police and God knows what else. We consider him family now too. And he's brought our Belle home. So let's give him a Seven Dials salute that can be heard right back in France.'

The cheering went on and on, so loud that Belle and Mog put their hands over their ears. Noah looked embarrassed, but Jimmy and Garth grabbed him, lifted him up on to their shoulders and joined in the cheering.

For Belle it was both heaven and hell. While it was wonderful to see her return creating such joy, and for Noah to have the appreciation he deserved, what she really wanted was to be alone with Mog, and Jimmy too, to sit down comfortably and talk. Not to be trapped in a smoky bar with a whole lot of strangers making such a din.

Noah was put down, Garth went behind the bar to hand out drinks, and suddenly Jimmy was there, putting one arm around Mog, the other round Belle.

'Go on through the back,' he said. 'You've got two years of catching up to do.'

Mog did exactly what Belle had imagined all the way home. She made a pot of tea. The noise from the bar was only marginally quieter in the kitchen but she appeared not to notice it.

'It feels so strange,' she said as she got a fruit cake out of a tin and put it on a plate. 'Since I've known you were coming home I rehearsed everything I would say, thought of all the questions I wanted to ask, but now you're here I can't think of anything to say.'

'It's the same for me,' Belle admitted. 'There's not even the familiar things around from the old house to prompt me.'

'Don't you like it?' Mog sounded so anxious Belle couldn't help but laugh.

'It's much, much nicer,' she said. She was speaking the truth. The old kitchen had been the only home she'd known, but it had been too big to be cosy, and it had always felt gloomy because it was a semi-basement. It was now dusk outside, but there was still light coming through the large window by the sink, and it looked as if the lemon-coloured walls had only recently been painted. There were yellow checked curtains at the window and a tablecloth to match. By the stove was a rag rug and two easy chairs with patchwork cushions. The dresser was full of pretty china, and even the shelves that held rows of glass jars containing everything from flour to brown sugar and rice had a little scalloped edging that had been painted yellow too.

It was clearly all Mog's work. Belle remembered she was always titivating things back in the old place for she was a born homemaker, but perhaps because Annie was reluctant to spend money on anywhere which wasn't seen by her 'gentlemen', there could only be small improvements.

'It was a hell hole when I first came here,' Mog said. 'Men living alone are such pigs!'

'So tell me about the fire and even more importantly about Garth. Noah tells me you are getting married.'

With that the ice was broken, and Mog talked animatedly about coming here to live, cleaning up the place and finally falling for Garth and his proposal of marriage.

'We're two of a kind,' she said with a loving smile that showed how happy she was with him. 'Or maybe I should say that we were both only half a person until we met and became one. He isn't the bad-tempered thug people used to claim, and I've found that I'm not the doormat I used to be. I never thought I'd ever find love, I just assumed it wasn't for women like me.'

Belle felt herself getting choked up with emotion and asked when the wedding was going to be.

'Well, now you're home we can arrange it as quick as we want,' Mog said, as she poured Belle yet another cup of tea. She had already offered all kinds of food, but Belle wasn't hungry. 'I think I must've known deep down that you would be found because I have kind of stalled on it. But my happiness is complete now you are back where you belong.'

'And what about Annie?' Belle asked. 'Noah told me what she was doing, and how you two just went your separate ways. Does she know I'm back?'

'She knows you were found. I went to see her, but we didn't know then how soon you were coming home.'

'And?'

'She was delighted to hear you were safe, but you know what she's like. Won't show any emotion, can't praise anyone or offer any sympathy. I used to think that it was somehow my fault she was that way, but to be honest, Belle, I can't be doing with it any more. If she wants to grow into an embittered old woman then that's her funeral. I'm done with running around for her and making excuses for her. She knows where I am and where you'll be. We'll just have to see if she turns up.'

Belle had hoped that her being away for two years would have made her mother softer and more caring, but she supposed that was too much to anticipate.

'But I want to know about you,' Mog said, changing the subject. 'Now, start at the beginning and tell me the whole story. No leaving bits out you think will upset me.'

*

An hour and a half and two more cups of tea and a ham sand-wich later, Belle had finally reached the point in the whole sorry story where Etienne rescued her. Mog's eyes had been as big as saucers for much of it, and she'd broken down in tears several times.

'How can you still look as fresh and lovely?' she asked.

'I have had ten days in Paris to be fattened up again and for the bruises to fade, with the kindness of people like Noah, Etienne and Gabrielle to help me over it,' she said. 'And Philippe sent me over a beautiful silk blouse and some French perfume before I left.'

'Have you been, you know, checked out?' Mog asked very gently.

Belle smiled at Mog's reticence to say 'pox'. She looked and sounded like a little suburban housewife now; no one would ever guess she'd been a maid in a brothel for half her life.

'Yes, while I was in the nursing home. There was no sign of any disease, but the doctor did warn me that it can be some time before symptoms show themselves. But then, I won't be going down that road again!'

Mog blushed and Belle laughed at her. 'We can't pretend I'm still a little innocent,' she said.

'To me you'll always be my little girl,' Mog said, her lip quivering. 'I can't bear to think of what you've been through.'

'It's all over now. Telling you all about it was the last hurdle. I've got a good bit of money, and I'm going to open a hat shop. The first hat I make will be for your wedding.'

Jimmy peeped round the door. 'If you want me to go away I will,' he said.

'Of course we don't,' Belle said. 'Come on in and join us. Are there many left in the bar? It's become a lot quieter.'

'Most of them have staggered home now,' Jimmy said.

'Garth said he's closing up any minute. Noah left some time ago. He said to tell you he had a letter to write.'

Belle grinned at that, and explained about Lisette to Mog and Jimmy. 'I hope she will come to England, he's really smitten with her. She deserves a better life, she is a good, kind woman, and very pretty too.'

She could see Jimmy wanted to know her whole story as well, but she knew she'd have to give him a censored version and that would take a day or two to plan. She was suddenly exhausted too, the travelling and all the excitement had drained her. 'May I go to bed now?' she asked. 'I'd like to stay up and talk some more but I'm just too tired.'

'Of course,' Jimmy said. 'Just to know you are safe upstairs is enough for Mog and me. We can talk tomorrow.'

Chapter Thirty-six

Sharp-eyed and brown-toothed Police Inspector Todd and his constable were just leaving the Ram's Head after interviewing Belle when Todd turned to her.

'Thank you for your valuable assistance, Miss Cooper,' he said brusquely. 'We shall have both men in custody by this afternoon. We've had them under surveillance since Mr Bayliss sent us word you had been found.'

Belle's mouth gaped in shocked surprise. The two men had been questioning her for over an hour, but as if she was a criminal, not a victim of crime. She didn't understand why they hadn't told her this at the start of the interview.

Todd had made her explain every last detail of what occurred up in Millie's room at Annie's, and kept stopping her with more questions as if trying to trap her in a lie. At one point he even implied she'd hidden under the bed for some reason other than being scared of getting caught upstairs. He clearly didn't believe she hadn't really understood what went on there.

When he got her to tell him about her abduction he wore a cynical expression as if he thought she'd climbed into that carriage with two strangers for an adventure. It was only when she finally got to the part about what happened to her at Madame Sondheim's, and she started to cry, that he softened a little.

He had shown her a long list of other girls' names and asked if she had met any of them or had heard anything about them. Some of the names were ones Noah had mentioned, but Belle knew nothing about any of them. That was something else he hadn't appeared to believe.

She was sorely tempted to tell Inspector Todd what she thought of him, but she bit back an angry retort. 'How clever of you,' she said, and masked her sarcasm with a brilliant smile.

'We will need you to make a formal identification of the two men once we have them in custody,' Todd said, clearly immune to sarcasm. 'And once your statement has been written up we will ask you to read it through and sign it. Meanwhile, may I say I am very glad you were found in Paris and brought back to your family and friends.'

Belle went back inside, once the policemen had gone, and found Jimmy waiting in the kitchen, an anxious expression on his face.

'Did it go all right?' he asked.

'I can understand why the majority of people around here don't want to help the police or even ask for their assistance. They sit on their hands for two years, then when I finally get back, after no help from them, they treat me as if I'm a liar,' she ranted. 'That man Todd has about as much sensitivity as a cockroach. But he did finally say they are going to arrest both Kent and Sly today. Let's hope they actually manage it.'

Jimmy looked sympathetic. 'The word around here is that no one will shield Kent now, not even if he tries to bribe them,' he said. 'Not just because of Millie or taking you, but for the terrible conditions he forces his tenants to live under, the other missing girls and the violence he metes out to anyone who stands in his way. He's had his day – even the men who were once his most staunch allies have abandoned him. He'll hang, I'm sure of that, and if Sly lives up to his nickname he'll talk to save his own neck.'

'I just hope those other girls can be found and brought home,' Belle said. 'But I expect most of them are beyond saving now.' She slumped down on a chair feeling completely dejected.

'Uncle Garth said I could have the rest of the day off. He thought you'd be a bit down and suggested I took you out somewhere to cheer you up,' Jimmy said. 'Would you like that?'

'It would be lovely,' she replied gratefully. She didn't want to spend the rest of the day indoors mulling over how unfairly the police had treated her, or dwelling on the fate of the other girls.

'It's such a nice sunny day we could take a boat to Greenwich, or go to Hampstead Heath or even Kew Gardens.'

'I'd like to go to Greenwich,' she said.

His face lit up and he said he'd go upstairs and change his clothes as he'd been working in the cellar earlier.

Belle stayed in the kitchen and washed up the tea cups. Mog had gone to the market to buy some vegetables, and she could see Garth through the window stacking up barrels and crates of empties for collection in the back yard. Going out with Jimmy for the day was an ideal way of talking things through with him; she knew she hadn't been very fair to him so far in avoiding doing so.

Yesterday she hadn't got up till late, and then Mog had commandeered her for the rest of the day, taking her to a dressmaker to see about getting a dress made for her wedding. Belle could have come home after that and talked to Jimmy, but instead she encouraged Mog to stay out with her for the afternoon shopping in Regent Street. During the evening Jimmy was behind the bar, so they had only had brief, snatched conversations.

What made it even harder to talk to Jimmy was that both Mog and Garth obviously had high expectations for them. She could see it everywhere. A bedroom on the top floor had been prepared for her with pretty flowery wallpaper, flouncy curtains, and the kind of new double bed with a fancy carved headboard that a newly married couple might choose. The room next to her bedroom was empty of furniture, and Belle was sure this was because it had been earmarked as a living room for her and Jimmy if they did get married.

While she knew that these types of assumptions and plans were commonplace in families where there were two young people considered ideally suited for each other, she found it oppressive and unrealistic. She really liked Jimmy; he had every quality that any girl would want in a husband. In fact if she hadn't been snatched away at such a young age, she had no doubt that they would have become sweethearts and might even have been married by now.

But Mog and Garth weren't taking into consideration that she wasn't an ordinary, innocent young girl any longer, and that her experiences had created a huge gulf between herself and Jimmy. She felt Mog and Garth ought to be able to see this for themselves, but because they'd found love, they had this rather sweet but potentially dangerous idea that Jimmy's devotion to Belle could wipe out her past.

Belle took Jimmy's arm as they walked down Villiers Street towards the Thames Embankment to catch a boat a little later that morning.

'Remember that day we came running down here in the snow?' he said.

'I used to think about it all the time when things were bad,' she admitted. 'It's so strange to find ourselves all grown up now; we've both changed so much in two years.'

'I don't think I have,' he said, grinning at her. 'Grown a couple of inches, built up a bit of muscle, but that's all.'

'No, there's more than that,' she said. 'You are a man now, you've developed confidence in yourself. You were still a boy grieving for your mother when I met you.'

He pulled a face. 'You make it sound as if I was drippy.'

Belle laughed. 'I didn't mean it like that. I was fairly drippy too, I didn't know anything then, I'd hardly been out of Seven Dials.'

They continued to chat as they joined the long queue for a boat to Greenwich. Belle's spirits were rising because Jimmy wasn't attempting to make her talk about the two missing years. He was telling her stories about neighbours, some of whom she remembered and some she didn't, but they were all funny. He was a good raconteur, descriptive, yet veering towards cynicism as if he'd studied the people he was talking about quite closely. She found herself laughing easily, and by the time they got on to a boat and found seats up by the bow, she was feeling very glad that they'd come out, and very comfortable with him.

There was a big mix of people on the boat: young couples like them, families, old people and quite a few foreigners on holiday in England. The sun was very warm, making the river sparkle, and everyone was jovial and friendly in anticipation of a good day out.

'I always wanted Mog to take me on one of these boats,' Belle said as the crew cast off and the boat began to chug away downriver. 'I used to think she was mean because she didn't, but I suppose Annie never let her have a whole day off.'

'She told me once that she asked Annie if she could take you on a little holiday to the seaside,' Jimmy said. 'Annie refused. She said she thought at the time it was because your mother was just being mean-spirited, but later she realized it was because she was jealous of the bond between you.'

'I don't know why Mog didn't leave, Annie was so nasty to her sometimes,' Belle said reflectively.

'Because of you, of course,' Jimmy said. 'But I think too she was very attached to Annie. She told me that the woman who owned the place before her was always on her back, but Annie stuck up for her. Mog isn't the kind to abandon anyone who has been good to her.'

'I don't think she had much idea of her own worth, even though she was the one who kept everything together,' Belle said. 'Tell me about how they came to split up. Didn't Annie want Mog with her at her guest house?'

'Annie just made her plans for herself,' Jimmy said. 'At the time I thought it was shabby of her, she didn't seem to care about Mog at all, but as it turned out, it was for the best.'

'I wonder when she'll deign to come and see me. Or do you think she's expecting me to go to her?'

Jimmy shrugged. 'She's a difficult woman to fathom. I've never told anyone this before, but I went to see her at the time Noah discovered you'd been sent to America. Apart from relaying that information, I suppose I just wanted to get to know her better, but she was very curt with me. She said that wherever you were, you surely could have written to her. Well, I pointed out you could very well have done so, but as the old place was burned down the letter wouldn't have been delivered.'

'I did send a card from New York,' Belle said. 'It never crossed my mind that they might not still be there. I used to imagine them in Jake's Court, Mog hanging out the washing, Mother sitting at the kitchen table over dinner with the girls. And you too of course, running errands for your uncle. I thought about writing a proper letter once I was in New Orleans, but I didn't because I thought it would be worse for Mog and Annie to know the truth about what had happened to me.'

'I can understand that,' Jimmy said. 'But I couldn't understand Annie's attitude, she just made me angry. She turned everything around to make out she was the wronged one. I said as much and she told me to get out.'

Jimmy went on to tell Belle all the different things he'd done to try to trace her. She smiled as he described breaking into Kent's office and his house down in Charing.

'Didn't you think that house was strange?' she said. 'I only saw the hall and a living room, but it was so pretty and nice, not the kind of house you'd expect a monster like him to live in.'

'I thought just the same. I wonder if we'll ever find out why it was like that,' Jimmy said thoughtfully. 'Could he really have been planning to take Millie there?'

Belle got a mental picture of Millie locked in an upstairs room and shuddered. 'Don't let's talk about that, it makes me think of Pascal. I think he and Kent were two of a kind.'

'I promise that one day you will wake up and see that you gained something from your experiences, however horrible the past couple of years have been for you,' he said.

Belle raised her eyebrows quizzically. 'That's as unlikely as me finding out I'm actually King Edward's love child,' she said with a giggle.

Jimmy smiled. 'Well, it happened to me. I was so upset when you disappeared, you were my only friend, and suddenly you were gone. But miraculously my life got better because of it. Mog came to stay after the fire, my uncle became happier with her around, and trying to find you gave us all new purpose and brought us all together. Even the pub is doing better because of it.'

'Yes, I can see how it improved your life,' she said. 'But I don't think I'll ever get to the point where I can say I'm glad I was sold into prostitution.'

'No, not that, but out of it came other things. I can only see it for myself when I look back. It was awful seeing Mog's grief, I was beside myself with worry too. It was a dark, horrible time. Yet without it, would I have come to like and respect my uncle? I don't think so. I gained Mog whom I adore, and found a first-class friend in Noah. They in turn gave me confidence, and I became good at running the pub. I feel I have a real family now and a future. And it isn't just me, look how happy Mog is now, and Uncle Garth. Three people whose lives were changed for the better.'

'Then I suppose I shall have to look back and see if I can find something I've gained,' she said.

'It's too soon for that yet. You are still dwelling on your lost innocence, the people who hurt you. But I bet there were people you are glad you met, things you've seen that have changed your thinking. One day you will wake up as I did and be glad for that.'

'Maybe,' she said. The only person who she was truly glad she met was Etienne, but she couldn't say that, and changed the subject to something lighter.

Belle found Greenwich enchanting with its quaint little old houses and pubs close to the river front, and the elegant Georgian houses further back. She thought the Royal Hospital School and Naval College looked splendid with such lush green lawns before them. After pie and mash from a stall by the river front, they climbed up the hill to look at the Observatory and sat on a bench to enjoy the view of the river.

'Henry VIII was born here in the Palace,' Jimmy said – he always seemed to know about history. 'It burned down though. And where the Observatory is now was Greenwich Castle where he used to keep his mistresses. It must have been quite a sight when kings and queens sailed upriver in the royal barges. And it's odd to think this is where time is measured, and longitude so people can sail by it all over the world.'

'Are you happy to carry on running the Ram's Head, or have you got other plans?' Belle asked. They had talked about so much. Jimmy had told her about the funeral of King Edward and then the coronation of George V a year later, when he'd stayed up all night to get a good spot to see the royal procession come past. He explained what the suffragettes had been doing in her absence, how many of them were force-fed in prison, and how one was killed when she threw herself under the King's horse at Epsom race course. He said Mog and Garth had had some very heated arguments about them. Mog admired them but Garth thought they should stay at home and look after their families and leave politics and voting to men.

They discussed the sinking of the *Titanic* on her maiden voyage too, which had happened on 15 April while Belle was still recovering in the nursing home in Paris. Noah told her that one thousand, five hundred people were lost when the ship hit an iceberg, but perhaps thinking it would make her upset he didn't say much more, and she couldn't read the French newspaper accounts of the tragedy. But Jimmy knew all of the story and related it to her in such detail that anyone would have thought he'd been on the ship.

Belle noticed that although Jimmy had talked a great deal about current affairs, neighbours and Mog and Garth today, he hadn't answered her question about his work. So she asked him again about it.

'I think once Uncle Garth and Mog are married, they'll be very keen to get out of central London,' Jimmy replied. 'I suppose I could stay on and run the pub myself, but I don't really want to. We all went out to Blackheath for the day at Easter, a while before we heard you'd been found. They talked of nothing else at the time but trying to find a pub there, but that's been forgotten since you came home.'

'Where is Blackheath?' Belle asked.

Jimmy pointed behind them. 'Just the other side of Greenwich Park. The road down to Dover goes through there, and with so many people getting motorcars now it would be a good place to choose. And they are building lots of new houses out that way too. If Garth found the right pub they could have paying-guest rooms as well. I think it is a brilliant idea. The Heath is lovely, with ponds, and there was a fair on when we were there. They play cricket up there in the summer, and the village is really pretty.'

'Sounds like you really want to go there,' Belle said. 'Would it be a good place for a hat shop?'

She had told Jimmy and Mog that she learned hat-making while she was in America and that she wanted to open a shop, but because of all the excitement of her being back, and the business with the police, they hadn't reacted to the idea at all.

'It would be ideal,' Jimmy said. 'It's that kind of a village, very middle-class with lots of men who work in the City, and wives who pride themselves on being fashionable and well dressed.'

Belle felt a surge of excitement at the idea of starting out somewhere where no one knew about her. But almost immediately she felt deflated because as a chief witness in a murder trial, her history would follow her.

'What is it?' he said when her face fell.

She explained.

'People don't keep things like that in their heads for long,' he said soothingly. 'They use the old newspaper to light the fire, and that's it, over and done with. It's only family and close friends who find it hard to forget. But you could change your name, then no one would connect you with the trial.'

Belle thought about that for a while. 'I can't imagine myself as anything but Belle Cooper,' she said eventually.

'You could be Belle Reilly if you married me.'

Belle had been afraid of him pressing her in some way, but the flippant way he'd made that remark made her giggle. 'A girl is supposed to agree to marry someone for much deeper reasons than changing her name,' she said.

'That's true,' he said equally lightly. 'But if we all moved to Blackheath where it's terribly respectable, I'd have to pretend to be your brother to avoid people talking. And that would become very complicated. It would be much easier to introduce you as my wife. And easier for you to get a shop – landlords are very prejudiced against lone women taking on a lease.'

Belle thought she ought to be nervous at the way this conversation was going, yet she wasn't. Everything he'd said was quite true.

'I meant husband and wife in name only,' he said quickly, before she'd even thought how to reply. 'I do realize after what you've been through that the last thing you would want is another man taking over your life.'

She felt his complete sincerity and was deeply touched by it. 'That wouldn't be fair on you, Jimmy,' she said quietly.

'You mean if you didn't want to share my bed?' he asked bluntly.

'Well yes, and not feeling that way about you,' she said awkwardly. 'I like you such a lot Jimmy, I trust you too and we could be the best of friends, but . . .' She paused, not knowing how to round it off.

'Listen to me,' he said, taking one of her hands in his. 'I've made a suggestion, nothing more. All I really want is for you to recover from what you've been through. To be your friend and support whatever you decide to do.'

She looked into his tawny eyes then and saw exactly what she'd seen the first time they'd met. Honesty.

They walked on up through Greenwich Park right to the iron gates at the far end, and he told her that the huge expanse of grass in front of them was Blackheath. There were some children sailing boats on the pond, the boys in sailor suits, the girls in pretty dresses, watched by their mothers, some with perambulators, sitting on benches.

Beyond the Heath she could see a church with a spire. The scene was so far removed from the hurly-burly and squalor of Seven Dials that she felt choked up.

'My mother brought me here once when I was about that boy's size.' Jimmy pointed out a boy of about seven. 'She never said, but I felt she wished we lived somewhere like this and I could sail boats instead of playing in the street. She had to work so hard to keep us. But she never complained.'

'Is that why you'd like to come and live here?' Belle asked.

'I suppose it is, well, partly. I'd like to have children one day and bring them over here to sail boats and play cricket with them. But mostly I'd like to live in a place with wide open spaces like this, to wake up each morning and hear birds singing, and just be happy.'

'I think that's a lovely ambition,' Belle said, and it struck her that she shared it.

In the days that followed, in between helping Mog with the chores, Belle often found herself thinking of the sun-drenched Heath, the pond and the sailing boats. She had already realized it would prove risky trying to open a hat shop anywhere close by Seven Dials, when there were already so many places to buy a hat in Oxford Street and Regent Street. Blackheath sounded perfect, and imagining her shop lifted her away from thinking about how she'd lived for the past two years, and what the immediate future had in store for her once Kent and Sly were arrested.

But so far the police had failed to catch the men, and every day Belle was growing more tense because of it. She knew it was perfectly possible that if Kent had heard she was back in England, he'd seek her out and kill her. She knew this was on Garth and Jimmy's mind too, just by the vigilant way they locked up at night and insisted she was accompanied every time she went out.

Jimmy was kept busy most of the day and evenings, but when the bar closed, he and Belle would sit by the stove in the kitchen and talk. Bit by bit, Belle told him about New Orleans, Faldo, and going to Marseille. At first she censored it, telling him only the amusing parts, or related it as if she'd been a mere bystander. But gradually, as she realized he wasn't easily shocked, she told it as it really was.

'That lad's got a wealth of understanding,' Mog remarked on the day Jimmy had accompanied Belle to Bow Street police station to read and sign her statement. 'I suppose working in the bar he's got to hear all sorts – living around here you don't stay innocent for long. But he don't judge, I think that's what I like about him the most.'

Belle could only agree. She even teased Jimmy that he would make a good priest.

'I could do the listening in the confessional all right,' he laughed. 'But I couldn't cope with all that praying and stuff.'

Belle wondered if by 'stuff' he meant being celibate. She knew he had walked out with a couple of young women while she was away, but she suspected he was still a virgin. His proposal lurked at the back of her mind, popping up at the oddest times. She thought it would be the easiest thing in the world to accept it; at a stroke she'd make everyone happy, even herself in many ways because as each day passed she liked him more. But while she was still thinking about Etienne and hoping against hope he'd come to claim her, it wasn't fair on Jimmy to lead him on to think she might be coming round to it.

But there had been no letter from Etienne. She had been back in London for two weeks now, and although she told herself mail from France might take longer than that to arrive, in her heart she knew there was no letter on its way.

Garth didn't allow women in his pub. His attitude wasn't unusual; except in hotel bars, or saloons close by theatres, most landlords were the same. Mog occasionally helped serve at lunchtime, but never in the evening, and Garth referred to the women who sometimes tried to come in as 'ladies of the night' and refused them entry.

His euphemism wasn't apt, for in Seven Dials they didn't wait for night, they were out there on street corners from nine in the morning. They had been on the street corners all of Belle's childhood, yet she had barely noticed them then. But she not only noticed them now, she felt deeply for them: dirty, raddled, some with wrinkled breasts barely covered, hair that hadn't seen a wash for weeks, and thin because they chose to buy cheap gin instead of food for the oblivion that came with it.

So when Belle and Mog heard strident female voices coming from the bar one evening as they were sitting in the kitchen, Belle looked up from her sketchpad in surprise.

'What's going on in there?' she asked.

Mog put her sewing down and looked out of the window. 'Well, it's not raining, that's when they usually try to make Garth let them in. Something must've happened out on the street. I'll go and see.'

She only went as far as opening the door through to the bar and peeped round it. 'Jimmy!' she called. 'What's going on?'

Belle couldn't hear his reply, but Mog came back and sat down. 'He said he'd come through in a minute and explain. But there's a crowd of girls in there, they look like the ones from Pearl's, and Garth's given them all a drink. So something must have happened there.'

Pearl's was a brothel a couple of streets away. Mog had mentioned it a day or two ago because it was rumoured to be owned by Kent.

'Maybe the police raided it to find him?' Belle suggested.

'If it was that, surely they'd have taken all the girls down to the station,' Mog said, and frowned anxiously.

It was frustrating hearing the voices growing louder and louder, but not knowing what was happening. Mog went over to the door several times to listen but couldn't make head or tail of what was being said. Then they heard the bell ring to warn everyone to drink up as it was closing time, and gradually the noise abated as everyone began to leave.

Finally Garth came through. His face was grim.

'What happened?' Mog said, going over to him and putting her arms around his waist.

'The police raided Pearl's,' he said. 'Kent was in there, but he had a gun and shot one of the policemen and legged it out the back window. The whole of Seven Dials is in an uproar. The girls came here to tell me because of Belle.'

Chapter Thirty-seven

Belle tossed and turned all night, very aware of Mog in the bed beside her, and that Jimmy and Garth were taking it in turns to stand guard downstairs.

Jimmy had pointed out before they went to bed that having shot a policeman there would be little point in Kent trying to kill Belle too, for he'd hang regardless of whether she was a witness to his crimes or not. Garth said that Kent would be much more concerned with getting out of the country, and both men were being logical. But Belle felt logic didn't come into it with men like Kent or Pascal.

They had looked out of the bedroom window before they turned in and seen two policemen patrolling Monmouth Street. Mog had said there would be more all over Seven Dials and pointed out how quiet it was everywhere, none of the usual drunks and whores wandering around.

Belle must have dropped off to sleep eventually for she woke with a start at someone knocking on the door downstairs, and she saw it was daylight.

Mog leapt out of bed like a scalded cat, pulling a shawl around her shoulders. 'Stay here,' she ordered Belle. 'I'll just go out on to the stairs and see if Jimmy or Garth is answering the door.'

Belle looked at the clock and saw it was six-thirty. Knowing she wouldn't be able to go back to sleep anyway, she got up and dressed.

Mog came back into the room. 'It's Noah,' she said. 'Jimmy has let him in.'

Belle hurried downstairs to find Jimmy fully dressed in the

kitchen with Noah, and Garth wearing only his trousers and vest, yawning sleepily.

'Noah's been at the police station getting the latest news,' Jimmy said.

Belle put the kettle on. Sometimes she thought she was turning into Mog, because she always did that in a crisis.

'Sorry to call so early, but I thought you'd want to know. Sly was arrested yesterday afternoon,' Noah said. 'I suspect he sang his heart out because it's the only way the police would've known Kent was due to go to Pearl's last night to collect the takings. Why they didn't catch him before he went in is anyone's guess, damn fools. Anyway, they charged into Pearl's like the cavalry. To be fair to them, I don't suppose they'd expected him to be armed with a gun. Kent was in an upstairs room he apparently uses as an office. He heard the noise, tried to climb out the window, and as the constable went in, he shot him.'

'Is he dead?'

'As a door nail,' Noah said glumly. 'A young man with three small children too. You can imagine the confusion in there, by all accounts the place is like a rabbit warren with narrow passages and small rooms. What with all the girls screaming, men trying to get back into their clothes and get out before the police questioned them, it must have been mayhem. Kent succeeded in getting away through the window and on to the roof, and from there it seems he went along the whole street and escaped the police who were stationed outside Pearl's.'

'So he's still at large?' Belle asked nervously.

'Yes, but there's a huge manhunt going on. Every policeman in London is out; there's nothing that motivates them quite as much as one of their own being down.'

'If they knew he owned Pearl's, why didn't they stake it out before?' Jimmy asked.

'I don't think they did know that. Pearl has been arrested. I dare say we'll find she was too scared to turn him in.'

Mog had come into the kitchen, her face was pale with fright. 'Where have all Pearl's girls gone?' she asked.

Noah shrugged. 'No idea, but as I came past there the police had it cordoned off. If the girls have got any sense they'll stay away for a while.'

'That's their home, Noah,' Belle reminded him, remembering how it was when Millie was murdered: so much hysteria and fright, yet at least the girls were allowed to stay in the house. 'All their belongings will be in there and most won't have anywhere else to go.'

'Do you think we should go away somewhere?' Mog asked.

Garth looked at her, saw how scared she was and went over to her and put his arms around her protectively. 'I can't leave here even if I wanted to,' he said. 'The place would be broken into as soon as we'd left the street, and I'm not letting you or Belle out of my sight. But Kent won't dare come here. He's not a fool or he'd have been caught days ago. So we stay, business as usual, only we keep vigilant.'

'We'll all sit down and have breakfast,' Belle said. She lifted the frying pan down off the hook, knowing that would spur Mog into laying the table.

Some fifteen minutes later they were all sitting around the table eating bacon and eggs, and calm had returned.

'I meant to come round last night,' Noah said as he took another slice of bread. 'We got a telegraph yesterday at the office from Paris saying the police have found the other girl's body. But I was there so late working on a piece about it, it got too late to call here.'

'Was she buried in Pascal's garden?' Belle asked. She could feel goose bumps popping up all over her.

'No, they dug all that up but found nothing. It was on some waste ground round the back of the Sacré-Coeur. A workman found it when they were levelling out the ground to pave it. They identified her by a necklace her grandmother had given her.'

'How did she die?' Garth asked.

'Must we talk about this as we eat?' Mog said, her voice shaking.

Noah apologized, but went on regardless to say the girl had been strangled.

'But can they prove Pascal did it?' Belle asked.

'They found some items of her clothing in his house,' Noah said. 'They were ones she was wearing on the night she disappeared. That seems to be enough to convict him.'

'If I was one of the police there I'd beat a confession out of him,' Garth said darkly.

'I would be surprised if they hadn't already done that,' Noah smirked. 'His trial will be set any day now. I shall go to Paris to cover it.'

'Will I have to go too?' Belle asked.

'I doubt it very much. Philippe said when we were there that your statement was enough for them. They have arrested Madame Sondheim too. They might need you there for her trial, but that's a way off yet. They are still gathering more evidence about her crimes and of course the others' in the chain.'

'What about Lisette?' Belle asked. 'Will she give evidence?'

'You'll be able to talk to her about that yourself, she's on her way here.' Noah smiled broadly, excitement showing in his eyes. 'I got a letter from her just two days ago. She and her son were in Normandy then with her aunt, and they will be arriving in Dover in a week's time. I'm going to look at a place for her later today. It's close to where I live.'

'Will Etienne know all about this?' Belle had to ask about him, she just couldn't help herself. She felt Jimmy's eyes on her and hoped he hadn't picked up on her eagerness and guessed he'd got a rival.

'He might not have been told about the body by the church, but he'll know about Madame Sondheim – by all accounts he's been of great help to the French police. He's a brave man, and a marked one now. But he struck me as a man with a mission to stop the vile trade in young girls, and I suspect he's long given up on concerning himself with his own safety.'

Belle expected Jimmy to make some kind of waspish remark, but he didn't. He went up another peg in her estimation.

Later that night, when the bar had closed, Jimmy reported back that all the conversation in the bar had been about Kent shooting a policeman.

'They all make out they know Kent so well,' Jimmy fumed. 'But when we were trying to find him two years ago, not one of the gutless halfwits knew anything about him.'

Belle just laughed. She found it funny to see mild-mannered Jimmy getting so het up. 'I doubt they know him at all, that's just what people are like. I bet half the population in London is claiming to have a relative or friend that went down on the *Titanic* too.'

Jimmy agreed with her. 'The day that news broke it was all we heard. I bet when Jack the Ripper was up to his tricks there were hundreds of girls who claimed they'd managed to escape his clutches too.'

'Are the police still patrolling the street?' Belle asked. Garth had forbidden her even to put her nose outside the door.

'Yes, they are everywhere, and people are even complaining about that. The shopkeepers are saying it's stopping people shopping, the street girls can't get punters, and the pickpockets have got no pockets to pick.'

'Has the pub had fewer customers then?'

'No, that's a funny thing, we're busier than ever. We even got folk in tonight that don't live around here.'

'We got a surge of extra business at Annie's when Queen

547

Victoria died,' Mog said impishly. 'Now, you tell me why anyone would get a surge of lust because the monarch is dead.'

All three of them started to laugh, and once started they couldn't stop. For Belle it was especially funny because she could imagine the frantic behind-doors scenes in the brothel. She wasn't sure what tickled Jimmy so much.

But having a good laugh made them all feel better.

Since getting back to London Belle had taken it upon herself to clean the bar each morning, leaving Mog to do other chores. One of the advantages of the job was that she always got to pick up the mail. She was aware Jimmy might be hurt if she received a letter from Etienne, and Mog would probably want to know too much, so she'd rather they didn't see any letter.

Now, still without one over two weeks since her return to London, she was almost at the point of giving up on Etienne. But when she went into the bar that morning and saw a white envelope on the floor beneath the letter box she flew over to it. To her delight it was for her. Putting it in her apron pocket, she nipped upstairs to read it in her room.

There was no stamp on it, French or otherwise, but she ripped it open eagerly, half expecting that Etienne had come to England and was letting her know. But she was disappointed to see the address at the top of the single sheet of paper was in King's Cross. It was from her mother, and she felt a bit guilty at her disappointment.

'Dear Belle,' she read. 'I am so glad you are safely back in England. Please forgive me for not calling on you, but there is some bad feeling between Mog and myself, and I really can't come there. I slipped this through the door on my way to the market this morning, in the hope that you could meet me later this morning in Maiden Lane, in the café there. Don't say anything to Mog, she has always liked to keep you all to herself and she'll try and stop you coming. I'll be there at 10.30.

Your loving mother.'

Belle read the letter several times before tucking it back in her apron pocket. Despite her deep love for Mog, she was mature enough now to see that Annie had never had a chance to be a real mother because Mog took over that role.

Now that she knew from Noah that Annie had been forced into prostitution, it gave her new perspective on why she could be so cold and distant. But Belle had never gone hungry as a child, no one was cruel to her, in fact she had fared better than most of the girls she'd been at school with who had two very respectable parents.

If she had got pregnant while she was in New Orleans, would she have been a good mother? She couldn't answer that, no one could until it happened to them. But she felt she must go to her mother. They had common ground now, and with that they might find they could be friends.

The problem was, she knew Garth, Mog and Jimmy were not going to let her go out. If she didn't turn up at the café she knew her mother would feel it was because she wanted nothing to do with her. Belle felt she must go to her, if only to explain about Kent being on the loose.

It was just on nine now. It was Mog's day for changing the sheets on the beds and Jimmy would still be working in the cellar until about half past ten. Garth could be anywhere; he didn't go in for set routines. If she finished cleaning the bar really quickly she could shoot out of the side door at quarter past ten, and they'd all still think she was in the bar for at least another half-hour.

As she worked, washing and drying glasses, polishing the bar mirrors and the bar itself, then mopping the floor, she considered the risk involved in going out alone. As so many people had said, now Kent had shot a policeman he wasn't likely to be hanging around here. And even if he was, he'd be holed up somewhere, not out in the streets or in a café.

She would give as her excuse when she got back that she wanted to get some materials to make a hat. Hopefully they might not have even missed her.

Belle washed her hands and face when she'd finished the bar, combed her hair and hung her apron on the back of the kitchen door. She wished she looked smarter to meet Annie. Mog had given her the green cotton dress she was wearing, as all her other clothes were too good to clean in, but it was dowdy and too big for her and made her look like a kitchen-maid.

Garth was out in the back yard, Mog was upstairs, singing as she changed beds, and Belle could hear clanking noises coming from the cellar, so she knew Jimmy was down there. She would go now while she could.

Luckily the side door had the kind of lock which didn't need a key to lock behind her, so there was no open door to give her away. Once out in the street, she ran through an alley opposite and came out in Neal Street. She saw four police-men before she even got to the market, but whatever people had been saying last night in the bar, everywhere looked just as busy as it had always been. Belle heard a clock strike the half-hour just as she was approaching Maiden Lane.

Maiden Lane had become even muckier than she remem-bered. The left-hand pavement was blocked by scaffolding on a building, and there were piles of sand and heaps of bricks on the pavement, so she crossed over to the right. The theatres in the Strand had their back doors opening on to this street and there were overflowing dustbins and piles of cardboard boxes. She couldn't see a café, but then, some of the buildings jutted out further than others, so she kept on walking down the street to look.

Suddenly a man grabbed her from behind, and a hand was clamped over her mouth. She knew in that instant that she'd been tricked, but before she could even react to that she found herself being dragged forcibly into a building.

She tried to kick back at her assailant, but he threw her against a wall, then kicked the door to the street shut. There was little light but even so she knew it was Kent, just by his shape and smell. She screamed at the top of her lungs until he silenced her with a punch in the face.

'I should've killed you in the first place, I knew you'd be trouble,' he snarled at her, thrusting a foul-smelling rag into her mouth to silence her. 'I'll finish you off this time though, but first you'll be my ticket out of London.'

Her eyes were growing used to the gloom now and she saw him pick up a length of cord to tie her hands behind her and round her ankles in much the same way he had the first time he captured her. When he'd trussed her up, he flung her over his shoulder and carried her up some stairs.

The smell of the place made Belle's stomach heave. It was the same kind of smell that wafted out of the most squalid tenements: human waste, mice, damp and plain filth. Like downstairs, it was very gloomy, with just a faint glow of light coming from the far end of a big room. She could see broken chairs lying amongst other debris and she thought it must have been a club or a dance hall at some time, but more recently desperate people had been living here.

Kent dropped her to the floor, which jarred every bone in her body, and with that walked away in the direction of the faint glow of light at the end of the room.

As Belle lay there amidst the stinking squalor, her face stinging from Kent's blow, it occurred to her that she was always regretting things. Why hadn't she taken notice of Garth's instructions not to go out? But even bigger than that regret was the horror that her own mother had lured her here. Why would she do that?

That hardly mattered now though, in the face of what Kent was going to do to her. He had nothing to lose and he was an intelligent, cunning man. She couldn't imagine how he thought she would be his ticket out of London, but he must have a plan.

Chapter Thirty-eight

Jimmy came up from the cellar and went into the bar, expecting Belle still to be cleaning. She had already finished, everything was gleaming and the floor still wet, but she wasn't there. Assuming she was upstairs with Mog, he ran up, but Mog was alone, gathering up dirty bed linen.

'Where's Belle?' he asked.

'Cleaning the bar,' Mog responded.

'She's finished that and she's not in the kitchen,' Jimmy said, then opened each of the bedroom doors to check she wasn't in one of them.

'Out in the yard with Garth?' Mog suggested.

Jimmy opened the window and called down to his uncle who was sitting on an upturned crate smoking his pipe, 'Is Belle out there with you?'

His uncle shouted back that she was in the bar.

Jimmy replied that she wasn't. He was growing worried now.

'Where else can she be?' he said to Mog, and ran off downstairs again to check the parlour that they rarely used.

He was standing in the kitchen looking anxious when Mog came down a few minutes later. 'I don't like this,' he said. 'Do you think she might have gone out, even though we said she mustn't?'

'Maybe she needed something urgently.'

'Like what?'

'I don't know, Jimmy,' Mog said. 'But girls get ideas into their heads. I expect she thought it was urgent.'

'At half nine I popped up for some hot water and I could hear her sweeping,' Jimmy said. 'Did you see her after that?'

'Well, I called out that I was going to change the sheets, and she made a joke about me not going back to bed,' Mog said. 'That was at ten.'

'She must've gone out the side door,' Jimmy said. 'Garth has been in the back yard all along so she didn't go that way.'

'Fancy her being so sneaky,' Mog said. Then, looking at Jimmy's stricken face, she went over to him and patted his arm. 'Stop worrying, she probably needed hairpins, or she saw someone she knew out the window and ran out to chat to them. She won't have gone far.'

'I don't like it, Mog,' he said. 'Look, she's taken off her apron, she wouldn't do that if she'd just popped out to speak to someone. Besides, she's been gone half an hour now.'

Mog looked round at the apron hanging on the door. Just that it was hanging up was unusual as Belle normally left it on a chair, anywhere but on the hook. She went over to it and felt it – the only time Belle hung it up was when it was wet.

'It's bone dry,' she said. But as her hands skimmed over it she felt something stiff in the pocket. She reached in and pulled the letter out, and as she read the contents her face turned pale.

'What is it?' Jimmy asked.

'A letter from her mother,' Mog gasped out. 'Only it isn't Annie's writing, and whoever did write it wanted to meet up with Belle.'

Jimmy snatched it out of her hand and read it. 'But that's Annie's address,' he said. 'Are you sure it's not from her?'

'Of course I'm sure. I saw Annie's writing every day for over twenty years, and that's not it.'

'But surely Belle would know that?'

'Her mother never wrote her a letter; the most Belle would've seen was a few scrawled shopping lists. She'd not even seen that for over two years. And I don't think Annie would say that about not wanting to come here; she's a lot of things but she isn't a coward.'

Jimmy looked at the letter again. 'Maiden Lane, that's where I broke into that office. It was a club then, but they closed it down eighteen months ago.' He looked at Mog, his eyes suddenly sparking with fire. 'This is Kent's doing. He's got her there. You tell Garth, and get the police to come down to Maiden Lane. Tell him it's the old club next to the back door of the theatre. I'm going there now.'

'No, Jimmy, he's got a gun!' Mog said in horror, but she was too late. He was already rushing for the door, stopping only to pick up a cudgel Garth kept for threatening would-be troublemakers.

He ran down through the market like the wind. He heard people shout to him but he didn't stop or even shout back. There was only one thought in his head: he had to save Belle.

At Maiden Lane he was forced to stop for a moment as he had a stitch and was out of breath. He bent till the stitch went, then went to the door of the old club. He could see by the refuse around it that it wasn't in regular use any more. It was his guess that James Colm, the man who used to run the club, had given Kent a key to hole up in here until the heat died down. Even though the police did know Colm was involved with the trade in young girls, they probably hadn't considered Kent might be here as the club had been closed down for so long.

The door didn't look very strong, but as Jimmy lifted the cudgel to smash it in, he realized Kent would hear him and he'd be ready and waiting with his gun. He might even shoot Belle too.

There was nothing for it but to climb up the front of the building and go in through the window.

He ran round to the Strand, remembering how the last time

he'd gone in there he was afraid of being seen. That didn't matter now, but he did hope that anyone watching wouldn't create a hue and cry so that Kent was alerted something was going on.

Tucking the cudgel into his shirt, Jimmy began to climb. He was much stronger now than he had been back then, and he shinned up the drainpipe effortlessly and stepped on to the window sill of the old office. The windows were so black with grime it was hard to see in, but standing well back to the side and hoping the curtains he remembered were still hanging to hide him, he rubbed enough of a patch on the glass to peer in.

The office was in a shambles. He could see an old mattress on the rubbish-strewn floor. The filing cabinets were gone, but the desk remained, and Kent was sitting at it, poring over what appeared to be a map.

He was facing the window: one sound from Jimmy and he'd look up. Jimmy peeped through the hole again, hoping to see the man's gun. But if it was lying somewhere in that room it was out of his line of vision. There was no sign of Belle but then she was probably out back in the old club.

Jimmy shrank back as he considered what to do. He thought of climbing down and asking someone in one of the shops below to go round the back and hammer on the door. That might make Kent go to investigate and he could smash through the window once his back was turned. But Kent would almost certainly pick up his gun and take it with him. Jimmy wasn't prepared to run the risk of Belle being hurt.

He peered in again and marvelled at how calm the man appeared to be, sitting there studying his map as if he was merely planning a holiday. But he wasn't looking dapper the way he had been when Jimmy had spied on him two years earlier. Back then his hair had been dark, only grey at the temples, but now it was all grey and so long it hung over his filthy, collarless shirt. He hadn't shaved for some time, but not long enough to have grown a beard. His once neatly trimmed military-style moustache was like a bush, virtually concealing his lips.

A few people on the pavement were gathering now to look up at Jimmy. He could hear the hum of their voices, and guessed they thought he'd been locked out and was trying to get in through the window. He heard one woman call out, telling him to be careful as he'd break his neck if he fell.

All at once an idea came to him. If those people made enough noise Kent would get up to look and see what was happening. The desk was nearer the second window, and there appeared to be less clutter there too, whereas Jimmy could see there was a pile of boxes beneath the window where he was. So Kent would take the easiest route to look out, and as he did so, Jimmy could smash his way in and hopefully knock Kent out before he could grab his gun.

It certainly wasn't a foolproof plan; all it had in its favour was the element of surprise. And he'd have to synchronize smashing the window and jumping through, plus bashing Kent with the cudgel before he had a chance to gather his wits.

But it was the only idea Jimmy had, and while he stood on the window sill considering the virtues and dangers of it, Belle was in there, in mortal danger.

So he half turned and began flapping his arms around and pretending to slip off the sill. He knew the people below wouldn't realize how deep the sill really was, and he willed them to start shouting at him.

'Stand still, we'll get help!' someone shouted.

All at once the murmur of voices became a hubbub, growing even louder as others stopped to join in. Quickly Jimmy put his eye to his spy-hole and saw Kent getting up. To make sure the man went right to the window, Jimmy pretended to slip again, and the gasps and calls for him to stay still were so loud that he knew Kent must be looking out.

Jimmy had put the cudgel on the window sill when he first

climbed up. Now he snatched it up, swung it back, and with all his strength crashed it into the glass. At the moment of impact he hurled himself forward, eyes closed. He felt shards of glass scrape his head and cheeks, but still held on to the cudgel and only opened his eyes as he hit the floor. He staggered, then spun round to see Kent was still at the window, but he'd turned round and his eyes were wide with shock.

Lifting the cudgel above his head, Jimmy leapt towards the man and brought it crashing down. The blow landed on Kent's shoulder and he reeled back with a howl of pain. Jimmy lifted it again, and with even more force hit him again on the side of his head.

Kent slumped to the floor like a sack of potatoes.

Jimmy was half blinded by blood. He wiped his eyes on his sleeve to clear them, then looked around. Kent's jacket was lying on some boxes, the gun sticking out of the pocket.

He snatched it up, tucked it into the waist of his trousers, kicked Kent to make sure he was unconscious, and when he didn't move, went to find Belle.

She was lying on the floor right up by the staircase door, trussed up with a gag in her mouth, her eye blackening from a blow.

'It's all right, you're safe now,' Jimmy said as he removed the gag from her mouth. 'Kent's out cold and I have his gun. But I've got to go back in there to make sure he doesn't wake up. Just wait a few more minutes, the police will soon be here.'

'So it was you,' she said in wonder.

Jimmy chuckled. He wanted to untie her and hug her, but he had no knife on him to cut the rope and he was afraid Kent might come round. 'Yes, it was me, but hold on, sweetheart. I can't untie you now.'

Belle watched as he walked back towards the light at the end of the room. He had such a light, lithe step, and it reminded her of the day he'd slid on the ice as they went down to the Embankment Gardens in the snow. That seemed a lifetime ago.

She had been in such abject terror lying here on the floor that she'd wet herself. She'd been able to see Kent sitting with his back to her right at the end of the room, but he was just a dark, unmoving shape. She didn't know what he was doing but she was convinced he was preparing to kill her. She had no hope of rescue. No one would think of looking for her here.

After trying vainly to free herself she gave up. It seemed to her that it was her fate to die through violence, and she'd just cheated it by being saved from Pascal. Then all at once there was shouting coming from the front of the building. She hoped it was the police, but with that hope came even greater terror because she knew Kent wouldn't simply give himself up. He would either start shooting or use her as a hostage. Either way she knew that she would die, whether here or somewhere else.

She saw Kent move from his seat, and then heard that incredible crash and tinkling of glass. Light suddenly streamed in and she saw a silhouette of another man with something big and heavy in his hands, then heard a thump and a howl of pain. Another dull thump and the man walked towards her.

The light was behind him so she didn't know it was Jimmy, not until he spoke. She thought of how an entire police force hadn't been able to catch Kent and arrest him, yet Jimmy had managed it all on his own.

'My Jimmy, a hero,' she murmured to herself.

He was shouting now to someone below the window. He was telling them to come to the back door. 'Smash it down!' he shouted. 'I can't leave this bastard. And one of you cut Miss Cooper loose when you get up here. She's tied up.'

Suddenly the stink of this place and the terror she'd felt disappeared. It was almost as if she was floating among clouds, and she could look down and see her past spread out before her. Kent was the man who had caused everything, and now he was caught, she was free. Free to put it all behind her, free to make a life of her own choosing.

Jimmy was right in saying that one day she'd find herself realizing that some good things had come out of all she'd been through. She knew about people now, the wicked and the good and all those in between who were a bit of both because they'd been damaged by the bad things that had happened to them. She understood how greed could distort people's thinking, and how lust without love would never completely satisfy anyone.

Truly wicked people were quite rare, she realized. Kent was one, Madame Sondheim and Pascal another two. But people like Martha, Sly and perhaps Madame Albertine in Marseille had probably become bad through greed and association with wicked people.

Yet on balance there were many, many more good people. Aside from Mog and Jimmy, there were Lisette, Gabrielle, Philippe, Noah, Garth and Etienne. Maybe some would argue that like herself, most of them were not entirely pure, but they stood up for right when it was needed.

Belle heard the sound of wood splintering, then the comforting tread of heavy boots on the stairs. It was all over now: she and Jimmy could go home very soon, and she could start her new life.

Chapter Thirty-nine
Epilogue

The Wedding March began, and as Belle turned to look at Mog coming into the church on Jimmy's arm, her eyes began to prickle with emotional tears. She'd already seen Mog in her finery when she'd helped her to dress earlier. She'd fastened the long row of tiny buttons down the back of her pale blue dress, and placed the blue and white hat she'd made on Mog's head, but to see her now, blushing and smiling like a young girl as she walked towards her man, was very moving.

It was early September and a glorious warm, sunny day. Outside All Saints Church on Blackheath families were having picnics; courting couples were strolling together, and old folks sitting on benches in the sunshine. And down the road, just waiting for Garth and Mog to become Mr and Mrs Franklin, was the Railway Inn, the public house of their dreams.

For three months now Mog and Belle had been living in a couple of rooms in Lee Park, a quiet, tree-lined road, so that Mog and Garth could be married here in Blackheath. Garth and Jimmy had remained at the Ram's Head, not only to sell it and to wait for the legalities of the Railway Inn purchase to be finalized, but for propriety's sake. Back in Seven Dials, no one worried much about such things. But they were all aware that starting a new venture in a very respectable area meant they must be seen to be respectable too.

Belle had thought she and Mog might find conforming to polite society's mores very difficult, but to their surprise it wasn't that hard. If asked, Mog told people she had been a housekeeper and Belle had been a maid in the same household. When they were alone they often laughed about this for in many ways it was true. Mog had always been rather genteel and she had brought Belle up to be the same, so there weren't too many pitfalls for them to tumble into. The only thing they found really difficult was getting used to their landlord and other men they came into contact with treating them as if they were delicate little flowers without a brain in their heads or an opinion of their own. Yet three months with little more to do than go for walks, read and sew, had given them both time to study the middle classes, adjust their behaviour accordingly, and have a well-earned rest while they planned for the future.

But now, as Belle watched Mog walk up the aisle to the altar rail where Garth was waiting with his best man, John Spratt, an old friend, she knew Mog would be delighted that the enforced idleness had come to an end. At last she could turn the rooms above the pub into a real home and have Garth beside her for ever.

'Mog looks lovely,' Annie whispered to Belle. 'And her hat looks as if it came from Bond Street. You really have a flair for millinery. And you look so pretty too!'

Belle glowed at her mother's praise. She was wearing a pale pink artificial silk dress with ruffles at the hem, and a white hat, all of which she'd made herself. She knew she would never become as close to Annie as she was to Mog, but they were both trying hard.

After that terrible day with Kent, Garth had gone to Annie and insisted that she came and saw her daughter to explain her part in it. Belle had seen a different side to her mother then: a vulnerable woman who had built a hard shell around herself, believing that by staying aloof, she could protect herself from further hurt.

It transpired that a man who had known Annie in the past had come to stay as a guest in her boarding house. Because this man knew so much about her anyway, and he seemed so kindly, Annie confided in him about Belle, and also told him that she hadn't seen her daughter since she got back from France.

Once Annie was told about the letter which was supposed to have come from her, she realized her guest must have been an associate of Kent's, sent to her with the sole intention of getting information about Belle. He clearly relayed this to Kent, who then forged an appropriate letter from her.

Annie admitted she should have come straight to the Ram's Head when Belle returned from France, but some of the sentiments in that letter were based on truth. She was ashamed she'd abandoned Mog and thought only of herself, but a year ago, when Jimmy had upbraided her for this, she felt everyone was against her.

'I couldn't bear to think that you would be submitted to the same terrible things as I was as a young girl,' she sobbed to Belle. 'It was less painful to think you were dead and had been saved the torment I went through. Each time Jimmy, Mog or Noah came to see me, I felt they were opening up my wounds again. I couldn't believe, as they did, that you would be found.'

Belle understood. Perhaps if the bond had been as strong between them as it was between herself and Mog, Annie might have known in her heart she was alive. She felt her mother was to be pitied, not to be pilloried further by being shut out of her daughter's life. Since then Belle had visited her in King's Cross every two or three weeks. As Annie had shared so many similar experiences in her past to Belle's in her two years away, they discussed them, sometimes crying, sometimes with laughter. Belle felt it had been very good for both of them to confide in each other.

She couldn't help but admire her mother's head for business and how hard she worked. Her two houses offered clean and comfortable rooms, and she offered breakfast and an evening meal for her guests. She did all the cooking herself and a great deal of cleaning too as she had only a maid-of-all work to help her, yet she seemed far happier than she had been in the old days back in Seven Dials.

Annie had been the one Belle turned to for advice when Etienne finally wrote to her, because Mog's loyalty would have been with Jimmy.

Etienne's letter was an odd one, not just because he found it hard to write in English, but because Belle felt he was hiding his true feelings for her. He said how he had given what evidence he could to the French police about the trade in young girls, and Madame Sondheim and many others in the chain had been arrested and were awaiting their trials. Pascal too was still awaiting his, and Etienne thought there was no doubt he'd go to the guillotine.

Etienne went on to tell Belle about his small farm, and that he had chickens and some pigs and was planting lemon and olive trees, and he had made his cottage more comfortable. He had read in the newspapers that Kent had been arrested, tried and found guilty of murdering three girls, Millie and two others, and he asked how Belle felt now that Kent was to be hanged. He wound up the letter by urging her to put the past away, that she was in his heart, and he wished her every success in the future.

Annie studied every word of the letter carefully. 'I'd say he does love you,' she said at length, 'but he knows he is not the right man for you. He is an honourable man and feels that he can only bring you more unhappiness. I think by the way he describes his little farm, he knows too that he couldn't settle in England and that you wouldn't want to live in France. But reading between the lines I'd say he is hoping he is in your heart.'

'Should I go to him and see?' Belle asked.

Annie shrugged her shoulders. 'If you were to do that I'm

sure he would welcome you with open arms, and that for a time you could be very happy. But you would have to pay a high price, Belle. He is well known in France, and because of his past you would be tainted with that too. Then there is the problem of his deep sorrow at losing his wife and children. Could you live alone in isolation with such a man and never regret leaving the people who love you here? Or your dream of having your own hat shop?'

Belle was touched that her mother had not ridiculed the idea of her feeding pigs and chickens, of watering Etienne's trees and living the life of a peasant. She felt that Annie even understood her physical desire for him, yet she didn't say that was not enough to keep her happy there.

'I believe you can feel the way you do about Etienne with a man who can give you all the other things you want too,' Annie said gently. 'I fear you have shut your mind to that. But you have to open it, be receptive and let love in.'

Kent's trial had taken place just before Belle moved to Blackheath. She was called as a witness to the Old Bailey, but because of the two other murders, and a dozen or more other witnesses, including Sly who had turned King's Evidence against his old partner, her role in the trial was less important than had been anticipated. Because of her tender age and being as much a victim of Kent as Millie had been, she wasn't subjected to rigorous cross-examination, and with Noah's connections with the leading newspapers, very little was said about her by any of the journalists who covered the trial.

Kent was hanged a couple of weeks after he was sentenced, and Belle made a point of not reading any of the newspapers at that time. She didn't want to hear his name again, much less read about him.

Now here in the church, listening to Mog and Garth making their vows to each other, all that darkness and brutality seemed a lifetime ago. Belle was the happiest she'd ever been, every day seemed to bring new joy, and she felt her heart was open again.

She looked at Jimmy up ahead in the front pew, straight-backed, his dark red hair looking like burnished copper in a ray of sunshine slanting in. He was several inches taller than the men near him, with wider shoulders, and was stronger and kinder than anyone else. He made her laugh, she could talk to him about anything, and he had proved that day he leapt through the window that he was every bit as valiant and tough as Etienne. He still had little scars on his cheeks and neck to remind her; some of them had been so bad he'd spent two days in hospital having pieces of glass removed from the wounds and having them stitched.

He knew everything about her, but she was still finding things out about him. He certainly wasn't just the devoted puppy dog trailing after her that she'd first thought when she came back to England.

Annie nudged her, and Belle came to with a start, suddenly aware that while she had been daydreaming, Mog and Garth had completed their vows, and everyone was getting down on their knees for prayers.

She quickly followed suit, but peeped though her eyelashes at Noah and Lisette and little six-year-old Jean-Pierre across the aisle. Jean-Pierre wore a white sailor suit and looked ador-able. He had the same dark hair and big dark eyes as his mother. Lisette looked beautiful in a silver-grey dress and the matching feathery hat which Belle had made for her. She loved her new life in London and had taken a job as a nurse in a small nursing home in Camden Town. She was most definitely as much in love with Noah as he was with her, and Belle thought it was only a matter of days before he would announce when they were going to be married.

Noah had become a very successful journalist. He'd made

his name this year with his hard-hitting articles about human trafficking. Thanks to his dogged persistence and motivating others, three of the girls he'd had on his list of those abducted by Kent and his cronies had been found in Belgium and were now reunited with their families. Now he was writing a series of articles about survivors of the *Titanic*. He'd told Jimmy recently that he was also writing a novel, but couldn't be drawn as to what it was about.

The other twenty or so people here today were Mog and Garth's more respectable friends from Seven Dials, shopkeepers, other publicans, a lawyer and a doctor and their wives, but Garth and Jimmy had thrown a riotous leaving party a week ago back at the Ram's Head so that the rest of their old customers wouldn't feel left out by not being invited today.

Two days ago a carter had brought all their furniture and belongings over to the Railway Inn, and Mog and Belle had arranged it in their new home. Tonight and for the next four days Jimmy would stay there alone, while Mog and Garth had a honeymoon in Folkestone. Belle would stay in Lee Park until then too. She smiled to herself at Mog's insistence that she and Jimmy should not be alone under the same roof. Considering Belle's former career that seemed ludicrous, but since they moved to Blackheath, Mog had become a stickler for her having a chaperone. She said it was to safeguard her reputation.

The final hymn, 'Love Divine All Love Excelling', was sung, and Mog, Garth, John Spratt and Jimmy went off to the vestry to sign the register. The organist was playing something gentle and there was a low buzz of conversation.

'I've got something to tell you,' Annie said. 'I'll say it now before all the hoo-ha of people kissing one another and photographs being taken. I want you to go into the solicitors Bailey and Macdonald in Montpelier Row on Monday or Tuesday, to sign the lease for that shop.'

Belle frowned. 'I told you they wouldn't let me have it as I was single.'

She had seen the empty shop in Tranquil Vale, the main street in Blackheath Village, a few weeks ago and got the agent to show it to her. It was perfect, a small shop complete with a pretty bow-fronted window, and a room behind big enough for a workroom, plus a lavatory outside in the back yard. The rent was reasonable too. But Belle had been turned down flat as a tenant.

Annie smiled. 'They will now, I persuaded them to let me guarantee the rent. As I own a property and they think I'm a widow, they couldn't really refuse.'

If it hadn't been for the bride and groom coming down the aisle with the widest of smiles on their faces, Belle would have thrown her arms round her mother. Instead, she quietly squeezed her hand in thanks and whispered that they'd talk later.

The wedding breakfast was in the Railway Inn. It was a traditional old pub with slate floors, a huge fireplace and a long curved bar. It had been neglected over the years, but once Garth had taken it over he closed it for a few days before the wedding to smarten it up.

He'd got in a team of people who scrubbed the floor, revarnished the bar, doors, tables and chairs, and repainted the smoke-stained walls in cream. Now, with gleaming mirrors behind the equally shiny bar, arrangements of flowers and new chintz curtains at the windows, it looked a different place. A local catering company had laid up two long tables in a 'T' shape, and placed the two-tier wedding cake made and iced by Mog as a centrepiece. Belle had been in from six that morning making little flower arrangements for the table to match Mog's posy of daisies and pink rosebuds and she'd also made all the gentlemen's carnation button-holes.

'It won't look or smell as pretty as this once we open for

business,' Garth joked as he directed the caterers to give everyone a glass of champagne before sitting down to eat.

'If you think I'm going to let you turn it into a rough house, then think again,' Mog retorted. 'And there'll be none of that "men only" business in here either. As I understand it, some of the ladies in Blackheath like to come into the snug for a glass of sherry.'

She had re-upholstered the cushions on the settles in the snug, which was separated from the main bar by a partition with attractive stained glass at the top.

'Now we're married, Mrs Franklin,' Garth said, looking at her tenderly, 'you'll do as I tell you.'

Everyone laughed, for it was patently obvious that Garth worshipped Mog and consulted her about everything.

'It's difficult to believe those two are the same people we lived with when we first met,' Jimmy whispered to Belle. 'My uncle was so fierce and grumpy and she was like a little grey mouse.'

Belle giggled. She had only known Garth then by repute, but it was said that if anyone upset him he'd boot them out into the street. Mog had been old beyond her years, she wore dowdy clothes and rarely contradicted anyone.

Love had made Mog blossom and gain confidence, and since Belle came back she'd encouraged her to wear more fashionable clothes that showed off her neat little figure. She no longer scragged back her hair so severely, it was as glossy as new conkers and fixed in a much softer chignon. When she let it down and brushed it to go to bed she looked no more than twenty-five.

Lisette came up to Belle just before they sat down to eat. 'You look so chic today,' she said in her delightfully accented English. 'It is no wonder Jimmy has eyes for no one else.'

Belle laughed. She had told Lisette about Jimmy at the time she was ill in the nursing home after her ordeal at Madame

Sondheim's and Lisette was convinced they were meant for each other. 'There aren't any other unattached women here to compete with me,' she said.

'That is true, but if there were, you would still have all his attention,' Lisette insisted.

'How is Jean-Pierre settling in at his new school?' Belle asked. Both Noah and Lisette were always saying such things about Jimmy and it was a little wearing.

'He is so 'appy there,' she said with obvious delight. 'His English is as good as mine now. He is reading well and likes to do sums.'

'And are you happy you came to England?'

'Oh yes, I do not miss France, except perhaps for the good wine and food. The butcher the other day say to me, "You Frenchies are too fussy."'

Both of them laughed. Noah often said how she picked over vegetables and fruit in the shops. By an unspoken agreement they never talked about how they really met. They both implied that Noah had introduced them, and only Mog, Garth and Jimmy knew the truth.

'Well, it's good English fare today,' Belle said. 'Roast beef with all the trimmings.' She went on to tell Lisette that her mother had secured the lease for the shop she was after. 'You must come to the opening,' she said. 'You can turn your French charm on the Blackheath ladies and show them how to wear a hat with style.'

Lisette leaned forward and kissed Belle on both cheeks. 'The bad times are over for both of us now,' she whispered. 'You brought me Noah, and I hope you will soon see Jimmy is the one for you.'

Almost three hours later after a hearty meal and a great deal of wine, all the wedding guests accompanied Mog and Garth to the station to wave them off on the train to Folkestone. Mog looked like a fashion plate in a cream costume with a peplum waisted jacket and a straight skirt which just skimmed her new brown patent leather ankle boots with a small heel. Belle had made her cream felt hat with a plaited band of cream and brown ribbon.

As the train pulled out of the station, all the guests dispersed, mostly on to the other platform to await a train back to Charing Cross.

Jimmy and Belle walked back to the Railway Inn to pay off the caterers whom they had left clearing up.

'It will be strange going back to Lee Park alone,' Belle said as they walked out of the station. 'I've got so used to Mog being there all the time.'

'I think Annie hoped you'd ask if you could go back with her,' Jimmy said. 'She looked a bit forlorn when she said goodbye.' Annie had left earlier, as she had to make dinner for her boarders.

'I don't think it was that, she was a teeny bit jealous of Mog. But wasn't it lovely of her to make the shop happen for me?' She'd told just about everyone about it during the wedding breakfast, and apart from her own delight it was good to be able to show her mother in a more flattering light.

'No more than you deserve,' Jimmy said. 'You won't know yourself, having so much room to make hats in. They are beginning to take over Lee Park!'

Belle had begun hat-making in earnest about six weeks ago, and with half a dozen sitting on blocks and boxes of trimmings and other materials piled all around, the living-room looked like a workshop.

They walked into the pub to find the caterers ready to leave. Jimmy paid them and thanked them for everything, then locked the door behind them.

'Help!' Belle made a pretend-horrified face. 'I'm alone with a man!'

'And I've locked the door,' Jimmy said with a leer. 'Now I'm going to ravish you.'

'Please don't, kind sir,' she said, running out into the kitchen. 'I'm just an innocent maid, and if you ruin me, who will have me?' she called back over her shoulder.

He came running after her and caught her in his arms. 'Unhand me, sir,' she said.

She knew he was only playing, but his arms around her felt so right that her body just moulded into his and she put her hand on his neck, drawing his head down to kiss him.

His lips were tantalizingly warm and soft, and as the tip of his tongue flickered against hers, she felt a surge of desire she hadn't expected. One kiss went into another, then another, and time seemed to stand still as they devoured each other.

It was Jimmy who broke away first. He was flushed and breathing heavily. 'And you, maiden, must unhand me,' he said, 'or take the consequences.'

'And what might those be?' she asked, smiling coyly at him.

'You will have to marry me.'

His offer to marry her months ago on the day out to Greenwich had been made lightly, and he'd said nothing more about it since. Since she and Mog had moved into the rooms in Lee Park and only saw Jimmy and Garth on a Sunday, Belle had really missed Jimmy, but she refused to believe he could ever be more than just a good friend.

But now, in the light of how his kisses had made her feel, she was no longer so certain of that.

'I love you, Belle, I always have,' he said softly. 'I met other girls while you were away, but they meant nothing, you were the one that was always on my mind. But it's time I walked you home now, I dare say we've both been affected by the wedding and drunk too much, and I'm not going to make a bigger fool of myself by pestering you.'

'You aren't making a fool of yourself,' Belle said. 'Just kiss me again before we leave.'

He swept her into his arms and kissed her until she felt she was going to faint with wanting him.

'Home now,' he said, taking her hand and leading her to the door. 'I think you need time on your own to think this through.'

Belle tossed and turned that night, unable to think of anything but Jimmy's kisses and how they had made her feel. She'd kissed only five men in her life – Etienne, Serge, Faldo, Clovis and Jimmy. Serge didn't count at all, for blissful as his love-making had been, she had never been under any illusion that it was anything other than sex. Faldo didn't count either for she'd felt nothing but a vague affection for him. Clovis was someone she regretted deeply. As for Etienne, she was still just a child when he kissed her, and after all she'd been through just before she met him it was likely she became infatuated because he was so kind to her.

She'd written back to him just before she and Mog moved to Blackheath, and told him about her life back in England, about Lisette and Noah, and how Mog and Garth were getting married. She'd said she hoped he'd find true happiness on his little farm, but said nothing of her feelings for him.

She realized now that her letter had finalized it for her. She'd met him at a desperate time in her life, and his kindness and wisdom had helped her through it. Looking back, it was hardly surprising that she'd put him on a pedestal. On top of that he was the one who rescued her from Pascal. What woman wouldn't love him for that? Yet in the past three months of being secure and happy she'd rarely thought about him, and when she did it wasn't with sadness for what might have been, only gratitude he'd been there when she needed someone.

Yet if Jimmy was to go out of her life she knew she wouldn't forget him in a hurry. He was part of her past, of the present, and she wanted him there in her future. Did she love him?

If someone was your best friend, someone you never wanted to lose, and you desired them, if that wasn't love, what was it?

She tried to think about her shop, to imagine how she would decorate and arrange it, and display her hats in the window. But her mind kept slipping back to Jimmy.

Everyone she knew would be delighted if they married. Even her mother had said that he was a diamond.

What was she waiting for? Did she expect a thunderbolt from the heavens to make her see it was meant to be?

She got out of bed, and as she so often did when she couldn't sleep, she picked up her sketchpad and a pencil.

But instead of drawing a hat, she found herself drawing a veil, and that led to a wedding dress.

It was barely light when she began, and she became so engrossed in the detail, her own face beneath the veil, the beading on the dress, a train sweeping out behind, even a frothy bouquet of roses and orange blossom in her hands, that she lost all sense of time.

As she finished it she glanced at the clock and was surprised to find it was nine o'clock.

She looked down at the finished sketch and smiled. 'That's the closest you're going to get to a thunderbolt,' she murmured. 'So I think you should go and tell him.'

Read on for a taste of Belle's
further adventures in *Belle's War*,
to be published by Michael Joseph
in spring 2012.

Chapter One
July 1914

The name 'Belle' in gold italic writing above a shop window made Etienne Carrera stop in his tracks and his heart beat a little faster. It was raining hard so he sheltered under a haberdasher's shop awning to look across the street at the little bow-windowed hat shop. It had to be her shop, it surely couldn't be mere coincidence when he had come out to Blackheath for the sole purpose of finding out how she was.

Etienne could see two ladies silhouetted inside the shop; their hand and head movements suggested they were excited by the hats on display. If the shop belonged to his Belle then he knew he should be satisfied that she'd achieved her ambition to become a milliner, and could go back into London happy that life was treating her well. But just the thought that she might be less than twenty yards from him sent a tingle down his spine.

A vivid image came into his mind, of saying goodbye to her over two years earlier at Gard du Nord in Paris. Her train to Calais was about to leave, doors were slamming, people were rushing frantically to get aboard and smoke was belching from the engine. Belle looked up at him, dark curls escaping from a little pink hat, her lovely eyes brimming with tears. She had pleaded with him to say something to her in French.

He couldn't remember his exact words now, only that they came straight from his heart. He said something like he would face any perils, walk through fire and floods just to be with her.

He should have simply said that he loved her, for her

French wasn't good enough for her to understand much more than that simple phrase. She tried to smile as the guard blew his whistle, and then ran to get on the train.

He remembered that she waved from the window until he could no longer see her.

Why had he been such a fool? They had shared so much and he knew women well enough to know that she had felt the same for him. He should have followed her to London within a day or two and told her, in English, what she meant to him. But he didn't because he'd believed he was doing the right thing for her by staying away.

Weeks passed before he even wrote to her. He found it difficult to write in English and he guessed his letter was stilted and lacking in warmth. She replied, but her writing too was very formal, without any hint that she had hoped for more from him.

Turning, Etienne looked at his reflection in the shop window behind him. Old friends back in France claimed he'd changed in the last two years, but he couldn't see any difference in himself. He was still lean and fit – hard work on his small farm kept him that way – and his shoulders were broader and more muscular than before. But perhaps his friends meant that his angular features had softened and made him look less dangerous.

There was a time when he had delighted in being told his blue eyes were icy, and that just a look from him was enough to strike fear into people. But back then he'd needed to be tough and ruthless, for that was all part of his work. While he knew he was still capable of violence if threatened or provoked, he wasn't part of that world any longer.

He'd come to England on business and, on a whim that he was almost regretting now, he'd gone to the address where Belle had lived when she got back from France, a public house in London's Seven Dials. But the public house had changed hands, and he was told the old landlord and his nephew had moved to Blackheath in south London.

So he took the train out here, asked the ticket collector if he knew Garth Franklin, and was directed to the Railway Inn. As it was closed until five-thirty he'd taken a walk up the hill towards the Heath, and here he was, looking across the street, hungry to know more about Belle.

A plump, rosy-faced matron, struggling with an umbrella which had blown inside out, joined him under the awning to shelter from the rain. 'If it don't stop soon we'll all get webbed feet!' she remarked jovially as she tried to turn her umbrella back the right way. 'I don't know what possessed me to come out in it.'

'I was thinking the same myself,' he replied, and took the umbrella from her to straighten out the spokes. 'There you are.' As he handed it back to her, he added, 'But I expect it will do the same again in the next gust of wind.'

She looked at him curiously. 'You're French, aren't you? But your English is very good.'

Etienne smiled. He liked the way English women of her age didn't hold back from questioning complete strangers. French women were much more reserved.

'Yes, I'm French, but I spent some time in England when I was young.'

'Are you here on holiday?' she asked.

'Yes, visiting old friends,' he said, for that was partially true. 'I was told Blackheath was a very pretty place, but I didn't pick a good day to explore it.'

She laughed and agreed that no one would want to walk on the Heath in such heavy rain.

'You must live in the south of France,' she said, looking at him appraisingly. 'Your face is very brown. My brother has holidays in Nice, he always comes back as brown as a conker.'

Etienne had no idea what a conker was, but he was glad

the woman seemed prepared to chat. He hoped he might learn something more about Belle from her.

'I live near Marseille. And that shop over there reminds me of the French milliners,' he said, pointing to the hat shop.

She looked over to it and smiled. 'I believe Belle learned her trade in Paris. All the ladies in the village love her hats,' she said, with real warmth in her voice. 'I'd have popped in there myself today if the weather wasn't so bad. Such a lovely young woman! She's always got time for everyone.'

'So she has good business then?'

'Yes indeed, she gets ladies coming from all over to buy from her, I'm told. But you must excuse me, I must make my way home now, or there won't be any dinner tonight.'

'It was a pleasure talking to you,' he said, and helped her put her umbrella up again.

'You should go over there and buy your wife a hat,' the woman said as she began to walk away. 'You won't find a better shop, not even up in Regent Street.'

After the woman had gone he continued to look across the street, hoping for a glimpse of Belle. The older woman's praise for her was evidence that the more scandalous episodes of her past hadn't followed her here, and that she was liked and respected in this genteel village. His mission had been accomplished and he knew he ought to go straight back to the station and catch a train into London.

The tinkling of a doorbell alerted him that someone was leaving Belle's shop. Both the ladies he'd glimpsed inside emerged – he guessed that they were mother and daughter for one looked to be in her forties, the other no more than eighteen or so. The younger one ran to a waiting automobile with two pink-and-black striped hat boxes in her hands, the older woman looking back into the shop as if saying goodbye. Then, suddenly, he saw Belle in the doorway. Slender and as lovely as he remembered, wearing a very demure high- necked pale green dress, her dark shiny hair piled up on her head with just a few curls escaping around her face.

At once he knew he had to speak to her, just one last time. Rumblings of war had become increasingly loud in the last year, and since the Archduke Franz Ferdinand of Austria had been assassinated back at the end of June, war seemed inevitable. Germany was bound to invade France and Etienne knew when that happened he would have to fight for his country, and might never get back to England again.

The two women got into the automobile and were driven off. Belle closed the shop door, and on impulse Etienne darted across the street through the rain. He paused to look through the window before going inside. Belle had her back to him, arranging hats on little stands. There was a row of tiny pearl buttons down the back of her green dress, and he felt a pang of jealousy that he would never be able to unbutton them for her. She bent forward to pick up a hat box from the floor and he caught a glimpse of shapely calf above pretty lacy ankle boots. When he rescued her in Paris he had seen her naked and felt nothing then but concern for her, yet now even a few inches of her exposed leg was arousing.

She turned as the doorbell tinkled and on seeing him her hands flew up to her mouth and her eyes opened wide with surprise. 'Etienne!' she exclaimed. 'What are you doing here?'

He immediately saw the wedding ring on her finger and realized that she must have married Jimmy Reilly, the child-hood friend she'd so often spoken about and who he knew had settled in Blackheath too.

'I'm flattered that you remember me,' he said lightly, hiding his disappointment. 'And you are looking even more lovely. Success and married life clearly suit you.'

He took a couple of steps nearer her, intending to kiss her cheeks, but she blushed and backed away as if nervous. 'How did you know I was here in Blackheath?' she asked.

'I called into the Ram's Head in Seven Dials. The new landlord there told me Garth and Jimmy had moved here, and as you'd told me in your letter that Garth was going to marry Mog, I expected that you'd be here too. I had a day to spare before I left England, so I caught the train out here. I meant to go into The Railway and introduce myself to Garth, but it was closed, so I walked up here and to my delight I saw your shop.'

'Forgive me, I should have written to you again and told you about Garth and Mog's wedding, and told you that I married Jimmy,' she said, looking both anxious and flustered by his sudden appearance. 'But . . .' she faltered, making a little gesture with her hands that implied she hadn't known how to.

'I understand,' he said lightly. 'Old friends do not need to explain. I am just happy that things worked out for you all. Do you and Jimmy live above the pub too?'

'Yes, we do, and my mother helped me get this shop. Do you like it?'

Etienne glanced around at the pale pink and cream decor. 'It's lovely, very feminine and chic. A woman out on the street told me you couldn't get better hats even in Regent Street.'

She smiled then and visibly relaxed. 'Why don't you take off that wet raincoat and I'll make us both a cup of tea?'

She went into a little room at the back of the shop, and called out to him, 'Are you still on your farm?'

Etienne hung his coat on a hook by the door, and brushed back his wet, fair hair with his hands. 'I am, but I also do a little translating, that is the reason I came to England, to meet with a company I have done work for in the past,' he called back.

'So your life is about more than chickens and lemon trees now?' she said as she came back into the shop. 'Please tell me you *have* kept to the straight and narrow?'

Etienne put his hand on his heart. 'I promise you I am a pillar of polite society,' he said, his voice grave but his eyes twinkling.

Belle giggled as if she didn't entirely believe him.

'Do you doubt my word?' he said with a boyish grin. 'Shame on you, Belle, for having so little faith in me. Have I ever lied to you?'

'You once told me you'd kill me if I tried to escape,' she retorted. 'And you later admitted that wasn't true.'

'That's the trouble with women,' he smiled. 'They always remember the little, inconsequential things.' He reached out and touched a pink-feathered hat on a stand, marvelling that her determination and talent had paid off. 'It's your turn to tell the truth now. Is your marriage all you hoped for?'

'Much more than I hoped for,' she said, just a little too quickly. 'We are very happy, Jimmy is just the very best of husbands.'

'Then I am happy for you,' he said, and gave a little bow.

Belle disappeared to the back of the shop once more and reappeared with two cups of tea. She sat on a stool behind her counter and Etienne sat down on one of the chairs.

'And what about you?' Belle asked. 'Do you have a lady in your life?'

'No one special enough to settle down with,' he replied.

She raised her eyebrows questioningly.

He smiled. 'Don't look like that, not everyone wants marriage and stability. Especially now, with war threatening.'

'It won't come to that, surely?' she said.

'I think it is only weeks away.'

'That's all men talk about these days,' Belle sighed.

Etienne smiled. Women in France made the same complaint. 'And what do women talk about?'

'In here it is mostly about fashion, children and domestic things, but we are all worried our men may have to join up and fight. I don't see why England has to get involved, it's nothing to do with us.'

He shrugged. 'France is more vulnerable than England. We may be invaded, you are safer here across the Channel. But enough of war, tell me about your family. You say your mother helped you get the shop. Does she live near here, and how are Mog and Garth?'

'Things are better with my mother, but she lives over in King's Cross and I only see her about once a month. Garth and Mog are very happy, they were made for one another. But why don't you come home with me and meet everyone? I know they'd be delighted.'

Etienne looked at her thoughtfully for a moment. 'All things considered, I think it is best I do not meet them. When you moved here you also left the past behind.'

Belle wanted to protest, but she knew in her heart he was right. On the day she married Jimmy she had firmly closed the door on her time in America and Paris. Etienne may have opened it again by coming to see her, and she was glad he had, but Jimmy might not see it that way.

'Maybe you are right. But what about Noah?' she asked. 'You will surely go to see him, you became such good friends? Lisette is expecting a baby and they have a lovely home in St John's Wood now.'

'I am having lunch with him tomorrow, near his office,' Etienne said. 'We will always be friends, but I don't call at his home; we both feel Lisette needs no reminders of the past, especially now.'

Belle gave a rueful smile. 'Respectability has a high price. Noah and Lisette come to see us now and again, we have all been to their home too. But we are always careful to avoid talking about how and why we met. Sensible as that is, it also prevents us from being really close.'

'Does the past affect your relationship with Jimmy?' Etienne asked, his eyes boring into her, daring her to lie to him.

'Sometimes,' she admitted. 'It's like having a splinter in your finger which you can't get out, and you can't help touching it.'

Etienne nodded in understanding. 'For me too. But in time a splinter works its way out and the hole it leaves will become filled with new memories.'

Belle laughed suddenly. 'Why are we being so gloomy? All of us – you, me, Jimmy, Mog and Lisette too. We all have so many good things now, far more than we ever expected. Why are humans so perverse that they choose to dwell on previous bad times?'

'Is it the bad times we dwell on, or the beautiful moments that lifted us up during those times?' Etienne asked, raising one eyebrow quizzically.

Belle blushed, and he knew she remembered only too well the moments they'd shared. She changed the subject quickly, moving on to ask him about his farm. Etienne found little funny stories to tell her about it to lighten the mood.

Then Belle got off her stool and began tidying up the shop. 'If you're sure you really don't wish to come and meet Jimmy, I must close the shop and go home,' she said. 'We always like to have a meal together before he opens the bar for the evening.'

Etienne got to his feet and took his tea cup out to the tiny kitchen. 'Yes, of course, it must be difficult to have a family life with a bar to run. And I have a train to catch.' He reached for his wet coat and put it back on.

'I think you should leave before me,' Belle said apologetically. 'I don't want anyone remarking that I was seen walking down the street with a stranger.'

He understood what she meant, and he suspected she wouldn't tell Jimmy he'd called in.

'I found what I was looking for,' he said softly, taking her hands in his. 'That you are happy and secure. If France goes to war, as it surely will, I may never get back to England again. Stay happy, love Jimmy with all your heart, and I hope one day I will hear through Noah that you have a whole brood of children.'

He lifted her hands to his lips and kissed them. Then turned quickly and walked out of the door.

As the door closed behind Etienne, Belle murmured, '*Au revoir.*' Her eyes prickled with tears for there was so much more she would have liked to say to him, so much more she wanted to know about his life.

She'd done her best to erase Etienne from her mind: how hard it had been to say goodbye to him in Paris, the yearning she had felt for him for so long after. Why did he have to drive that particular splinter back into her now?

She had told him the truth. She and Jimmy were very happy. Jimmy was her best friend, lover, brother and husband all rolled into one. They shared the same goals, they laughed at the same things, he was everything any girl could want or need. He had healed the horrors of the past and in his arms she had encountered exquisite tenderness and deep satisfaction, for he was a caring and sensitive lover.

Yet she couldn't help but ask herself why, if everything was so good for her, did she feel there was something missing in her life? Why, when she read about suffragettes in the newspaper, did she feel envy that they had the guts to stand up for rights for women in the face of hostility? Why did she feel a little stifled by respectability? And above all, why was it that Etienne's voice, his looks and his lips on her hand still had the power to make her shiver?

She wished she could have told Etienne how wonderful it was to see him again, that he had been in her thoughts so often over the last two years and that she owed him so much. But a married woman could not say such things, and neither could she encourage him to stay in her shop any longer. Blackheath was a village, people were small-minded and nosy, and there would be plenty of them glad to gossip about seeing a handsome man talking to Belle in her shop.

She shook herself out of her thoughts, replaced some hats on their stands, dusted off the counter and picked up some stray tissue paper from the floor. Opening the drawer in which she kept the day's takings, she emptied the money into a cloth bag and pushed it into her reticule. She secured her straw hat to her hair with a long hat pin, flung her cloak over her shoulders and took her umbrella from the stand.

Standing by the door, she paused before turning off the lights, and reminded herself of when she opened her shop for the first time. It had been a cold November day, just two months after Mog and Garth's wedding, and she and Jimmy were due to be married just before Christmas. Everything had been new and shiny that day. Jimmy had indulged her by buying the small but expensive French chandeliers and the glass-topped counter. Mog had found the two button-back Regency chairs and had them re-upholstered in pink velvet, and Garth's present to her was paying the two decorators who had done such a fine job of turning the dingy little shop into a pink and cream feminine heaven.

She had sold twenty-two hats that first day, and dozens of other women who came in to browse had since been back to buy. In the eighteen months that the shop had been open, there had been fewer than seven days in total when she hadn't sold one hat, and those were all in bad weather. The average weekly sales worked out at fifteen hats, and though it meant she had to work very hard to keep up with the demand, and use an out-worker to help her, she was making a very good profit. During the summer she'd bought in plain straw boaters and then trimmed them herself, and that had proved very profitable. Her shop was a resounding success.

'As is everything in your life,' she reminded herself as she turned out the lights.

Etienne went straight to the station, but having found he'd just missed a train and had twenty-five minutes to wait for the next one, he stood at the window by the ticket office and looked at the Railway Inn nearby.

He had never quite understood English public houses: the rigid opening hours, men standing at the bar drinking huge quantities of beer then staggering home at closing time, as if they could only face their wives and children when drunk.

French bars were far more civilized: they weren't seen as a kind of temple to get drunk in, for they were open all day and a man wasn't considered odd if he drank coffee or a soft drink as he read the newspaper.

The Railway at least looked inviting, with its fresh paint and sparkling windows. He could imagine on a cold winter's night it was a warm, friendly haven for men to gather in.

As he looked at it, a big man with red hair and a beard came out of the front door. He was wearing a leather apron over his clothes, and Etienne guessed that this was Garth Franklin, Jimmy's uncle. He was looking up at water spurting out of a broken gutter and running down the front of the building, and he called out to someone inside, presumably asking the unseen person to come and look too.

A younger man joined him, and Etienne knew immediately that this was Jimmy, Belle's husband. He was bigger than Etienne had imagined, as tall as his uncle and with the same broad shoulders, but clean-shaven and with darker red hair, more auburn than fiery red. The pair, who looked like father and son, stood there gazing up, discussing the broken guttering, seemingly oblivious to the rain.

Then Jimmy turned suddenly, his face breaking into a joyful smile, and Etienne saw it was because he'd seen Belle coming towards them.

She was struggling to hold the umbrella over her and keep her cloak around her shoulders, but she ran the last few yards towards the men. As she reached them, her umbrella tilted back and Etienne noted that her smile was as bright as her husband's.

Jimmy took the umbrella from his wife with one hand and with the other he caressed her wet cheek, then he kissed her forehead. Just those small, tender gestures told Etienne how much the man loved her.

He had to turn away. He knew he should feel at peace to realize Belle was truly loved and protected, but instead Etienne felt only the bitter pangs of jealousy.

Lesley Pearse

ABOUT LESLEY

Lesley Pearse is one of the UK's best-loved novelists, with fans across the globe and book sales of nearly four million copies to date.

A true storyteller and a master of gripping plots that keep the reader hooked from beginning to end, Lesley introduces readers to unforgettable characters about whom it is impossible not to care. There is no easily defined genre or formula to her books: some, like *Rosie* and *Secrets*, are family sagas, *Till We Meet Again*, *A Lesser Evil* and *Faith* are crime novels, and others such as *Never Look Back*, *Gypsy* and *Hope* are historical adventures.

Remember Me is based on an astounding true story about Mary Broad who was convicted of highway robbery and transported on the first fleet to Australia, where a penal colony was to be founded. The story of the appalling hardships that faced the prisoners there, and how courageously determined Mary was to gain a better life for her children is one you are unlikely to forget.

Passionately emotive *Trust Me* is also set in Australia, and deals with the true-life scandal of the thousands of British children who were sent there in the post-war period to be systematically neglected, and in many cases, abused.

Stolen is a thriller – the first of her books with a contemporary setting – and was a Number One bestseller in 2010.

Painstaking research is one of Lesley's hallmarks; first, Lesley reads widely on the subject matter, and then she goes to the place she has chosen as a setting. Once there, digging up local history, the story begins, whether it is about the convicts in Australia, the condition for soldiers in the Crimean war, the hardships facing gold miners in the Klondike or the sheer jaw-dropping courage of the pioneers who forged their way across America in covered wagons.

History is one of Lesley's passions, and mixed with her vivid imagination and her keen insight into how people might behave in dangerous, tragic and unusual situations,

'Lesley introduces readers to unforgettable characters about whom it is impossible not to care'

she is soon able to weave a plot with many dramatic twists and turns.

'It wasn't until I was working on my sixth or seventh book that I became aware that my heroines had all had to overcome and rise above emotional damage inflicted upon them as children,' Lesley points out. 'I have had to do this myself; my childhood certainly wasn't a bed of roses, but the more people I get to know, the more I find that most have some kind of trauma in their past. Perhaps this is why so many of us like to read about triumph over adversity.'

Lesley's colourful past has been a very useful point of reference in her writing. Whether she is writing about a grim post-war orphanage, about a child that doesn't quite fit in at school, about adoption, about a girl who leaves home too young and too ill-equipped to cope adequately, about poverty or about the pain of first love, she knows how it feels first hand. For as Lesley laughingly puts it, 'my life has had more ups and downs than a well bucket.'

But the sadness and difficulties in Lesley's life are in the past now. With three grown up daughters, and two much loved grandsons, the latest one, Harley, born in March 2010, Lesley feels her life is wonderful.

'Painstaking research is one of Lesley's hallmarks'

'I live in a pretty cottage in Somerset, with my two dogs, Maisie and Lotte, and my garden there is an all consuming passion,' she says. 'I feel I am truly blessed to wake up each morning with such lovely choices: writing or gardening. They fit so well together; if I'm stuck for an idea in the latest book, I go out and dead head the flowers, mow the lawn or weed. Often I'm writing until two or three in the morning as there is complete silence then and no distractions like the phone to disturb my concentration. I have to confess to wasting a lot of time on Twitter though. It's like having a whole bunch of invisible friends, many of whom are writers too; we comment on things, tell each other what we are up to, and sometimes we get into conversations that are so funny I'm sitting there howling with laughter.'

Friends are very important to Lesley; some of them go right back to ones she met at school and as a teenager.

They are her life blood and she likes nothing better than a girl's day out with shopping and lunch with a group of them.

'I love it too when I'm invited to give a talk; sometimes these are in libraries, where I get to meet my readers; sometimes as a guest speaker at lunches or dinner for a charity function. A writer needs to have direct contact with people – without it they would be working in a vacuum. The feedback you get is so valuable, which book they liked best, or least, and why. It's also a great opportunity to get out of my wellies and old gardening clothes, dress up in something glamorous and visit a part of the country I haven't been to before.'

Lesley's storytelling abilities are even more evident when she is speaking to a group of people, for she can trawl through her past and tell hilarious anecdotes that have her audiences in fits of laughter. One suspects she might have made a good actress if she hadn't drifted from job to job as a young girl. As it was, she was a nanny, a Bunny girl, a dressmaker, and spent many years in promotion work, along with more mundane temping office work. 'The companies I was sent to as a temp were usually glad to see the back of me,' she laughs. 'I was a distraction because I talked to everyone and I was an appalling typist. Funny that I now type fast and accurately. But back then I was always tempted to put my own words into letters I was asked to write, just to pep up the dullness of them.'

Lesley is also the president of the Bath and West Wiltshire branch of the NSPCC – a charity very close to her heart because of physical and mental abuse meted out to her as a child.

'In my ideal world all children would be wanted, valued, loved and cared for,' Lesley says. 'I know from research that child abuse is an evil as old as time, and the only way to stamp it out is through education. I wish every school would put parenting on the curriculum and drum into teenagers the importance of taking care to ensure that they are in stable loving relationships before embarking on having a baby.'

'Lesley's colourful past has been a very useful reference point in her writing'

ABOUT *BELLE*

What was your inspiration for *Belle*?

While researching *Gypsy* and *Never Look Back*, I kept finding details about the thousands of young women who became prostitutes during the Californian and Klondike Gold rushes. The common preconception is that these women were forced into it through dire poverty or brutality. Some of them undoubtedly were, but there were many more who went into it willingly, even joyfully. Some led very colourful lives; the ones at the top end of the market were almost celebrities.

I found myself drawn into a shadowy industry which, although morally reprehensible to some, did in fact provide much needed fun, comfort and respite for gold miners who had to endure terrible hardships in their search for gold.

The stories of these women stayed in my head, and although I didn't want to write another book set in a gold rush, I found myself drawn to create a heroine who, although initially forced into prostitution, decides to embrace the life and make it work for her.

A key theme in the novel is the contrast between Belle's hometown of Seven Dials in London and her new home of New Orleans. What made you choose these two locations?

I often stay in a hotel in Seven Dials, and although it is now a very fashionable part of London, it was once a festering slum area where every kind of vice abounded. The appallingly squalid rookeries that once housed countless thieves, beggars, prostitutes and the poorest in Victorian and Edwardian society have long since been demolished. Classy shops selling designer goods and smart restaurants, elegant pubs and wine bars have taken the place of the old gin palaces, dingy ale houses and pawn shops. Yet it is still possible in the remaining narrow streets and tiny courts to get a glimmer of how it was in the days of gas lighting and hansom cabs. As I've wandered about looking at the remaining old buildings I can imagine the brothels, the street traders, and the ragged waifs that grew up in such a harsh environment.

One evening while making my way back to my hotel through a rather poorly lit street, I imagined a young girl brought up in one such brothel, and the seed of the idea for Belle was sown.

I chose New Orleans as the other main location in the story because the infamous Storyville, where prostitution was legal, was at its height in the early 1900s. I went to New Orleans to research it further and although Storyville had been torn down and rebuilt as social housing, the French Quarter is still as it always was, beautiful, bawdy, sensuous, alight with music and all the ghosts of its wicked past. I felt that Belle could have easily embraced the life of a courtesan there.

The trafficking for prostitution is an important issue affecting many women and children today as well as several characters in *Belle*. This must have been a difficult topic to research. What similarities did you find between the trade now and then? Do you think there is anything we can learn from looking at the trade in recent history?

Then, as now, trafficking of women and children for the sex trade is a furtive but hugely profitable trade. Had I been trying to research the present day trade I doubt if I would have had much success. The people who mastermind it are probably running it from behind a legitimate business, or from a country where officials are being paid off to keep quiet. They certainly wouldn't talk about it to someone like me! Their victims are the kind who cannot seek help: illegal immigrants and those who fear retaliation against their family back home if they speak out.

Back in the time my book is set, pretty young girls could be snatched off the streets for this trade, or lured from their homes with a promise of a job in service. They were often sent to another country, so that their inability to make themselves understood and the lack of funds to make their way home kept them captive. Once pressed into such work, even if they were able to escape from their captor, there was such a stigma against 'ruined' women that most would stay in the trade out of a sense of shame. Their lives were mostly short: disease, drugs and drink saw to that.

Sadly I don't think anything has changed much, despite a better equipped and trained police force, or better education. The victims of trafficking might be from Eastern Europe, Thailand or Africa, rather than English country girls, but trafficking appears to be on the increase rather than slowing down. Strip clubs, pole dancing clubs and massage parlours abound in every major city – the soft end of the sex trade which we've all grown used to seeing. Young girls and boys sell themselves to buy drugs, or even to support themselves while at university. Every now and then we read about paedophile rings being broken up, but for every such ring which is exposed, and those involved sent to prison, there are probably dozens more still active.

I did discover in my research that in Paris alone in the 1900s, four out of five women used prostitution as a way of making a living. Some of these were only part time, using it as a last resort to buy food or clothing as and when they found it necessary, but for the rest it was their only source of income. The proportion of active prostitutes is of course much lower now, but that is only because there are many forms of employment open to women now and unemployment benefits are available.

'Amongst Friends'

The Lesley Pearse Newsletter

A fantastic new way to keep up-to-date with your favourite author. *Amongst Friends* is a regular email with all the latest news and views from Lesley, plus information on her forthcoming titles and the chance to win exclusive prizes.

Just go to **www.penguin.co.uk** and type your email address in the 'Join our newsletter' panel and tick the box marked 'Lesley Pearse'. Then fill in your details and you will be added to Lesley's list.

THE BOOKS

GEORGIA
Raped by her foster-father, fifteen-year-old
Georgia runs away from home to the seedy
back streets of Soho ...

TARA
Anne changes her name to Tara to forget her
shocking past – but can she really become
someone else?

CHARITY
Charity Stratton's bleak life is changed for ever
when her parents die in a fire. Alone and pregnant,
she runs away to London ...

ELLIE
Eastender Ellie and spoilt Bonny set off to make
a living on the stage. Can their friendship survive
sacrifice and ambition?

CAMELLIA
Orphaned Camellia discovers that the past she has
always been so sure of has been built on lies. Can
she bear to uncover the truth about herself?

ROSIE
Rosie is a girl without a mother, with a past full of
trouble. But could the man who ruined her family
also save Rosie?

CHARLIE
Charlie helplessly watches her mother being
senselessly attacked. What secrets have her parents
kept from her?

NEVER LOOK BACK
An act of charity sends flower girl Matilda on a trip
to the New World and a new life ...

TRUST ME
Dulcie Taylor and her sister are sent to an
orphanage and then to Australia. Is their love strong
enough to keep them together?

FATHER UNKNOWN
Daisy Buchan is left a scrapbook with details about
her real mother. But should she go and find her?

TILL WE MEET AGAIN
Susan and Beth were childhood friends. Now
Susan is accused of murder, and Beth finds she
must defend her.

REMEMBER ME
Mary Broad is transported to Australia as a convict
and encounters both cruelty and passion. Can she
make a life for herself so far from home?

SECRETS
Adele Talbot escapes a children's home to find her grandmother – but soon her unhappy mother is on her trail ...

A LESSER EVIL
Bristol, the 1960s, and young Fif Brown defies her parents to marry a man they think is beneath her.

HOPE
Somerset, 1836, and baby Hope is cast out from a world of privilege as proof of her mother's adultery ...

FAITH
Scotland, 1995, and Laura Brannigan is in prison for a murder she claims she didn't commit.

GYPSY
Liverpool, 1893, and after tragedy strikes the Bolton family, Beth and her brother Sam embark on a dangerous journey to find their fortune in America.

STOLEN
A beautiful young woman is discovered half-drowned on a Sussex beach. Where has she come from? Why can't she remember who she is – or what happened?

LESLEY PEARSE

GYPSY

Liverpool, 1893, and tragedy sends Beth Bolton on a journey far from home ...

Fifteen-year-old Beth's dreams are shattered when she, her brother Sam and baby sister Molly are orphaned. Sam believes only America can make their fortunes so, reluctantly leaving Molly with adoptive parents, brother and sister embark on the greatest adventure of their lives.

On board the steamer to New York there are rogues aplenty. But Beth's talent with the fiddle earns her the nickname Gypsy – and the friendship of charismatic gambler Theo and sharp-witted Londoner Jack. And after dodging trouble across America, the foursome head finally for the dangerous mountains of Canada and the Klondike river in search of gold.

How far must Beth go to find happiness? And will her travels lead this gypsy to a place she can call home?

'Lose yourself in this epic saga' *Bella*

LESLEY PEARSE

REMEMBER ME

Cornwall, 1786, and twenty-year-old convicted felon Mary is to be transported to Australia ...

Mary Broad is a mariner's daughter who makes the biggest mistake of her short life when she steals a silk hat from a passer-by. Soon she's sent far from home across cruel seas – and it will take all her courage to survive both the horrific conditions aboard ship and the unknown country that awaits her. But Mary is determined to make something of herself in the hope that one day, she will return ...

Based on a true story, *Remember Me* brings Mary Broad vividly to life in this moving story of a woman triumphing against overwhelming odds.

LESLEY PEARSE

FAITH

1995, Scotland. The prison of Cornton Vale.

Laura Brannigan is in jail for murder. For two years she's been battling for justice – insisting that she didn't kill her best friend, Jackie. Yet with her spirits at their lowest ebb, she receives a letter that takes her back to a different time and memory of an old love …

Twenty years ago was a heady time for Laura: she'd escaped an abusive home and together with new best friend Jackie she'd made a fresh start. The pair had sworn to be sisters for ever. And Stuart had come into their lives – giving Laura a brilliant summer of love.

So what went wrong in the intervening years? And why is Stuart writing to Laura now? Does he have faith in her innocence? And can he help free Laura from prison – and her past?

'An emotional and moving epic that you won't forget in a hurry' *Woman's Weekly*

LESLEY PEARSE

ROSIE

Somerset, 1945, and motherless Rosie Parker is desperate to be saved from her brutish half-brothers …

Rosie thinks she's found a friend in the form of cockney housekeeper Heather Farley, who her father one day brings home to their farm. But soon enough Heather vanishes, abandoning Rosie to her fate. When kindly Thomas Farley comes to find his sister several years later, Rosie learns the terrible truth about Heather – and her family – and runs away from the farm.

Alone in a cruel world, she must somehow come to terms with her shocking past. Yet pursuing Rosie is the man who brought ruin on her family. Is it really possible that he could also bring her happiness?

LESLEY PEARSE

NEVER LOOK BACK

London, 1842, and one good deed takes Matilda Jennings from the dirty backstreets of London to the bright lights of America ...

Matilda was a poor Covent Garden flower girl until the day she saved the life of Tabitha, a minister's daughter. Drawn into the bosom of Tabitha's family, Matilda is given the opportunity of a lifetime.

She is taken from the London slums to the darkest corners of New York, then the plains of the Wild West and San Francisco's gold rush. Streetwise and strong-willed, Matilda forges a new life for herself and Tabitha, and encounters Captain James Russell – a man she knows she can truly love. Yet a war is raging and they must brave not only separation but also the birth pangs of a new nation.

But all Matilda knows is that she must carry on – and never look back.

LESLEY PEARSE

CHARLIE

Devon, 1970, and one glorious summer's day, sixteen-year-old Charlie Welsh sees her mother brutally attacked by two strangers ...

With her father away, Charlie must do all she can to protect her mother from further attacks. And somehow she must find out who would want to hurt her family – and why – without losing faith in her beloved parents. Luckily, Charlie is not alone. She meets kind, funny student Andrew, whose strength she'll desperately need.

Can the couple unravel the mysteries of the past that haunt Charlie's family? Or will facing up to those mysteries destroy their love for each other?

'Characters it is impossible not to care about' *Daily Mail*

LESLEY PEARSE

FATHER UNKNOWN

West London, 1990, and the death of Daisy's adopted mother reveals a family secret that threatens everything she's ever known ...

As Daisy tries to come to terms with her devastating loss, her secure existence is thrown into turmoil after the discovery of a scrapbook full of her mother's memories. Suddenly she is confronted with the knowledge that her real mother was a farmer's daughter from Cornwall – but her biological father's identity remains a mystery. Daisy drops everything to go in search of her roots, but in doing so she risks hurting not only her adored Dad, but also her relationship with her policeman boyfriend, Joel.

As a gripping story of greed, misery and corruption unravels, how will she cope with the truth about her real parents – and the real Daisy?

LESLEY PEARSE

HOPE

Somerset, 1836, and baby Hope is cast out from a world of privilege as living proof of her mother's adultery ...

Smuggled away from the Harveys and Briargate House to a nearby village, Hope grows up in the arms of the warm and loving Renton family, her true identity a secret. But her idyllic childhood comes to an end when she is taken into service by the Harveys, setting in motion a chain of events that will see her blackmailed into leaving her beloved family for ever. Destitute on the streets of Bristol, Hope nevertheless finds the courage to nurse those dying of cholera and soon her new-found talent for healing sees her heading for the horrific battlefields of the Crimea.

But the secrets of the past are not yet done with Hope Renton and she must return to England to face the legacy of her birth ...

'Characters it is impossible not to care about' *Daily Mail*

LESLEY PEARSE

A LESSER EVIL

Bristol in the 1960s and young Fifi Brown defies her parents to marry a man they think is beneath her ...

Determined to follow her heart, Fifi moves with Dan to London where they rent a seedy flat in Dale Street, Kennington. Shocked by the squalor yet exhilarated by her freedom, Fifi is curious to know what goes on behind her neighbours' shabby front doors.

One family holds particular fascination. At number 11, the infamous Muckles terrorize the neighbourhood and scandalize the street with rumours of criminal depravity. When Fifi tries to help the Muckles' youngest child, she risks not only her marriage and her family – but the lives of all the inhabitants of Dale Street ...

'An epic tale of endurance and triumph' *Woman & Home*

LESLEY PEARSE

SECRETS

Kent in the 1930s and when her mother is declared insane, sweet-faced Adele is sent to a children's home …

Yet her new home masks a terrible secret that forces Adele to run away to Sussex and seek out the grandmother she has never known. Unsure at first of a warm welcome, Adele soon makes a life for herself in the beautiful Rye Marshes, where she meets dashing Michael Bailey. Over time their friendship blossoms into love, as he joins the RAF and she becomes a nurse.

But just as Adele thinks her troubled past is behind her, war breaks out and her mother appears – bearing shocking family secrets. Suddenly, all Adele's hopes for the future seem ready to crumble …

LESLEY PEARSE

TILL WE MEET AGAIN

Bristol, 1995, and Susan Wright walks into a busy doctor's surgery and guns down two members of staff, then calmly waits for the police ...

Beth Powell is the lawyer assigned to defend Susan. She finds her client uncooperative until both women realise that twenty-nine years earlier, they were childhood friends. As the evidence against Susan mounts up, both she and Beth begin to talk about the secrets and the traumas that sent them down such different paths in life.

Their friendship grows stronger, but for one of them, there can be no happy ending ...

'Riveting ... examines the intricate relationship of two childhood friends' *Hello!*

LESLEY PEARSE

TRUST ME

South London, 1947, and when young Dulcie Taylor loses her parents, she is sent far, far from home ...

Deprived by tragedy, little Dulcie and her sister May are sent first to an orphanage and then shipped off to begin new lives in Australia. But the 'better life' the sisters are promised turns out to be a lie. It seems everyone who ever said 'trust me' somehow betrays that trust. But then Dulcie meets Ross, another orphanage survivor, and finds a kindred spirit.

Can Dulcie ever get over the pain of the past and learn to trust again? And does she have the strength to fight not only for herself, but also for her sister?

He just wanted a decent book to read ...

Not too much to ask, is it? It was in 1935 when Allen Lane, Managing Director of Bodley Head Publishers, stood on a platform at Exeter railway station looking for something good to read on his journey back to London. His choice was limited to popular magazines and poor-quality paperbacks – the same choice faced every day by the vast majority of readers, few of whom could afford hardbacks. Lane's disappointment and subsequent anger at the range of books generally available led him to found a company – and change the world.

'We believed in the existence in this country of a vast reading public for intelligent books at a low price, and staked everything on it'
Sir Allen Lane, 1902–1970, founder of Penguin Books

The quality paperback had arrived – and not just in bookshops. Lane was adamant that his Penguins should appear in chain stores and tobacconists, and should cost no more than a packet of cigarettes.

Reading habits (and cigarette prices) have changed since 1935, but Penguin still believes in publishing the best books for everybody to enjoy. We still believe that good design costs no more than bad design, and we still believe that quality books published passionately and responsibly make the world a better place.

So wherever you see the little bird – whether it's on a piece of prize-winning literary fiction or a celebrity autobiography, political tour de force or historical masterpiece, a serial-killer thriller, reference book, world classic or a piece of pure escapism – you can bet that it represents the very best that the genre has to offer.

Whatever you like to read – trust Penguin.

Direct Action Against Drug Dealers may have executed a
pedlar of heroin and other filth to our children, one Francis
Deauville, on Thursday morning. Sources indicate that
DAADD also attempted the execution of a drug dealer in
Larne on Tuesday night. Francis Deauville of Sunnylands
Estate in Carrickfergus was a smuggler and supplier of
heroin. Sunnylands Estate lies in the domain of Loyalist
crime lords who were doing nothing to prevent Deauville
carrying out his activities. Our sources indicate that brave
volunteers from DAADD stepped up to the breach and
executed Deauville. He had no children or dependants but
the children of Ireland will be saved from the scourge of
heroin by the removal of this human scum. DAADD have
frequently put all drug dealers on notice to leave Ireland
now before it is too late. DAADD will not tolerate your
activities and will find you anywhere! Our day will come.

I put the paper down. It's what Strong wanted. He'd be happy,
and a happy Chief Superintendent was a tide that would raise
all the boats. But it didn't get us off the hook, we'd still have to
find out who killed him. I said as much to Crabbie. He nodded
but we both knew the pressure would be somewhat alleviated.
The police, the newspapers and the general public all knew that
DAADD was an IRA front organisation. No one was going to
come forward to testify against anyone from the IRA and no
doubt, as the Chief Super predicted, there would be another
IRA murder along in a few days to absorb the public's attention.

I handed the article to Lawson. "Thoughts?"

"Uhm. I've looked into the statistics and if this is true, it's the
fifth alleged drug dealer the DAADD have murdered in the last
twelve months; but this one is a bit unusual in its geographical
location and murder weapon. They've never killed anyone with
a crossbow before and only once before have they come into
Protestant territory to kill an alleged drug dealer."

"But they have come into Protestant territory before?" Crabbie asked.

"Yes. They went up Sandy Row in December to kill a cocaine dealer. Alleged cocaine dealer I should say. No formal claim of responsibility because it was enemy turf."

"So if we know the group and why they did it, the only thing we have to explain is the murder weapon," Crabbie said.

"They've used it twice now. Once successfully. Once unsuccessfully. It seems a very odd choice for an organisation that is awash with firearms," I said.

"It could be a new tactic to set DAADD apart from the IRA proper, or it could just be the idiosyncrasies of one particular DAADD volunteer, I'll look into it," Lawson said.

"Good. But, Lawson, don't use the word 'volunteer' – that's their language. It's an innocuous word which they have appropriated."

"What should I say?"

"Anything else, but not that. It makes you think of the International Brigade going off to fight Franco, not some gangland hood driving about in a car shooting people out the window with his shiny new crossbow."

"Who's Franco?"

"Jesus wept. For a smart kid there are serious deficiencies in your knowledge, son."

"Sorry, sir."

"Don't apologise. Read some George Orwell. *Homage to Catalonia* would be a good start. Now, what about the Deauvilles' theoretical/hypothetical lock-up garage?" I asked.

"Nothing from the people watching the residence."

"Mrs D. didn't leave her house?"

"Not yet," Crabbie said.

"Disappointing. OK, Lawson, do me a favour and call up the shops selling crossbows and tell them we're on our way over."

"Yes, sir."

When Lawson had gone, Crabbie walked me over to his desk and handed me a couple of newspapers.

"What's this?"

"It's about our case," he said.

I shook my head. "They take us to task, do they? I don't want to read it."

"No! It's good news. Neither the *Irish News* nor the *Newsletter* have followed up on the *Belfast Telegraph* story, so we may have dodged a bullet," Crabbie said, handing me both morning papers which had only covered the story in capsule form:

CARRICKFERGUS MURDER

Francis Deauville, 43, a suspected drug dealer, was shot in the Sunnylands area of Carrickfergus on Thursday morning. Police are investigating.

MURDER IN SUNNYLANDS

A murder in Sunnylands estate, Carrickfergus, in the early hours of Thursday morning is being investigated by the RUC. The victim, Francis Deauville, originally from Bangor, was rumoured to have associations with drug dealers in the area.

Neither tabloid had run with the idea of Carrick CID's incompetence, nor had they reprinted the photo of the unattended body lying in the driveway.

"This is fantastic!" I said.

"I don't know what happened, Sean. You'd think after the *Tele* story yesterday the tabloids would have been all over us," McCrabban said.

"I know what happened. Chief Superintendent Strong, or should I say acting Assistant Chief Constable Strong, said he was going to sort this out for me," I exclaimed. "And it looks like he has. He's used his influence and killed the bloody lede."

"We owe him," Crabbie said.

"We owe him big time, mate. Does he smoke cigars?"

"Dunno."

"I'll get him a bottle of whisky. Good stuff." I looked at Crabbie for a moment and shook my head. "Not that it'll make any difference in the long run if you're quitting and I'm quitting, although I have to say that the prospect of getting a job with Beth's father seems to have vanished."

Crabbie nodded and kept his mouth firmly shut. He didn't want to ask if there was more trouble on the home front and I didn't feel like going into it just now.

"We still have to try and find the murderer. Let me get a cup of coffee and we'll get to work."

I went to the coffee machine and pressed the chocolate and coffee buttons at the same time. What came out was a surprisingly drinkable concoction that for many years I thought I'd invented until I heard tell of a "mocha".

I read through the complete witness-canvassing statements from Mountbatten Terrace, but no one had heard or seen anything. I read Mrs Deauville's full statement, but it was no help either.

I read the forensic report and called up Frank Payne to ask how exactly you could tell if all the crossbow bolts were fired from the same crossbow. He spun me some shite about score marks on the aluminium paint that I decided to believe.

Lawson's inquiries got nowhere and we took a tea break to read the paper.

"Is it better to reign in hell or serve in heaven?" Lawson asked, looking up from the *Daily Telegraph*.

"Reign in hell," I said.

"Reign in hell," he agreed.

"Serve in heaven," McCrabban dissented grimly and not completely convincingly.

At 10 o'clock Lawson and I drove to Belfast to check out the two archery shops in Northern Ireland that sold crossbows. We showed them Mr and Mrs Deauville's photographs, but no one remembered either of them buying a crossbow. We asked them questions and the more facts we got the more we were disheartened by what we heard. Combined, the two shops had sold well over two thousand crossbows in the last three years to target shooters, hobbyists and even hunters. Since crossbows were entirely legal neither shop kept a list of who had purchased them. Reselling crossbows was also legal and unregulated. The particular bolts that had killed Francis Deauville were nothing special and could be fired from any of their weapons. Again, they did not keep records of who bought these bolts.

"How close would you have to get to kill someone with a crossbow?" I asked Jake of Jake's Archery Stores on Anne Street.

"The average hunting range is fifty, maybe sixty yards. You can obviously go beyond that – even an eighty-yard shot would still be powerful enough to kill medium and even big game. The real question here is whether you can land the shot with perfect precision and penetrate the vital organ(s); most people can't do so with consistency. Which is why most crossbow hunters will prefer to take a shot from a maximum of thirty-five yards away . . ."

Thirty-five yards was much further than I'd been expecting. Deauville and Morrison could have been shot from the far side of the street.

"How long does it take to get good at firing a crossbow?"

"Most people can get reasonable accuracy with a few days' practice. Even out of the box you can be pretty accurate first time out. There's no technique. You just look down the iron sights and shoot."

"And if you had some experience with the weapon?"

"You'd be deadly. And, of course, the advantage of a crossbow over a gun is its silence. Doesn't make any appreciable noise at all. As you probably know, Inspector, even a suppressed pistol will make some noise," Jake said.

"And suppressors can affect accuracy," Lawson said.

"So a crossbow is accurate at considerable range, a barbed bolt will penetrate all manner of clothing and leather, it's completely legal and it's silent," I said. "I'm surprised more paramilitaries don't use them."

"That surprises me, too, to be honest. A hundred quid will get you a decent starter package," Jake said.

We drove back to Carrickfergus RUC and told Crabbie this unhelpful news. While I'd been out Strong had called the switchboard looking for me, so I went into my office to call him back.

He wasn't in his office and I didn't feel comfortable calling him at home so I left him a message saying that I'd been in and out of the office all day.

We spent the rest of the morning doing old-fashioned police work, combing through arrest records for crossbow offences, looking up similar crimes in the UK, Ireland and further afield and going through the evidence we'd taken from the Deauville residence.

Helpful and/or stupid criminals often kept their receipts and this was how we found the lock-up garage.

A receipt dating back to the previous December for a shed on an allotment out in Eden.

I called Harry Mulvenny from the canine unit and we went out there in the Land Rover. While Crabbie and Lawson went up front I sat in the back with Harry and his two bitches Cora and Louise. I closed the partition to the front, so we could have some privacy.

"No pun intended, Harry, but I have a bone to pick with you," I said.

"What have I done?" he said in his just-off-the-boat Scouse accent.

"You were at Deauville's house?"

"Yeah, we didn't find anything."

"You were there when Dalziel sent McCrabban to the hospital

and when forensics fucked off?"

"Yeah, so?"

"Dalziel left and when you left that meant Lawson was there by himself."

"And how is this my fault? I'm a canine officer."

"You're a sergeant in the RUC. You should have taken command. Acted on your initiative. Lawson is a detective constable with barely two years under his belt. You should have stepped up, assumed command, got forensics in, secured the crime scene until Crabbie got back."

Harry knew I was right. "Are you going to report me to McArthur?"

"No. I'm the fall guy on this debacle and there's no point getting anyone else in the shit . . . But next time remember you've got those stripes on your shoulders for a reason."

We got out of the Land Rover at a squalid little bit of waste ground near Kilroot Power Station. If this was an allotment there wasn't much evidence of anything growing.

We found Deauville's shed and the dogs were going crazy before we even opened the door.

Lawson broke the padlock with a pair of bolt cutters and inside Harry discovered a dozen bags of refined heroin. Pounds of the stuff. Not ounces, pounds.

I went back to the Land Rover and got put through to Chief Inspector McArthur.

"Sir, if you want to make someone in the drug squad happy and owe you a big future favour you should get them out here. We found a couple of pounds of heroin. It's a major score so it'll be a drugs squad case, not Carrick CID."

"I'll call Chief Inspector O'Driscoll."

"He'd be perfect, sir. And I think you should come out yourself, sir. Some good PR for the station."

"I think I will do that. Very good PR for the station after yesterday's black eye."

The rain came on, so I left Lawson at the shed and waited in the Rover until the drugs squad and McArthur arrived. Seamus O'Driscoll was another rare Catholic detective in the RUC and he'd brought with him seemingly half the narcs in the force. Twenty men and women in white evidence-gathering boiler suits.

"If it isn't Sean Duffy as I live and breathe," O'Driscoll said, offering me his hand. He was a tall, unhinged looking fellow with red hair and bad teeth, but he wasn't a bad sort. We went back aways and I could possibly have liked him if he hadn't been two years and nine months younger than me and already far ahead of me on the chain of command. We had come up together, though, so there was no question of me calling him "sir", or of him demanding it.

"O'Driscoll drove with a song, the wild duck and the drake," I said but the illiterate eejit just give me a funny look, so I dropped the Yeats.

"This is quite a big score you've given me here, Sean, I'll owe you," he said.

"You don't owe me anything. My gaffer thought you'd be the best man for the job and I agreed."

O'Driscoll grinned from ear to ear. Not a pretty sight, so I decided to put an end to it. "You could give me one big hand though. I've had a couple of men watching Mrs Deauville's house in the hope that she would lead us to her husband's lock-up. But now that we've found it by other means I'm going to take the men away. I've been paying their over-time out of the CID budget. If you want to keep up the surveillance can you pay for it out of your budget?"

"No need for surveillance. I'll just arrest her."

"Oh, OK, fair enough. Well do me a favour, Seamus, go easy on her. We don't think she killed her husband and she's pretty torn up about it."

"I'll be gentle."

"At least bring in a WPC. We did and we're not exactly cutting-edge."

"Isn't the purpose to get her to talk?"

"No, the purpose is 'to protect and serve,'" I said, giving him the motto of the LAPD.

"Oh yeah, sure, of course it is."

"I'll get Lawson to give you over the files and you can photocopy them. Standard division of duty: you handle the narco aspects, we'll do the homicide, OK?"

"Sounds good. I heard this wife of his was a foreigner?"

"Bulgarian, but don't believe any nonsense she tells you about not speaking English. She's fluent."

Chief Inspector McArthur had arrived with a reporter from the *Carrickfergus Advertiser*. I shook his hand and took my leave. Didn't need any more press attention today.

Back to the barracks on Shanks's mare.

Of course it began to rain and then hail and I was out only in my T-shirt and thin leather jacket.

Soaked when I got back to the office.

Sandra brought me tea and biscuits while I huddled in front of the single bar of the heater.

The phone rang just as I was thinking of calling Beth again.

"Hello?"

"Ah, Duffy, been trying to reach you all day."

It was Chief Superintendent Strong. A friendly voice in a cruel world.

"Sir, I've been meaning to talk to you, too. I want to thank you for whatever you did to keep yesterday's story out of the morning papers today."

He cleared his throat. "I'll admit that I did make a few phone calls into the shell-like ears of a few people who have had occasion to rely on the police for scoops and tips in the past."

"Well, I'm most grateful, sir."

"Forget it, Duffy. Tell me about the developments in the case," he said eagerly. I was a little surprised that one of the Greats of Mount Olympus would be interested in muckety-muck police work, but he had stuck his neck out for me, so no wonder he was keen.

"Well we interviewed the wife and released her."

"Released her?"

"It was our feeling that she was not a suspect or a material witness."

"What did she tell you?"

"Nothing, really. She doesn't know who killed him or why."

"She saw nothing?"

"Apparently not."

"And you definitely don't like her for it?"

" . . . uhm, like I say, I'm not completely sure, sir. But my instincts and the evidence tend to suggest that she is not to blame."

Not to blame for the murder, anyway. She'd almost certainly been smuggling in Turkish heroin – somehow – but that wasn't my concern and if CI O'Driscoll couldn't pin that on her it was no skin off my nose.

"I'd like to see the transcripts of your interview."

"I'll have Lawson fax them to you, sir."

"What else?"

"At the time of the arrest we didn't find Mr Deauville's heroin laboratory on site so it was reasonable to assume that it was at an off-site location and that she might lead us there in an attempt to destroy evidence."

"And did she?"

"No. But we found the lab by other means. An old receipt he'd kept."

"Good work! Were there drugs in it?"

"Oh yes, sir. A lot of drugs. A couple of pounds of heroin. More than we could handle, sir, so we called in the drug squad."

"Brilliant, Duffy. Who was the drug-squad liaison?"

"CI O'Driscoll, sir."

"How do I know that name?"

"Maybe from the poem, sir?"

"What poem?"

"The Yeats poem, sir. O'Driscoll drove with a song the wild duck and the drake—"

"Jesus man, I didn't tell you to start reciting it."

"Sorry, sir."

"What else, Duffy? What's this I hear about a DAADD connection?"

"Uhm, you've heard about that, sir, have you? Well, it's slightly unusual, DAADD have not claimed responsibility for the killing with a recognised codeword, but there was a story in *Republican News* strongly suggesting that they did it."

"The bastards. So it really wasn't the wife at all?"

"It's looking unlikely."

"Tell me, Duffy, do we ever catch any of those DAADD murderers?"

"If they're IRA men and there are no witnesses or forensic evidence I'd say it's going to be very tricky, sir."

"So not totally unprecedented if they get away with it, eh? If the Chief Constable starts breathing down our necks asking—"

"The Chief Constable?" I asked with alarm.

"Relax, man, I'm your shield, remember?"

"Yes, sir, thank you, sir."

"So what's going to happen next in the case?"

"CI O'Driscoll is going to arrest Mrs Deauville for the drugs smuggling."

"Maybe I'll watch it through the glass."

"The interview, sir?"

"Yeah, why not. I've taken an interest in this case and I'd like to see it through to the end now."

"That's fine by me, sir. And I'm sure Chief Inspector O'Driscoll won't mind. I believe he's based at Antrim RUC."

"Very good, Duffy, you've done well today, better than yesterday. Have a good night."

He hung up and I called O'Driscoll to warn him that acting ACC Strong might swing by to watch him work his interview magic, which alarmed him nicely. I went home, fed the cat, called Beth and got the engaged tone. I called again and I got Beth's mum, who said that Beth was out with "some old friends" and that Emma was sleeping.

I made a pint glass vodka gimlet, easy on the ice, lime and soda, heavy on the vodka.

I called up Belfast International Airport and checked to see if there were any direct charters to Bulgaria. Of course there were. Two a week from Belfast to Varna on the "Black Sea Riviera". That's how she smuggled the drugs. You bribe the officials at the Varna end and confidently walk through customs and immigration at the Belfast end. There was a chance of a random pat-down, but I knew that the immigration officers at Belfast's ports and airports were on the alert for known terrorists and the sniffer dogs at the airport were the ones who'd been trained to look for explosives not drugs. Northern Ireland's drug problem wasn't of sufficient concern yet to have narco canine teams and officers at the airports. Eventually it would be, but not yet.

I thought about telling O'Driscoll this information, but decided against it. It was his case to make and no concern of mine. I was doing the murder, he was doing the drugs. And I felt sorry for Elena Deauville.

I looked out "Fantasia on a Theme by Thomas Tallis", stoked the peat fire in the living-room grate and lay down on the floor to listen to it.

The cat crawled onto my stomach.

By the second vodka gimlet and the second iteration of the concerto much of the bad shit was going away.

Of course the real bad shit was still to come but I didn't know that then.

At midnight the phone rang.

Beth?

"Hello?"

"Sean, it's Seamus O'Driscoll, just wanted to let you know that we've arrested Mrs Deauville and taken her to Antrim RUC."

"It's midnight, Seamus."

"I thought you would want to know."

"Fine. Thanks. But there's no need to call me with further updates. You can call DS McCrabban at the station. I think he's duty detective."

"I will. Listen, Sean, Chief Super— I mean Acting Assistant Chief Constable Strong's here right enough, how do I handle him?"

"Jesus, mate, it's not Cardinal Ó Fiaich. He's just another dozy peeler."

"I'll tell him you said that."

"Goodnight, Seamus."

"Night, Sean."

The cat was looking at me expectantly and since no one else wanted to hear it I gave him the last two stanzas of "The Host of the Air":

"O'Driscoll scattered the cards/And out of his dream awoke:

Old men and young men and young girls/Were gone like a drifting smoke/But he heard high up in the air/A piper piping away,

And never was piping so sad/And never was piping so gay."

The cat yawned, not very impressed by this at all. "I learned that when I was eleven. Give me some credit," I said. "I suppose it's too old-fashioned for you, is it?"

But the wise little creature was already asleep.

10: DEATH ON THE ROCK

Sunday morning. No girlfriend, no baby girl, cold house, rain so hard it was bouncing eight inches off the pavement. Coronation Road was wet and empty and I felt isolated and alone.

With the family around and the sun shining and the kids out playing, this street seemed to lie at the centre of the earth, as Jerusalem does on medieval maps. The living room of #113 Coronation Road was the centre of the centre and the record player spinning Peetie Wheatstraw's "Police Station Blues" was the axis around which the whole universe curved.

But not today. Today #113 Coronation Road was just a cold little ex-council house with ashes in the grate and a hungry cat whining in the kitchen.

I called Beth but Hector answered the phone and claimed she was down at Larne Marina working on their boat the *Grania*.

"At this hour? In this weather?"

"Yes. You know Beth, she loves sailing."

First I knew about that, I nearly said. "Yeah, I know. She's not out on the water though, is she? It's supposed to storm later."

"Of course not."

"OK, I'll try her later. Tell her to call me and tell her I miss Emma."

I lit the fire in the living room, found a record, put it on, and thanked God for Ella Fitzgerald and a case to occupy my brain and keep away the blues.

The IRA proxy group DAADD were sort of claiming the Deauville murder and we could yellow this file soon enough but there were a few things about the case I did not like.

I took a hit on my asthma inhaler and had a cup of coffee and settled in front of the fire to think.

Think until ten anyway when I would try Beth again.

Item #1: would the IRA or its DAADD proxy really have driven deep into a Loyalist area like Sunnylands Estate to kill some random drug dealer?

Item #2: would they really have used a weapon as exotic as a crossbow when they were plenty of guns available in Ulster?

Item #3: what did Elena Deauville know about the murder that she wasn't saying?

I considered the problems one at a time:

Item #1: on the surface it didn't make a whole lot of sense for the IRA to come to a housing estate in Carrickfergus. The IRA's preference was always for soft targets. Would they really drive deep into a twisty Loyalist housing estate to kill a random pusher? The only reason they would do such a thing would be for the PR value: to prove that they could go where they pleased. Bam! We drive into Protestant Larne to shoot a drug dealer. Bam! We drive into Protestant Carrickfergus the very next night. Look at us, we can be anywhere! Yes, that worked as a reason, but then why not claim it with a recognised codeword and shout it from the rooftops? You don't want to antagonise the Loyalists and jeopardise a truce, fair enough, but then why kill Deauville and shoot Morrison in the first place? So maybe you shoot Morrison to establish a pattern, then you shoot Deauville, then you tell *Republican News* that this was the DAADD and they believe it. Everyone's happy: the press is happy, the RUC detectives are happy, parents concerned about evil doers selling drugs to their kids are happy . . . And of course the real killer is happy because he or she has gotten away with it . . .

Item #2: the crossbow is weird. Sure, the shop man could talk about its effective range and its silence, but still, why wouldn't the killer use a gun? The IRA had plenty of guns. Was it really because of the noise?

Item #3: Elena Deauville. The more I thought about it, the more I didn't like her testimony. That little look she gave. That hesitation. She was hiding something. Something important. Something beyond the fact that she was a brilliant heroin mule.

I called the station and asked for the duty detective.

"CID," Crabbie said.

"Fill me in," I said.

"On what?"

"Didn't they re-arrest Elena Deauville last night?"

"Yeah, your mate Seamus lifted her. You want the details?"

"If it's not too much trouble."

"You seem to be in a mood."

"I'm not . . . And Seamus isn't my mate. He's just a Catholic. Not all us Catholic peelers are buddy buddies, you know?"

"I thought you came up together," Crabbie protested.

"What if we did? What's the story with Mrs D., Crabbie?"

"They arrested her, took her to Antrim RUC and interviewed her. Do you want to come in and read the transcript? CI O'Driscoll faxed it over."

"No, you can summarise it for me."

"They asked her about the lock-up. She denied all knowledge of its contents. She denied all knowledge of her husband's drug dealing and she said she had nothing to do with any smuggling."

"Did Seamus believe her?"

"No. He asked how her husband could be a heroin dealer and she not know about it. He said it wasn't credible."

"And what did she say to that?"

"She said that if she knew her husband was a heroin dealer why hadn't she gotten rid of the evidence as soon as she found him dead?"

"What did Seamus say to that?"

"Seamus said that if she'd gone all the way to the lock-up in Eden and left her husband's body in her driveway after she discovered it, it would have been very suspicious and after she'd been released from custody she couldn't do it because she must have seen the policemen watching her house."

"That makes sense to me. What do you reckon?"

"She was completely hysterical after the body was found. She was in no fit state to think rationally about concealing evidence. And after she was released, as CI O'Driscoll says, she must have seen the men watching the house. They were ordinary PC's so that wouldn't surprise me."

"Anything else interesting from the interview?"

"She gave him nothing, Sean. Less than she gave us, even. Deny, deny, deny. Of course she had a Legal Aid solicitor with her this time."

"Did she ask for a lawyer?"

"Apparently she did."

"So they had to give her one."

"Aye."

"So O'Driscoll's keeping her up at Antrim for further questioning, is he?"

"No. He thinks he has enough evidence already for a prima facie case. She's already been formally charged at Antrim Magistrates Court."

"That *is* fast work. They set bail?"

"5,000 pounds."

"Steep for a guilt-by-association case."

"O'Driscoll told the court that she was a flight risk so they confiscated her passport and set a big bail. Her Legal Aid solicitor was furious, saying she was a poor widow living in a council house on benefits, but apparently the magistrate was unmoved."

"I take it no one has paid the bail."

"No."

"Unless they find her prints on the stuff I think it's going to be a tougher case to make than O'Driscoll thinks. No chain of causation, no real proof that she knew anything about the drugs. A jury might let her off. If it were me I'd offer her a deal. But then again, that's not our problem, is it?"

"No."

"Any developments on our side of the case?"

"Nothing. That story in the *Republican News* is as good as a DAADD claim of responsibility, as far as the media is concerned. Didn't make any of the Sunday papers. I don't think we'll even have to have a press conference."

"Thank God for that."

"What *will* we do next?"

"We'll appeal for witnesses. Maybe have poor Mrs Deauville go through a third police interview."

"You think she was lying to us?"

"Of course she was lying to us, she's a bloody drugs smuggler, but there was one question in particular that's been bothering me. Do you remember I asked her if she'd seen anyone following them and she sort of hesitated before she answered?"

"Aye, and she sort of stared at that Bulgarian bloke and then at us before saying no."

"Did she?"

"Yeah."

"What do you think that was about?"

"Just nerves, I thought."

"Could be," I said reflectively.

I looked at my watch. "Don't you have church soon?"

"I do indeed."

"I'll come in and take over for you."

"It's Lawson's rota."

"I'm at a loose end. Beth. You know?"

"How is everything with uh, uh . . ." Crabbie began, immediately regretting the sally. But I wasn't going to let him off the hook that easily, the poor bastard.

"So glad you asked, mate. She's staying with her parents. We had a wee row and I thought it was no big deal but apparently I freaked her out. And her da swings by yesterday and says she's switching to business administration, whatever the hell that is. And now she's away working on the family yacht like the Proddy gentry. You never had a boat as a child, did you?"

"No I—"

"Course you didn't. Son of the soil like you. Who has a boat? Nobody. I don't know what's going on, mate. Maybe this whole row about the house was a mere pretext. A *casus belli* you know?"

"Sean, I'm sympathetic, but I have to get back to—"

"Casus belli and now we're talking Latin maxims, here's one even you'll remember from your Ballymena Academy days: *contra principia negantem non est disputandum.* How can I argue with her when she's denying there's even an argument and she keeps changing the rules?"

"Sean, I have to go."

"Go then. We'll talk some more when I come in in a bit."

I dressed in a sports jacket, white shirt, red tie, black jeans, DMs. Clocked myself in the mirror, killed the fucking tie.

Under the BMW for bombs. No bombs, just the diffraction iridescence of a drop of oil floating in a puddle of rainwater.

Into the Beemer. Second gear. Third. A hard turn at Victoria Road and another onto the A2. Up to 60 mph going past the Fisherman's Quay. Going so fast the turn into Carrick police station was impossible.

As I say the Beemer, like a greyhound, needs its morning workout.

Into the harbour car park in a squeal of breaks.

Out of the car for the first cigarette of the day.

Dog walkers. Church goers. Some of them know me. Nod a hello and stand on the pier looking down into the black water of Carrick harbour. Behind me was the big Norman Castle and in that castle the well of Fergus Mor Mac Erc, King of Dalriada, the King who brought the stone of Scone from Ireland to Scotland and that sits under the Coronation Throne to this very day. The King who started all this Thucydidian bollocks if you want to go back that far. I didn't. I didn't give a shit about any of it any more. "Fuck it," I said and stamped out the ciggie and got back in the Beemer.

A kid letting his collie piss against the back wheel.

"Oi! You! That's my car."

"Sorry, mister, but when she has to go she has to go."

"What's her name?"

"I have no idea, but we call her Susie."

Everybody's such a smart ass these days. "Tell Susie to piss somewhere else."

Grumbling, I drove back to the station. When I got there Crabbie had legged it in case I laid any more of my personal stuff on him. Said morning to Lawson and went up to my office and read through the transcript of Mrs Deauville's second police interview. Crabbie was quite correct, she'd given O'Driscoll even less than she'd given us.

I wanted to know more about DAADD's murderous ways so I called Marcus Finn in Special Branch intel and although he wasn't in on a Sunday a young DC called Kenny Clarke said he was starving and would fill me in if I got him lunch.

"Lunch where?" I asked suspiciously.

"I'm not picky."

"I'm not even in Belfast. I'm in Carrick."

"Well then, I'm sorry. I'm not authorised to give out this kind of information over the tele—"

"Meet me at the Europa Grill in twenty minutes."

"What do you look like?"

"A depressed policeman."

"Aren't all policem—"

Click. Twenty minutes of hardcore Beemer driving later.

"Ah, Inspector Duffy, I believe," an amiable-looking eejit of a man in a red jumper said.

We sat in the window overlooking Great Victoria Street. He ordered the most expensive steak they had and I got one too. I'd put it on CID expenses.

"So tell me about DAADD," I said.

"He was a kindly man, but he just couldn't cope with family life so he left when I was eight to seek his fortune in Australia."

"You're hilarious."

"Wow, tough room. You don't have much of a sense of humour, eh?"

"No. DAADD?"

"Well, they're your standard IRA front organisation. Not much to them really. They've been growing in the last few years, of course, because intel-wise we've been on the back foot in so many areas."

"Back foot how?"

"Remember that chopper crash on the Mull of Kintyre?"

"I remember reading something about it."

"Very clever idea. Get all your top MI5 and Special Branch agents with expertise in the IRA and put them all in one heli-copter and then fly that helicopter into a mountain in Scotland. Great thinking. Anyway we've been struggling since then and that coupled with all the new money and weapons flooding in . . ."

"What new money?" I asked as the steaks came. Both of them overcooked.

"Tons of new money. Money from Americans and Libyans and Russians . . . And then, of course, there are the general intelligence failures. So many IRA spectaculars in the last five years: the Maze Escape, the Brighton Bombing, Enniskillen."

"What does it all amount to?" I asked.

"What indeed? What indeed? A lot of our informers have turned up dead. Even some of our agent handlers."

"Smart guy like you must have some theories."

"Oh, there are lots of different theories."

"Like what?"

"Incompetence."

"That one makes sense. What else?"

He lowered his voice. "There's the theory that the IRA have a mole in the higher ups in the RUC or MI5."

I laughed. "Next?"

"There's the theory that Thatcher is deliberately letting the situation spiral out of control so she can wash her hands of Ulster, unilaterally withdraw and let the UN or the Americans take charge."

"I hadn't heard that one. She wouldn't do that."

"Wouldn't she? Only Nixon could go to China, remember. And it would be immensely popular in England. A few Tory right wingers would be furious for a while but they love her."

This was getting pointless. Bored intel guys and their speculations. I was an actual detective who had actual work to do.

"Tell me about DAADD."

He told me everything he knew. DAADD had attacked forty-two alleged drug dealers in the four years since they'd been calling themselves DAADD (before that they simply called themselves the IRA). Twenty-five of these alleged drug dealers had been successfully killed with a variety of weapons: pistols, rifles, shotguns, carbines. They'd never used crossbows before, but as an ad hoc group loosely under IRA command a crossbow attack wasn't out of the question.

"Really? I thought it was a completely bizarre choice of murder weapon considering the number of guns available in Ulster," I said.

"Guns yes. We estimate that the Libyans alone have given the IRA about eight hundred AK-47's and—"

"Eight hundred?" I said, aghast.

"Oh, maybe I shouldn't have said that. You won't repeat that, will you, Inspector Duffy? Wouldn't want to generate alarm."

"No. We wouldn't want that, would we?" I said, imagining the prospect of eight hundred armed IRA men descending en masse on Carrick police station – it would be a massacre. Thank you Colonel Gaddafi.

"But a machine gun makes a bit of a racket doesn't it? Even a hand-gun makes noise. No, a crossbow could be quite an effective little weapon for a group like DAADD. Differentiate them from their mother organisation. Especially when non-lethal force is required or you're doing a punishment attack. I was fascinated by the attack on Mr Morrison and since the second on Mr Deauville I've been eagerly awaiting a third. If there is one we can consider that a pattern and I'll write a paper on it. I'll send it to you if you want."

"Thanks. Well, look, I'm sorry but I must dash," I said, pointing at my wrist watch.

"You haven't got pudding."

"You get one," I said, getting up and leaving two twenty pound notes on the table.

"Where are you going?"

"Work. You've been very helpful, thanks, mate," I replied, found the BMW in the Europa Car Park, checked underneath it for bombs and drove back to Carrick RUC.

I spun Lawson my worries about the case and Constable Clarke's attempts to bat away at least one of them regarding the murder weapon.

We had nothing else on so we worked the evidence until two o'clock, processing tips from the Confidential Telephone and reading and rereading Mrs Deauville's statement. For want of anything better to do, I drove us to Mountbatten Terrace where we canvassed the neighbours again, but nobody had seen or heard anything and if they had "they wouldn't be telling the bloody peelers".

We went for an afternoon tea break at the Old Tech on West

Street and sat by the fire. The tea was warm and the shortbread was home-made. While we were in the restaurant the rain stopped, the wind changed and the snow began.

Carrickfergus lies far to the north on the 55th parallel, which also crosses the Alaskan peninsula and the city of Novosibirsk. I went to a lecture once where Jo McBain said that a hundred centuries ago Carrick and all of the north of Ireland lay under a mile of ice. But now the snow came only for a few days a year in February and March and the sea never froze. It was a miracle really, but as Dr McBain said, surely the ice *would* come again and all these pubs and houses and power stations and people would be wiped clean from the land.

No need for peelers then. No need for anything.

"Sir? . . . Sir?"

Lawson staring at me.

"What?"

"You were lost in thought."

"Aye, I was."

"Were you thinking about the case?"

"I was thinking about ice."

"I was just saying we should get back to the station."

"Yeah."

We went back to the station, where much to my surprise Crabbie was there to meet us.

"What are you doing here?"

"Wife has the kids down to visit her sister in Fermanagh."

"The house felt a bit lonely?"

"You said that, not me."

"You are allowed to admit to human emotion, you're Presbyterian, not Vulcan."

"Well . . . " Lawson said.

Crabbie and I both grinned. "Times have changed, eh, Crabbie? When you or I were at his tender age we wouldn't have dared raise an eyebrow to our elders and betters, would we? Next he'll be saying that the music of 1988 is better than the music of 1978 or 1968."

Crabbie shrugged, having no interest in the topic. As the saying goes, he liked both kinds of music: country and western. The day the music died for him was March 5th 1963 when Patsy Cline's plane had gone down.

"Here's a thought, gents. I know the weather's not good but don't you think it's about time we went down to the Glasgow Rangers Supporters Club and asked a few questions? Last place Mr Deauville was seen alive. Probably should have gone there yesterday," I said.

"It was a Saturday yesterday, they all would have been at the Rangers game in Scotland," Crabbie said.

"Do they go to every game then?"

"Oh yes. Over on the ferry to Glasgow every Saturday," Crabbie said.

"I suppose you're a Celtic supporter, sir?" Lawson asked. An innocent enough question everywhere else in the world except for Belfast and Glasgow, where the wrong response could get you a punch in the face.

"I don't give a shit about Scottish football, Lawson. As far as I'm concerned there's only one football team in the world."

Crabbie nodded in agreement. "Liverpool FC?" Lawson groaned.

I ruffled Lawson's blond locks. "The kid has learned something under our tutelage. All right lads, let's go, wrap up warm," I said.

I didn't trust the Beemer without snow tyres so we decided to hoof it. Exercise would do us good. Dr Havercamp would be proud of me. I'd been following his regimen fairly strictly. Asthma inhaler every morning. Cut down my smoking. Cut down my drinking. No pot. Stress was through the roof, though and that couldn't be good: Beth taking Emma to her parents and the *Belfast Telegraph* trying to crucify me . . .

We walked out in the snow to the Glasgow Rangers Supporters Club which was located near the bird sanctuary between the railway lines and Carrick Leisure Centre. Lawson was wearing a parka, Crabbie and me were both in duffle coats.

Until a few years earlier this had been marshy wasteground but the local council had formed an artificial lake and now it was a mini birders' paradise with quite the collection of ducks, kittiwakes, common gulls, crows, magpies, guillemots, fulmars, razorbills.

Not everyone was as enthused by our avian friends as I was.

"They make a bit of a racket, don't they?" Crabbie said.

"A racket to the uninitiated, but to me—" I began and as I explained how to differentiate the different bird calls I saw Lawson put on his Walkman headphones and tune me out – the cheeky wee skitter.

It was pretty back here behind the leisure centre. I should take Emma here in her stroller, she'd like that, I thought. Emma. Didn't Beth know what she was putting me through, taking her away from me?

If we separated now would I even get visitation rights? Family law, even in benighted medieval Northern Ireland, gave scant regard to the rights of the dad . . .

My conversation dried up and Crabbie wasn't exactly a chatterbox.

We walked around the lake.

It was a Japanese woodblock print.

Us. The snow. The water.

Lawson's Walkman, the sound of birds, and the soft airy snow falling onto the supine lake surface like a Basho poem.

We reached the Glasgow Rangers Club tucked behind the trees. This place was not from a woodblock print: a utilitarian breeze-block building bedecked with union jacks, Scottish saltires and painted representations of – presumably – famous Glasgow football players of the past. There were grilles on the windows to prevent petrol-bomb attacks and a heavy metal door.

I pounded on the door while Crabbie attempted to light his pipe and Lawson took his Walkman off.

"What were you listening to, Lawson?" I asked him.

"The usual."

"Zeppelin, Floyd, Sabbath?"

Lawson gave a little half-smile to convey the fact that I'd committed yet another generational crime.

"Not exactly," he said.

"Who then?"

"I just bought the Morrissey solo album, *Viva Hate*, not even out until next week, but I got an early release from KragTrax," Lawson said.

"Morrissey? The Manky lad who pulled out of Wogan at the last minute?" McCrabban said, astounded.

"I think that's Boy George," I said.

"No that's the one," Lawson clarified.

"Is the record any good?"

"It's not as good as the Smiths, but it's pretty good."

"Going back to our earlier conversation, don't you think the 80s has sort of reached a musical nadir after the heady days of the 70s?"

The young detective constable shook his boyish head. "Totally disagree," he said. "Popular music today is more interesting on nearly every front than the stuff that was being pumped out in the 70s. All that big boring corporate rock and—"

I pounded on the door again. "Open up in there!"

"Who is it?" a voice from within inquired.

"Inspector Duffy, Carrick RUC," I said.

"The poliss?" the voice from within asked.

"Just bloody open up!"

The door swung open and we went inside the Rangers Club. It was cold, stark, dimly lit and there was a sawdusty vinegary smell. The club was utilitarian on the inside, too, with a long crude bar that served only Harp and Bass on tap. The chairs were stacked on the tables, giving the place an even more desolate appearance. The voice from within belonged to a skinny but tough-looking thirty-year-old bloke with beady brown eyes and a misshapen shaved head which made him resemble one of the Talosians from the original series of *Star Trek*. He was wearing a Rangers away shirt and dungarees, which was an odd and unattractive combination.

"What can I do you for?"

I told him why we were here. He said his name was Teddy Pendergrass and he was the barman/janitor/bouncer for the establishment.

"Were you working here Wednesday night into Thursday morning?"

"I was."

"And do you remember serving Mr Deauville?" I asked, showing him Deauville's photograph.

"No . . . I don't think I've seen him, uhm, in here before," he said looking anywhere but at the three of us.

"You're a terrible liar, Teddy. Don't ever go into the confidence game. Now, Deauville was here on Thursday night and you remember him, don't you?"

"No, not really."

"Christ, Teddy, do you want us to lift you? Is that what you want? Now, do you remember him or not?"

"Aye, maybe."

"Was he a regular?"

"Aye, I think he was."

"Why would he come here of all the bars in Carrick to drink at?"

"Subsidised beer for club members. 50p a pint."

"He wasn't selling drugs out the back was he? Selling drugs out the back and giving you a cut of the action?"

"No! He wasn't!"

"So if I was to bring Sergeant Mulvenny and his K9 team down here they wouldn't find anything, would they?"

"What people do in the privacy of the stalls is their concern. I don't know if they're smoking dope back there or not."

"We'd have to close the place down, wouldn't we, Sergeant McCrabban?"

"Oh yes, Inspector Duffy, we'd have to. Under the Proceeds Of Crime (Northern Ireland Order) and under the Asset Forfeiture Act (Northern Ireland Order) we'd have no choice but to shut this place down and seize the assets of anyone who works here," Crabbie said, playing along.

"But here's the thing, Ted, we're not the drugs squad, we're investigating a murder. If you can help us solve our crime the drugs squad doesn't have to know about any of this and Sergeant Mulvenny's dogs don't have to come out into the cold."

Ted was desperate now. "What do you want to know?"

"Who did Francis Deauville associate with in here and who was he drinking with on Wednesday night?"

"Deauville only joined a couple of months back. He mostly drank by himself but occasionally people would go up to his table and he'd go to the bogs and sell them product. At least I assume he did. I never asked about it."

"What people?"

"All sorts of people, young, old, you name it."

"And how do you know he would sell them product if you never asked about it?"

"I never asked and I told him I didn't want to know. I didn't want to be involved and get myself kneecapped or worse."

"So how do you know he was selling drugs?"

"I'm not stupid, so I'm not. And at the end of a night he would give me a wee tip."

"How much?"

"It depended on how well he'd done, I suppose. Sometimes twenty quid, sometimes a hundred."

"Tell me about Wednesday night."

"What do you want to know?"

"His customers on Wednesday."

"He was only in for an hour or so on Wednesday before last orders."

"And who did he sell to?"

"The place was empty. You know what the weather was like."

"I don't know what the weather was like. I was in Donegal."

"Freezing so it was. And wet. I don't think he had a single customer."

"Have you ever listened to Lou Reed? The weather is no deterrent to the determined junkie looking for a fix."

"That may be the case but Frankie was drinking alone all night until his friend came in."

"What friend?"

"Some old fella. His age or older, wearing a flat cap."

"Describe him better."

"I didn't really look at him. Just an old guy, tall, wearing a flat cap over his face. They sat in the corner."

"He kept the cap on inside?"

"Aye."

"And how long did he and Deauville talk for?"

"About fifteen minutes. Frankie got him a whisky. Bells, I think."

"And then what?"

"Then the old guy left and Frankie sat there for a bit, finished his pint and he left too."

"Ever see the old guy in here before?"

"I don't think so, but it's hard to tell because his hat was down over his face."

"Do you have CCTV cameras in here?" Lawson asked.

"No."

"Did Deauville seem agitated or nervous, anything like that?"

"Nope. He seemed fine. Just like he was having a drink with an old friend . . . There was one thing, though."

"What was that?"

"Well, when I called last orders Frankie comes up to the bar and gives me fifty quid like he's just had a massive score. But he hadn't. He hadn't sold anything really."

"Did you ask him why the money?"

"No, like I say, no questions. Better not to know."

"You're going to have to come down the station with us and give our sketch artist a drawing of this guy," I said.

"He didn't look like anything. It's just a hat and a coat."

"What type of coat?"

"Just a heavy raincoat. He may have had a wee beard or that could have just been the shadow. No, there's no point getting me to draw anything."

"Regardless, you're going to have to come with us."

We took him back to the station with us and he did indeed produce a very unhelpful drawing with the sketch artist. A tall well-built man with a hat pulled low over his face. Possibly a beard or prominent sideburns. It was interesting, though. Direct Action Against Drug Dealers didn't usually meet with their victims before they shot them. Then again, maybe this was just an old friend of Deauville's right enough. Or maybe it bloody wasn't.

The snow continued to fall and at five o'clock everyone was keen to get home as driving on some of the country roads was bound to be treacherous.

I called Crabbie and Lawson into my office.

"OK lads, we'll all head home, but I think tomorrow we'll go up to Antrim RUC and ask Mrs Deauville if she's seen this mysterious stranger around, what do you lads think?"

"It's not much of a picture," Crabbie said.

"It's the best lead we've got," I countered.

"It's the only lead we've got," Lawson said.

I went into Chief Inspector McArthur's and filled him in on the details. He couldn't care less. This was a DAADD murder and those never got solved and the press wouldn't care if we didn't bring anyone in for it so therefore it wouldn't affect his career. And in a couple of months he'd be free of me forever.

I drove home carefully along the seafront and even more carefully up the unsalted Victoria Road. Irish people weren't used to driving in snow and the eejits were going far too fast, slipping and sliding every which way. Still, I got the Beemer in front of #113 in one piece.

As I was coming in the phone was ringing. I dropped everything and picked it up.

"Hello?"

"Hello Sean, I'm so glad I caught you. You were right, Emma misses you, she wants to hear your voice."

"I miss her. Put her on."

"Dadda!" Emma said.

"Emma honey."

"Story dadda! Story!"

"Story . . . Well, once upon a time there was this naughty little girl with blonde hair who was always breaking into people's houses. She was what we policemen call a recidivist so the local peeler, a very nice, generous, forgiving and intelligent police-man called Sean, told her she had to go and live in the woods for a while. She went out into the woods and she saw a cute little house there with the smell of porridge coming out the open window. Not just ordinary porridge but those steel-cut oats and honey that Daddy makes. Now this girl who we'll call—"

"Emma!"

"Goldilocks, immediately decided she would get up to her old tricks again by breaking into the house of a nice bear family . . ."

When the story was finished Emma yawned and Beth said she had to put her to bed.

"When are you coming back? You know I'm sorry, right?"

Beth lowered her voice. "To be honest, I'm getting a bit fed up here. Dad's always going on about business administration and how I'm wasting my time doing an English degree."

"Come back then! I'll come down tonight and get you both."

"In this weather?"

"It's no problem."

"No. My Auntie Anne and Uncle Robert are coming over on the ferry tonight. They haven't seen the baby. They'll be staying for a couple of days and by then I'll be thoroughly sick of it here. Can you come and get me on Tuesday morning? I've got a tutorial on Wednesday and I can get the train up to Belfast and you can watch Emma, yeah?"

"So you'll come back and stay here?"

"We'll have to have a serious talk about our future."

"Of course! I'm all about serious. You know me. And like I say, I'm willing to move whenever you want."

"And there will be no more shouting or stress?"

"Listen, Beth, that morning you went down to Larne I had my RUC medical and I've been told to cut down on the drinking and the smokes and the stress and I've been doing it. I'm a new man."

"Sure you are, Sean Duffy."

"What's with you and the boats?"

"I've always sailed. You didn't know that?"

"No."

"I've got all these hidden depths you don't even know about. Some cop you are. This is Dad's new boat. It's a restoration job. I was going to take it out today, but it was impossible with the weather."

"We'll go out in the summer. I've never been sailing before. I imagine it'll be fun," I said, lying like a trooper.

"OK, Sean, I'll call you."

"Bye, Beth."

I hung up feeling happy. Two good phone calls with Beth in a row. DAADD getting us off the hook by sort of claiming responsibility for the Deauville murder, a possible eyewitness

. . . things were looking up.

I made a hot whisky, heated up some soup for dinner, put on Ella Fitzgerald and sat in the living room with the TV on mute.

I quickly unmuted the telly. Something had happened in what looked like Gibraltar.

People had been killed. The killers had been, who? Men in balaclavas. Terrorists? No. No, the killers had been SAS soldiers and the people they'd shot were an IRA active service unit.

Damn it, I was going to have to pay attention to this. I put down the whisky and got my notebook. The BBC was being cagey with the details but RTE from Dublin were jumping right in. They said that the IRA unit had comprised two men and a woman and that they'd been planning to blow up some sort of British army post while the guard was being changed. RTE didn't know the men's names but the woman was a young girl from Northern Ireland called Mairéad Farrell.

The BBC said that the IRA unit had been killed in a gun battle. RTE were saying that they had been executed while attempting to surrender.

"Jesus, I don't like the sound of this," I said to the cat. "Thank God the weather's terrible." Snow and rain would deter the rioters, but for how long?

I turned the TV off and listened to comfort music while I drank hot whiskies and had only my second and third ciggies of the day.

Comfort music? Standard stuff: Schubert, Mozart, Mendelssohn.

I lit the paraffin heater and went to bed.

While the snow fell I found myself dreaming of Spain. I dreamed of palm trees and beaches and copper-haired Mairéad Farrell spread-eagled on the street in a white martyr's blouse and Red Army Faction flares.

I dreamed of the nameless, faceless SAS men celebrating in their army barracks in Hereford. Woodbines and Carling

Black Label and rugby songs. I dreamed of Tariq ibn-Ziyad, the Conqueror, and I dreamed of the great rock named forever in his honour, Tariq's mountain, Jabal Tāriq: قراط لبج

I dreamed of Molly Bloom, transported to grey Dublin, lying in her marriage bed, day-dreaming of her past erotic adventures in a sunlit Gibraltar.

A dream within a dream.

. . . and the sea, the sea crimson sometimes like fire and the glorious sunsets and the fig trees in the Alameda gardens yes and all the queer little streets and the pink and blue and yellow houses and the rosegardens and the jessamine and geraniums and cactuses . . . Yes. Oh yes. Yes.

Mairéad and Molly. Molly and Mairéad. Two lost girls. The blood coiling under Mairéad's twisted body, merging with the scarlet of her hair; Molly's hair splayed over the white of her wedding sheets.

I woke before the dawn and lay in the darkness watching the indigo flame of the paraffin heater. I was unsettled by the dream and annoyed at myself for dreaming it as I trumped down the stairs wrapped in the duvet to stoke the fire. I put on the kettle and took a puff on my inhaler. As if completing a conversation I explained things to the cat. "As you well know when your legs twitch after your phantom mice it's only a silly dream, lacking divinatory or prophetic or any other content, and a cat of your standing in the feline community and a man of my age should not be vexed by the foolishness of dreams."

The foolishness of dreams which, in this bellicose corner of this malicious little island, had the ability to change instantly into nightmares.

11: THE LADY VANISHES

Nothing under the Beemer. Careful drive along Coronation Road to the station. Everyone in the barracks full of the talk of Gibraltar. Undisguised triumph. *We got three of those IRA bastards, that'll learn them.* No appreciation that this small tactical success will have strategic consequences. As soon as the weather improves there will be riots in West Belfast and when the coffins come back for burial there will be three massive IRA funerals. So often in Ulster a tactical success led to a strategic reverse and vice versa.

I flicked through the morning papers. Mairéad Farrell did not, in fact, have red hair. It was more of a chestnutty brown. She seemed like a nice girl. They all seem like nice girls. If the SAS and MI6 were telling the truth they were plotting to blow up the changing of the ceremonial guard. Twenty young men and God knows how many civilians. *If* the SAS and MI6 were telling the truth. I'd met spooks and blades and they lied like they had invented the concept.

I'd only just taken a sip of my coffee when Chief Inspector McArthur came in with a huge grin on his face.

"Did you see the *Newsletter* this morning, Duffy?"

"No."

He handed me the paper. The headline and pages one to three were all Gibraltar, but lo and behold there was a big picture of him on page four taking the heroin out of Francis Deauville's lock-up.

"This is great for us, Duffy. For the whole station. No more scary phone calls from the Chief Constable now, eh?"

I let him speak and smiled and nodded in the right places. He was right, though – better to have the press off your back than on. When he was gone I rounded up Lawson and McCrabban for the drive to Antrim RUC. We had a picture to show Mrs Deauville now and maybe she would remember something.

Lawson made the courtesy call to Antrim RUC to let them know we were on our way but when he put the phone down he looked puzzled.

"What's the matter?" I asked.

"She made bail," he said.

"Mrs Deauville?"

"Yeah."

"Who paid it?"

"Her legal aid solicitor got an envelope full of fifty pound notes and a typed note that explained that this was for Elena Deauville's bail."

The envelope full of fifties and the note were standard paramilitary procedure, but why would the paramilitaries bail her? Perhaps she or her husband had set up this arrangement for herself in the event of her arrest?

"We better go talk to Mrs Deauville and find out who her mysterious benefactor is. At what time was she bailed this morning?"

Lawson looked pale. "It was last night. At 9pm. The solicitor wanted her out pronto so she walked the bail money over to the barracks."

"And the police just released her?"

"They had to."

"And no one told us?"

"Nope. But in their defence last night everybody was pretty

preoccupied by the news from Gibraltar."

"How is that a defence?"

"Uhm, well—"

"What if she's skipped?"

"They took her passport, didn't they?" McCrabban said.

"Why are we talking? Let's get over there."

We got in a Land Rover and drove up to Sunnylands estate but of course she wasn't there.

The police evidence tape was still across the door and I had to use my skeleton key to get in. There was no evidence of packing, her jewellery was still in the box upstairs. At the back of one we found a semi-secret drawer filled with twenty pound notes. She wouldn't have forgotten that.

"Don't think she's been home at all," Lawson said.

"She hasn't. Come on. Let's find out where she did go."

Back to the barracks. I left a reservist at her house in case she did return. No direct flight to Bulgaria today but via London or Paris no probs with a duplicate passport. I circulated her description to the ports and airports. I called up O'Driscoll to get his take but he seemed to think it was no big deal.

"So what? She made bail. She'll still have to appear in court in two weeks."

"You don't get it, mate. She's not at home. She's flown the coop."

"And lose five grand bail? No way. They're in a council house living from benefit cheque to benefit cheque."

"They're major heroin smugglers, Seamus, for all we know they have fifty grand stashed away."

"You've always been a worrier, Duffy. She'll show up in court, you'll see."

I hung up on him. Seamus was a decent bloke but he had never been a top-quality peeler and his horse sense was way off on this case. There was something seriously wrong here.

"Get me her solicitor on the phone," I said to Lawson.

The solicitor was an old pro called Carol McCauley out of McCauley and Wright in Antrim. She filled me in on the bail envelope and the note. This was not the first time she'd had such an unusual bond payment and if these Troubles went on it wouldn't be the last.

"I'm not interested in the money, Carol, in fact I'm not even that interested in your client's career as a heroin smuggler—"

"She's been charged with obstruction of justice. That's all. There's no evidence of anything else."

"Which explains why the bail was a mere five grand."

"The magistrates listened to a load of circumstantial evidence from the RUC drugs squad—"

"Carol, look, as I say, I couldn't give a shit about the drugs or the bail money. I'm investigating her husband's death. Mrs Deauville may be in danger. She may have been a witness in her husband's murder. That's all I care about."

"So what is it you want to know?"

"What did she say to you about the murder?"

"She never spoke to me about the murder."

"And what did she say about the bail money? Where did it come from?"

"She said that she had no idea. She said that maybe some of Frank's friends had helped her out."

"That seems unlikely. He was an independent operator. After you got her out last night where did she go?"

"She asked to be left at Antrim bus station."

"And is that where you left her?"

"It is."

"And she got on a bus?"

"Uhm, no, I didn't actually see her get on a bus."

"Well you've been very helpful, we'll take it from there."

"Is everything all right? Do you think she's OK?"

"I have no idea but she didn't come home last night. If we're lucky she's just skipping out on the bail."

"And if we're unlucky?"

"She's dead."

I filled in Lawson and Crabbie and got them working the phones.

Yes, there was a 9.30pm bus from Antrim to Belfast, delayed until 10pm because of the snow. But there were only two passengers on that bus and both of them were men.

There were no trains running because of the snow.

We got in the Land Rover and drove up to Antrim. We showed Mrs Deauville's mug shot around the bus station and to the taxi drivers at the taxi rank. No one recalled seeing her. The bus station had a good CCTV system and because of all the hijackings in the early 80s all the Ulsterbuses did now too. A scan of the buses leaving Antrim between 9pm and midnight revealed no Elena Deauville.

"She didn't get a bus, she didn't get a taxi, she didn't get a train. What did she get?" I asked Crabbie.

"It's time we got serious. Up the alert level at Interpol and you and I will have to go through the security footage at Larne harbour from last night until this morning."

We drove to Larne Harbour and went through their tape. It was hard to say for certain but it seemed that no one resembling Elena Deauville got on the one ferry that had left last night before weather had cancelled the sailings. Because of the rough seas the boat had only attracted thirty passengers. Ten of those were women and none of those women resembled Elena.

"She could have been wearing a wig or disguised herself," Crabbie said and we went through the tape again to double check.

No Elena.

No Elena at the airport either.

There were many ways to get over the land border between Northern and Southern Ireland so it was possible that she'd slipped across to Eire. But who had driven her and where had they crossed on that snowy night with so many country roads closed?

"I don't understand it," Lawson said.

"I think I do," I said.

"Me too," Crabbie said.

"Well you first then, Crabman," I told him.

"Her husband's killer sent the bail money. And when she was bailed he followed her to the bus station in his car. It was snowing and the buses were delayed so he offered her a lift to Carrick."

"And then what?" Lawson said.

"He killed her," Crabbie said.

"Why?" Lawson gasped.

"He didn't like the fact that she was spending so much time in police custody? He was worried that if the charges started to mount up she would tell what she knew?" he suggested.

"What did she know?" Lawson asked.

"I have no idea," I said.

"She may have just skipped," Crabbie added. "Staying with a friend on a cold night. Maybe she'll show up tomorrow large as life."

"I hope to fuck she's gone to Bulgaria. We'll follow her and I'll charge three first-class plane tickets to Carrick RUC and when Kenny Dalziel comes back from his holidays he'll have a heart attack," I muttered.

We sat in the Incident Room to await developments.

There were no developments.

I called Beth's ma and told her I was gonna be at the station.

We watched TV. *Miami Vice* repeat on BBC2:

Brenda: "How do you go from this tranquillity to that violence?"

Sonny Crockett: "I usually take the Ferrari."

I sent Lawson home after the show and I went to my office to check on the border crossings. No sign of Elena Deauville.

Crabbie came in to see me before he went home.

"Any news of Mrs Deauville?"

"No. You want a drink?"

He shook his head.

"What do you think, Crabbie?"

He sat down opposite me. "My take: she didn't run. She's in a sheugh somewhere with a bullet in her."

"My take too. She knew something. I should have gotten it out of her."

"Don't blame yourself."

"I do."

He shook his head and stood up. "I hate to ask, but, uhm . . ."

"It's better. It was all a misunderstanding. She's coming back. I think."

"Well that's good."

"It is good. Joni Mitchell, you know?"

"What?"

"Big Yellow Taxi."

"What?"

"You better go, mate. Those roads are going to be bad tonight again."

"Aye. See you."

He left. More TV. An *Open University* programme on quince:

Guy with a beard: "Most varieties of quince are too hard, astringent and sour to eat raw unless 'bletted' (softened by frost and subsequent decay)."

I found myself falling asleep in my office chair. Doing that a lot lately. Probably because of repeated head trauma. I'd been knocked out more than the average peeler. Head trauma, asthma, stress – a bomb under your car: occupational hazards for your Northern Irish cop.

Woke up at one. Checked all the crossings and hospitals for Mrs Deauville. Nothing. Checked with the constable at her house. Nope.

Out to the car.

Talk radio.

DJ spouting bullshit about the Gibraltar killings without the ballast of anything resembling facts.

Pulled in to Coronation Road, nearly killing the cat.

I parked the Beemer and picked him up. "Used one of your nine lives, there, mate," I said.

Took the cat indoors and fed it and watched the snow come on again.

Joyce again: Dubliners snow. The snow general all over Ireland. Falling on Coronation Road and Carrick Castle and all over County Antrim.

Falling on the grave the honest men of Milltown Cemetery were digging for Mairéad Farrell.

And on the grave that a bad man of unknown origin was digging for Elena Deauville.

12: THE ANGRY FATHER

The next morning Lawson came into my office with a file.
"What's this?"

"Remember you asked me to look into all the recent heroin overdoses?"

"Yeah."

"Here's one for you that I missed initially. In Bangor last November young lad called Joshua Redmond has what in the papers is called a cocaine overdose. But nobody dies from a cocaine overdose – very few anyway – so I looked into the case. He actually died from a cocaine–heroin speedball. Father had an angry outburst at the funeral 'against drug dealers and their protectors'. Said they should all be killed. Few days later our friend Francis Deauville is told to leave Bangor by the UDA and the UVF."

"Tell me about this angry father."

"Lorry driver. Criminal record for GBH. Six three and in one of the mugshot photos he had prominent sideburns."

"Tell me about the GBH."

"Bar fight in Newry four years ago. Put a bloke in the hospital with a broken collar bone and another man with a fractured neck."

"He beat up two men?"

"Yup."

"Tell me about the kid."

"The kid was only fifteen. The parents were divorced and he was living with his mother in a different part of Bangor from his dad."

"It's got the feel of a wild goose hunt. Let's go see him anyway."

Beemer to Bangor through the North Down suburbs. A gentle part of the province with the nickname: "The Surrey of Northern Ireland".

Mr Redmond's flat, however, was in the Kilcooley Estate, which judging from the terrifying murals of gunmen everywhere was firmly in the control of the UDA.

Redmond's place wasn't hard to find: it was the one with the big rig parked outside.

Doorbell.

Game faces.

Barking Alsatian dog.

"Who the fuck is it?"

"It's the police. Carrickfergus RUC."

"Is this about my road tax?"

"No, it's about Francis Deauville."

He opened the door and kicked the dog behind him into a living room where it came to the window and salivated, growled and barked at us. Redmond was a big, hairy man who looked like Giant Haystacks, the wrestler from off the telly without Haystacks's charm and charisma. Bereaved father, though, so I was prepared to cut him a lot of slack.

"We're homicide detectives looking into Francis Deauville's death," I said.

"That scumbag?"

"You knew he was dead then?"

"Oh yes, I knew. Had a few beers that night."

"After your son died you threatened to kill the drug dealers who sold him the heroin."

"I did," he said grimly. "But I didn't kill that fucker Deauville. Wish I had. Wish I'd thought of it."

"Where were you last Wednesday night?"

"France, driving me lorry."

"Can you prove that?"

"Mais oui. Let me show you the paperwork."

He showed us the paperwork and yes he was in France at a weigh station in Dijon at midnight on the night of the killing.

"How do these weigh stations work?"

"You have to be there in person. They check your licence and weigh your vehicle."

I didn't even have to look at flight schedules to see that it was impossible to get from Dijon to Belfast in the time available. Mr Redmond was not the killer.

"What do you think?" he asked snatching the documentation back.

"You have a pretty good alibi," I said. "Maybe you hired someone to do it?"

"Do you have any children, Inspector Duffy?"

"A little girl. Emma. Not yet one."

He nodded from big sad brown eyes. "Wish I *had* killed Deauville. He was filth in human form. Off the record?"

"Off the record."

"If you find the killer tell me who it is and I'll buy him a drink," he said, his voice cracking.

I looked at Lawson, but Lawson was seeing what I was seeing. This was the face of an innocent man unless he too had rehearsed this scene for the benefit of the police, which it must be said, some people do.

"I'm really sorry about your son," I said and he could see that I was.

"Off the record again?"

"Sure."

"I loved my boy. He was a good lad. Fell in with a bad crowd round here. His mother couldn't cope. If I'd had custody I would have took him driving with me all over Europe. Shown

him another way. Another world. I shouldn't have said anything
at the funeral. Should have kept my mouth shut and bided
me time. There's talking and there's action, isn't there? Knew
a driver years ago in Birmingham. His daughter was beat into
a coma by her boyfriend. Lovely wee lass. Smart, funny, very
pretty. Now she's in a wheelchair, brain-damaged. Can't feed
herself, can't talk. This guy – my mate – says nothing at the
trial. Says nothing after the verdict. Nothing to the press. Just
a humble wee man content to accept the justice of the court.
The boyfriend gets three years in prison. His daughter has a
life sentence. Their family is destroyed. So he waits. He waits
and waits and of course the boyfriend is released after two years
for good behaviour. Again my mate waits so it's not obvious. He
finds out where the boy lives and he watches him and he waits.
A year goes by after the boyfriend is out of prison and then he
and his brother visit the boy in his new flat. They knock on his
door and the lad opens it and they go to town on him with tire
irons . . . That's the way to do it, Inspector Duffy. No threats,
no outbursts at funerals. Don't draw attention to yourself. You
wait and wait and when the time is right you strike. You'd do the
same if someone harmed your Emma, wouldn't you, Inspector?"

"I would," I said immediately.

"We all would. You – the police, the courts, your job is to rob
fathers of our right to natural justice. If I'd kept my mouth shut
I could have murdered Deauville in due course. But somebody
did it for me."

"Someone you know?"

"No."

"The wife, though. Killing her's not so easy is it?" I said.
"Would you kill her as well?"

He shook his head. "Have a good day, Inspector," he said and
closed the door.

On the ride back to Carrick I let Lawson drive while I thought.
A vengeful parent might kill Deauville but you wouldn't kill him

and then wait a couple of days and kill the wife too. Not out of revenge. Not after the blood pact had been fulfilled and honour satisfied. You'd kill Elena for different reasons. Because she knew something: she'd witnessed the killer stalking them, she'd seen the killer's car parked outside her house, her husband had confided in her that he'd had threats . . . something like that.

I went back to the station and read the transcripts of her two police interviews but there was nothing new in them.

O'Driscoll's Q&A had been about the drugs so that was excusable. This was on me. I had botched this one. I had had her in my interview room and I had let her go home without telling me everything she knew. It was my fault that the killer was going unpunished. It was my fault that Elena Deauville was dead.

13: THE PAPER, THE SCISSORS AND MICHAEL STONE

You know what I'm talking about. You've seen it before. You work the case from every angle but the case still dies. Like a cardiac team in casualty with the family just outside the glass we did everything we could for the Deauvilles. But Mr Deauville's murder went unsolved and Mrs Deauville's disappearance went unsolved. At any other time perhaps we could have generated some interest in the media but for the public in Belfast it was all Gibraltar all the time. The IRA, ahem, *volunteers* were being shipped home from the Rock – the funerals were going to be the biggest thing since Bobby Sands.

Things weren't so bleak for me, though. Beth returned with Emma no questions asked. If it had been a punishment it had been an effective one. If it had been Beth just getting a little breathing room it also had been effective. She seemed happier and I was relieved.

"So we'll start looking at houses then, shall we?" Beth said.

"We will."

My Coronation Road days were numbered.

I was relieved too that for now my name was out of the papers and I was down to four ciggies a day: after breakfast, lunch, dinner and before bed. Find me the Catholic RUC man that can do better.

But nothing changed the fact that the case was dead-ending.

No forensic or eyewitness testimony on Francis Deauville. Nothing at all about Elena. We dug into her background and through Interpol the Bulgarian police gave us what they had, which turned out to be very little. Ordinary childhood and high school. Excelled in English and history, had indeed met Francis Deauville where she claimed she had met him (at the ruins of a Roman town) and apparently fallen madly in love.

Francis's CV had more scope for enemies. All those heists over the water. Crooks always fell out over who fucked up in the jobs that went wrong and who got more than his share of the loot in the jobs that went right. Francis must have made many enemies in England. Any one of them could have come over on the boat to kill him.

But that wasn't it either.

This was local. This was personal. This was something specific about Francis himself. All my instincts told me that and the little clues told me that too.

So the days went on and the nights went on and there was no change. We were a small department and there were other cases. It wasn't time to put the Deauville file away but pounding the beat and working the phones was giving us nothing. Although I was wary of journalists I did a couple of interviews for the papers including an English-language Bulgarian paper called *The Sofia Echo*.

Ordinary day in the barracks. The snow long gone. Rain now. Warm drizzle.

"Phone call for you, Inspector Duffy," Sandra said.

"Lads, I better get this. To be continued."

I went to my office and picked up the receiver.

"Duffy, Carrick CID," I said.

"Hello, Sean. It's Pytor Yavarov."

"What can I do for you, Pytor?"

"I'd like to talk to you about the Elena Deauville disappearance."

"Do you have information?"

"I would prefer it if we talk in person."

"I can be in Dublin in two hours."

"I am already in Belfast. I do not want any nosy inquiries from my colleagues in the embassy if I am seen talking to a stranger who then turns out to be a Northern Irish policeman."

"OK, we'll meet in the centre of Belfast. But it's going to have to be a quick meeting. Those IRA funerals are this afternoon and traffic will be a nightmare."

"Do you know of a discreet place?"

"Let's meet in the last snug on the right of the Crown Bar in half an hour. OK if I bring Lawson and McCrabban?"

"Do you trust them?"

"With my life."

"I will see you in half an hour."

Twenty-seven minutes later Lawson, Crabbie and I walked into the Crown Bar and ordered three Guinnesses and three Irish stews.

Yavarov was waiting for us in the snug, huddled over a lager and vodka chaser. He was nattily dressed in a wool raincoat and a tweed jacket with a red cravat underneath. He declined a Guinness and a stew, even though we explained that that's what you ate and drank in here. The Crown was a Victorian saloon that still had its original gas lights and fixtures and fortunately for our purposes was equipped with many individual booths or "snugs" that allowed one privacy.

"So what's this all about?" I asked Yavarov.

"I read about Mrs Deauville's disappearance in *The Sofia Echo*," he began. "It is fortunate that I did so. No one told us in the embassy that she had gone missing."

"I contacted Interpol and I assumed they would have contacted you," I said, quick to defend my reputation against a charge of professional misconduct.

"Interpol did not contact us."

"Well, you know now. She's been missing for a week and there's no sign of her anywhere. We've checked the ferry ports and the airports and we're certain she didn't get out of Northern Ireland that way. The border's another matter. There are hundreds of unofficial crossing points and she could have used one of those."

"She could be alive?" Yavarov asked.

"She could be. She was last seen at a bus station in Antrim but she didn't get on any of the buses. Who knows, maybe a friend drove her over the border and she hid out in the Irish countryside before getting a plane somewhere."

"Why would she run away?"

"Because she was worried she was going to be charged with heroin trafficking? That's five to ten years in prison," Crabbie said.

"You had no evidence of her direct involvement in the drug trade," Yavarov said.

"So why do you think she ran?" I asked.

"If she ran it was because she did not trust the police to protect her," he said definitively.

"Protect her from what?"

"In Bulgaria the police can be bought and sold for a few Lev."

"The RUC is incorruptible," Crabbie said.

"That is not what I hear. I hear you work with Protestants to kill the IRA. I hear you let the IRA and the UVF divide up Belfast between them for the purpose of selling drugs and running protection rackets. I hear you let Protestant and Catholic gangsters kill drug dealers who do not pay them protection," Yavarov said.

Some of that, of course, was true.

"That may happen. But not in my manor. There are no free passes for murder in Carrickfergus," I insisted.

"You I trust to do the right thing, Duffy. Perhaps I would have kept this information to myself if I did not trust you," Yavarov said and finished his vodka. He took a sip of the nasty-looking lager.

"You have tried Harp?" he asked.

"Yes," we all said together.

"It is good, no?"

"Maybe it's an acquired taste," I said to be polite. (Belfast pub Harp was an acquired taste like coprophagia or getting pissed on by hookers.) "Now, Mr Yavarov, you've come a very long way this morning to tell us something. Why don't we end the small talk and you just tell us what it is you think we should know."

"When I met Mrs Deauville before you began your tape recording she told me something she did not wish to tell you."

"What?"

"The day her husband was killed Mrs Deauville and her husband were in the pub in Carrickfergus for a drink. When they walked home Mrs Deauville thought that someone was following them in a car. Mr Deauville told her that she was talking nonsense but she grew up in Bulgaria in the bad days. She knew when she was being followed."

"What car?"

"A blue Ford Escort."

"That's not as helpful as you think it is, Mr Yavarov. There must be 5,000 blue Ford Escorts in Ireland," Crabbie said.

"Perhaps this will help," Yavarov said, sliding across a piece of paper.

When I opened it it was a licence number: AIU 9785.

"That's a Derry licence plate," Crabbie said.

Yavarov looked at us and shrugged. "It may not mean anything."

He had nothing more to add but this was bloody gold.

"We'll certainly investigate it, Mr Yavarov. Now if I were you I'd get home, the IRA funerals for the three volun– people who were killed in Gibraltar are due to start in half an hour and I imagine the trains are going to be packed and the city is going to be one huge traffic jam."

He stood up. "I hope you will be able to find Elena Draganova."

I shook his outstretched hand. "I hope so too."

We saw Yavarov across the station and headed home in the Beemer before the funeral procession began.

When we got back to Carrick RUC we went straight to the computer in the Incident Room. Finding out who drove AIU 9785 was the work of a moment. A few mouse clicks on the Macintosh and a sift through the National Vehicle Registry database.

The car belonged to one Harold Selden, forty-five, who lived in the Scissors Area of the Creggan Estate, Derry.

"What's a lad from Derry doing all the way down in Carrickfergus?" McCrabban asked.

"What's a *Catholic* lad from Derry doing all the way down in a Protestant housing estate in Carrickfergus?" I countered. For if he lived in the Creggan he was definitely a Catholic as all the Prods had been driven out of that part of the city two decades ago.

"I think we can guess why he was so far out of his territory," Crabbie said.

"What?"

"Scouting a hit for the DAADD?" Crabbie suggested. "Smart play. Bring in an assassin from the outside who won't be recognised down the chip shop later."

"Maybe some eccentric assassin who likes to shoot his victims with a crossbow?" Lawson mused.

"Look him up on the criminal database, Lawson."

That also was the work of a moment. "No criminal record," Lawson said, with obvious disappointment.

"That doesn't necessarily mean he hasn't done anything," Crabbie said. "It could just mean that he's a good criminal who doesn't get caught."

"Who fancies a trip to Derry?" I said cheerfully.

This suggestion was not met with universal enthusiasm.

"Now?" Crabbie said.

"Why not. What else are we going to do?"

"It's such a hassle to get up there and the day's nearly over," Crabbie said.

"You're afraid, aren't you?"

"No. I'm not afraid of Derry. I've been there before."

"You can admit it. There's parts of Belfast that scare me, but Derry's great. Derry people are wonderful. Love to go back to Derry. Derry's my home."

"Yeah, cos nothing bad's ever happened in Derry," Lawson muttered.

"What's the matter? Are you afeared too?"

Lawson shook his head. "No, but Crabbie's right. It's getting late. Those big funerals are on. Shouldn't we let the local peelers bring him in for questioning?"

I shook my head. "Look at the pair of you. Well, I'm going out to the car. You're free to join me if you want."

Of course they both traipsed after me but I saw Crabbie check his sidearm twice and Lawson looked as pale as William Joyce when they took him to the drop box at Wandsworth Prison.

"If you're worried about the hour let's see if we can't light up the Glenshane Pass, eh?"

"Sean, don't kill us. I have three kids and Lawson's got his whole life ahead of him."

"Sensible speed boys. You know me."

It was eighty miles from Belfast to Derry on the M2 and the A6. A one hour and twenty minute run according to the Automobile Association. I did it in 59 minutes dead. The BMW 535i lapped it up like a kitten licking cream.

We stopped outside Harry Selden's house, a nice wee three-bedroom semi-detached job in the Scissors area of the Creggan. One of the nicer parts of the sprawling estate. By the murals all around this was heavy IRA land, but there were few wee muckers or watchers on the streets today.

"Maybe there's a football game on?" Crabbie suggested.

"Nah, around here everyone's glued to the telly watching the funerals."

We knocked on Harry Selden's door.

"Go away!" he said.

"It's the police," I said.

"The police? Now?"

"Yes."

We heard Mr Selden trump down the hall and violently open the door. I couldn't help but like Harry as soon as I saw him because he was a rotund man in a cardigan with thinning black hair and a jovial shine to his cheek. He had very dark eyes and little brown caterpillar eyebrows. He was about my height and we would have made a good Laurel and Hardy standing together if we'd put on 30s garb and he'd grown a bristle moustache. I brought to the forefront of my mind the possibility that he had murdered both Elena Deauville and her husband Francis and that took the edge off my admiration.

"Mind if I ask you a few questions, Mr Selden?"

"You know the funerals are about to start?"

"Sorry, I thought they'd be over by now."

"No. I was watching it. They're just finishing the service. Have you got any identification?"

I showed him my warrant card.

"You're a Catholic?" he said accusingly after reading my name.

"Yes."

He pointed his finger at me. "You as good as killed those kids in Gibraltar. That wee girl. You work for them uns that have done it. You know what you are?"

"A policeman come to ask you some questions?"

"A traitor."

You'd think they'd be more original with their dialogue. Like

I hadn't heard this a million times since I'd joined the force.

"Where were you on Wednesday the 2nd of March, Mr Selden?"

"I was in the hospital getting me appendix out."

"What hospital?"

"Altnagelvin."

"When did you enter the hospital?"

"The previous Friday. I took ill in the *council* chamber. It was an emergency."

"And on the Wednesday you were still in the hospital?"

"I was nearly in a bloody coma. I had septicaemia."

"You seem better now."

"Yeah, they finally let me out last Saturday. I was in hospital for an entire week. Missed a week of *council* business. What's this all about?"

"Can we come in and talk? Maybe a cup of tea?"

"No, you can stand there or you can fuck off. You're not coming in and you're not getting any tea. What's this about?"

"On Wednesday March 2nd your Ford Escort was seen in Sunnylands Estate, Carrickfergus, following a man who was murdered on Thursday morning. How do you explain that, Mr Selden?"

"I explain it very easily, Mr Duffy. My car was stolen from right in front of my house while I was in the bloody hospital."

"And did you tell the police it was stolen?" Crabbie asked.

"Oh, it speaks, does it? Does the wee blond one speak as well, or is he your ventriloquist's dummy?"

"Can you answer Sergeant McCrabban's question?"

"Why didn't I report my stolen car to the police? Because I have no truck with the police. I don't recognise the RUC as a police force. It is an arm of the British state. An occupying army. No, *Sergeant McCrabban*, I will never report anything to the police or go into a police station for any reason."

"That's convenient. So you say your car was stolen but there's no proof that it was stolen," I said.

"Who said there was no proof? I never said that. I just said I never told the police. I told the insurance company, though. And I've got the claims forms to prove it. Just hold on a wee minute there and I'll get them."

He slammed the door in our faces and returned a moment later with the insurance form that certified the fact that he had reported his car stolen on March 5th, the day he had gotten out of hospital. Northern Ireland was one of the few places in the world where you didn't need a formal police report for stolen property because so many people refused, like old Harry, to have anything to do with the RUC.

"So you get out of hospital and you notice your car was gone and you immediately called the insurance company, is that right?" I asked.

"That's right. But my mother who lives with me noticed that the car had been gone for about four days. She doesn't remember when. She hasn't been too well herself. A stroke."

"I'm sorry to hear that."

I showed the form to Crabbie, who read it and nodded. He passed it to Lawson who also read it.

"Now, do you mind, I want to watch the TV and me mum will want her tea."

"I just have a few more questions," I said.

"Do you know who I am?" Selden said, snatching the form back from Lawson.

"Harold Selden of the Creggan Estate?"

"*Councillor* Harold Selden of Derry City Council. And your harassment will not go unnoticed at the next Derry City Council meeting, Inspector Sean Duffy of Carrickfergus CID."

Another door slam.

"What was that you were saying about Derry people being wonderful, sir?" Lawson said.

I turned to McCrabban. "He's developing quite the lip, young

Lawson, isn't he?"

"Aye. I don't entirely approve of that," Crabbie said.

Quick drive to check on Selden's story at the hospital. Ruptured appendix, blood poisoning, finally released from the hospital on the Saturday morning – a full 48 hours after Deauville's death.

"Pretty good alibi that, in a coma, in hospital, in Derry," McCrabban said.

"Indeed," I agreed.

Silent drive home in the car.

Snow flurries. No radio reception to speak of.

"He doesn't look a bit like the artist's sketch, anyway," Crabbie announced as we neared Carrick. "The strange, tall DAADD assassin who eccentrically has drinks with the person he later assassinates."

"Aye, none of it really fits," I agreed and dropped the lads at the station before heading up Coronation Road.

Beth met me in the hall with a can of Bass. Now that I had formally committed to leaving this street, she was much happier. This estate, these people, were only temporary constructs to be put up with for a while. My class-war comments had hurt her too and she was pretending not to be mortified by these DUP-voting, country-music-listening, self-immolating-in-chip-pan-fire Proddies.

"Did you take your inhaler?" Beth asked.

"I did."

"And no cigarettes?"

"No. Only two. Thank God I've been busy, how does anyone quit smoking when you've got nothing to occupy your mind?"

"Don't ask me, I never started. How'd the funerals go in Belfast?"

"Don't ask me. I was only there for half an hour and then we went up to Derry."

"Derry? Really?"

"Yup."

"That was a fast run there and back."

"Thank you. Glad somebody appreciates it. What have you been doing all day?"

"Watching your offspring. Reading. Which I'm going to get back to. Watch Emma, will you?"

"My pleasure."

I sat in the living room by the fire and played with Emma. Put the record player on. "This, Emma, is Luigi Boccherini, now people are going to tell you that he's courtly, old-fashioned, even boring, but you just listen to the warmth of that melody, eh?"

Emma was ignoring me and trying to choke herself to death on a Lego brick. I removed the brick from her gob and helped her make a tower. Warm house, girlfriend, baby girl and kitty – what more could a man ask for? Yeah, the missus was a bit on the high-maintenance side but I was fighting an age gap. Nah, take your pleasures where you find them and this was the good life.

At 6pm I made us some dinner, put on the BBC news and my jaw dropped.

It was on every channel.

I called Crabbie immediately. "Are you watching this?"

"I was just going to pick up the phone and call you," he said.

The IRA funerals at Milltown Cemetery in Belfast had been attacked by a rogue, presumably deranged, Loyalist gunman called Michael Stone. He had fired an automatic pistol into the crowd of mourners and thrown hand grenades at Gerry Adams and Martin McGuinness. Three were dead and dozens were wounded. It could have been many more. And what made it worse, somehow, was that the whole thing had been captured live on television. Michael Stone had thrown his grenades and run towards the motorway where the crowd had caught up with him and almost beat him to death.

It was the worst incident of the Troubles since the Enniskillen bombing back in November when the IRA had blown up a dozen civilian mourners at a Remembrance Sunday service. That had been a bad one. The father of a nurse who'd been murdered – Marie Wilson – had gone on Irish television and publicly forgiven the bombers in an act of Christian charity. This had shamed the IRA and since then the bombings had wound down and we thought things were actually going to change. But I suppose nothing ever changed in this three-hundred-and-fifty-year-long blood feud.

Beth came into the living room. "What's happened?" she asked, seeing my face.

I told her. And we watched the news footage. "I hate this whole fucking country," she said and I could do nothing but nod my head in agreement.

14: A TASTE OF HONEY

The next morning we had to report for duty as normal but nothing felt normal about that day. We knew there were going to be riots and if the Belfast police were overwhelmed they would be calling for support from the surrounding districts.

I had a little meeting with Crabbie and Lawson in my office. "I imagine they'll be looking for officers to do riot duty. It'll be over-time and danger money but I don't want either of you doing it. I'm not banning you from doing it, but I'm telling you it's fairy gold. You can get seriously hurt. And we're detectives. A cut above the ordinary peeler, you know?"

It was the same speech I gave every year during Marching Season. There was an element of hypocrisy in it because sometimes I did riot duty and crowd-control duty when I wanted to (when Muhammad Ali came) and sometimes you couldn't help it, when we were ordered into a DMSU team; still, when we had the choice I preferred not to go and not to let my men go.

"It's easy money," Lawson said. "And some of them boys on the nights get triple and even quadruple time! That's barrister's money!"

"Let them get their triple time. We've a murder and a disappearance to solve."

"No one gives a crap about this particular murder. Everybody wants it to go away," Lawson grumbled.

What age was Lawson now? Twenty-one? Twenty-two? How did he get so old so quick?

"You're dismissed, Lawson."

After he'd left the office I poured Crabbie a glass of the sixteen-year-old Bowmore. "You really want to quit and leave him in charge? Dalziel running the station and him running CID?"

"I thought you liked him."

"I do like him, but if we both go this place is doomed."

Crabbie looked out the window at the rain lashing the Belfast docks. "It's all doomed anyway."

The phone rang.

"Inspector Duffy, CID," I said.

"This is Stephen O'Toole from the *Belfast Telegraph*, we're running a wee story this afternoon about police harassment of elected Sinn Fein councillors, care to comment?"

"Not much to say about that, Mr O'Toole, we here at Carrick RUC have excellent relations with all the elected representatives in Northern Ireland."

"So you're denying that you have a policy of harassing Sinn Fein councillors?"

"There is no such policy. Sometimes we have to question councillors or judges or even journalists in the course of an investigation but that's all. I don't have the time or inclination to harass anyone."

"Thanks very much, Inspector Duffy."

"Anytime."

He hung up. Crabbie gave me the old raised left eyebrow. "Trouble?" he asked.

"I hope not."

The story, when it appeared that afternoon, did not mention my name at all, but if I'd been a bit smarter I would have realised that this was merely a shot across the bows. Harry Selden was a man with pull.

Two days after the Michael Stone incident there was another

horrific encounter on live TV. Two British army corporals from the signals regiment took a wrong turn into another IRA funeral. When they tried to reverse out of the street, the crowd seized them, pulled them from their cars, stripped them and lynched them on live TV.

That night the Protestant and Catholic districts of Belfast *both* came out in riot.

Beth was shocked. She had only hazy memories of the early 70s. She didn't know things could get this bad.

"Maybe building this house is a bad idea, Sean, maybe what's best for Emma is to get out of Ireland completely."

"What do you mean?"

"Everything's falling apart. All the smart people are getting out. Both my brothers have gone, Dad's thinking of selling the business."

"I'll admit to having had similar thoughts."

"Is it too late for you to get into the Met?"

"The Metropolitan Police? Yeah, it's too late. I'm thirty-eight now. They don't take new recruits aged thirty-eight."

"But you're not a new recruit, you could join as a detective, as a detective inspector."

"I knew one guy who managed to pull that off," I said thinking of Tony McIlroy. "But for that to work you need influence."

"Daddy's rich."

"I mean influence over the water. The Met's not going to take me . . . What would you do in London?"

"Anything. As long as it was safe. Look at Kenneth Branagh's parents. They did the right thing. They got him out."

"You might be right, Beth," I said reflectively. "I've done my bit here in Northern Ireland and I've achieved nothing."

Next day I let Crabbie and Lawson volunteer for this mythical quadruple-time riot pay while I drove up to Derry again and parked the car just down the street from Councillor Selden's house.

I followed him on his rounds to the Sinn Fein Advice Centre and to the Spar Supermarket and to the butchers. Nothing interesting. Nothing untoward. But a couple of times he doubled back to see if he was being followed, which *was* interesting.

I drove over to the infamous Strand Road police station, introduced myself and asked for the intel officer. A Detective Sergeant called Linda Quinn (a woman *and* a Catholic no less) gave me some interesting stuff about Selden that wasn't in the files.

"Oh yes, we're pretty sure that Selden's a player," she said with satisfaction, in a soft County Armagh accent.

"IRA?"

"IRA indeed."

"How high up?"

"Oh, not very high. He's getting on a bit. Forty-three, I think. If you haven't made command by forty you sort of take a back seat."

"What about DAADD?"

"What's that?"

"Direct Action Against Drug Dealers."

"Oh yes, those fellows. No, they don't have much of a presence in Derry. For the moment anyway. DAADD's more of a Belfast group. Up here the IRA just kills or kneecaps the drug dealers that have upset them. They don't need a cover organisation in Derry, they've already got the public on their side."

"I know, I almost joined myself after Bloody Sunday."

"So that's something you and Selden have in common, then."

"What?"

"He was in the police. He joined the IRA after Bloody Sunday."

"He was in the police?"

"Didn't you know that?"

"No."

"Well, not the real police, the B Specials."

"The B Specials?"

"They were a reserve force in the 1960s. They were notorious for—"

"I know what they are. This is too weird to be a coincidence."

I explained that Francis Deauville, my murder victim, had also been in the B Specials.

"Maybe not that weird a coincidence. There must be thousands of people who served in that force," Linda said.

"Where would I find the records of people who served in the B Specials? They're not in the RUC service files."

"You'd have to go to the records office in Belfast. All those old paper files. Probably all falling apart. In fact, you'll probably find they have all been, quote, damaged in a flood, unquote, in case there's anything embarrassing in them."

"It's embarrassing enough that an ex B Special became an IRA player."

"There's more than you think. Bloody Sunday changed everything up here. But I'm glad I'm here, in Derry, not in Belfast with all that rioting. That's where you are, isn't it, Inspector Duffy?"

"Carrickfergus. But close enough." Hmmm, Harry Selden in the B Specials, just like poor old Francis Deauville. I thanked Sergeant Quinn and drove back to the Creggan to sit in front of Selden's house and think.

I'd only been there fifteen minutes when he came out of his house holding a paper cup and walked it over to the Beemer.

I wound down the window.

"I brought you a cup of tea, Inspector Duffy. It's a cold day to be sitting out here," he said.

"Thanks," I said taking the tea and putting it in the cup holder.

"Now, if you're interested I'll be home for about half an hour and then I'll be walking to the Sinn Fein Advice Centre for my weekly advice clinic. Then I'll be picking up some sausages for me mother at the Spar."

"How's she doing today?" I asked.

"Oh she's a little bit better today. She's improving rightly just like the doctor said she would."

"You do right by your mother, Mr Selden. It's nice to see," I said.

"You have to stick by your loved ones."

"Especially women. The way women are treated in this country. It's positively medieval."

"That's true. Look at poor Mairéad Farrell, shot by your friends in the SAS," he said.

"And look at poor Marie Wilson. Blown up by an IRA bomb while laying a wreath for those who fought against Hitler . . . oh, silly me, I forgot, the IRA was on the same side as Hitler. They conveniently forget that little fact in the Sinn Fein manifestos, don't they?"

His lips thinned and he did not reply.

"B Specials, eh?" I said.

"What's that?"

"You were in the B Specials."

"Where did you get that information?"

"Is it true?"

"For a very brief time before the Troubles began I had a part-time job as a—"

"Do your friends in the IRA know about this curious career choice of yours?"

"I don't have any friends in the IRA. I'm a Sinn Fein councillor, in case you have forgotten."

"My memory would really have to be going bad – you've reminded me of it often enough."

"A councillor cannot be harassed by a policeman, not if the policeman wants to stay out of the newspapers."

I laughed at him. "Do your research! It's a bit late for that. Tell me, did you serve with Francis Deauville in the Specials? Is that how you know him?"

"I don't know any Francis Deauville."

"Sure you do. He was on the six o'clock news. The IRA shot him because he was a heroin dealer. Interesting that you would deny knowing him, though. Interesting that your car would make its way from this safe little street all the way down to the twisty dangerous streets of Sunnylands Estate in Carrickfergus," I said.

"What are you implying, Inspector Duffy? Are you implying that I crawled out of my sick bed, somehow got all the way to Carrickfergus to murder a man I don't know for reasons that are oblique and all this without any of my doctors or nurses noticing?" Harry asked, his plump jovial face assuming a sinister aspect. He'd been getting gradually bigger and paler as the conversation had gone on and now when he leaned back on his heels he wasn't Oliver Hardy at all. Now he was Mr Potter from *It's A Wonderful Life* or maybe even Sydney Greenstreet from *The Maltese Falcon*. Like many big, heavy men he was light on his toes. Dainty, almost. I liked that. I opened the car door, got out and stood facing him.

"I'm implying that you had something to go with Francis Deauville's death. I'm implying that had something to do with Elena Deauville's disappearance. Another woman who was not treated well on this fair isle."

"Me? You're accusing me, a councillor on Derry City Council?"

"I'm accusing you, a player in the IRA."

"That's a serious charge."

"I'm a serious man."

He stared at me for a minute and then walked away in disgust. Halfway across the street he turned to face me. "I'm a serious man too," he said.

When he'd gone back indoors I threw the tea out the window. If it hadn't contained piss, spit or poison I was a Chinaman.

I looked at my watch. It was nearly three. Might as well have a quick pint and call it a day and go home for me tea. No point staking out Selden's house any more, not when he'd made me and probably already had his goons following me.

I drove to a phonebox and called Beth.

"Hello?"

"Beth, it's me, I'm up in Derry, but it's a bust up here so I'm coming home."

"Thank God you're not in Belfast. There have been terrible riots. It's on the news."

"I think Lawson's up there. I hope he's all right."

"Lawson, yes. We really should have all your colleagues round for dinner some night. We've never done that and we should. And your boss too."

"Sounds like the sort of thing married couples do."

"It does," she agreed.

"Is that a proposal? I think you missed Leap Day."

"I did, didn't I?"

"I can't keep track of you. One minute you're for leaving the country and having me join the Met and the next you want my boss round for tea so we can brown-nose him."

She bit her lip and nodded. "You're right. I have to make my mind up. We both have to do a lot of thinking about the future. Anyway, I have to go, Sean, Emma's at Jollytots and it's after three. I'm picking her up but I'm having Janette Campbell watch her while I go to the library to work. OK to get your own dinner tonight?"

"That's fine. Maybe I'll make us something."

"Ooh, I'd like that. Bye."

"Love you."

"Love you too."

Love you too, eh?

The whole province can go to hell but I got an "I love you too." Those few days at her parents' had maybe been her "Big Yellow Taxi" moment too.

I drove to the Joyce Cary pub for a quiet pint before hitting the bleak treeless joys of the A6 again.

The place was deserted but it would fill up at quitting time.

I ordered a Guinness. "You wouldn't have any food, would you?" I asked.

"*An rud a lionas an tsuil lionann se an croi,*" he said.

"Well I've an eye for grub if you've got any."

"There's only the lentil soup left. Vegetarian. Vegan, actually, if you can believe it."

"Sounds horrible. I'll take it."

I ate the soup and drank the Guinness. A pretty young woman with what appeared to be a black eye came in, ordered a gin and tonic and sat by herself in the corner.

A few minutes later, from a different part of the pub, a young man came over to the bar to order a drink, but when he noticed the young woman he left the bar and sat down at her table opposite her.

I sighed inwardly. Men. They were all fucking clueless.

The young man started pestering the young woman, who was actually shaking now. I put down my soup spoon and walked over.

"Oi mate, take it easy, she just wants to be left alone," I said.

"How is it any of your business, pal?"

"Come on, mate. Just head on. You really don't want to do this."

If it was Carrick, or even Belfast, I would have flashed my warrant card but you didn't do that kind of thing around here.

"Do you want to go outside and discuss it?" he said.

"No, I don't. Move on, son, look at her, she wants a bit of peace and quiet, OK?"

One of his fingers poked me in the chest right in the middle of my Che Guevara T-shirt. His big greasy paw on my T-shirt? I grabbed his wrist with my left hand and bent the finger back with my right. He gasped in pain.

"Just go home, son," I whispered.

"OK, OK, let go!"

He scurried out of there and I said "excuse me" to the girl and returned to the dregs of my pint.

Five minutes later she was standing next to me at the bar. In the Jameson mirror I could see that she'd been very attractive before the punch in the face. Very attractive after the punch in the face. Dark curly hair, blue eyes, pale. A very Derry look. She had a handbag and a shopping bag and nothing else.

"That was kind of you," she said. "I didn't need that aggravation after the day I've had."

"Do you have a place to go tonight?"

"Yes, I'm going to stay with my friend Siobhan. If he comes looking for me he'll never look for me there. He'll think I'm with my mum and dad but I won't be. I'll be at Siobhan's. She's a friend from work. He doesn't know her."

"That's a good plan," I said.

"Siobhan's ma is a social worker and she's got connections with the police. She can get me one of them what do you call them things? Restriction order?"

"Restraining order."

"Aye, one of them."

"Yeah, that's the way to go about it. Stay with someone he doesn't know and let the courts and the police handle the whole thing. Smart thinking."

"I'm Mary, by the way."

"I'm Sean."

She gave me a frail, ashamed smile. "I couldn't ask you for one more big favour though, Sean, could I?"

"How much do you need?"

"Oh, it's not that. I just want to go home and get some clothes for work. He probably won't be there. He doesn't knock off *his* work until five. But if he is home he'll fucking give me a hammering, so he will."

"Where is this place?"

"Dungiven Street. Round the corner. Do you know it?"

"Aye, I know it."

I looked at my watch. It was nearly 4 now.

"If we're going to do this we need to do it right now. Can you be in and out in fifteen minutes? I really don't want a confrontation."

"I can be in and out in five."

"That's good. Where does your friend Siobhan live?"

"Siobhan . . . Oh, she's out near Altnagelvin."

"I know where that is, too. I can run you over."

"I don't want to put you to any trouble."

"It's no trouble, it's on my way back to Belfast. Let me call home first."

I put fifty pence in the bar phone and called home.

Janette Campbell was over babysitting. "Hello?" Janette said.

"Janette, it's Sean, there shouldn't be any hassles but I may be a wee bit delayed in Derry. Can you tell Beth?"

"You're in Derry and might be delayed. Is that the message?"

"Yeah. I should be home on time, but you never know."

"OK, Sean."

I hung up and walked back over to Mary. "Come on, love, let's get this show on the road before your husband gets back."

"He's not my husband. I wouldn't marry the likes of him. Just my boyfriend. Ex-boyfriend."

We walked out to the Beemer. I pretended to drop my lighter and looked underneath it for bombs. No bombs. We drove out to Dungiven Street. Quiet little residential block of redbrick back to backs. We walked to the front door and she gingerly took out her key and put it in the lock. She turned the key and leaned in the doorway with a whispered "Nate? Nate?"

She turned to me "No Nate," she said.

I looked at my watch again. "Fifteen minutes, mind. It'll be better for all of us if he never knew you were here."

I followed her into the hall.

They did it very professionally indeed.

A man was waiting behind the door with a sawn-off shotgun. Another man came out of the side room with a pistol. Both men were wearing balaclavas. Both guns were pointing only at me. Mary walked along the hall, into the kitchen and straight out the back door of the house without turning her head once to look at me.

"Don't move," the man with the pistol said. "When we tell you to, we want you to lie down on the floor."

There was no play that wouldn't result in my immediate death. I put my hands up and when ordered to I lay down on the floor with my hands behind my back.

They stripped me of my weapon.

They handcuffed me and took my wallet and the knife in my sock.

Classic honey trap. Oh Duffy. Eejits fell for honey traps, not you. Not an experienced peeler like you.

15: THAT PETROL EMOTION

Things are different in the movies. When the IRA take a policeman or a soldier hostage in the pictures what follows is an often philosophical and historical argument about the British presence in Ireland and the crimes the Brits have committed against Irish rebels. In real life what happened was what had happened to the two corporals in West Belfast: the hostage is stripped and beaten and then summarily executed. There's no philosophy, no history, just a savage beating and then a bullet in the brain.

If the IRA want specific intelligence from the hostage then there will, of course, be graphic physical torture until the victim tells them everything he or she knows. Hundreds of tortured victims had been found over the years lying by the side of the road or buried in shallow graves.

I had seen bodies where the paramilitaries had drilled into victims' kneecaps, wrists and ankles. I'd seen bodies where the eyeballs had been gouged out, where the victim's feet had been blowtorched, or where the victim had been castrated and forced to eat their own genitalia until they'd choked to death. None of this was necessary. That initial blow torch to the feet would make anyone talk. The rest was just for the sadistic pleasure of the torturers.

I knew all this and I knew there was absolutely no point trying to lie.

Truth right from the start, that was the way to go.

It wouldn't stop them hurting me. It wouldn't stop me from being terrified but it was a *tactic* and in a situation like that you need to cling to something. I decided to cling to truth.

A hood was thrown over my head and I was bundled outside to a waiting car. I was chucked in the boot and driven a short distance.

Taken out, dragged to a house and sat on a chair in the middle of a room with several people already in it. I could hear a petrol can being sloshed around in the background. Dousing someone in petrol and threatening to burn them alive was another old torturers' trick. I didn't want that, either.

"There's no need for the petrol or anything else. I'll tell you everything you want to know," I said.

"OK. What's your name?" a voice asked.

"Sean Duffy of Carrickfergus RUC."

"So you're admitting that you're a policeman then?"

"I am."

Grumbling and muttering from those assembled in the room. He's admitted he's a peeler: what else needs to be said?

"Why were you in Derry?" a different voice asked.

"I was investigating the murder of Francis Deauville and the disappearance of Elena Deauville in Carrickfergus."

"Who are they?"

"Francis Deauville was a heroin dealer probably executed by DAADD. Elena Deauville was his wife, who went missing."

"What's the Derry connection?"

"A car belonging to Harry Selden was spotted in the vicinity of Deauville's house shortly before his murder. The car was following Deauville."

"Harry Selden?"

"Aye."

More muttering from the men in the room. Four distinct voices, possibly five.

"Don't lie," a voice said.

"I'm not lying."

"We won't hesitate to torture you if we have to to get you to tell the truth."

"I believe you," I said.

"We've got a can of petrol here and we're in a derelict house. We could just pour this over you, light a match and leave."

"I smell the petrol. I know you could do that. Please don't! I'm telling you the truth!"

Silence and this was more terrifying than the questions. There could be a gun at my temple right now and I wouldn't even know it.

I was afraid of the darkness.

Afraid of the pain.

My whole body began to tremble. I was having trouble breathing.

"I'm having trouble breathing," I said.

"You'll be having more trouble breathing in an hour or so," a voice said.

A few guffaws.

"You know Harry Selden's a councillor, don't you?" a voice said, a different voice, higher-pitched but vibrating with authority. It was a voice I recognised from the TV. This was almost certainly ****** ***********, the IRA commander in the city and a prominent leader in Sinn Fein.

"He may have mentioned that to me," I said.

"What exactly is his connection to this murder case?"

"All we know is that his car showed up in Carrick and he may have been following the victim. But Selden says his car was stolen."

"Was his car stolen?"

"Apparently it was. He put in an insurance claim, although he didn't report the car stolen to the police."

"He wouldn't go to the police."

"That's what he said."

"It sounds to me, Inspector Duffy, that this wee trip up here was a wild goose chase," ****** ********** said.

"That may be the case."

"You're a very brave man driving around the Bogside in an unmarked police car. Very brave or very stupid."

"Very stupid it turns out."

"You're from Derry though, are you? That's a Derry accent is it?"

"I went to school here."

"And you're Catholic."

"Yes."

"A Catholic policeman."

"Yes."

"You know there's a bounty on Catholic RUC men."

"I know."

"You don't seem particularly scared."

"I'm fucking terrified. I have a wife and a kid. A little girl. She's just begun talking and walking."

"We all have wives and kids . . . All right, time's a factor here. I don't think we need to send a message with this one. He won't give us any trouble . . . You won't give us any trouble, will you, Sean Duffy?"

"I won't be any trouble."

"So you'd appreciate it if we didn't set on you on fire or didn't beat the shit out of you?"

"I'd very much appreciate that."

"Are your parents alive?"

"Yes."

"I'm sure your mother would be happy to know that you didn't suffer."

"Yes."

"There's plenty here who would love to use you to get revenge for what happened in Gibraltar and what happened at Milltown Cemetery."

"I know."

"But if you're a good lad and just do everything everyone tells you and don't play silly buggers I can promise you a quick and painless death and a body that won't upset your wife or mother if it ever gets found. That's the best offer you're going to get today. Fair enough?"

I swallowed hard. I had one play and it wasn't much of a play. I'd been to school with Ken Kirkpatrick who was now the IRA quartermaster in Derry. And I'd been Deputy Head Boy to Dermot McCann when he was Head Boy. Dermot was an IRA martyr who'd nearly killed Mrs Thatcher in Brighton (fortunately no one knew my part in that affair).

"Look, I don't know if it'll help but Ken Kirkpatrick knows me. He knows I'm not a bad guy."

"You know Ken Kirkpatrick?"

"I went to school with him. I went to school with Ken Kirkpatrick and Dermot McCann."

"Dermot's no longer with us."

"I know, but if you talk to Ken—"

"We're not talking to anybody! I'm in charge here. Now, I've offered you a nice little arrangement. You be quiet and do as you're told and you go gentle into the good night. If you start to get on my nerves it's the petrol can. Fair enough?"

"Fair enough," I said.

"Right, well I'll say goodbye then, Sean. Another team will be along in a few hours to take you out of here. The big lad here will be watching you until they come. His instructions are very clear: if you cry out or move from that chair he'll shoot you on the spot. If you try to bribe him or try to talk your way out of it or ask for a glass of water or open your mouth at all he'll shoot on the spot. That's clear, isn't it?"

"Very clear."

"Good. Come on, lads."

Everyone left the room except for the Big Lad. I could hear

him breathing and turning the pages of a newspaper. I waited for a count of two hundred after they'd gone before I tried speaking to him.

"What are you reading?" I attempted.

"Sport."

"Oh yeah? I'm a big Hugh McIlvanney fan myself."

"Not that. *Roy of the Rovers.*"

I wanted to connect with the Big Lad but I wasn't exactly a regular reader of *Roy of the Rovers.*

"Haven't read it for a while. Is Ben Galloway still Roy's manager?"

"Ben Galloway?"

"Yeah, sort of a Bill Shankly figure?"

"Bill Shankly?"

"The Liverpool manager?"

"Are you a Liverpool fan?" he asked.

"Yeah, are you?"

The Big Lad got up from his chair and leaned real close to my head. "I'm Man United. Fucking hate Liverpool. And I fucking hate you, Duffy."

He banged the jerry can off the side off my head. "You want this petrol all over your fucking face?"

"No."

"One more word out of you and it's human torch time. Get me?"

"Aye. I get you."

Several hours later a different five-man team took me from the Big Lad and threw me in the boot of a big Volvo Estate.

There was much discussion and some argument and finally they got going and drove me way out into the middle of nowhere into the yellow dark, the red dark, and the deep blue dark . . .

16: OUT HERE IN THE WOODS

I had fallen and I couldn't breathe and they were going to shoot me. All I had to do was close my eyes and await the nothingness. How easy that would be.

And I was so tired after all these years of this.

Being a peeler.

Being a peeler in the police force with the highest mortality rate in the world. Hated by all sides. Your life on the line every day. It was no surprise that it was ending this way. In a shallow grave in the woods. Killed by half-baked, unprofessional PIRA volunteers: a geography teacher, a stupid young man and a silly girl.

Close my eyes, check out, leave them all behind . . .

But Emma.

Emma's face.

And Beth.

Open my eyes. Hoist myself up onto my knees. In front of me black soil and under it a line of chalk and under that . . .

"You have to give me a moment to make my contrition!" I demanded.

"What did you say?" the woman asked.

"You have to give me a moment to make my contrition. And then you can shoot me in a State of Grace," I said, breathing deep, clearing my lungs and clasping my hands together in prayer.

"He's a Catholic?" the woman asked, shocked.

"Didn't you know?" Tommy said.

"No. I thought he was a Prod."

"He's the lowest form of life there is that walks this earth. A Catholic RUC man," Tommy snarled.

"Allow me to make my peace, for God's sake," I said.

Hard-to-read expressions behind balaclavas, but she seemed upset and the other kid wasn't too happy either.

"Please! I'm from Derry, like you. Please. You have to give me a chance to make my peace," I said, breathing in hard again, clearing my lungs and shuffling closer to the chalky ground.

"No, pal. There's going to be no last-minute confession, no contrition, no State of Grace for you," Tommy said and raised the revolver.

"What would Dr Martin say about that?" I attempted, naming the headmaster of St Malachy's where Tommy could have been a teacher.

The revolver twitched. Tommy's eyes widened under the mask.

A lucky guess.

The woman looked at Tommy and then back at me.

"What did you say?" she asked.

"We know all about you Tommy, who you work for, we've been watching all of you," I said.

"You've been watching us?" the woman said, aghast.

"What else does he know?" the young man asked.

"He doesn't know fucking anything!" Tommy said. "He's just playing for time."

I put my hands together in prayer. They were still sore from the handcuffs but I'd been uncuffed for almost ten minutes now and the blood had returned to my fingertips. "It's too late for me, I can see that," I began. "But you'se are all going to go down for killing me. For certain. Now if you don't mind I'm just going to compose myself: *actiones nostras, quaesumus Domine, aspirando*

*praeveni et adiuvando prosequere: ut cuncta nosta oratio et oper-
atio a te semper incipiat et per ta coepta finiatur . . ."*

The woman was looking at me, appalled, she would have
been even more appalled if she knew that this was the prayer
before action, not the prayer before death.

I leaned forward towards the big piece of flint lying there in
the chalk.

Strange stuff, flint. No one really knows how it's made or
where it comes from. Without it the Neolithic revolution in the
British Isles wouldn't have happened. No hand axes, no spears.
No Newgrange, no Stonehenge.

Flint.

The young man took the .45 from her and walked towards
me. He pointed it at my head.

"Shut the fuck up with them words! Now talk. How do you
know all this shit about Tommy and him being at St Malachy's
and Dr Martin?"

I looked at him. "You know what the penalty is for killing a
peeler? You get an automatic life sentence and they'll give you a
thirty-five-year tariff before they can even consider parole. You
won't be out of prison until 2023. How old will you be then?
Sixty?"

Tommy looked at the others and shook his head. "He's bluff-
ing. He has no idea who we are and no one else has any idea
either."

"Your whole plan has been fucking compromised, if there
even was a plan. I only arrived in Derry yesterday. Isn't a honey
trap usually planned well in advance? This was a last-minute
operation. And since when did the IRA kill coppers and bury
them in the woods? You disappear traitors. You bury informers
in the woods but policemen you *display*, don't you?"

"Yeah, what the fuck are we doing up here? Why didn't we
just shoot him and leave him in a sheugh outside of town?" the
young man asked.

"They want me vanished forever. No murder inquiry, no body, they want me wiped from history. Why is that? Who are you really doing this bit of dirty work for?"

The young man let the .45 drop to his side and turned to face Tommy. "Aye. This whole thing's a big bollocks, so it is. Answer us, Tommy. What are we doing up here in the mid—"

The edge of the flint thumped into his calf and he went down like a poleaxed gazelle. He fell sideways and I threw the big piece of flint at Tommy and hurled the spade after it. The kid was screaming so hard I must have severed a tendon. I jumped on top of him, rolled him, easily grabbed the .45 from his hand and kept rolling, expecting the .38 slugs to come roaring towards my head.

But Tommy was too slow. Glacial. Standing there flinching, trying to compute his comrade's cry of pain, trying to under-stand the flint's trajectory, trying desperately to grasp what had just happened.

The big piece of flint and the spade missed him by a mile and when he finally understood what was happening and his eyes cleared, he saw me on one knee pointing the black army-issue .45 at him. He raised the .38 and was surprised again when a hole appeared in his sport jacket under the pocket. A small hole in the front and a massive exit wound in the back through which came bits of ribs and lungs and heart.

A heart shot from a .45 at this range was almost instant death but I shot him again anyway in the head and his skull shattered like a coconut ventilated by a claw hammer.

The young man was clearly paralysed by the flint but to be on the safe side I shot off his right knee cap.

Only her left, but foolishly she started to run and I had no choice. The first shot missed but then I nailed her in the back and she went down like poor dead Mairéad Farrell falling for-ever in that car park back in Gib.

I got to my feet and walked towards her. The round had taken her in the left-hand side near the small of the back. I turned her over and I saw that she was bleeding out to the right of her belly button. There was no place to put a tourniquet. She looked at me desperately but I shook my head. Keeping an eye on her writhing, screaming friend, I knelt beside her and took her hand.

"You fucking fuck, Duffy," she said.

"Yeah."

"You fucking bastard," she said, sobbing.

"I'm sorry."

"Like fuck you are," she said squeezing the hand, hard.

"Do you want a benediction?"

"No . . . Yes."

I took off the balaclava. She was a blonde with green eyes. About twenty-eight years old. She looked nice and intelligent too. Such a fucking waste.

"What's your name?"

"Karen."

I made the sign of the cross and said quickly: "Here lies Karen. *Ave Maria, gratia plena, Dominus tecum. Benedicta tu in mulieribus, et benedictus fructus ventris tui, Iesus. Sancta Maria, Mater Dei, ora pro nobis peccatoribus, nunc, et in hora mortis nostrae.*"

I thought she would be dead by "mother of God" but amazingly she was hanging in there. I looked at the exit wound again.

What the hell? The blood was oozing out rather than haemorrhaging. The big .45 round had somehow missed all the major blood vessels. It had winged her, catching only fat and stomach. She must be under the fucking protection of St Jude. I ran back to Tommy, picked up the .38 and ripped the jacket off his back. I ran back to Karen. "I think you're going to live," I said and pushed the jacket down hard on the exit wound.

"I don't believe you," she groaned, her eyes wide, wanting to believe it.

I took her hand again and squeezed. "I think you're going to make it. By all rights a big calibre round like that should have torn you up inside but somehow it missed all the major blood vessels."

"I'm bleeding like fuck!"

"Of course you are but it's not arterial bleeding. Hold that jacket over the wound and don't try to move."

I let go of her hand.

"Don't leave me!"

"I have to go. Your mates will have been expecting one gun shot, perhaps two, but not four. The .45 made a racket that you could hear for miles."

"Don't leave me!"

"You'll be OK. Keep the pressure on the wound, OK?"

"OK."

"Now listen to me: when they come they're probably going to want to move you. If they move you you'll start to haemorrhage and you'll bleed to death before they can get you to a hospital. Do you understand?"

"I understand."

"What's your blood type?"

"B positive."

"OK, I'll go and get help."

"Duffy . . . Sean, what if . . . what if, they want to just finish me, so I don't talk, so they can get out of here?"

"Are they the sort that would do that?"

"I don't know."

I thought about it for a second.

"All right. I'll leave you the .38. If they try any funny business just fucking shoot them. And don't fucking shoot me as I'm running off."

"I won't shoot you," she said.

I put the .38 in her right hand and for a split second the barrel was pointing right at me but she didn't pull the trigger.

"Hang tight. And tell your young friend there to hang tight.

He'll live too," I said and ran off into the forest, circling round through the trees to the right, well off the trail.

Going downhill without a gun in your back made this little trek an entirely different experience.

My asthma didn't play up in the slightest.

A lovely old wood – in spring it would be full of bluebells.

When I reached the fire-break at the bottom of the hill, I could see two men arguing with one another.

Both of them were carrying shotguns. Nope, correction, one of them was carrying an AK-47.

I decided not to try to intercept them or attack them or arrest them. If anything went wrong and that guy opened up with the AK I was toast. Burnt-soda-bread-full-of-holes toast lying in the bottom of a sheugh.

Arrest would be nice in theory. But they would never talk. No one ever talks. And I wasn't going to push my luck.

I drifted deeper into the forest and kept going south until I reached the car park.

No one was here now, but there was the big stolen Volvo estate they'd brought me in. I looked through the window and didn't find a key but the door was open and those big Volvos from the late 70s had an easy-to-smash plastic dash and steering column.

In a manner that would have impressed the best teenage car thief, I had smashed the plastic, sparked the car and got the steering lock off in under two minutes.

I took a sniff of the dangling Pine Barrens air freshener to get the smell of blood and death out of my nostrils.

I drove out of the car park and headed north until I saw a road sign for Derry. It was so early that traffic was non-existent and in fourth gear I managed to get the big old diesel Volvo up to 75 mph. I tried Radio 1 but it was all Whitesnake and Billy Ocean and George Michael and Cheap Trick.

I drove to Strand Road RUC like a banshee on her broom

and was about to go into the station when I thought better of it, accelerated past the cop shop, drove up Asylum Street and towards the Bogside.

Squeal of breaks and a three-gear down shift and I stopped at a house in Heaney Street. I ran down the drive and rang the bell. I kept ringing it until Ken Kirkpatrick opened the door holding an ancient-looking pistol.

He recognised me immediately, even though it had been nearly fifteen years.

"Sean Duffy," he began. "I never thought I'd see the likes of you again. Not after you'd taken the King's shilling."

Arses like Ken Kirkpatrick were always coming out with old-timey phrases like "taken the King's shilling", but I had no time for his bullshit today. Ken Kirkpatrick was the Provisional IRA quartermaster general for Derry and as such was the number 3 or number 4 IRA man in the whole city.

"Kitchen, now," I said and marched into the house.

"What do you want, Duffy?" Ken said following me into the back kitchen.

"Listen, Ken, I got lifted last night by an IRA active service unit, taken to a derelict house, interrogated and then they took me out to Glenblane Forest to shoot me this morning. They fucked it up. I killed one of your men and shot one of them in the knees and a wee lassie in the back. There's two more of them up there. The woman is bleeding to death. She needs a couple of pints of B positive blood and she needs to go to a hospital. If you go now you can get a team there and save her."

"What?"

I slapped my hand on the kitchen table. "Fucking wake up, Ken! Glenblane Forest. One of your ASUs tried to kill me. I turned the tables and there's a girl called Karen bleeding to fucking death. B positive blood. Did you get all that in your skull?"

"Yes, I got it!"

"Make some fucking phone calls! I'll leave the room. If you need more details I'll be in the bloody lounge."

I went into the living room and sat on a musty leather sofa.

Quiet in here. Ticking grandfather clock, old bookcase full of nineteenth-century hardbacks, family portraits . . .

Exhausted.

So very tired . . .

Don't go to . . .

Don't . . .

A hand on my shoulder.

Ken shaking me awake.

"Sean, here's a mug of tea. Way you like it. Milk, two sugars, am I right?"

"That's right. Thanks. Was I asleep?"

"You've been asleep for an hour."

I sipped the tea and looked at Ken. Pale as a ghost, chubby, his ginger hair now almost entirely gone. He had run to fat and baldness like his da.

"Can I ask you something, Sean?"

"Sure."

"Why didn't you go to the police?"

"Is everything sorted? Did you get the girl?"

"We got her. We brought the team in. The lad's going to be fine too. They're both in Altnagelvin Hospital."

"What did you tell the hospital?"

"We'll say it was a punishment shooting gone wrong, we found both of them by the side of the road."

"What'll you say about the dead man?"

"We'll think of a cover story. Accidental discharge of a firearm, something like that. Why didn't you go to the RUC, Sean?"

"The police would have taken all day to comb the forest for the ASU. They probably would have waited until they could get army back-up. The girl would have bled to death."

"What's that to you? They were trying to kill you, weren't they?"

I shook my head. "I don't know, Ken, I've seen enough death. Been responsible for enough death."

"But you'd be a big hero in the RUC. Not many peelers survive hits like that."

"Who wants to be a hero? And hero at the expense of some wee lassie's life?"

"This is yours," he said, handing me my wallet, police ID, watch and even my gun.

"Jesus! I wasn't expecting . . . thanks," I said. "Where did this come from?"

"It was dropped off. By the uh . . . at the highest levels."

"I appreciate it."

"So what will you tell the police about what happened today?"

"Not much I can tell them after coming here."

"You're not going to mention any of this to anyone?"

"I won't if you won't."

"We won't."

"Then I won't. I'm compromised now. Coming to your house. Not going to the station. Nah, I'd rather this whole little operation went away. Better for the cops not to be even more suspicious of me. And better that I don't become a fat revenge target for the Derry brigade of the IRA," I said, emphasising these last words.

Ken nodded slowly. "Even though you killed one of our operatives I think the consensus in Derry will be that the local brigade of the IRA is in your debt."

"Thanks, Ken. I don't want to become a *special project* of the dead man's family."

"I'll see that you don't. No one from the Derry Brigade or from Tommy Flaherty's family will be looking for revenge. Sound OK?"

"Sounds OK."

I could tell there was something else he wanted to say but Ken's mouth closed and he didn't finish the thought.

I drank the mug of tea and put it on the coffee table. I yawned and stretched.

"Can I call you a taxi or do anything else for you, Sean?"

"A taxi would be great, Ken. I've got my car parked on Dungiven Street."

He made the call and he walked me down the hall when the taxi arrived.

"I know we're on opposite sides, Sean, and the circumstances aren't the best but it was good to see you. You seem to be good at what you do. You're what the old men would call a *worthy opponent*."

I grimaced. "Getting caught in a rookie-mistake honey trap? I'm a worthy nothing. I'm a fucking eejit, Ken."

Again Ken's mouth opened and closed again. I looked him in the eyes but I couldn't figure him out.

The taxi honked.

I opened the front door.

Ken waved to the taxi driver and held up two fingers, meaning two minutes. He took my sleeve and led me onto the porch. He lowered his voice so that whoever was sleeping upstairs couldn't possibly hear:

"Funny thing that honey trap, Sean. I looked into it. Whole thing was organised in minutes. Do you know how long these things normally take? Weeks of preparation. Weeks."

"That is strange."

"And can I tell you something else. The order to lift you came from Dublin."

"Dublin?"

"From the top brass. From the Army Council."

"What are you talking about?"

"You've strayed into some deep waters, Sean. Operations in

Derry are always handled by the Derry Brigade but the order to lift you came from the IRA Army Council in Dublin. The top boys here weren't too happy about that, which is why it wasn't difficult to get you your wallet and gun back."

"Deep waters? What deep waters? I'm investigating a murder of a drug dealer."

"Could you have antagonised somebody in the course of your investigation?"

"I certainly annoyed the hell out of Harry Selden."

Ken shook his head. "Harry's not a major player. He doesn't have the authority to order what happened to you."

"That's what I thought. So am I in any immediate danger? I have a kid now."

"Oh?"

"A wee girl, Emma. Walking and nearly talking. I wouldn't want anything to happen to her."

Ken rubbed his chin. "There will be an internal inquiry about what happened to you. A post-mortem. It'll take a few weeks to sort everything out. I imagine you'll be safe until after that's concluded but if someone in the Army Council wants you dead I wouldn't want to be in your shoes."

I grinned at him. "Like many other people before now, Ken, this person will learn that killing me isn't so fucking easy."

We both smiled sadly at this bit of bravado.

Ken opened the front door and stepped back inside. "You didn't hear any of this from me. OK?"

"OK."

"Write down your telephone number and if I hear anything I'll give you a call."

I gave him my card and walked out to the taxi.

"Where to mate?"

"Dungiven Street."

Dungiven Street.

A really thorough look under the Beemer for bombs. A big

hit on the asthma inhaler from the glove compartment.

"I'm alive," I said.

The Beemer didn't understand but growled in sympathy when I put the key in the ignition.

I drove to Waterside Railway Station car park and pulled the Beemer into an empty spot. Early yet. Only a few people around.

I took out the picture I had in my wallet of *Michael Tramples Satan* by Guido Reni and gave a prayer of thanks to Saint Michael the Archangel, the Patron Saint of Policemen, and then another to Mary the Mother of God, who had had her hands full watching over me for the last few years.

I took out my emergency hip flask filled with a 1967 Balvenie Vintage Cask – a gift from my father on Emma's birth (we all should have such fathers). Twenty-one-year-old whisky and the removal of the imminence of death: no man on that morning anywhere in Ireland felt as glad to be drawing air as I did then.

I got out of the car and walked to the Waterside Train Station wall, and then, like Elizabeth Smart in her memoir, I sat down and wept. Ten minutes of tears. Ten solid minutes of them. The refrain of "Big Yellow Taxi" playing deep in my hippocampus.

They would have killed me. They really would have done it. And that poor man . . . that poor stupid geography-teaching man.

"Are you OK, son?" a passing nun asked me when I had just about recovered.

"Thank you, I'm fine, sister," I said, getting to my feet. "I was just having a wee moment."

She looked at the hip flask and my crumpled Che T-shirt.

"Are you a married man?" she asked, a little impertinently.

"In a way," I replied.

"Get away home to your wife then, and stay away from the

strong liquor. It is the curse of Ireland, is the strong liquor."

"Yes, sister."

Back to the Beemer.

I looked underneath it for bombs, didn't find any and put the key in the ignition. The big throaty, comforting engine roared into life. I drove cautiously out of Derry and then gunned it on the A6. By the Glenshane Pass I was doing my usual ton and change and I reached 115 mph by Maghera.

When I made it back to Coronation Road it was 8.00 but Beth was still in bed.

I stripped and climbed in beside her.

"Sean?" she said sleepily.

"It's me."

"I'm furious with you."

"Why?"

"Jeanette said you'd be late, but I didn't think you'd be out all night."

"Sorry."

"Where have you been? I was worried sick. I called John McCrabban and he thought you might be on a stake-out."

"Aye. It was something like that."

"You have to call me and let me know. Anything could have happened. I was worried, Sean!"

"I know."

"I'm serious!" she said.

"Next time I will."

"You better. I was so worried. I called John."

"You said."

"Did you have car trouble?"

"No."

"You stink of petrol."

"Oh. Yeah. Had a bit of trouble with a jerry can. Might have got some petrol on me. It was a long night."

"You'll have to shower."

"I will. Listen, Beth, I'm just going to shut my eyes for a minute. Let me lie in if I manage to drift off, will you?"

"Do you think you *can* drift off? It's a very sunny morning."

And if she said anything more I didn't hear it for sleep has always been a friend to lucky men and drowned men and those very lucky men indeed who are pulled living from the sea.

17: THE OLD FILES

I woke at noon plus forty and schlepped myself downstairs for the 1 o'clock news. Can a Mick schlepp? *I* can, so fuck off.

Beth was in Belfast, Emma at Jollytots. Don't care what Dr Havercamp said, this was a day for herb. I'll give him Lawson's piss if he does a random.

Shed. Moonshine. Resin. Joan Armatrading.

Back inside.

Cold shower. Shave. Shirt. Blue sweater. Sports jacket. Black jeans. DMs. Lucky Che T-shirt lying on the bedroom floor. Still lucky. Pet the cat. Under the Beemer for bombs. Really good look today.

Somebody in the IRA Army Council wants you dead. Why? I'm nobody. On a dead-end investigation. Had to be a reason, dig deep, dig all the way to boiling iron at the centre of the earth.

Along the sea front to Carrick RUC.

Crabbie in the Incident Room, Lawson making coffee, down-hearted because there wasn't any riot duty scheduled for the day.

"Case conference."

Crabbie and Lawson sat down and I closed the door.

"What I'm about to tell you doesn't leave this room, OK?"

"Why?" Crabbie asked suspiciously.

"I made some questionable calls in the course of an

investigation yesterday. I did it with the best of intentions to save a young woman's life."

Crabbie sighed. "I'll get us some tea and biscuits and when I've got them why don't you tell us everything, Sean?"

When I was done with the explanation Lawson's eyes were wide. Crabbie's only display of emotion had been to fill, empty and re-fill his pipe.

"So what do you think?" I said.

"I'm happy that you're still with us, Sean," Crabbie said. "That was a close one."

"It certainly was."

"But you should have gone to Strand Road police station," he said firmly.

"I concur, sir," Lawson said. "They could have at least attempted to round up the cell that kidnapped you."

"You know they would have demanded army back-up to go off on a manhunt in the forest and by the time the army had arrived the girl would have been dead and the rest of the cell probably would have escaped anyway," I said.

"But it would have been the right thing to do," Crabbie said.

I nodded. Crabbie was a policeman who would never manu-facture evidence or take fruit from the jurisprudential poison tree or knowingly break the law. Crabbie had doomed-Edward-ian-expeditions-to-the-Pole concepts of rectitude and discipline.

But he was also an old friend now and I could see the emotion behind his eyes. If he'd known Ken Kirkpatrick he would have done exactly the same thing. He would have saved the girl too.

"How much danger are you in now, do you think, Sean?" he asked, blowing pipe smoke towards the ceiling.

Lawson said nothing, his head still spinning from all of this.

"I don't know. I really don't know. Ken Kirkpatrick says there will be an internal inquiry following yesterday's events. He says I'll probably have a week or two until this person in the Army Council is able to act again. She's only just come back, but I'm going to ask Beth to take Emma away and stay with her parents."

"A sensible precaution for starters," Crabbie said. "But maybe for your own good you should report what happened to Special Branch."

"You know what they'd do to me. Disciplinary proceedings and then the sack. And then possibly criminal charges for aiding and abetting a terrorist suspect."

"That's probably true," Crabbie said. "But if the IRA are gunning for you?"

"The IRA are gunning for all of us, all the time, and as a Catholic peeler I've had that bounty on my head for fifteen years."

"Do you want to come and stay with me? Way out on the farm no one can get close without us hearing their car."

"That's the one advantage I have of living on Coronation Road. It would be the bold IRA team that comes down there trying to kill me deep in Loyalist turf."

"Aye, although don't forget Francis Deauville. Somebody got him. Somebody got him with medieval technology," Crabbie said.

"First things first, I'll get Beth and Emma to safety and then I'll weigh up my options."

"We need to figure out what this all means," Lawson said.

"We bloody do," I agreed. "And quick."

"As I see it the honey trap was not a random crime of opportunity. It wasn't designed to lift a policeman, it was designed to lift a specific policeman: you. And there's only one reason why, really, because you were getting too close to Harry Selden."

"Which means that Harry, despite being in a coma, was somehow involved in the murder of Francis Deauville," Crabbie said.

"We're sure he was definitely in the hospital?" Lawson asked.

"Yup, we are. Interviewed his doctors and his nurses. It was him and before you ask, no, he doesn't have a twin brother, or any other brother for that matter," I said.

"And on Harry Selden's say-so the IRA Army Council ordered a hit on you? Is Selden really that important?" Crabbie asked.

I shook my head. "I don't understand it. Ken Kirkpatrick says he's only a minor player. He says he's not even a particularly big cheese in Derry. And he's certainly not on the IRA Army Council like ****** ***********."

"So what could this be about?" Crabbie asked.

"It's *something* to do with Selden. And it's something to do with this case we're working on. And it's something to do with Selden and Deauville working together in the B Specials all those years ago."

"We better get moving then, Sean. This is urgent, I'll get my coat," Crabbie said.

I smiled at him. "Where do you think we're going?

"I think we're going to Belvoir Park Records Office where they keep the files on the B Specials and after that I think we're all driving up to Derry to talk to Mr Selden."

"What say you, Lawson?" I asked.

"You know my motto, sir: all for one and one for all."

"My motto is: don't trust whitey and whitey is everywhere in this fucking town. Let's keep all this quiet for now."

BMW. Radio 3. A2. M5. South Belfast.

The nice part of Belfast.

Parks, the Lagan, trees, attractive houses spilling down to the water's edge. You'd hardly think there was a war going on.

"You'd hardly think there was a war going on," I said.

"This is what it's like on my farm," Crabbie said. "If we didn't have TV we could be living in the good old days."

Belvoir Park Records Office was in the same complex as the Belvoir Park Forensic Science Laboratory. A top-notch, modern, state of the art facility for processing evidence from all the criminal cases in Northern Ireland and even some cases from Scotland and the Republic of Ireland too.

A few years after our visit a 3,000-pound IRA truck bomb,

that you could hear up to twenty miles away, reduced the entire structure to rubble, but that was in the future and on this particular March morning everything was shiny, sparkling and new.

The B Special records were in a sub-basement in old cardboard files that were covered with dust and mildew. If someone in RUC Clerical had really cared about preserving these records they would have been transferred to microfiche, but no one gave a shit about the B Specials, who'd been in them and what they had done.

The librarian, an ancient WPC called Fogerty, took us to the shelf stacks and explained that the records were alphabetised by last name.

"That should be easy enough to sort out," I said.

But, of course, it wasn't.

Harry Selden's cardboard file was there all right, under S, but the paper documentation inside the file was missing. Francis Deauville's cardboard file was there all right, but the paper documentation inside the file was also missing.

WPC Fogerty was perplexed. "I don't understand it," she said. "Even if they never made a single arrest or ever even turned up for duty, at the very least there should be date of birth, height, weight, home address, total pay, date of swearing-in and date of discharge."

I showed her the empty files. "There's not even a blank piece of paper. There's nothing at all. Is that usual?"

"I don't know. I've never really looked through these files."

"Let's do some random sampling."

We looked through thirty or forty random B Special personnel and not a single one of them was completely empty and most had several pages of documentation detailing the reserve policeman's arrests, etc.

"This is most unusual," WPC Fogerty said.

"Who has access to these files?" I asked.

"Anyone who has access to the records building. As soon as

you're inside all you have to do is walk down the stairs to the basement."

"And who has access to this building?"

"Anyone with a police, army or grade 4 civil service ID would have access," she said.

"So that would be how many people in Northern Ireland?" I asked.

"Thousands," she said.

"Tens of thousands," Lawson corrected.

"If you wanted to take a file with you, how would you do that?"

"Oh, you can't take these files out of the building. You can photocopy them if you want but they can't leave the building. I make sure everyone's aware of that and you have to come past the librarian's desk when you leave."

"But what's to stop you just walking out with the contents of the files rolled up in a newspaper or shoved in your pocket?"

"No one's ever stolen a file," she protested.

"Au contraire, WPC Fogerty. Someone indeed has stolen the files of Francis Deauville and Harry Selden. What about CCTV cameras on the front gate?"

"Well yes, but we have 200 personnel in here and we get thousands of visitors to the RUC, RIC and army records rooms upstairs."

"Would you have any idea when these files could have been removed?" I asked.

"No. They could even have been taken from the old RUC HQ building before we moved here a year ago. And the records department there was open access. No cameras. Just flashed your ID to the security guard."

"So even if I got young Lawson here to go through the CCTV footage from the front gate checking every single visitor you've ever had in this facility—"

"Why me?" Lawson protested.

". . . ever had in his facility to see if any of them are suspicious, and I don't even know how he would possibly determine that, it wouldn't actually make any difference because the files could have been removed from the old RUC HQ building, where there were no CCTV cameras in the records department?"

"That's right."

I sighed. "And there are no copies anywhere else?"

"No," WPC Fogerty said.

"Thank you very much WPC Fogerty, you've been very helpful," I said.

Outside to the Beemer. Even in the police forensic lab car park I got down on my knees to check for mercury tilt switch bombs.

We had an early lunch in Belfast and then decided to drive up to Derry for what felt like the millionth time in this investigation.

Brave face on it for the lads, but the fear.

The fucking fear.

Deep waters.

Hits ordered in from Dublin.

Hit pieces in the newspapers.

What kind of a case was this? Who wanted it to end? And why?

Need time. If I have time.

Get Beth and Emma out of the house and think.

Think, think, think.

Drive and think.

Crabbie was sitting next to me in the front seat going through his notes. He didn't like what he was reading there.

"What's the matter, mate?"

"I just don't see a way through this. We're in an information void. Whatever Harry Selden and Francis Deauville were up to in the B Specials will forever be a secret because Selden won't tell us and Deauville's dead."

"Do you think Deauville told his wife and that's why she's disappeared?" Lawson asked.

"That's what the killer thought, anyway. Even if she didn't know. The poor wee lass was silenced because she might have known," Crabbie said.

I was fed up with the same old roads, so at Claudy I cut over onto the Longland Road to go into the city via Strabane and the A5. It was on that lonely stretch of nothingness through the bleak treeless foothills of the Sperrins that I noticed a car on our tail.

"We're being followed," I said.

Crabbie looked in the mirror. The car was a black Ford Escort XR3i. We both knew what that meant. "Aye I see it," he said.

"Oh my God! Is it the IRA? Are they going to get us?" Lawson said, alarmed.

I patted the Beemer's steering wheel. "I'd like to see them try to get us. But no, it isn't the IRA, son, it's the bloody Special Branch."

"It's policemen? Maybe it's just the traffic police."

"No, it isn't traffic. They're in plain clothes. Now why are they following me do you think, Crabbie?"

"I wouldn't like to speculate," Crabbie said.

"Me neither. Look at them. They think they're being terribly discreet. Is there a seat belt back there, Lawson?"

"Yeah."

"Put it on. I'm going to lose the bastards in Strabane."

"Sean, is that wise?" Crabbie asked.

"If any of us were wise we would have chosen a different profession. Now be a good 'un and click my seat belt for me, will ya?"

Crabbie clicked in my seat belt and did his own belt too.

"What are you going to do, Sean?" he asked.

"I'm just going to lose them. We don't need meddling from those boys."

"If you say so. How will you do it?"

"Just before Strabane proper there's a wee road through a

housing development, I think it's called the Wood-something Road – there's a hill that obscures the view and at the end of that there's a sharp turn onto the A5 going into Derry. If you know what you're doing you can lose them on the Wood-something Road, scream onto the A5 and be halfway into Derry before they know what's hit them."

"If you're going to do that slow down now. Get them accustomed to a lower speed in top gear," he suggested.

"Good idea, mate, I'll cruise along in third."

"What are youse doing? You're running from Special Branch? That can't be a good idea," Lawson said.

I downshifted to third gear and reduced my speed to 40 mph. The Ford Escort reduced its speed and dropped way back to avoid being seen.

We came to a small hill just after the village of Artigarvan. We were a mile and a half from the A5 turn. This was the moment. On the reverse slope of the hill I'd gun it.

I crested the hill and as soon as the Ford disappeared in the rear-view mirror I pushed down hard on the accelerator pedal. The BMW screamed up towards 60 mph. I hit fourth gear and now we were doing 70. The outskirts of Strabane went past in a blur and the A5 turn came faster than I was expecting.

A Tayto Crisps lorry was coming towards the junction. I could either hard-brake, stop and let it pass or try to beat it. If we stopped the goons would catch us.

"A lorry!" Lawson screamed.

"Damn it," I yelled and gunned the engine and drove through into the junction in a horrible fishtail of screaming tyres and honking horns. I accelerated hard away from the crisps lorry, waved a friendly apology to the driver, switched to fifth gear and in thirty seconds we were going north east at 100 mph.

The Ford Escort was nowhere to be seen.

"All right back there?" I asked Lawson.

He tried to reply but couldn't quite manage it. McCrabban

showed no visible change of emotion.

I parked the BMW outside Harry Selden's house but when I rang the doorbell his mother, who appeared to be in rude good health, said that he was at a council meeting. We found him at his office in the Guildhall and a pleasant young secretary told us we could wait and that he would be along presently.

Harry Selden was not pleased to see us when he eventually showed up.

"Inspector Duffy and I see you've brought a couple of body-guards with you," he said mirthlessly. He was wearing a blue checked seersucker jacket and checked trousers over a shirt that seemed too tight on him. His tie was black like his fucking heart. Definitely no Oliver Hardy vibe today but perhaps there was a hint of northern working-man's-club comic. I asked if we could talk in his office.

"You can have five minutes," he said. "I'm a busy man."

We went inside his office, which was a tastefully decorated job overlooking the River Foyle. Big comfy leather chairs, nice big desk, nice watercolours. You could do good work sucking money out of the Brits in this office.

"So what is it now?" Selden asked.

"I suppose you already know that after we had our little chat I was abducted by the IRA."

"I don't know what you're talking about," he said, looking me, rather impressively, straight in the eye. He held my gaze but only for a three count and then his gaze shifted to his feet.

Christ, the guy was no poker player. Give me two days with him in an interrogation suite and I'd have him singing "When The Saints Go Marching In" and the name of every girl he necked in the back row of the Regal Cinema. Lifting a Sinn Fein councillor wouldn't be easy though, without any evidence. Not impossible, of course, but not easy.

"Well, as you can see, your chums weren't able to give me a hole in the back of the head."

"No? How'd you escape? Magic powers?"

"Just a bit of luck, actually."

"You should write fiction, inspector."

"Fiction is redundant around here, don't you think? Reality is so much worse. I was kidnapped, probably at your orders."

"You've a great imagination, pal."

"I've got a terrible imagination. That's why I'm living in Northern Ireland in the 1980s. Anybody with any imagination would have hightailed it out of here long ago."

"Yeah, well, you can piss off now."

"What's the next trick? Another smear attack in the press, or you going to try and get to me in Carrick?"

"I despair, really, I do," Harry said and gave Lawson and McCrabban a sigh. "Can youse talk sense into him? I've looked into this case of yours. I don't for the life of me see why you are trying to drag me into it. I was in hospital in Derry with blood poisoning when they shot this drug dealer fella in Carrickfergus. Teleportation is not one of my gifts."

"Your car was in Carrick tailing the dead man."

"My stolen car."

"There can't have been many Catholics in the B Specials back in 1968," I said.

"Oh it's back to this again, is it?"

"It's back to this again."

"You're one to talk about Catholics in the police."

"Touché, Harry. What did you and Frank Deauville get up to together in the B Specials in 1968?"

"I never heard of this Frank Deauville before you started bleating on about him."

"That's not what your file says," I attempted.

A smile flitted across his lips.

He knew. He fucking knew the files were gone. His file. Deauville's file. Harry knew.

"What file's that?" he asked.

I said nothing and as I guessed he would, he filled the dead air with more nonsense: "Are you talking about my old police records? What do they say?"

I got up from the comfy leather sofa. Lawson and McCrabban got up too.

"We'll see ourselves out," I said.

"Is that it?" he asked.

"You'll be hearing from us again," I said.

"No I won't. That's harassment. Next time you want to talk to me, you can talk to my solicitor first."

I nodded, said goodbye to the secretary and walked down the stairs with Lawson and Crabbie.

When we were safely back in the Beemer, Crabbie shook his head and lit his pipe.

"Aye," he said.

"Yeah," I agreed.

"What?" Lawson said. "What did I miss?"

"He knew about the missing file. The question is how?" McCrabban said.

"How indeed?"

18: INFERNAL AFFAIRS

Home to Coronation Road. Emma excited to see her Da-da-da, Beth in good form reading *Ubik* while I made the tea: spagbol for everyone, Chilean red and garlic bread for me and B.

After dinner we took Emma up the road for a walk.

"The man in that house builds ships. The man in that house was a prisoner of the Japanese. The man in that house has a pet lion," I said.

"The woman in that house makes gin in her bathtub. The woman in that house is divorced and has a huge crush on Daddy," Beth said.

I put Emma to bed and when I came downstairs Beth was thumbing through my albums.

Time for The Talk.

Don't mention the kidnapping or the promise of being burned alive or the dead man or shooting a girl in the back.

Don't mention the fear.

The fear in the chair.

The fear in the walk up the hill.

The fear that the men will, in due course, try it all again.

Secrets.

Secrets were poison. Especially in the six counties: a fake world built on fantasies, secrets and dissimulation.

But sometimes you needed to dissimulate.

"Is this Steve Reich any good?" she asked, holding up a record.

"Do you like xylophones?"

"God no!"

I took the record from her. "Listen, Beth, there's this threat thing that has come down from intel. It's against my life. Nothing to get panicky about but it's against me personally not just against the police in general. We don't know if it's real or not, but I'd prefer it if you and Em moved back in with your folks for a few days. "

"We only just moved back here!"

"I know."

"This isn't your way of kicking us out, is it? I didn't like being away from you, Sean. I tried it and I didn't like it."

"That's good to hear. I'm not kicking you out. I hate being away from you and Emma, but this is some scary stuff."

She nodded and bit her lip. She understood.

"One question. If it's too dangerous for us to stay here, why are you staying here?"

"It's not too dangerous. Nothing's going to happen. This is just a precaution. If someone is lunatic enough to drive by the house and maybe try and have a go I want you and Emma well out of it. Nothing is likely to happen, but I'd be able to handle everything better knowing that both of you are safe."

She was tearing up now. She put her arms round me. I hugged her and carried her to the sofa. "How long for?"

"I don't know. A few weeks maybe. Until I put this investigation to bed. I've stirred up something strange, something deep."

"When do we have to move?"

"You'll have to go by the weekend. The threat becomes a bit more imminent after the weekend."

"What does that mean?"

"I can't really explain, but you should go sooner rather than later."

"I have my last tutorial tomorrow and then we're off for the term. I could have my dad come with one of his vans the day after."

"You don't have to take all your stuff. But, yeah, the day after tomorrow is a good idea."

"OK, Sean, if that's what you want," she said sadly.

"Don't worry. It's probably nothing. We get this sort of thing all the time. It's always bollocks."

"And after that I want to look at permanently moving away from here."

"I've already agreed to that. I'm a man of my word."

She kissed me on the lips. "That you are," she said.

The next day I got up early and made everyone pancakes for breakfast. I dropped Emma off at Jollytots and Beth down at the train station.

I drove to the barracks feeling gloomy.

Lawson was waiting for me with a cup of coffee in the car park. Whenever Crabbie sent Lawson down to the car park to wait for me with a cup of coffee it was invariably because there was bad news waiting for me upstairs that he wanted to warn me about.

"Oh shit, what now? I haven't failed another physical, have I?"

"No. It's not that, sir. There are two men in your office."

"What two men?"

"They wouldn't say."

"How'd they get in? What if it's an IRA hit squad or one of those stripograms?"

"They're policemen."

"All stripograms are policemen."

"I think they might be Special Branch."

"So ugly stripograms."

I was trying to get a smile out of Lawson but it wasn't working.

"Gimme that coffee."

Coffee. Asthma inhaler. Stairs.

Four men in my office: two goons from the internal investigation unit of Special Branch (one called McWhirter and a
Jock called Nelson whom I'd encountered before); our ineffec-
tual union rep, Sergeant Price, and Chief Inspector McArthur.
McWhirter had a flasher vibe about him – skinny and pale and
I'll bet his hands sweated something chronic. Nelson had a face
like Brian Clough getting sodomised with a pineapple.

"Were you boys having a séance?" I asked.

"Maybe for your days as a free man," Nelson said.

"That doesn't make any sense," I said, shooing him out of my
good swivel chair.

"This is serious, Sean," McArthur said.

Nelson handed me a manila envelope.

"Is this an invitation to your birthday party?"

"Open the envelope and then we'll see who's laughing,"
Nelson said.

I opened the envelope. It was a series of photographs of me
going into Ken Kirkpatrick's house.

"A known IRA man. An old friend of yours from Derry. You
show up at his house at five in the morning. Stay for 90 minutes
then head out again. Lots of handshakes at the door," Nelson
said.

I handed the photographs back to Nelson.

"You want to explain yourself, Duffy?" McWhirter asked.

"Nope."

"I think photographs of you consorting with the IRA quartermaster for Derry is pretty fucking serious," Nelson said.

"Yeah well you shouldn't think so much, Nelson, you might
break your head."

"A plain clothes undercover team took photographs of you
going into Ken Kirkpatrick's house," McWhirter said.

"Where are the plain clothes undercover teams when you
really need them, eh?" I muttered.

"Duffy, I think you have to explain this. It looks very bad with all this talk of IRA infiltrators and—" Sergeant Price said.

"You think I'm an IRA mole? Me? I don't know whether to laugh or cry. This is what you geniuses in internal affairs have come up with?" I said, addressing the two Special Branch goons.

"A Catholic boy from Derry, who we know attempted to join the Provisional IRA after Bloody Sunday," Nelson began. "Know that for a fact from a number of sources. Who we know has had numerous disciplinary and other offences, yet mysteriously manages not to get the sack even when I personally get him to give me his resignation. Whose case files have never involved the prosecution of a single IRA man. Not one. For anything. Not so much as a parking ticket. Maybe instead of attempting to join the IRA in 1972 you did in fact—"

"March zipped by, didn't it? I didn't realise it was April the first already," I said.

"Did in fact join the IRA and have been working for the Provisionals ever since," Nelson said.

"If I were a mole wouldn't it be smarter to have me prosecute a few low-ranking IRA guys and have me rise up the ranks in the RUC? Wouldn't it be more efficacious for me to join the intel branch or, here's a thought, Special Branch?"

"You might not be the only one. There might be dozens of you," Nelson said.

I looked at Sergeant Price and McArthur.

"You don't have to say anything without a solicitor present, Sean," Sergeant Price reminded me.

I pulled out a bottle of whisky from my desk drawer. "Can all of you gentlemen please leave my office? I have work to do."

"Sean, these men have come all the way from Castlereagh to put these allegations to you," McArthur said.

"And they can go all the way back to Castlereagh."

"You're not even going to attempt an explanation?" Nelson said.

"An explanation? I was doing police work. You should fucking try it some time."

"Why did you evade us yesterday?" McWhirter asked.

"What do you mean?"

"We were following your car on the Strabane Road," McWhirter said.

"Were you? I never noticed. You must have been doing an amazing job. Normally I'm pretty observant about these things. Now listen, I'm a busy man, so unless you've got an arrest warrant in another brown envelope, which I don't think you have . . . well then, you know, fuck off."

Nelson stood and put the manila envelope under his arm. "This time it won't be you getting the sack, pal, it'll be you getting the sack and then going to the old grey bar hotel. You could be looking at twenty years, Duffy. But don't worry, I hear they treat policemen really well inside. We'll be talking again," he said.

"I don't think we will."

Nelson and McWhirter left and I waved Sergeant Price away with them.

That only left the Chief Inspector. He took the seat opposite me and refused a drink when offered.

"What's all this about, Sean?"

"This guy in Derry, Harry Selden, he's up to his neck in the Deauville murder case. I went to an old friend of mine, Ken Kirkpatrick, to get the lowdown on Selden."

"Is this Kirkpatrick chap in the IRA?"

"He is, but he's a friend of mine who has helped me out with info in the past. He gave me some good stuff about Selden."

"Well?"

"Selden is a low-level IRA commander and a medium-level Sinn Fein politician. Ken filled me in on all that."

"What does he have to do with the Deauville case?"

"Quite a lot, I think. Deauville and Selden served together

in the B Specials. And Selden's car was seen following the Deauvilles shortly before Mr Deauville's murder. He claimed it had been stolen. He wasn't driving it because he was in the hospital, but I don't like the coincidence."

"Who *was* driving the car?"

"We don't have eyewitness testimony because our eyewitness, Elena Deauville, has vanished."

"What about that artist's sketch you have?"

"Looks nothing like Selden."

McArthur leaned back in the chair, put his head in his hands and sighed. "Special Branch thinking one of my men is an IRA infiltrator? The timing is awful," he muttered.

"Yeah I know, I'm sorry, sir, what with your promotion board coming up."

He hadn't meant to say that out loud and he was embarrassed now. He stood up, straightened his tie.

He leaned on the desk and looked at me. "Man to man, you're not an IRA mole are you, Duffy?" he asked.

I almost laughed in his face. Laughter of despair this time. If senior policemen thought moles could be found by simply asking them outright it was pretty worrying. And if even McArthur thought I might be a mole, what the fuck had I achieved here at Carrickfergus RUC? What had I achieved in my entire police career? Nicking a few villains here and there while all around me King Chaos ran his Carnivale.

"No, sir, I'm not the mole."

"Good show, Duffy. I believe you."

"Thank you, sir."

"Maybe you should lie low for a bit, take the rest of the day off, couple of days maybe?"

"Won't that look rather suspicious?"

"Everything you do will look suspicious from now on but why stir the pot?"

When he'd gone I called the only influential friend I had left.

"Hello?"

"Sir, it's me, Sean Duffy, I'm sorry to bother you."

"What is it, Duffy?" the brand new Assistant Chief Constable Strong replied.

"I've just had a rather unpleasant encounter with an internal affairs team from Special Branch. Did you know about this?"

"Of course not. What's going on, Duffy?"

"They've got photos of me coming out of Ken Kirkpatrick's house in Derry. They think I'm some sort of IRA agent. It's absolute rubbish, sir. There's this Jock sergeant who's got it in for me . . . Anyway, sir, you're the only important friend I've got, I don't want to be railroaded here. They're talking about sending me to prison."

"What is this about, Duffy? What were you doing in Derry?"

"I was investigating the Deauville case."

"Have you made any progress?"

"Some. I've learned that Harry Selden and Deauville were in the B Specials together. Selden's car was seen near to Deauville's house just before the murder. The two of them are linked somehow."

"How?"

"I don't know."

"Why would this Selden character drive all the way to Carrickfergus to murder this Deauville fellow?"

"I don't know, sir."

"Do you have any eyewitnesses to the killing?"

"None, sir."

"So what exactly have you got?"

"Uhm, only the fact that Selden's car was seen following Francis Deauville before the murder."

"Who saw this?"

"Mrs Deauville."

"Hasn't she gone missing?"

"Yes, sir."

"This wasn't in her statement."

"No, sir. She told the Bulgarian translator that she saw a car following them and wrote down the number plate."

"So this is all hearsay evidence. Completely inadmissible in court."

"Yes, sir."

"Let me see if I understand you, Duffy. DAADD has claimed responsibility for this killing but instead of pursuing that angle you're following some insane lead from hearsay evidence? Is that what you're telling me?"

"Sir, they haven't actually claimed responsibility. Not formally. There's also the B Special angle. We know both men served in the B Specials because it's in their criminal record file, but when I went to look at the B Special files for Deauville and Selden to see if they had served together or done a joint arrest or anything like that, well, the files were gone, sir! Total dead end, sir."

A long silence.

"Hearsay evidence and missing files, is that what you're telling me, Duffy? And now you've been seen going into a known IRA man's house at five in the morning? And you wonder why Special Branch is interested in you, with your extremely patchy service record?"

"Sir, I—"

"Son, I'm going to have to tell you how it is. Clearly no one has told you how it is for years so I'm going to have to be the man to do it. I'm an Assistant Chief Constable now. I'm very high up the food chain. I can't afford to be dragged down by a man like you, Duffy. You've had some successes in your career but also some notable failures. If you're going to fuck this case up like you've fucked up in the past I'm going to have to cut you loose. Do you understand me, son?"

"I think so, sir."

"Can I give you a piece of advice, Duffy?"

"Of course, sir."

"File the Francis Deauville murder as an unsolved DAADD killing. Case closed pending further developments. File the Elena Deauville disappearance as a bloody missing persons case. Case closed pending further developments. Move on to other business. Don't go back to Derry. Keep your head down. Do you hear me, Duffy?"

"Yes, sir."

"Now I will see what I can do about these Special Branch detectives. But I won't be able to get the ants off your back while you're sticking your arm into the ant hill."

"Thank you, sir. I appreciate anything you can do, sir. Got a lot on my plate at the moment."

"Have less on your plate, Duffy. Close those cases, move on, don't make pointless fucking waves."

"Yes, sir, I understand sir."

"Goodbye, Duffy. Don't call me again. It's always a long-distance call up here at ACC rank. I don't think you can afford the charges."

Dialtone.

Another friendship burned. Well done, Sean. Well done.

19: LIFTED

Living room, mulling it all over. Gears turning. Patterns forming. Something told me that I'd been given everything I needed to solve the equation. It was all there. It was a complicated equation but somehow I knew that it was all there. A better detective would have put it together now. Where was Miss Marple when you needed her?

Knock at the front door. Early morning. Post-milkman but pre-starlings.

Looked through the peephole. Two goons. Didn't recognise them. One was wearing a raincoat and a dark grey suit. He had a moustache, copper hair and beady brown eyes. He was about forty. The other one was a woman about five years younger than him, with her hair in a blonde ponytail. She was wearing the uniform of an RUC Superintendent. She had odd yellowish goblin eyes.

I unhooked the lock and opened the door with my foot, coffee cup in one hand, Glock in the other.

"Yes?"

"We'd like you to come with us, Inspector Duffy," the woman said. "I'm Detective Superintendent Baker, this is Detective Sergeant O'Neill. Would you mind not pointing that gun at me?"

"I'll keep the gun pointing at you until I see some identification," I said.

They showed me two warrant cards that seemed convincing enough.

"What's this about?"

"We'd like to ask you some questions."

"What about?"

"Personnel stuff. Your record."

"Am I about to win police officer of the year?"

"Not exactly."

"Specifically what questions about my record?"

"Allegations of corruption and about your connections with the IRA," Baker said.

"I'll need to get dressed," I said.

"Can we come in?" Baker asked.

"No, you can wait in your car. I'll be five minutes," I said and closed the door.

I pulled on a pair of jeans and a sweater and left a note for Beth. "Police business. Should be back in a couple of hours."

I went to the car. Of course the anti-corruption unit was driving a brand new Mercedes Benz. No irony or integrity worries there.

"I'll sit in the front seat if you don't mind, I need to stretch my legs out," I said.

"That's fine," Baker said and got in the back.

I sat in the plush Merc seat. O'Neill checked for mercury tilt switch bombs and got in beside me. There was a tape of Willie Nelson's "Pancho and Lefty" in the player and it kicked in when he turned the engine on.

"What's the last thing you want to hear after you've given Willie Nelson a blow job?" I asked O'Neill.

"I dunno," he said.

"'I'm not Willie Nelson'," I said.

O'Neill grinned until he caught Superintendent Baker's face in the rear-view mirror.

Divide and conquer, Duffy. That's how you'll beat them. That and keeping a cool fucking head.

We drove up to Castlereagh Holding Centre and they led me down to a sub-basement interrogation suite.

Tape recorder spooling.

Water flowing in pipes.

Baleful dungeon noises.

Creepy distant heathen laughter.

The corruption stuff was bullshit and they knew it. Chicken shit rule-breaking, fiddling the over-time claims . . . it wouldn't wash, but that was only the starter.

"So, Inspector Duffy, how long have you been friends with the top brass of the Derry Brigade of the IRA?" Baker asked.

"I know a lot of people in Derry. Some of them are in the police, some of them are in the IRA, some of them actually work for a living. It's a small city. Everybody knows everybody else. Contacts are useful for a policeman, especially for a detective. Good to keep all the channels open."

Baker nodded, put a box file on the table, opened it and began looking through its contents with a bit of theatrical tut-tutting.

"What we can't figure out, Duffy, is whether you're incompetent, unlucky or whether you're working for the other side," Baker said.

"Duh, duh, duh . . . " I said, making a fake organ noise.

"The Tommy Little case no arrests, no convictions. The Lizzie Fitzpatrick case no arrests, no convictions. The Lily Bigelow case, one arrest but you allowed the suspect to escape the jurisdiction . . . do we need to continue? I think you see the pattern here," Sergeant O'Neill said.

"In 1972 you joined the IRA, didn't you? You've been working for them ever since, haven't you?" Baker said.

I held out my wrists. "That's brilliant. Absolutely brilliant. It's a fair cop, gov. Take out your notebook. I'll tell you everything."

Sergeant O'Neill did in fact take out his notebook. Baker frowned and her little goblin eyes twitched.

No one said anything and the silence worked me. I was actually getting a bit concerned now.

I attempted an ingratiating smile, which I'm sure looked ghastly.

"Come on, guys, you can't be serious. I've worked with MI5. Why don't you ask them about my loyalty!"

"Yes, MI5, that's another interesting one," Baker said, taking a photocopy of the story about the crash in the *Irish News* and pretending to read it. "Apparently you were supposed to get on that helicopter with all the top MI5 agents in Northern Ireland, that helicopter that flew into the mountain on the Mull of Kintyre. Got off at the last minute, didn't you, while all your friends in MI5 died?"

"That's not what happened. I broke my leg and the pilot wouldn't let me fly."

"Hmmmm," Baker said.

This was getting annoying. "We all know the real collusion problem in Northern Ireland," I said.

"Oh yes and what's that?" Baker asked.

"That's between Special Branch and its informers in the Loyalist paramilitaries. One day there's going to be a reckoning for all the civilians, all the Catholic civilians, you've let die in Loyalist attacks, to protect your agents."

I stood up and headed for the door.

"Where do you think you're going?" Baker asked.

"I don't have time for this. This may be how you get your kicks but I've an actual job to do. Next time you want to question me you better have an arrest warrant. And my solicitor and my union representative will need to be present. If you come to my home again I'm going straight to the newspapers. I can just see the *Guardian* headline now. 'Catholic RUC Man Harassed by Protestant Police Establishment'."

"I'm a Catholic!" O'Neill protested.

"You're an Uncle Tom, that's what you are," I said.

"You haven't heard the last of this, Duffy," Baker said.

"I don't know how things work here, but in CID before we even think about bringing a case to the Director of Public Prosecutions we have to have witnesses, chains of causation, motivation, forensic evidence. You've got none of that. You've got nothing."

"If you're a mole we'll get you."

"I'm not the bloody mole."

Door slam. Stomp along the corridor. Upstairs. Another dramatic exit.

Asthma inhaler. Played it badly. As always. Hothead.

Downstairs.

Desk Sergeant. "Can you call me a taxi, mate?"

Outside into the cold air.

Hands shaking.

Cigarette. Fucking stress.

Taxi back to Carrickfergus.

Thinking.

Thinking . . .

Newspapers . . .

Upstairs to my office. A fifth of whisky.

I called Carrick Library to confirm a fact about their collection.

I summoned Crabbie and Lawson into my office, gave them a summary of the internal-affairs accusations and what Assistant Chief Constable Strong had suggested we do with the case.

"So what are we going to do with the case?" Crabbie asked.

"I've been mulling that over. There were three prominent local newspapers printed in Belfast in the 1960s: the *Belfast Telegraph*, the *Irish News* and the *Newsletter*. There's three of us. We'll look up the names Deauville and Selden in the indexes and if nothing comes up we'll look up every incident involving the B Specials from say 1966–1969."

"That was when the Troubles were kicking off. The B Specials will be mentioned all the time. We'll practically have to read every single issue of every single paper," Lawson said.

"We better read every single issue of every single paper just to be on the safe side," Crabbie said.

"I've just checked with the librarian. Carrickfergus Library has all three papers in either hardbound or microfiche edition," I said.

"Take us weeks," Lawson said.

"We better get cracking then," Crabbie said. "I'll take the *Newsletter* if you don't mind. Good farming stories."

"I'll take the *Irish News* cos it'll be shorter than the *Telegraph*," I said.

"I'll take the *Telegraph* then," Lawson said gloomily because, as we all knew, the *Belfast Telegraph* had more pages.

"When do we start?" Lawson asked.

"No time like the present."

Seven hours library time later, exhausted and bug-eyed and without finding anything helpful I drove back home to Victoria Estate.

It was raining.

Coronation Road was quiet.

It wasn't destined to stay that way.

20: OUT OF THE SILENT PLANET

Beth had already changed into her PJs and was reading a CS Lewis science-fiction novel from the 50s. Lewis was from Belfast but you wouldn't know that if you'd ever heard him talk in the poshest voice in the world on the BBC, explaining the existence of evil or how God is able to listen to a million people praying at the same time. (God exists outside time and thus has an infinite amount of time and patience to listen to our prayers, poor sod.)

Emma was asleep upstairs. I was reading *Tristes Tropiques*. The music on the record player was Chopin.

Drizzle outside.

I looked at Beth. I wanted to tell her about my troubles but the Derry stuff would only upset her and the Special Branch investigation was nonsense. Her legs were curled up underneath her and she sat there: elfin, boyish, coiled, quiet.

Jet the cat came in and rubbed against me. With a great deal of hassle I had installed a cat flap in the back door so he could go out at night but he seldom ever went out after dark. He'd been Lily Bigelow's cat and had lived most of his life in her flat in London and wasn't that confident about patrolling these streets at night. Streets of Carrickfergus that abutted the Irish countryside and were therefore full of the smell of other cats, stray dogs, foxes and God knows what else. I petted the cat and looked at Beth.

She caught me looking.

"What?" she said. "You look worried."

"I'm not worried."

"Sean, please, come with me to my parents tomorrow. I know you're not a fan of Larne, but we don't really live in Larne, it's more Ballygally."

"I'm not worried. I've got a two-week window before I should be worried and even then I can't see anyone coming onto Bobby Cameron's turf to knock off a peeler without his permission."

"What *are* you thinking about then?"

The lie of the previous sentence? Special Branch railroading me into a jail cell? The fact that ACC Strong and CI McArthur could no longer be counted on to back me up against the bureaucrats and bullshit artists . . . Take your pick.

"CS Lewis was a good friend of Louis MacNeice, who grew up just round the corner from here. MacNeice would come back to Carrickfergus often to visit his parents and sometimes he'd bring WH Auden or CS Lewis with him. They would walk around Carrick together, maybe they even walked down this very street."

"Really?"

"Cool, huh?"

"It is, actually."

And thus distracted, Beth returned to her book.

We went to bed at midnight, checked on the girl, left food for the cat. Slept.

Three am is when they come. The Devil's Hour. When most terminal patients slip away in hospices and hospitals. When the human body is at its weakest. When even the bakers and milkmen are still asleep.

Drizzle on the quiet street and the hills beyond.

No watchers. No dog walkers. Nothing.

Cloudless night. Sickle moon. Constellations rotating about Polaris. Orion. The Great Bear. The Little Bear. Everyone asleep. But not me.

Living room. Staring at the embers. Worries. I looked for something gentle to put on the record player.

Peggy Lee. Peggy Lee singing about *Enttäuschung* – nothing more comforting than that.

Then an odd thought came to me. Something ACC Strong had said: *Hearsay evidence and missing files, is that what you're telling me, Duffy? And now you've been seen going into a known IRA man's house at five in the morning?*

If he didn't know about the Special Branch investigation until I mentioned it, how did he know that I'd arrived at Ken Kirkpatrick's house at five in the morning? Had I said that to him? I didn't think so.

Was it possible that Strong was my secret persecutor? Had he set Special Branch on me? Is that how it worked in the upper levels of the RUC? You prove your ability to command by being prepared to sacrifice your own men?

What motivation could he have for doing that? Would my scalp and a few other scalps and a vigorous internal anti-corruption campaign help prove to Mrs Thatcher that he was the one she should appoint as the Chief Constable's successor?

It was strange, too, that Internal Affairs were coming after me at the same time as the IRA's Army Council and the bloody papers.

Strange, but not, perhaps, a coincidence?

My head hurt.

Phone ringing in the hall.

At this hour!

Probably the Carrick switchboard and I was *not* duty detective tonight.

I picked up the receiver. "What is it? You've probably woken the baby!"

"Get out of the house, Sean! They're coming for you. Get out now!"

I believed it instantly. It was Ken Kirkpatrick from the Derry IRA.

"Beth and Emma are with me!"

"That won't stop them. Get them out, Duffy. Now!"

I slammed down the phone and looked through the hall window. A Ford Transit van was parking itself right outside the gate.

I ran upstairs, three steps at a time.

I shook Beth awake and put my hand over her mouth.

"Mmmfff?"

"IRA hit team. They're going to kill us all. We have to get out!"

I ran into Emma's room, scooped her up, took Beth's hand and stopped at the top of the stairs.

Too late.

A sledgehammer smashed through the front door and it came off its hinges.

If we went down the stairs we were all dead.

Once before my home had been invaded but I'd had more time then. Time to think. Time to move the paraffin heater. I had no time now.

No time. No gun. And a wife and child to protect.

I opened the bathroom door and pushed Beth inside.

Emma began to cry.

"Up there!" a voice said from the bottom of the steps.

I closed the bathroom door as I heard men charging up the stairs. "We'll go out the bathroom window onto the wash-house roof and into the back garden," I whispered.

The window had recently been painted. Would it open?

I tugged and it wouldn't budge.

Men nearly at the top of the stairs.

I gave Emma to Beth, took off my T-shirt, wrapped it around my fist and smashed the window through. I lifted Beth and Emma up and shoved them through.

"He's in there!"

A bullet came through the bathroom door. And then two more bullets. I jumped head first through the bathroom window, scraping my back on the broken glass as a machine gun tore through the bathroom door's handle and lock.

I got half a hand up to stop myself landing face first on the wash-house roof but I still bashed my nose.

Blood in my mouth. Ringing in my ears. I turned to see a man in a balaclava standing in the bathroom with an AK-47. Another man behind him.

Beth had already jumped down into the garden with Emma. I rolled off the roof, fell, landed on the wet grass with a thump, got up and dragged them towards the hedge separating us from the Bridewells' garden.

Machine gun bursts and tracer set the night on fire.

I shoved Beth and Emma over the hedge and dived through the bush after them.

Bullets buried themselves in the garden path where I had just been standing.

The gunman and his companion jumped down onto the wash-house roof. Another gunman came through the back door. The man on the roof jumped down. At least three of them in the back garden now. All of them with machine guns.

And I had nothing.

I ran Beth and Emma through the Bridewells' garden and we smashed through the wooden picket fence between us and the McMurtrys' house.

More tracer and machine gun fire in terrifying parabolas of red death behind us.

"This way!" I said and we ran across the McMurtrys' back yard and vaulted the low wall between the McMurtrys' and the Ferrins'.

"There he goes!" a voice said and all three men emptied their clips after us.

A pause while they reloaded.

The air filled now with car alarms and burglar alarms, dogs barking, birds squawking, Emma screaming.

We ran through the Ferrins' vegetable garden, demolishing their tomato plants on bamboo runners and I helped Beth climb the metal fence between the Ferrins' and Bobby Cameron's house.

"When you get over to the other side bang on Bobby Cameron's back door until he opens up!" I said to Beth. The fence was seven foot tall but Beth was limber. When she dropped down on the other side I passed Emma over the top to her. Beth took her and looked at me through the wire mesh. Bobby's was the last house on the terrace and there was no way out of his back garden but the way we'd come.

"What if Bobby doesn't open the door?"

"He has to. If we try to go to the street they'll kill us."

I started climbing the fence.

The men had all reloaded now and I was an easy target. The machine guns danced and I threw myself over the lip of the fence and landed in Bobby Cameron's garden. Beth was nowhere to be seen.

"Beth!"

"She's inside," Bobby said, running out the back door naked and holding an M249 light machine gun.

"Violet will look after her and the baby. Here," he said handing me a revolver.

I took the gun and as the hit squad ran from my garden into the Bridewells' garden we opened up on them.

The M249 is a belt-fed weapon that fires from an open bolt. When the trigger is pulled, the bolt and bolt carrier move forward under the power of the recoil spring. A cartridge is stripped from the belt, chambered, and then discharged. A simple weapon. Simple but very, very effective. The M249 can fire 200 rounds a minute. Before it was taken out of service in the US

Army to be safety-featured it was known as the SAW because it could saw through just about fucking anything. Bricks, armour plate, humans . . .

An AK-47, even three AK-47s, were no match for this wall of death.

The SAW demolished the Ferrins' greenhouse, the McMurtrys' wall, my hedge. I fired the revolver at the three gunmen but it was redundant and unnecessary in the face of the M249's devastating blanket of fire.

Brass cartridges spewed all over the garden, the SAW sang and Bobby yelled with delight: "Come on! Come and get it! Come on!"

He hadn't hit any of the IRA hit team, but he didn't need to. They weren't fools. The SAW was the gateway to hell and the man wielding the M249 looked like a fucking maniac.

They ran back into my house and when the cartridges finally ran out of the belt on the machine gun I heard the Ford Transit van accelerate away down Coronation Road.

Bobby stood there, holding the smoking gun, naked, happy, the SAW's echoes bouncing off the houses as far away as Fairview Park.

I went into Bobby's house to check that Beth and Emma were unhurt.

I hugged them and told them it was over and then I dialled the station and told Mary to tell RUC command to set up a roadblock. It probably wouldn't be quick enough but you never knew.

Back to the girls.

Emma and Beth were terrified but unharmed.

I hugged and kissed them both again and held them *tight*.

"It's OK, it's OK, it's OK, baby girl. We're safe. The bad men have gone," I said to Emma as I held her.

Beth said nothing. She was in shock. Violet waved me away and put a blanket round her. She gave Beth a cup of sweet tea while Bobby led me out to the back garden where the smell of gunpowder and war was prehistoric and rusty and terrible and beautiful.

"Friends of yours?" Bobby asked.

"IRA hit team."

He nodded. "No Loyalist would dare come onto my street."

"I thought no IRA team would either."

"They'll know better next time. Now, listen Duffy, we have a bit of a problem. The police will be here in five minutes. This machine gun—"

"I'll say the IRA team dropped it when they followed me out of the bathroom. I picked it up and ran with it and then turned it on them. Wipe your prints off it. And I'll get my prints on it."

Bobby wiped down the machine gun and I picked it up. It was so hot it seared my wrists and I immediately dropped it again. Prints imprinted. Job done.

Everyone in Coronation Road and Coronation Crescent and Victoria Estate was out now in their nightshirts and pyjamas, amazed, scared, excited, incredulous at this turn of events.

For the kids this was better than a chip pan fire or when Paisley came electioneering in his open-top car and camel-hair coat.

This would be a night they would tell their children about. When the demons came to Coronation Road and fled.

Now the excitement was over the shakes were starting. And the chills. Need a blanket and a cup of tea to ward off shock.

"Good woman, your Beth," Bobby said.

"She feels like nobody likes her on the street. You couldn't encourage them to be a wee bit friendlier, could you?"

"Aye."

"Not that she'll be staying here for a while."

"This kind of thing is enough to put you right off the neighbourhood."

"Yes."

"I suppose I better go inside and get some clothes on," Bobby said.

"Aye," I agreed and stinking of cordite, sweat, gun oil and adrenalin I waded through the fire, shell casings and massacred tomato plants, back over the walls and hedges into my own garden, where Peggy Lee was still singing about disappointment, where the cat was yawning and where, faintly in the distance, I could hear the sirens from cop cars, Land Rovers and ambulances Dopplering their way onto the stave of the night's music in a manner that was not displeasing to me at all.

21: AFTERMATH

Street full of people. Safe now. Army helicopters flying in big curves above Carrickfergus. Above them the Great Bear drooping his protective paw over all of us.

Cops, soldiers, press. Press – *like to see you fuck with me now Special Branch, yeah, maybe in due course, but not now.* And you too, Dr Havercamp. I dare you to put me on restricted duty. I double dare you.

Kids looking at me in wonder. Bobby Cameron smoking a cigarette and drinking a can of Bass, *no officers I didn't see anything, I slept through the whole kit and caboodle.*

A solitary crow on the telegraph wire.

A solitary crow with a knowing, sleekit black eye.

Cut to:

Larne. Next morning. Saying goodbye to Beth and Emma. Safe now in her father's house. "How long will we have to be here, Sean?"

"Not long. I feel it. Things are coming to a head."

Cut to:

Carrick RUC. My office. A report that the getaway Ford Transit had been found burned out in Eden Village next to the skid marks of an Audio Quattro.

Cut to:

Carrick RUC. Chief Inspector McArthur's office. Chief Inspector McArthur reading the story about me surviving a gun attack on my home in the *Belfast Telegraph* and "it's also in three of the London papers! Three of them, Sean. Maybe they'll give you the Queen's Police Medal."

"I already got one of those."

"Maybe they'll give you the George Cross!"

"Maybe they'll give me the Victoria Cross."

"Oh no, they can't do that, you have to be in the army or the—"

Cut to:

Coronation Road. The workmen installing the iron front door and bullet-proof windows at #113. "They'll need a rocket launcher to take you out now, mate."

"Don't give them any ideas."

Cut to:

Beth looking at houses for sale in Scotland. "I've had it with this bloody country."

"I don't blame you."

Cut to:

Ownies Pub. Crabbie, Lawson and me at the table upstairs overlooking the lough and the Marine Gardens and the Castle. Three Guinnesses in front of us. Three whisky chasers already gone.

We'd done good work in this pub. Case conferences, strategy, working out our plans.

"The papers think this was a random attack on a Catholic peeler and that's good. I don't want the Army Council to know that I know that this was personal."

"But why, personal?" Crabbie asked.

"It's because of this case. Something about Selden and Deauville and the B Specials. Ken Kirkpatrick hinted I was close to something."

"But you say Selden is only a mid-level player. Intel says he's only a mid-level player," Lawson said.

"Exactly. That's what makes it so bloody weird. The Army

Council isn't going to risk an operation in Carrickfergus because I got on the nerves of Harry fucking Selden."

"So what do we do?" Crabbie asked.

"Only two things we can do: 1) Drop the case and let it be known that we are dropping the case, or 2) Keep digging through the newspapers and following up on the other leads until we find out what the connection is. I'm not going to make you guys go with me here. If I'm in jeopardy, you're in jeopardy. I'll take a majority vote."

Lawson was the first with his hand in the air. "There is a third possibility, sir. We tell everyone who asks that we've yellow-filed the case but we keep digging. That's what I think we should do."

"Yeah, that's smart." I agreed. "Crabbie, are you in?"

Crabbie looked at me. "Do you even need to ask?" he said indignantly.

Cut to:

Carrick Library. Reading through old newspapers.

Cut to:

My office. Following up on the other leads.

Cut to:

Beth's parents' house in Larne. Any other girl would have gone to pieces. Hospital time. Shock. PTSD. But as I said: hidden depths, bottom, holding it together – for now – for the sake of Emma and me.

"How are you doing, sweetie?"

"I feel like we're in the bottle city of Kandor."

"The what?"

"Your knowledge of Superman is as bad as your knowledge of Philip K. Dick."

Her turf-blown features, looking at me, right through me. Elizabeth of the waves. Elizabeth of the holding it together.

I kissed her.

She tasted of red wine and tears. No wonder for either.

"Where are your folks in this great pile?"

"They're in the front room with Emma."

"Who's upstairs?"

"Nobody."

"Come on."

"Sean, no, we can't, your car's running, I—"

We ran up to the bedroom.

Ten minutes was enough.

You want the best sex in the world? Ever? Have three men in balaclavas fire Kalashnikovs at you and your girlfriend and miss. And fucking miss.

Cut to: Carrick Library.

Long days, long nights and then:

Lawson staggering towards me from the microfiche machine. He had a box of film and a photocopy in his hands. He looked terrified.

"I found it," he said in an awed whisper. "It was here all along."

Here all along, like an unexploded bomb from 1968. You can kill a man and disappear his wife and disappear the files but you can't unmake what happened.

History knows.

And Morrigan knows.

And Death knows.

"What is it?" I asked.

"We can't discuss it here. I've photocopied the story and put the microfilm back in the box."

"You certainly win the tinfoil-hat award. OK, then, if we can't talk here we'll go to my office."

"We can't go to your office, sir. We'll have to go to Ownies or somewhere neutral like that."

"What are you talking about?"

"We can't go anywhere near a *police* station."

"Oh shit," I said.

"Oh shit indeed," Lawson replied.

22: WHATEVER HAPPENED TO THE LIKELY LADS

It was 1968. That Wunderjahr *when bliss was it in that dawn to be alive and to be young was very heaven.* The kids had had enough of their parents' wars and their parents' rules and, most of all, their parents' music. Paris was erupting, London was erupting, San Francisco was erupting and even dear old Stone Age Belfast was erupting.

After fifty years of discrimination over jobs and housing, Catholics had taken a leaf out of Martin Luther King's playbook and begun demonstrating for equal treatment in the state of Northern Ireland. Demonstrations had led to riots and counter-demonstrations from the likes of Ian Paisley and his rabble. Violence descended like a black cloak over Ulster and twenty years later it was still here. In 1968 one of those little acts of violence was the shooting of a couple who had rammed a police checkpoint. A police checkpoint manned by auxiliaries, by the B Specials, who had shot at them with their .303 Lee Enfield rifles left over from the war.

The story itself barely got a mention, and the coroner's inquest a hasty month later only gleaned a couple of paragraphs and two sad little black-and-white snaps of a boy and a girl.

The young couple were Maria McKeen (seventeen) and Patrick Devlin (nineteen), driving Patrick's father's Morris Minor. It was the same week a dozen other people died. The overburdened coroner was brief and to the point. *The young couple were going to the Grand Opera House for a show. They were late, but that was no reason to charge through a police checkpoint, especially in these troubled times. The police had no choice but to assume they were terrorists fleeing justice. A tragic case indeed, but no criminal charges were necessary.*

The three B Specials manning the checkpoint were Francis Deauville, Harry Selden and, wait for it, one John Strong who later transferred to the RUC and began rising up the ranks.

Rising up the ranks to Assistant Chief Constable.

John Strong. Read the name, but don't even say it out loud.

"What does this mean?" Crabbie asked in a whisper.

"Let's go find out. Don't mention this to anyone. No one. If anyone asks what we're working on tell them that post office robbery from 1986."

"What's that thing you're always saying about paranoia, Sean?"

"Not me. William Burroughs. A paranoid man is a man who knows a little about what's going on."

"That was it," Crabbie said.

Don't trust whitey and whitey is fucking everywhere.

We walked out of Ownies and went to the station to research the case.

There was no case.

No criminal charges. Nothing in the files.

"We need to talk to the parents," I said.

The electoral records told us that although the Devlin family had moved to England the McKeens were still here, living way up the coast in Cushendun.

BMW.

A2.

The causeway road.

James McKeen had had a stroke and had good days and bad days but Judith McKeen was clear-eyed and angry and sharp as a tack.

"Maria was a mezzo soprano. Very cultured wee girl. Very beautiful. Such a voice. They were going to the Grand Opera House to see *Tristan and Isolde*. Patrick had got his father's car especially. Such a good boy. The idea that he could ever have a run a checkpoint . . ."

"Even if they were late?"

"Even if they were late."

"What do you think happened at that checkpoint?" I asked across the tea cups in that little house in Cushendun village.

"Old Jackie Finnerty the undertaker told James that she'd been interfered with. Now James never told me that at the time. I suppose he thought that it was better I didn't know, but it came out years later on one of his bad mornings. Jackie Finnerty was ninety by then but when I put it to him he said it was true."

"I'm sorry to be so indelicate but what do you mean interfered with?"

"She was raped. Raped by those three B specials is my belief."

I looked at Crabbie and Lawson. Both of them would normally be scribbling in their notebooks, but notebooks can be seized by Special Branch and by your station chief.

"I'm sorry to press the point but how do you know it wasn't Patrick who did it?"

"Patrick wasn't that sort of boy. Patrick was a very shy, very good boy. And it wouldn't make sense, would it? He rapes her and then she goes on with him to the opera house?"

"Definitely rape, not just ordinary sex?"

"Jackie Finnerty is dead now but he saw a lot of bodies in his time and he said rape. He said you always know."

"Why didn't you go to the coroner with this story?"

"My husband James did go to the coroner but the coroner said that she'd probably had sex with Patrick and did he really want his daughter's reputation dragged through the mud? And that was that. James wasn't a fighter and I didn't know at the time."

Judith McKeen looked at us and we looked at her. Her strong dark eyes and her thick grey hair and her strong bony hands.

"Are youseuns looking into this?" she asked.

"We are," I said.

"The police investigating the police?" she said sceptically.

"The police investigating the police," I insisted.

"Can I tell you what I think happened?" she said quietly.

"Please do."

"They were drunk. The three of them. Drunk on duty. The coroner said there had been some 'light drinking on duty', whatever that meant. And they stop this car on the coast road and Maria's all dressed up to the nines, looking gorgeous and one of them touches her and Patrick yells blue murder and they shoot him and rape her."

"Would you give us permission to have Maria's body exhumed? Recently there have been a number of successful prosecutions following the recovery of what is known as DNA evidence. That seems very unlikely in a case like this but you never know what—"

"When they had to move the cemetery to Ballycastle because of the new road James said he didn't want poor Maria to be all dug up and jiggered about and reburied miles away from all of us. So we had her remains cremated and scattered in the sea just out there. When my time comes that's what I want too."

"I see," I said.

"We have no one here now. Maria's brother, Kevin, is in Canada. He has a hotel in Calgary. We never see him. He's very busy."

"Grandchildren?"

"Not yet. Not ever, I think. It'll be a lonely few years when James goes."

I looked at Lawson and McCrabban to see if they had any questions but neither of them had anything.

"Where are these men now? The men who done this?" Judith asked.

"One of them's dead and we're investigating the other two," I said.

She nodded.

"You'll do your best. I can see that. All three of you," she said. "Now I better go see to James. This has been one of his bad afternoons."

"Will you do me one more favour?" I asked at the door.

"What's that?"

"If anyone asks you about this conversation I'd prefer if you didn't say anything about it," I said.

"They've got you afeared these men? Have they?"

She could see it in my eyes, so there was no point in denying it. "There is an element of risk in this investigation so it's probably best if we keep it quiet until we're sure of the facts," I said.

We drove back to Carrickfergus RUC along the coast road, to give us plenty of time to talk.

"Thoughts, gentlemen?" I said.

Lawson leapt right in. "They were drunk, like Mrs McKeen said. They were probably patting her down or grabbing her arse or something, the boy goes for them and they shoot him. In for a penny in for a pound, rape the girl, and then kill her."

"And then what?" I said.

"They concoct their story, everyone believes it, they get off," Lawson said.

"That's not what he means. He means how has this led to Deauville's death?" Crabbie said.

"Any thoughts?"

"Do you have a hypothesis, sir?" Lawson asked.

I looked at both of them. "I believe I do have a working hypothesis that fits with the information we have available."

I didn't say anything and continued to drive along the road.

"Well go on then, sir," Lawson said.

"Unfortunately I have zero evidence for any part of my hypothesis. Nothing I can present to the DPP, nothing that I could take to any of our superiors."

"Go on, Sean, you have to tell us what you're thinking."

I pulled over to the side of the road and we walked to a pub in the picturesque village of Waterfoot in the Glens of Antrim. Quite the dissonance between the story percolating in my brain and the beauty of the surroundings.

A pint. A cigarette. A think. I made sure we got a table outside in the empty beer garden where our only listeners were the cows staring at us over the stone wall.

"They didn't plan on rape. Not at first. The rape comes near the end. They've been drinking but they don't consider themselves to be bad men. Three concerned citizens working as reserve policemen. Salt-of-the-earth types. Two Prods and a Catholic. Just like the three of us."

"Very different from the three of us," McCrabban said, with as grave a voice as I've ever heard him use.

"Young couple stop at the checkpoint, impatient to get going. Cops are being overbearing and a little lascivious. Just light banter. Maybe the girl gives the policeman lip. Maybe the boy. They take the boy out, rough him up, one thing leads to another. The girl goes for them. They point the rifles at the boy and one of them has the bright idea to teach the wee lassie a lesson. She won't talk, and if she does no one will believe her. Teach her a lesson and let them go. This is Ulster: whatever you say, say nothing. They take turns and she's screaming and the shy boy finally cracks. Tries to take down one of them. But it's no go and they shoot him. And then they feel they have no choice and they have to shoot her. And then it's a pact in blood between the three of them: Deauville, Selden and our good friend and lord protector Assistant Chief Constable Strong."

I took a sip of my Guinness and continued.

"The years go by. The B Specials are disbanded. Strong joins the RUC proper but Selden and Deauville take very different paths. Deauville goes to England and drifts into a life of petty and not so petty crime. Selden moves back to Derry and when Bloody Sunday happens, like every other Catholic man in the city he attempts to join the IRA. They take him in. He slowly moves up the ranks. He's a plodder. Not a gunman or a planner or a thinker. Just a plodder. He'll never go anywhere, but then he has an idea. What about his old friend John Strong who he's heard has joined the RUC. What's he up to these days? And he finds out that John Strong has made quite a career for himself. He's going places. And he arranges a not-so-accidental meeting with John Strong. And he tells Strong that all this beautiful life you've made will end if I tell people what really happened to Maria McKeen and Patrick Devlin back in 1968."

Crabbie filled his pipe. "I don't like where you're taking this, Sean," he said.

"And at first Selden just asks for a few bits of information here and there, maybe a tip-off or two about an upcoming raid. And maybe it even goes two ways, maybe Strong gets information from the IRA as he moves up the ranks and the IRA high command realise that they have a very important operational asset indeed. Both men help each other. Both careers blossom. Selden does in fact become something of a player and as a reward gets to be a councillor."

"But no one in Derry knows this, only the Army Council itself," Lawson said. "That's why your mate Ken thought Selden was a nonentity."

I looked at Crabbie and he knew it was possible, maybe even probable. There *was* an IRA mole and that mole was John Strong.

"An Assistant Chief Constable who belongs to the IRA," Lawson said, gasping over his drink.

"An Assistant Chief Constable, maybe Chief Constable in waiting who is their creature to his very boots. What a coup that would be."

"And everything's just peachy for a few years but then

Deauville returns from England with a new wife and a new game," Lawson said.

"And he spots his old friend John Strong in Carrick. Maybe at the Rangers Club," Crabbie suggested.

"And Deauville's not like the IRA. He's not subtle. He's not interested in the long game. He sees that Strong is a wealthy man, an important man and he asks for money. A lot of money. If Strong pays him a handsome cheque every month poor Elena won't have to risk life and limb smuggling heroin from Bulgaria every six weeks," I said.

"And after this chance meeting with Deauville, Strong tries to contact his handler immediately. But where is Harry Selden? Harry's in the hospital. So Strong decides to act on his initiative. I'll shoot the blackmailing bastard myself. Can't use my service revolver but it's dead easy to buy a crossbow somewhere. And then I'll get Harry to get the IRA to claim the hit. End of problem."

"But the IRA didn't want to claim the hit, they're pretty protective of their and other groups' kills, aren't they? And it was only with reluctance that Harry got that DAADD claim out into the press," Lawson said.

We finished our drinks and stared at the sea.

"We have no proof and we're not going to get any proof," McCrabban said. "Strong is far too clever to admit anything."

"What if we wore a wire and confronted him? I mean you, sir, you confront him?" Lawson asked.

I shook my head. "Crabbie's right. Those Jedi tricks aren't going to work with him. Overtly or covertly he won't admit anything to me. And we'll have played our hand. He's a very dangerous opponent. The most dangerous opponent we've ever had and he'll destroy us all if we bring him in and only wound him."

"And what if we're wrong? What if we bring him in and accuse him and we're just dead wrong?" Lawson said. "The high jump for all of us."

"I don't think we're wrong. Strong told me to drop the case. He needs it gone. He's come at me on two fronts, through Special Branch and through the IRA."

"He can't know that we suspect him. You have to tell Strong that we're yellowing the file. DAADD claimed the kill and we're letting it drop for lack of evidence. Similarly with Mrs Deauville, we're letting the case lapse," Crabbie said.

"Then what?" I asked.

"Then you write a letter to Harry Selden on official stationery telling him too that the case is closed and that the RUC regrets any inconvenience it may have caused," Crabbie said.

"Agent and handler both get the good news and both think they're in the clear. I officially move on to other work, meanwhile we try harder than ever to nail the fucker," I said.

23: THE ACC

First things first. Letter off to Selden. Full-throated apology. Regret any inconvenience. Blah, blah, bloody blah. Then wait for the other shoe to drop.

Two days later the phone rang in my office.

"Hello?"

"Duffy, it's John Strong."

"Sir, I wasn't expecting to hear—"

"It's a pleasure to talk to you, son. I don't want to embarrass you but you're quite the hero now, after what happened to you at your home," ACC Strong said.

"From zero to hero, isn't that the expression, sir?"

"Now, now, Duffy. Don't be facetious, I always knew you were a good policeman. And I hear you're in the running for a medal?"

"Another medal, sir. That'll be my second."

"You are in a cocky mood this morning. So, uhm, what are you up to these days?"

"Nothing much, sir, a post office robbery from a few years ago that we can't seem to crack."

"Whatever happened to that case you were working on with the French name?"

"Oh, the Deauville case? You were right, sir. There was no juice to it. DAADD murdered the poor chap and we've no eye-witnesses or forensic evidence of any kind so we're dropping it.

Moving it to the yellow file. Moving onto other business."

"I think that's probably for the best, don't you?"

"Yes, sir. I'm sorry to have let you down, sir. It's yet another homicide case that goes unsolved, sir, and it won't do my reputation any good for bringing DAADD or IRA men to justice but—"

"No need to finish that sentence, Duffy. You're doing the right thing. And there's some of us up here that know you're a good policeman. Special Branch still causing you problems?"

"They're still investigating me, I think, sir."

"I'll see what I can do to get them off your back."

"Thank you, sir, I'll get you a drink next time you're down the police club."

"I won't get there as often as I'd like now, not with all my new responsibilities."

"Of course, sir."

"Bye, Duffy. Good to see you've decided to become a company man again."

"Yes, sir. Straight and narrow for me from now on . . . Sir, I'd like to get you a wee something for all your help, though. You're a Rangers man rather than Celtic, am I right?"

"Of course!" he said, laughing. "But you don't have to get me anything."

"I'll find something nice, sir. Tickets to an Old Firm game or something like that."

"You don't have to do anything, Duffy. Just keep your nose clean. Bye, Inspector."

"Bye, sir."

He hung up.

A Rangers fan who goes to the Rangers club and is seen there by Francis Deauville? Yeah, that would work.

The IRA Council would get the message from two different sources now. Their mole was safe. *Yeah don't worry, lads, Duffy's not as smart as he thinks he is and he's safely neutered.*

A third Army-Council-sanctioned attack on Sean Duffy seemed an unlikely possibility.

Time for Duffy and crew to get working.

We told the Chief Inspector we were running down leads on the PO robbery and started doing leg work. We took Selden and Strong's photographs to the crossbow shops, but no one remembered either man. At the Rangers Club the barman liked the look of Strong as the tall man in the flat cap but wasn't completely convinced it was him and "wasn't completely convinced" was not something you could take to court.

We tried to look up the coroner on the McKeen–Devlin deaths but that old complacent lying bastard had died ten years previously.

We ran the missing persons reports on Mrs Deauville but there was no give there either.

We discreetly accessed John Strong's personnel file but all that was in there was a hagiographical ascent to glory.

We looked into the possibility of exhuming Patrick Devlin and examining the wounds on his body but the family wasn't in the country any more and an exhumation was not something you could keep quiet about. And even if we did pull up poor old Patrick Devlin from his final resting place, only a pistol shot in the back of the head could possibly be strong enough probative value to indict a high-ranking policeman – every other gunshot wound could be turned by a good lawyer into the kind of wound you get in a melee from running a roadblock. Attempt to take down Strong with evidence like that and we'd be blowing up all our careers and putting our lives in jeopardy. The exhumation of Patrick Devlin would have to be a last desperate roll of the dice.

We did finally find Harry Selden's "stolen" car burnt out and forensically dead in a wrecker's yard in East Belfast. No help at all on that score.

Days like this.

Nights like this.

The Troubles simmered in the background, an entire generation scarred by the brutal murders of the two corporals and the
three IRA funeral mourners on live TV.

Throw in the "punishment" shootings and the firebombings
and the attacks on cops and soldiers.

Old news now. Most of that stuff wouldn't make page one of the
Irish papers and wouldn't get mentioned at all in the British ones.

My old gaffer and one of John Strong's mentors, Superintendent
Bertie Hare died of coronary heart disease. Dress uniform for
his funeral in the rain at Victoria Cemetery. ACC Strong didn't
show up. Busy man. A Church of Ireland priest telling the men
gathered round the grave that he was "confident in the resur-
rection of the flesh".

I was glad someone was confident.

Fortunately we had a few real minor cases that allowed us to
hide the big case: a shoplifting gang, joyriders, coal thieves.

March advanced into April.

Beth grew more and more agitated at her parents' house.
More and more depressed about living in Ulster at all. "That
house Dad's building for us feels like it's a prison."

"Then we won't move in there."

"But Northern Ireland feels like a prison."

"Ulster as existential prison. I've had those thoughts. Many
times."

"They do my exact masters course at Glasgow University.
It's better, actually. They have teachers there who'll let you do
comic books as well as contemporary fiction."

"Glasgow University? Sounds good."

"I'd transfer my work done. I could finish the whole thing in
under a year."

I'd lost one girlfriend to a Scottish uni. Could I lose two?
That's the way history goes, says Nietzsche. Wash and repeat.
Until all feeling is gone and everything fades into nothing. Wash
and repeat.

Walking insomniac around Carrickfergus.

Down Coronation Road, Barn Road, Taylor's Avenue. The dream engine spilling vowels on Victoria Estate. An audiobook on my Walkman. Poems. Berryman. Huffy Henry and Amy Vladeck. Huffy Henry and Louis MacNeice.

Others lines from other poems:

The blots on the page are so black they cannot be covered with shamrock . . .

The falcon cannot hear the falconer . . .

And this from the opera the dead couple in 1968 did not get to see:

Frisch weht der Wind/Der Heimat zu
Mein Irisch Kind/Wo weilest du?

Where indeed?

He was out there, like a spider at the centre of a web. A dangerous opponent. One mistake, one false move, and me and Lawson and Crabbie were all going to go down. How can you mess with a man who has the IRA *and* the police on his team?

Even a clown like Dalziel assumes a new light. You're an eejit, Kenny, a complete fucking eejit, but at least you're not a traitor.

24: DRIVING MUSIC

Belfast does weather well. Especially rain.

One night I grabbed the lock-pick kit, the Glock and the raincoat and walked down the path of 113 Coronation Road in a downpour from Ezekiel 38.

Lightning danced around the occult chimney at Kilroot and the yellow cranes above the dry dock at the shipyard. Thunder boomed across the lough. I looked under the BMW for mercury tilt switch bombs but the brave boys who plant such things were all abed tonight.

It was late.

Stupid o'clock.

I drove up Coronation Road and turned right on Victoria Road. The estate was deserted. The Beemer purred down Victoria Road past the graveyard and the butchers, past Lawson's house and the supermarket.

We came to a rest at the newly installed traffic lights, which, of course, were red, even though there wasn't another car around for miles.

I put one of Lawson's CDs in the player. It wasn't the LA rap one that he and all the kids at the station and even John Peel were calling a classic. It was a band called The Butthole Surfers from Texas. I looked at the CD case while the light stayed red. The album was called *Hairway to Steven*.

The light went green and I turned right.

The BMW wanted to stretch itself.

Up the Marine Highway, heading for the city.

Belfast: beautiful in its brokenness.

All cities will look like this in the far future: ruined and fractured, walled and utilitarian. This is Earth's only city. A Belfast that vibrates in the present and the past and in the days to come.

Burned-out cars. Bomb sites. Wet horses tied to girders. Dead televisions in the rubble.

Like the man said. The dead man in the forest outside Derry with his strange map and his interesting opinions. We were once creatures of the savannah, whose lives were mapped by the journeys of the great migrating herds across the rift valley. We can't live like this. Stationary, on top of one another. It's bad for our mental health.

It was so windy the cranes were swaying at the shipyard and the army helicopters had been grounded. Good night for a smash-and-grab raid somewhere with the choppers down and the police huddled in their barracks. Remember that if Special Branch forces me to resign and I'm looking for a career change.

I drove up the Antrim Road, past Our Lady of Lourdes, past the zoo, and then I curved down again through the empty city streets to the Shore Road.

I knew where I was going.

The address from the personnel file.

I parked the car outside the Assistant Chief Constable's house on the Belfast Road. A big granite three-floor job on the water's edge of Belfast Lough. I put on gloves and a balaclava. I took the Glock from the passenger's seat and put it in my raincoat pocket. I examined the lock-pick kit to make sure everything was in order.

I got out and walked to that big iron gate.

Rain was pouring down my neck between my raincoat and my Che T-shirt.

Sea spray was splashing against the gable wall.

Lightning again hit the power-station chimney.

I looked at the Beware of the Dog sign.

"Dog better beware of me."

I climbed over the gate and dropped down the other side.

Way to deal with an attack dog is to offer it your left arm. He'll bite it and hold on and then you punch him in the eye with your right fist. No need for a gun. Amateurs and farmers shoot dogs.

I stood there, waiting.

No dog.

I walked down the long driveway past the rose bushes.

Onto the porch with its empty milk bottles and a garden gnome in an English bobby's uniform. Strictly against regulations, that. Standing order 222, "Display nothing in your car or your house that might indicate that you are a member of the RUC."

Have to have a word with him about it.

Yale 1970s front door lock. Easy peasy. Leaky tumblers. Pick it with a screwdriver if I needed to. Lock-pick kit it anyway. Tension wrench in bottom of lock, pick in top. Feel for the tumbler, turn, hey presto the door is open.

Safety chain behind the door.

Pliers from lock-pick kit could snip through it in a second but there was no need. It had been placed too close to the catch, with too much slack, and it wasn't that tricky to lift it off with my gloved fingers.

I stepped into the house.

I walked into the hall and then into the living room with its big windows and the view over Belfast and North Down.

I caught my balaclavaed reflection in the glass.

Why are you doing this, Duffy? Why do you always have to be so fucking theatrical? You weren't always this way. Don't you remember that row you had with your philosophy tutor at Queens when he was recommending the stance Camus takes in *The Myth of Sisyphus*? Melodramatic and narcissistic and false you called it. You were right then, you're wrong now.

I mean just look at you: raincoat, gloves, gun, balaclava. It's pathetic. Age hasn't matured you. It's made those traits that were ticks in the twenty-five-year-old into full-blown affectations in the thirty-eight-year-old. And affectations is putting it politely. Haven't you grown up at all? You have a child, for Christ's sake, isn't that supposed to wise a man up?

I stood there looking in the window glass, saying nothing. Frozen there half in and half out of the rain, an image flickering in the lightning like a ghost.

I sighed, gently closed the front door and sat down on the sofa.

I was disgusted with myself, sitting here in Assistant Chief Constable Strong's living room at midnight, getting his carpet all wet.

The bold move would be to put something on his stereo. Something loud, Beethoven if he had any. He comes down in his dressing gown, bleary-eyed, holding his service revolver in front of him and I'm sitting there on the sofa waiting for him, like a stone cold motherfucker.

I take off the balaclava and he sees it's me.

"It's all right, Margaret," he says to the wife and then comes over to the stereo and turns it off.

"What's the meaning of this, Duffy?" he says.

And I stand up and I tell him that I know what he's done. I let it all out. "You had me lifted in Derry! You gave me up to the IRA! Your own man. To protect your arse!"

Yeah something like that.

I put my head in my hands and sighed.

I looked at the Glock in my right hand.

I got up and, still dripping, walked over to the stereo, rifled through the CDs. There wasn't any Beethoven anyway. No classical music at all, in fact.

A black Alsatian walked into the living room from the kitchen.

It wasn't expecting to see me and after a moment's shock came over and sniffed my hand. I took the glove off to let him better get the measure of me. An intruder who deserved to get bitten or a friend of the family?

He must have smelt *cop* because he licked my wrist and lay down on the living-room rug. I rubbed his belly and he liked that.

It was time to go now, time to flee, but Dozy Duffy didn't go. Dozy Duffy found himself walking upstairs.

He opened the door at the top of the stairs which was a bathroom. Another door which was a child's bedroom, with a fifteen-year-old boy sleeping in a race-car bed that was nearly too small for him. Another bedroom was a spare room and another bedroom was the master bedroom.

Moonlight was illuminating the face of Assistant Chief Constable Strong and the long red hair of Mrs Assistant Chief Constable Strong, whom I'd met once at the police club in Kilroot.

Look at you two lying there. You don't know how close you are to death, how close that boy is to losing a father. I'm boiling with fury. I'm an avenging angel for my own daughter who, but for a stroke of luck, would be fatherless.

And Maria McKeen and Patrick Devlin and all the others you have betrayed.

Look at you. A killer by proxy. A coward.

I have come for you, Strong.

I shook my head again.

No.

Theatrical. Ridiculous.

I closed the door, walked back onto the landing and down the stairs. I patted the dog and went out into the rain. I carefully closed the front door behind me. There was no way to put the safety chain back on the hook but chances were they wouldn't notice that, or they'd think they'd forgotten to do it. Or they'd think it was elves.

The dog was watching me through the frosted glass part of the door. It began to bark.

Of course.

I ran down the path, climbed the gate, quickest ever look under the Beemer, got in and drove; I was a good bit away when I saw the bedroom light come on in the rear-view mirror.

"That was a close one."

I accelerated up the A2 and kept accelerating as the dual carriageway became the M5. I drove into Belfast but the city was deserted. I don't know what I was expecting or hoping for. An ambush? A riot? None of those things.

Back out of the city along the Shore Road. To Carrickfergus. The North Road and finally up to Knockagh Mountain. It always comes back to here.

I got out of the Beemer and walked around the monument and watched the lightning stab great red electric forks over the glacial valley. Some strikes as far away as the Galloway hills in Scotland.

The rain poured down onto me.

And I was not baptised and I was not cleansed and my anger did not abate.

But a thought was growing.

A plan.

A way of getting the bastard. A way of getting all of them.

What was the thing that they feared the most?

Blackmail. Blackmail had started this ball rolling.

Yeah, it would be theatrical and I'd just renounced theatrics in that big speech to myself. But fuck it. Foolish consistency/ hobgoblin, all that jazz.

I grinned and took a hit on my asthma inhaler. I got back in the BMW, stuck in NWA's "Fuck Tha Police" and for the final time in this case I drove to Derry.

25: THE OFFER

I parked the Beemer two roads over and checked the street for Special Branch observation teams. Last thing I needed was internal affairs dicking with me now. No vans, no Volkswagen campers, no eejits sleeping in cars.

Harry Selden couldn't believe it when he came downstairs to wonder why his stereo had suddenly come on and he saw me standing there listening to *Willie Nelson Live* in his living room. He was wearing a navy blue dressing gown and slippers and holding an ancient-looking shotgun that would probably take us both out if he squeezed the trigger.

"What the hell?"

"Put the gun down, Harry, I'm unarmed and I've important things to discuss with you. Do it now, before I'm forced to tell you my Willie Nelson joke."

He turned off the stereo and lowered the shotgun.

"Get out of my house. My mother's sleeping upstairs."

I sat on the sofa. "I'll take a cup of tea."

His really rather adorable visage contorted into the sort of rage Oliver Hardy contorted into when James Finlayson started smashing up his car in *Big Business* (1929).

"No tea, Duffy, get the fuck out of my house before I call the police."

"I thought you had no truck with the police."

"Get out, Duffy!"

"Lower your voice, Harry. Mother's sleeping upstairs."

"What the fuck is the meaning of this? You're going to be in all the papers tomorrow."

"No, I don't think I will. To quote Bugs Bunny, it's mongoose season, and you're the fucking mongoose."

"Have you lost your—"

"I know everything, Harry. I know about you and Strong and Deauville and that couple you murdered back in 1968. Maria McKeen and Patrick Devlin."

He was momentarily taken aback but he recovered himself quickly enough. "We didn't murder anyone. We were exonerated by—"

"It doesn't matter. I don't care. 1968? Might as well be 1868 or 1690 or May 29th 1453, I don't give a flying fuck."

He seemed confused now. I supposed he'd been expecting moral indignation and he wasn't getting any.

"Go and make the tea and be quick about it."

He made the tea and came back with a mug and a couple of digestive biscuits. I dipped the biscuit and sipped the tea.

"Have you seen my personnel record, Harry?" I asked.

"No."

"Well, your friend John Strong has, and sorry reading it is, too. The shit I have had to put up with over the years. You wouldn't believe it, mate. Promotion holds, demotions, suspensions without pay . . . And now they're going to put some fucking connected Proddy bastard called Dalziel over me. Best years of my life I've given to the RUC. For what? So I can look under my car every day for bombs, so I can walk about with a big fat target on my back?"

"I don't understand, what is it—"

"I want what John Strong has. I want a pay cheque every month from the IRA into a Swiss bank account. Nothing extravagant. Nothing you can't handle. Let's say 10 grand a month. Gaddafi gave you five million dollars so I know you're good for it. Or pay me direct from Noraid in America if you want."

"I don't know what you think you're—"

"I'm not done! And I want Strong to forward my career in the police. Immediate promotion to Chief Inspector and eventual promotion to Chief Super. Strong will become my mentor and he'll make sure I rise up through the ranks with him."

"Duffy, what—"

I took out my Glock and pointed it at his face. "I'm not fucking done," I snarled. "And I want an end to attacks on my family. A permanent end. I want it to be known on the Army Council that I am one of the good guys now. I am not to be touched."

"You're wearing a tape recorder," Selden said.

I shook my head.

"Search me, top to bottom, I don't care."

I held the gun in the air and he searched me for a wire and found nothing.

"Now we can talk, right?" I said.

But still he was suspicious. "I don't know what you think you know—"

I yawned. "So tired of this shit. You blackmailed Strong into becoming an IRA agent because of what happened in 1968 and since, oh I don't know, maybe the last decade or so you've been running John Strong as your agent. The most important agent the IRA has in the police."

"That's fantastic. Ridiculous, I—"

I pointed the gun at him again. "I'm in no mood, Harry. I'm just tired. Tired of all the nonsense. I'm as good as married. I have a wee girl who you tried to kill. You'll pay me until I hit my twenty years in the police in 1994 and then I'll retire with the rank of Detective Chief Superintendent and maybe an MBE and I'll move to Spain and live on my pension and on the considerably higher sum you've put in the Swiss bank account."

I finished the tea. Hopefully there wasn't rat poison in it.

"You've got 48 hours to think it over. If you choose to decline my generous offer I'll have to go public with my allegations. And my proof."

"Proof?"

"Proof."

"What proof? Proof of what?"

"You'll see. Maybe no one'll believe it, but fuck it, I don't care. Look at my eyes. Look at them. I'm done. Done with all this bullshit. So what if I pull the temple down about our heads? I'm fucking exhausted by all of you."

I stood up.

"It's too risky for me to come up here, what with intel watching you and IA watching me. I never want to have to drive onto this bloody street again. From now on you'll be servicing me . . ."

"Wait a minute, Duffy, we haven't discussed anything. I haven't committed to anything. I don't know if any of this is possible. I—"

"Here's the first step. You and me and Strong are going to meet. None of us can ever be seen together so it's got to be somewhere safe at night. On my turf. Somewhere I control. At that first meeting I'll bring my Swiss bank account number. You two will bring nothing. No IRA hit team, no bodyguards, no guns, nothing. Understood?"

"I haven't agreed to any—"

"Furthermore, you will not discuss our little conversation today with anyone except John Strong. I want the deal to be in place before the Army Council is approached. I don't want them thinking I'm some rogue fucking lunatic like Deauville who is going to ruin everything for them. I want them to see me as a friend of John's and yours and a potentially valuable asset in my own right. Is that clear?"

"Duffy, look, what you're saying is all very well but—"

I got close to his face. "Rule number 1: only discuss this with John Strong for now. Rule number 2: only the two of you at the first meeting. Rule number 3 is the same as rule number 2: no bodyguards, no minders, no drivers, nothing like that. I will be alone. And if anything happens to me before the meet, you're all up the spout."

He nodded. He was beginning to process it all now, beginning to figure out the angles.

"About this proof," he said.

Ah, so that was the line that was really worrying him.

"Proof that the pair of you murdered Deauville and disappeared his wife."

"What is it?"

"You'll see it. And after the first meeting, when we've established some trust, you and I will never have to meet again. The money will go into my bank account and Strong and I can meet socially or at work."

"How will we ever be able to trust each other?" Selden asked.

"Mutual blackmail. I've got a hold over you and as soon as that first cheque goes into my bank account from the IRA you've got a hold over me. It'll be in both our interests to keep quiet. Everybody wins."

"And the Deauville case?"

"Yellowed. No one gives a shit about a fucking drug dealer and his fucking heroin-smuggling wife."

"And the McKeen–Devlin case?"

"Old news. No one gives a shit about that either."

Selden looked me up and down. "I don't know, Duffy," he said slowly. "This doesn't seem like you."

"Doesn't it? From the boy who tried to join the provisionals in 1972 but was turned down by Dermot McCann? From the young man who has realised that dirty cops and Loyalist thugs are the real enemies of the people of Ireland? But ultimately from the old man who's just sick and tired of all of it and the only thing he wants is a quiet life? Let me finish my career in safety and get my pension and move abroad. Ten grand a month? Small price to pay for keeping one of your prize assets in place and keeping a lippy peeler off your back."

He nodded.

"Well?" I asked.

"Perhaps something can be arranged," he said.

"Good. It's the smart play for all of us. Now this is where we meet. There's an abandoned factory in Carrickfergus called Courtaulds. I know it well and it's close to my house. It's my turf and it's safe. Tomorrow night at midnight in the turbine room. That'll give you nearly two days to think it over. If you're not there by 12.05 there's no deal and fuck it, I'll go to the press. Yes, I know Strong will try to bring me down and probably he will bring me down but no one will ever really trust that fucker again and they'll be watching him like a hawk."

"Tomorrow night. Midnight. Courtaulds factory, Carrickfergus," Selden said, still not completely convinced.

"No guns, no surprises. Just you and Strong. I'll bring my bank account number and my proof of your complicity and we'll take it from there," I said.

"I'll talk to him."

I laughed. "He's not going to be happy."

"We've had many such difficult conversations," Selden said.

"I'll bet you have. This is the beginning of a beautiful friendship," I said and offered him my hand.

He shook it tentatively. I walked to the front door and turned. "No tricks! I am not a problem. A problem is something that can't be solved with money. I can be solved with money. OK?"

"OK."

I drove out of Derry just as the sun was coming out of the bit of the Atlantic Ocean that embraces the coast of Western

Scotland. On a whim I drove east to Tor Head and followed the trail to the top of the promontory.

From here it looked like I could see the whole world.

With no one around for miles and miles I allowed myself a clenched-fist cheer. Just one. They were only half in the bag.

I followed the A2 back to Carrickfergus, driving right past Judith McKeen's house in Cushendun.

Back to Coronation Road.

Fed the cat and went to sleep on the living-room sofa.

No one came to kill me in the night and if they were going to come it would have been last night.

Probably.

Hit the bricks. Look under Beemer. Crabbie and Lawson in my office. I told them what I'd done and then I told them the plan.

"Strong and Selden have to come to see what this proof is. They'll be expecting me to come alone but I won't be alone. They'll check that I'm not wearing a wire before we talk and I won't be wearing a wire, either. But Lawson, you'll be there in the corner with the boom mike and the high-gain antenna hooked up to the tape recorder. Almost as good as a wire."

"And you'll get them to incriminate themselves?" Crabbie said.

"I'll try to."

"And what if it's a double cross and they bring a couple of gunmen with them?" Crabbie asked.

"You know that factory. We can see for miles round there. If we don't like what's coming we can get out of there. But anyway, you'll be there with a Heckler and Koch MP5, as will Lawson and me . . ." I suddenly realised I'd been getting ahead of myself. "Uhm, that's if you lads are in. I should have—"

"Of course we're in, sir," Lawson said matter of factly.

Crabbie nodded vigorously. "Oh aye. We're in. Do you think there's anyone else we can trust though? For back-up."

"I doubt it," I said. "What do you think?"

"We'd have to lie to them. As soon as we mention that we're trying to trap ACC Strong . . . well, alarm bells will be ringing. And if we lie to them and Strong shows up . . . Confusion, to say the least."

"In house," Lawson said. "The three of us. We'll take him down."

26: THE FACTORY

The abandoned factory was a movie trailer from an entropic future when all the world would look like this. From a time without the means to repair corrugation or combustion engines or vacuum tubes. From a planet of rust and candle power. Guano coated the walls. Mildewed garbage lay in heaps. Strange machinery littered a floor which, with its layer of leaves, oil and broken glass was reminiscent of the dark understorey of a rainforest . . .

Yeah, I know.

Circles.

That's why I'm getting out. I wasn't joking about retirement, but I have a slightly different plan, one that won't involve me selling my soul to the paramilitaries.

Crabbie signalling me with his torch.

The torch on and off and on and off to tell us that a car was coming.

A momentary ellipse. A fragment of a second. But enough to move us from prologue into body . . . This was it. I was confident. I had prepared the ground. Walked the terrain. I had sent home the aged night watchman, telling him that there was a police operation underway. I had gotten the best bullet-proof vests and Heckler and Koch MP5s from the armoury. I had taken Crabbie and Lawson to the UDR base in Woodburn and gotten two hours' range time shooting the MP5s. Shooting, reloading, shooting until they were utterly familiar with the gun. Lawson was the more—

Crabbie was running towards me.

"What is it?" I said.

"Two vehicles. One of them is a van, one of them is a car. I don't like it."

"We can abort. We can get out of here before they pull up," I said.

"I don't know," he muttered.

"Let's see who gets out of them," I said, running to the broken window.

I checked my watch. It was five to twelve.

Sure enough it was a van, but there was only one man in it: Selden, wearing an anorak and carrying a torch. The other car was a white Bentley Mulsanne Turbo – Strong's car. How did we not twig that he was on the take? Jesus.

"False alarm," I said to Lawson. "Everything's going according to plan."

Lawson was hiding in the deep shadow in the corner of the factory with his sound-recording equipment.

It was all deep shadow in here, perfect for vanishing men. There was only one working light from an arc light the night watchman had set up. The only ambient sources were the street lights on the dual carriageway below us and the stars and moon. Lawson was next to the arc light switch and at the first sign of trouble was to kill the light. Would he know what trouble meant? He'd have to.

Selden and Strong walked up the path to the factory entrance together. Thick as bloody thieves.

"OK, Crabbie, get in the corner over there and cover me," I whispered.

I zipped up my leather jacket.

Leather jacket, bullet-proof vest, jeans, Adidas gutties, lucky Che T-shirt again.

When they came in the door it was Selden, the handler, who said: "Hello?"

I let them walk in a little further before I answered: "Gentlemen, it's good to see you."

"About this—" Strong began, but Selden cut him off.

"Come over here, Duffy, I need to know that you're not recording this."

"Why would I do that? It's going to incriminate me as much as it'll incriminate you."

"Nevertheless."

I walked over, carrying the machine gun.

"I thought you said no guns," Selden said.

"No guns for you, but I'm not meeting the two of you without protection. Get on with your search. I'm wearing a vest but it's loose enough for you to look underneath it."

Selden patted me down and found no wire.

"He's clean," Selden said.

Strong looked around the factory. "Are you alone?"

"I'm alone."

"What about the redoubtable Sergeant McCrabban?" Strong said suspiciously.

"You'd think he'd believe one bad word about you? He worships you. All the men do. They'd throw me down a well if I lifted a finger to you . . . What about you, though, did you keep your side of the bargain? You kept the Army Council out of it?"

"Of course!" Selden snapped. "I wouldn't dare present them with a problem like you for a third time. I'd be the one making that trip out to the forest."

"Good. Then everyone kept their word."

"Now, what about this proof of yours?" Strong said.

"An eyewitness saw you and Deauville talking in the Rangers club. He drew an uncannily accurate picture of you and when I showed him your photograph he confirmed it. He'll never think of it again until I go public with revelations but then he'll be able to back me up 100 per cent."

"What's his name?" Selden demanded.

"No, no, no. Now it's your turn. What happened March 22nd 1968? Quid pro quo."

"Quid pro quo is you giving us your informant's name."

"Quid pro quo is us both trusting one another and being able to fuck one another, now what happened March 22nd 1968?"

A long pause before Strong shrugged.

"If there's no wire what difference does it make?" Strong said.

"Tell me."

"Not much to tell. It wasn't even our fault. It was Frank Deauville. It was all him," Strong said.

"What did he do?"

"We stop the car. They're not suspects, they're not anything, Harry says to wave them on but Frank says no, the wee lassie might have something concealed under her dress."

"And then what?"

"Well, we'd all been drinking a bit. It was a cold night."

"What happened?"

"Frank looked under her dress, or tried to, and she slapped him and then he lost it. He dragged her out of the car and then the boy comes running round and he's on top of Frank . . ."

"What happened?" I asked.

"Frank threw the boy off and swung his rifle round and shot him. The bullet went through his heart, killed him on the spot."

"The whole thing was an accident," Selden said.

I shook my head. "No, it wasn't an accident. The girl was raped."

"Frank's blood was up. He was furious. We couldn't stop him," Selden said.

"Couldn't or didn't want to?" I asked.

Strong shone his torch in my face. "How do you know all this?"

"I'm a detective. I find shit out."

"OK, now you know what happened. What's the name of this eyewitness?"

"Who shot the girl?"

"What's got into you, Duffy?" Strong said, his radar pricking up by my insistence on the details.

"Who shot the girl?" I asked again.

"Frank insisted that we all shoot her. He would have shot us if we didn't," Selden said.

"My rifle jammed," Strong said.

Aye, maybe so, but you pulled the trigger, didn't you?

I turned to Selden. "And when did you recruit John into the IRA?" I asked.

Selden shook his head. "We all drifted apart after that. I didn't know what any of them were doing until I saw Frank's name in the paper in '83, I think. He'd solved some kind of big bank fraud case."

"And that's when the blackmail started?"

"Blackmail's an ugly word . . . We scratch his back and vicey versey, like you said," Selden said.

"Who is this eyewitness?" Strong demanded.

"I've written down their name and address on a piece of paper. I've also written down my bank details and I've put them both in this envelope," I said, reaching into the inside pocket of my leather jacket.

Strong took the envelope and shoved it into his sports coat pocket.

"And you haven't told anyone else what you know?" Strong said.

"Nope."

Strong looked at Selden and nodded. Selden took a step back away from me. "There's been a change of plan, Duffy," Selden said.

"What change of plan?"

"Well, you were right," Selden said. "I couldn't go to the Army

Council with a third request to kill you in as many weeks. I'd be a joke. In fact, worse than a joke, I'd be fucking dead. So I had to keep my mouth shut about our little talk. No help coming from the high command."

"And obviously I couldn't bring in any of *my* colleagues," Strong said.

"But for heaven's sake, this is Ulster. It was easy enough to round up four men in Derry who would kill somebody no questions asked."

"What four men?"

"Us four men," they said, coming in the door.

They'd obviously been in the back of van, waiting for their cue. Double cross. He was going to take the envelope and kill me.

The leader was a pale, beady-eyed man who was an odd amalgam of a Staffordshire bull terrier and Charles Hawtrey. The other three were archetypes: an old one, a tall one, a skinny young one. You can think of them as *Carry On* actors too: Syd James, Bernard Breslaw, Jim Dale. No Kenneth Williams, I'm sorry to say. But it's OK. You don't really need to think about them at all. In forty-five seconds all four of them would be dead.

The men were carrying assorted weapons: an AK47, double-barrelled shotguns, a revolver.

Strong and Selden pulled pistols from inside their jackets.

"Six against one. Seems a bit unfair, no?" I said.

"Fuck me, Duffy, what a headache you were. It's your own fucking fault, you know, you just wouldn't let it lie, would you?" Strong said.

The seven 'p's.

Proper preparation and planning prevents piss poor performance.

Hands into fists. Drip of endorphins soothing the lizard brain.

Again that old, old thought: *fear is power*, son, *fear is the precursor to action*.

A look of alarm in Strong's eyes. "Why are you smiling, Duffy?"

"Kill the light!"

The light went out.

It was pitch black.

I hit the deck and immediately all six men fired into the space where I had been.

I crawled through the rubble.

Fire above me.

A terrifying noise bouncing off the walls.

I crawled in a diagonal, away from the gunfire. The shotgun men shot both their barrels immediately, the AK man went through his clip in a few seconds, the men with pistols fired intermittently into the darkness.

Ping! Ping! Ping! all around me. "Jesus!"

I kept crawling through glass and muck and oil.

Something hot screamed past my face.

"Return fire for fucksake!"

Were they dead?

Oh fuck, had I killed them too?

Two muted flames shooting towards the gunmen.

Crabbie was behind a turbine in one corner. Lawson was behind a cast iron door in another. Both of them had suppressors on their MP5's, not just for the noise but to screen the muzzle flash.

"Return fire!" I screamed unnecessarily.

They knew what they were doing and they had targets to shoot at: the dusty yellow flames from the barrels of the men shooting at me.

Crabbie fired.

Lawson fired.

Turning round and lying on the ground in sniper mode I fired.

The range time paid off.

Range time always pays off.

Three men went down.

We all shot again and two more men went down and one made a bolt for the back door.

"Lights!"

The lights came on and I got to my feet and pointed the MP5 at the vacuum where the baddies had been standing. Jim Dale, Haughtrey, Breslaw and James were all dead. Selden was bleeding out from a hole in his chest the size of an orange.

"Is everyone OK?" I screamed.

"Not a scratch," Lawson said.

"Crabbie?"

Silence.

"Crabbie!"

"I think I was hit."

I sprinted over to him. "Where were you hit?"

"I'm fine. Go after. Strong, Sean! He's getting away," Crabbie said.

"Are you OK?"

"I'm all right. It was just a scratch. Go after Strong."

Lawson came over to the pair of us.

"Run with me to the car!" I said and we ran through the factory. "Did you get everything on tape, son?" I asked.

"Yes, sir."

"All right. I want you to call Special Branch, not the regular police. Tell them what happened. If they can find Superintendent Baker get them to send her. Play her the tape if necessary."

"What are you going to do?"

"I'm going to try to catch Strong before he does anything stupid."

27: RUNNING FOR THE BORDER

I dashed out to the BMW. Strong was getting away in his Bentley Turbo making for Belfast.

"Your family's back that way!" I yelled after him, but he was gone. He wasn't going back to be with his wife and kids while the cops closed in. He was trying to get away.

The 1988-89 Bentley Mulsanne was a mean piece of equipment. 400 brake horse power, twin-turbo 6.75 litre V8, top speed of 140 mph.

I got in the Beemer without looking underneath it for bombs.

"Here we go," I said and drove out of the factory and onto the onramp for the dual carriageway. At this time of night there was almost no traffic.

Perfect. Just me and him.

The Bentley was a mile ahead now. He was making for the M5, heading for the city and a million ways to escape after that. Yeah, that Bentley turbo was some car all right. Look at it go.

I laughed.

I was driving the BMW 535i sport with a 5-speed Getrag manual transmission. I knew the specs off by heart: 0–60 mph in 6.5s. Top speed (computer-limited): 128 mph. Top speed (without computer limit): 146 mph. Needless to say, I had showed my warrant card and had the dealership remove the computer limit.

The Bentley was about to get fucking crucified.

We reached the hill coming into Newtownabbey. The mercury tilt bomb under my car did not go off because there was no mercury tilt bomb.

Don't make a habit of this, Sean.

I grinned at myself in the rear-view. I was alive. And the killers were dead.

I was alive and the killers were dead but the man who had sent the killers was getting away in a souped-up Bentley. Smile gone. Shit, I couldn't even see him any more.

Surely he couldn't outrun me in that big boat?

I turned on the police scanner.

Reports of a white car doing over 100 mph at Mullusk.

He was already at Mullusk?

I'd have to shovel some more coal on to catch him.

I ate the tarmac on four wheels.

I ate the M5 and the M2 coming into Belfast.

I ate the motorway out past Dunmurry.

I ate Ballyskeagh and Moira.

The BMW's speedometer nudged upwards.

110 mph. 120 mph. 125 mph. 130 mph.

Christ, this thing could fly. I pushed the accelerator all the way to the floor.

150 miles per hour.

Portable siren on. Roof light flashing. Lane ahead cleared. On the big diagonal across Ulster.

The motorway was a relatively recent development and this BMW was brand new, so it was possible that this was the fastest anyone had ever driven in Northern Ireland outside of the Ulster Grand Prix circuit and even there . . .

Screaming down the M1 and then the A3 towards Armagh.

What traffic there was moved aside.

Cars blurred.

I couldn't risk fiddling with the tape deck at this speed so I turned on Radio 1 and prayed for something good.

John Peel was on repeat but Peelie was playing something way out of his comfort zone.

"This isn't really my cup of tea, but I think this might be the beginning of a new form in metal music. Or not. Send the kiddies to bed, get headphones for granny. Here for your delectation is Slayer and their song 'Raining Blood'."

I cranked the volume, which turned out to be a good move.

Ulster dematerialised.

I was flying over it.

I was seeing it from the air.

I was peering through the Mir space station window.

I was unfolding one of poor dead Tommy's secret maps.

I knew exactly where he was going. He was on the A3 now, the Monaghan Road, he was heading for the border just ten miles from Armagh.

Traffic cops didn't have the juice to catch us in their Ford Sierras and Ford Escorts.

After Slayer came Motorhead's "Ace of Spades".

Perfect.

Armagh. Milford. Madden. Middletown. He was heading for the Irish Republic all right. There was a checkpoint at the formal border where the A3 became the N12. But the checkpoint didn't matter because he was going to ditch the Bentley somewhere along here where the road ran parallel to the border and where there were no boundary walls or fences or anything of the—

I hit the brakes.

The Beemer screeched to a halt, fishtailed, thought about rolling, decided against it, fishtailed the other way and stopped.

There was the car. Ditched in a sheugh. Or sheughed in a ditch if you preferred.

Door open, Strong gone, out into the night.

Where was this place?

I got bearings. Typical border landscape. Boggy sheep fields rolling down the hills to a river.

The river. Yes. That's where he'd go.

And then I saw a trail through the grass. No blood. Just a big heavy running man.

I got out of the Beemer and followed him across the grass to a stream that I learned later was called the River Cor. The other side of the river was the Irish Republic. A place beyond my jurisdiction.

The moon came out from behind the clouds. And I saw him at the top of the rise beyond the river.

"You can't touch me, Duffy! This is the border! I'm over the border!"

"What are you going to do? Run and hide for the rest of your life?"

"Fuck off back to Belfast!"

"We'll extradite you from whatever rat hole you bolt to!"

"Oh you will, will you?"

Hadn't he learned anything about me from my file? Maybe not the greatest copper in these islands, but everybody, even my worst enemy, would agree that I was a stubborn son of a bitch. I'd fucking nail him if he went behind the Iron Curtain or a beach in Brazil or the Amundsen-Scott base at the South fucking Pole.

I looked at the tiny river separating him from me.

Was I going to be stopped by this . . . puddle?

Fuck that.

"What are you doing, Duffy? This is the Irish Republic!"

I waded into the river. It only went up to my knees. If he'd had more bottle he could have driven his car over. No need to abandon a decent car.

Strong pulled out his gun.

He shot once.

Missed.

Shot again.

Missed.

Click.

Click.

Click.

"I think you'll find it's empty," I said, crossing the stream into Southern Ireland.

Reverse the shot.

Him looking at me wading the river. Nemesis.

Back to me, looking at him.

He still could have run. Run to the top of that hill, jumped the little barbed-wire fence, gone on through the sheep shit and the bog.

But he knew he was beat.

He put his hands up.

"You can't touch me, Duffy. It's illegal."

I got to within six feet of him, took out the Glock and pointed it at him.

"You know why Death lets me live, John?"

"No, Duffy, I don't."

"Because I give him so much business."

Hammer back.

"Please! No!"

"As I see it, there are four possibilities. Number one, I let you run. You run. You probably get caught but you might escape and assume an identity and live out your life on an IRA pension. That might be a good punishment for you. Always worried, living in fear. Number two, I shoot you. I shoot you and pick up the shell casings and carry your body back across the river. Fireman's lift. Easy. What happened? Oh, he was making a run for it. Didn't quite make it. I shot him in Northern Ireland, no diplomatic incident, no need to involve the Guards."

"Please, Duffy—"

"Possibility three. I slug you across the face, drag you back across the river, deny you ever made it over and bring you in for trial. And then there's possibility number four. We'll get to that one in a minute, but first you talk."

"What do you mea—"

"Tell me about the crossbow. We couldn't figure that one out."

"The crossbow?"

"The crossbow."

"I was fucked, Duffy. Deauville saw me at the Rangers Club and my only contact was in the hospital. Deauville was going to start blackmailing me. I had to end it. I had to kill him before anything got going. My son had a—"

I put my hand up to stop him.

"I get it. Francis Deauville pops up out of nowhere with his big mouth just when you were on the verge of promotion to ACC. You couldn't shoot him with your gun because it would be traced back to you. You couldn't get the IRA to get you a stolen gun because your IRA contact was in the hospital gravely ill, but your son had a crossbow. You take the crossbow, practise with it in that big back garden of yours. Get good at it. Shoot that guy in Larne to establish a pattern and then you shoot Deauville, toss the weapon in the sea, and when Harry is out of intensive care he tells his mates in DAADD to call it in as one of theirs."

"You see, Duffy—"

"I'm not done, Strong. Never interrupt Columbo when he's doing his final fucking speech. But DAADD refused to admit to the killing lest it start a turf war, so Harry got that story printed in *Republican News*, which was good enough for us. The car. I should have paid more attention to the car. You couldn't follow Deauville and shoot some tosser in Larne in your big fucking Bentley so you took the train to Derry and borrowed your mate Harry's car. And squared it with him when he got out of the hospital. Am I right?"

He nodded. "You've solved it. You've figured it out as you always do, Sean."

"Who bought the crossbow? We showed your photograph at

the archery shops."

"My wife bought it for Teddy."

"Your wife. Should have thought of that."

Still keeping the gun on him I sat down on the grass and took my leather jacket off and opened the Velcro on the bullet-proof vest.

"That's better. Sweating like a bastard in that thing."

"Who were those men with you?" Strong asked.

"Lawson and McCrabban."

"I knew it! I told Harry that you'd tell them, that the whole thing was a set-up."

"But Harry was sceptical about your psychic ability?"

He took the envelope out of his jacket pocket. "It's a blank piece of paper in here, isn't it?"

I nodded.

"Tell me about Mrs Deauville," I said.

"Oh, I had nothing to do with that. Harry was out of the hospital then. He took care of all that."

"Took care of it how?"

"I didn't ask."

"Took care of it how?" I asked and waggled the gun in his direction for emphasis.

"Killed her. Abducted her from the bus station in Antrim," he said.

"Why'd you do it, John?"

"She knew too much."

"I don't mean that. Why did you do all of it? Work for the IRA, betray your friends, the police, everything?"

"I had to do it! Harry was blackmailing me. It would have been the end of everything. And it wasn't so much. They never wanted so much. It's like the red telephone, isn't it? The red telephone between the Kremlin and the White House. A line of communication. That's what I told myself. We have a mole in their upper echelons and they have moles in ours. We keep each other honest."

"So you were doing the police a favour?"

"In a way, yes. Besides, all this . . . what's the point? You know. You're a Catholic. You know. It's all a sham. What's that line, 'On the dunes and headland sinks the fire' . . . You know the rest. Smart boy like you."

What eejit can refuse quoting memorised poetry:

"'On dune and headland sinks the fire/all our pomp of yesterday/is one with Nineveh and Tyre.' Is that what you mean?"

"That's the one, Duffy," Strong said, sitting down on the grass.

"That's the reason you sold us out? Apart from the money and the fear? And you as the red telephone?"

"You've had those thoughts too, Duffy. We've all had the same conversations. What's the point to any of this?"

I took off my vest and let it drop next to Strong. "Aye, I've had those thoughts. You ever watch that Carl Sagan bloke on TV?"

"I've seen him."

"Civilisations rise and fall and rise and fall, and eventually the sun goes out and the earth dies and then all the suns go out, and all the civilisations die and eventually entropy maximises, the second law of thermodynamics wins, and there's nothing in the universe, no light, no atoms, nothing . . . But just because the world's ending, doesn't mean you give up. It was the great heretic Martin Luther who said 'If the Apocalypse was coming tomorrow, today I would plant a tree.' Wise words. And that's how we win: by sticking up a middle finger to the darkness closing in. I'd love to shoot you, John. For all your crimes and lies. I'd love to do that. But I'm not going to. And I'm not going to arrest you, either. On your feet. Back over the border. Any funny business and it's a bullet in the brain. Pick up my vest and leather jacket. Hold them out in front of you."

He picked up my gear and started walking towards the river.

"What *are* you going to do?" he asked.

"We're going to spin this as a mad vendetta by a clearly unstable Harry Selden against the Carrickfergus RUC who had been hassling him about a dead drug dealer and a missing persons case. Your name won't come up. I made sure Harry didn't tell the IRA Army Council that you'd been compromised. They all still think you're pure."

"What *are* you going to do?"

"We're going to run you as a double agent, John. The IRA will get you a new handler and you'll tell them you had no idea what Harry was up to. You'll tell them everything we want them to know from now on, but this time you'll be working for the good guys. If you're worried about Special Branch not believing me, don't be. I've got your whole confession on tape. Lawson recorded it with the high-gain antenna. You don't need wires when you have one of those."

"Shit," he said. "Where are you taking me now?"

"Special Branch. There's a Superintendent Baker that I may have offended with a joke about Willie Nelson. You might help me get on her good side."

Strong looked down. "I'm sorry about all this," he said.

I had no compassion for him at all. "You will be, mate. You will be."

We walked back across the River Cor and I handcuffed him at the car and put him in the back of the Beemer.

"We'll get your car out of the sheugh and fixed and back to your house. Appearances will be everything here. You didn't know what Harry was up to and you were home the entire evening. Savvy?"

"Savvy."

I patted the BMW's roof and drove north.

The radio crackled back into life when I got within range.

"Inspector Duffy! . . . Inspector Duffy! . . . Inspector Duffy!"

"This is Duffy, what's up, Lawson?"

"Oh sir, it's Sergeant McCrabban, sir, he's dying!"

28: DETECTIVE SERGEANT JOHN 'CRABBIE' MCCRABBAN

The Royal Victoria Hospital.

Casualty.

John McCrabban in emergency surgery for an AK 47 slug in his stomach.

Lost a lot of blood in the ambulance.

Should have been with him.

Should have been there with him instead of chasing down a traitor.

Screech of brakes as the BMW pulled into the ambulance bay.

"You can't park that here!" a policeman said.

I showed my warrant card. "Inspector Sean Duffy, RUC. If that man in the back of the car gets out I've told him you'll shoot him, so you'll have to shoot him. He's very dangerous."

"Yes, sir."

Inside the hospital.

Doctors and nurses in the trauma wards. A busy night for the RVH.

Lawson saw me at the Reception Desk.

"Sir!" he said.

He'd been crying.

"How is he?"

Lawson shook his head. "I'm so sorry, sir. I didn't realise

how badly he was hurt. I was checking the bodies and waiting for Special Branch like you said. I didn't realise Sergeant McCrabban was unconscious until Superintendent Baker showed up and I went looking for him."

"How was he in the ambulance?"

Lawson sniffed. "Haemorrhaging. He's lost so much blood. I don't think . . . The men in the ambulance said he wasn't . . ."

"Oh God."

I turned to the nurse at the desk. "Where's John McCrabban?"

"He's in the OR."

"Where is that?" I demanded.

"Sir, you can't go in there. It's a sterile environment. You'll have to wait here."

I waited.

And waited.

Helen and the boys arrived.

I hugged Helen. I hugged the boys.

Beth and Emma arrived. Beth was in tears. "Oh my God, Sean."

We paced the corridor.

Waited.

Lawson talking to me at the Coke machine.

"I didn't realise he was hit, sir. I didn't know he was down. He told you to go. I thought it was just a scratch, I—"

"Ssshhh. It's going to be OK. How can a bullet kill John McCrabban? It would be like a bullet trying to kill a fucking oak tree."

Beth, Emma and I played with Crabbie's boys.

We got Helen a cup of tea.

Seizing a moment when the kids were quiet, I went to the Catholic chapel and had a heart-to-heart with the Virgin.

"Yeah, I know. I know. I fucking know, OK? But this will be the last time. Just this last time and I won't ask any more," I said.

29: THE CHIEF CONSTABLE

If you really have to get shot, Belfast is one of the best places to do it. After twenty years of the Troubles and after thousands of assassination attempts and punishment shootings Belfast has trained many of the best gunshot-trauma surgeons in the world.

After four hours Crabbie was discharged from the OR and given into the hands of some of the best nurses in the world.

The head surgeon talked to Helen.

She hugged him and turned to us. "They think he's going to pull through."

Tears.

The complete waterworks from all of us.

From the OR to the recovery ward.

There was Crabbie. Bandaged. Sedated. Plugged in.

Only Helen allowed in to see him at first. But then the rest of us permitted to stand by his bed "as long as we were quiet".

"How is he?" I whispered to Helen.

"He hasn't spoken a word, but the doctor says he should be—"

"Sean, is that you?" he asked, opening first one eye and then the other.

"It's me."

"Did we get him?"

"We got him . . . But don't worry about that now. Helen's here and the boys—"

"Is Helen here?"

"Of course I am!"

He looked at Helen. "You're here, Helen?"

"Yes!"

"And the boys are here?"

"Yes, Dad, of course we are."

He shook his head and frowned. "If you're all here, who's looking after the farm?" he said dourly.

Back to Carrickfergus RUC.

The farm remark already legendary.

Upstairs to my office.

Me falling asleep at my desk while typing up the report.

A knock on my door.

"Sean?"

The door opened. Chief Inspector McArthur was standing there with another man, the Chief Constable of the RUC, Jack Hermon.

I snapped to my feet.

"Sir, I had no idea—"

Hermon waved me down.

"How's your man, Duffy?"

"Sergeant McCrabban, sir? He's on the mend."

"Good to hear it. You probably need to get some sleep, don't you?"

"I haven't finished the report, yet, sir, I was just typing it now. We, uhm, need to get the story . . ."

Hermon turned to Chief Inspector McArthur. "I'd like to talk to Inspector Duffy, alone, if that's all right."

"Oh . . . Yes, of course," he said and left the room. Hermon sat down in the chair opposite.

"Help yourself to a whisky," I said, gesturing towards the drinks trolley.

"Little early for me," he replied.

"Yeah. What time is it?"

"Not quite noon . . . This has been a terrible business," he said.

"Yes. It has."

"Glad McCrabban is on the mend."

"Yes, sir."

"But, Strong. Dear, oh dear. I trusted that man. I thought he was an up-and-comer."

"If my, our, plan is going to work, sir, you'll have to continue to trust him, sir. At least in public."

"Perhaps I will take a wee dram," Hermon said and poured himself a fifth of the sixteen-year-old Jura – the best whisky on the drinks trolley.

"Look, Duffy, I'll need a good man to be one of Strong's handlers. Someone intimate with the details of the case, someone who can bully him when he needs to be bullied and someone who can—"

"Let me stop you right there, sir. I'm very flattered but I don't know if I'm that man. I'm thinking of quitting, actually. Moving to Scotland in a year or so. My girlfriend, Beth, wants to go. She doesn't feel safe here, obviously. And we have a child together, so I need to go with her."

Hermon smiled. "I read about your girlfriend Beth on that attack on your house. A remarkable young lady, it seems."

"Oh, you wouldn't think it to look at her, but she's a toughie," I said.

Hermon stood up. "Scotland's not so very far away," he said. "In fact, if I'm not mistaken that's it, there, that blue line on the horizon."

"Yes, sir, I believe it is," I said and couldn't stop a massive yawn.

"We might be able to arrange something for you even if you lived over there. The part-time reserve perhaps. How many years until your twenty-year-pension, Duffy?"

"I've actually quite a bit to go, sir, 1994 will be my twenty years and you can't accumulate pension years in the part-time reserve."

Hermon frowned and looked into his whisky glass. "Exceptions can be made. Exceptions are made all the time in special circumstances."

"And for McCrabban too? He's thinking of retiring as well."

"For John McCrabban, a good man, yes, for him too."

I thought about what other concessions I could ask for. "And if I do stay here even part-time I don't want Kenny Dalziel to be my gaffer. I like Chief Inspector McArthur and I get on well with him. He's due a promotion but perhaps he could get the bump in salary and still, somehow, keep his job."

Hermon nodded. "All of that can be sorted out in due course. The first thing we have to do is, as you say, get our story straight."

Two hours later. Outside to the BMW. Exhausted. Need my bed. But not home. Not yet. Into Carrick to visit a jeweller's shop.

Down the A2 to Larne.

Knock on Beth's door. Her parents and her in the kitchen. Giving them the public version of the previous night's events.

Her father shaking my hand.

Later. In the playroom with Emma.

"Glasgow University, eh?"

"Yeah, it's super modern. The English department, anyway."

"In about a year from now?"

"I think that's how long it would take to get everything sorted."

"Have you heard of a thing called the part-time police reserve?"

"I've heard of it."

"You're a reservist in the RUC but not the full-time reserve, I wouldn't be on call. I'd only have to come in seven days in a calendar month. I could get it all over in a week or I could do two shorter stints."

"What do you mean?"

"I can retire with a full pension in 1994. If we live in Scotland I can get the ferry over and do my seven days a month easily.

The rest of the time I'll be a stay-home dad and look after Emma."

"Will you still be a detective?"

I shook my head. "No, that's not going to be possible. You can't be a part-time detective. But it won't matter. Crabbie's probably going to do the same thing. He wants to concentrate on his farming, so he'll be moving to the part-time reserve too."

"Who will run Carrick CID?"

"Lawson will do it. They'll promote him to Detective Sergeant and maybe get him a DC. It'll take me a while to train him up. Me and Crabbie. It'll take us that year and then we can both jack it in for the reserves."

Beth bit her lip and pushed a gorgeous line of golden hair from her face. "And we'll be out of all of this in our house over the water."

"We'll be out of it in our house over the water."

"And in the meantime?"

"Bobby Cameron is having the council install speed bumps and a one-way system on Coronation Road. No more drive-bys. And the man who had the vendetta against me in the IRA is dead. Oh, and I think you'll find the neighbours are a bit friendlier now too."

"Is that everything?"

"One more thing."

I started to get down on one knee.

"Let me put a stop to that straight away, mister," she said, pulling me back up again.

"Don't you wanna—"

"No!"

"But your dad . . ."

"Yeah, he'll be annoyed, won't he?" she said happily. "Can you cope with us just living in sin, you big Catholic weirdo?"

"I can cope with it," I said.

She grabbed the ring box. "At least let me take a look at it to see if you're a cheapo as well as a weirdo . . . Nope, not a cheapo. Very impressive."

"You want to try it on?"

"No, I don't."

"Shall I return it?"

"Keep it in a safe place."

30: O MASTERFUL BLEAK COP

A café just outside of Newry in the shadow of the Mourne Mountains. Thunder rumbling in from the Irish Sea. Rain lashing the windows. It's early. The café is deserted but for a couple of long-distance lorry drivers wolfing down Ulster fries and mugs of tea.

I've got my back to the door, a cup of coffee and *The Times* cryptic crossword.

Fourteen down: "The rich and powerful fear you, o masterful bleak cop."

Hmm. What can they mean by that?

The café door opens and a big heavyset man in a raincoat and a flat cap barges in. For a second he looks like trouble and I reach for the revolver in the pocket of my leather jacket.

"Some weather!" the man says, takes a table on the opposite side of the café and orders bacon and eggs.

I watch him for a minute but he's soon lost in the football pages of the *Sun*. I leave the revolver alone and go back to the cryptic crossword.

I still can't get the clue. My brain isn't working this early in the morning.

The door opens again and Assistant Chief Constable Strong comes in looking harassed and afraid. His tie is askew and he hasn't brushed his hair. He's buttoned his anorak with the wrong buttons. This will never do.

I wave at him and he comes over to the table and sits down opposite me.

"Fix your coat and run a hand through your hair," I tell him.

"I can't do this, Duffy!" he wails.

I grab his knee under the table and squeeze it, hard.

"Lower your voice and calm down," I tell him.

"I can't do this," he whispers.

The bored, sarky, pretty waitress comes over. "What can I get youse?"

"He'll have the same as me. Toast and a coffee," I tell her.

"Marmalade or jam?"

I look at Strong.

"Uhm, uhm . . ."

"He'll take the marmalade, love," I tell her.

"I can't do this, Duffy, if they find the wire I'm a dead man," Strong says when the waitress is gone.

Today is his first meeting with two members of the IRA Army Council in a pub in Newry. He's wearing a mike and a tape recorder, both of which are in his no doubt very sweaty underpants. MI5 are watching his every move but I'm the last person he wanted to see before driving the last part of the journey in his Bentley. I'm his handler. He thinks if he can convince me that he's not ready I'll call the operation off.

But I won't do that. I would never do that. One slip, one really thorough pat-down search and Elena Deauville and Maria McKeen will get the justice they deserve.

"They're not going to search you. They trust you. And if they do search you they'll never grab your bollocks – they're far too shy for that," I tell him.

"I can't do this, Sean."

"You can do it. It's what you've been doing for years. Except now you're going to be telling them what *we* want them to know."

When the coffee comes I slip him an aspirin.

"This is a Valium, it will calm you down and give you confidence and make you more alert," I lie.

He believes me and swallows the pill.

I spend the next ten minutes talking him down from the ledge. He doesn't touch his toast.

I look at my watch.

"It's time to go. Follow me to the loo in a minute and I'll check your gear."

He follows me into the bathroom and I fix his tie and check the mike and the tape recorder. It's all fine.

Back to the table. I make him take another sip of the coffee.

"Just do exactly what we told you and everything will be OK," I tell him.

He gets to his feet and nods.

He walks out of the café as if he's on his way to an execution, which, in truth, he might be . . .

I return to the cryptic crossword.

"The rich and powerful fear you, o masterful bleak cop," I say to myself.

O masterful bleak cop is a weird thing to say, it must be an anagram of something, maybe a—

"Peter Falk as Columbo," I say and fill in the clue. The final remaining clues tumble in pretty easily.

When I've paid the bill and gone back outside the rain has ceased but a cold wind is blowing in from the sea and the mountains are caught in its bitter grip. The southern rim of the sky is thinning from grey to black. The rush hour is over and the road is quiet and in the dense empty silence you can hear the alarms of wood pigeon and the cries of hawks.

I walk to the Beemer, look underneath it and get inside.

A spook called Wilson taps on the passenger's side window. I unlock the car and let him in.

"Did you gentle his condition, Duffy?"

"He's as good as he's going to get," I tell him.

"If he doesn't have a heart attack he might be quite a useful little asset," Wilson says with satisfaction.

"We'll see. You'll take it from here then, will you?"

"Aye. We'll take it from here."

"I'll be off then."

"Safe home."

Up along the motorway and into Carrickfergus. I drive to #113 Coronation Road where there is a giant For Sale sign on a board in the front yard.

I go inside, where Beth and Emma and Jet the cat are waiting.

Beth is poring over the forms for Glasgow University, where her potential supervisor has said that it would be fine for her to study Frank Miller's *Batman* as a response to Henry Miller's *Air Conditioned Nightmare*.

"Oh, I got sent some estate listings today. What do you think of this place?" Beth asks, handing me an estate agent's brochure. It's for a house overlooking the sea in Portpatrick, Scotland," she says.

I look at the house with its falling gables and ivy-covered windows and overgrown garden and path down to the water. It's practically a ruin but the location is terribly romantic.

"It'll be perfect. Let's go take a look at it."

31: SILENCIO

Blue. Big sideways swathes of blue. A universe of blue. A great blue engine. A machinery of blue.

Beth was manning the tiller, showing Emma how it worked.

I was up front in all that blue.

We had left Carrickfergus early, at five am, just as the sun was coming up as it is wont to do in August, at this hour, in these latitudes.

It was a straight run across the North Channel with only one tack. McCrabban and Lawson were sitting gingerly in the back, wondering if it was really a good idea to let an infant steer the boat. Wives and children had been invited but Helen was no sailor and didn't trust the little boys on board and Alex didn't have a steady girlfriend yet. It was warm already but Crabbie was dressed for an expedition to Ice Station Zebra with a massive windbreaker and multiple layers under that.

"Are we in any danger?" Crabbie asked nervously.

I shook my head. "It's a gorgeous day, not a cloud in the sky. We should be fine."

Gorgeous indeed.

When we cleared Belfast Lough Beth decided to hoist the big green spinnaker sail.

"You boys need to help," Beth said to Crabbie and Lawson. "Alex, you pull on that sheet over there and Crabbie, you pull on that sheet here."

"What sheets?"

"The ropes. The blue rope and the red rope."

We raised the spinnaker and the main and a curly-haired, freckled-faced, deeply concentrating Emma steered the *Deirdre* out of the lough and into the Irish Sea.

We were heading for the Scottish coast. Carrickfergus was behind us now, even the castle looking small and grey on the shoreline. Jet the cat came up on deck after falling asleep on a rope coil. He decided that the moving watery realm was not for him and went back down below.

"How's the farm going?" I asked Crabbie as I handed him a cup of tea.

Crabbie, unlike every farmer on the face of the earth, did not spend the next ten minutes complaining about how difficult it was to be a farmer.

"It's all right," he said.

"And your health?"

"Mustn't grumble," he said.

"Does he ever grumble?" Beth asked and Lawson and myself both shook our heads.

"He doesn't grumble but his frown could fell a gazelle at fifty paces," Lawson said.

Yeah, that frown. Last week McCrabban and I had driven to Judith McKeen's house in Cushendun and told her that the two men who had shot her daughter were both dead. Both themselves shot. She nodded and when she asked if the third B Special had had anything to do with it I had said no, that he was innocent, and that was when Crabbie had frowned. It was a lie, a necessary lie, but a lie nonetheless.

"What type of boat is this?" Alex asked.

It was a small Bermuda-rigged two-masted ketch with a cabin and bunks for four. It was a carvel-built design from Harry Brace's private yard on the Clyde. The planking was teak, which was extremely rare for a Scottish yard. 1947 or possibly

1948, although the man who'd sold it to Beth claimed it was from the 60s because he thought – wrongly – that its venerable age would decrease its value. It was only thirty-two foot long but the design was such that it looked much roomier when you were down below. It was a beautiful-looking craft with its sleek hull, weathered teak decks and brass fittings. By far the stand-out craft in any marina filled with 1980s white fibreglass mono-hulled cruisers and ugly speedboats.

"It's a ketch," Beth and I said together.

Two and a half hours later we dropped the sails and motored into Portpatrick harbour. I threw a stern line to a helpful kid on the shore and he tied us up onto a cleat while I jumped onto the pontoon and ran a line forward. Portpatrick couldn't compare with Oban or Port Ellen or Tobermory but it was a lovely little place nonetheless and I could see that the lads were delighted by the whole experience of getting up early and sailing over to Scotland for lunch.

We ate at a fish restaurant and found the house for sale on a cliff just outside of town. It had once been a lovely three-bed-room, but that once was probably about 1910. The roof looked none too stable and it had a garden full of weeds and nettles. However, the view across the water to Ireland was to die for.

"It'll certainly take some fixing up," Beth said and I could tell that she loved it. The lads agreed that it was just the place for us.

I put in an offer there and then and the estate agent told us that the current owners would almost certainly take it.

After thoroughly exploring "our" house we took Emma to a park back in town.

"There's Kilroot Power Station there across the sea. It's hard to believe that we live so close. I should get a little boat, myself," Lawson said, like me, now thoroughly convinced by a nautical existence.

"There's an old joke: the two best days of a boat owner's life are the day he buys his boat and the day he sells his boat," Beth told him, but I could see he didn't believe her. The hooks were in. It had been that big green spinnaker sail.

We stayed for dinner in Portpatrick and it was late when we headed out of the harbour again.

On the journey back Crabbie joined me on the foredeck and we talked tactics.

"They'll take my recommendation that Lawson pass for sergeant and be promoted to head of Carrick CID," I said. "I think he'll be ready to take over in about a year or so."

"Yes, that sounds about right," he agreed.

"And we'll both resign as detectives and move to the part-time reserve," I said.

"That will suit me down to the ground," he said. "I can concentrate more on the farm."

"We'll teach him everything we know and let the new generation handle things for a while."

"Aye."

The sun began sinking behind the Irish coast.

The yellow dark, the red dark, the deep blue dark . . .

Stars in swirls. A sickle moon. Silence.

Between Ireland and Scotland not a ship or a plane or another vessel.

Just the night itself and the flat black sea that makes a noise like singing.

The cat asleep. Emma asleep. Beth reading Frank Miller and allowing Lawson to hold the tiller.

Yes, the plan would work out fine.

We'd train Lawson and we'd move to Scotland and I'd finish out my time as a reservist. One more year of murder cases that don't get solved and missing girls who never come back and, as a sideline, handling the flighty, paranoid, highly strung Assistant Chief Constable Strong – an absolute menace of a man whom I would have to keep on a very tight leash.

And after that just a few more years of commuting to Belfast by plane and ferry, doing humdrum police work so I didn't blow my agent-handling cover: foot patrols, traffic work, paperwork.

It was nothing I couldn't handle.

I had Beth and Emma.

A boat called *Deirdre*.

Two excellent friends.

It would be a good life.

Good enough.

ADRIAN McKINTY'S SEAN DUFFY THRILLERS

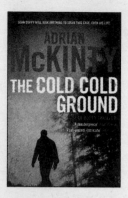

THE COLD COLD GROUND

Book one in the Sean Duffy series
Adrian McKinty

'If Raymond Chandler had grown up in Northern Ireland, *The Cold Cold Ground* is what he would have written' *The Times*

Two dead.

One left in a car by the side of a road. He was meant to be found quickly. His killer is making a statement.

The other is discovered hanging in a tree, deep in a forest. Surely a suicide: she'd just given birth, but there's no sign of the baby.

Nothing seems to link the two, but Detective Sergeant Sean Duffy knows the links that seem to be invisible are just waiting to be uncovered. And as a policeman who has solved six murders so far in his career, but not yet brought a single case to court, Duffy is determined that this time, someone will pay.

'Told with style, courage and dark as night wit' Stuart Neville

'An exciting new voice' Ian Rankin

ISBN 978 1 84668 823 2
eISBN 978 1 84765 795 4

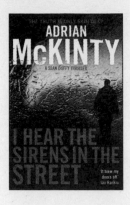

I Hear the Sirens in the Street
Book two in the Sean Duffy series
Adrian McKinty

'The ever-excellent McKinty is on great form . . . characteristically fast and thrilling' *Mail on Sunday*

1982. The year of a world cup, the Commodore 64 and the Falklands War. In Belfast, there's just more rain and more Troubles.

After an injury in the line of duty, Sean Duffy's back at work, ready for his first case: a torso in a suitcase dumped in an abandoned factory. And a single clue. A tattoo: 'No sacrifice too great'. Somewhere, there is a missing 't'.

Duffy knows there's always a bloody trail leading from a body to its killer. And no matter how faint, he will find it. So from businessmen to beautiful widows, old police notes to ambassador's records, country lanes to city streets, Duffy works every angle. And wherever he goes, he smells a rat . . .

'One hell of a story. Sean Duffy is a great creation, and the place comes alive' Daniel Woodrell

ISBN 978 1 84668 819 5
eISBN 978 1 84765 929 3

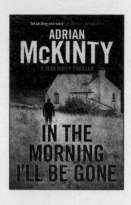

In The Morning I'll be Gone

Book three in the Sean Duffy series
Adrian McKinty

'Begins and ends spectacularly' *The Times*

Sean Duffy's got nothing. So when MI5 come knocking, Sean knows exactly what they want, and what he'll want in return, but he hasn't got the first idea how to get it.

Of course he's heard about the spectacular escape of IRA man Dermot McCann from Her Majesty's Maze prison. And he knew their paths would cross. But looking for Dermot leads Sean to an old locked-room mystery, and into the kind of danger where you can lose as easily as win.

From old betrayals and ancient history to 1984's most infamous crime, Sean tries not to fall behind in the race to annihilation. Can he outrun the most skilled terrorist the IRA ever created? And will the past catch him first?

'Creeps up on you and explodes like a terrorist bomb . . . places McKinty firmly in the front rank of modern crime writers' *Daily Mail*

ISBN 978 1 84668 821 8
eISBN 978 1 84765 931 6

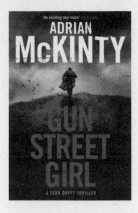

GUN STREET GIRL
Book four in the Sean Duffy series
Adrian McKinty

'Reminds me of Iain Banks' jaded-but-idealistic narrator-heroes'
Guardian

Duffy's back to blow a closed case wide open . . .

Belfast, 1985. Gunrunners on the borders, riots in the cities, *The Power of Love* on the radio. And somehow, hanging on, is Detective Inspector Sean Duffy.

The usual rounds of riot duty and sectarian murders are interrupted when a wealthy couple are shot dead while watching TV. Their son jumps to his death, leaving a note claiming responsibility. But something doesn't add up, and people keep dying.

Soon Duffy is on the trail of a mystery that will pit him against shadowy US national security forces, and take him into the white-hot heart of the biggest political scandal of the decade.

WINNER OF THE 2014 NED KELLY AWARD

'One of the great crime series . . . brilliant' *Sun*

ISBN 978 1 84668 982 6
eISBN 978 1 78283 051 1

Rain Dogs

Book five in the Sean Duffy Series
Adrian McKinty

'McKinty has all the virtues: smart dialogue, sharp plotting,
sense of place, well-rounded characters and a nice line in what
might be called cynical lyricism . . . Gateway McKinty: you
won't stop here' *Irish Times*

A death in a historic castle, locked up overnight. It almost looks
like a suicide, but then Sean Duffy pulls on a few little threads,
and the whole Establishment could come undone . . . It's just
the same things over and again for Sean Duffy. Riot duty.
Heartbreak. Cases he can solve but never get to court. But what
detective gets two locked room mysteries in one career?

When journalist Lily Bigelow is found dead in the courtyard
of Carrickfergus castle, it looks like a suicide. But there are
just a few things that bother Duffy enough to keep the case
file open. Which is how he finds out that she was working on a
devastating investigation of corruption and abuse at the highest
levels of power in the UK and beyond.

And so Duffy has two impossible problems on his desk: who
killed Lily Bigelow? And what were they trying to hide?

'A treat and an education' Val McDermid

ISBN 978 1 78125 457 8
eISBN 978 1 78283 162 4

McKINTY & DUFFY
PARTNERS IN CRIME
@
WWW.ADRIANMCKINTY.COM

A NEW CRIME SCENE HAS
BEEN DISCOVERED

There's a lot of criminal activity happening on Adrian McKinty's website: competitions, giveaways, news and events, gallery, blogs, personal updates from Adrian and the chance to read his next book. Adrian would love to hear what you think of his books.

You'll discover what DUFFY is up to next . . .

KEEP UP TO DATE AT WWW.ADRIANMCKINTY.COM
JOIN ADRIAN McKINTY ON TWITTER:
@ADRIANMCKINTY